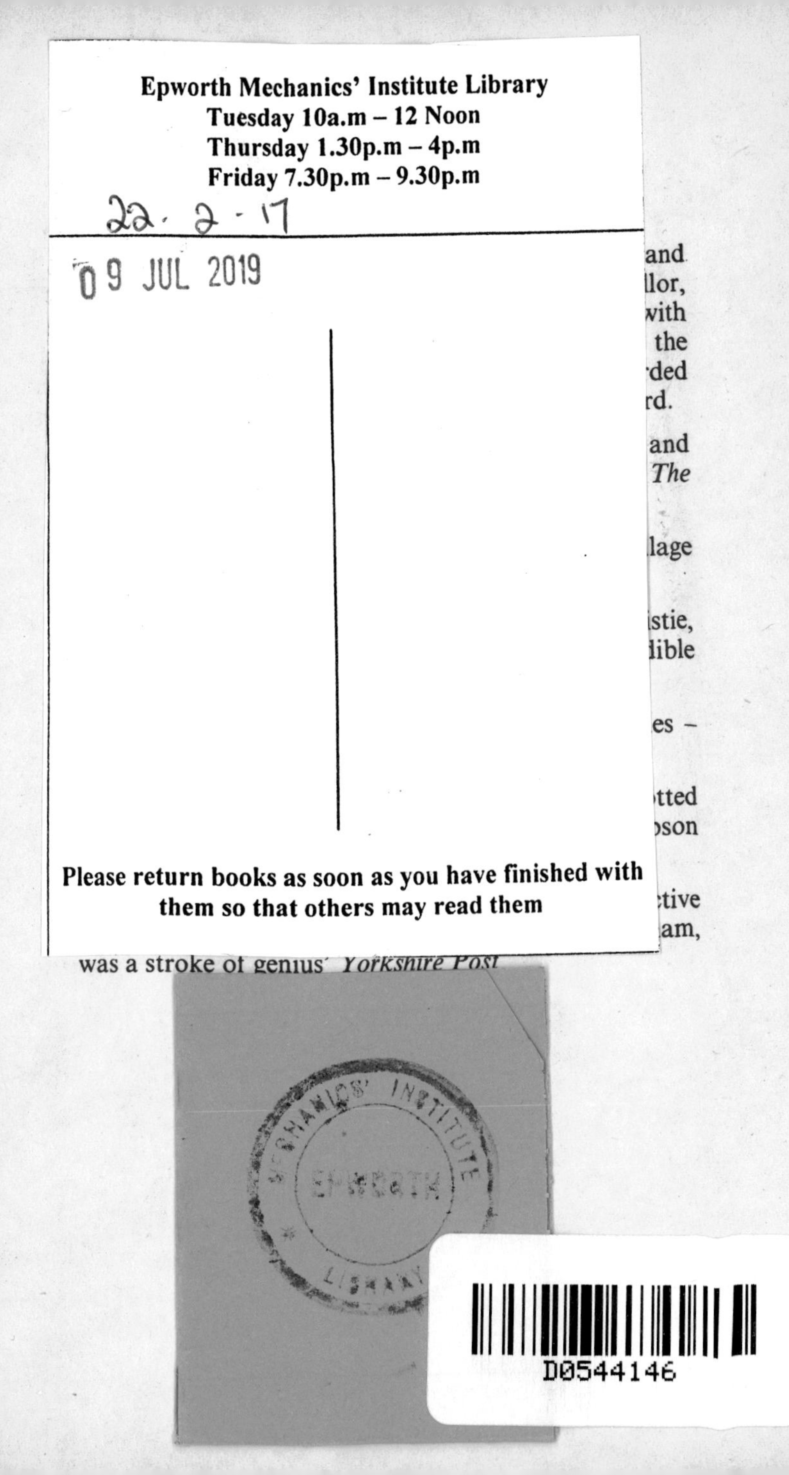

Epworth Mechanics' Institute Library
Tuesday 10a.m – 12 Noon
Thursday 1.30p.m – 4p.m
Friday 7.30p.m – 9.30p.m
22. 2 - 17
09 JUL 2019
Please return books as soon as you have finished with them so that others may read them
and
llor,
with
the
rded
rd.
and
The
llage
istie,
dible
es –
tted
oson
ctive
am,
was a stroke of genius' Yorkshire Post
MECHANICS' INSTITUTE
EPWORTH
LIBRARY
D0544146

Also by Dorothy Simpson

HARBINGERS OF FEAR

Inspector Thanet Series

THE NIGHT SHE DIED
SIX FEET UNDER
PUPPET FOR A CORPSE
CLOSE HER EYES
LAST SEEN ALIVE
DEAD ON ARRIVAL
ELEMENT OF DOUBT
SUSPICIOUS DEATH
DEAD BY MORNING
DOOMED TO DIE
WAKE THE DEAD
NO LAUGHING MATTER
A DAY FOR DYING
ONCE TOO OFTEN

INSPECTOR THANET OMNIBUS
SECOND INSPECTOR THANET OMNIBUS
THIRD INSPECTOR THANET OMNIBUS

DOROTHY SIMPSON

THE FOURTH INSPECTOR THANET OMNIBUS

WARNER BOOKS

A *Warner* Book

This edition first published in Great Britain by Warner Books in 1999
Reprinted 2001

Previously published separately:
Doomed To Die first published in Great Britain in 1991 by Michael Joseph Ltd
Published by Warner Books 1992
Reprinted 1999

Wake The Dead first published in Great Britain in 1992 by Michael Joseph Ltd
Published by Warner Books 1993
Reprinted 1993 (twice), 1994, 1995

No Laughing Matter first published in Great Britain in 1983 by Michael Joseph Ltd
Published in 1994 by Warner Books
Reprinted 1994, 1995 (three times), 1997, 1998, 1999, 2000

A CIP catalogue record for this book is available from the British Library.

ISBN 0 7515 2523 5

Printed and bound in Great Britain by Clays Ltd, St Ives plc

Warner Books
A Division of
Little, Brown and Company (UK)
Brettenham House
Lancaster Place
London WC2E 7EN

www.littlebrown.co.uk

DOOMED TO DIE

To Emma and Allan

ONE

On the evening of the day Bridget left home Thanet took Joan to the cinema. He hoped that the distraction would help him to forget that image of the train pulling away from the station platform, taking his beloved daughter out of his life. But it was no good, throughout the film the sense of loss remained, a dull persistent ache lurking at the back of his mind, ready to ambush him whenever he allowed his guard to slip.

One of the advantages of living in the small Kentish town of Sturrenden is that everywhere is within easy walking distance, and the Thanets had decided to leave their car at home. Outside it was a crisp, dry autumn evening with a hint of frost in the air. Joan shivered and turned up her collar, then glanced up at Thanet and took his arm.

'Come on, darling. Cheer up. She'll be home again at Christmas.'

Bridget had for many years been set on a career in cookery and now, at the age of eighteen, had left for a year's cordon bleu and housekeeping course at a well-known cookery school on the far side of London.

Thanet gave a shamefaced grin. 'I know. Stupid, isn't it? We spend all these years equipping them for independence and then when they finally achieve it we're sorry we succeeded! No, I don't mean that, you know I don't.'

Joan squeezed his arm. 'I know.'

'It's just that the break seems so final, somehow.'

'Not final in the true sense of the word. But I know what you mean. There is a sense of finality about it because it's the end of an era, isn't it? And however pleased we might be for her, because she's doing what she's always wanted to do, we can't help feeling sad for ourselves because our lives have lost a dimension.'

'That's it, exactly!' said Thanet. He sighed. 'Time seems to go so quickly. One minute they're toddlers, underfoot all the time, the next they've gone.'

Joan gave his arm a little shake. 'Come on, cheer up. It'll be another four years before Ben goes to university.'

'If he gets in.'

'My goodness, you are gloomy tonight! Of course he'll get in! He's unusually bright, he's working hard...'

The ache had eased a little and Thanet was able to leave the subject alone. They walked on in companionable silence, their footsteps echoing through the quiet streets as they passed the familiar squares of lighted windows behind which people were eating, sleeping, watching television, arguing or sharing jokes in the rich emotional chaos that is family life.

Ben heard the key in the front door and came to meet them.

'Sergeant Pater rang. Said it was urgent. I told him you'd ring back.'

The Station Officer. And at this time of night ... In a flash the last vestiges of Thanet's depression had vanished as the familiar tingle of excitement pricked at his scalp. 'Right, thanks.' He went straight to the phone.

Joan pulled a face and headed for the kitchen. 'We all know what that means.'

Thanet dialled. 'Bill? Sorry, I've only just got in. What's up?'

'Report of a suspicious death, sir. Timed at 9.40 p.m.'

Thanet glanced at his watch. Ten-twenty. Someone should have reported in from the scene by now. 'Heard anything more?'

'Victim's a woman in her thirties. Looks like murder. Scalp wound and plastic bag over the head.'

'Right. What's the address?'

'Barnewell Oast, Melton.'

Pater's tone made Thanet pause. Melton is a couple of miles out of Sturrenden, on the Cranbrook road. And of course, Barnewell Oast was where Mrs Broxton lived!

Vanessa Broxton was a barrister, known to many of the police at Sturrenden because of her work for the Crown Prosecution Service. Hence that note in Pater's voice. Thanet had himself worked with her on a number of occasions. She was in her late thirties, able and ambitious; he had been surprised when, a couple of years ago, she had started a family, and unsurprised when she had been back in Court a short time after the baby was born. This year she had taken another brief break to have a second child. Presumably Mrs Broxton herself was not the victim or Pater would have said so.

'I see. Mrs Broxton's place. Who rang in?'

'She did, sir.'

'She all right?'

'Sounded a bit shaken, naturally, who wouldn't be?'

'I'll get out there as soon as I can. Everyone else organised?'

'Yes, sir. Sergeant Lineham is already there and Doc Mallard is on his way. So are the SOCOs.'

'Good. Got any directions?'

Thanet scribbled them down as Pater talked. When he put the phone down Joan was holding out a Thermos flask. 'You'll be needing this.'

He kissed her. 'Thanks, love. Don't wait up.'

With so little traffic about it took only ten minutes to drive to Melton, a few minutes longer to find the Broxton house.

Barnewell Farm and the converted Oast which had originally belonged to it stood in a quiet lane on the outskirts of the village. The two houses were about a hundred yards apart, the boundary between them delineated by a row of young silver birches. Thanet recognised Lineham's Ford Escort and the police surgeon's cherished old Rover among the cars already parked in the wide gravelled drive. Mrs Broxton's distinctive red Scimitar was presumably in the garage.

He got out of his car and stood for a few moments taking in the geography of the place. Over to his right, behind the delicate tracery of the birches, he could see the lights of the farmhouse and, at an upper window, the motionless silhouette of someone watching the police activity next door. A potentially useful witness?

Ahead of him the twin cones of the oast houses, linked by a barn, peaked against the sky. The lower roofs of a series of smaller farm buildings attached to them extended left and then forwards in an L shape. The one nearest to him, he noticed, had triple garage doors, but the rest had obviously been incorporated into the house.

As he crossed the drive, feet crunching on the gravel, the front door opened and Lineham came out with the uniformed constable who had been on duty there when Thanet drove in.

'Ah, there you are, sir. Packham came to tell me you'd arrived. The doorbell doesn't work.'

'Hullo, Mike. What's the story?'

'Don't suppose I know much more than you, yet. You know it's Mrs Broxton's house?'

'Yes. Pater told me.'

'She's pretty upset, of course, so I thought it best to leave questioning her until you arrived. A WPC is with her.'

'Has her doctor been sent for?'

'Yes. He was out on a call but he'll be along as soon as he can.' Lineham turned to lead the way inside.

Thanet nodded a greeting to Packham as they went by. 'I

gather it was Mrs Broxton who found the body, Mike?'

'Yes. It's her nanny who's been killed.'

Thanet looked at him sharply. 'The children all right?'

Lineham nodded. 'Fast asleep, upstairs.'

'And it looks like murder.'

'Not much doubt about it, I'd say. Well, you'll see for yourself.'

Thanet paused, ostensibly in order to look around, but really to give himself a moment or two to brace himself for the ordeal ahead. Even after all these years he still could not face the prospect of that first sight of a corpse with equanimity. Somehow he always managed to conceal the complicated jumble of emotions which invariably assailed him – pity, anger, horror, sadness, but he had never managed to come to terms with the way this particular experience affected him, or to understand why he felt the way he did. And in this case, well, scalp wounds in particular could be messy, very messy ... He forced himself to take in his surroundings.

This was presumably the barn which linked the twin oasts. He was standing in a spacious entrance hall which soared two storeys high right up into the exposed roof timbers. On the floor of polished stone flags oriental rugs created pools of glowing colour, and handsome pieces of antique oak stood here and there against the creamy walls. To the right a wide staircase of polished oak boards led up to a galleried landing.

'Impressive, isn't it?' said Lineham admiringly.

Thanet gave an inward smile. He could guess what was coming.

'But then, we knew they couldn't be short of a penny.'

Guy Broxton was a successful businessman and the Broxtons' combined income must indeed be substantial.

Thanet concealed his amusement with difficulty. Confront Lineham with any house bigger than a semi and his reaction was always the same.

'We're not here to study the Broxtons' life-style, Mike. Which way?'

Lineham gestured. 'In the kitchen.'

The diversion had helped and Thanet followed the sergeant along a short corridor leading off the hall on the right, as ready as he was ever likely to be for what was coming.

Lineham pushed open a door. 'In here.'

This was the ground floor of one of the oast houses and unusual in that it was an oval not a circular oast. In the days when home-brewed beer had been the norm and every sizeable farm had its own oast house, this was where the hops would have been dried. The kitchen, which had been built into it following the curves of the walls, was every woman's dream, of a type familiar to Thanet from the illustrations in Joan's favourite magazine: custom-made wooden units, a green Aga cooker set into a deep chimneybreast of mellow brick, glass-fronted wall cupboards containing an attractive array of china and glass, a floor of polished terracotta tiles, a central pine table and chairs and an old pine dresser displaying a carefully designed clutter of plates and jugs. Cream linen curtains patterned with sprays of wild flowers hung at both windows. The activity in the room was a shocking contrast to what Thanet imagined to be its normal atmosphere of warmth, light and decorative richness. The Scenes-of-Crime team was busy taking samples and photographs and Doc Mallard, bald head gleaming, was kneeling beside the body, which was huddled on the floor beyond the far corner of the table on the same side of the room as the Aga.

Thanet approached. 'Hullo, Doc.'

Mallard glanced up over the top of his gold-rimmed half-moon spectacles. 'Careful, floor's slippery. Spilt milk. Better come round the other way.'

Glad of the momentary delay Thanet paused to inspect the pool of milky liquid and the small saucepan lying on the floor against the base of the wooden units before walking around the table and approaching the body from the far side. He steeled himself, looked.

For a flicker of time he couldn't make sense of what he saw. In his dread of this moment he had temporarily forgotten the plastic bag which Pater had mentioned, and the unnatural sheen of blood-smeared plastic encasing the woman's head caught him unawares. Then his brain reassimilated the information and he saw that she was lying on her side, her face partly obscured by the mass of curly fair hair which had fallen across her cheek. She was small and slender, neat buttocks encased in tight green corduroy trousers stained now by the voiding of the rectum common in cases of suffocation, her tiny feet encased in fashionable brown suede laced ankle boots. Her knitted jacket was a glorious kaleidoscope of greens, browns, creams and near-black neutrals. If he hadn't already been told that she was in her thirties, from what he could see of her he would have guessed that she was much younger, even in her teens, perhaps. The richest years of her life should have lain ahead.

Thanet welcomed the familiar surge of anger, the anger which invariably spurred him on and gave an edge to his determination to succeed in each new murder investigation. No one, under any circumstances, had the right to deprive another human being of the most precious gift of all, life.

Mallard put a hand on the floor to heave himself up. 'We could turn her over now, if you like. I didn't want to move her until you'd seen her.'

Thanet glanced at Trace, the SOCO sergeant. 'Got all the photographs you need?'

'Yes, sir. Sir...'

'What?'

'The back door. I thought you'd like to know. It's unlocked.'

'Is it, now? Interesting. Thanks.' Thanet studied the position of the body for a moment longer, then glanced at Lineham. 'Give me a hand, Mike.'

Together they bent down and gently rolled the woman over. Her bulging eyes stared sightlessly up at them, her congested features further distorted by the plastic. Her trousers were spattered with the spilt milk, Thanet noticed, the heel and side of one boot still wet with it. He stood back while Mallard continued his examination and tried to work out what had happened. Careful not to touch he bent to inspect the corner of the kitchen table nearest to her. It was smeared with blood. He pointed it out to Lineham.

'There must've been a quarrel,' said the sergeant, 'in the course of which the saucepan of milk was knocked over. She stepped back, slipped in the greasy liquid and fell, banging her head on the corner of the table. Then someone decided to put the bag over her head and finish her off.'

'Looks like it,' agreed Thanet. 'What d'you think, Doc?'

'That's your department,' said Mallard, levering himself to his feet again. 'We'll know more after the PM, of course, but on the face of it, yes, the fact that the head wound bled so much indicates that she was alive when she hit her head, and it would seem pretty obvious that she was then suffocated.'

'When did it happen, d'you think?'

'I was waiting for that one.' Mallard glanced at the Aga. 'It's warm in here, so it's tricky.' He considered. 'You know how I hate committing myself at this stage but, well, say within the last four hours, to be on the safe side.'

Thanet glanced at his watch. Ten-fifty-five. Some time between 7 and 9.40, then, when Mrs Broxton had rung in.

Mallard snapped his bag shut. 'Right, well, I think that's about it for the moment. I'll let you know when we fix the PM.' He held up a hand as Thanet opened his mouth. 'Don't bother to say it. Yes, it will be as soon as possible.'

Thanet grinned. 'Thanks, Doc.'

'Bridget gone yet?' asked Mallard, as Thanet escorted him to his car.

Helen Mallard, his wife, was a professional writer of cookery books and had for a number of years encouraged Bridget in her choice of career. She and Bridget regularly met to dream up new dishes and it was through Helen that Bridget had first landed a commission to write a children's cookery column in the *Kent Messenger*.

Thanet grimaced. 'Saw her off this morning.'

'Helen will miss her.'

'So will we! Oh, give Helen our congratulations, by the way. I saw her latest book in Hatchards in Maidstone this week. *Eat Yourself To Life*. Good title.'

'We thought so. I'll tell her. Thanks.'

After several attempts the Rover's engine coughed into life.

'You never know,' said Thanet through the car window, 'if it makes enough money you might even be able to afford a new car.'

Mallard was always having to put up with good-natured teasing on the subject of his car.

Mallard switched his lights on and engaged first gear with a flourish. He raised his chin in pretended affront. 'I will ignore that remark, or this could be the end of a beautiful friendship.'

Thanet gave the Rover an affectionate pat as it went by and stood for a moment smiling indulgently at its vanishing tail-lights. He had known Mallard since childhood and he and Joan had always been fond of him, had remained loyal friends during the bad years after the lingering death of Mallard's first wife from cancer. The tetchy, irritable, scruffy Mallard of those days was virtually unrecognisable in the spruce, buoyant man he had become since he met and married Helen, and Thanet never ceased to marvel at the transformation.

Back in the house there was a lot to do. Briskly he issued

instructions, sending the solid, reassuring Bentley, accompanied by a WPC, to interview the owner of the silhouetted figure glimpsed at that upstairs window in the farmhouse next door, in case it turned out to be a woman living alone. He hoped it would. Solitary women often took a lively interest in the affairs of their neighbours.

Finally he turned to Lineham. 'Right then, Mike. Let's go and see what Mrs Broxton has to tell us.'

TWO

Vanessa Broxton was huddled miserably in a corner of one of the deep, soft sofas in the drawing room, feet tucked up beneath her, discarded shoes on the floor. WPC Barnes, who had been keeping her company, stood up as Thanet and Lineham entered the room.

'D'you want me to stay, sir?' she asked quietly.

'Yes, please.'

Mrs Broxton glanced up. 'Hullo, Inspector Thanet, Sergeant Lineham.' She grimaced. 'I never thought we'd be meeting under these circumstances.'

'No. May we . . . ?'

'Yes, of course.'

She swung her legs to the floor, tugging the hem of her skirt down, and slipped her shoes on.

Thanet chose a chair opposite her and Lineham retreated to one slightly behind him and off to one side. This room, the ground floor of the other oast, was also oval. Floor-length curtains in shades of apricot and turquoise hung at the windows, the colours echoed in the apricot fitted carpet and sofas and chairs upholstered in shades ranging from deep cinnamon to peacock blue. Between two of the windows a floor-to-ceiling bookcase revealed that this was a literate household where the printed word was considered just as important as the ubiquitous small screen – more so, perhaps; the television was conspicuous by its absence. Silk-shaded lamps cast warm pools of light on furniture that glowed with the unmistakeable patina of age.

Vanessa Broxton was wearing a straight charcoal grey skirt and white tailored blouse, part of her workaday uniform, no doubt. Slung loosely around her shoulders was a thick blue knitted jacket and as Thanet watched she crossed her arms and tugged it more closely around her, hugging herself as if to contain the shock she must have sustained. He had never seen her look so vulnerable before. Of medium height, she seemed to have shrunk since he last saw her, and her usually immaculate short straight dark hair was dishevelled as though she had been running her fingers through it. Her long narrow face was striking rather than beautiful, with heavy dark brows and prominent nose, and her best feature by far was her eyes which were a very dark brown, almost black. In Court Thanet had seen them glitter like anthracite but tonight, as they watched him, waiting for him to begin, they were soft, bewildered and, not surprisingly, afraid.

'Do you feel up to answering some questions?'

'Yes, of course.' She sat up a little straighter, bracing herself.

'The dead woman was your children's nanny, I gather.'

'Yes. No. Well, not exactly.' She ran her fingers through her hair and gave an embarrassed little laugh. 'Sorry, I'm sounding positively incoherent, aren't I? Let me explain.' She took a deep, ragged breath. 'My usual nanny, Angela – Angela Proven – has been with me ever since I had Henry – that's our first baby, he's twenty months now – but yesterday she was rushed into hospital for an emergency appendectomy. This left me in a terrible fix. My husband is away in Brussels on business and I had a case starting in Norwich this morning. I have a housekeeper who comes in daily, but she has two children herself and can't be here at night. As it was a Sunday none of the staffing agencies was open, of course, and neither my mother nor my mother-in-law lives close enough to take the children. I just didn't know what to do. You'll appreciate the problem with my particular line of work, Inspector. It's not like an office where if you take a day off you can catch up later. If a barrister fails to turn up in Court on a day when there is only one case in the list, not only the judge but the Court officials, the jury, all the witnesses, everyone has to go home ... And apart from the fact that it doesn't help your career to acquire a reputation for unreliability, this particular case was important to me. Work is always slow to pick up after such a long break and this was my first decent case since I started back after Alice was born. It was expected to last about three weeks and involved my staying away from Monday to Friday in Norwich ... I'm just trying to explain how it came about that I asked Perdita to look after the children for me.'

'That would be Perdita ... ?'

'Perdita Master. I've known her for years, we were at school together. Not that we've ever been close friends, but living in the same area we've run into each other from time to time and kept up with each other's news. So when I met her at the hospital, it seemed like an answer to a prayer when I found she'd just left her husband and was looking for somewhere to stay for a few days while she sorted herself out. Sorry, I forgot to say, she was a trained nanny, before she got married –'

'I'm sorry to interrupt, but you said, at the hospital ...'

She raked her fingers through her hair again. 'Yes. Oh God, I'm not doing very well, am I, I feel such a fool ...'

'You've had a severe shock ... I assume you accompanied Miss Proven, when she was admitted to hospital.'

'Yes. Well, she went by ambulance and I followed by car, with the children – as I say, I had no one to leave them with ... Anyway, I waited for a bit and then Angela was taken into the theatre and it seemed pointless hanging around for hours, especially with the children, so I decided to go home and on the way out I ran into Perdita. She'd been visiting her mother, who was in for some tests. Naturally we each explained what we were doing there, and when she heard about the fix I was in she suggested we could do each other a good turn. If she came and looked after the children until the weekend, when I could interview for a temporary nanny until Angela gets back, she could have a few days respite in which to sort out what she was going to do...'

'She'd just left her husband, you say?'

'Yes, on Saturday, the previous night. There'd been a frightful row, I gather, and she'd walked out on him. She'd gone to her mother's, but Giles had followed her there and –'

'Sorry, would that be Giles Master the estate agent?'

She nodded. 'Yes.'

The firm of Master and Prize was one of the larger estate agents in the town and had been founded by Giles Master's father, who had died a few years previously. Thanet knew most of the businessmen in Sturrenden by sight and some of them quite well; like Master, who was a few years younger than Thanet, many of them had attended the same school as he. He hadn't liked Giles much as a boy and had had no reason to change his opinion since.

'Anyway, as I was saying, when she walked out he guessed she'd go to her mother's house and followed her there, made an awful scene banging on the door and shouting because her stepfather wouldn't let him in. So when I saw her on Sunday afternoon she was trying to think of somewhere to go – not too far away, because of her mother being in hospital – where he wouldn't be able to find her ... He's terribly jealous and possessive, she's had a hell of a time with him, poor girl...' For a moment the flow of her narrative halted as the memory of Perdita's fate caught up with her again. Then she shook her head, took another deep breath and went on. 'Anyway, we both thought it would never occur to him to look for her here...'

'You think that's what happened?'

Mrs Broxton hesitated, frowned down at her lap. 'How can I say?'

She paused and Thanet waited. She had remembered something, he was sure of it, and was debating whether or not to tell him.

'I don't actually know anything other than what happened to me.'

So she had decided against it. Could he have been wrong? He decided to go along with her, for the moment. 'And what was that?' Thanet had been wondering: if Mrs Broxton was supposed to be on a three-week case in Norwich, what was she doing here, at home? Unless the case had gone short, of course.

'My case went short,' she said. 'After the mid-day adjournment the defendant entered a plea. So naturally I decided to come straight home – well, I had to go back to the hotel to collect my stuff and pay the bill, of course. Anyway, I got away about three. I didn't bother to ring Perdita, I thought I'd easily be home between five and six.' She grimaced. 'Unfortunately my car broke down on the M11.' She ran her hand through her hair again. 'Oh God, what a day! There wasn't much traffic about and no phones in sight. I didn't dare get out of the car and set off to walk to the next one.'

Thanet nodded sympathetically. Ever since the motorway murder of Marie Wilkes, a young woman who had been seven months pregnant at the time and who had had to walk only a few hundred yards in broad daylight to telephone for assistance, women travelling alone whose cars broke down on motorways had been advised to lock the doors, stay inside and wait until help arrived, however frustrating the delay.

'It really does make me so angry, that women have lost the

freedom to behave normally.' Briefly Mrs Broxton's eyes flashed with remembered fury and frustration. 'I was kicking myself for not having had a phone put in the car, or at least getting one of those emergency kits I read about, with a sign one can put up in the back window. I thought no one was ever going to stop, but eventually a police car pulled up and sent for the RAC. But it was another three-quarters of an hour before they arrived ... I assure you I really heaved a sigh of relief when I at last arrived home. And then, of course –'

'Sorry, what time was that?'

'About half past nine, I think.' She waited a moment, in case Thanet had a further question, then went on, 'When I got to the front door I could hear Henry screaming. He always insists on having his bedroom door left open at night and with the galleried landing sound tends to carry, you can hear him if he so much as whimpers. Inside, I called Perdita, but there was no reply so I went straight up to the nursery. He was in a terrible state, practically hysterical...'

'Presumably he still sleeps in a cot.'

'Yes, thank God, or...' She shuddered and put her hands over her eyes, as if to blot out the images conjured up by her imagination.

'What about the baby? Alice?'

The first hint of a smile, there. 'Sound asleep, thank God. She sleeps like a log, always has. Fortunately she's in a separate room, so that there's no chance of Henry disturbing her. He does tend to wake in the night and make a fuss until someone comes.'

'Right. So you comforted Henry...'

'Yes. I thought he'd take ages to go to sleep, he was in such a state, but in fact he went out like a light, within minutes. I think he had cried himself to the point of exhaustion.'

'So then what did you do?'

'Well, naturally, the first thing I did was go and look for Perdita – that is, I glanced into her room, it's across the corridor from Henry's . . .'

'Is that normally Miss Proven's room?'

'No, that's next door to Henry's – well, between Henry's room and Alice's, actually. This is just a spare room, Angela sometimes has a friend to stay and she'll sleep in there . . . Anyway, Perdita wasn't in there, I didn't for a moment think that she could have been, and not heard Henry screaming . . . So then I went downstairs . . .'

Suddenly, as if impelled from her seat by an invisible force, Vanessa Broxton stood up and walked around to pick up a cigarette box from a sofa table behind the settee upon which she had been sitting. She opened it, peered inside then slammed it down in frustration. 'Oh God, I'm sorry, has anyone got a cigarette?'

Thanet looked at Lineham and WPC Barnes, both of whom shook their heads. 'Go and see if you can find one,' he said to the woman police constable.

Vanessa Broxton had returned to her seat. 'I haven't had a cigarette for over two years, I gave up when I was pregnant with Henry.'

'I think, under the circumstances, you can allow yourself a little laxity,' said Thanet.

WPC Barnes returned with a packet of Silk Cut and offered it to her.

'Thank you. There's a lighter on the table there . . .' Mrs Broxton put the cigarette to her lips with a hand that shook and inhaled deeply, closing her eyes. 'That's better.' She opened her eyes and gave a shamefaced grin. 'It's disgusting, but it helps.'

Thanet smiled, content to wait. He knew she was bracing herself for the worst part of her story.

THREE

After a few more puffs Vanessa Broxton pulled a face, reached for an ashtray and stubbed the cigarette out. 'I think I can manage without this after all. Sorry, where was I?'

'You went downstairs ...'

'Ah, yes. I glanced in here, first. I thought perhaps she'd fallen asleep on the settee, or had been listening to music with headphones on, but the room was empty. So then I went to the kitchen ... and ... and found her. Well, you saw for yourself ...'

'Did you move the body at all?'

'No.' She shuddered, compressed her lips. 'I did touch her, though. I felt her pulse, just to be sure ... But I could see she was dead ...' She shook her head. 'I couldn't believe it. It seemed like a nightmare, there in my own kitchen ...'

'Did you touch anything else?'

'I don't think so, I may have done.' She pressed her fingers to her temples again. 'I don't really know. I'm sorry.'

'So then what did you do?'

'Went straight to the phone, of course, to ring the police.'

'That would be the phone in the kitchen?'

'No. I couldn't ... Not with Perdita ... I used the one in the hall.'

'Mrs Broxton, when I asked you just now if you thought

Mrs Master's husband had found out she was here, I had the impression you remembered something...'

She gave a wry smile. 'One thing I should have remembered is that nothing much escapes you, Inspector. Yes, there was something... I suppose I was just giving myself time to make up my mind whether to mention it or not ... I didn't want to be unfair to Giles. But of course, it's not a matter of being unfair, is it? Apart from the fact that if I don't tell you someone else is bound to, with the work I do I really ought to know that I *have* to tell you everything, down to the last detail...'

'So what was it, that you remembered?'

'Well, yesterday, when Perdita and I came out of the hospital, we could see that Giles was waiting for her, by her car. I suppose he'd guessed she'd probably visit her mother some time during the day and had decided to hang around so that he could catch her on the way out. At this point Perdita and I separated. Perdita was going to drive to her mother's house to collect her things, and then come on to mine. She and Giles had a brief argument, then she got into her car and drove off.'

'Did he follow her?'

'No. Not to my knowledge, anyway. He stood looking after her for a moment or two, then went to his car. He was still sitting in it when I left.'

'So what are you suggesting?'

'I'm not suggesting anything, Inspector, merely telling you what happened.'

But it was clear why Mrs Broxton had thought the incident could be significant. Master didn't sound the type to give up easily: if he had decided to try again, later in the day, to see his wife, had gone to her mother's house only to find that she was not staying there any longer ... He could well have remembered seeing her with Vanessa at the hospital and put two and two together.

'Mr Master knows where you live?'

'Yes, he does.' She ran a hand wearily through her hair again. 'Oh God, what a mess...'

The brown eyes were dulled now, almost glazed. Shock was beginning to catch up with her.

'We've nearly finished, Mrs Broxton, then you can rest. I wonder, do you happen to know the address of Mrs Master's parents? We'll have to let them know what's happened.'

'Oh God, yes. As if they didn't have enough to cope with as it is, with her mother so ill in hospital...'

'We'll tell her stepfather, first, I think, and leave him to break the news to his wife when he feels she can cope with it. If you could just give us his name?'

'It's Harrow. They live in Wayside Crescent, Sturrenden. On the Pilkington estate. I don't know the number, I'm afraid.'

'Not to worry, we can easily find out. The next thing I wanted to ask you was this. These keys were in Mrs Master's pocket. Do you recognise them?' Thanet held them out.

She leant forward to inspect them. 'Yes. They're the keys to this house. I gave them to her. Front door, back door.'

'Why d'you think she would have been carrying them?'

Vanessa Broxton shrugged. 'She probably took the children out for a walk this afternoon and didn't want to carry a handbag. I've done the same myself.'

Thanet nodded. A reasonable enough explanation. 'Yes, of course. The next point is, do you happen to have noticed if there is anything obviously missing from the house? There seem to be no obvious signs of forced entry or disorder, I don't suppose you've even thought to check, in the circumstances...'

She again ran a hand through her hair, glanced about the room. 'Oh God, no, I haven't. It just didn't occur to me, everything seemed to be in order, as you say...'

'Tomorrow, perhaps, when you have time.'

'Yes, of course.'

'I only ask because I don't know if you realised ... Your back door was unlocked when we arrived this evening.'

This brought her head up with a jerk, eyes now alert and wide open with shock. 'Was it? Oh God, I never thought to check ... What a *fool* ... He could still have been out there, after I got home. All I could think of was getting away from ... getting out of the kitchen, ringing the police, getting somebody here, anybody ...' Her hands were clasping, unclasping, kneading each other in her agitation.

There was a knock at the door. WPC Barnes opened it and went out, came back a moment later. 'Mrs Broxton's doctor is here, sir.'

Just at the psychological moment, by the look of it. Thanet stood up. 'Good. Bring him in.'

The doctor was short, middle-aged, brisk. He nodded at Thanet then went straight to Mrs Broxton, took both her hands in his. 'Vanessa, my dear, what a terrible business. How are you?'

'Better for seeing you, Peter.' She gave him a wan smile. 'But I think the appropriate expression in the circumstances is, "As well as might be expected."'

'I'd better take a look at you.' He glanced at Thanet, raised his eyebrows.

'Yes, we've finished here for the moment,' said Thanet. Then, to Mrs Broxton, 'WPC Barnes will stay here tonight, so if you need anything ...'

'Thank you, Inspector. You've been very kind.'

At the door Thanet turned. 'Oh, just one small matter ... We'd like to take a look at the room Mrs Master was using ...'

Vanessa Broxton waved a hand. 'Please, whatever you need to do, just do it. Anything, anything at all ...'

'Thank you. If you could just tell us where it is?'

'Up the stairs, turn left, then straight along the corridor. It's the second door on the right. The children's rooms are opposite and Henry's door is open, so if you could be as quiet as possible...'

'Of course.'

Outside in the hall Perdita Master's body was just being removed by two ambulancemen. Thanet watched them leave before going in search of the dead woman's bedroom.

'If the back door was unlocked it could have been an intruder, couldn't it?' said Lineham as they mounted the stairs.

Thanet shrugged. 'Or whoever killed her unlocked it to get out.'

'You think it might have been the husband, and she let him in herself?'

'Early days, Mike. Early days. Let's not start speculating too soon.'

'In any case, it's odd that Mrs Broxton didn't think to check that the back door was locked, before ringing us, don't you think?'

'Oh, I don't know. I think it's quite feasible that she was too shaken to be thinking clearly.'

On the galleried landing Thanet paused to look around. Above him massive honey-coloured oak beams lit to dramatic effect by strategically-placed spotlights rose in graceful curves, horizontals and diagonals. Below, the generously proportioned hall added a further dimension of light and space.

Lineham was concentrating on more mundane matters. 'But she's not stupid. In the circumstances you'd think her first thought would be to make sure the house was secure. After all, as she says, for all she knew the murderer could still have been around.'

Thanet shrugged. 'You know as well as I do, Mike, that people don't always think or act logically in situations of stress.'

They turned left as instructed along a broad corridor. More ancient beams straddled the ceiling and at one point they had to duck to pass beneath. Ahead of them, on the left, a door ajar indicated that they were approaching Henry's room and Thanet glanced at Lineham and put a finger to his lips. Henry had had enough traumas for one evening.

The room which Perdita Master had so briefly occupied was pleasant and comfortable, with a green fitted carpet, cream-washed walls and sprigged floral curtains. Double doors on a fitted cupboard opened to reveal a neat washbasin built in to one half, hanging and shelf space for clothes in the other.

She had brought very little with her: toilet things, several changes of underwear, another pair of cord trousers, cream this time, a couple of blouses, a pair of flat shoes. The most interesting item was a sketchbook on the bedside table. It was relatively new, the first pages taken up by sketches of flowers, grasses and trees. The last ten or twelve were a different matter. One was full of quick studies of two children, a small boy and a baby – Henry and Alice? – the last two of more detailed portraits of a man, drawn from several different angles.

He showed them to Lineham.

'Her husband?' said Lineham.

Thanet shook his head. 'I know Master. That's not him.'

'Perhaps Mrs Broxton will know who he is.'

They both stared at the sketches. The subject was in his late thirties or early forties, Thanet guessed, with straight hair worn rather too long for Thanet's taste and a narrow, sensitive face. The eyes were deepset, depicted with a distant, somewhat contemplative expression, the mouth rather weak.

'A lover?' said Lineham.

'Could be.' Thanet was still looking at the drawings, admiring now the skill of the artist. 'She was good, wasn't she? I wonder if she was a professional.'

'Mrs Broxton said Mrs Master was a trained nanny, before she got married.'

'Before she got married. Exactly. I can't quite see Giles Master allowing his wife to play nursemaid as a career.'

Lineham raised his eyebrows. '"Allowing"? Like that, was it?'

'Perhaps I'm judging him too harshly. Anyway, you'll see for yourself soon, no doubt.' Thanet tapped the sketchbook. 'If she wasn't a professional she was a very gifted amateur. If the other drawings are of Henry and Alice, then as these come afterwards we can only assume she must have done them since she got here yesterday.'

He could imagine Perdita sitting propped up against those pillows, lamplight turning that mass of fair hair to spun gold, totally absorbed in her task and finding solace in it. He tried to put himself in her situation. The break-up of a marriage is always traumatic to both partners, regardless of which one is choosing to initiate it. Perdita would still have been shaken, emotionally bruised by the row with Giles and having so precipitately left her home. She was at a major turning point in her life, living in a kind of limbo. What more natural than in that state her thoughts would have turned to her lover, if she had one? He would have been her life-line to the future.

'Mrs Broxton said that Mr Master was very jealous and possessive, sir. That Mrs Master had a "hell of a time" with him. If it was only on Saturday night that he discovered she had a lover . . .'

'Quite.'

'Looks as though this could turn out to be pretty straightforward, doesn't it?'

'Perhaps.'

'Mr Master next, then?'

'Yes. Someone will have to break the news to him anyway. Looks as though in this case it had better be us.' This was one task which, like every policeman, Thanet hated above all others. 'Better take a look at her handbag before we go.'

On a demure little easy chair covered with the same

sprigged material as the curtains lay a bulky brown leather shoulder bag. Lineham emptied its contents on to the bed and sat down beside them.

Thanet continued to study the drawings. He would know this face again when they met it. And if this were Perdita's lover, here was a second person about to receive a crushing blow. Thanet wondered if the man were married, had a wife and family...

'Doesn't look as though there's anything of any significance here, sir. Just the usual stuff.' Lineham was putting things back into Perdita's bag.

'Right. Let's go, then.' Thanet tucked the sketchbook under his arm. If Vanessa Broxton was still around he wanted to show her the portraits. But in case she wasn't, first of all...

Outside in the corridor he paused outside Henry's room. Silence. With a gesture to Lineham to remain where he was Thanet pushed the door open a little wider and tiptoed in. A nightlight in the shape of a red-spotted mushroom with a rabbit perched on top illuminated the cot. Henry was sound asleep, flat on his back with arms outflung in the careless abandon of childhood. One glance was enough to tell Thanet that this was indeed the small boy in the sketches. Perdita had been very talented, there was no doubt about that.

He returned to the corridor. 'The drawings are of Henry,' he whispered to Lineham.

On the galleried landing they met Mrs Broxton's doctor and WPC Barnes coming from the opposite direction. Presumably the Broxtons' bedroom was on the first floor of the far oast.

'Would it be possible to have a quick word with Mrs Broxton?' said Thanet.

The doctor shook his head. 'Sorry, she shouldn't be disturbed again tonight. I've given her a sedative. Constable Barnes has kindly agreed to listen out for the children.'

Thanet gave a resigned nod. Too bad. Identification of the

man in the sketches would have to wait until morning.

Downstairs Bentley had just returned from interviewing the neighbour.

'Any luck?' asked Thanet.

'She's a Mrs Barnes, sir. A widow. Says she was putting the cat out at about 8.30 this evening and heard some kind of commotion over here – someone hammering on the front door and a man shouting, she says. She couldn't hear what he was saying, but after a few minutes the shouting stopped. She went back indoors then and just happened to go upstairs.' Bentley grinned. 'The landing window overlooks the drive of this house, so I'd guess she went up deliberately, to see what was going on. Unfortunately, she's got arthritis in both hips, so it took her some time to get there and by the time she did all she saw was a car driving away.'

'Any description of the car?'

Bentley shook his head. 'Nothing of any use. Big and dark in colour, that's all. And it was too dark for her to see who was driving, or how many people were in it. One interesting point, though. She did say she was aware of an unusual number of cars around this evening. She noticed because it's usually pretty quiet at night here.'

'What did she mean by "around"? Did she mean driving past her house, or coming into the drive of this one?'

'She couldn't be sure. Her sitting room is on the front corner nearest to the drive of the Oast, so it would have been difficult to tell.'

'And what did she mean by an unusual number?'

Bentley shrugged. 'She couldn't be very specific. When I pressed her she said between four and six.'

'Close together, or spaced out?'

'Between the incident we spoke of and the time the police cars started arriving.'

'Between 8.30 and, say, 10, then ... Could mean anything or nothing.'

'She said she'd wondered if there was one of those supper safaris – you know, when a group of people have the first course at one house, the main course at another and the dessert at a third. They tend to go in for that sort of thing around here, apparently.'

'Remember to ask the men to check that, when you're doing house-to-house enquiries in the morning.' Thanet glanced at his watch. Ten past twelve. 'It's too late to start tonight. Lineham and I are going now to break the news to Mrs Master's husband, and I'd like you to do the same with her stepfather.'

A shadow flitted across Bentley's round, normally placid face. 'Right, sir.'

Thanet left Lineham to check the number of the Harrows' house and also the Masters' address in the telephone directory, while he went to see how the forensic team was getting on in the kitchen.

Five minutes later they were on their way.

FOUR

Outside Thanet shrugged deeper into his overcoat and shoved his hands into his pockets. The temperature had dropped still further and the roofs of the cars were frosted over. The sky was thick with stars.

'Shall we go in separate cars, sir?' said Lineham.

'Where does Master live?'

'Nettleton.'

'Ah.'

They knew Nettleton well, from a case they had worked on together some years ago. Carrie Birch had been an apparently innocuous middle-aged cleaning woman, whose body had been found crammed into an outside privy behind a cottage near where she lived. Nettleton was only a couple of miles from Melton and it shouldn't take more than ten minutes to get there at this time of night.

'We'll go together in yours and pick mine up on the way back.'

'Right.'

Lineham sprayed de-icer on to his windscreen. 'The Super isn't going to like this, is he?' he said as he got into the car.

'You mean, because Mrs Broxton is involved? No. It could be tricky.'

Superintendent Draco, a fiery little Welshman, had arrived

to take charge of Sturrenden sub-divisional headquarters a couple of years previously, full of zeal and enthusiasm to make his patch the best-policed area in the South of England. The ensuing period of change and adjustment had been painful for all concerned, but the results had been impressive: the record of arrests had gone up, morale had improved dramatically and although everyone grumbled about the demands Draco made upon time and energy he was universally accorded unqualified respect and even a grudging affection.

'Come to think of it, though, it's odd he hasn't turned up tonight, don't you think, sir?'

Draco liked to have his finger on the pulse of his division and the previous year had even gone through a period of turning up unexpectedly during the course of an investigation and sitting in on interviews with witnesses. Thanet had not enjoyed having the Superintendent breathing down his neck and had heaved a sigh of relief when Draco had turned the spotlight of his attention elsewhere. It was certainly unusual for him not to have been present for something as important as the start of a murder investigation, especially as the crime had been perpetrated at the Broxtons' house. Draco prided himself on good relationships with other professions concerned with the maintenance of law and order.

There had been so much to take in this evening that Thanet had not noticed Draco's absence until now. 'Yes, you're right, Mike. It is. Actually, I was thinking the other day ... Don't you think he's been rather subdued, lately?'

'Now you mention it, yes, I have. I wonder...'

'What?'

'Well, Louise said she saw Mrs Draco in town the other day and she didn't look at all well. Louise wondered if we'd heard anything. I meant to ask you.'

'No, I haven't heard a word. But if she is ill, it would explain a lot.'

Thanet would never forget the first time he had met Angharad Draco. Shortly after Draco's arrival in Sturrenden the Thanets had been invited to a Rotary dinner and during the preceding reception Joan had nudged him.

'Who is *that*?' she'd whispered.

Following the direction of her nod Thanet had beheld one of the most beautiful women he had ever seen in his life. Tall and willowy, with a cloud of gleaming copper-gold hair and flawless complexion, the woman Joan had indicated was surrounded by a crowd of admiring males. She was in her early thirties, he guessed, and her lovely body in its simple floor-length sheath dress of sea-green silk would have had any sculptor reaching for his tools.

'No idea. Good grief – look!'

The group of men around the woman had shifted slightly, revealing the shorter man who stood beside her, smiling up at her. As the Thanets watched she put a proprietorial hand through his arm and returned his smile.

'Draco,' breathed Thanet. 'Surely that's not his wife.'

But it was. Later in the evening the Thanets had been introduced to her by a Draco whose uxorious smile held a distinct tinge of amusement; he was clearly used to the effect Angharad had upon others, and to the politely concealed disbelief that he should have won such a prize. It had been obvious then that he adored her and that his feelings were reciprocated.

Thanet had eventually come to understand that in fact the Dracos complemented each other: she needed his ebullience and volatility as much as he needed her cool, calm reserve. They had no children and apparently did not feel the lack of them; in such a mutually exclusive relationship any third person would perhaps have been superfluous.

Now, if Angharad were ill, if there were something seriously wrong with her ... How would Draco bear it? Thanet remembered Doc Mallard's long years of near-disintegration, and shivered inwardly.

'I'll ask Louise to keep her ear to the ground,' said Lineham.

His wife was a trained nurse and had many friends in the medical profession, having worked for some years as a Sister at Sturrenden General Hospital.

'How is Louise, by the way? I haven't seen her for ages.'

Lineham did not reply immediately. Thanet thought that this was because they were approaching a T-junction, but after slowing down, waiting for a car to pass and turning left, Lineham still said nothing. Perhaps he hadn't heard?

Thanet glanced at him. It was dark, of course, but even so the dim illumination from the dashboard was sufficient to reveal the grim expression on Lineham's face. Thanet revised his opinion. The sergeant had heard, and either he didn't want to reply or he didn't know what to say. In either case Thanet had no intention of repeating the question.

But Lineham, it seemed, had merely been considering his answer. 'To be honest, sir, I think she's a bit confused.'

This was unexpected. Louise was a very decisive sort of person, with positive views on pretty well everything and a black and white outlook on life which Thanet would personally have found very difficult to live with. 'Oh?' he said, warily. Dare he ask what about? Was Lineham expecting him to?

Thanet decided to follow one of his own rules: when in doubt say nothing. If Lineham wanted to pursue the matter, he would. But if so, he would have to make up his mind quickly. Another half a mile or so and they would be in Nettleton. Having been brought up in this area Thanet knew most of the roads around Sturrenden. He knew, for instance, that the camber was wrong on the next bend ahead, that if Lineham didn't slow down a little the car might well drift across the centre line...

Lineham slowed down.

'About going back to work, that is.'

'I'm not sure what you mean,' said Thanet, cautiously. He

knew from his own experience what a minefield the question of working wives could be.

'Well, you know how keen she's always been, to get back to work when both the children are at school, how difficult she's found it to adjust to staying at home, while they were small?'

'Yes.' Only last year Louise's restlessness had almost resulted in Lineham leaving the force; unable to find a satisfying outlet for her own energies she had for a while tried instead to persuade her husband to strike out in a new direction. Fortunately Lineham had found the strength to resist and on Thanet's advice had, instead, persuaded Louise to find a part-time job for the few hours a week when Mandy, their youngest, had been at playgroup.

'Well, as you know, Mandy will be starting school at Easter and I thought Louise would be over the moon at getting back into nursing, but no, now she's saying she's been out of the profession too long, that she's lost touch with all the latest developments in medicine, that she wouldn't be able to cope . . .'

'But surely there are refresher courses, for people in her position?'

'That's what I say to her. But I don't know . . . I think the truth is, she's lost confidence in herself.'

'That's not unusual. In fact, I understand it's quite common for women who've been at home for a few years to feel like that. Joan did, herself.'

'Did she?' said Lineham eagerly. 'I didn't know that.'

'Oh yes, she certainly did. Look, if it would be any help, I'm sure Joan would have a chat with her.'

'Would she?' Lineham's tone was still eager, but it changed as he said doubtfully, 'I'm not sure that Louise would be too pleased if she thought I'd been talking to you about it. Unless Joan could bring the subject up casually, without her knowing . . .'

'I'm sure she could. She's pretty good at that sort of thing.'

'Yes, I know.' Lineham was silent for a few moments, then said, 'D'you think you could ask her, then? If the situation arises, that is, when she could do it tactfully?'

'Of course.'

'Thanks. I really would appreciate it. Nothing I say seems to make any difference. Perhaps Louise will listen to someone from outside the family who's been through the same thing herself.'

Lineham pulled up at the main Sturrenden to Maidstone road, then crossed it to enter Nettleton. It was now just after midnight and apart from a single light in the bedroom of one of the cottages the village was dark and silent.

'D'you know where the house is?' said Thanet.

'In Wheelwright's Lane. It's a turning to the right, just past the post office.'

The black and white timbered building, formerly a private house, which housed the general shop and post office loomed up on their left.

Lineham signalled and turned right. Wheelwright's Lane was narrow and winding, with a scatter of cottages which soon gave way to open fields and clumps of trees, their branches etched black against the night sky.

'Now,' said Lineham, leaning forward to peer through the windscreen, 'if it's where I think it is ... Yes, it'll be one of these.'

Ahead lay a cluster of buildings: a pair of cottages on the right and several larger, detached houses strung out along the road on their left.

'What's it called?' said Thanet.

'Applewood House.' Lineham slowed down as they came to the first drive entrance.

'This is it,' said Thanet, peering out. The name was stamped in black letters on a white board attached to the right-hand gatepost.

Lineham reversed, then drove in, wheels crunching on the gravel.

Despite the hour there were lights on in the house, a sizeable red-brick house of relatively recent design, with white-painted window-frames which gleamed in the darkness.

There was no knocker and after a moment or two of groping and peering Lineham found an iron loop which he thought must be the bell. He pulled it.

No response.

'Try again,' said Thanet.

A minute or two later a man's voice called out, 'Who is it?'

'Police.'

The scrape of a key, the rattle of a latch and the door swung open. A man peered out.

'Mr Master? It's Inspector Thanet, Sturrenden CID.'

Master swayed. 'Ah, Thanet, yes ... What is it? What's the matter?' The words were slurred and it was clear that he had been drinking.

'If we could come in for a moment...'

Master stepped back unsteadily to let them in and led them through a small, square hall into a room on the left. Inside he turned slowly to face them. 'What is it?' he repeated.

A thrill of interest and curiosity coursed through Thanet's veins at his first clear view of Master's face. He was familiar with Master's conventional good looks, well-cut tweed suits and generally well-groomed appearance; he and the estate agent were both out and about a lot in the area in the course of their work. Tonight, however, Master sported a black eye and severe bruising of the left cheek. His tie was loosened and his usually sleek brown hair was dishevelled. He was clearly in no condition to receive such news as this – if news it was. On the other hand, if he were innocent, perhaps the fact that his perceptions were blunted would help to cushion the blow.

In any case, Thanet had no choice. 'Won't you sit down, Mr Master?'

Master simply stared at him with alcohol-dulled eyes.

'Shall we all sit down?' Thanet moved decisively to the nearest armchair and sat.

Following Thanet's nodded instruction Lineham stepped forward and, putting one hand gently under Master's elbow, guided him to a chair and lowered him into it.

Master continued to stare blankly at Thanet.

Come on, get it over with, thought Thanet. 'I'm afraid we have some bad news for you.'

No change in Master's expression.

'It's ... it's about your wife. She ... I'm sorry, there's no way I can make this easier for you ... She was found dead earlier this evening.'

Master continued to stare and it was a full minute before a glimmer of comprehension and disbelief crept into his eyes. 'Dead?' he whispered. His voice grew louder, thickened. 'Perdita? She's not. Can't be.'

'I'm sorry. It's true.'

'No!' Master rubbed his hands over his face, his eyes, shook his head violently as if to clear it. 'Must be mistake. All right s' evening.'

'You saw her this evening, then?'

'Just said so, didn't I?' Master raked his hair with his hands, made an obvious effort to pull himself together and speak clearly. 'There must be some mistake,' he repeated stubbornly.

Thanet shook his head. 'I'm afraid not.'

There was a brief silence, then Master muttered, ''Scuse me,' and blundered out of the room.

At Thanet's nod Lineham followed him. The sergeant left the door open and it was soon clear that Master had merely crossed the hall to a cloakroom; from the sound of it he was dousing his head in water.

Thanet glanced around. A dying log fire smouldered in the hearth and a near-empty bottle of whisky and half-full glass showed where Master had been sitting. A television set still murmured in a corner and Thanet crossed to switch it off before studying the room more closely. It was large, and spacious, with windows on three sides, French doors which presumably opened on to the garden and a high ceiling decorated with plaster mouldings. Interestingly, however, despite the big, soft sofas and chairs and tastefully disposed antique furniture, the impression was curiously chilly and impersonal. Thanet frowned, trying to work out why. Perhaps it was absence of clutter – books, newspapers, magazines? Or perhaps the predominance of blue? Blue and cream carpet, deep blue or cream upholstered chairs, cream brocade curtains ... Only one bright pink chair and a brilliant explosion of colour in a picture on the wall opposite the fireplace redeemed the room from coldness. Thanet crossed to take a closer look at the painting, which had caught his eye earlier. Indeed, it could hardly fail to catch the eye. A thought occurred to him: perhaps, if Perdita Master had painted it, the room had been designed around it, to accord it just this degree of prominence?

It was, he realised as he drew closer, a watercolour, not an oil painting as he had at first thought. He was no connoisseur of art, and had always supposed that such vibrancy of colour could only be associated with oils. This was, he supposed, a painting of a garden, or of a flowerbed, depicting a waving forest of brilliant fuchsia-pink exotica – lilies, perhaps? – in a dense, lush undergrowth of writhing greens and purples. And yes, it had been painted by Perdita Master; her signature was in the lower right-hand corner.

He was still studying it when Lineham returned, followed a moment or two later by Master, whose hair was wet and roughly combed. The estate agent certainly looked more alert, and Thanet wasn't sure whether the glazed look residual in his eyes was due to shock or alcohol. It shouldn't take too long to find out.

Master plumped down in his armchair, automatically picked up his glass, looked at it, then slammed it down again so forcibly that the liquid slopped over on to the table-top. 'Oh, sit down, for God's sake! No point in standing there like a couple of tailor's dummies.' He buried his face in his hands, shaking his head and massaging his forehead with hooked fingers.

They sat.

'I really am sorry,' said Thanet gently.

Master looked up. 'Are you?' he said fiercely. Then he leaned back, closed his eyes. 'Oh God, I'm sorry. It's not your fault...' His eyes snapped open, suddenly dark with apprehension. 'You haven't told me yet what happened, how she...'

There was no way Thanet could soften the blow. 'Your wife was found dead in the kitchen of Mrs Broxton's house. And I'm afraid it was no accident.'

Master stared at him, trying to take in the implication. 'No accident? What d'you mean? Are you saying...?'

'I'm sorry. Yes. She was killed, deliberately.'

Master's eyes were wide with shock. 'Murdered?' he said, his voice rising. 'You're saying Perdita's been *murdered*?'

If the man was acting he was carrying this off superbly. But then, he would have a lot to lose ... Thanet nodded. 'Yes.'

'But how...?'

'It looks as though there was an argument, a quarrel ... So far as we can tell at the moment, Mrs Master fell, knocking herself out –'

'And the bastard just left her there to die!'

Master's voice was hoarse with outrage and Thanet did not contradict him. If Master were innocent there was no point in turning the knife in the wound by giving further details.

Master moaned and again buried his face in his hands. From time to time he shook his head in disbelief or despair.

Thanet sent Lineham to make some coffee. 'Hot and strong.'

When Lineham returned Master accepted the mug of steaming liquid and sipped at it as obediently as a small child. Eventually he said wearily, 'I suppose you'll be wanting to ask me some questions.'

'When you're ready.'

'I'm as ready as I ever will be.'

'Very well ... You say you saw your wife earlier on this evening?'

A nod.

'Would you tell us about it?'

The man hesitated, clearly marshalling his thoughts. 'You obviously know that she was staying with Mrs Broxton ...' He waited for Thanet's nod. 'Well I got there about half past eight, twenty to nine ...'

'I'm sorry to interrupt, but was this meeting prearranged?'

Master looked uncomfortable. 'No. I just called in on the off-chance ...' He waited, but Thanet remained silent. 'Anyway, she agreed to come out for a drink with me ...'

'What about the children?' said Thanet.

Master waved a dismissive hand. 'Oh, that was all right. They were sound asleep.'

Thanet's face must have shown his disbelief, because Master burst out angrily, 'If you don't believe me you can ask the landlord of the Green Man in Melton. There weren't many people there, he should remember us.'

Master must be telling the truth, the story could so easily be checked.

'I think it only fair to tell you that Mrs Broxton said your wife had left you.' Thanet paused, but Master said nothing. 'She also says that you have since attempted to talk to Mrs Master on at least two occasions, once on Saturday night, when you followed her to her parents' house, and once on Sunday afternoon, at the hospital. She says that Mrs Master had gone to stay with her in the hope of a few days' peace when she could sort out what she wanted to do ... You must see that in the circumstances I find it very difficult to believe that she willingly went for a drink with you this evening, especially as it would have meant leaving the children alone in the house at night.'

'No, well ...' Master was realising that some explanation would have to be given. His hand moved to pick up his glass of whisky, stopped. 'Oh hell, what's the point of pretending. The truth is, I made her come with me ... Don't look at me like that! Don't you see, I *had* to talk to her. And she wouldn't let me in.'

Thanet could understand why. Once Master had got his foot over the threshold there would have been no way that Perdita could have got rid of him.

Abruptly, Master stood up and began to walk about. 'She was my *wife*, for God's sake! Surely a man's entitled to talk to his own wife!'

'Mrs Broxton's neighbour has told us that around 8.30 there was some sort of commotion outside Mrs Broxton's house. A man shouting, she said. I assume, from what you're saying, that that was you.'

Master swung around and faced Thanet. 'I told you, Perdita wouldn't listen! And don't think I can't see where all this is leading, Thanet.' He advanced until he was standing only a few paces in front of Thanet, looming over him threateningly.

Bracing himself in case of attack, out of the corner of his eye Thanet was aware of Lineham also tensing in readiness for action.

Master was pointing an admonishing finger, punctuating practically every word by stabbing the air. 'Just get this into your head, will you? I did *not* kill my wife. I wouldn't have harmed a single hair of her head...' His tone suddenly changed. 'Can't I make you understand? I loved her!' His belligerence had evaporated and he now sounded more bewildered than anything else. 'I loved her more than anything on earth, and now...' Abruptly he plumped back down into his chair and his eyes filled with tears, which began to spill over and trickle down his cheeks. Tugging a handkerchief from his pocket he dashed them away impatiently.

Only the most consummate actors can cry at will. The man's distress was genuine, Thanet was sure of it – but based on what? Grief at the news of the death of his wife, or remorse at having brought it about? Thanet was as aware as the next man that the most likely culprit in a case of domestic murder is the husband or wife, and this fact had caused him some of the most uncomfortable moments in his career. Always, in this first interview with a bereaved partner, he was torn between compassion in case the suspect were innocent and determination that if he were guilty he couldn't be allowed to get away with it.

'Look, Mr Master, you shouldn't jump to conclusions. I assure you that at the moment we have a completely open mind on the subject. I'm just trying to get you to see that you have to be frank with us –'

'All right, all right, you've made your point!' The man's natural aggression was already beginning to reassert itself. He blew his nose loudly and put the handkerchief away.

'So let's start again from the beginning, shall we? You got there at about 8.30...'

FIVE

At a signal from Thanet, Lineham took over the questioning. It was some time before the full story emerged.

Master had arrived at the Broxtons' house between 8.30 and 8.40. In response to his knock Perdita had come to one of the front windows, being understandably wary of opening the front door at night in such a quiet country area when, apart from the children, she was alone in the house. At first, seeing that it was Giles, she had simply gone away, but he had persisted, banging more loudly on the door until she had come to the window again and this time opened it.

'Giles! Stop making all that noise, you'll wake the children. Go away!'

'Let me in! I have to talk to you.'

'I've got nothing to say to you. We said it all on Saturday night.'

'Perdita, please . . . I won't stay long, honestly.'

'I'm sorry, Giles, I just don't feel I can trust you to keep that promise.'

Thanet guessed that she had also felt she couldn't trust her husband to keep his temper.

'But I will! I will, honestly ... OK, look, in that case, let's go down to the pub in the village, for a quick drink. We won't stay long, I promise. You can leave whenever you like ...'

'And leave the children alone in the house? Don't be ridiculous. It's out of the question!'

And she had closed the window and gone away again.

'So then what did you do?' said Lineham.

'Well I wasn't going to give up, was I? No way!' Master shook his head. 'After all, as I say, all I wanted to do was talk to her, for God's sake! So I thought, Right, if that's the way she wants it ... If she doesn't mind the children being woken up, that's fine by me. And if Mrs high-and-mighty Vanessa Broxton doesn't like having the police called around to her house, then that's just too bad.'

'So what did you do?'

'Hammered on the door and shouted fit to wake the dead,' said Master with retrospective satisfaction.

It was perhaps the fact that the word was at the end of the sentence that made it seem to hang on the air, reverberate. The brief animation which Master had displayed while he recounted this incident fell away and his expression changed as he returned to the present with a thud. 'Oh God ...'

Thanet waited for a minute or two before saying, 'This needn't take much longer, sir. If you could just finish telling us ...'

Master nodded, took a deep breath, then expelled it slowly. 'She didn't hold out long, of course. I knew she wouldn't.'

After a few minutes Perdita had returned to the window and reluctantly agreed to talk to him outside. A moment or two later she had come out, shutting the front door behind her.

Presumably so that her husband wouldn't force his way in, thought Thanet.

Master had stopped.

'Then what?' said Lineham.

'I was hopping mad,' said Master sullenly, 'at the way she was treating me. After all, she was the one who was in the wrong. She was the one who'd walked out on me, not the other way around...'

Lineham said nothing, waited.

'I didn't see why it all had to be on her terms.'

'So?'

'I told you, I was furious with her...'

Thanet guessed that Master was ashamed of what he had done next, and this was why he was prevaricating. He could also guess what was coming.

Lineham was still waiting.

'I made her get into the car,' muttered Master shamefacedly.

Lineham opened his mouth, shut it again.

Thanet imagined the sergeant had been going to say, 'Made her? How?' and had thought better of it. Sensible perhaps to gloss over the use of force at this point. But it wouldn't have been difficult. Perdita had been small and slight, Master must be a good fifteen stone.

'Then what?' said Lineham.

Master shrugged. 'I'd left the keys in the ignition, so it was easy. I just took off. We went to the pub, as I said.'

Lineham was shaking his head. 'Sorry, sir. After all that I can't see Mrs Master meekly going along and having a drink with you. How did you manage to ... persuade her?'

Master shot him a venomous look. 'All right, so I'm not very proud of myself now...'

Lineham raised his eyebrows.

Master jumped up and went to stand in front of the fire, his back to them. 'Oh hell...' He swung around to face them. 'I simply told her that if she didn't I'd just keep on driving, and the kids would be left alone all night. But if she agreed,

I'd guarantee to get her back to the house in half an hour.'

It had been Hobson's choice for Perdita.

All this had taken no longer than ten or fifteen minutes and they had arrived at the Green Man in Melton at about ten to nine. In the event, it had been a pointless exercise. Perdita had remained adamant. She refused even to consider going back to him and had repeated that nothing would change her mind about seeking a divorce. In the end he had given up. He took her back to the Broxtons' house, arriving there at about twenty past nine and had left at once.

'You didn't go into the house?' said Lineham.

'No. I didn't bother to ask. She'd only have refused. Anyway, there would have been no point. Her mind was made up. I just dropped her off then drove away.'

Lineham glanced at Thanet, eyebrows raised. *Anything else you want to ask?*

Thanet nodded and picked up the plastic carrier bag in which he had put Perdita's sketchbook. He took it out. 'We found this amongst your wife's belongings.' He flicked through it, held up the full-face sketch. 'Can you identify this man?'

The muscles of Master's face froze but he couldn't control the expression in his eyes. Shock, pain, anger, all were there. 'Yes. That's our next-door neighbour, Howard Swain.'

'Drawn by your wife, I assume?' Thanet glanced at the painting on the wall. 'She was an artist, I gather.'

'Yes. She's . . . she was, very talented.' Master nodded at the drawing and said, with an attempt at lightness, 'She was always persuading friends to sit for her. She preferred to draw people she knew than to hire a model. I imagine those are preliminary sketches for a portrait.'

Thanet didn't believe him. The fact that these had been drawn in such detail and probably from memory strongly suggested an emotional involvement on Perdita's part. But if so, Master was doing his best to play it down. Why? Because he couldn't bear to think of her having a lover? Or because knowing that she had a lover would give him a stronger motive for killing her, in the eyes of the police? It was interesting that Swain was their next-door neighbour. Perhaps he, too, was sporting a black eye.

Master looked exhausted. His eyes seemed to have receded deeper into their sockets, the pouches beneath them to have become more pronounced.

Thanet took pity on him. If the man were innocent he needed a respite; he had suffered enough for one evening. And if he were not . . . well, it was obvious that at the moment nothing would shake his story. Further questioning would have to wait until they had something specific to go on. He stood up. 'About the formal identification . . . I'll send someone to pick you up, in the morning.'

Master's lips tightened. 'What time?'

'Nine o'clock?'

A nod. 'Right.'

At the front door Thanet paused. 'That's a nasty black eye you've got there, sir. What happened?'

Master's mouth tugged down at the corners. 'Believe it or not, I walked into a door. I feel such a fool . . . Got up to go to the bathroom during the night, didn't switch the light on . . .'

That old chestnut! In Thanet's opinion Master would have had to run into a door at top speed for the impact to have had that effect. But he merely nodded, murmured his thanks and left.

'Walked into a door!' said Lineham as they got into the car. 'I bet this chap Swain was the reason she was leaving him and after the row on Saturday he went steaming around there and they had a fight.' He peered through the windscreen at the house next door, which was all in darkness. 'Are we going to see Mr Swain now?'

Thanet glanced at the dashboard clock. Nearly one a.m.

'I don't think we've got enough evidence to justify hauling him out of bed at this hour. No, he'll keep till tomorrow. I think we'll call it a day.'

Next morning, he and Ben were having breakfast when the phone rang.

'I'll get it,' called Joan, who was on her way downstairs.

'Yuk!' said Ben, surveying the array of cereal packets on the table. 'Bran, bran and more bran. Oh, sorry, bran, bran, muesli and more bran. Why can't we have rice crispies, or sugar puffs, or even cornflakes . . . ?'

'Stop grumbling,' said Thanet, with only half his attention on the conversation. The phone call was probably for him. 'High fibre is good for you.'

The door to the hall was ajar and he heard Joan say, 'Oh, no! When was this?'

Her tone told him that this was bad news. His stomach lurched. Bridget. Something had happened to Bridget. He got up and went to the door.

Joan was facing him, clutching the phone in both hands. Her expression confirmed that this was serious. In a series of lightning vignettes his ever-fertile imagination presented him with a succession of images, each more horrendous than the last: Bridget lying in the road, injured and bleeding; Bridget flying through the windscreen of a car, her face cut to shreds; Bridget lying, as he had seen so many people lie in premature death, sheeted in the morgue, a label on her toe the only vestige of her identity . . . Joan covered the receiver, whispered, 'My mother. Heart attack.'

The relief was only momentary. Thanet was very fond of his mother-in-law, had got to know her particularly well when she had come to live with him and the children while Joan was completing her training for the Probation service. He put his arm around Joan's shoulders. 'She's not . . . ?'

Joan shook her head.

This time the relief was heartfelt.

Joan said, 'I'll get there as soon as I can.' She put the phone down. 'That was Mrs Parker, Mum's next-door neighbour. They were supposed to go shopping together in Maidstone this morning and wanted to leave early, to get in before the rush. She went out to get the milk at half past seven, noticed Mum's curtains were all still drawn, no lights on. There was no answer to her knock so she let herself in, she's got a key...'

'What's the matter?' Ben was standing at the kitchen door, listening. 'Is it Gran?'

Joan nodded, biting her lip.

'She's not...?' said Ben, echoing his father.

'No, of course not! She's...' Joan hesitated, clearly wondering how much to tell him.

'What?'

Joan glanced at Thanet. *Shall I?*

'Oh *Mum*!' said Ben. 'Come on! I'm not a baby, you know. What's the matter with her?'

'She's had a heart attack.'

Ben's fingers tightened on the doorpost. 'Oh...' He put the question that Thanet had been waiting to ask. 'How serious is it?'

'Mrs Parker didn't know. But fortunately it seems to have happened not long before she got there – Mum had just got out of bed, they think... Mrs Parker called an ambulance and they got there very quickly. They've taken her to Sturrenden General.'

The muscles of Joan's shoulders were rigid with tension beneath Thanet's arm.

'I must go,' she said. She put her hand to her head. 'Let me think. What have I got to do, first? I'll have to let them know, at work...' She glanced at her watch. 'But that'll be all right, I can do that later.'

'I'll do it for you, if you like.'

'No, it's all right, I'll have to speak to Janice myself, get her to reorganise my day. Fortunately there's nothing especially . . . Oh no . . . There was one particularly important appointment this morning. With Sharon . . .'

Sharon Strive was a young single parent with two small children who after a long history of shoplifting was making a serious attempt to go straight. Joan had been working with her for some time.

'She's not on the phone, either, there's no way of getting in touch with her.'

'Someone from the office will go around and explain, I'm sure. She'll understand, in the circumstances. First things first.' He pushed Joan gently towards the stairs. 'Go on, get ready.'

'I just hate letting people down, especially someone like her, who hasn't got anyone else.'

'Get your coat,' said Thanet. 'I'll see to everything here. And I'll ring the hospital and get along as soon as I can.'

'No, don't worry, I'll ring you as soon as I find out the position. You'll be so busy today, with this new case. How long will you be at the office?'

Thanet thought rapidly. 'Till about 9.30, I should think.'

'Right.' Joan hurried upstairs and Thanet went to move his car out of the drive, so that she could get hers out of the garage.

For once Thanet arrived in good time at Draco's morning meeting. Very little of interest had come in overnight and he had left Lineham to organise various tasks for the team: a preliminary, low-key call at the Swains' house, an interview with Mrs Broxton's housekeeper, house-to-house enquiries in the vicinity of the Broxtons' home. The PM had been fixed for that afternoon.

Draco was standing at the window when Thanet entered, looking out at the forecourt, hands clasped behind his back.

'Ah, good morning, Thanet. Take a seat. Sorry I couldn't get along last night.'

He offered no explanation, Thanet noted.

Draco sat down heavily at his desk.

There was definitely something wrong with him, thought Thanet. All the Superintendent's usual bounce and verve had drained away. The jet-bright blackness of his eyes was dulled and even his crisp, dark, springing hair seemed more limp and lifeless than usual. Perhaps it was Draco himself who was ill, or at least well below par.

Chief Inspector Tody, Draco's deputy, sidled in in his usual irritatingly deferential manner, followed soon afterwards by Inspector Boon of the uniformed branch, a long-time friend and colleague of Thanet.

The meeting began as it always did with a brief summary of the previous day's proceedings by each of them. The murder of Perdita Master at Melton was by far the most serious crime to report, and of necessity Thanet's report was the longest. Draco would normally have peppered Thanet with questions, but today his interest was little more than cursory. Apart from a brief flare of interest at the fact that the murder had taken place at Vanessa Broxton's house ('You'll have to be careful not to tread on too many toes there, Thanet'), he said little until Thanet had finished. Then, with a visible effort, he said, 'Not much to go on at the moment, then?'

'No, sir. Only the polythene bag.'

'Well, you never know what we might learn from that. Every contact leaves a trace, remember, Thanet. Every contact leaves a trace.'

'Yes, sir,' said Thanet, suppressing his irritation. He did wish Draco wouldn't treat him like a raw recruit half the time! Boon's ironic wink made him feel a little better.

'Right,' said Draco, laying both palms flat on his desk.

This was the usual signal for the meeting to end and all three men began to rise.

'Er ... There's just one other thing,' said Draco.

They subsided into their chairs again.

Draco picked up a pencil and began fiddling with it, tapping on the desk and turning it in his fingers. 'Er . . .'

Thanet and Boon glanced at each other. What was coming? Draco was usually positive, decisive, the words tumbling over each other in his haste to get them out, or rolling forth in the sonorous, measured cadences of a Welsh preacher.

'I had hoped it wouldn't come to this, but . . .' Draco compressed his lips. 'I'm afraid, however, that it looks as though I am going to have to make somewhat heavier demands than usual upon you, so . . .'

He glanced at each of them in turn, his gaze sombre, assessing.

'It seems likely,' he said carefully, 'that in the near future I shall have to take time off occasionally.' He lifted his chin, almost pugnaciously, as if preparing himself to meet whatever blows fate had in store for him. 'My wife is ill, and she is going to have to go to London for time to time for treatment. Naturally I shall go with her . . .' He was looking at his desk, unable to meet their gaze, afraid perhaps that the sympathy in their eyes would unman him.

There was a moment's silence while his three subordinates glanced at each other, united in shock and sympathy. Then Tody cleared his throat and said, 'We're very sorry to hear that, sir. We hope the treatment will be effective very quickly and meanwhile, please, don't worry about what will happen at work. I know I speak for all of us when I say we'll be only too willing to stand in or work overtime whenever it's necessary.'

Draco risked a glance at them. 'Thank you.'

It was obvious that his self-control was precarious and in unspoken agreement his three subordinates rose and left the room. Outside they conferred in low tones. 'Sounds serious,' said Tody gloomily.

'If it is, it'll hit him hard,' said Boon.

'Don't talk as though she's dead already!' said Thanet. 'We don't know what's wrong yet. Could be something that'll respond to treatment.'

Boon shrugged. 'Let's hope so.'

When Thanet told Lineham the sergeant snapped his fingers. 'I forgot to tell you ... Louise told me this morning that she'd run into one of her friends from Sturrenden General yesterday and she'd told her that Mrs Draco has leukaemia.'

'Oh, no ... How serious is it? Aren't some types of leukaemia curable nowadays?'

The phone rang: Joan, with news of her mother. Mrs Bolton was in intensive care and the nursing staff would say no more than that it was too early to tell. Joan was going to stay at the hospital all day, if necessary.

'I'll probably have to see someone in the hospital later on this morning,' said Thanet. 'I'll try and get along to see you at the same time.' He wouldn't tell Joan about Angharad Draco at the moment.

'Oh good. See you then.'

Thanet put the phone down. 'Bit of an avalanche of doom and despair this morning, eh, Mike?'

'I expect we'll survive, sir. We usually seem to. Meanwhile ...'

Meanwhile, thank God, there was work to be done.

'Who first, then, sir?'

'Better go and see Mrs Master's parents, I suppose.'

'Not Mr Master? Or Mr Swain?'

Thanet shook his head. 'Mr Master is doing the identification at the moment. And anyway, as I said last night, I want to see if we can get something a bit more concrete before we go back to him. With any luck Perdita Master confided in either her mother or her stepfather. And Mr Swain can wait. He won't run away.'

'We hope,' murmured Lineham *sotto voce*, as they picked up their coats and headed for the door.

SIX

In comparison with today's sprawling conurbations the Pilkington estate in Sturrenden is positively cosy, consisting of no more than a few pleasant tree-lined streets of 1930s houses. Wayside Crescent backs on to school playing fields and Perdita Master's mother and stepfather lived in one of the few detached houses. It was typical of the era, with generous bay windows upstairs and down and an arched entrance porch floored with quarry tiles. The place was spick and span, with neat front garden, weed-free drive, fresh paintwork and shining windows.

The man who opened the front door was, Thanet guessed, usually equally neat, the type who feels most comfortable in suit and tie and whose only concession to leisure wear would be to discard his jacket in favour of a knitted cardigan. This morning the suit was appropriately sombre, dark grey worsted, with white shirt and black tie. The tie, however, was ill-knotted, a shoelace on one of his highly polished black shoes was trailing, and there was a small whitish patch on his jawline where he had cut himself while shaving and dabbed the spot with a styptic stick.

'Mr Harrow?' Thanet introduced himself and Lineham.

Harrow's jowls quivered as he clenched his teeth. 'I still can't believe it . . .' He stepped back. 'Come in.'

He was in his mid-fifties, shortish and plump, verging on fat, with a round face, double chin, pale watery blue eyes and a few strands of hair trying to conceal the fact that he was virtually bald.

He led them into a stiflingly hot sitting room which was neat if somewhat insipid, with pale green walls, deeper green curtains and a fitted carpet in shades of green and beige. It was comfortably furnished with settee, matching armchairs, and bookshelves in the alcoves on either side of the gas fire with its imitation logs. The most striking feature was the painting on the opposite wall, one of Perdita's, Thanet guessed. Here was a night-time garden, the pale disc of the moon floating through swollen, swirling masses of sombre cloud. In the foreground was a forest of white lilies, ghostly in the moonlight, their pale, delicate trumpets upturned as if in worship of the silver goddess of the night.

Harrow acknowledged Thanet's evident interest. 'Perdita painted that. A birthday present for my wife. Do sit down.'

Excess flesh strained against fabric at shoulder, thigh, stomach and crotch as Harrow lowered himself into an armchair.

Thanet sat on the settee, deliberately choosing to turn his back on the painting. It had a kind of magnetic power, drawing the eye and nailing the attention, altogether too distracting while conducting an interview. Even so, he could visualise it, almost *feel* it on the wall behind him, exerting its strange fascination.

Lineham took the other armchair. He and Thanet preferred not to sit next to each other at interviews. It was important for them to be able to see each other's face. Unspoken communication was an essential part of their routine.

'Such a waste,' said Harrow, shaking his head.

Thanet was already beginning to feel uncomfortably hot. How could people live in such a temperature?

Lineham was also feeling the heat. Like Thanet, the sergeant had already removed his overcoat and was unbuttoning his jacket.

'I'm very sorry about your stepdaughter. It must have been a terrible shock to you.'

Harrow inclined his head. 'Yes. And the worst part of it is, I've still got to tell my wife. She's in hospital.'

'Yes, I know.'

Harrow leaned forward anxiously. 'You haven't told her yourself, I hope?'

Thanet shook his head. 'We thought it best to leave it to you.'

'Good.' Harrow pulled a face. 'I say "good" but I'm dreading it. She's got enough on her plate to cope with as it is. Anyway, I guessed you'd come around this morning so I thought I'd wait to visit her in case you had any news. Have you?'

'It's too early yet, I'm afraid. We came to see you to fill in a little of the background.'

'In what way?'

'It's important that we should understand what has been going on lately in your stepdaughter's life.'

'You're not saying she was ... that this has happened ... that someone she *knows* was responsible for her death? I assumed it was some maniac who had broken in ... One hears so much of that sort of thing these days.'

'At this stage we simply don't know. So if we could ...'

Harrow heaved himself up out of his armchair and began to walk about. 'But that's impossible! Ludicrous! Unless ...'

Abruptly, he stopped walking and turned to stare at Thanet.

'Unless what?'

Harrow shook his head. 'Nothing.'

'Oh come, Mr Harrow. Obviously a thought struck you, just then.'

But Harrow again shook his head, stubbornly. 'It was nothing, really.'

Thanet guessed that Harrow was thinking of Perdita's husband, of the quarrel. He decided not to press the point at the moment. 'Anyway, it's essential that at this point we take as broad a view as possible, and gather some background information. So if you could answer a few questions . . .?'

Harrow returned to his chair, sat down again. He lifted his sausage-like fingers in a gesture of surrender. 'Of course. Anything to help.'

Thanet was beginning to sweat. 'I wonder if, before we begin, we could perhaps have the door open?'

'Of course.'

Lineham jumped up with alacrity, opened it as wide as it would go.

'Sorry,' said Harrow. 'I always forget how hot people find it. I've got used to it by now, of course. It's my wife. She can't stand the cold, always has to have the place like a hothouse. Only yesterday, in the hospital, she was complaining about the temperature in there. All the other women were sitting up in frilly nighties and she was practically shivering. When I went back in the evening I had to take a woollen bedjacket in for her. Sorry, I'm rambling . . . I can't seem to think straight this morning . . . What did you want to know?'

As arranged, Lineham began the questioning and they soon learnt that Perdita's father had died when she was ten and that her mother had remarried two years later. The young girl had been very fond of her father and despite every effort on Harrow's part had found it difficult to adjust to having a stepfather.

Harrow shook his head sorrowfully. 'I'm afraid she never really forgave me for taking her father's place. I've often thought it was just as well Stephanie didn't come along until we'd given up hoping she might – that's our other daughter. She's thirteen now.'

Perdita would have been in her twenties by then, Thanet worked out.

'I think Perdita would have found it even more difficult, if she'd had to share her mother with a baby. As it was, by the time Steph arrived Perdita had been away to college and when she did come home to visit she was more like a mother than a sister to her.'

'How is Stephanie taking the news of her death?'

Harrow compressed his lips. 'She doesn't know yet. I haven't been able to pluck up sufficient courage to tell her.'

'What did you tell her last night, after my men had called? Or didn't she wake up?'

'She wasn't here. She's staying with a friend while her mother's in hospital. You know what girls of that age are like. Any excuse to stay at one another's houses...'

Thanet grinned. 'My daughter was just the same.'

'It's very convenient, really. My hours are rather irregular. I'm Deputy Head at St Michael's Primary and I often have to get to school early, or leave late. Steph goes to Sturrenden High and it's always Ros – my wife – who does the school run. So when Stephanie suggested staying with Diana...'

Thanet nodded. Harrow didn't exactly fit Thanet's image of a deputy head, but then the man couldn't be expected to be at his best this morning.

'Steph was here over the weekend, of course. Actually, that was another reason why I was glad she suggested staying with Diana. If Giles – that's my son-in-law, Perdita's husband – was going to keep coming around here causing trouble ... I didn't like the idea that he might come when I was out and Steph was here alone. I'm not sure she'd have been able to cope ... You did know that Perdita and her husband had separated?'

'Yes,' said Thanet. 'And we knew Mr Master had come here once, on Saturday night, but you said, *keep* coming around and causing trouble ... He came more than once, then?'

'He came back on Sunday and then again on Monday.'

Thanet glanced at Lineham. 'Let's take it in sequence, go back to Saturday night.'

'What, exactly, did happen on Saturday night?' said Lineham.

Briefly, so briefly that Thanet wondered if he had imagined it, some memory or thought flickered in Harrow's eyes, was quickly suppressed. Then he ran his hand over his head, gingerly patting the carefully layered strands. 'Perdita arrived at about – let me see – ten o'clock or thereabouts. She didn't say much, just that she and Giles had had a row and could she have a bed for the night? Naturally I said yes. She had just gone upstairs when Giles rang to see if she was here. Perdita refused to speak to him and asked me to tell him she didn't want to see him. The next thing we knew he was banging at the door, demanding to be let in.'

'And did you let him in?'

'No, of course not.' Harrow contrived to be both brusque and self-righteous. 'If Perdita didn't want to see him, that was that, as far as I was concerned. He kicked up a dreadful row, half the street was on the doorstep wondering what was happening . . . In the end I said if he didn't leave I'd call the police. So he went away. But he was back by ten the next morning. Fortunately Perdita had already gone out, so he went off fairly quietly.'

'Where had she gone?'

Harrow shook his head. 'No idea. I got up late and she had already left.'

'Had she taken her stuff with her?'

'No, not then. Not that she had much, just a small grip. She came back and collected that in the afternoon.'

'Did she say where she'd been?'

'To visit her mother in hospital, she said. I knew she was going, we'd arranged it the night before – that she'd go in the afternoon and I'd go in the evening.'

'What about Stephanie?'

'She was going on a school trip to London on Sunday afternoon, some exhibition at the Barbican ... When her mother was unexpectedly called into hospital Steph said she wouldn't go, but my wife insisted that nothing would be happening, medically speaking, on a Sunday and it was pointless Steph missing her trip for no good reason.'

'Did Mrs Master tell you where she was going, when she collected her bag?'

'Yes. She said she'd run into an old school friend of hers at the hospital, and she was going to stay with her for a few days. She gave me the address and telephone number, in case I needed to get in touch with her about her mother, and asked me not to tell Giles where she was.'

'And did he come back?'

'Yes. He was knocking on the door at eight o'clock next morning. He was furious that I wouldn't tell him where she was.'

'So Mrs Master left here on Sunday morning some time before ten o'clock and didn't get back until ... ?'

'About four.'

'And apart from the time she spent visiting her mother, you've no idea where she was or who she went to see?'

'No idea at all.'

Lineham glanced at Thanet. *Anything else?*

Once again Thanet produced the sketch.

Harrow frowned at it, holding it at arm's length. 'I'm pretty certain – yes, that's Perdita and Giles's neighbour. Swain, that's his name. Howard, I think. Arty-crafty type. Knits.'

Lineham's eyebrows shot up. 'Knits?'

Harrow waved a hand. 'Calls himself a knitwear designer. His wife's something high-powered in TVS.'

'Were he and Mrs Master anything more than friends?' asked Thanet.

Harrow looked taken aback. 'Were they having an affair, you mean? I've no idea. It's possible, I suppose. They both worked at home, so there was plenty of opportunity. But if so, it's the first I've heard of it ... Perhaps that's what the row was about, on Saturday night.'

'Did you know that Mrs Master was asking for a divorce?'

Harrow's plump lips pursed into a silent whistle. 'No wonder Giles was in such a state! He's always been somewhat, shall we say ...' He broke off, aware perhaps of the potential significance of what he was saying.

'Possessive?' said Thanet. 'Jealous, even?'

Harrow looked uncomfortable. 'He's always been very fond of Perdita ... Look, Inspector, if there's nothing else ... I feel I really must get along to the hospital as soon as possible, in case my wife hears about it from someone else.'

'Don't worry. Your stepdaughter's name is not being released until this afternoon.'

Harrow looked relieved. 'Oh good. But still ...'

Thanet hesitated. He very much wanted to go to the hospital himself, to find out how his mother-in-law was. He had intended to go later, after seeing Swain. But perhaps it would be useful to talk to Mrs Harrow, first, if she were well enough to be interviewed. Thanet's guess was that if Perdita and Swain had been having an affair, it might well have been Swain she went to see on Sunday morning. If she had confided in her mother when she saw her on Sunday afternoon Mrs Harrow might be able to confirm this. He made up his mind, stood up. 'We'll come along to the hospital with you.'

Harrow looked alarmed. 'You're not going to talk to my wife? She won't be up to it. She was very fond of Perdita, this is really going to hit her hard.'

'Don't worry,' said Thanet. 'If your wife doesn't want to talk to us, she needn't. It'll be entirely up to her. I have to go to the hospital anyway, for another reason.'

Harrow was still looking doubtful. 'I wouldn't want to put

any pressure on her. She's got enough on her plate at the moment, without this.'

'Don't worry,' said Thanet gently. 'We're not inhuman, Mr Harrow. We won't do anything to distress your wife, I assure you.'

Harrow stood up reluctantly. 'I'll get my coat.'

SEVEN

'How is she?' said Thanet.

He had gone straight to intensive care, leaving Lineham with Harrow. On the way to the hospital it had been agreed that Harrow should see his wife alone to break the news to her as best he could, and that they would then enlist medical opinion to try to assess whether or not she was up to talking to Thanet and Lineham.

Joan's smile of greeting faded as she shook her head. 'Conscious. I've seen her ... She's holding her own at the moment but we won't know for some time, apparently, whether she's going to be all right. She could have another attack at any time, we just have to wait and see ... The risk is greatest, apparently, in the first twenty-four hours.'

Thanet comforted Joan as best he could. She and her mother – her father had died some time ago – had always been close and this was very hard for her, he knew. Then, after a brief glimpse of his mother-in-law alarmingly surrounded by wires and machines, he made his way through the labyrinthine corridors of the hospital to the women's medical ward, where he found Lineham leafing through a tattered copy of *Homes & Gardens* in the waiting room.

'He's still with her,' said Lineham, tossing the magazine on to a low table. 'He said he'll tell her we'd like a word with her and see how she reacts. The Sister is being very helpful, she understands the situation. She says there's no reason why we shouldn't talk to Mrs Harrow as long as she is willing.'

'Good.' Thanet was relieved. He had meant what he said to Harrow: if Mrs Harrow didn't want to talk to them, then that would be that. All the same, he hoped that she would agree to do so. He very much wanted to learn more about Perdita Master.

'What, exactly, is she in for?'

'A whole battery of tests. Harrow says she's never had very good health but this time she's apparently been ill for months with one of these mystery viruses that no one can identify. Now they're making one final attempt to get to the bottom of it.'

A few minutes later a pretty young coloured nurse came into the room. 'Sister says you can talk to Mrs Harrow now. We've transferred her to one of the side wards.'

The Ward Sister met them at the door. 'I've told Mrs Harrow that it's up to her to say when the interview is to stop.'

Thanet nodded. 'That's fine by us.'

His first sight of Rosamund Harrow shook him and he at once understood the general aura of protectiveness which seemed to surround her. She was sitting in a chair beside the bed, wearing a thick woollen dressing gown. On top of that, around her shoulders was draped a blue woollen bedjacket, presumably the one Harrow had brought in the previous evening, and over her knees was a tartan rug. Even so, despite all this camouflage, nothing could disguise her emaciation. The ankles which protruded from beneath the rug were mere sticks, the hands bundles of bones, the head little more than a skull encased in skin stretched tight. To him it looked as though this was a hopeless case, that disease had already almost won the battle against medical science. If he had known she was in this condition he wouldn't have dreamt of interviewing her unless it were absolutely essential. However, it was too late to back out now without causing her embarrassment. Harrow was sitting beside her, one arm around her shoulders.

'Mrs Harrow, I really am sorry to trouble you.'

Her lips quivered and she pressed them hard against each other for a moment before speaking. 'I...' She cleared her throat, tried again, 'I do understand that it's necessary. In the...' She shook her head as tears began to spill over and trickle down her cheeks.

'Look, let's just forget this, shall we? It's not essential that I speak to you at the moment. I'll come back later, when you've had a little time...' Privately, Thanet was resolved not to come back at all unless it were absolutely unavoidable. It had been stupid anyway, even to consider interviewing a sick woman five minutes after she'd heard her daughter had been murdered. What could he have been thinking of?

She shook her head, wiping her eyes with a balled-up handkerchief. 'No. It's all right, really. I'd like to help, if I can.'

Thanet was already at the door. He hesitated, glancing at Harrow.

Harrow said, 'I think my wife really would prefer you to stay.'

'Yes, I would. Please, Inspector, do sit down – if you can find something to sit on, that is.'

'You're sure?'

She nodded.

Thanet felt he had no choice. 'Fetch us a couple of chairs, would you, Sergeant?'

Lineham disappeared, returning a few moments later with two plastic-topped stools.

'If you feel you've had enough at any point, just say the word.'

She nodded, attempted a smile. 'Thank you. You're very kind.'

Thanet didn't feel in the least kind, he felt a monster. 'It's just that we thought you may be able to fill us in a little on your daughter's background.'

She waited, her brown eyes huge in their sunken sockets.

'We understand Mrs Master came to see you on Sunday afternoon?'

She nodded. 'Yes. She ... She wanted me to know that she and Giles – her husband – were splitting up, that she'd asked for a divorce.' Mrs Harrow gave Harrow an apologetic glance. 'She also told me that she'd fallen in love with someone else. I'm sorry, love, I couldn't tell you that before, she asked me not to say anything to anybody at the moment.'

'Did she say who the man was?' said Harrow.

His wife shook her head. 'No. But I certainly can't blame her, after what she went through with Giles, can you?'

'So,' said Thanet, 'her news didn't exactly surprise you?'

'Only in that I couldn't believe she'd actually plucked up the courage to tell him. No, I knew she hadn't been happy with Giles for a long time.'

'Why was that, do you know?'

'Several things, really. Giles had always been, well, difficult.' She glanced at Harrow.

'I told you,' said Harrow. 'Jealous. Very possessive.'

Mrs Harrow sighed. 'Oh, incredibly. You wouldn't believe ... He had to know every single thing she did. Perdita even had to account to him for every penny she spent. She loved pretty things, nice clothes, but Giles ... He always seemed to think she was dressing to attract other men. I remember once he even tore up a new shirt she'd bought, said it was too revealing, too transparent. I don't know how she stuck it as long as she did.'

Talking seemed to have calmed her down and Thanet was beginning to feel more comfortable about the interview. 'So when she told him she wanted a divorce ... ?'

'He went berserk. Locked her in the bedroom. Would you

believe, she had to get away by climbing out of the window? Luckily there's a little extension at the back and she was able to drop down on to the roof, or she'd have been stuck there.'

'It sounds as though you were really quite relieved to hear they were splitting up.'

'Well, when your daughter's unhappy like that, over a period of years, it's very hard to bear. No, she knew I'd be pleased, that's why she wanted to tell me, and especially about the fact that she'd found someone else.'

'And she really gave no hint as to who he was?'

'No . . . though I think I can guess. But perhaps I shouldn't have said that. He's married and now that she's . . . I wouldn't want to make trouble for him. Perdita wouldn't want me to, I'm sure.' Mrs Harrow shook her head, the tears welling up and spilling over once more. She dabbed them away. 'It seems so unfair. She's had such a rotten time of it and now, just when it seemed . . . It wasn't just her husband, you see, it was her mother-in-law too. She made everything ten times worse.'

'In what way?'

'She couldn't stand Perdita. To tell you the truth, I don't think she could have accepted anyone Giles married. He's an only child, you see.' Mrs Harrow frowned, skin creasing against bone in slack folds. 'The trouble was, it was all done so . . . subtly, I don't know that Giles was even aware of what was going on half the time. But Perdita knew. Oh yes, Perdita knew, all right. And Mrs Master knew she knew.' Mrs Harrow shivered and hugged the dressing gown more tightly around her. 'Horrible woman.'

'I'm not sure I quite understand what you mean.'

'Well, that's the trouble, it's so difficult to explain . . . It's just that whatever Perdita did – or didn't do, whatever she said – or didn't say, Mrs Master would somehow twist things to show that Perdita was wrong, or her method was unsuitable or inferior or naïve or *some*thing. And Perdita herself was too sweet-natured to retaliate. She just put up with it. It used to make me so angry ... And as I say, I'm not sure whether Giles genuinely had no idea of what was going on, whether he knew but chose to ignore it, or whether he did nothing because he simply didn't know how to deal with it. Though I think he did get fed up with his mother always being on their doorstep. She was always round there in the evenings and at weekends.'

'She's a widow, I believe?'

'Yes. A pity, I've always thought, as far as the young people were concerned. If she'd had a husband of her own to look after ... Though I understand she's always been very possessive about Giles. She doesn't seem to have much of a life of her own, does she, Ralph? – no close friends, so far as I know, or other interests.'

Harrow was nodding. 'Could never stand the woman, myself.'

Thanet was aware of Lineham shifting uncomfortably beside him. Perhaps all this was a little too close to home for the sergeant's comfort. He too was an only child and had had to suffer the claustrophobic attentions of a widowed mother.

'She and Giles didn't have much of a social life, either – virtually none, in fact. Giles almost invariably said no to invitations and in the end people stopped asking them. I don't think he could stand the way other men looked at her. Perdita was always very attractive to men, you see. I don't know what it was about her, but right from the time when she was in her teens she used to have a string of boys after her. Actually, when she started work it was a nuisance – she never stayed long in any one job because sooner or later her employer would start hanging around her and either she'd get fed up with it and move on or the wife would get suspicious and give her the sack.'

'Did she enjoy all this admiration?'

'Well it was flattering, of course, when she was younger,

but no, I think she found it more of a nuisance than anything else, especially after she was married, with Giles being so jealous. No, I think the only reason she was able to stick with the marriage so long was because she found her satisfactions elsewhere – in her painting, chiefly, and in her garden. She loved her garden.'

'I've seen some of her work,' said Thanet. 'She was very talented.'

'She was always mad on painting and drawing, right from the time she was a little girl. She should have gone to Art School. She could easily have gone to Maidstone College of Art, or Medway, but no, she had to go and train as a nanny. I know she always loved kids, but it seemed such a waste . . . I blame myself really. She was at the age when if I said "Black", she'd say "White". I was always on at her to go to Art School but the more I pressed the more determined she became not to go. I should have seen what was happening and just shut up, let her go her own way. If I had, I think she would have gone.'

'She never had any children of her own?'

'No. That was a great disappointment to her. Though now, perhaps it's just as well –' Mrs Harrow suddenly clutched at her husband's hand. 'Ralph! I've just thought! Stephanie! Does she know yet?'

'No. I wanted to tell you first.'

'You must go. At once. I couldn't bear it if she heard from someone else. She'll be so upset, she was so fond of Perdita . . .'

Harrow patted her hand. 'It's all right, don't worry. She won't hear from anyone else. The police are not releasing details until this afternoon, are you, Inspector?'

Thanet shook his head. 'No.'

'Oh. But you will make sure . . . ?'

'Of course I will. I promise.'

'Sorry,' she said to Thanet.

'If you'd like to stop, now?'

Mrs Harrow shook her head, slowly, as if her thin neck could not sustain too vigorous a movement. 'No, it's all right. It's just ... No, if there's anything else you want to ask ... I'd rather get it over with.'

'Very well. Her husband, Mr Master, did he mind not having children?'

Her answer was what he expected.

'No. I think he was glad, really. He preferred to have her all to himself.' Her lips quivered again, but she took a deep breath and continued. 'It's so sad, really. I think she was very relieved to have come to a decision, to have actually managed to tell Giles she was leaving him. She looked happier and more optimistic than I'd seen her in years ... Looking back, you know, I don't think she ever really got over her father's death.' She glanced at her husband, squeezed his hand. 'Not that it's any reflection on you, Ralph, but she never did accept you, did she? She'd always been a Daddy's girl, you see, and she changed a lot. Became, well, withdrawn and gloomy. I thought she'd get over it, but she never did. I remember once...' She stopped and her eyes darkened with pain at some memory.

'What?' said Harrow.

She shook her head, sorrowfully. 'I was just thinking ... At one time, in her teens, she used to be obsessed with death. She was forever asking questions about it, questions I couldn't answer. And then, a few years ago, when she was going through an especially difficult patch with Giles, she said to me, "Still, I don't suppose it matters much, does it, Mum? I don't expect I'll have to put up with it much longer." And when I asked her what she meant, she told me that she'd always thought she would die young.' Mrs Harrow's face was becoming even more skull-like, as if the thin layer of flesh upon it were melting away before their eyes. She was staring at her husband without seeing him, looking back into the past and relating it to the present in a way which was evidently almost too painful to bear. 'It's almost,' she whispered, 'as if she knew . . . that she was doomed to die before her time.'

Abruptly she turned her head into Harrow's shoulder and began to weep, harsh, racking sobs which were painful to witness.

Thanet glanced at Lineham. *Time to go.*

Unobtrusively, they withdrew.

EIGHT

Outside in the corridor, Thanet said, 'If I'd known she was in that condition ... Why didn't anyone warn us?'

Lineham shrugged. 'Doesn't sound as though Mrs Master had much of a life, does it? If you ask me we won't have to look much further than her husband. If he could tear up her new blouse simply because he couldn't bear to think of other men seeing her wear it, imagine how he'd react if she told him she'd fallen for someone else! He'd go berserk! I bet you anything he got that black eye in a fight with Swain on Saturday night. I bet that's why he locked her in the bedroom, so that she wouldn't be able to get away while he was beating Swain up. He didn't reckon on her climbing out of the window though, did he?' The thought evidently gave Lineham satisfaction.

'I agree, he does seem the best bet so far. I wonder if forensic will come up with anything useful on that polythene bag. That's what bothers me as far as –'

He stopped as they turned a corner and ran into Vanessa Broxton, casually dressed in jeans and knitted jacket. Her eye shadow was unevenly applied, her mascara smudged, her eyes anxious in their shadowed sockets. The strain of the last twenty-four hours was taking its toll.

She had left the children with the housekeeper. 'I don't

think Angela's really up to having Henry bounce all over her yet,' she said, with an attempt at lightness. 'How are things going, Inspector?'

'Too early to tell at the moment, I'm afraid.'

'If you need me, I'll be at home. I'm not going back to work until I find a reliable temporary nanny. Fortunately, the fact that my case went short means that I'm free at the moment.'

'Have you managed to get in touch with Mr Broxton yet?'

She grimaced. 'No. He's moving about, it's difficult. I expect I'll hear from him this evening, though. He rings every other day, when he's away.'

Back at the car there was a message on the radio. The men who had been to interview Howard Swain reported that Swain appeared to have been in a fight; he too was sporting a black eye.

'Told you!' said Lineham triumphantly. 'Do we go and see him next?'

Thanet nodded. He was curious to meet the third person in the triangle which had seemingly brought Perdita Master to her death. He was inclined to agree with Lineham. It was looking more and more likely that Master was their man. Though, as he had been about to say when they ran into Vanessa Broxton, the polythene bag puzzled him. It seemed out of character. He could see Master losing his temper with his wife, lashing out at her in a jealous rage, but he would have thought that having knocked her down, Master would then have been more likely to be overcome with remorse rather than resort to such a cold-blooded and calculated way of finishing her off. Still, time would tell, no doubt.

Meanwhile, Thanet was content to enjoy the brief drive out to Nettleton. It was a glorious autumn day. The frost which had lain thick upon the grass when he got up this morning was long gone and the sun, now high in a sky of pure unblemished blue, illuminated the glowing colours of the foliage in trees and hedgerows: the gold of oak, the lemon, butter-yellow and apricot of field-maple, the scarlet of hawthorn berry, the frothy cream of old man's beard, all set against the tender green of winter wheat and the rich chocolate furrows of newly-ploughed fields. Thanet loved the gentle, rolling curves of the Kentish landscape, the undulating skyline of the North Downs, the sense that the countryside was gradually preparing to settle down into its winter sleep.

Apart from the occasional tractor the roads were quiet, Nettleton asleep in the noonday hush. As they approached the Masters' home Lineham slowed down so that they could take a better look at it by daylight. It was a substantial house, built probably in the sixties, Thanet guessed. Its proportions were good, the windows generous and the grounds extensive and well maintained. They glimpsed a man with a wheelbarrow raking up leaves on the lawn.

'Full-time gardener by the look of it,' said Lineham.

'I doubt it. Her mother said that Mrs Master loved her garden and implied that she spent a lot of time in it. He probably comes in once or twice a week to do routine maintenance.'

'What would two people want with a house that size anyway? And I wonder how he got planning permission?'

Thanet didn't respond. He was used to Lineham's twinges of envy over other people's life-styles.

'This'll be the Swains'.'

A five-barred gate stood open at the entrance to another gravelled drive, but the house was very different, a long low black and white timbered Elizabethan dwelling with a tilting roof-line and leaded windows.

'Ve-ry nice,' said Lineham as they got out of the car.

The Masters' house, Thanet guessed, had been built in part of the original grounds of this one, perhaps replacing a range of stables or outbuildings. No one would get away with that these days. In the country old was now considered sacred.

Thanet often thought that it was a pity the same principles had not been applied to the towns. The county town of Maidstone, for instance, had been ruined by the wholesale destruction of old buildings replaced by characterless blocks of offices and ugly warehouse-style temples to consumerism.

But the charm of a house like the Swains' would never fade. It sat in the landscape as if it had grown there, the very materials of which it was constructed hewn from local timber, culled from local tilefields, local earth. Thanet's own preference was for brick and tile-hanging, but he couldn't help admiring such a picturesque tribute to the skill of Elizabethan craftsmen.

Lineham was already wielding the heavy iron ring-knocker on the front door, the hammer-like blows reverberating in the still, sun-drugged air. Thanet walked across to join him, admiring the late-blooming yellow roses trained across the front of the house, the well-tended borders crammed with cottage-garden plants. Here was another keen gardener, it seemed. Perhaps that was how Perdita Master and Swain had first got to know each other well – over the garden fence, so to speak.

'Yes?'

A shock of recognition. Despite the purple and yellow bruising around Swain's left eye, the strip of plaster along his jawbone, he was immediately recognisable as the man in Perdita Master's sketches. She had captured exactly his air of sensitivity, the impression of a mind engaged elsewhere in some aesthetic activity.

'Oh, not again,' said Swain, when they introduced themselves. 'I've had you lot around once this morning already.'

'Yes, I know, I'm sorry. But I wouldn't trouble you if I didn't think it necessary.'

Swain stood back with ill grace. 'You'd better come in.'

The room into which he led them was low and square, with massive overhead beams and a huge inglenook fireplace.

It was comfortably if conventionally furnished with chintz curtains and matching loose covers on chairs and sofa. Through an open door at the rear Thanet caught a tantalising glimpse of a kaleidoscope of colour: floor-to-ceiling shelves on one wall held a rainbow of coloured cones of wool, and the other visible wall was a huge pinboard covered with vivid sketches, designs and samples of knitted swatches trailing multi-coloured strands.

Here was more common ground between the two. Perdita and Swain were both artists, united in their love of beauty, colour and form.

Swain himself was presumably wearing one of his own creations, a rugged masculine heavy-knit sweater in an abstract design of muted earth colours – browns, greens and a deep, rich aubergine.

'I don't know what more I can tell you,' he said as they all sat down.

'Perhaps I ought to show you this,' said Thanet. He took out Perdita's sketchbook and opened it, held it up.

The shock showed in the clenching of Swain's fists, the tightening of his lips, the determined effort he made not to betray emotion. It was clear that he had recognised not only himself but the hand of the artist.

'We found it amongst Mrs Master's possessions, at the house where she was staying. And it's clear, from the preceding sketches, that these were done from memory. An excellent likeness, I'm sure you'll agree.'

'She . . .' Swain paused to clear his throat, take a deep breath to steady his voice. 'She had brilliant recall.'

'Interesting that during her very brief stay at Mrs Broxton's house, Mrs Master should have spent most of her spare time drawing you.'

Swain said nothing, just shook his head slightly, perhaps to deny involvement with Perdita, perhaps to hold emotion at bay.

'It's only fair to tell you that we know Mrs Master wanted a divorce because she had fallen in love with someone else.'

Still Swain did not speak. Perhaps he couldn't trust himself to do so.

'We know too that she told her husband of her intentions on Saturday night, and that they had a row about it ... And of course, we find it very interesting that both you and Mr Master have obviously been involved in a recent fight.'

This time Swain opened his mouth, but Thanet held up a hand, forestalling him. 'Please, don't insult us by telling us that you, too, walked into a door. We're not idiots, Mr Swain. The inference from all this is quite clear, and sooner or later the truth is bound to come out. It would be easier all round, I think, if you were frank with us now.'

Swain was looking down at his hands, rubbing the side of one thumb with the other, his jaw muscles clenched.

Thanet waited, to give the man time to think it over, and then said softly, 'Don't think that we don't understand your position, Mr Swain. It must be an unbearable strain on you, to have lost the woman you loved and not be able to mourn her openly.' He meant it. Although in his heart he could not condone adultery, he could recognise and sympathise with suffering when he saw it.

Compassion prevailed where reason had not. Swain made a small, choking sound and jumped up, went to stand with his back to them at one of the windows, his shoulders jerking with stifled sobs. After a few moments he took out a handkerchief and furtively wiped his eyes, blew his nose.

Why were so many men ashamed of showing emotion? Thanet wondered. What could be more natural than to show grief at the death of a loved one? The tradition of the stiff British upper lip had a lot to answer for. Far better to mourn openly, acknowledge and come to terms with a sense of loss, than to drive it underground to fester perhaps for years to come.

At last Swain turned to face them again. 'I must apologise, Inspector.'

'Please don't. It would be presumptuous to say I know how you feel, because I've never been in your position. Shall I just say that I find your reaction entirely natural.'

Swain managed a faint smile of gratitude now, and returned to his chair. He blew his nose once more then put his handkerchief away, in control of himself again. 'You're right, of course. What's the point of denying it? Perdita and I were in love...' Briefly his voice wavered and he took another deep breath. 'We had planned to marry, eventually, when we were free...'

Thanet waited, willing for Swain to set the pace. Now that the man had begun to talk he would go on.

'She had a terrible time with him, you know. He was impossibly, insanely jealous. He wanted her all to himself, all the time. He didn't want her to go out or do anything, ever, except with him. She was becoming virtually a prisoner in her own home. It hadn't got to the stage where he actually locked her in, but she could see that coming, in the not-too-distant future. He'd ring her up at all times of the day, to make sure she was there, and if she wasn't, when he came home he'd question her. Where had she been? Who had she seen? What had they done? What had she bought? Which shops had she been into? It was as if he wanted to be with her physically or vicariously twenty-four hours a day, and as you can imagine she was suffocated by it.' Swain shook his head. 'I'd have gone mad, if someone had invaded my privacy to that extent ... I often wondered why she chose me, you know, and I suppose the answer is quite simple. I was *there*.'

Thanet risked a question. Swain was well launched now. 'Wasn't Mr Master suspicious of you, living next door and working at home?'

'Oh God, yes. In fact, Perdita and I had to pretend we couldn't bear the sight of each other. In public we treated each other with icy politeness, no more. We knew that if either of us showed even the slightest sign of interest in the other Giles would up sticks and go, and then Perdita would have been totally isolated ... And that wasn't all she had to put up with. There was his mother, too. She couldn't stand Perdita. Well, I don't know if that's strictly true. What she couldn't stand was the thought of her son having a wife, with first claim upon him. Especially if he was as obsessed with her as Giles was with Perdita. Not that she showed it overtly, mind. On the surface she was all sweetness and light, but she never missed a chance, by innuendo, to underline Perdita's failings and make her miserable. But it was all done so subtly that I don't think Giles was even aware of it ... Anyway, it got to the stage where we were both sick and tired of the situation, and decided to pluck up the courage to tell our respective partners simultaneously, on Saturday night. We were both dreading it, but Perdita especially, as you can imagine. She was afraid of what he might do. I begged her to let me be with her when she told him, but she was adamant that she wanted to do it alone. She said she owed him that much, not to humiliate him in front of me ... So we arranged that I would be here and that if there was any trouble she would ring me ...'

He paused, gave Thanet a rueful glance. 'You've guessed what happened, or some of it, anyway. There was an almighty row and Giles dragged Perdita up to their bedroom and locked her in. Fortunately there's an extension below their window, and she managed to climb out and get away while he was here. He came around straight away, of course, as soon as he'd locked her up. The second I opened the door he came bursting in, knocked me flying. I tried to retaliate, but he's much bigger and stronger than me and it only took a few blows to floor me.' Swain's hand went up and gingerly touched the strip of plaster along his jawline. 'I hit the back of my head on something and passed out. Apparently he just stood there shouting at me to get up and fight like a man, but when he saw I was out cold he gave me one final kick in the ribs and stormed off.' This time Swain's hand massaged the left side of his rib cage. 'I've got the most psychedelic bruise you ever saw, down here.'

'You said, "apparently". Your wife was a witness to all this?'

'Yes. It was she who told me what happened after I passed out. The whole thing was a nightmare.' Swain rubbed a hand wearily across his eyes. 'Thank God the children are away at boarding school.'

'And it was presumably Mrs Master who told you how her husband reacted when she broke the news to him.'

'Yes, when she rang me on Saturday night, from her mother's house. We arranged to meet on Sunday morning, to discuss what she was going to do next. Obviously she couldn't go home again...'

So that was where Perdita had gone. Her stepfather had told them that she had already left when he got up on Sunday morning. Thanet was pleased that they were gradually building up a picture of her movements over the last couple of days before she died. 'How long did you stay together?'

'Until after lunch. She was going to visit her mother in hospital in the afternoon. Mrs Harrow has been ill for some time, and they've never succeeded in finding out exactly what is wrong with her. She's been waiting for a bed at Sturrenden General so that they could take her in and really try to get at the root of it. Apparently they rang up on Saturday morning to say that a bed had unexpectedly become available and could she come in straight away. She didn't tell Perdita because she didn't want to worry her. She knew Perdita was having a bad time at home, and she was only going to be in for a few days. It wasn't as though they were going to operate...'

'So when Mrs Master went to her mother's house on

Saturday night she didn't know Mrs Harrow wouldn't be there?'

'No. She didn't find out until she got there.'

'Was she upset, that she hadn't been told?'

'Yes. And angry with her stepfather, that he hadn't let her know in spite of her mother's wishes.'

Remembering how ill Mrs Harrow had looked, Thanet wasn't surprised. If Perdita had been fond of her mother, as apparently she was, she would have wanted to know exactly what was happening, however worrying it might be.

'So when you parted, after lunch on Sunday, Mrs Master had no specific plan in mind?'

'No. She said she'd probably go and stay in a hotel for a few days, give Giles a chance to calm down and get used to the idea that she'd meant what she said, about a divorce. She said she'd be in touch, when she found somewhere. But then later, oh, it must have been about six, she rang to tell me she'd run into an old friend at the hospital, Mrs Broxton. She said Mrs Broxton was in a fix because her nanny had been rushed into hospital with appendicitis and she herself had a case starting the next day which involved her staying away from Monday to Friday – she's a barrister, well, you must know that by now, of course. So they'd agreed to help each other out. Perdita would look after the children until Saturday, while Mrs Broxton tried to find a temporary nanny. Perdita thought that Giles would never find her there . . .'

The implication was strong. *But she was wrong, wasn't she?* Here was someone else who was convinced of Master's guilt.

Thanet would have loved to know how Swain's wife had taken all this, but felt that it would be better to find out for himself. It could be highly relevant. Mrs Swain could be considered to have as good a motive as anyone for getting rid of her rival. Harrow had said she was 'something high-powered in TVS', so presumably she wouldn't be the type to take this sort of situation lying down. Yes, a visit to Mrs Swain should come fairly high on the agenda, depending on how the next interview with Master went.

Meanwhile, there was one more question he wanted to ask and there was no way of putting it tactfully. 'Did you see Mrs Master last night?'

'Last night?' Briefly, something flickered at the back of Swain's eyes, then he shook his head. 'No, I didn't.'

The statement was so unequivocal that Thanet felt there was no point in pursuing the matter at the moment. He was in no mood for a patient breaking down of Swain's resistance at this stage of the interview. But he was left wondering: what was the question he should have asked?

NINE

'Why didn't you ask him where he was last night?' said Lineham, as they walked to the car.

Thanet shrugged. 'Didn't seem much point. He was so positive about not seeing her it would have taken a lot of pressure to get him to change his tune. And frankly, I wasn't prepared to exert it at that stage. I felt he'd had enough for today. Anyway, I really don't think he's involved. What possible motive could he have?'

'With respect, sir . . . What are you grinning at?'

'You. Every time you say, "With respect, sir", I know you're going to disagree. And before you go on, just put through a call to headquarters, will you? Get them to fix up an appointment with Mrs Swain at TVS at 2.30 or thereabouts.'

This took a little longer than expected, owing to the fact that at work Mrs Swain was apparently known under her maiden name of Edge. When the appointment was at last arranged Thanet suggested having lunch at the village pub before seeing Master again. 'We could do with a break.'

'Good idea. I must admit I'm feeling a bit peckish.'

When they had collected their beer and sandwiches and were seated in a quiet corner Thanet picked up their interrupted discussion, quoting Lineham with a grin. '"With respect, sir . . ."'

Lineham grinned sheepishly. 'It's just that I don't necessarily agree with you about Swain. Just say, for example, that he and Mrs Master arranged to meet at the Broxtons' house last night. When he gets there she tells him she's decided not to go ahead with the divorce after all, that she can't face all the hassle it would involve with her husband. They're in the kitchen, she's about to make a hot drink. They have an argument, he grabs her, she pulls away, knocking the saucepan of milk off the cooker. She's off balance and, as we said before, she slips, knocking her head on the corner of the table –'

'And when he sees she's passed out, instead of trying to revive her he whips a handy polythene bag out of his pocket, slips it over her head and waits until she's stopped breathing before leaving. Oh yes, highly credible, I must say!'

Lineham said nothing, just looked slightly crestfallen and took a large mouthful of ham and tomato sandwich. He chewed for a few moments and then shook his head. 'It's that polythene bag that's the trouble, isn't it?'

'Yes. Mind, even if there were no polythene bag I find it difficult to imagine Swain resorting to violence. He's just not the type.'

'I'm not talking about violence, sir. Not really. Just a heated argument which got out of control.'

'Yes, I appreciate that. It was the wrong word to use, for the scenario you were describing. Nevertheless . . .'

'I still think it's possible. We all know that even the mildest of men can get pretty worked up, given the right circumstances. And in this case' – Lineham leaned forward in his eagerness to convince – 'in this case, if she was telling him the affair was over . . . I mean, he'd naturally have been upset wouldn't he, if he was in love with her? And pretty angry too, going through all that for nothing!'

'All that?'

'Telling his wife he wanted a divorce, for one thing. She

might have known nothing about the affair until he told her, on Saturday night. And getting beaten up by Master, for another ... All, as I say, for nothing!'

'I suppose so.' But Thanet was still doubtful. 'This is all wild guesswork, of course. But even if you're right, it's still, as you say, that polythene bag that's the problem. Not so much in terms of availability, it could well have been lying around to hand somewhere in the kitchen, but in terms of the murderer's behaviour. There's a world of difference between causing someone to slip and fall during the course of an argument and cold-bloodedly putting a plastic bag over her head to finish her off. I'm not sure that I could see Master doing that either.'

'I disagree with you there! He's a nasty bit of work, if ever there was one. I can just see him standing there looking down at her and saying to himself, "If I can't have her, no one will." He might regret it afterwards, when he had time to think about it, but at the time ... For that matter, I found it difficult to swallow that after taking her back to the Broxtons' last night he just went meekly home.'

'I'm not so sure. He could have decided to give her a few days to cool off, before trying again.' Thanet opened up his beef sandwich, and peered inside. 'They've been a bit light-handed with the mustard.' He took another bite, chewed. 'The impression I've got is that he wasn't going to give up easily. If he didn't succeed in persuading her one day, he'd just come back the next. And the next. No, I think that whoever killed her truly wanted her dead. And I don't think you could say that about either Master or Swain.'

'Truly wanted her dead,' repeated Lineham thoughtfully. 'The only person I can think of who might possibly fit that description is Mrs Swain.'

'"Might" is the operative word. For all we know she's been longing to get rid of her husband for years and Mrs Master is the last person in the world she'd want dead. No doubt we'll find out when we see her this afternoon.' Thanet drained his glass. 'Finished, Mike?'

'We're still going to see Mr Master next?'

'Of course. Despite what I said about the polythene bag he's still top of our list. Statistically, he has to be.'

There was a silver-grey Peugeot 205 parked in Master's drive alongside his Mercedes.

'Visitors,' said Lineham, as they got out of the car. 'I wonder who.'

'From what we've heard about her, could be his mother.' Thanet hoped it was. He was curious about Mrs Master senior.

While they waited for the door to open he looked around at the garden. Here again was evidence of devotion, skill and artistry. Carefully trained climbers clothed the walls of the house, tubs of winter-flowering pansies stood on either side of the front door, and mixed borders of shrubs and perennials curved away around the beautifully tended lawn, each group of plants a harmonious composition of colour, form and habit.

The door opened.

Not Mrs Master senior, then. This woman was in her mid-forties, a good ten years too young. She was slim, elegant in black and grey silk dress, expensively-styled dark hair curling around her narrow, sharp-featured face. Her reception was cool. 'Yes?'

'Could I have a word with Mr Master, please?'

'He's not seeing anyone at the moment. Can I help? I'm his mother.'

Astonished, Thanet looked again more carefully, but she still didn't look any older to him. No one's idea of a mother-in-law, this.

She was evidently used to this reaction. She was watching him with a spark of amusement in her eyes.

He introduced himself.

'How can I help?'

'We really do need to see Mr Master, I'm afraid.'

'Really! Must you bother him at a time like this?'

'I wouldn't be asking if it weren't essential, Mrs Master.'

'Well I think it's disgraceful! He's shattered, poor lamb, absolutely shattered. He's only just got back from identifying the . . . from the mortuary. I believe it was you who arranged it, Inspector.' The implication was clear. *I'm blaming you for the state he's in and the least you can do is leave him alone.*

'I know. And I'm sorry. But we really must talk to him again.'

She frowned, deep creases appearing between the neatly plucked eyebrows. 'Couldn't you at least leave it till later?'

'I'm afraid not. We have a great deal to do, as I'm sure you can imagine. And now we're here . . .'

She hesitated for a moment longer, clearly debating whether to hold out, calculating her chances of success. She was obviously used to getting her own way. Then she sighed, capitulated. 'Oh, very well, if you must. But do try not to upset him any further.'

Reluctantly she stood back and let them in. She indicated a door at the back of the hall. 'In the kitchen. I was just trying to persuade him to eat. He's got to keep his strength up.'

She followed them into the room and Thanet did not demur. He was eager to observe the relationship between mother and son. Perdita had apparently found it very difficult to cope with. Thanet wasn't surprised.

Master was sitting head in hands at the kitchen table, which was laid for two: silver cutlery, crisply folded napkins and shining crystal wine glasses. Again, the message was clear. *She's gone, but I'm still here to look after you.* The arrangement of yellow chrysanthemums in the centre of the table was a small explosion of colour in the room, which was all white – white ceramic tiled floor, white units, white furniture. It was, Thanet thought, as clinical and impersonal as an operating theatre. Perdita's choice? he wondered. If so, what did it say about her? Apart from the painting in the sitting room he had as yet seen nothing of her personality imprinted anywhere in the house. Yet she had lived here for years ... It was as if she had deliberately chosen to hide herself from public view. Perhaps she'd had some private corner to which she could withdraw and truly be herself. Of course, her studio! No doubt she had one. If so, Thanet determined to see it.

'It's the police, Giles. They insisted on seeing you.' Frosty disapproval in Mrs Master's voice.

As Master raised his head she edged around the two policemen to stand behind his chair and rest her hands on his shoulders.

Thanet saw the barely perceptible flinch. Mrs Master must have felt it too for her forehead creased and she withdrew her hands, sat down beside Master instead.

So his mother's attentions were unwelcome. A brief glance at Lineham's face told Thanet that the sergeant had missed none of this.

'They're only doing their job, Ma.'

Mrs Master's lips tightened, but she said nothing, merely flicked her hair back from her face with an impatient gesture and folded her hands in her lap. The knuckles were white, Thanet noticed.

'May we sit down?'

Master waved a hand. 'Help yourself.'

'How cosy!' The muscles along her jawline tightened. 'Am I supposed to offer you a drink, Inspector? Or lunch, even?'

'Ma, please! What did you want to ask me, Thanet?'

Master looked haggard. His eyelids drooped as if he had not slept at all last night, and the extensive bruising to his left cheek didn't help. He had cut himself shaving and there was a smear of blood on the collar of his shirt – the same shirt that he had been wearing last night, Thanet realised.

The jacket of fine tweed draped over the back of Master's chair was also the same, Thanet now noticed. It looked as though the man hadn't even bothered to go to bed.

There was no doubt about his grief and once again Thanet suppressed the twinge of compassion. A woman had been murdered and it was his duty to get to the bottom of it.

'I think that you were perhaps less than frank with us last night, Mr Master.'

'What do you mean?' Wary.

'We've just interviewed your next-door neighbour, Mr Swain.'

Master's eyes darkened, his teeth clenched. 'So?' Slowly he straightened up. Despite his distress his instinct for self-preservation was asserting itself.

'So he too is sporting a black eye.'

Master shrugged. 'Coincidence.' It was a poor attempt at nonchalance. He must realise that Swain would have had no reason to conceal the truth.

'That's not what Mr Swain says.'

'Really, Inspector!' Mrs Master cut in, eyes flashing. 'What are you implying? That my son and this . . . person, have been in some sort of vulgar brawl?'

'Ma, please! If you're going to keep interrupting –'

'I am not "keeping interrupting"! It's the first time I've spoken! And I was merely pointing out the unlikelihood –'

'Ma,' said Master wearily. 'Shut up. And if you can't shut up, perhaps you'd better go. You don't know what you're talking about.' He waited for a moment to see if she would follow his suggestion, but she didn't move, just compressed her lips as if to prevent errant words escaping and sat back in her chair folding her arms. *Nothing will make me leave if I don't want to.*

Thanet was interested. He wondered just how much Master had told his mother. He had obviously not confided in her.

Master turned back to Thanet. 'I take your point, Inspector. I can see there's no point in denying it. Yes, Swain and I did have a fight. On Saturday night.' He cast a warning glance at his mother, who had just opened her mouth.

She shut it again.

He picked up one of the table napkins and begun rolling the corner between his fingers.

His mother could restrain herself no longer. Her hand shot out to grasp his arm, red talons digging into flesh. 'Why?' she demanded fiercely. She gave his arm a little shake. 'Why did you have a fight?'

She looked eager, Thanet thought, as if she were about to receive some news for which she had been waiting a long, long time.

'Oh, for God's sake!' He erupted out of his chair, tossing her hand off his arm so violently that she rocked back in her chair. 'Can't you guess what all this is about? They were having an affair! Perdita and Swain were having an affair! Perhaps now you'll be satisfied!'

She too jumped up and stood facing him. In profile, thus, the family resemblance was unmistakeable. Her expression was of apparent disbelief. But she was a bad actress, Thanet thought. He could almost feel the satisfaction which was vibrating through her, lending her words of denial a spurious passion. 'Satisfied? What do you mean, satisfied?'

'You never did like her, did you? Ha! That's putting it mildly. You couldn't stand her, could you? You may have thought I didn't realise what you were up to, but don't think I didn't know you were always looking for ways to put her down! No wonder she got fed up with it, fed up with me! I should have had more sense, should have realised just how much it upset her, and told you I wouldn't put up with it! Well, now you've got what you always wanted. She's gone, dead, finished!'

Master appeared to have forgotten that Thanet and

Lineham were there. Either that, or he was past caring.

'Giles! You don't know what you're saying! That simply isn't true! Perdita was a sweet girl...'

'Mother, for God's sake, stop playing the hypocrite. I *know* how you felt about her, I tell you. What's the point in pretending any more?'

Mrs Master clearly didn't know what to say, how to react. It looked as though this was the first time her aversion for Perdita had ever been brought out into the open. She shot the two policemen an embarrassed glance. 'I'm so sorry, Inspector. My son is overwrought.'

'Overwrought?' shouted Master. 'OVERWROUGHT? Of course I'm overwrought! What do you expect? My wife has been murdered, she's lying there now stretched out on a marble slab... Oh God, I can't bear it...' He plumped down into his chair, put his elbows on the table and lowering his head clasped his hands over the top of it as if to cling on to his sanity.

Thanet glanced at Lineham. The question in the sergeant's eyes was clear. *Don't you think we ought to go?*

Thanet shook his head. *No.*

To witness this degree of distress in another human being was always painful, but he could not allow embarrassment to deflect him from his task. He had to remember that the cause of Master's distress could be not simple pain at the death of a beloved wife but remorse at having brought that death about. Jealousy is a fearsome emotion, violent and uncontrollable, and despite Thanet's doubts about the polythene bag he had to remember that Lineham was right. A dog-in-the-manger attitude was not uncommon. *If I can't have her, no one else will.*

Mrs Master was still standing and now she put out her hand as if to rest it on her son's bent head in a gesture of sympathy. But she thought better of it. The hand hovered for a moment and was then slowly withdrawn. She shot Thanet a venomous glance. *Now look what you've done.* It was clear that she was not in the habit of accepting responsibility for the consequences of her behaviour.

'Mr Master,' he said gently. 'Look, I know how painful this is for you, and I'm sorry. I have no wish to cause you more distress. But if I am to find out what happened to your wife, I must know everything, absolutely everything, about the circumstances leading to her death. Now I can, if you wish, leave this for the moment and come back another time. But I think it would be better, don't you, if we could get it over with. Then we can go away and leave you in peace.'

Silence. Master shook his head and then unclasped his hands, slowly sat back, eyes shut as if he could not bear to reveal the naked emotion in them, see the effect his ravaged face was having upon them. 'I suppose so.' His voice was dull, exhausted. He opened his eyes and glanced up at his mother. 'I think it would be best if you went.'

There was a note of finality in his voice. She opened her mouth to object, glanced at Thanet and then, without a word, marched to the door, high heels clacking on the polished tiles. Outside the sound ceased abruptly as she moved into the carpeted hall.

Thanet wouldn't have put it past her to listen at the door and he glanced at Lineham, nodded at it. *Go and check that she's not there.*

The sergeant rose and, moving quietly in his rubber-soled shoes, crossed the room, opened the door and glanced outside. Satisfied, he returned. *All clear.*

Now that Master was in a cooperative state of mind it didn't take long to find out the facts. This time he held nothing back, confirming what until now had been hearsay, information gleaned from others.

After Perdita had broken the news to him on Saturday night he had grabbed her by the wrists and dragged her upstairs, locked her in their bedroom. In a furious temper he had then left the house immediately to confront Swain. After the fight he had returned home to find Perdita gone. Realising that she had probably taken refuge at her mother's house he had followed her there, but Harrow, her stepfather, had refused to let him in. Frustrated he had gone home and drunk himself into a stupor.

On Sunday he had woken late with a fierce hangover and because of this had missed Perdita, who had already left by the time he got to Wayside Crescent. Harrow had answered the door and when Giles had asked to see Perdita's mother in the hope of enlisting her aid in persuading Perdita to come back to him, he learnt for the first time that Mrs Harrow had gone into hospital the previous day.

Realising that Perdita would no doubt visit her mother some time that day he had driven straight to the hospital and waited there for hours. He had seen her arrive, but had bided his time until she came out, telling himself that she might be more willing to talk to him if she were not anxious to get away and see her mother.

When she did come out he had been annoyed to see that she was with Vanessa Broxton and the children, but they had separated and he had had the chance of a few words with her. She had refused to talk with him at any length, however, and he had decided that it would be best to let her simmer down for a while and speak to her the next day, Monday.

On Monday morning he had again gone around to Wayside Crescent and had been bitterly disappointed to hear that she had returned there to pack her bags on Sunday afternoon and had then left, saying that she was going away for a few days. Harrow wouldn't tell him where she had gone, but Master remembered seeing Perdita with Vanessa the previous day and on the off-chance that Vanessa might know had rung the Broxtons' house. A woman had answered the phone.

'Hullo?'

'Mrs Broxton?'

'No, she's not here.'

'Could you tell me when she'll be back?'

'Who's speaking, please?'

'My name is Master, I'm the husband of a friend of...'

'Oh, it's Mrs Master you want to speak to?'

'Ah ... Yes. Is she there?'

'I'll fetch her.'

But Perdita had told him once again that she had no intention of coming back. And no, she would not meet him in the meantime to discuss the matter. Vanessa was away for the week and she had promised to look after the children until Friday evening. So he had decided to go to the Broxtons' that night after the children were in bed.

The rest they already knew.

Thanet was nodding. The picture was gradually becoming clearer.

Master leaned back in his chair and closed his eyes. He looked exhausted. Perhaps the retelling of the events of Perdita's last days had had a cathartic effect upon him, and now he would be able to sleep.

'I don't understand it.' Master was shaking his head in bewilderment. 'I really don't understand.' Suddenly his eyes snapped open and with one last spurt of energy he leaned forward, clasping his hands together so fiercely that his fingers made indentations in the flesh. 'What did I do wrong, Thanet? I gave her everything, everything she wanted.' He waved his hand, encompassing kitchen, house, garden. 'And I never so much as looked at another woman.' Suddenly he unclasped his hands and thumped the kitchen table so hard that Thanet and Lineham jumped, the glasses rocked, the cutlery clattered. The series of tiny noises drew his attention to the two places so carefully laid by his mother and with a small, inarticulate sound he laid his forearm on the table and swept everything off. Silverware crashed on to the floor, glasses smashed and one napkin ring flew across the room to hit the wall before rolling into a corner.

He was surveying the mess, face expressionless, as his mother burst into the room. 'Giles! What happened?' An accusatory glance at Thanet and Lineham. Perhaps she thought they had been resorting to strong-arm tactics. In any case, it was bound to be their fault.

'Don't fuss, Mother. A slight accident, that's all.' He looked at Thanet. 'Have we finished?'

'Almost. One question for you, Mrs Master.'

She had begun to pick up the debris and she straightened up, table napkins in hand. 'For me?' She was looking at Thanet as if he were a bad smell.

'Yes. Did you see Mr Master at any time, over the weekend?'

'Naturally.' She was picking up knives, forks, spoons, now. 'We see each other most days, don't we, dear?'

Master gave a resigned nod.

'When, exactly, would that have been?'

She dumped the handful of cutlery on the table with a clatter. 'Would you mind telling me what is the point of all this?'

'I'm just trying to build up as complete a picture as possible of the movements of everyone connected with your daughter-in-law, over the last few days before her death.'

'I can't see what possible relevance this could have . . .'

'You must allow me to be the judge of that,' said Thanet sharply.

'Very well. Giles came around for Sunday afternoon tea, as usual. He and . . . They always do . . . did.'

'That was when he told you Mrs Master had left?'

'Yes.' Her lips tightened.

Thanet could see her thinking. *Good riddance to bad rubbish*. And yes, buried deep but nevertheless discernible was a glint of elation in her eyes.

'And on Monday?'

'I popped around here late in the afternoon. Naturally I was anxious about my son.'

'Did he on that occasion tell you where your daughter-in-law was?'

'Yes, of course. With that Broxton girl.'

So Mrs Master senior had also known where Perdita had 'hidden' herself. Who hadn't? Thanet wondered.

He stood up. 'I'm afraid there's just one other matter I must trouble you with, Mr Master. I shall need to examine your wife's things. And I imagine she had a studio . . . ?'

Master was looking sick. Thanet wasn't surprised. The thought of a complete stranger pawing through his wife's belongings would be enough to upset any man, but for a jealous one the idea would be purgatory.

'I suppose it's essential . . .'

'It is. If you would just show us where to go, we needn't trouble you any further. We'll try to be as unobtrusive as possible.'

'Very well.' Wearily Master stood up. 'Where first?'

'Perhaps we could begin upstairs?'

TEN

On the landing Master turned left towards the front of the house and stopped outside a door. 'This one.'

He blundered back down the stairs.

Thanet and Lineham watched him go.

'Poor devil,' said Lineham. 'Doesn't know whether he's coming or going.'

'Not like you to be sorry for a murder suspect, Mike.' Thanet opened the door and light streamed into the corridor.

'Must be going soft in my old age,' said Lineham with a grin. 'Anyway, you must admit he's got a lot to put up with, with that mother of his.'

Ah, so that was the reason for Lineham's sympathy, thought Thanet as they walked into the Masters' bedroom. It was understandable that the sergeant should identify with Master in this respect.

'I must say, I'm glad she's not my mother-in-law.' Thanet thought of Joan's mother, lying in intensive care. *Please, God, let her be all right.* As soon as he was finished here, he'd ring the hospital to see if there was any news.

The room was spacious, light and airy, with luxuriously soft fitted carpet and floor-length curtains. The effect was comfortable but curiously impersonal, as if it were a hotel room temporarily occupied by tenants who had failed as yet to stamp their personalities upon it. The colours were muted, safe – predominantly pale green and cream. Thanet would have expected something a little more inspired from an artist, a woman to whom colour would surely have been one of the most important factors in her life. He was becoming more and more convinced that Perdita had not cared enough either for her husband or her home to employ her talents wholeheartedly in beautifying it.

He noticed that the duvet on the bed was tossed into an untidy heap on one side of the bed, as if someone had pushed it aside when getting up. It looked as though Master might have lain down fully dressed and tried to sleep. There was a damp patch on one of the pillows, Thanet noticed, and the other one lay part of the way down the bed, askew. He had a sudden, painfully vivid vision of Master giving vent to his grief in the early hours of the morning, clutching the pillow upon which his dead wife's head had rested . . .

Thanet shook his head and the image shattered, dissolved. 'What did you say, Mike?'

'Stacks of jewellery here. Look.'

Thanet joined Lineham at the dressing table. Standing amongst a clutter of expensive-looking perfume bottles, Perdita Master's jewel box was a sumptuous affair of soft white leather lined with red velvet, and it was crammed with necklaces, brooches, earrings, rings in every conceivable stone.

'Must be worth a fortune,' said Lineham. 'Let's hope he's got it insured.'

Thanet picked up a gift tag which had slipped down flat against one side of the box. '*To my darling wife. Jewels to a jewel.*'

He showed it to Lineham. 'Makes you wonder what it must be like, to be loved so . . . overwhelmingly.'

'As Mr Swain said, suffocated,' said Lineham with feeling. 'Desperate to escape.'

Well, Perdita Master had escaped, and enjoyed two brief days of freedom. And look at the price she had paid for it.

'I wonder *why* he was so jealous.' Thanet knew that violent jealousy is supposed to arise from a poor self-image. The theory is that you place so little value on yourself that you can't possibly believe that the object of your affections can love you. But Master's mother obviously thought the sun shone out of him. His father's influence, then? Jealous perhaps of his wife's attitude towards the baby, and taking it out on the child by constant denigration?

While they talked they had been looking around. There was a stack of glossy art books on one of the bedside tables and Thanet glanced through them. These, too, were presents from Master to his wife. *To darling Perdita, Christmas 1989. Happy birthday, darling! To my darling wife on our 15th anniversary*. How terrible unrequited love must be, thought Thanet. Popular opinion agrees that it is better to have loved and lost than never to have loved at all, but he wasn't sure that this was necessarily true. To love a woman with all your heart and to have to live with her indifference, year after year . . . To do everything in your power to please her, to win her, and to live always with the knowledge that you have failed . . . It must be soul-destroying.

And he, he told himself briskly, must be careful. He was becoming maudlin, and in danger of feeling too sorry for Master. All the same, this brief inspection of their bedroom had, he felt, given him a valuable glimpse into their relationship.

'There's nothing here, Mike. We'll go back down.'

Master had pointed out the door to Perdita's studio as they passed through the hall earlier. Downstairs all was silent and Thanet wondered what Master and his mother were doing. Eating a silent lunch in the kitchen? Or had Master retreated to his study, if he had one, to mourn in solitude?

Lineham led the way. He flung open the studio door and

Thanet stopped dead, momentarily overwhelmed by the impression of light, space and visual richness. He had been seeking an imprint of Perdita's personality and here, at last, he had found it.

This room had been built along the back of the house, facing north, and was flooded with the clear, flat light so necessary to the serious artist. The wall facing the garden was glass from floor to ceiling and huge skylights had been set into the sloping roof. Along the back wall of white-painted brick hung panels of material, some plain, some richly textured and patterned in brilliant colours. Beneath them ran a long wooden bench cluttered in places with a diversity of objects doubtless used by Perdita in her paintings: curiously shaped pieces of wood, shells, pots and vases of all sizes and descriptions, fans, feathers, pebbles and stones, even pieces of bleached bones, including a skull. At intervals, in cleared spaces, a still life had been set up. Along one of the side walls were racks holding finished paintings and sheets of watercolour paper, and along the other, shelves stacked with reference books, sketchbooks, notepads, jars of pencils and brushes, paints, all the paraphernalia of the working artist. Draped over a chaise-longue was a dazzling variety of shawls, scarves and pieces of fabric. There were two easels, one freestanding and the other a large adjustable table model set up on a worktable at right angles to the tall windows. Thanet crossed to look at the painting taped to it.

Perdita had been working on another night-time landscape, a powerful disturbing work of rich, sombre hues. Distorted shadows were cast by the moon which floated behind the stark, silhouetted branches of trees and in the foreground was a tangle of undergrowth which only partly concealed the bleached bones of some long-dead animal.

'Wow!' Lineham brought Thanet out of his absorption with a jolt. The sergeant was standing in the middle of the studio, revolving slowly. 'Some place, eh?' He crossed to peer over Thanet's shoulder. 'Wouldn't like to hang that on my wall.'

'She was good, though, wasn't she?'

'I'm no judge of that, I'm afraid. But she certainly didn't lack for equipment.'

Thanet thumbed through some of the numbered sketch-books ranged along the shelves. Book after book was filled with pencil drawings and watercolour sketches, some bold and rapidly executed, some fragmentary, some meticulously detailed, and covering every conceivable subject. It was obvious that to Perdita a pencil or a paintbrush in the hand had been almost an extension of her body. Thanet shook his head, sighed. What a waste of talent. And how desperate she must have been to get away, to have left all this behind her.

'Don't seem to be any personal papers here,' said Lineham.

'Depends what you mean by personal.'

'Letters, documents, that sort of stuff.'

'Wait a minute.'

Thanet had spotted something. Covered by one of the vivid shawls which Perdita had loved, a futuristic design of whorls, squiggles and geometric shapes, was what Thanet had taken to be a table and now realised was a filing cabinet. But if they had hoped for personal revelations they were disappointed. It merely contained a drawer of indexed photographs and immaculately kept business records: receipts, details of sales, exhibitions, letters from galleries and from Perdita's accountant. Having seen the power of her work Thanet was not surprised to see how successful she had become. She would certainly have been able to support herself, and Thanet wondered if Master in fact realised that by providing her with this elaborate cage and encouraging her to develop her gift he had unwittingly handed her the means to escape from him.

'Look at this! Two thousand quid!' Lineham was holding a receipt in his hand, looking dazed. 'She was getting two thousand quid for one painting!'

'Frankly, having seen her work, I'm not surprised. Don't look so astounded, Mike. People will pay, you know, for a fine work of art.'

Lineham was still shaking his head. 'But two thousand pounds ... How can anyone afford that sort of money – and for a modern artist. I mean, it's such a risk, isn't it?'

'Depends on whether you're acquiring the painting as an investment or simply because you like it. Anyway, I don't think there's anything more to see here. It's gone two. We'd better get a move on, if we're going to be in time for our appointment with Mrs Swain.'

There was still no sign of either Master or his mother and they let themselves quietly out of the house.

They stopped at the telephone box in the village for Thanet to ring the hospital. No change in his mother-in-law's condition.

As he got back into the car Lineham said, 'I've been thinking ... What you said, about someone truly wanting her dead, what about Mr Master's mother? She certainly seems glad to see the back of her.'

'Mrs Master senior doesn't seem to be shedding any tears, I agree. But what motive could she have had? After all, Perdita was gone. She'd left her husband and no doubt her mother-in-law was delighted. But why bother to kill her?'

'To make sure she didn't change her mind, come back?'

'A bit thin, Mike.'

'Maybe, for a normal person. But Mrs Master is obsessive as far as her son is concerned and as you're always pointing out, people with obsessions don't behave normally.'

'I can't see that she'd have had any reason to go and see her.'

'She did know where young Mrs Master was. She admitted it.'

Thanet was shaking his head. 'I still think she'd have left well alone. I think she'd have been well satisfied just to know that Perdita was out of the picture. If there'd been any positive indication that Perdita was considering coming back, now, well, that would be different. But Master says that when he talked to his wife on Monday evening she was still determined not to do so. And I really can't see that he'd have any reason to lie about that, quite the reverse. I'd be much more inclined to think he was lying if he was trying to pretend that everything was all right between them.'

'True ... Unless, of course, he was trying to protect his mother.'

'If she'd killed his wife! I should think he'd have been much more likely to turn on her with his bare hands! No, you're pushing this too far, Mike.'

'I was only going by what you said, about whoever killed her truly wanting her dead!'

'I know. I just don't think there's any point in pursuing this line of thought for the moment. If something turns up to make me change my mind, fair enough, we'll reconsider.'

The traffic was thickening and slowing down as they approached the section of the A20 where the new M20 motorway was being constructed. Alongside the old road excavations and earthworks disfigured the landscape, with their attendant turmoil of trucks, diggers, cranes and workers' caravans.

'What a mess!' murmured Thanet.

'The A20'll be much quieter when it's finished.' Lineham was a great fan of motorways.

Thanet merely grunted. He hated what was happening to Kent. Along with most of the other inhabitants of the county he bitterly resented the fact that the so-called garden of England was being turned into a through road to Europe. The Channel Tunnel was a blight on the county. For miles inland the coastal areas had been devastated to provide approach roads and loading depots, the M20 motorway link had laid waste a great swathe of countryside, and the dreaded

High-Speed Rail Link was the worst threat of all. In order to match the High-Speed Link through France, where relatively uninhabited countryside made construction far easier, British Rail was intending to slice through ancient Kentish villages with a total disregard for history, tradition or the lives of the people who lived in them. Property values close to the proposed route had slumped and many had found their houses unsaleable. Driven to desperation, the placid inhabitants of Kent had taken drastic measures. There had been protests, marches, petitions to Parliament, they had even burnt an effigy of the Chairman of British Rail, all apparently to little avail. But lately there had been whispers: the cost of the Link had soared and it could prove too expensive an undertaking. Thanet fervently hoped that this would prove to be the case.

He glanced at his watch. Twenty past two. They were going to be late. At a snail's pace they crawled through Lenham then on past Harrietsham. Then came a glimpse of the battlements of Leeds Castle before they arrived at Hollingbourne corner. Here the traffic became virtually stationary as at the double roundabouts two lanes reduced to one. By now it was twenty to three.

Lineham thrummed his fingers on the steering wheel. 'Come on, come *on*.'

Thanet could sympathise. He too hated being late. 'No point in getting worked up about it, Mike. There's nothing we can do.'

At last they reached the Maidstone turn-off and were clear of the congestion. A couple of miles further on they turned right to the TVS Studios.

'Ever been here before, Mike?' said Thanet as the barrier was raised and they drove in.

Lineham shook his head. 'Nope. I must admit, I'm quite looking forward to it.'

TVS, which serves the densely populated South East, is an

immensely successful Independent Television company. The modern building which houses its Maidstone studios has been built in the former grounds of a small country house, Vinters Park.

'Don't suppose we'll see much of it, Mike. We're hardly likely to get a guided tour.'

Thanet was right. Perhaps in retaliation for their lateness Ms Edge/Swain made them wait fifteen minutes in the foyer before she arrived. She then led them a short distance along a corridor before turning into a small room furnished with a low round coffee table and a few chairs.

When they were seated she glanced at her watch. 'Right, Inspector. How can I help you?'

A clear message. *I'm a busy woman. Don't waste my time.*

Thanet had already apologised for being late, though she had not. He had no intention of being pressured or rushed through this interview.

'As I've no doubt you've gathered, we are investigating the murder of Mrs Perdita Master.'

Her lips compressed and the muscles along her jawbone tightened as she clenched her teeth. She was a complete contrast to Perdita, tall and heavily-built with straight blond hair cut very short and a broad, high-cheekboned, almost Slavic face which seemed incomprehensibly familiar to Thanet. He was sure he had never actually met her before or seen her on the box. She was wearing brown corduroy trousers, chestnut-brown leather boots and a beautiful mohair sweater in an abstract design of browns, neutrals and black – one of her husband's creations, Thanet assumed.

He wondered how she had felt about her husband's bombshell on Saturday night. Or perhaps it hadn't been a bombshell at all, maybe she had already known about the affair, or at least suspected it. Did she love her husband? he wondered. Perhaps she hadn't cared. She would at least have been able to support herself, jobs in television were notoriously well paid. But if she had cared, yes, she would be a formidable opponent. Capable of murder, to hold on to what she wanted?

He looked again at the firm, square jaw, the pugnacious blue eyes. Thanet could see what Harrow had meant by 'high-powered'. He could well imagine that many people would find her intimidating.

However, she wasn't going to intimidate him.

'I'll come straight to the point, Mrs Swain. We have been to see your husband and he has been very frank with us. He has told us that he and Mrs Master were having an affair, and that on Saturday night he informed you that he was going to leave you, for her.'

She picked up the huge soft brown leather shoulder bag that she had deposited on the floor beside her chair, opened it and took out a packet of cheroots. Taking her time, she lit one and exhaled slowly, leaning back in her chair and blowing the smoke towards the ceiling. She smiled. 'My, we don't pack our punches, do we, Inspector. Are you saying that I am suspected of killing my rival?'

'That might be putting it a little too strongly. But clearly, you have a motive and therefore we have to consider the possibility.'

She took another puff, exhaled again. Then, suddenly, she leaned forward. 'Let me make my position quite clear, Inspector. Frankly, I'm glad that Perdita is dead. I never did care for her, I can't stand that boneless, helpless little woman type and she was always the same, even at school. Men like it, of course.' She rolled her eyes, cast them up to heaven in mock despair. 'They really go for it, and my husband was no exception. He thought I didn't know what was going on, but he was mistaken. I'm not blind and I'd seen it coming, for months.'

Briefly, her composure slipped and Thanet glimpsed the pain behind the façade. So she had cared. Deeply. His interest quickened.

'But, Inspector, and believe me, it's a very big "but", I did not kill her. I knew that in the end, you see, my husband wouldn't have had the...'

Guts? supplied Thanet.

'He wouldn't have been able to bring himself to leave. He enjoys his little comforts and I earn far more than he does. When he'd got around to the nitty-gritty, he'd have worked out that he couldn't afford to leave me and continue living in the style to which he has become accustomed.'

Thanet sensed rather than saw Lineham shift on the seat beside him. What had discomforted the sergeant? The note of contempt in Mrs Swain's voice, when she spoke of her husband? Thanet knew that Louise, Lineham's wife, could be pretty scathing at times. Was Lineham going to find himself in the position of identifying with yet another suspect?

'I'm not so sure of that, Mrs Swain. Mrs Master had become pretty successful, you know.'

She waved her hand and a worm of ash fell on the carpet. She put out her foot and rubbed it in. 'She may have sold a painting or two. But it's a pretty precarious living.'

Thanet was amused to find himself indignant on Perdita Master's behalf, had to restrain himself from arguing with Mrs Swain. Was she genuinely ignorant of Perdita's success? he wondered, or was she deliberately misrepresenting the facts? Perhaps it was simply wishful thinking on her part.

'Just now you said, "Even at school", Mrs Swain. You were at school with Mrs Master?'

'We both went to Sturrenden High.'

Of course, that was why Mrs Swain looked familiar!

Thanet's brain had produced a fleeting, vivid image: a group of girls walking along the pavement outside Sturrenden High, chattering, laughing and casting sidelong glances at the boys hanging around on the opposite side of the road hoping for just such a glimpse as this. In those days approaches to members of the opposite sex had been much more hesitant, tentative. She had always been in the same group, had stood out because she was a good head taller than the rest. Her hair had been glamorously long, then, had swung to and fro like a golden bell as she walked, a magnet to the boys' attention. He suddenly realised that there was a rich vein of information he had not yet tapped – Joan. She, too, had been at Sturrenden High, and although she was a year or two older than Perdita and this woman, she might well know something about them. And about Vanessa Broxton too. Joan had been in bed when he got home last night and this morning there had been no opportunity to talk before the phone call about her mother took precedence over everything else. He hadn't even told Joan the name of the murder victim.

'So you know Mrs Broxton, too.'

She blew smoke again. 'Naturally. Cosy, isn't it? We were all in the same form.'

'Friends?'

She grimaced, shook her head. 'No. Vanessa was too much of a swot, and Perdita ... Well, Perdita was always a bit of an outsider.'

'Why was that, d'you think?'

She shrugged. 'How should I know?'

There was a knock at the door and a girl put her head around it. 'Oh, sorry.' She withdrew.

'If she was an outsider, she must have been different. In what way?'

Another shrug. 'She always seemed to live in a world of her own. You felt that half the time she didn't really see you even if you were standing bang in front of her. As if you were invisible or something. And who likes to feel invisible? No, she just didn't seem very interested in having friends, doing things with other people. She was always stuck in a corner by herself, drawing.' Briefly, a reminiscent smile touched her lips. 'She used to do some pretty good caricatures of the staff, I remember.'

'But this didn't make her any more popular?'

Mrs Swain shook her head emphatically. 'I told you, she just wasn't interested.'

'Unusual, in a teenager.'

'And of course,' said Mrs Swain, blowing a smoke ring and watching Thanet with a glint in her eye, 'she was pretty, well, for want of a better word, retarded.'

'Retarded?' Thanet's eyebrows rose. Then he realised that her choice of word had been deliberate. She had wanted to jolt, to shock.

'Don't look so astonished, Inspector. I don't mean mentally. Sexually.'

'She just wasn't interested in boys?'

'Exactly. Pretty rare, in an adolescent, wouldn't you say? Of course, to begin with she was a late developer. Small, skinny. She was in the fifth form before her periods started. We all knew, because she was never excused gym. We used to joke about it.'

And pretty cruel such teasing could be, Thanet thought.

'We'd all had boobs for years before Perdita began to sprout them. And then, suddenly, we realised that the boys were sniffing around her. We could never understand the attraction.' She smiled, a slow, lazy, almost seductive smile. 'A mystery, isn't it? S. A.?'

'Sex appeal?'

Again the smile, with a hint of appraisal as well as amusement in it as she glanced at Lineham, who always seemed to emanate a prudish disapproval when sex was openly discussed, even after all his years in the force. 'Don't you like talking about sex, Sergeant? That must make life difficult for you.' She raised her arms above her head and stretched, her heavy breasts lifting beneath the soft, caressing surface of her sweater. 'Me, I find it highly stimulating.'

Lineham, apparently impassive, made a note and Thanet read it, out of the corner of his eye.

Likes sex!

Thanet suppressed a grin. It might be misinterpreted. 'And Perdita had it, you say? She was sexually attractive?'

'She must have been, mustn't she? Why else would the boys suddenly have been around her like bees around a honeypot? As I say, we could never understand it.'

'And she encouraged them?'

'That was the interesting thing. No, she didn't. But it sure didn't put them off, no sirree. Back they came for more. And yet, the odd thing was . . .'

'What?'

She leaned forward, stubbed out the cheroot. 'Well, you know what it's like when you're at school. You're always being asked what you want to do when you leave, having to make subject choices, filling in questionnaires . . . We all envied Perdita in that respect because we thought she'd be saved all the agonising. It seemed so obvious that she'd go to Art College, be a painter, or a designer, or an illustrator. We just couldn't believe it when it came out that she intended to train as a nanny.'

'She never once said she wanted to go to Art School?'

'Not to my knowledge. So off she went to some college and got herself trained. Not that she was a great success, by all accounts.'

'Why not? Wasn't she good at it?'

'I assume you're just pretending to be naïve, Inspector? Oh, she was great with the *children*, or so I understand. It was the daddies that were the problem. I heard on the grapevine that she had real problems there. Never stayed in any one job more than six months.'

'Because of this mysterious attraction for the opposite sex.'

'Precisely. Galling, isn't it? The rest of us spend a fortune on clothes, make-up and hairdos trying to make the best of what Mother Nature gave us, and Perdita did it without lifting a little finger. She really didn't give a damn and yet they all came running.'

Including your husband, thought Thanet. And I can imagine how you felt about that.

'You really didn't like her very much, did you?'

'I don't go around murdering people I don't like, Inspector. Otherwise I'd have been put behind bars years ago.'

Maybe. But it was time, now, to put the all-important question. 'Nevertheless . . . Perhaps you could now give us an account of your movements last night?'

ELEVEN

Mrs Swain smiled that slow, lazy smile again. 'Last night? Why, I was at home with my husband of course, Inspector. Like a good little wife.'

'Little' was scarcely the word he would apply to Mrs Swain. This was precisely the answer he had expected, of course. She must have realised that she would come under suspicion, in the circumstances. And there had been plenty of time for Swain to ring and warn her that they had been around to the house asking questions and to arrange that he and his wife should alibi each other. 'Could you be a little more specific?'

'Well, let me see. We had supper about 7.30, as usual. Pork and apple casserole, in case you're interested, followed by gooseberry fool. Afterwards we watched television for a while, then I did some work. Then we went to bed.'

Pointless to ask which programmes she had watched. Working in TVS she would be certain to own a video. Gone were the days when people could be caught out because they had lied about their viewing habits.

'Did you know that Mrs Master was staying at Mrs Broxton's house?'

'Not until your men came around this morning. My husband would hardly have been likely to tell me where his mistress had flown to, would he?' Her voice suddenly deepened in a passable imitation of her husband's. '"Oh, by the way, darling, Perdita's gone to stay with Vanessa Broxton for a few days."'

'Perhaps not.' He rose. 'Well, I think that's all for the moment, Mrs Swain. But we might need to see you again.'

She stood up, grinned. 'Is that a threat or a promise, Inspector?'

'You're not planning any trips in connection with your work?'

'No. And if I do, I promise I'll let you know in advance, like the dutiful citizen I am. Cross my heart.'

'Thank you.' At the door he paused. 'Do you see much of Mrs Broxton these days?'

She grimaced. 'Vanessa? No. We were never particularly friendly, as I said, and anyway she's far too busy with her children, her work and her husband, in that order, to have much time to nurture friendships.'

'In that order? You surprise me.'

'Oh, make no mistake about it, her children come first with Vanessa. She's got all sorts of problems looming, I'm afraid, when they start going to school and want her to watch their Christmas plays and egg and spoon races.'

'Perhaps they'll go to boarding school.'

'Is that a dig at me, Inspector? If so, I suppose it's justified. Yes, I did take the easy way out. I couldn't stand all that guilt, you see, it's not my style. But Vanessa is a different matter. Funny, I'd never have thought she was the maternal type, but I've seen it happen before, especially in career women who leave it late to have a baby. They just fall in love with the child, and find themselves in an impossible position, torn between work and missing those few, short years of infancy. And of course, even when the children start school it's always the woman who has the ultimate responsibility for them. No one expects the father to take time off from work if a child is sick, it's always the mother who has to make excuses or frantically look around for someone to sit in. I tried it for a few years when my children were young. My husband wasn't working at home then and believe me, it was hell. It's the one area in which women will never achieve equality. It's choices, choices all the way, and compromise most of the time. And then more often than not you end up by pleasing nobody.'

This was true. Thanet had often heard Joan bemoaning the fact. And he had sympathised with her. But he didn't really see that there was much that could be done about it. He knew that in some households, where the man worked at home or in a job where flexible hours were possible, he would occasionally assume responsibility for the children. But this was rare and it was generally the woman who had the unenviable task of juggling the demands of home, children and career against each other. Vanessa Broxton's dilemma when her children's nanny had been rushed into hospital was typical, and had in a way led directly to Perdita's death. If she hadn't been desperate to find someone to look after them, if Perdita hadn't been looking for a sanctuary, if she and Vanessa hadn't met on the steps of the hospital ... If, if, if, he told himself irritably as they walked back to the car. Always a pointless exercise.

'Cool customer,' said Lineham.

'You didn't like her.'

'Did you, sir?'

'Not particularly, no.'

'Think she was telling the truth about last night?'

Thanet shrugged. 'Difficult to tell. I imagine she's a good liar. But I have a feeling that no, she wasn't.'

'You think she might have done it, then?'

'She has a motive. And the nerve. I can just imagine her going around to have it out with Perdita ...'

'She's got the build, too. If they had an argument she could have knocked her flying quite easily.'

And yes, Thanet could imagine Mrs Swain coolly stooping to examine the unconscious woman, then grabbing a plastic bag and slipping it over Perdita's head.

Lineham had obviously been thinking along the same lines. 'Perhaps we'll find some nice juicy prints on that bag.'

'Mmm. Well, we'll have to wait and see. Meanwhile, we'll put Bentley on to questioning the other householders in Wheelwright's Lane. If either of the Swains did go out that night, someone might have seen them.'

Back at the office Thanet reported briefly on the day's findings to a still subdued Draco. There was no word from Mallard about the post mortem; presumably nothing unexpected had emerged. No doubt the written report would arrive tomorrow.

He and Joan had arranged that Ben should spend the evening at a friend's house, so Thanet went straight from work to the hospital. He found Joan sitting in the small waiting room near the intensive care unit, head back, eyes closed. She looked exhausted. He sat down beside her, laid his hand gently on her knee.

She opened her eyes and gave a weary smile.

'How is she?'

'So far, so good. I've been allowed to look in on her from time to time and they say that the more time that elapses without a second attack, the better the prospects.'

'Good. Excellent. Will I be able to see her?'

'Oh yes, I'm sure you will, shortly. The doctor's with her at the moment. Have you finished for today?'

'There's someone I have to see, here at the hospital, then yes, I have. Will you be coming home, soon?'

'Probably, yes, depending on what the doctor says.'

'You look tired.'

'Yes I am.' She rubbed her eyes and smoothed back her hair. 'If we can just get through today . . . How has your case been going?'

'So-so. I didn't have a chance to tell you, last night. Do you remember a Perdita Master – sorry, no, that's her married name. I don't know what her maiden name would have been. Her stepfather's name is Harrow, but she might well have kept her father's name ... Anyway, a Perdita somebody, at school?'

'Perdita Bly?'

'Could be.'

'I only remember one Perdita. It's an unusual name. She's two or three years younger than me. Small, slight, with lovely fair hair. She's an artist, she's getting quite well known now.'

'Was, I'm afraid. *Was* two or three years younger than you.'

Joan's eyes opened wide in shock. 'Luke, you don't mean she's the one who's been killed?'

'I'm afraid so.'

'How *awful*. How dreadful.'

'I'm sorry, perhaps I shouldn't have told you yet. You've got enough on your plate at the moment.'

'No, it's all right. I mean, I was never particularly friendly with her. It's just that when it's someone you know ...'

Thanet nodded, understanding.

'What happened?'

'Are you sure you want to hear all this just now?'

'Yes. It'll take my mind off Mother. Oh dear, that does sound callous, but you know what I mean.'

Thanet had always talked to Joan about his work. It made such heavy demands upon him and therefore upon his marriage that he had always felt it important to share it with her and she, he knew, appreciated the fact that he trusted her enough to confide in her. She listened intently as he talked, her clear grey eyes fixed on his, a small frown of concentration between her brows. He noted the spark of recognition as he mentioned Vanessa Broxton's name and then, when he came to Ms Edge/Swain, she interrupted for the first time.

'Does she work at TVS?'

'Yes. I'm not sure what she does, exactly. She's tall, heavily-built, fair . . .'

'Victoria Edge. How extraordinary, Luke! They were all in the same form, at school.'

'So I gathered. Can you tell me anything about them?'

Her eyes glazed in thought and she was silent for a minute or two. 'Not much that'll be of any help, I shouldn't think.'

'Tell me what you remember.'

But Joan was right. She couldn't tell him much that was new. Not having been in the same year she hadn't come into close contact with any of them. But she did remember them, partly because each of them had in her own way stood out from the crowd, and partly because none of them had moved away from Sturrenden as had so many of their contemporaries and inevitably Joan had run into them from time to time – Vanessa Broxton, especially, in Court. Vanessa, she said, had always been serious, had already, by the time Joan left school, been acquiring a reputation for intellectual ability; her name had always been prominent at prizegivings.

Victoria Edge had stood out by virtue of her size, but also because she had had a talent for getting herself into hot water and it had occasionally fallen to Joan, as a prefect, to reprimand her.

Joan grimaced. 'Not that she ever paid any attention. She was pretty much a law unto herself.'

Now that was an interesting comment, thought Thanet. 'A law unto herself.' Did this mean that Mrs Swain regarded it as her right to do as she pleased, even if it were outside the law? And if so, how far would she go, in applying this principle? To murder?

'And Perdita . . .' said Joan. 'Well, I remember Perdita because she was always by herself, usually in a corner with a sketchbook in her hand. I used to feel sorry for her. She missed so much, I felt, by cutting herself off from the others.'

'You think it was a conscious choice on her part? She was a loner because she wanted to be one, not because she had resigned herself to the inability to make friends?'

'I would say so, yes. I certainly never got the impression, as you do with some people, that she was hanging around wistfully on the edge of things, hoping to be asked to join in. She was very self-contained. And forever drawing, as I said. It always seemed to me that she was doing what she wanted to do. I could be wrong, of course. Maybe she gave that impression because it was less humiliating than admitting she couldn't make friends, but I didn't think so and neither did anyone else, to my knowledge.'

'I see. And you never thought that there was any connection between the three of them?'

'No more than there always is between members of the same form. They were so different, I wouldn't have said they had anything in common.'

But they did now, thought Thanet grimly. Perdita's death had linked them for ever. It was the nature of that link that intrigued him. Or was he trying to read too much into the situation? Perhaps it had been sheer coincidence, nothing more. There was one thing that still puzzled him, though, as it had puzzled other people. Perdita's mother had mentioned it and so had Victoria Swain. He had intended to discuss it with Lineham, but had forgotten. Why had Perdita, so engrossed in her painting and drawing that her career seemed a foregone conclusion, deliberately turned her back on art and chosen instead to train as a children's nanny? He put the question to Joan.

She frowned. 'I didn't know she had. I assumed she'd studied art. I lost sight of her for years, but then I began to notice her name cropping up in local exhibitions. Then a couple of years ago the *Kent Messenger* ran a feature on her. Apparently for several years running she'd managed to get a painting hung in the Royal Academy Summer Exhibition and was beginning to exhibit regularly in galleries in London.'

Thanet was nodding. 'I thought you'd have heard of her, even if you didn't remember her from school.' He knew that Joan, who was very interested in art, kept a close eye on what was going on in the area. 'She was becoming very successful and I'm not surprised, having seen her work.'

'Yes, it's really good, isn't it? I've been wishing for ages that I'd bought some of her paintings years ago, when she was still unknown. They're way out of our price range now, of course.'

'I'll say!' Thanet was hearing Lineham's voice. '*Two thousand quid for one painting!*'

'Anyway, to get back to what you were saying, yes, I am surprised that she didn't go on to study art. A children's nanny! It seems so . . . inappropriate, somehow, for someone like her. Not that there's anything wrong with being a children's nanny, it's just that . . . Well, I'm more than surprised, I'm astounded.'

'Her mother says that she was going through a rebellious stage, that perhaps it was because it was taken for granted that she would go to Art College that she had to go off and do something entirely different.'

'Mmm. Could be, I suppose. Were there any children by the second marriage?'

'Not at that stage. There is a stepsister, but she's only thirteen now, so Perdita would have been in her twenties when she was born. And according to the stepfather Perdita was very fond of her.'

'So at the point when she was having to make up her mind what she was going to do, she was still an only child . . . Were she and her mother close, do you think?'

'I would say so, yes. I think Mrs Harrow would have liked Perdita to have gone to Maidstone College of Art, or Medway.'

'Perhaps that's your answer. Perhaps Perdita felt that what

her mother really wanted was for her to stay at home. And with two Art Colleges so close she might have felt her mother would have been hurt if she'd said yes, I want to study art but I want to leave home to do it. Perhaps she needed her independence and felt that the only way to get it without upsetting her mother was to choose a career where she would have to go away to do her training. Seems a bit drastic, though, doesn't it?'

'I don't know. Mrs Harrow is desperately ill at the moment and I understand her health has been poor for years. Perhaps Perdita has always felt protective towards her.'

'Could be. Anyway, I don't suppose you'll ever know, now. The only person who could really explain it would be Perdita herself.'

'Incidentally, talking about Mrs Harrow's illness reminded me . . . You know I said the Super has been somewhat subdued lately? He told us this morning that his wife is ill, that she has to go to London for treatment. And apparently Louise told Mike that Angharad Draco has leukaemia.'

'Yes, I know. It's terrible isn't it? I heard this morning. I ran into Louise when I went into the town to buy some odds and ends for Mother.'

Thanet remembered his promise to Lineham, to ask Joan to have a word with Louise. But Joan, it seemed, had pre-empted him. She was telling him now that Louise had seemed rather low herself, and that with only a little prompting she had confessed to feeling depressed and nervous about going back to nursing when Mandy started school.

'Had you told her about your mother?'

'Yes.'

It was typical of Louise, Thanet thought, to spill out her troubles during such a brief encounter when she must have realised Joan was pressed for time and anxious to get back to the hospital, and he experienced, not for the first time, a spurt of resentment against her self-centredness and insensitivity. He didn't know how Lineham managed to put up with it.

'Don't look like that, darling.' Joan knew how he felt about Louise and could read him only too well. 'I did rather bring it on myself, you know.'

And that too, he thought, was typical. Joan always seemed willing to attempt to carry the troubles of the world upon her shoulders.

'Anyway, I was surprised,' said Joan. 'I'd always thought she was raring to get back to work. I told her it was perfectly normal to feel like that, that I'd felt like that myself, that we all did after taking a long break to look after the children. I said I was sure that if she did a refresher course she'd get her confidence back in no time.'

'Good. That's exactly what I told Mike. D'you think it helped?'

'Well, she certainly seemed more cheerful when we parted ... Ah, there's Doctor MacPherson.'

A tall, lanky Scot, with sandy hair and brows, the doctor had a reassuring air of authority. It was good news. He was increasingly confident now that Joan's mother would be all right. If all went well, in the morning she would be moved out of intensive care and there was even a chance that by afternoon she might be allowed home.

Joan was radiant. 'What a relief. Oh, thank you, doctor. Everyone here has been wonderful.'

'She was a lucky lass, that her neighbour found her almost immediately. Tomorrow we'll have a wee chat, and discuss the course of treatment she'll have to follow. It will mean changes in her life-style and of course it would be best if there were someone to keep a close eye on her for a few days, at least.'

'We can arrange something, I'm sure,' said Joan. 'I can take a few days' leave. She can come home to us, to begin with.'

'Excellent. The heart has tremendous powers of regeneration and there is no reason why she shouldn't get back to living a perfectly normal life.'

'That really is great news. Thank you so much. Can we see her again, now?'

'Just for a wee while. Then she should rest.'

Mrs Bolton was looking much more her usual self. She looked pale and tired, of course, but that was to be expected. Her body was recovering from a major trauma.

Thanet took her hand. 'How are you, Margaret?'

She smiled. 'Fine, thank you.'

'You certainly look better than when I came in this morning. You gave us all a few nasty moments there.'

'Me too!' She glanced at Joan. 'You really must go home, dear. You look exhausted.'

'Don't worry about me!'

'Did the doctor tell you? He thinks I'm going to be all right.'

'I know. What a relief!'

'So you will go and get some rest now, won't you?'

'For goodness' sake, Mother, do stop worrying about other people! It's the last thing you should be doing. Just relax and concentrate on getting better.'

'Don't worry, I shall. But –'

'Mum,' said Joan, taking her mother's other hand, 'if it'll stop you fussing I'll go, very soon, I promise. But there's someone Luke has to see, here in the hospital, so I'll just sit with you quietly until he's finished, OK?'

'All right. This a case you're working on, Luke?'

'Yes. I'll be back as soon as I can.'

Visiting time was not yet over and most of the beds in the women's surgical ward were surrounded by small family groups. Unlike most of the other patients, Angela Proven, Vanessa's nanny, looked remarkably bright and cheerful. She had just one visitor, a young woman of her own age.

'I'll be off then, Ange,' said the girl, when Thanet introduced himself. 'I'll try and get in again tomorrow.'

'OK, Ros, thanks.'

Curtains were drawn around the bed and they were left alone.

TWELVE

'I think you're here under false pretences,' said Thanet, smiling, as he sat down.

'What do you mean?'

'You look much too healthy to be in hospital. Positively blooming, in fact.'

She grinned. 'I didn't know police officers were allowed to pay compliments.'

She was solidly-built, verging on plumpness, with a mop of dark curly hair, round face and bright dark eyes. She was wearing a nightshirt with rows of ladybirds marching across the front. She would be good with children, Thanet thought, practical, reliable, but with a sense of fun.

Her eyes clouded. 'I suppose you're here about that poor woman.' She shivered and rubbed her arms, where gooseflesh had suddenly appeared. 'To think it might have been me...'

'I think we have to reserve judgement on that, for the moment, Miss Proven –'

'Angela,' she cut in.

'– Angela.'

'But why? It was a burglar, surely?'

'That is a possibility, yes. Though nothing was taken.'

'Only a possibility? You mean, it might have been someone she knew? That it was *deliberate*?' She shivered again. 'That's even worse.'

'We really don't know yet. That's what I'm trying to find out.'

'I don't see how I can help. I never even met her.'

'I'm aware of that. But part of my job is to talk to everybody who is even remotely connected with the crime. And as it took place in Mrs Broxton's house and that is where you work . . .'

She shrugged. 'Go ahead, if it'll do any good.'

Thanet sat back in his chair. It was important to look relaxed, somewhat difficult in the circumstances. Despite the spurious air of privacy induced by the curtain this interview was in fact taking place in public and within the hearing of anybody who cared to listen. His tone was casual as he said quietly, 'You've worked for Mrs Broxton for some time, I believe?'

'For nearly two years – well, twenty months, to be precise. I came when Henry was born.'

'You obviously get on well with her – with them.'

'She's pretty good to me. Treats me fairly – sees I don't get landed with all the housework, for example, makes sure I get my time off. And they've provided me with a Mini. I know it's so that I can go shopping with the children and take them out, but even so, I have the use of it in my spare time, and that's great. Especially living where we do. Some employers never think you might not like being stuck out in the country with no means of transport. And she doesn't try to undermine my authority with the children, that's another thing. You wouldn't believe how some mothers carry on.'

'She's very fond of the children, I understand.'

'Potty about them. She absolutely hated having to leave Henry, when she went back to work after having him. "Angela," she said to me, "for two pins I'd chuck it all in."'

'But she didn't.'

'Well, it's difficult for someone in her position, isn't it? I mean, you spend years building up your career and then you have children and you've got to decide whether to stop altogether or try to keep things ticking over. I think she knew that if she opted out she'd be very bored later on, when they didn't need her so much. But it wasn't easy for her, I can tell you.'

A bell rang and at once there was a scraping of chairs, a sudden heightening in the buzz of conversation up and down the ward. Goodbyes were said, footsteps receded, silence seeped back.

Thanet lowered his voice still further. 'How did Mr Broxton feel about this?'

She frowned. 'I really can't see where all this is leading.'

Thanet grinned. 'To be honest, neither can I. But can you bear with me? Believe me, the only way to proceed in a case like this is to gather as much information as possible and keep sifting it through. Most of it is irrelevant, but you never know.'

She grinned back. 'OK, you've convinced me. As long as you don't expect me to gossip about my employers . . .'

'Not gossip, no. What I would value is straightforward information, or conclusions based on your own observation. If you really feel you don't want to answer a question then fine, that's all right by me.'

'You mean that?'

'I wouldn't say it if I didn't.'

'OK, then. Not that there's anything to hide, but . . .'

The curtain suddenly swished back and there was some confusion while Thanet explained to a startled nurse that no, he was not a visitor trying to get away with extending visiting hours and the Sister came bustling up to clarify the situation. Those patients who were not comatose watched with interest. What was going on?

Finally they were left in peace again.

'You were saying, Angela, about Mr Broxton . . .'

A teasing look. 'You were asking, you mean . . . Well, Mr

Broxton is a busy man. He really doesn't have much to do with the children. A lot of men aren't very interested in infants. Later on, when they're older, he'll probably find them much more rewarding. But I think he was quite keen for Vanessa to resume her career. I think he realises that she's the sort of woman who needs to use her brain.' Angela grinned. 'Not like me.'

'Now here's a question you might take exception to.' And if you do, thought Thanet, you'll have answered it just the same. 'Is everything all right between Mr and Mrs Broxton?'

'You mean, does he have a bit on the side? Not to my knowledge. No, they get on pretty well, really. They have the occasional argument, but no monumental rows or anything like that. He's very fond of her I think, in his own way.'

But Angela evidently wasn't as taken with Guy Broxton as with his wife, thought Thanet. Her tone was definitely lukewarm. Relevant? Most unlikely, he thought.

'Was Mrs Broxton friendly with Perdita Master?'

The mop of hair swayed to and fro as Angela shook her head. 'Not so far as I know.'

'So Mrs Master never rang up, came to the house . . . ?'

'No.' She hesitated.

'What?' Thanet prompted.

'I did hear Vanessa mention her once, though. She and Mr Broxton were discussing some exhibition they'd been to. Vanessa had wanted to buy one of Mrs Master's paintings, but Mr Broxton hadn't liked it.'

'It just isn't to my taste, that's all.'

'Well I thought it was excellent.'

'I'm not disputing its quality. I agree, it was a very fine painting. I just don't want to have it hanging on my wall.'

'But why not?'

'It was too . . . dark.'

'How can you say that? There was a lot of colour in it.'

'I didn't mean visually. I meant in mood. Perhaps "dark" wasn't the right word. "Sombre", then.'

'I just think we ought to buy one soon. She's getting so well known, the prices will go sky-high and we'll be kicking ourselves for not buying earlier.'

'I thought we agreed we'd never buy anything for the house just because it's a good investment.'

'But if we like it and *it's a good investment, that's a bonus, isn't it?'*

'Yes. If. But that doesn't apply here. Perdita Master is, I grant you, a very talented artist, and her work may well, as you say, appreciate in value. But I find it depressing, not uplifting, and I don't want to have to look at it every morning when I come down to breakfast. Now if you want to buy that painting and hang it in your study, then go ahead, that's fine by me.'

'And did she?' said Thanet.

Angela shook her head. 'No.'

'And that was the only time you heard either of the Broxtons mention her name?'

'Until yesterday, yes. It stuck in my mind because we read *A Winter's Tale* at school, and I always thought Perdita such a sad name. Lost. The lost one.' The corners of Angela's mouth tugged down at the corners. 'And now she is, isn't she? Poor woman.' She looked on the point of tears.

Thanet was surprised, but reminded himself that robust as she may appear Angela had not only just undergone surgery but had sustained a nasty shock. She must have felt that she had had a narrow escape when the woman who replaced her had been murdered in the kitchen which by now must feel as familiar to Angela as that in her own home. He hurried to reintroduce a brisk note of commonsense back into the conversation. 'Mrs Broxton never mentioned that she had a friend who trained as a nanny?'

'No.' Angela shrugged. 'There was no reason why she should. It's not as though we ever met.'

There was no more to be learnt here, it seemed.

At the intensive care unit Joan was back in the waiting room. She stood up when she saw him. 'She's asleep now. It's what she needs most of all, they say. Rest.'

'Good. You're ready now, then?'

He helped her on with her coat. 'An early night for you, love. We'll pick up something to eat on the way home.' He held the door open. 'Do you think you'll be able to arrange a few days' leave?'

'Oh yes, I've already made tentative arrangements.' Joan tucked her arm into his as they set off along the corridor. Now that all the visitors had gone the place seemed virtually deserted. 'There's nothing the others can't deal with.' She pulled a face. 'Except, I suppose, Sharon. It's taken so much hard work to get her into the right frame of mind to make a real effort to kick the habit of shoplifting, I'm afraid she might revert if she feels I've let her down, walked out on her.'

'She'll understand, surely, if you tell her why.'

'With her head, yes. But not with her heart. By now her reaction to rejection is automatic, virtually outside her control. People have been walking out on her all her life – mother, father, boyfriends, husband . . . It's really tough being a single parent. It's difficult enough trying to work with two young children if you have the support of a husband, but when you're on your own . . . It must seem so much easier to her just to go out and steal the things she needs, especially when there they are, spread out all around her every time she walks into a shop. And she's offended four times already. It was only because of the children that she was given probation last time. I've got a nasty feeling that next time she might get six or nine months inside. And the children will be taken into care.'

'Yes, I can see that. What time are you seeing Dr MacPherson tomorrow?'

'Eleven o'clock. After he's finished his rounds.'

'In that case, couldn't you fit in one visit to Sharon tomorrow morning, first? Then if you arranged another appointment for, say, Friday, that would probably see her through the week. I'm sure we could find someone to sit with your mother for an hour or so on Friday.'

A door they were passing opened and a man stepped out without looking where he was going, bumping into Thanet. Thanet put out a hand. 'Look out ... Oh, it's Mr Harrow, isn't it?'

Perdita's stepfather was almost unrecognisable in heavy tweed overcoat and fur hat pulled down over his ears. Presumably years of living in a hothouse had made him especially vulnerable to chills when he went out. He looked dazed, disorientated, and looked at Thanet without recognition.

'Inspector Thanet. We met this morning ... And this is my wife.'

Harrow looked at him for a moment longer before his eyes cleared. 'Ah, yes. Of course. I'm sorry, I ...'

'Are you all right?'

Harrow frowned. 'It's hot, isn't it?'

He put his hand up to his head and tugged his hat off, looked at it as though he'd never seen it before. His face was red and his forehead wet with perspiration. 'Sorry, Mrs Thanet, you must think me very rude. How do you do?'

Joan smiled as they shook hands.

They all began to move along the corridor.

'I've just been having a word with Sister, about my wife ... Are you here visiting someone too, Inspector?'

'Yes. How is Mrs Harrow?'

Harrow frowned. 'If only they could find out what's the matter with her ... Ah, there's Stephanie.'

So this was the Harrows' daughter, Perdita's young stepsister. The corridor had widened out into a waiting area and the girl sat there alone in an attitude of dejection, head bent, thin shoulders bowed. She looked up as they came into view and Thanet was disturbed by her expression. She's afraid, he thought. Terrified, in fact.

Harrow advanced on her, smiling. 'Sorry I was so long, Steph.'

The girl stood up. Small, slight, with a froth of frizzy fair hair, she looked disturbingly like her dead sister. She glanced at the Thanets, dismissed them as of no importance. 'What did she say?' Her tone was urgent.

That, no doubt was the reason for her fear. She thought her mother was going to die.

And, thought Thanet sadly, remembering the pitiful state that Mrs Harrow was in, she was probably right.

Harrow shook his head. 'She had nothing new to tell us. We've just got to be patient, that's all. Steph, this is –'

'Patient!' Stephanie looked frantic. 'How long do we have to go on being patient? Until Mum is . . .' But she couldn't bring out the word, choked on it. 'All this stuff about advances in medical science! It's been months now, and they can't even tell us what's wrong with her!'

'I know. Hush.' Harrow put his arm around her but she flung it off, grabbed up her anorak and began putting it on. 'Let's get out of here!'

She marched off along the corridor still struggling to get her arms into the jacket. With an apologetic glance at the Thanets Harrow followed her.

Thanet watched them go. He felt desperately sorry for both of them, sorry most of all, perhaps, that they didn't seem able to turn to each other for comfort.

'Poor girl,' said Joan, looking after them. 'It's not surprising she's in such a state. Her sister murdered, her mother . . . Is there really a possibility that Mrs Harrow might die?'

'More than likely, I should think.' Thanet was grim. He had encountered enough misery for one day. He put an arm round Joan's shoulders. 'Come on. Home,' he said.

THIRTEEN

When Thanet looked out of the window next morning he thought for a moment that it had been snowing. Trees, shrubs, lawn were all covered with a filmy blanket of white. Then he saw that it was merely an exceptionally heavy frost. Although it was warm in the bedroom he shivered at the prospect of going out. He hated the cold. Winter could never pass too quickly for him.

Lineham invariably arrived at the office first, Thanet was never quite sure why. Was the sergeant an insomniac, or an early bird by nature? Was it simply that he loved his work (true) and couldn't wait to get to his desk each morning? Or was it a need to get away from his family that drove him out of the house betimes each day?

In any case, whenever Thanet arrived first as he did this morning he felt quite smug. Should he as a reward indulge himself in a pipe before Lineham arrived? Perhaps not. He had been trying to cut down lately and, besides, the sergeant hated pipe smoke. Lineham was bound to be upset at being – Thanet consulted his watch – yes, a good ten minutes late, without having to suffer what he claimed was near-asphyxiation.

Thanet sat down and hunted through the stack of reports on his desk for the one on the PM. It wasn't there. Perhaps

Mallard intended to bring it up himself, later. There was nothing from forensic yet, either. He must remember to give them a ring.

The door burst open.

'What a moron!' Lineham exploded. 'Idiots like that should be put off the road, banned from driving!'

'What's the matter, Mike?' Thanet could guess, in view of the weather conditions this morning. He himself had seen three cars at the side of the road with smashed wings and dented bumpers.

'Why on earth can't people keep their distance when the roads are icy? I could see this ... this ...' Words failed him. Lineham hated swearing. '... this IDIOT behind me, driving much too close, but there's nothing you can do except let cretins like that go past, and we were in a line of traffic, so I couldn't. And of course, the car in front of me braked unexpectedly ... I was all right, I was far enough away to slow down in time, but this moron ...' Lineham dropped into his chair and thumped his desk so hard with a clenched fist that the various objects on it jigged and rattled. 'I could kill him!'

Lineham had always been keen on cars and his Ford Escort was dear to his heart.

'How much damage is there?'

Thanet let him talk the incident out of his system. He knew he wouldn't get much sense out of him otherwise. Eventually the sergeant wound down. 'Sorry, I should have asked. How's your mother-in-law?'

'Better. They're moving her out of intensive care and say the risk of a second attack should now be past.'

'When'll she be allowed home?'

'Might even be today. We won't know for certain until the doctor's seen her this morning. She's coming to us for a while. Joan's going to take a few days' leave.'

'By the way, thank Joan for having that word with Louise, will you? She seems happier about things now.'

'Actually, that was purely fortuitous. I hadn't actually spoken to Joan about it.'

'Well I'm grateful, anyway. It really helped her to know that someone like Joan had felt exactly the same. She's already decided to take her advice and do some refresher courses.' Lineham shook his head in mock despair. 'I don't know. Women! You can tell them things till you're blue in the face and they don't take a blind bit of notice. Then along comes some outsider – no offence meant, of course, sir – and there they are falling over themselves to do precisely what you were suggesting in the first place . . . Anything interesting come in overnight?'

'Haven't had a chance to find out yet.'

A sheepish grin indicated that Lineham was back to normal. 'I did get a bit carried away there. Sorry. But honestly . . .'

Lineham looked all set to start sounding off all over again and Thanet had no compunction in interrupting.

'Mike!' He glanced at his watch. Eight-forty. 'Look, it's time to go down to the morning meeting.' He handed the reports over to Lineham. 'You'd better make a start on these, or we're never going to get anywhere today. And give forensic a ring, find out what's happening.'

But the meeting was quickly over. Draco had rung to say he couldn't make it and Tody took his place. It wasn't until Draco was absent, Thanet thought, that you realised what a difference his presence made. Irritating he might be – infuriating, occasionally – but he did make the place hum, there was no doubt about that.

Mallard arrived soon after he got back to the office. 'What happened to your car, Lineham?'

Lineham opened his mouth but Thanet held up his hand. 'No. I absolutely refuse to hear it all again. Let's just say someone ran into the back of it.'

'Oh, bad luck.' Mallard peered at Lineham over his half-moons. 'You're all right, though?'

'Yes, *I'm* fine. Wish I could say the same about my car.'

'Good.' Mallard turned back to Thanet. 'Thought I'd just pop up with this.' He handed over the report.'Not that there's anything very startling in it. Asphyxiation, following a blow on the head, just as we thought.'

'No ifs or buts?'

'Perfectly straightforward.'

'Not one single, minute revelation?'

'None. Sorry. I heard about your mother-in-law, by the way, Luke. How is she?'

Thanet once again gave a brief account of the situation.

'If she's over the first twenty-four hours the imminent danger should have passed. But I expect she'll have to make some changes, as far as diet and exercise are concerned.'

'So we gather. Doctor MacPherson's going to have a chat with her and Joan this morning.'

'Good. You make sure she follows his advice. The most important thing is that she shouldn't regard herself as a permanent invalid.'

'Not much likelihood of that, I shouldn't think.'

'And make sure you don't treat her like one, either. So many people still think that if they've had a heart attack they've got to languish the rest of their lives away in an armchair.' Mallard snorted. 'Lot of nonsense. The more they keep their circulation going the better. Exercise is the answer, Luke, and you make sure she gets it. Plenty of exercise. When she's had two or three weeks to recuperate, of course. But it's important to start in a small way as soon as possible, and build up the programme.'

'Don't worry. We'll see she does as she's told.'

'Good. Anyway, how's the case going?'

'Slowly, as usual.'

Mallard grinned and slapped Thanet on the shoulder. 'Patience, Luke. Patience. The older you get the more you realise how important it is to cultivate it.'

Thanet smiled back, remembering the years when Mallard's short fuse had been notorious. 'You're an example to us all, Doc.'

When Mallard had gone Thanet read through the post mortem report before handing it to Lineham. 'He's right. Doesn't help at all. Did you get anywhere with forensic?'

Lineham shook his head. '"Soon", that's all.'

'I'll believe that when I see it. Anything interesting in the other reports?'

'Not really. The landlord of the Green Man confirms Mr Master's story. He and Mrs Master arrived there at a quarter or ten to nine, stayed half an hour or so. He remembers them because they spent the whole time arguing. In the end she walked out, and he followed.'

'Hmm.' Nothing new there. 'What about that supper safari the Broxtons' neighbour suggested might be going on that night, to account for all the cars she heard?'

'Not a whisper about that. I think we can take it there wasn't one.'

'So whose cars were they, I wonder? Anything else?'

'Routine stuff, that's all.'

'Have you gone right through them?'

'Just a few more.'

'Pass a couple over.'

A few minutes later Lineham said, 'Mrs Broxton's cleaning woman confirms the phone call Mr Master told us about. And . . .' His tone suddenly changed and he sat up. 'Listen to this. At around 9.15 on Monday morning she heard Mrs Master talking to someone called Howard on the telephone. She was arranging to meet him that evening.'

The night she died. Swain had denied any such meeting.

Thanet held out his hand. 'Let me see.'

He skimmed the report. *I heard Mrs Master say, 'See you tonight, then. Soon after nine.'*

'He was lying,' said Lineham with satisfaction. 'I knew it.'

And, as they had suspected, so was Mrs Swain. No doubt she and Swain had cooked up their mutual alibi between them.

It was what they needed, the first discrepancy, their first break. It was only a small matter but enough to open up new lines of enquiry. If a case was static, it was dead. All the same, Thanet knew it was important not to get carried away. 'Don't read too much into it, Mike.'

The phone rang. Bentley, who was doing the house-to-house enquiries in Wheelwright's Lane.

'Thought you'd want to know right away, sir. I've just interviewed a Mrs Marsh. She lives in one of the semi-detached cottages opposite where Mr Master and the Swains live. Her neighbour, an old lady, is away visiting her son, but Mrs Marsh has got a baby who's teething and she spent most of Monday evening in his bedroom walking about with him or sitting in the chair by the window, rocking him to try and get him off to sleep –'

'The bedroom's at the front?'

'Yes. There was no light on in the room, she'd just left the door from the landing open, and she drew the curtains back because she was bored stiff. So she had a good view of the houses opposite.'

'And?' Thanet knew he was being impatient but couldn't help himself. With any luck . . .

'She says they *all* went out during the evening – Mr Master, Mr Swain and Mrs Swain.'

'The Swains were together?'

'No, they left separately. Mr Master left some time before them, between eight and half past, she thinks, and then Mr Swain, around nine. Mrs Swain followed immediately afterwards.'

'Followed? You mean she got the impression that Mrs Swain was actually following her husband?'

'Yes. She says that as soon as Mr Swain's car had driven

out, his wife came out immediately and went off in the same direction. Towards the village.'

And thence to Melton? 'If it was dark, how did she know which of them left first?'

'She knows the cars and both the houses opposite have security lights which come on automatically as soon as anyone comes out of the front door and crosses the drive. She saw them quite clearly, she says.'

'Did she see any of them come back?'

'Mr Master got back at around 9.30. Then a bit later, around a quarter to ten she thinks, Mrs Swain got back.'

'Before her husband?'

'Yes.'

'She's certain of that?'

'Seems to be. Says Mr Swain arrived home about half an hour after his wife. Says all the coming and going livened up her evening no end.'

Thanet could hear the smile in Bentley's voice. 'Well done, Bentley. Thanks for ringing in right away.'

'I thought you'd want to know.'

Thanet put the receiver down. 'Did you hear all that?' He recounted the conversation to Lineham.

'A witness!' said Lineham. 'Terrific! It's obvious, isn't it? Mr Swain arranges to go over to Melton to see Mrs Master soon after nine. Mrs Swain guesses that's where he's going – where else would he be going at nine o'clock in the evening? –'

'The pub?' said Thanet.

Lineham glared at him.

'All right, sorry, Mike. Go on.'

'– and decides to follow him.'

'Why?'

'Because she's curious to know where Mrs Master is? She's a pretty forceful type isn't she, Mrs Swain. Maybe she decided she wasn't just going to sit back and let Mrs Master take her husband away without a fight. So she decides she's going to tackle her. But she can't if she doesn't know where she is. She may even have asked her husband, but he refused to tell her. Anyway, the moment Mr Swain's car has driven off she's after him.'

'And then?'

Lineham paused. 'I haven't had time to think it through yet.'

'So think it through now. Go back to the point when Master arrives at the Broxtons'.'

'Well, let's see. Mr Master claims he got there at 8.30. After the argument about whether his wife will go with him or not, he drags her into the car and then drives off. He blackmails her into agreeing to have a drink with him, on the basis that if she won't he'll just keep on driving and the children will be left alone for hours. They arrive at the Green Man in Melton around 8.45. At around nine Mr Swain leaves Nettleton, followed by his wife –'

'If she did follow him, it would have been a bit tricky to avoid being spotted. The lanes around Melton aren't exactly thronged with traffic at that time of night.'

'That would have made it all the easier for her!' said Lineham triumphantly. 'She could have kept her distance, she'd have been able to see the glare of his headlights some way ahead. And if she didn't actually get close enough for him to recognise the car – and as you pointed out earlier, it was dark – then she'd have been in no danger of him spotting her. After all, he'd have no reason to suspect he was being followed. I don't suppose she made a habit of it.'

'All right. So they're both in Melton. He turns into the oast house, she presumably hangs back or drives past.'

'Right. He knocks at the door, but Mrs Master is out at the pub with her husband, so he gets no reply.' Lineham stopped, frowned. 'This is where it gets complicated.'

'Yes. Because if he did it, it must mean that he hung around until after she and Mr Master got back at – 9.20, was it?'

Lineham was consulting his notebook. 'Yes. Nine-twenty.'

'Well, let's say, for the sake of argument, that Master did exactly what he claims to have done, brought his wife back and then left. And let's say Swain did hang about waiting in case she came back. He sees them arrive, watches Master leave, then knocks on the door...'

Thanet paused, indicating that Lineham should continue the scenario.

'She takes him into the kitchen,' said the sergeant, 'and, for whatever reason, they have an argument, some sort of scuffle and she slips, bangs her head on the corner of the table, passes out.' He stopped, looking rueful. 'And that's where we come unstuck, isn't it, sir? I agree, I just can't see him putting that polythene bag over her head.'

Thanet was shaking his head. 'No, it just won't work, will it? For one thing, I can't really see why Perdita and Swain should have had an argument at all. Anyway, I don't think he did go into the house.'

'Why not?'

'Think, Mike! He's her lover. They've arranged to meet. He's hung around in the hope of seeing her and finally she gets back and he waits until her husband's gone then she lets him in. Even if, for the sake of argument, we say he did kill her, I can't see a disagreement blowing up to murderous proportions between them *and* his getting away, all in the space of ten minutes.'

'Why ten minutes?'

'Because that's when Mrs Broxton gets home.'

'But she didn't go straight into the kitchen!' said Lineham triumphantly. 'She went upstairs because Henry was screaming.'

Thanet frowned. 'I'd forgotten that.'

'She didn't ring in to report finding the body until 9.40. So he would have had twenty minutes.'

Thanet waved his hand irritably. 'Ten minutes, twenty minutes, what's the difference? It's still not long enough. No, I don't think he went in at all.'

'But his wife might have!' said Lineham. 'Say Swain didn't wait, say he gave up and left before the Masters arrived back. *But say his wife didn't.*'

'You mean she might have been so geared up to having it out with Mrs Master that now she'd found out where she was staying she was determined to sit it out, no matter how long she had to wait.'

'Well, it would be quite in character, don't you think, sir?'

'Right. Say she did. Go on.'

'Mrs Master arrives home. Henry couldn't have been crying at that stage because if so she'd probably have picked him up and been carrying him when she answered the door to Mrs Swain. And she'd hardly then have taken him back up and plonked him in his cot while she talked to her, would she?'

'No.'

'So when she came in she probably either popped up to reassure herself that the children were all right or went to the foot of the stairs and listened to see if either of them was crying. In any case, she then went into the kitchen to make herself a drink of Horlicks or something. She puts the milk on the stove and then hears someone knocking at the front door. Mrs Swain knows that Mrs Master is in because she saw her arrive back and she's not going to give up easily. When she doesn't get any response from ringing the bell she hammers on the door – that's probably what woke Henry up, come to think of it. He might not have started crying immediately, so Mrs Master has taken her into the kitchen by the time he starts, and doesn't hear him. Then they have the argument and everything happens just as we've suggested.' Lineham looked at Thanet hopefully. 'What d'you think, sir?'

Thanet was looking for loopholes. 'What about Mrs Broxton?'

'It could all have been over by then. An awful lot can happen in ten minutes, or even five. Oh, I know what you said about ten or even twenty minutes not being long enough for a quarrel of these proportions to have blown up between Mr Swain and Mrs Master, and I tend to agree with you. They were lovers, after all. If she was going to break off with him she'd do it gently, lead up to it ... But Mrs Swain is a different matter. She isn't going to hang around making polite conversation, is she? So it happens just as we've said and then, just as it's all over, Mrs Swain hears the front door slam. She realises she's got to get away fast, and lets herself out through the back door ... Of course! That would explain why it was unlocked!'

'Could be ... And it's only a ten-minute drive to Nettleton, she could still have been home by a quarter to ten ... But if it did happen like that, why did she get back before her husband?'

'Perhaps he didn't feel like going home straight away, went to a pub, had a few drinks?'

'Possible, I suppose. Well, we mustn't get carried away by all this but it's certainly the most likely scenario we've come up with so far.' Thanet had jumped up, begun putting on his overcoat as he talked. He was eager now to tackle the Swains again, put this new theory to the test. 'Come on, Mike, let's go.'

FOURTEEN

The mid-morning traffic was light and they were soon clear of the town. They had decided to talk to Swain first, see if they could get anything more out of him before driving to TVS at Maidstone. Thanet's spirits rose. He was looking forward to the interview with Mrs Swain. She was a formidable opponent and he enjoyed a challenge. Interviewing was the part of his work that he enjoyed most, when mind and intuition were stretched to the limit and the skills he had built up through years of experience were fully employed.

Although the sun was high in the sky the temperature had still not risen much above freezing, and in the shade of trees and hedges frost still crisped the grass. The ground, Thanet guessed, would still be rock-hard, furrowed ridges in ploughed fields only just beginning to soften as the warmth began to penetrate. Persuaded by these early frosts that winter was upon them, soon now the trees would shed their remaining leaves, the glorious autumn colour would melt away and the woods become no more than dark smudges delineating the graceful curves of fields and Downs.

For a while both men were silent, thinking. Then, picking up the conversation where they had left it, Thanet said, 'I bet he doesn't even know she went out that night. She left after him and came back before him.'

Lineham grinned. 'I can't see she'd have told him she followed him.'

'No. In which case, if it was her suggestion, when they heard about the murder, that it might be a good idea to say they'd both been home all evening, he'd assume she was trying to protect him rather than herself.'

Lineham gave a cynical grunt. 'Typical, I should think.'

'You really don't like her, do you, Mike?'

'You said you weren't too keen on her either.'

'That's true. But I do find her stimulating. Pity she's at work. I'd like to have interviewed them together, seen how they interact.' Thanet was always fascinated by the way in which people can change in the presence of their partners. The bold become muted, the shy can blossom, the strong become weak and the weak strong, as if the chemistry which attracted them to each other in the first place is most evident when they are together.

Nettleton, as usual, seemed asleep. Thanet wondered if it ever woke up. They turned into Wheelwright's Lane and a minute or two later Lineham slowed down as they approached the cluster of houses. Thanet glanced at the cottage where Mrs Marsh their witness lived.

'Stop short of the Swains' drive, Mike.'

Lineham pulled up and they both got out of the car. It was immediately obvious that anyone in the front bedroom of either cottage would have an excellent view of the Swains' front drive directly opposite. The cottages were close to the road, the front gardens tiny, and there were no trees to obscure the view.

'Can't be much more than fifty, seventy-five yards to the Swains' front door,' said Lineham. 'And with security lights on . . .'

'The sightlines into the Masters' drive aren't as good, though. That tall beech hedge gets in the way.'

'True. But that really doesn't matter so much, does it, sir?

He's already admitted going to see his wife, and the times tally with Mrs Marsh's statement.'

'Quite. Might as well leave the car here. There's plenty of room to pass.'

The neatly clipped yew hedges on either side of the five-barred gate had obscured their view of the garden and it was not until they were halfway to the front door that Thanet spotted Swain working in one of the flower borders over to the left, at the far side of the lawn. He was bent double cutting down spent herbaceous plants and the wheelbarrow beside him was piled high with autumn debris.

Thanet called his name and Swain straightened up, secateurs in one hand, a clump of dead flower stalks in the other. When he saw who it was he laid the stems on top of the heaped barrow and began to walk towards the two policemen, stripping off his gardening gloves as he came. He was wearing ancient corduroys, an old anorak and wellington boots. The picture of a healthy countryman was belied as he came closer by the pallor of his face, the dark smudges beneath his eyes. He obviously hadn't been getting much sleep lately. Guilty or innocent, not surprising in the circumstances.

'Sorry to trouble you. I wonder if we could have another word?'

Shoulders drooping with resignation Swain turned and led them along the narrow paved path at the side of the house around to the back door. Here he stopped, pushed it open and paused to lever off his boots, stepping in stockinged feet on to the doormat inside. Thanet and Lineham followed him in. Swain pulled out a chair and sat down, indicating that they should do likewise.

Thanet waited until Lineham was settled, notebook at the ready, then folding his hands together on the table leaned forward. 'We don't take very kindly to people who lie to us in murder enquiries, Mr Swain.'

Swain's response puzzled him. First there was what Thanet

could have sworn was a genuine look of surprise, almost immediately overlaid by comprehension. But Swain's tone was firm. 'I haven't lied to you, Inspector.'

'There are, shall we say, sins of omission as well as commission.'

Swain hesitated. You could almost see him thinking, *How much do they know?*

'Mr Swain, when I asked you if you had seen Mrs Master on Monday night you said no. What would you have said, I wonder, if instead I had asked if you had *arranged* to see her on Monday night?'

Swain opened his mouth to reply and Thanet had to make a lightning decision: should he give Swain the opportunity to lie? If he did, time would be wasted and a tactical advantage lost. 'And before you say anything, I should warn you that we have a witness who overheard that arrangement being made.'

Once again Swain's reaction puzzled him. This time the look of comprehension in his eyes was immediate, but almost at once was overtaken by confusion. Why? If Perdita had told him that the cleaning woman had overheard the call, why should he now be feeling confused? Unless . . . Yes, that must be it. Perhaps Swain had first thought that his wife might have listened in on his conversation with Perdita, but had at once realised that it couldn't have been she who had told the police. It would have made nonsense of their agreed alibi.

As he watched Swain trying to make up his mind what to say he decided he would lose nothing by putting him out of his misery and might, perhaps, gain. Let off the hook, Swain would, as Lineham would have put it, owe him one. He explained about the cleaner, watching comprehension leach into the man's expressive eyes.

Swain made an embarrassed gesture. 'Yes, well, I'm sorry, Inspector, if I misled you. But I wasn't lying. I really didn't see her, you know.'

'Well, well . . .'

The unexpected, lazy drawl from the doorway startled Thanet, engrossed as he was in the way the interview was going.

'The third degree, and in my own kitchen! Who would have believed it?'

Victoria Swain stepped forward, moved indolently to stand behind her husband and rest her hands on his shoulders in a brief caress. Then she slid into a chair beside him. This morning she was wearing narrow black trousers, a silky pale blue blouse and a black knitted jacket with a design of huge pansies in shades of mauve and blue. Another Swain creation, Thanet presumed. Her blue eyes mocked him across the kitchen table.

Well, he thought, you wanted to interview them together, and here they are.

'Not at work today, Mrs Swain?'

'Sorry to disappoint you, but no, Inspector. As a matter of fact I'm working at home. I thought I heard voices, so . . .'

'I'm not in the least disappointed. In fact, I'm delighted. It will save us that tiresome journey through the M20 roadworks, to Maidstone. We were coming to see you next.'

'Really. How convenient.' She raised her hands, palms up. 'Well, here I am. Do your worst – or should I say, your best?'

Thanet saw Lineham shift slightly and guessed what the sergeant was thinking. *She really gets up my nose.*

Swain gave his wife an apologetic glance. 'It's no good, Vicky. They know.'

Know what? wondered Thanet.

'Know what?' said Mrs Swain. *Be careful*, her frown said. *Give nothing away unless you have to.*

'That I arranged to see Perdita on Monday night. The cleaning woman at Vanessa's house overheard Perdita on the telephone.'

'Oh dear, oh dear, what a calamity!' She raised an eyebrow at Thanet, inviting complicity. 'Servants have always been the bane of the middle classes, wouldn't you agree, Inspector? No privacy.'

'Well, now you're here, Mrs Swain, I will say to you what I said to your husband. We don't take very kindly to people who lie to us in murder enquiries.'

The blue eyes opened wide, baby-innocent. 'Lie to you, Inspector? Who's been lying to you?'

'As I also said to your husband, there are sins of omission as well as commission. He may have been guilty of the first, but you are most certainly guilty of the second.'

'Oh?' The innocence overlaid by wariness, now.

'Yes.' Thanet allowed the heavy monosyllable to hang on the air, the silence to stretch out. No harm in making her sweat a little. This wasn't a game and the sooner she realised it the better.

'All these tales of a cosy evening at home. Pork and apple casserole, wasn't it, as I recall? Followed by gooseberry fool. Then a little work, television and bed.'

'My, you have got a good memory, Inspector. Didn't even need to refer to your notebook ... But, as a matter of fact, that was precisely what we did have for supper on Monday night. Down to the last detail.'

Thanet was tired of sparring. 'Was that before or after you both went out?'

Their expressions changed. Thanet was certain that it was the word 'both' which caused Swain's eyebrows to rise and the look of enquiry he turned on his wife.

Victoria Swain, however, did not even blink. 'I think you must be misinformed,' she said icily. The blue eyes were frosty now but Thanet thought that deep within them he detected the first flicker of unease.

'Reliably informed, as a matter of fact, and by a witness who could have no possible reason to lie.'

At the word 'witness' she tried to conceal her dismay, but failed. She shifted uneasily on her chair and Thanet could see that she was struggling against the temptation to look at her husband and gauge his reaction to all this.

'Witness, Inspector?' said Swain.

Thanet glanced at Lineham and nodded at the sergeant's notebook. Lineham obediently began to thumb through it. Both men knew that as Bentley had given the report by telephone there would be no written report in its pages. Thanet hoped the sergeant would make it sound good.

'Let me see ... Here we are ...' Lineham held the book up as if to see it more clearly. '"On Monday evening Mr Swain drove off towards the village at about nine o'clock and Mrs Swain followed immediately afterwards ..."'

Swain's head snapped around to look at his wife and Victoria Swain burst out, 'How could anyone possibly say that, even if it were true. It was pitch dark by then.'

'"I could see clearly because they have security lights which come on automatically as soon as anyone comes out of the front door and crosses the drive ..."'

Mrs Swain simultaneously thumped the table in frustration and stood up. 'Must be that old biddy across the road, damn her eyes. Twitching her net curtains all day long, and nothing better to do than spy on her neighbours ...' She marched across the room and stood with her back to them at the window, folding her arms tightly as if to hold her anger in, prevent it getting out of control. Her back was rigid and her head turned slightly to one side, so that from where he sat Thanet could see the muscles of her jaw working.

It was a tacit admission. But why so violent a reaction? he wondered. Was it because she had lost face, been caught out in a lie? Because she was going to have to bear the humiliation of admitting to her husband that she had followed him? Or was there a more sinister reason? Was she in truth the murderer, faced now by the fact that her alibi had crumbled?

She swung around to face him again. 'No!' she said, startling him. Had she read his mind?

But she was merely contradicting herself, it seemed. 'No, it couldn't have been her. She's away, isn't she? I saw her son carting her off plus suitcase on Saturday morning. So it must have been little Mrs butter-won't-melt-in-my-mouth Marsh.'

'Does it matter who saw you? The fact is, you were seen, both of you.'

'Of course it matters!' she said savagely. She glanced at her husband. 'For God's sake stop looking at me like that, Howard! I had a right to know where you were going, didn't I? I am your *wife*.'

'You mean, you actually *followed* me?'

Thanet saw her realise, too late, that she could have claimed to have gone somewhere else. It was unlike her to miss a trick. It could only be because the shock of being discovered had temporarily affected her judgement. He watched her collect herself and prepare to make the best of the situation. How would she do it? he wondered. And who would she tackle first? Himself, or her husband?

She glanced at Thanet. 'I should like to speak to my husband alone.'

He shook his head. 'You've had plenty of time to talk to him, if you wished, and there'll be plenty of time after we've gone.'

The blue eyes flashed ice at him but she did not hesitate. Swiftly she crossed to sit once more beside Swain, half turning her back on the two policemen as if to shut them out.

So her husband took priority. That was interesting. Had he in fact been mistaken? If Mrs Swain had truly felt herself to be in danger, would she not have tried to save her own skin, first? Was she innocent after all?

Thanet glanced at Lineham. The sergeant's eyes were sparkling. He was enjoying this.

Victoria Swain laid her hand on her husband's arm. 'I just wanted to know what was happening,' she pleaded. 'You can't imagine what it's like, being left in the dark...'

No response.

'I just thought, if I could talk to her . . .'

Swain's eyes narrowed. 'You saw her?'

'No. How could I? You know yourself that she wasn't there.'

Swain glanced quickly at Thanet, then back at his wife. Calmly, deliberately, he shook her hand off his arm, a telling gesture of rejection.

She drew back as if stung. Anger sparked in her eyes and her tone changed. 'Well what did you expect me to do? Sit back and do nothing while you ran after that little –' With an effort she stopped herself, glowered at Thanet. *Now look what you've done.*

Thanet didn't mind being blamed if the results were so fruitful.

'Well,' he said pleasantly, 'I think we're beginning to get somewhere. Correct me if I'm wrong, won't you? On Monday evening you, Mr Swain, set off for Mrs Broxton's house to see Mrs Master and you, Mrs Swain, followed. What interests us is what happened when you got there.'

They looked at each other.

'Nothing,' they said simultaneously, united at least in this.

'Could you be a little more specific?'

Swain shrugged. 'I rang the bell several times, but there was no reply.'

Lineham was scribbling something. He held his notepad out for Thanet to see. *Bell out of order*, he had written. Thanet nodded. He hadn't forgotten.

'Did you knock?'

'Yes, but there's no knocker and it's a great big thick door, so I doubt that anyone would have heard.'

Unless, like Master, you had been determined to make as much noise as possible, thought Thanet.

'So what did you do then?'

'I didn't quite know what to do. I couldn't understand it.

There were lights on in the house and anyway I knew the children would be in bed, so she couldn't have gone out. I thought she might be in the bathroom or something, and failed to hear. So I hung around for a few minutes more then tried again. When she still didn't open the door I gave up. I thought she might have fallen asleep or something, she'd had a pretty exhausting couple of days, but since then . . .' He faltered. 'I've wondered, since . . . Perhaps she was . . . Perhaps she'd already been . . .'

But he couldn't say it. He gave Thanet a beseeching look. 'D'you think that's possible? I couldn't bear it if I thought she was . . . if I could have helped her, and she . . .'

If the man was lying he was putting on a pretty good performance, thought Thanet. He shook his head. 'It's impossible to be precise about time of death, Mr Swain. What did you do then?'

'I . . .' Swain avoided looking at his wife. 'I went for a drink.'

'Where was that?'

'The Dog and Fiddle, in Barton.'

'How long did you stay there?'

A shrug. 'I'm not sure. I had a couple of drinks. Half an hour, perhaps.'

'And you got home when?'

'Around a quarter past ten, I think.' For the first time Swain looked at his wife. 'Something like that, wasn't it?'

As Mrs Marsh, prisoner at the nursery window, had confirmed.

Victoria Swain was nodding.

'So let me be quite clear about this. You left here around nine, arrived at Mrs Broxton's house some ten minutes later and stayed only five minutes or so. So you would have got to the pub at about . . . say, nine thirty, and left around ten. Is that right?'

'More or less.'

Thanet glanced at Lineham to check that he had got everything down, then turned his attention to Mrs Swain. 'And what about you?'

She shrugged. 'More or less the same.'

'I should like a little more detail, please.'

'Oh God, if you must have chapter and verse . . .' She took a deep breath and launched into her story, rattling it off without hesitation and without once glancing at Swain. 'I left here immediately after my husband. When we got to Melton and he turned into the Broxtons' drive, I realised that that must be where Perdita was hiding out. I was a bit surprised, she and Vanessa have never been particularly friendly, as I told you, but I couldn't think of any other reason why Howard should go there. So I drove past and parked at the entrance to a field just beyond the house next door. Then I walked back. When I got there Howard was still standing by the front door, ringing the bell. Eventually he gave up, got back into his car and drove off – past me, actually. I had to duck behind a hedge.'

Thanet had been beginning to wonder if Swain and Master might actually have passed each other in the lane between the pub in Melton and the Broxtons' house. The timing was very close. But here was the answer. When Swain left he had gone the other way.

'I was worried in case he'd recognise my car, but he didn't,' Victoria Swain was saying. 'I'd parked well back, of course, and turned off the lights. But by the time I'd got back to it and got it started I realised I'd probably lost him.' She shrugged. 'So I came home.'

'And what time did you get back?'

Another shrug. 'Twenty, a quarter to ten?'

'Why did it take you half an hour to do a ten-minute journey?'

'Ah. The sleuth moves in for the kill! Sorry to disappoint you, Inspector. I wasted a little time driving around trying to see if I could pick up my husband's tracks.' She gave Swain a shamefaced grin. 'I'd make a rotten detective. And it was the first and last time, I promise.' She put her hand on his and this time although he did not respond he did not cast it off but let it rest. A spark of hope kindled in her eyes.

She really does care about him, thought Thanet. And although one would never have guessed it, meeting them as individuals, he is the one with the power and she is the supplicant. The question is, how much does she care, and how far would she go to keep him? As far as eliminating her rival?

One thing was certain, as he said to Lineham on the way back to the car, Victoria Swain was still high on the list. She had motive and opportunity aplenty.

FIFTEEN

When they reached the gate Thanet paused. Of its own volition his hand had found its way into his pocket and come out holding his pipe. He realised how much he was longing to smoke it and Lineham hated him smoking in the car. Besides, a thought had just occurred to him. 'Let's walk along the lane a little way, Mike.'

He took out his pouch, fed tobacco into his pipe and lit it, hunching his shoulder and turning away from the slight breeze in order to shelter the flame.

Lineham waited patiently. He was used to this ritual.

'I was just thinking...' Thanet paused to strike another match. 'The way you described the murder happening ... D'you realise that everything we've said about Mrs Swain could equally apply to Master? By the time they got back he must have been pretty angry and frustrated. He could have forced his way in when she opened the front door...'

'Or gone around the back, even. No, it's highly unlikely the back door would have been unlocked.'

'Oh, I don't know...'

'What, when she was out there in the country alone in the house at night with two small children?'

'Not for any length of time, I agree. But say, for instance, that once she had satisfied herself that the children were all right she went straight to the kitchen as you suggested to make herself a hot drink. She puts the milk on to heat, rinses out the bottle, and opens the back door to put it out. This could all have taken the same length of time as it would have taken Master to decide he wasn't going to let the matter rest and make his way around to the back door. So as she opens it, there he is, waiting...'

It seemed all wrong to be discussing murder out here in the peace of the countryside. Ahead of them the lane curved to the left, flanked by brown ribbons of dead leaves and hedges glowing with autumn colour. Here and there the bright red hips of the wild rose mingled with clusters of blackberries shrivelled by the frosts.

His pipe still wasn't drawing very well and he took it apart, blew through the mouthpiece and put it together again. That was better. 'For that matter, I suppose we could say exactly the same about his mother. You said yourself that if we were looking for someone who wanted Perdita dead, her mother-in-law certainly qualified.'

'And *you* said it couldn't have been her because there was just no reason why she should have gone to see her.'

Thanet shrugged. 'Say I was wrong. Say there was a reason, and we just don't know about it yet? She's admitted that she knew where Perdita was staying...'

'I can't imagine how we're ever going to find out what that reason was, if there is one. She's not exactly going to hand it to us on a plate, is she?'

'Mmm. That's a tricky one, I agree. Any bright ideas, Mike?'

'Not a glimmer.' Lineham grinned. 'You'll just have to play it by ear, as –'

'I know – as usual.' It was true, Thanet thought, he did play it by ear. It was all very well to plan a strategy, to know which points you wanted to cover in an interview, but it was equally important to listen to what was not being said, to try to work out what was going on beneath the surface. Call it intuition, empathy, whatever, it was a vital skill in the policeman's repertoire and the most difficult one to acquire.

'Fancy having a go yourself, Mike?'

'No thanks. I think I'll pass, on this one.'

'Oh come on! You like a challenge, you know you do.'

'I just think you'd be much more likely to get somewhere with her than I would. You're good at worming things out of people.'

'So are you, when you put your mind to it.'

Lineham said nothing, just compressed his lips and shook his head.

A battered old Mini came around the bend in the lane ahead much too fast and they both had to jump back almost into the hedge. Lineham scowled after it. 'Idiot!'

Thanet decided to stop teasing. He didn't want to make Lineham feel awkward about refusing. He knew quite well why the sergeant – usually very keen to take an active part in interviewing – was so reluctant to take on Master's mother: she reminded him too much of his own. 'It's OK, Mike. I was having you on. It's just the sort of problem I like to tackle, you know that.'

Lineham looked relieved. 'When are you going to have a go then, sir? She's round at Mr Master's house now. I saw her car in the drive as we passed, earlier. It's still there, I could just see it through the hedge.'

'Yes, I know.'

'So what are we waiting for?'

Lineham wheeled around and set off back down the lane at a brisk pace, leaning slightly forward like a tracker dog scenting its quarry. With an indulgent smile Thanet followed. Lineham's eagerness and enthusiasm were two of his most endearing traits.

When they reached the car Thanet stopped and looked at his watch. 'I think I'll just ring in and see if there's a message from Joan.'

He and Joan had arranged that, depending on the time at which her mother was discharged from hospital and whether or not she was transported by ambulance, Thanet would try to be at the house when they arrived in case help was needed.

It was just as well he'd rung. The message was that no ambulance was available and Joan would appreciate it if he could manage a brief visit home between 2 and 2.30. Probably to help get his mother-in-law up the stairs, Thanet thought. He could ask Lineham to give him a hand. He checked the time. Twenty past twelve. Plenty of time.

Lineham was standing by the gate to Master's house, waiting, and as Thanet approached he held up his hand. 'Listen.'

One of the windows in the sitting room was open and angry voices floated out across the drive.

'Mr Master and his mother,' said Lineham. 'They're really having a go at each other about something.'

'Are you thinking what I'm thinking, Mike?'

Lineham grinned. 'Be interesting to know what it was about, wouldn't it?'

Avoiding the gravelled drive they moved quietly alongside the hedge to the house and then across to the open window.

'... have expected you to understand.' Mrs Master's voice.

'Oh, for God's sake, Ma, why can't *you* understand? How can you expect me to be interested in what's happened to a piece of jewellery when I've lost my *wife*.'

'But it was my mother's! The loveliest thing she ever owned! I should never have let you talk me into giving it to Perdita. And now ... You can't imagine how it upsets me, to think I might never see it again.'

'Don't talk nonsense, Ma. I keep telling you, it can't just have vanished into thin air. It'll turn up.'

'How? It's not here, I'm certain of that, I've been through her things half a dozen times to make sure. The police assure me she wasn't wearing it, and Vanessa Broxton swears it's not at her house –'

'Will you stop going on about it! I'm sick and tired of hearing about it. I just couldn't care less, is that clear? I simply don't want to know!'

A door slammed and there was silence. Master had obviously stormed out of the room and Thanet didn't blame him. Mrs Master senior wouldn't win any prizes for sensitivity, that was certain.

He raised his eyebrows at Lineham and nodded in the direction of the front door. They both crouched double to pass the open window before straightening up.

'Wonder what it is that's missing,' said Thanet.

'She said she'd asked the police . . .'

'So it would be legitimate for us to be asking for further details.'

They exchanged smiles. Things were looking up, thought Thanet. If Perdita had been given a piece of family jewellery to which Mrs Master senior was particularly attached, might her mother-in-law not have gone to see her on Monday night to try and get it back? It would be in character. Mrs Master struck him as being very much the sort of person to cling on to things as well as people. If Giles had told her Perdita had left him she might well have thought the piece would be lost to the family for ever if she didn't make an attempt to retrieve it. Then if Perdita had refused to hand it over . . . Thanet had anticipated a difficult time trying to winkle out of Mrs Master a possible reason why she might have gone to see Perdita on Monday. Now it looked as though it might have been handed to him on a plate.

When she opened the door it was obvious that she was still ruffled after the row with her son. Two bright spots of colour burned in her cheeks and her eyes glittered dangerously when she saw who it was.

'What do you want this time? We told you everything we knew yesterday. Can't you leave us in peace?'

Today she was wearing a grey, black and white pleated

skirt, a crisply tailored white blouse and a black silk scarf with a paisley pattern in grey, white and red. Despite her evident agitation she looked as well groomed as ever, and certainly not a day over forty. How did she do it? Thanet wondered.

'I understand you were enquiring about a piece of jewellery that seems to have gone missing?'

'Ah.' Her expression changed. 'I'm sorry, I thought...' She stepped back. 'Come in, won't you?'

She led them into the blue and cream sitting room. Today, with the sun shining in, the room looked less cold, less forbidding, but it was still Perdita's painting which drew the eye like a magnet, the pure brilliant colours glowing, seeming almost to pulsate in their neutral setting.

'I know you must all think I'm making a terrible fuss about nothing,' she said as they sat down. 'Especially in the circumstances. But it's the sentimental value as much as its actual worth. It was my mother's, you see...'

'How much is it worth, exactly?' Not wishing to betray his ignorance by direct questions Thanet was banking on the fact that sooner or later he would learn what 'it' was.

'Around five thousand pounds, as I said when I reported its disappearance. But that's not the point. As I say, it's the sentimental value that's important. It's well insured and I could easily buy another one, but it just wouldn't be the engagement ring my father bought for my mother.'

So it was a ring. Thanet tried to think back. No, Perdita hadn't been wearing one, he was certain of that. He would have noticed it, especially if it was as spectacular as it sounded.

'Could you describe it for me?'

Mrs Master looked irritated. 'I gave a full description when I reported its loss.'

'I'm afraid I haven't actually read the report myself. I just ... heard about it. So if you could bear with me...'

'It's a diamond cluster. Six perfectly matched diamonds. A really beautiful ring. I know you may think it terrible of me to be fussing about it at a time like this, but, well, it's such a desirable object ... It could so easily go ... well, go astray.'

'Are you questioning the honesty of my men?' said Thanet calmly.

'Oh no. No, of course not. It's just that ...'

'Because I can assure you that Mrs Master was not wearing the ring when we examined her and that it was not in her room at Mrs Broxton's house.'

He glanced at Lineham for confirmation and the sergeant gave an emphatic nod.

'Oh. Yes. I see. Well then, where can it be?'

'I really don't know.' *Nor do I care*, his tone implied. 'She might have left it at her mother's house. She stayed there overnight on Saturday, I believe.'

'Of course!' said Mrs Master senior, her narrow features showing the first signs of animation since they arrived. 'How stupid of me! Why on earth didn't I think of that?'

'It's understandable that you were worried about it,' said Thanet. 'It's obviously a valuable piece. Was that why you went to see your daughter-in-law on Monday night?'

It was the brief euphoria of relief that brought about her unguarded response, Thanet was sure.

'Yes, of course,' she said. And stopped, trying to hide her dismay. 'I mean ... Well, not on Monday, of course.'

So she hadn't given up hope of concealing the truth.

Thanet raised his eyebrows. 'When, then?'

'Sunday. It must have been Sunday.'

'Really? When, on Sunday?'

'Sunday evening.' She was beginning to get the trapped, panicky look of someone who feels that he is inexorably being driven into a corner and knows that he is going to be unable to get out.

'What time?'

'Er ... somewhere around nine, I suppose.' She reached across to the soft black leather shoulder bag which lay in the far corner of the settee, took out a wisp of handkerchief and crumpled it in her hand.

'Who told you that she was at Mrs Broxton's house?'

'Why Giles did – my son. I told you that yesterday.' Briefly she was defiant again, almost scornful. But almost immediately her expression changed. She became very still and her eyes widened in shock as she realised the trap she had dug for herself.

Thanet allowed the silence to lengthen, gave her time to realise that there was no way to extricate herself. Then he said softly, 'Quite. Your son didn't know where his wife was himself until Monday morning, did he?' Abruptly his tone changed, his eyes became steely. 'You must realise that lying to the police during the course of a murder investigation is a serious matter. Apart from holding things up it's bound to make us wonder what you're trying to hide ... So let's try again. What time on Monday evening did you go to see your daughter-in-law?'

She dabbed at her upper lip with the handkerchief. 'I told you, somewhere around nine.'

'You can't be more precise?'

She shrugged. 'It might have been a bit earlier than that.'

Thanet had to admire her resilience. Already her confidence was returning. It showed in the raised angle of her chin, the way she straightened her spine. Only the thumb and forefinger plucking at a corner of the handkerchief betrayed her tension.

'So what happened?'

'I rang the bell, but no one came. So I left.'

'Did you hear anything, see anyone?'

'Not see anyone, no.' She hesitated.

Was she genuinely trying to remember, Thanet wondered, or was she trying to think of something, anything, that would let her off the hook?

'I remember now. I could hear a child crying – well, screaming, actually. He sounded pretty upset. Yes. That was why I didn't wait. I thought Perdita would be trying to calm him down and it wasn't a good time to see her. I decided I'd come back some time during the week.'

True or not? It was possible, of course. If Henry had been disturbed by the commotion Giles had made ten or fifteen minutes earlier, he could well have worked himself up into a state of hysteria by then. In any case it was obvious that this time she was going to stick to her story and until they had some concrete evidence which disproved it they would have to accept it. He glanced at Lineham and stood up. The sergeant snapped his notebook shut and followed suit.

'Very well, Mrs Master. We'll leave it there for now. But I hope you've realised that there really is no point in lying to us. We always find out in the end ... You won't be going away at all, for the next few days?'

A flash of alarm. 'No ... But why ... ?'

'Good.'

Outside he said, 'No harm in frightening her a little. Well Mike, what d'you think?'

'If she was telling the truth, it means she was there while Mr Master and his wife were out at the pub.'

'If, yes. But if she knew they'd been out, because her son told her ... Say she did in fact go there later, after the Swains had left and before Mrs Broxton arrived home ... She would have realised that if ever she did have to confess to being there that night, it would be safest to say that it was during the period her son and his wife were out. Though what she said about the child crying sounded authentic enough.'

'Only because it was credible in the circumstances,' said Lineham eagerly. 'I mean, if she knew Master and his wife were out, it would be a likely thing to happen, wouldn't it? For the little boy to wake up and start crying? She didn't mention the crying at first, did she? And didn't you notice the long pause before she told us about it?'

'Yes, I did ... And another thing ... If Henry was yelling his head off at nine o'clock, and was still crying at 9.30, when his mother got home, why didn't either of the Swains hear him – or Master, for that matter, when they were there between 9 and 9.30?'

'I suppose he could have cried himself to sleep briefly, then woken up and started again?'

'Possible, I suppose. What we need, of course, is a definite lead. Let's hope that forensic report'll come through soon as promised, and that when it does it'll give us something definite to go on.'

'No wonder the elderly neighbour said she'd heard several cars,' said Lineham. 'It must have been like Piccadilly Circus there that night!'

As if Perdita were a magnet to which they were all being drawn, thought Thanet.

'Well, where now?' said Lineham as they got into the car. He looked at his watch. 'It's just before one,' he added pointedly.

'Feeling peckish, Mike? All right, we'll get a bite to eat in the village.'

After an excellent ploughman's lunch in the Green Man ('Three sorts of pickle *and* pickled onions!' said Lineham) they rang in to find out if the forensic report had come through.

'No joy,' said Lineham, shaking his head. 'Wish they'd get the lead out of their boots.'

'We'll call in at my house then, see if Joan needs a hand.'

Lineham had willingly agreed to help.

Joan came into the hall as they let themselves in. 'Oh good, Mike's with you. I was wondering how we'd manage to get her upstairs.'

'How is she?' said Thanet.

Joan pulled a face. 'Pretty weak. They provided a wheelchair to get her to the car and said that it was all right for her to walk from the car to the house if it wasn't too far. They said it's important for her to have a little regular exercise every day, and that in another week or so it should be all right for her to come downstairs as long as she doesn't climb the stairs more than once a day, until she's stronger. If you hadn't managed to get home I was going to make up a bed for her on the settee.'

'Right. Let's see what we can do.'

They all went into the sitting room. Margaret Bolton was lying on the settee with her feet up, looking alarmingly pale and fragile. Thanet supposed that the doctors knew what they were doing, but for the first time he appreciated fully the responsibility Joan had taken on. His mother-in-law was going to need a great deal of care and attention for some time yet.

'How are you feeling, Margaret?'

She attempted a smile. 'Hullo, Luke, Mike. A bit limp, I'm afraid.'

'Still, it's good news, isn't it? They must be satisfied that you're going to be OK now or they wouldn't have discharged you.'

'And,' said Joan, smiling at her mother, 'they say that there's no reason why she shouldn't get back to leading her normal life again before too long, didn't they, Mum?'

Margaret Bolton nodded. 'The sooner the better, as far as I'm concerned. I don't want to be a burden on you, Joan. You've got your work to think of, as well as your family.'

'Nonsense. Of course you won't be a burden. How could you? My office is quite happy for me to take a few days' leave and after that I'm sure we'll be able to get some help, if necessary.'

'Anyway,' said Thanet, 'we certainly don't want you worrying about it. That would be the worst possible thing in the circumstances. Now, let's see about getting you upstairs.'

'I've prepared Bridget's room for her,' said Joan.

'I assumed you would.'

Between them Thanet and Lineham easily managed to carry Mrs Bolton up the stairs and into the bedroom. The bed was made up, its covers invitingly turned back and Thanet couldn't help feeling a pang of loss when he noticed that the familiar clutter of objects had been cleared from Bridget's dressing table and bedside table and replaced by the things which Joan had unpacked from her mother's suitcase.

They lowered Mrs Bolton gently on to the edge of the bed.

'Anything else we can do?'

Joan shook her head. 'I can manage now. Thanks, darling.'

'See you tonight, then.' Thanet kissed her and left her to help her mother undress.

'Doesn't look too good, does she?' said Lineham, when they were back in the car.

Thanet shook his head. 'I was thinking just a few minutes ago, I hope the doctors know what they're doing.'

'When I told Louise, last night, she said that this is the best way to treat heart attacks in the elderly. She says it's essential to keep the circulation going and this is why they now get them up so soon and insist on regular bouts of mild exercise. And the recovery rate, she says, is excellent, if they survive the first twenty-four hours.'

'That's what Doctor MacPherson said. Let's hope he's right ... Anyway, we'd better get back to work. Give them another ring, see if that forensic report is in.'

It was.

'Good,' said Thanet. 'Back to the office, then, let's see what they have to say. Let's hope they give us something we can use.'

SIXTEEN

Superintendent Draco was just getting out of his car when Lineham pulled into the car park at Headquarters. Draco raised his hand in salute and waited for them.

Thanet thought that the Super looked terrible: all Draco's bounce had gone, the pouches beneath his eyes were soft and puffy and his sallow skin had an unhealthy pallor to it. Whereas he would once have bounded up the steps to the entrance door, now he plodded and Thanet and Lineham had to adjust their pace accordingly.

Thanet wondered whether to ask after Draco's wife, but couldn't bring himself to do so. He wasn't sure if he was being tactful or just plain cowardly.

'How's it going, Thanet?' Even Draco's voice lacked its usual vigour.

'Not too badly, sir. It's a bit complicated. Too many suspects, all with motive and opportunity. Trouble is, so far we haven't got a single piece of concrete evidence to tie any of them in with it.'

'Forensic report through yet?' But Draco didn't look as if he were really interested in the answer. Incredible for a man who had once told his team that if anyone so much as sneezed in his patch he wanted to hear about it.

'We haven't seen it yet, but it's just come in, sir.'

'Good.'

They parted in the foyer and on the way upstairs Lineham said, 'D'you think she's worse?'

'I couldn't pluck up the courage to ask.'

In the office Thanet eagerly skimmed the forensic report. He read it again more slowly, conscious of Lineham barely containing his impatience to hear what it said. Then he handed it to the sergeant and went to stand looking out of the window. Something was nagging at his memory. What was it?

Outside sun glinted off glass and chrome, leaves fluttered down from trees, people went about their business but Thanet saw it all only as a blur. His attention was wholly focussed elsewhere. What was it, that he was trying to remember?

Lineham's voice disturbed his concentration. 'Pretty disappointing, isn't it? Loads of smudged prints on the polythene bag but nothing clear enough to be of any use. Just one good print on that and we could have nailed him.'

'Not necessarily, Mike. Counsel would have argued that it could have been made at any time.'

'Maybe, but at least it would have pointed us in the right direction . . . What about this blue fluff?'

Blue woollen fibres had been found in the polythene bag.

'Perhaps we ought to concentrate on that, do you think, sir?'

'I should think only luck will help us there. Just think, Mike. Those fibres could have come from anywhere – from any piece of clothing or item of household goods, past or present, owned by any of the suspects or their families.'

Thanet became aware that he was massaging his right temple, that he had a slight headache – or perhaps not so much a headache as a build-up of pressure, as if the memory that was eluding him were physically trying to push its way out of his brain.

'Still, it's a starting point, isn't it, sir? If you don't mind me saying so, if we gave up before we began just because we didn't think we'd get anywhere, well, we never would get anywhere, would we?'

'Point made, Mike. So where do you suggest we begin?'

'We could systematically work through the wardrobes and cupboards of each suspect in turn.'

'Beginning with whom?'

Lineham shrugged. 'Mrs Swain?'

'That'll be fun when we get to Swain's workroom,' said Thanet, remembering his brief glimpse of the floor-to-ceiling shelves packed with cones of wool, the sample swatches trailing multi-coloured strands.

Lineham grinned. 'The lab boys'll go mad!'

'Anyway, perhaps it would be sensible to ask...' He stopped.

'What's the matter, sir?'

Thanet became aware of how he must look: dazed stare, mouth half open in astonishment.

'Mike! Just a minute.' Thanet sank down into the chair behind his desk. He needed a moment to readjust. It was as if he had been looking at the whole thing from the wrong end of a telescope.

'Are you all right?' Lineham's face loomed at him as the sergeant bent forward in concern and Thanet flapped him irritably away. 'Yes, yes! I just need to think, that's all.'

He watched Lineham retreat, trying unsuccessfully not to look hurt.

'Oh all right, Mike, I'm sorry. It's just that I suddenly realised...'

Lineham's face changed, became eager. 'What?'

Thanet leaned forward. 'We've been over and over the timing of all the suspects' movements on Monday night, trying to work out the sequence of events. We've queried all those timings, checking and crosschecking, believing or disbelieving. But there's one person whose statement we've never questioned.'

Lineham frowned. 'Whose?'

Thanet told him, and had the satisfaction of seeing the look of astonishment on his sergeant's face. 'Now you know why my jaw dropped just now.'

'Mrs Broxton?' Lineham was still looking incredulous.

Thanet nodded.

He recalled the image his memory had presented him with just now. As clearly as if she were sitting before him in his office he had remembered Vanessa Broxton as he had first seen her on Monday night. Huddled in a corner of one of the big sofas, feet tucked up beneath her, she had been wearing the clothes she must have worn in Court that day, a straight charcoal grey skirt and white blouse. And, slung loosely around her shoulders, a thick blue knitted jacket.

'Remember when we interviewed her on Monday? She was wearing a blue woollen jacket.'

'But that doesn't mean a thing. I mean, even if the fibres did turn out to be from that jacket, it wouldn't be any help to us. Counsel would argue that the bag in which the jacket had once been was lying around in the kitchen and the murderer just saw it and grabbed it.'

'Unlikely, Mike, with small children in the house. The danger of leaving plastic bags lying around is so well known by now ... I bet you and Louise don't, do you?'

Lineham shook his head.

'Well, I can't imagine Mrs Broxton doing so either. But she is the one person who'd be able to find one in that house in a hurry, isn't she?'

'But why would she want to?'

'Ah well, now that's what I suddenly realised. She did have a reason, a powerful one ... Just think, Mike. She's devoted to those children. Her nanny, Angela Proven, told me that she's "potty about them", that she absolutely hated having to leave Henry when she went back to work. That she'd even told her that for two pins she'd chuck it all in. I quote. And you remember what Mrs Swain told us? That Vanessa's children came first with her, that motherhood had overwhelmed her. She said she'd seen it happen before, especially in career women who leave it late to have a baby. They fall in love with the child, she said...'

'So? I'm sorry, I still don't get it.'

'Well don't you see, the one thing that would arouse Vanessa Broxton's fury is ill-treatment of her children. And Perdita leaving them alone in the house at night would certainly count as that, wouldn't you agree?'

Lineham nodded.

'So, just say Mrs Master senior was telling the truth. You remember she said she heard a child screaming while she was ringing the bell just before nine...'

The light had finally dawned, he could see it in Lineham's face. Lineham raked his hand through his hair. He looked stunned. 'Draco's going to love this.'

'So what? We've never treated her any differently from any of the other witnesses. Why should we, just because of her position?'

'True. So, you mean, supposing Mrs Broxton didn't return at 9.30 as she claimed, say she got back earlier, while Mr and Mrs Master were still out...'

'Exactly!'

'And Henry was in a real state, practically hysterical ... Yes, she would have been livid, wouldn't she? No, hang on a minute. That won't work. That means she would have been in the house when Mr Swain came knocking.'

'Not knocking, Mike, *ringing*. And the doorbell was out of order.'

'He did say he knocked as well.'

'But he also said the door was so solid that unless he had really hammered at it it would have been difficult to make much impact. And I don't suppose he would have liked to do that, not like Master who was determined to make as much noise as he could. No, if she was busy trying to calm Henry down she might well not have heard him. It's a big house and we've found this ourselves, haven't we, when we go to big houses, even when the doorbell is working and there's a knocker too. How many times have you heard people say, "But I was in, all the time"?'

Lineham nodded, conceding the truth of this.

'So, say all these people have been telling the truth: Mrs Master senior came and went away just before Mrs Broxton arrived home; Mr Swain came and left soon afterwards; his wife did just what she said she did, followed him, watched him leave and set off again without coming near the house . . .'

'And then the Masters arrived home.'

Thanet nodded eagerly. 'Quite. Now, just visualise it: this was at twenty past nine. Mrs Broxton has probably just managed to calm Henry down – you know how long it takes when a child is in a real state. And all the time she's seething. Where is Perdita? She hasn't had time to look all over the house, probably just had a quick look in the kitchen and the bedroom before attending to Henry. And then she hears the front door slam. Until now it probably hasn't even occurred to her that Perdita could actually have gone out and left the children alone in the house, but now . . . She spends another minute or two making sure that Henry is thoroughly settled and then she races downstairs, absolutely furious. Meanwhile Perdita, reassured by the silence from upstairs, goes into the kitchen to make herself a hot drink . . . And from then on it happens just as we've suggested.'

Lineham had been nodding from time to time but now he stopped. 'OK, say it did happen like that, they had a row, Mrs Broxton is so angry she goes to grab her by the shoulders to shake her, Mrs Master steps back, slips and so on . . . I still can't buy Mrs Broxton looking around for a polythene bag and deliberately finishing her off.'

Thanet stared at him in silence. Carried along by the

excitement and impetus of what had seemed a brilliant new explanation of what had happened he had chosen not to face that final stumbling block. He sat back in his chair and sighed. 'You're right, Mike. I can't see it either.'

'I think,' said Lineham, obviously determined to drive the point home, 'that she'd have been horrified when she saw Mrs Master lying there unconscious. She'd have been much more likely to rush to the telephone.'

'Yes, yes. You're right, you're right.' Thanet felt for his pipe. He was in need of consolation and for once he was going to ignore what Lineham felt about it. 'Ah well, back to the drawing board, as one might say. Pass that report back, will you, Mike, let me have another look at it.'

While he was studying it he lit up.

Lineham got up to open the office door.

'I do wish you wouldn't make me feel such a pariah, Mike.'

'Sorry sir.' Lineham glanced pointedly at the curls of smoke beginning to wreath their way towards him. 'It's just that...'

'I know, I know.' Disappointment was making Thanet unwontedly irritable. 'Well, I suppose we'd better do as you suggest about the fibres, beginning with the Swains.' He sighed. This was going to take for ever. 'Get a search warrant and put a team of four on to it. As you say, the lab boys are going to love this. But if it's the only way...'

'Right, sir.' Lineham was already lifting the telephone.

Meanwhile, where did they go from here? Thanet looked at the reports stacked on both his and Lineham's desks and groaned inwardly. He knew, really. They had reached the stage in a case that he disliked most of all, the point where they needed to have a thorough reassessment of everything that had come in. He and Lineham must now each work his way systematically through every single report. It was surprising how often some hitherto disregarded scrap of information could acquire a new significance in the light of subsequent findings, and it was also the only way to get a clear overall view. Always, in the first day or two, there was so much to try and assimilate, so many people to interview, that it was impossible to do anything but follow up one lead after another. But there usually came a point when the pace slowed, even ground to a standstill. And then . . .

He sighed, shuffled his chair closer to his desk, pulled the pile of reports nearer to hand and took the first one off the top.

He wasn't even aware that Lineham had been out of the room until the sergeant came back and said, 'Report time, I see.'

Thanet nodded.

Lineham pulled a face, sighed, sat down at his desk and was immediately engrossed.

For the next hour they worked steadily, the silence broken only by the occasional comment. Thanet shifted position from time to time, trying to ease the familiar dull ache which was the result of a back injury many years before. He was just beginning to wonder how Draco would react if he entered the room and found his Detective Inspector stretched out on the floor doing back exercises when there was a knock and Bentley put his head around the door. Thanet could tell at once that there was something up. The DC's usually placid face was animated, his eyes sparkling with excitement. 'Someone asking to see you, sir.'

'Who? Well come in, man, come in.'

'Mrs Broxton, sir. And her husband.' He paused, to give emphasis to his next words. 'And her solicitor.'

The atmosphere in the room suddenly changed as Thanet and Lineham exchanged glances. Had Thanet hit the nail on the head after all?

His lethargy of a moment ago was gone, the ache in his back forgotten. His stomach clenched with excitement. 'Send them up.'

SEVENTEEN

Vanessa Broxton wasted no time on preliminaries.

'I'll come straight to the point, Inspector.'

Superficially she looked as she always did in Court – well-groomed and confident. She was wearing a dark grey herringbone tweed suit with a black velvet collar, white blouse, high heels. Studying her more closely, though, Thanet could detect the signs of strain: the too rigid posture, the occasional tightening of her jaw muscles and the fear which lurked at the back of her eyes. Despite the latter, however, she looked – what was the word? – resolute, that was it. Yes, resolute.

The two men who flanked her were a complete contrast: her husband tall, fair, well built, striking; the solicitor short, dark, slight, nondescript. Thanet was not fooled by the man's appearance. Geoffrey Mordent was the senior partner in one of Maidstone's largest firms of solicitors, and widely respected for his ability as well as his humanity.

Vanessa Broxton was looking Thanet straight in the eye. *I have nothing to hide.*

Guy Broxton had been watching her. Now he turned an assessing eye on Thanet.

Mordent, too, had been looking at her. Now, as she glanced at him he gave a faint smile and nodded, encouraging her to continue.

'When you interviewed me on Monday night, Inspector, I'm afraid I was less than frank with you. No, to be blunt, I lied to you. I'll explain why in a minute, but for the moment suffice it to say that I now realise how very foolish I was. So I've come to tell you what really happened.'

She glanced at Mordent, who nodded again and said, 'Mrs Broxton is here entirely with my approval. I am in full agreement with her desire to be frank with you, and wish to make it clear that although I shall naturally protect her interests, I am present chiefly as a friend.'

Thanet nodded. 'Please continue, Mrs Broxton.'

She hesitated for a moment, then said, 'The first thing I lied to you about was the time. I said I arrived home at 9.30, but in fact it was half an hour earlier.'

Thanet restrained himself from casting a triumphant glance at Lineham. So he had been right.

'As I told you, the moment I opened the front door I heard Henry screaming – no, it was before that, even. I could hear him as I put my key in the lock. Then it happened just as I told you. In the hall I hesitated for a moment, calling Perdita, but I didn't wait to see if she was around, I rushed straight upstairs to Henry's room. As I said, he was practically hysterical, I'd never seen him in such a state before. So naturally I picked him up, walked about with him, did everything I could to soothe him, quieten him down. And all the time I was getting more and more angry, wondering where on earth Perdita was, wondering how she could possibly have let him get into such a state ... 'Anyway, he had just calmed down and I was on the point of putting him back to bed when I heard the front door slam. Up until then it had simply never occurred to me to think she could actually have gone out and left the children alone in the house...'

Her voice was beginning to rise in remembered outrage and she stopped, took a deep breath and waited a moment before continuing.

'I put Henry down in his cot, but of course this woke him up and he clung to me, started to cry again. Perdita must have heard him and she came straight upstairs and into the nursery. She looked pretty appalled to see me there, as you can imagine. She started to apologise, but I just hissed at her to go away, go downstairs and wait for me. It took a good five minutes longer to get Henry settled and all the while I was seething, thinking of what I was going to say to her when I saw her. Then suddenly Henry went out like a light. I suppose he was exhausted with all the crying. So I tiptoed out on to the landing, then ran downstairs.'

Thanet could visualise it all: Perdita truly appalled, as Vanessa Broxton had said, to find Henry in distress and Vanessa returned home unexpectedly. Still upset after her forced excursion to the pub with Giles, full of guilt, distress and self-justification, she would have been in a highly volatile state by the time Vanessa came down. Probably she had started to make a hot drink in an attempt to calm herself down by the familiar, soothing domestic task ... And Vanessa, churning with fury, boiling up for a confrontation, flying down the stairs and bursting into the kitchen ...

Vanessa Broxton's composure was slipping and her husband reached out and took her hand, clasped it tightly. 'It's all right, love. Keep going, the worst'll soon be over.'

She shook her head, her eyes bleak. *This will never be over, for me.*

'She was in the kitchen. She was holding a saucepan with milk in it. All I could think was, she goes out and leaves my babies alone and then calmly comes into the kitchen and makes herself cocoa!'

'What the hell d'you think you were doing?'
'It was ...'
'I come home unexpectedly and what do I find? Henry

hysterical and you're not even here! You'd gone out, for God's sake! Gone out and left my babies alone in the house!'

'It wasn't . . .'

'I don't care what you say, there can be no possible excuse, d'you hear me, no possible excuse!'

'But, Vanessa . . .'

'Don't Vanessa me! In fact, don't ever speak to me again. Get out of my house this minute, d'you hear me, get out!'

Vanessa Broxton buried her face in her hands.

Her husband put his arm around her and briefly she turned, rested her forehead against his shoulder. Then she looked back at Thanet. 'It was an accident, I swear,' she whispered. 'And even now, looking back, I can't really tell you what happened. I've thought and thought about it, and I've worked out what *must* have happened, but that's not the same, is it? I think I must have pushed her, but . . . All I really know is that one minute she was standing in front of me and the next she was . . . just lying there, on the floor. I vaguely remember hearing a crash, but apart from that . . . Her eyes were closed and her head was bleeding . . . I couldn't believe it. I knelt down beside her, calling her name. I felt for her pulse and it wasn't there . . . Dear God, it wasn't there . . .'

Vanessa Broxton shook her head in remembered disbelief. 'I realised she was dead and I'd killed her.' She bent her head in shame and contrition.

There was a moment's silence before Thanet said, 'And then what did you do?'

She looked up. 'I didn't mean to harm her, I swear it. It's just that . . . I'd never been so angry in my life before. I was beside myself.' She gave a wry smile. 'Never again will I disbelieve a client when he says he didn't know what he was doing.'

Thanet repeated his question. His calm acceptance of her account seemed to reassure her. Or perhaps she felt that she was now past the part of her story that was hardest for her to tell. In any case she made a visible effort to be brisk and matter-of-fact.

'Naturally I didn't know what to do. I was, well, stunned, I suppose, for the first minute or two. And then my first instinct was to call the police. Which is, of course, what I should have done. There's a phone in the kitchen and my hand was actually on the receiver when I thought, but if I do call them, and I'm arrested what will happen to the children? Angela was in hospital, my husband abroad . . . There were a couple of friends I could ring, but that would have involved getting Henry and Alice up out of bed and transferring them and I wasn't sure, if I were arrested, if the police would allow me to do that. And after the upset Henry had already had that night I certainly wasn't going to allow him to be frightened out of his wits by having a complete stranger do it.' She gave an apologetic smile. 'I wasn't thinking ahead at all, as you see. I was in a panic, I suppose. I knew I'd have to call the police eventually, but I just couldn't think straight and I realised I had to have a little while to myself, first, to work out what I was going to say to them.

'I went into the drawing room. I was still shaking and I decided to allow myself just one drink – no more, because I knew I couldn't risk not being able to think clearly. So I poured myself a stiff whisky and drank it, telling myself that as soon as I'd finished it I'd ring you. But I kept thinking about the children and worrying about what would happen to them if I was arrested. Then there was my work . . . If this all came out, I was finished. Even if I were acquitted I couldn't imagine many solicitors would be anxious to employ me . . . Then I suddenly thought, why own up at all? I could just say I'd come home and found her like that. It would buy me some time, give me a chance to pull myself together and sort something out for the children . . .' Vanessa Broxton stopped, shook her head and gave a wry smile. 'I can't believe it really, can't believe I was so stupid! Me, of all people, with the sort of work I do! It was a sort of madness and I'm deeply ashamed of myself, I assure you ... Anyway, that was what I decided to do. But I knew I'd have to make sure an intruder would have been able to get in, so I steeled myself to go back into the kitchen and unlock the door. Then I returned to the drawing room and tried to think calmly, work out exactly what I was going to tell the police when they arrived. Then I dialled 999 and reported the murder.'

There was a long silence. Thanet was aware that they were all looking at him expectantly, awaiting his reaction, but he was thinking furiously. Had Vanessa Broxton told him the whole story, or not? She had said nothing about the plastic bag and Thanet was inclined to believe her. Her story had the ring of truth to it. He could imagine it all happening as she had said, what he could not swallow was the possibility that she had then decided to finish Perdita off. Because if she had, it would have been a conscious, deliberate act, and he really didn't think her capable of calculated murder, however upset she might have been at the time. But if she hadn't...

Light suddenly dawned.

Of course!

How stupid, how blind he had been!

All along, as Lineham had said, that polythene bag had been the stumbling block. But if not one, but *two* people had been involved, the whole thing became comprehensible.

He could see it all: the murderer – faceless as yet – looking in through the kitchen window, seeing Perdita lying unconscious on the floor, trying the door and finding it unlocked and then, seeing his – or her – golden opportunity, seizing his chance ... It would have taken no time at all.

Lineham was frowning. He hadn't seen it yet, then. The sergeant glanced up, caught Thanet's eye, his gaze sharpening as Thanet's excitement communicated itself to him.

The silence in the room had become uncomfortably protracted. Broxton stirred, cleared his throat as if to remind Thanet that they were waiting.

'Mrs Broxton,' said Thanet, picking his words with care. 'Are you sure you have told us the whole story? I want you to think back now, and make sure that you have omitted nothing.'

There, he had given her one last chance to mention of her own free will that final act if she had indeed committed it.

She was frowning, puzzled, obviously aware that he had something specific in mind. She shook her head. 'Not to my knowledge, no. If there is something it's because I've just forgotten about it.'

'This is scarcely something you could have forgotten.' Thanet's tone was dry. If she were innocent, it was time to put her out of her misery.

The three of them were staring at him intently, trying to read his mind.

'Well?' said Broxton impatiently. 'Are you going to tell us what it is?'

'Mrs Master did not die from that fall. As she fell she did bang her head hard against the corner of the kitchen table, yes, and this knocked her out. But she died of asphyxiation.'

The astonishment on their faces – including Vanessa Broxton's – was, he would swear, genuine.

Then they all spoke together.

'Asphyxiation?'

'But...'

'I don't understand.'

'Someone,' said Thanet, 'took a polythene bag and pulled it over her head as she was lying there unconscious, and smothered her.'

He was watching Vanessa Broxton as he spoke. Her eyes opened wide in horror, the whites showing clear around the irises. One hand went up to her mouth and the other raked through her hair.

Her husband and Geoffrey Mordent had turned to look at her.

'But ... But that's impossible!' she whispered.

Thanet shook his head. 'I've read the post mortem report and I'm satisfied that that was the cause of death. And of course I saw the polythene bag over her head myself.' He glanced at Lineham. 'We all did.'

Lineham nodded.

Suddenly Broxton was on his feet. 'Now look here, Thanet, are you implying that my wife cold-bloodedly murdered that woman? Because if you are –'

Geoffrey Mordent reached across Vanessa and tugged at Broxton's sleeve. 'Sit down, Guy. We both know she would have done no such thing. And I don't believe that Inspector Thanet is implying anything, he's simply informing us. Besides, don't you see? As far as Vanessa is concerned, this alters the whole thing? *Someone else killed her*.'

'But I felt for her pulse,' whispered Vanessa. 'It wasn't there. She was dead, I tell you ...'

Thanet shook his head decisively. 'No. It's an easy mistake to make, one that's been made many times before, I assure you. The shock of it all would have blunted your perception.'

'But then, how ... who ...?'

'That, obviously, is what we yet have to discover. Tell me, when you arrived home, did you put your car in the garage before going into the house?'

She nodded. 'Yes, of course.'

So no one would have known she was there, thought Thanet. To all intents and purposes the place was deserted.

'Did you hear anyone knock at the front door?'

'No. No one. The doorbell isn't working, of course, and the door is so thick and heavy it's very difficult to make anyone hear just by knocking on it, unless you really hammer at it. And I was upstairs with Henry and he was crying most of the time. Even if he hadn't been, I don't suppose I would have heard, it's not as though I was expecting anyone and listening out for them. You mean . . . ?'

'Did you hear any cars outside?'

Again she shook her head. 'I was too preoccupied with Henry to have noticed . . .'

'And when you were downstairs, in the drawing room, after the incident?'

'No. I was in such a state I don't suppose I'd have noticed if a herd of elephants had thundered through the front garden.' For the first time she managed a faint, rueful smile.

Thanet was working it out. If Perdita arrived back at 9.20 it would have been 9.25 before Vanessa went down to the kitchen. The brief confrontation with Perdita would have taken only a minute or two, say until 9.30 at the latest. Vanessa had rung the police at 9.40 and they had taken a further ten minutes to arrive . . .

'You must have been in the drawing room for at least twenty minutes before the police arrived?'

She frowned, paused to work it out. 'I suppose so, yes.'

'And how long was it before you went back into the kitchen to unlock the back door?'

'Five, ten minutes? It's difficult to tell.'

So the murderer could have slipped into the kitchen either before or after that.

'Now think carefully: did you on that occasion look at Mrs Master's body?'

'You're suggesting that the murderer might already have come in by then?' She shook her head. 'I'm sorry, I can't help you there. I'm afraid I studiously avoided looking at her. I was aware of her lying there, of course, out of the corner of my eye, but I certainly didn't notice a polythene bag over her head, or obviously all this wouldn't have been such a shock to me.'

'That polythene bag . . . Might it have been lying around somewhere, in the kitchen?'

She shook her head emphatically. 'Absolutely not. Angela and I have always been very careful not to leave plastic bags lying around, and I'm sure Perdita would have done the same.' She frowned. 'Though until all this happened I would have sworn that she would never have left young children alone in the house ... I still can't believe that she did.'

Lineham shifted position and Thanet knew what he was thinking: why don't you tell her that Master forced his wife into the car, blackmailed her into staying with him?

Thanet said nothing. He had his reasons.

'Anyway,' said Broxton to his wife, 'you can now stop tormenting yourself. Someone else killed her.' He glanced at Thanet. 'You can't imagine what a relief it is, to know that.'

'But that's not true!' said Vanessa. 'Don't you see that, Guy? I killed her just as surely as if I had put that bag over her head!'

Broxton took her hand. 'Darling, don't be ridiculous! How can you say that?'

She was shaking her head vehemently. 'And how can you say I'm innocent? If I'd called an ambulance immediately, as I should have, and stayed with her until it arrived, Perdita would still be alive ... Don't you *see*?' she repeated. 'I helped him, didn't I? First I made her unconscious so she was helpless, didn't have a chance ... Then I unlocked the door to let him in and finally I left her alone and defenceless! I made it so easy for him!'

'Not intentionally!'

'That doesn't make any difference. Oh, it might make a difference legally, but morally, emotionally ... No, I'm as guilty as he is.'

Broxton cast a look of helpless frustration at Thanet. *Can't you make her see how wrong she is?*

But Thanet knew that nothing he could say would make any difference. Somehow Vanessa Broxton was going to have to come to terms with what had happened, but it would take time, a long time. Perhaps she never would get over it. He had seen this coming. This was why he had said nothing as yet about Perdita having been forced into accompanying her husband. It was, he knew, unfair to the dead woman to go on allowing Vanessa Broxton to think so badly of her, but if Vanessa knew she had misjudged Perdita, that if only she had allowed her to explain Perdita would still be alive, she would be feeling even more guilty. Assuming the murderer were caught she would have to find out eventually, of course, at the trial if not before, but perhaps by then she would be less raw, less in shock. No, the best course would be to take her husband quietly aside at some point, tell him the truth, and suggest he tell his wife if and when the time was right to do so.

Geoffrey Mordent was also trying to comfort her. He patted her arm. 'Guy is right, Vanessa. You didn't intend to harm her. As we've said all along, it was an accident, you must hang on to that. At least you now know that it wasn't you who killed her.'

'I know you're trying to be kind, Geoff, but it won't work. I know how I feel and nothing is going to change that.' She looked at Thanet. 'If you want me to make that statement, Inspector . . .'

She stood up.

'Sergeant Lineham will go with you. Thank you for being so frank with us.'

'What will happen now, Inspector?' said Broxton.

'At the moment, nothing. But we might well have to talk to you again, Mrs Broxton, so please don't go away without letting us know.'

Lineham opened the door and Vanessa Broxton led the way out, grim-faced, her burden of guilt only marginally lighter than when she had arrived.

EIGHTEEN

When Thanet let himself into the house that evening Joan was just putting the telephone down. She snatched it up again, listened, then pulled a face before replacing it.

'Oh, what a shame, I've been talking to Bridget, you've just missed her. I didn't want to upset her, when she's just settling in, but I thought she'd be furious if I didn't let her know about Mum.'

Bridget was very fond of her grandmother.

'She wanted to come home right away, but I said no. I thought it would be too unsettling for her, and now that the worst of the danger is past ... You do think that was the right thing to do?' she asked anxiously.

'Yes, I'm sure that was best. It would be pointless for her to come home at this stage. And I agree, if you hadn't said a word about your mother she'd be furious when she found out, later ... Your mother's still all right, then?'

Joan nodded.

'Good. How about Bridget?'

Joan wrinkled her nose. 'I'm not sure. We chatted for a while before I told her, and although she *says* everything's fine, I suspect she was just trying to reassure me.'

They went into the kitchen, where Joan had supper under way. She began peering into saucepans, stirring things.

'I wonder what's wrong,' said Thanet. He trusted Joan's intuition in such matters.

'Just the strangeness of it, that's all, I should think. We thought she'd be a bit homesick at first.'

'You think I ought to give her another ring? No, I suppose not. She'd realise why.'

'Or think we're fussing. No, best to leave it for the moment. Anyway, she said she might be going out.'

Out. Thanet blanked out alarming visions of smoke-filled pubs crowded with undesirable young men, of frenzied discos where drug-pushers and pimps lurked in the shadows on the look-out for just such tender prey as Bridget.

'Did she say who with?'

Joan shrugged, straining the water off the potatoes. 'Some of the other girls, I imagine. I didn't ask.'

Far better not to, they had discovered. Bridget was happy to volunteer information unprompted but presented with questions she became the proverbial clam. Most teenagers were the same, Thanet assumed. He would just have to get used to the idea that she was now out of his orbit, that the people with whom she was in daily contact were strangers to him, the places she frequented as unfamiliar as if she were in a foreign land.

Joan added margarine, black pepper and milk to the potatoes, plugged in the hand blender and switched it on. She raised her voice slightly above the noise. 'No point in worrying about it. She'll tell us soon enough if she wants to talk. She probably wants to feel she can cope with it by herself. And knowing her, she wouldn't want us to worry.'

'I suppose not.'

Joan glanced at his face, switched off the blender and put it down. Then she came to put her arms around him. 'She'll be all right, darling. Don't worry.'

Joan's hair was soft and silky against his cheek and smelt of summer meadows. 'I know.'

They kissed, a kiss of mutual reassurance. Their first chick had flown the nest and it was hard to accept that she was on her own now. They could only hope that they had equipped her well enough to face whatever problems came along without too much heartache.

Joan turned back to her preparations.

'I'll lay the table,' said Thanet.

'It's done.'

'Ben in?'

'He ate earlier, it's Judo night.'

'Of course. I'd forgotten it was Wednesday. Well, I'll just pop up and see your mother, then.'

'Right. You might well find she's asleep. I made some soup and gave it to her about half an hour ago, I thought it would be the best thing for her at the moment.'

Upstairs all was silent. Joan had left a small table lamp alight in Bridget's room and Thanet tiptoed in, suppressing the familiar sensation of loss that gripped him whenever he was reminded of her absence. Mrs Bolton was asleep, curled up on her side, only the top of her head visible above the duvet cover. Her breathing was shallow but regular. Reassured, Thanet moved quietly back across the room and down the stairs.

'Fast asleep,' he announced.

'Good. We'll eat, then.'

Supper was unusually good. Joan was an excellent cook, but with a full-time job she had neither the time nor the energy to spend on preparing food during the week. That was another way in which they were going to miss Bridget, Thanet realised. On her evenings off from the restaurant where she had been working for the past year, if she wasn't going out Bridget had often cooked the evening meal for the family, frequently experimenting with recipes she had gleaned at work. But today, despite the fact that Joan had had her mother to look after, she had obviously made a special effort and Thanet made appreciative noises as they ate the cream of celery soup (made with skimmed milk, as Joan was quick to point out) and chicken breasts cooked with a ragout of peppers, courgettes, onions and tomatoes. For pudding there was a selection of fresh fruit.

As they ate Thanet told her about the latest developments in the Perdita Master case.

'Poor woman,' said Joan, when he had finished telling her about the interview with Vanessa Broxton. 'How is she going to feel when she finds out that Perdita hadn't been neglectful of the children after all . . .? She must feel bad enough already. But to learn that it really wasn't Perdita's fault, that if only she'd given her a chance to explain none of this need have happened . . .'

'I know.'

'It's terrible to think your life can change so dramatically for the worse in such a short space of time. There she was, with everything any woman could wish for and then suddenly there comes this bolt from the blue . . . You know, I'm really surprised that she didn't give Perdita an opportunity to explain. She did know her, after all, knew that she just wasn't the kind of woman to walk out on two babies without some pretty compelling reason.'

'I think that half the problem was that when she got home she was feeling pretty fragile. For a start, she must have been disappointed that her first decent case for many months had gone short on the first day. Then she broke down on the motorway and had to wait ages for the RAC to arrive. To find Henry in such a state and then to discover that Perdita had apparently just walked out on them . . . It must have been the last straw.'

'Yes, I can see that.'

'At least her account helped me to understand what really happened. Until then I just couldn't seem to get it clear in my mind. Anyone can lose his temper, have an argument, and it was easy to see how Perdita had slipped in the spilt milk . . . But there's such a divide between something that happens in the heat of the moment and the deliberate act of killing someone with a plastic bag. The second I realised that two people must have been involved it all made sense. I can't think why I didn't see it before. I was just being particularly dense . . .'

They had finished eating and Joan began to gather up the dishes.

'Leave that,' said Thanet, taking them from her. 'I'll do the washing-up – no, no argument,' he said firmly as Joan began to protest. 'You go and put your feet up. Coffee?'

'D'you mind having tea?'

'Tea it shall be.'

'I'll just pop up and take another look at Mum. No, I must, really. Then I'll sit down, I promise.'

But Thanet had almost finished the washing-up before Joan came back downstairs. He could understand her need to keep checking on her mother, but he was concerned about her. She was looking very tired. The strain and anxiety of the last two days had taken their toll and he hoped she wasn't going to exhaust herself by over-zealous nursing.

When he took the tea in she was looking thoughtful. She accepted her cup with a word of thanks and then said, 'So who d'you think could have done it?'

Thanet sat down, adjusting a cushion in the small of his still-aching back. He lit his pipe. 'Ah, well that's the problem. There are several possibilities. But to be frank, I don't think it was either Master or Swain. Mike says he can imagine Master saying to himself, Well, if I can't have her no one will, and I suppose to some degree I can agree with that if the act of smothering her with that bag were done in the heat of the moment. But if Vanessa Broxton caused the fall, I can't imagine Master coming into the kitchen and cold-bloodedly murdering his wife. If he had seen her lying there on the floor

I think he'd have been much more likely to get into a panic, ring for an ambulance, and try to revive her. And the same goes for Swain. No, as I said to Mike, whoever killed her really wanted her dead.'

'So that leaves her mother-in-law or Swain's wife. Your back's playing up tonight, isn't it? Why don't you stretch out on the floor?'

'Perhaps I will, when I finish my pipe.' Thanet grinned. 'I was tempted to this afternoon, but I didn't think Draco would approve. He's been looking pretty grim today, by the way.'

'New developments?'

'I didn't like to ask.'

They were silent for a few moments, thinking of the Dracos. Joan sighed and then returned to their discussion. 'What's Mrs Master senior like?'

Thanet grimaced. 'Let's just say I'm glad she isn't my mother-in-law.'

'Which reminds me.' Joan put her cup down and started to get up. 'I'd better just...'

Thanet put his hand on her arm and gently restrained her. 'It's not ten minutes since you last went up.'

'I know, but I must. It won't take a minute...'

Thanet laid his pipe in the ashtray. 'I'll go this time.'

When he got down again his pipe had gone out and he decided to take Joan's advice, stretch out on the floor. Tired muscles protested at first as they came into contact with the unyielding surface and then, miraculously, as Thanet relaxed, the pain began to ease. 'Lovely,' he said, with a beatific smile.

Joan nudged him with her toe. 'Don't go to sleep. You still haven't told me. Why don't you like her? Perdita's mother-in-law, I mean? What's she like?'

'Well, I told you about the fuss she's making over the ring, so that gives you some idea ... Let me see, she's slim, elegant, looks a good ten years younger than she must be. Sharp, forceful, likes to get her own way, arrange the world as she wants it. Which includes having a firm grip on her son.'

'Poor man. A bit like Mike's mother in that respect, then.'

'Yes, Mike didn't like her, I can tell you. But Mrs Lineham is only a mild version of Mrs Master, I assure you.'

'And Mrs Master hated Perdita, you say?'

'The general opinion is that she would have hated whoever her son married. Apparently she never showed her dislike openly, presumably for fear of alienating Giles, but everyone agrees that she never missed a chance of getting at Perdita, making her feel inferior.'

'D'you think he really was unaware of what was going on?'

'No. That was obvious, from various things he said to his mother when we interviewed him yesterday. But I suspect he'd never actually brought it out into the open before.'

'So she's a real possibility, you think?'

'Yes. Though if she was telling the truth, she's in the clear. She says she arrived there somewhere around nine, perhaps a little earlier.'

'But you don't believe her?'

'Well, that's the trouble. There's one detail in her story which seems to bear it out. She says she could hear a child screaming, so she left, didn't bother to wait because she thought Perdita would be occupied with trying to calm him down.'

'So that would have been just before Vanessa arrived home.'

'That's right. Wait a minute, though!' Thanet rolled over on to his side then sat up, wincing. 'Just say all that was true, but that on the way home Mrs Master changed her mind. She desperately wants that ring back, you know. Perhaps she thought she'd been too hasty, should have waited. So she went back, arriving after Perdita's return. She couldn't make anyone hear, so she went around the back, looked in through the kitchen window, saw Perdita lying there, found the door unlocked and saw her chance...'

'You really think she'd be capable of that?'

Thanet thought for a minute or two before answering. 'Yes, I do.' He eased himself down on to the floor again.

Joan shivered. 'She doesn't sound my idea of the ideal mother-in-law either! What about Vicky? Victoria Swain,' she added to his uncomprehending look. 'She was usually called Vicky at school.'

'Yes, well, I'd say the same about her. It's interesting, really. To meet the Swains individually you'd say she's the one who wears the trousers, but when you see them together you soon realise that he does. She tries to hide it under that flippant devil-may-care attitude, but it's obvious that she adores him and would, I imagine, do anything to keep him. And the other thing is that her image is obviously very important to her. I should think she'd go to any lengths to preserve it. She sees herself as strong, successful, independent. She wouldn't enjoy being made a laughing stock in front of her colleagues, seen as a woman who couldn't keep her husband.'

'Well, as I told you, she was certainly a law unto herself at school. If she wanted to do something she did it, and if it got her into trouble then that was just too bad.' Joan grinned. 'I used to dread her doing something wrong while I was on duty. She'd just stand there with a mocking smile on her face and apologise sweetly while it was obvious to anyone watching that she was just making fun of you.'

Thanet shook his head and tutted. 'Oh dear oh dear! Very undermining of one's authority, that!'

Joan picked up a cushion and swiped him with it. 'You're supposed to be sympathetic!'

Thanet put up his arms to fend her off. 'I call this taking unfair advantage of a man while he's down. I was only joking!'

'Precisely!' But she put the cushion down, got up. 'I won't be a minute.'

'But . . .'

But she was already gone. She couldn't go on like this, she'd wear herself out. He'd have to talk to her about it and she wouldn't like that. He sighed. Joan could be pretty stubborn when she chose. He rolled over and eased himself to his feet. He couldn't argue with her from the disadvantage of a supine position.

When she came back down he was sitting on the settee.

'I thought you were supposed to be resting your back.'

'It's much better, honestly. Besides, this is more important. Listen, love, you simply cannot go on running up and downstairs every ten minutes.'

Joan was immediately on the defensive. 'I didn't while we were eating, did I?'

Thanet shook his head in exasperation. 'That's beside the point. You know what I mean.'

'I can't help it, Luke.'

'But you can. You must. I'm only thinking of you.'

'I realise that, but it won't go on indefinitely, you know. Once the first couple of days are over I'll feel better about leaving her alone for longer periods. I just have to keep on making sure she's all right, that's all. I keep thinking, if she had another attack and I didn't know ... It was different while she was in hospital. I knew then that someone was keeping an eye on her all the time. But here, there's only me. I'm the one who's responsible.'

Thanet could understand all too well how she felt. And knowing Joan, if he extracted from her some kind of promise which was against her conscience, that would worry her so much she'd be even worse off. Reluctantly, he conceded. 'I can see that. All right. But do try not to overdo it, love.'

'I will try. But it's true, what I said. I can't seem to help it. It's an inner compulsion which says Go and look, go and check, and I just can't not do it.'

'Well, I hope you're not going to worry yourself sick when we have to leave someone else in charge.'

'I don't think I will. I honestly believe I'll feel better about it with every day that passes.'

'We'll have to try and fix up some kind of rota for next week.'

Doctor MacPherson had apparently said that Joan's mother ought to have someone around for the next week or two, and Joan had volunteered to keep her with them for that period. Joan had been given a few days' leave, but next week would be difficult. There were various things arranged at work, including a three-day course at Canterbury which Joan was running. It had been fixed for months and she really didn't feel that she could back out at the last minute.

They discussed possible arrangements for a while and then Joan said, 'It's all very well talking about the next couple of weeks, but it's what happens afterwards that's worrying me. I know Doctor MacPherson says that she will quickly get back to normal, but I keep thinking about what happened this time because she was living alone. What if they hadn't happened to be going shopping and Mrs Parker hadn't found her when she did? Mum'd be dead by now. It doesn't bear thinking about.'

'What are you saying, love?' Though Thanet could guess.

She hesitated, flickered a brief, assessing glance at him. 'I was wondering how you'd feel if I suggested she come and live with us.'

Now it was Thanet's turn to hesitate. He should have seen this coming, earlier, have given it some thought. But he'd been so busy today, there really hadn't been time ... 'I certainly don't think it's something we ought to rush into.'

'Well we wouldn't, obviously. But that's not telling me how you *feel* about the idea.'

Thanet considered. 'It certainly doesn't fill me with dismay, if that's what you mean. I'm very fond of your mother, as you know, we've always got on very well together. I think that what I'd find hardest is the lack of privacy. There'd always be someone else around. I know that Ben still is, at the moment, but in a few years he'll be gone too, no doubt, and I must admit that for me the only consolation for losing both the children would be that we'd have more time to be together again, just the two of us. That's pretty selfish, I suppose...'

'No, I feel the same. But we wouldn't have to sacrifice that, you know. I was thinking ... We could always sell both houses, ours and hers, and buy a larger one, with a separate granny annexe.'

'You have been putting your mind to this, haven't you? Yes, that would be a possibility. But would it be the answer?'

'What d'you mean?'

'Well, consider. We're not talking about having your mother to live with us because she's lonely, or because she can't look after herself. She has plenty of friends, leads a very active, busy life, and until now her health has been good. And the doctor says she'll get back to normal quite quickly. The only reason for having her live either close to us or with us is that there'd be someone to keep an eye on her all the time, so that in an emergency help would be close at hand. But it wouldn't be, would it? She'd be alone all day during the week, and without the advantage of neighbours who know her and care about her.'

Joan sighed. 'I hadn't thought of it like that. That's true. And I wouldn't want to give up my job. Though that's pretty selfish, too.'

'Not at all! Can you imagine what your mother would say if you even suggested it? She'd never agree, you know that.'

'True ... What d'you think we ought to do then?'

'Wait,' said Thanet firmly. 'As I said, there's no need to rush into anything. Let's see how she is, in a month, three months, and then reconsider. I'm certainly not against the idea in principle, but I think that in any case we have to wait until she's well enough to discuss it with her, see how she feels. Because whatever we do, it's got to be a solution which is acceptable to her as well as to us.'

'You're right, of course. All right, that's what we'll do. Thanks.'

'For what?'

'For being prepared to consider the idea seriously. A lot of men would have been horrified at the prospect.'

'And a lot wouldn't. The reasonable ones, anyway.' He grinned. 'And I, of course, am a reasonable man.'

'Modest, too.'

'Of course.'

The phone rang. He got up, careful of his back. When he returned Joan took one look at his face and said, 'What is it, what's wrong? It's not Bridget ... ?'

He shook his head. 'No. That was the hospital. I asked them to let me know if there was any radical change in the condition of Perdita's mother. She died an hour ago.'

He sat down and put his head in his hands. 'I knew I shouldn't have interviewed her yesterday morning. I told you how ill she looked, didn't I? When I saw the state she was in I should have left her alone.'

'But you said she insisted on going on with the interview.'

'I know, but ...'

'Luke. Use your commonsense. You're not seriously suggesting that the fact that you interviewed her yesterday had anything to do with her death, are you? Because if so –'

'You didn't see how ill she was, Joan. If you had ... Anyone in that condition should be left in peace.'

'I still don't think you can blame yourself. If you ask me the blame lies with her husband. In his position I think I'd have insisted that she wasn't even told about her daughter's death. She was in no fit state to hear news like that.'

'Maybe it's because he knew she was dying that he felt she should be told, that she had a right to know.'

'Oh, I don't know, it's so difficult ... But in any case, I

think he should have warned you just how ill she was. And he didn't, did he?'

'No.'

'And I suppose, if I'd been her ... I think I'd have wanted to talk to you, to feel I'd done all I could to help you find out who'd killed my daughter. In fact, I think I'd have been pretty angry if I'd been prevented from seeing you, just because I was ill.'

'Terminally ill.'

'All right, terminally ill ... Do you think she knew she was dying?'

Thanet sighed. 'I don't know. I wouldn't be surprised. And I suppose you're right. She was very determined to tell me everything I wanted to know.'

'Well there you are, then. Stop blaming yourself. You talk about my conscience, but yours is just as bad!' Joan stood up. 'Come on, it's time we went up. I've got to give Mother her last dose of pills and settle her for the night. And I think you ought to have a hot bath, for your back.'

She was right. A hot bath would help. Thanet ran the water as hot as he could stand it and relaxed, staring mindlessly at the ceiling through clouds of steam. Unbidden, an image of Perdita's body floated into his mind, that pathetic, almost child-like figure, the face disfigured by the unnatural sheen of plastic. He'd read a novel once called *Little Boy Lost*. That's what Perdita had been, despite her actual age. Little Girl Lost. Although he could never recall seeing her in life he pictured her vividly now, a solitary figure in playground or classroom, bent over her sketchbook, absorbed in her drawing. Strange that she hadn't gone to Art School, had insisted instead on ignoring her abiding passion and following a completely different career. And sad that she had never had children of her own. Or perhaps not. Perhaps, together with the lack of joy in her marriage, it was her childlessness that had enabled her to channel all her creativity into her work and produce such haunting paintings, paintings with the power to imprint themselves on the mind of the beholder and linger in the memory. He could visualise them now, especially the one that hung in the Harrows' sitting room, the one of the garden of lilies at night. Why had it had such a powerful impact upon him? he wondered.

The water was cooling now and he sat up, ran some more hot, lay back again, still thinking about this. If the mind of an artist is revealed in his work, what did Perdita's tell him about her? What were the emotions which animated it? Anger, for a start, he realised, remembering the explosion of colour in the painting in the drawing room at her house. Anger against what, or whom? he wondered. And, of course, sadness. Sadness, melancholia, pessimism, whatever you chose to call it. But Perdita's pessimism had not been ill-founded. She had indeed died before her time, as she had always thought she would.

Doomed to die. It was almost as if she knew that she was doomed to die... Mrs Harrow's words wreathed and twisted their way through his thoughts like the wisps of steam which hovered just below the ceiling above him. Had Perdita known? Could she have known? Or was it possible that because of the strength of her conviction she had somehow, subconsciously, manoeuvred herself into the position where an early death was not only likely but inevitable?

He shook his head. No. He was becoming fanciful.

But the thought lodged in his brain, stayed with him. He had lain so long in the bath that by the time he got to bed Joan was already asleep. He yawned, stretched, relaxed. It shouldn't take long to get to sleep tonight. He was tired. So tired...

But perversely his brain refused to switch off. There had been so much to absorb over the last couple of days, so many people to see, so many assessments to make. Snatches of conversation kept swirling through his brain interspersed with fleeting, vivid images: Vanessa Broxton as he had first seen her on Monday night, huddled in a corner of the settee, then staring bleakly at her husband this afternoon: *Don't you see? I made it so easy for him, I'm as guilty as he is;* Giles Master's mother grasping her son's arm, red talons digging into flesh: *Why did you have a fight?* And Master: *Perdita and Swain were having an affair. Perhaps now you'll be satisfied;* Victoria Swain: *For God's sake stop looking at me like that, Howard! I had a right to know where you were going, didn't I? I am your wife.* And Swain: *You mean, you actually followed me?* Then the Harrows: Stephanie, pale and frantic, sister dead, mother dying, (dead, now, Thanet reminded himself. Poor kid): *How long do we have to go on being patient? Until Mum is...* Harrow himself: *My wife can't stand the cold.* And Mrs Harrow, her emaciated body encased in thick woollen dressing gown, woollen bedjacket draped around her shoulders: *It's almost as if she knew that she was doomed to die.*

Doomed to die...

The words echoed along the corridors of Thanet's brain. Desperate by now for sleep he turned over and snuggled up to Joan's comforting warmth, tried to fill his mind with soothing images of country walks, days at the seaside, anything to slow down his thought processes and take his mind off the case. Gradually it worked and he began to drift. Far far away at the end of a long tunnel was a tiny spot of light. He allowed himself to float towards it. When he got there he would, he knew, make an important discovery. Water suddenly began to flow through the tunnel towards him, carrying him backwards, away from his goal, and he began to swim, to strike out strongly. He had to get there, he had to. Water was getting in his eyes and his nose and his arms and legs were beginning to ache. But he couldn't give up, he couldn't, wouldn't. He was at the point of despair when suddenly the thrust of the water began to diminish, to ease.

Suddenly he was on his feet staggering towards the end of the tunnel, the light increasing with every second, searing his eyeballs and zigzagging into his brain.

Someone was shaking him. 'Luke, wake up.'

He opened his eyes. Joan was leaning over him, her face full of concern. A gentle light from the bedside lamp played on her hair, outlined the soft curves of her breasts. 'You were having a nightmare.'

He smiled up at her, shook his head. 'Not a nightmare.' He put his arms around her and pulled her close.

He felt marvellous, invincible.

At last he knew why.

And who.

NINETEEN

'So what d'you think, Mike?'

Thanet awaited Lineham's verdict with eagerness. He had just finished propounding his new theory. The sergeant had listened intently, frowning with concentration, fiddling with a paperclip which he had unbent and twisted until now it snapped in his fingers. He tossed it on to his desk and shook his head. 'It's a bit of a long shot, isn't it, sir?'

Thanet was disappointed. He had hoped for a more positive reaction than this.

'I don't think so, no, not particularly,' he said stiffly.

'But with respect, sir . . .'

'Oh, not again, Mike! I've said before, if you disagree with me, why not come straight out with it?'

Thanet was being unreasonable and he knew it. Another time he would simply have teased Lineham, as he often had on this particular subject.

At this point Lineham would usually look sheepish but now, stung perhaps by Thanet's tone he said, 'D'you really want to know, sir?'

Thanet had a feeling he wasn't going to like what he was about to hear, but if he wasn't to lose face he had no choice but to say, 'Of course.'

'It's because I know that if I do – come straight out with it, that is – I'll get my head bitten off.'

'That's not true!'

'Isn't it, sir? Be fair. You really don't like it when people disagree with you.'

It was true that he did like to be right. It was one of his major faults, Thanet knew. 'Oh come on, Mike. I'm always ready to listen to someone else's opinion, you know that.' He wasn't that unreasonable, was he? Surely not.

'Eventually, yes.' Lineham's grin took the sting out of his words and recognising the justice of them Thanet grinned back.

'All right, all right, so you've made your point. Can we now get back to what you were going to say. "With respect..."'

'Just that we've got no actual evidence. It's all, well, guess – er, surmise.'

'I'll ignore that attempt to be tactful, Mike. Yes, there is a certain amount of guesswork, I agree. Personally I'd prefer to call it intuition. But then, there always is, in police work, you know that as well as I do. The important thing is that it should always be based on fact and you have to admit that this theory does fit the facts as we know them.'

'Maybe.' Lineham still sounded doubtful. 'But as far as proving it is concerned, everything depends on matching that sample.'

'Exactly. So I want you to concentrate on that. Go and get hold of another sample to compare it with and then take it straight to Aldermaston. I'll give Bob Farley a ring, tell him how urgent it is that the tests are done immediately you get there, and he can get everything set up.'

Detective Sergeant Farley was the Police Liaison Officer at the Aldermaston lab and Thanet knew him well, having worked with him for several years.

'How long do you think it will take you?'

Lineham glanced at his watch. 'It's half-nine now. Say half an hour to collect the sample, an hour and a half to get there, half an hour to get the tests done, an hour and a half back ... Four hours or so, I should think.'

'I'll expect you between 1.30 and 2, then. Fine.'

'I could always ring you from the lab with the result, then you needn't wait for me.'

Thanet knew how much it must have cost Lineham to make this offer and he appreciated his generosity. The sergeant would be bitterly disappointed not to accompany Thanet when he made the arrest. Provided, of course, that the tests came up with the expected result. But he wouldn't think about that. He was right, he knew it, he felt it in his bones.

'No, Mike, I'll wait. I expect –'

The telephone rang.

Thanet lifted the receiver, listened. 'Put her on.'

Lineham raised his eyebrows interrogatively, but Thanet did not respond. All his attention was directed at what he was hearing. It was some time before he spoke. 'Yes. Yes, I see ... No, I'm not surprised, I suspected as much ... No, you can leave it in my hands now, I'll make all the necessary arrangements ... Yes, of course, we'll do our best ... That's an exceptionally generous offer, I'll tell them that ... I should think it will be late afternoon ... Yes, I agree ... Could you? That would be excellent ... Yes, I think that would be best ... Meanwhile, I'll ring you back later to let you know what's happening ... Yes. Thank you. Goodbye.'

He replaced the receiver and sat gazing at it for a few moments deep in thought, his face sombre. Then he looked at Lineham. 'I was right, Mike. Not that it gives me much satisfaction.' He recounted the conversation to Lineham, watching the sergeant's face change, become as grim as his own. At the moment this vindication of his theory meant very little to him. It was one thing to have suspected, another to have those suspicions confirmed. So much suffering, past, present and future...

'So it's all the more urgent to get that confirmation on the sample.'

Lineham rose. 'I'm on my way. I'll give you a ring from the lab in any case, when we know the result.' He hesitated. 'What are you going to do meanwhile, sir?'

Thanet was already reaching for the telephone. 'Make some phone calls. I want to get all this sorted out before you get back, if I can, so that we know exactly what the position is. But I want you with me when I make the arrest, so I will wait for you, as I said.'

'Thanks. I'd hate to miss that.'

There was much to discuss, much to arrange, and the rest of the morning passed swiftly. By twelve Thanet was waiting for Lineham's call, satisfied that he had done everything that could possibly be done at this juncture.

Now all he needed was confirmation from the lab. With that evidence he should be home and dry. Without it – well, things would be very much more difficult. Surely they should have finished the tests by now? He stood up and began wandering restlessly about the office, picking things up and putting them down without really seeing them. He became aware that the sky had cleared and the sun was shining. He had been so preoccupied he hadn't even noticed. He was crossing to the window when the telephone rang. In his haste to answer it he banged his knee on the corner of his chair. He snatched the receiver up, rubbing his kneecap.

'Lineham here, sir. We got a match!'

The relief was overwhelming, the pain forgotten. 'Terrific! How soon are you leaving?'

'Right away.'

'Good. Don't break your neck on the way home. I won't go without you.'

'Thanks.'

Elated, Thanet replaced the receiver. Then he remembered what would follow the arrest and his heart sank. When you were working on a case you couldn't think any further than solving it. It was only when that hurdle was surmounted that you really became aware of the aftermath. An arrest was never the end. The lives of friends and relations of both murderer and victim are often blighted for years. And in this particular case one innocent victim might perhaps never recover.

His knee was still aching and he stood up, tested it. No real harm done. He would go to the canteen and have some lunch, get a sandwich for Lineham to eat in the car. They wouldn't want to linger once the sergeant arrived.

By two o'clock they were on their way, tense and silent. Thanet was preoccupied with planning the crucial interview ahead, trying to anticipate possible obstacles, to decide how to counter possible lines of resistance. Despite the fact that they now had concrete proof of the murderer's presence at the scene of the crime, he knew that this did not necessarily mean that he would get a confession. And a confession was what he was aiming for. He wanted it over, done with.

Apart from a young mother pushing a pram Wayside Crescent was deserted.

Lineham glanced at the house as they got out of the car. 'Think he'll be expecting us?'

Thanet shrugged. 'Who knows?' All the curtains were drawn, he noticed, an almost obsolete way of announcing a death in the family. Oh God, in concentrating upon the murder he had ceased to think of Harrow as a widower of less than twenty-four hours. He remembered Harrow's protectiveness towards his wife. Whatever else the man was guilty of, his concern for her had been genuine. Thanet hardened his heart. He wasn't going to allow sympathy to get in the way.

In silence they walked up to the front door, rang the bell. Already, Thanet noticed, minute signs of neglect were beginning to mar the pristine perfection so noticeable on their first visit. Empty crisp packets and sweet wrappers had blown on to the front drive and muddy footprints defaced the shining surface of the quarry tiles in the porch. Footsteps sounded within, the door was unlocked and a blast of warm air came out to meet them, as if the gates of Hell had briefly opened.

'Mr Harrow? We'd like a word.'

Harrow looked at him dully, without recognition. He was wearing the same dark grey suit and black tie as on the last occasion they had visited him. But last time it had been to mark a different death, Thanet reminded himself. And that death was the reason why they were here.

'Detective Inspector Thanet and Detective Sergeant Lineham.'

Harrow's expression changed, became impatient, faintly hostile. 'Does it have to be now, Inspector? I'm just off to the undertaker's. I don't know if you've heard, but my wife died last night.' *You ought not to be bothering me at a time like this.*

'Yes, I did hear. I'm sorry. All the same, I'm afraid I must insist...'

Harrow hesitated a moment longer, then shrugged, stood back and ushered them into the stifling semi-darkness of the sitting room. Thanet had a brief glimpse of the lilies and the moon in Perdita's painting gleaming ghost-white on the wall opposite the fireplace before Harrow switched on the electric light and the sickly yellow glow of artificial light in daytime robbed the picture of some of its magic.

Harrow sat on the very edge of his seat, an obvious hint that he expected the interview to be brief.

Shock tactics, Thanet had decided, would be best and as soon as they were settled he nodded at Lineham and watched Harrow as the sergeant delivered the caution. Harrow's hands were resting on his plump knees and now he rubbed them back and forth as if his palms had begun to sweat. Thanet saw the muscles of his throat move in an involuntary though silent gulp of fear. But the man's face remained impassive. He must have lived through this moment in his imagination so often over the years and especially since Monday night that he had managed to armour himself against self-betrayal.

'Is this some kind of bizarre joke, Inspector? If so, I don't find your sense of humour to my taste.'

Thanet shook his head. 'No joke, Mr Harrow, as you know only too well. I don't treat murder with levity, I assure you.' The temperature in the room was so high that already he was conscious of the prick of sweat beneath his arms. But he couldn't remove his jacket, run the slightest risk of imparting an air of informality to the interview. He would just have to stick it out. He wondered if Lineham were equally uncomfortable.

Harrow stood up. 'Then I can only inform you that you are making a grotesque mistake. And now, if you don't mind...'

'Oh but I do,' said Thanet softly. 'I mind very much. I'm afraid you're going to have to resign yourself to hearing me out. Sit down, please.'

But Harrow was not yet ready to capitulate. 'I just don't believe this. When I've heard tales of police brutality or callousness I've always thought that people were exaggerating. But to barge into the house of a man who's just lost his wife, and prevent him from going to arrange her funeral...'

'You shall arrange it, I assure you. Soon. As for your accusation of callousness, well, I don't like this situation any more than you do, but as far as I'm concerned it has to be dealt with and that's all there is to it. So, please, sit down and let's get on with it.'

Harrow hesitated a moment longer and then returned to his chair. He sat back, folding his hands primly on his lap. 'I don't seem to have any choice, do I?'

Thanet had had enough. He wanted the whole distasteful business over with. 'It's pointless to continue with this charade of innocence, you know, Mr Harrow. We not only know exactly when and how you killed your stepdaughter . . .' He paused, to give emphasis to his next words. 'We also know why.'

For the first time Harrow's composure slipped. Fear flashed in his eyes and he unfolded his hands, rubbed them again against his bulging thighs. 'I don't know what you're talking about.'

'Oh yes you do! But just to convince you that I'm not bluffing, I'll spell it out to you, chapter and verse.'

This time Harrow said nothing. He stared at Thanet like a rabbit mesmerised by a stoat.

'What happened on Monday night was, as we now know, the climax of a long process which began many years ago, the gradual destruction of your stepdaughter. A process which ended as it was begun, by you.'

Harrow's fear was even more evident now. A sheen of sweat had appeared on his forehead and his jowls quivered as his teeth clenched.

'Things might have gone on as they had for years if it hadn't been for an unfortunate combination of circumstances. Perdita fell in love with someone else and eventually plucked up sufficient courage to tell her husband she was leaving him and, on the same day, your wife was unexpectedly found a bed in hospital. And so it came about that when Perdita sought refuge here on Saturday night you and Stephanie were alone in the house and Perdita found that history was repeating itself in the worst possible way. She caught you in bed with your daughter.'

Thanet paused and his last words hung in the air, the disgust in his voice ringing in his ears. The atmosphere in the room was heavy with condemnation.

But Harrow was not ready to give in. He had, after all, too much to lose. 'I should be careful if I were you, Inspector. Those are very serious accusations.'

'I am well aware of that, Mr Harrow. And I certainly

shouldn't have risked making them if they hadn't been corroborated.'

This time the fear in Harrow's eyes was stark, urgent, his voice so husky that he had to clear his throat, make two attempts to get the word out. 'Corroborated?'

'You must realise that I can only mean one thing. Yes, your daughter Stephanie has at last plucked up sufficient courage to lay evidence against you. Her mother can no longer be hurt by having to live with the knowledge of her husband's corruption of her daughter.'

'You realise that it's only her word against mine.'

'Oh, I don't think there'll be any problem there. In fact, I'm certain of it. But we won't waste time on that at the moment. Let's get back to the murder of your stepdaughter, or rather to Saturday night. Perdita, of course, was appalled. Having suffered so many years of abuse herself I'm sure she kept a watchful eye on Stephanie. But somehow Stephanie must have managed to reassure her that everything was all right. How did you manage to keep Stephanie quiet, Mr Harrow? Did you convince her that no one would believe her if she talked? Or that if they did believe her they would think she was the one to blame, for leading you on? Or paint a dire picture of what would happen to the family if it came out – you would lose your job, be put into prison, the house be lost because mortgage payments couldn't be kept up . . . And then, of course, there was the most powerful deterrent of all: what would it do to her mother – her mother who was so frail that such a shock would surely kill her?'

Harrow had lowered his head and was staring at the floor, unable perhaps now to meet Thanet's eyes.

'But I digress again. For Perdita this was the last straw. She saw now that she had been wrong to keep quiet about her own sufferings. By doing so she had simply ensured the same purgatory for Stephanie. I'm sure you begged and pleaded, but she realised that even if you promised never to lay a finger on Stephanie again, you were simply not to be trusted – the children at your school could well become your next victims. Quite simply, you had to be stopped, for once and for all, and she told you that as soon as your wife came out of hospital, she would tell her the truth.

'Nothing you could say would make her change her mind. She insisted that you arrange that while your wife was away Stephanie stay with a friend and she herself would stay only the one night. When, the next day, she arranged to go and look after Mrs Broxton's children for the week, she had of course to tell you where she was staying in case you had to get in touch with her quickly about her mother. So on Monday night you knew where to find her. You also knew that apart from the children – and you didn't think of them, did you, when you killed her? – she would be alone in the house. So you waited until late evening, then went. When you got there the place seemed deserted. You rang the bell but got no reply. You knew she must be in at that time of night because of the children, so you went around to the back of the house. The kitchen curtains were undrawn. You looked in and could scarcely believe what you saw. Perdita was lying on the floor. You tried the door. It was unlocked. You went in, saw that she was either unconscious or dead – I doubt that you even bothered to check – bleeding from a head wound. I don't know whether, up to that point, you had actually thought of murder, but now you realised that if Perdita were dead all your problems would be solved, and no one would ever suspect you of killing her. No one had seen you arrive, and you would make sure that you left no trace of your visit. But you had to act quickly. What could you use, to make absolutely certain that Perdita never woke again? Then you realised. In your pocket you had the perfect weapon. This.'

Harrow raised his head as Thanet felt in his inside pocket, took out his wallet, opened it and extracted a sample bag.

Inside, clearly visible through the plastic, was another plastic bag, folded up and labelled. The temptation now, of course, was to lie, to tell Harrow that there were clear samples of his fingerprints on the bag. Many of Thanet's colleagues, he knew, would not hesitate to do so if they felt that it would be useful, give them an advantage, and would think Thanet a fool for not doing so. But he hated such tactics. Victory was so much sweeter if fairly won. Anyway, in this case deception was unnecessary. He had another card up his sleeve. And knowing that there were no traceable prints on the bag he had no compunction in taking it out, shaking it, holding it up.

Harrow said nothing, simply stared at the bag as though he had never seen one before. Or perhaps, Thanet thought, he was staring through it, beyond it, into the past, seeing instead Perdita's body lying on the floor, watching his own hands ease this very bag down over her head...

Thanet shrugged. 'There's not much more to tell. The deed was very quickly done. You couldn't have been there more than a minute or two.'

He stopped, waited. There was no tension in him, only relief that the unsavoury tale was told, and a weariness that was a result of the telling. He sensed rather than saw Lineham look at him expectantly.

Harrow too looked up. He was showing more resilience than Thanet would have given him credit for. 'If you've quite finished, Inspector ... As far as the death of my stepdaughter is concerned, you have no proof of any of this. One plastic bag is, after all, just like any other plastic bag...'

So the fact that Thanet had not mentioned identifiable fingerprints had not escaped him.

'Ah, but that's where you're wrong, Mr Harrow. We do have proof.'

Once again Thanet took out his wallet, opened it. He laid another labelled sample bag on his knee. 'In here is a sample of woollen fibre, found in the plastic bag which was put over your stepdaughter's head.' He took out a third bag, laid it on his other knee. 'In this one is a sample of fibre taken from the woollen bedjacket which you took in to your wife on Monday evening before going on to see Perdita. Our forensic science laboratory has confirmed that they match.'

All three men stared at the two little plastic bags, the minute scraps of blue fluff inside them. It was against the rules to have borrowed them for this purpose, of course, but Thanet had been unable to resist the temptation.

Harrow looked up and Thanet could tell from the look in his eyes that he knew when he was beaten. 'What will happen to Stephanie?'

Thanet experienced a surge of anger and it was difficult to keep his voice level as he said, 'You should have thought of that before.'

TWENTY

'What's this Mrs Bonnard like?' said Lineham.

They were on their way to see Stephanie. Harrow had been charged, taken back to Headquarters and left to stew for the moment; as far as Thanet was concerned Stephanie's welfare now took priority. Mrs Bonnard was the mother of the friend with whom Stephanie had been staying and it was she who had rung Thanet that morning to tell him that Stephanie, released from silence by her mother's death and terrified that she would now be entirely at her father's mercy, had broken down and confided in her.

'She sounds very nice. Very concerned for Stephanie's welfare, even took the day off work to stay with her. She's known her for several years as a friend of her daughter and she's fond of her. She's very upset by all this, of course, could hardly believe it when Stephanie told her about the abuse ... Turn into Wayside Crescent, then first right, second left.'

'Poor kid,' said Lineham, signalling then turning the wheel obediently. 'She's had a rotten time, hasn't she. Years of putting up with that and then, this last week, a positive avalanche of disaster – her stepsister murdered, her mother dead, and now her father arrested ... I don't envy you the job of breaking that piece of news to her, I can tell you.'

They passed Harrow's house, its curtains still drawn as if

to hide its secret from the world. Thanet experienced a spasm of revulsion against those overheated rooms, which like a hothouse had nurtured the monstrous bloom of perversion that had flourished there. Harrow had turned off the heating before they left and by now the temperature should have dropped, perhaps symbolically, to something like normal. 'I don't think it'll be that much of a surprise, actually. I forgot to tell you ... Later on this morning, when I rang back to tell Mrs Bonnard about the arrangements I'd made with the Social Services, she said that she was convinced Stephanie was holding something back, something else to do with her father. She was sure that Stephanie wanted to tell her but couldn't bring herself to do so. I would guess that something Harrow has said or done since Perdita's death has made Stephanie suspect him. No doubt she witnessed the row between the two of them on Saturday night and heard Perdita tell him that she was going to report him to the police as soon as Mrs Harrow came out of hospital. She must have realised how powerful a motive this gave him, and put two and two together. This is the turning, I think. Yes, Meadow Drive.'

Lineham turned in. 'Number 14, wasn't it?'

'That's right.' Thanet was peering out of the window.

'Poor kid. If she did suspect her father, it must have been a great temptation to try and get him off her back by getting him arrested for murder, instead of sexual abuse. Much less of an ordeal for her. And yet she chose to do it the other way around. She's got guts, hasn't she?'

Guts, loyalty or a desire for revenge? Thanet wasn't sure, and didn't suppose that he would ever find out.

'She must be scared stiff about what will happen to her now.' Lineham was scowling, leaning forward to peer out of the window as if he were trying to read Stephanie's future.

'I know. She's very lucky that ... Ah, there it is.'

Mrs Bonnard's house was much smaller than the Harrows',

semi-detached with a cramped garden and no garage. She had obviously been looking out for them because the car had scarcely drawn up at the kerb when she opened the front door. Her smile could not disguise her anxiety. 'Inspector Thanet?' Her gaze went past him to Lineham, who had stayed in the car. 'He's not coming in?'

Thanet shook his head. 'We thought it would be a bit overpowering, if there were two of us. And as you're going to be present...' He gave her a reassuring smile.

She was in her forties, heavily built and fair-haired, with laughter lines at the corners of eyes and mouth. Thanet guessed that her usual expression would be one of good-humoured placidity – just what Stephanie would need in these appalling circumstances. Her clothes were clean but dowdy – a dark green sweater and brown Crimplene skirt. Thanet knew that she was a single parent, having been divorced ten years ago. She worked as a supermarket check-out attendant, and one of his anxieties regarding the tentative arrangements he had made for Stephanie's future had been that Mrs Bonnard's generous offer might have been prompted chiefly by mercenary motives. Now, although he had been with her for no more than a few seconds, Thanet was reassured. This woman was not out for what she could get, he was sure of it.

She paused in the hall and lowered her voice to a concerned whisper. 'Is her father...? Have you seen him?'

Thanet nodded, lowered his voice in response. 'Yes, but prepare yourself for a shock. He's been arrested and charged with Perdita's murder.'

She stared at him, her eyes opening so wide that the whites showed clear all around the irises. She was silent for a few moments absorbing the news and then she said, 'She suspected, didn't she, poor lamb. That was what she was holding back.'

Thanet nodded. 'Probably.'

'I wonder if this will ... She really worries me. She's bottling it all up inside, hasn't shed a single tear, even over her mother's death.'

Mrs Bonnard opened a door to the right of the narrow hall and led the way into the room. 'Inspector Thanet is here, Stephanie.'

Like its owner, this room was clean but dowdy. It looked as though it had been furnished to last. The predominant colour was a safe fawn, the carpet a practical all-over pattern, the three-piece suite covered in a hard-wearing uncut moquette.

Stephanie was sitting bolt upright in one corner of the settee, arms folded tightly across her chest as if to prevent herself from flying apart. Her face was pale, the delicate skin beneath her eyes bruised by insomnia and anxiety. She was wearing her school uniform of navy skirt and blue and white striped blouse, and the mass of curly hair so like that of her dead stepsister was tied back with a dark blue ribbon. She looked heartbreakingly vulnerable and much younger than her thirteen years.

'Hullo, Stephanie. We met once before, at the hospital.' He gave her only the briefest of smiles, feeling that she would find it inappropriate to be less restrained in the circumstances, but the genuine warmth and goodwill he felt towards her must have communicated themselves because her expression lightened just a fraction and she gave a stiff little nod of acknowledgement.

Mrs Bonnard sat down beside Stephanie and Thanet took an armchair facing them. 'I was very sorry to hear about your mother,' he began. 'I'm not just saying that, I really mean it.'

Her lips tightened and she nodded again, her knuckles whitening as her fingers dug harder into the striped material of her blouse. Still she said nothing. Perhaps she couldn't trust herself to speak.

'But of course, that's not why I'm here.' He paused. Stephanie would be expecting him to talk to her about the matter of her father's prosecution for child abuse, but first he had to surmount the hurdle of breaking to her the news of his arrest for murder. There was nothing he could do to soften the blow. 'First, I'm afraid I have some very bad news for you.'

Apprehension flashed into her eyes and she glanced at Mrs Bonnard, who patted her knee.

'Your father...' He had to say it. 'Your father has been arrested, and charged with the murder of your stepsister.'

She stared at him blankly. Had she taken in what he said? Mrs Bonnard was watching her anxiously.

'I have a feeling,' he said gently, 'that you might have been half expecting this.' He waited a few moments and then said, 'Am I right?'

Her lips tightened and then she gave a barely perceptible nod.

Thanet hadn't known that he had been holding his breath. Slowly he exhaled with relief.

So far, he realised, she still hadn't said a word.

Now her lips parted. 'Where...?' It was scarcely more than a whisper and she cleared her throat, tried again. 'Where ... Where is he?'

'In custody.'

Stephanie's arms had remained tightly folded throughout the interview so far, her body stiff with tension. Now, at last, she stirred, the grip on her upper arms relaxed and slowly her hands drifted down to her lap. She looked at them as if they did not belong to her and then, gently, began to massage one hand with the other. If her fingers had maintained that tight grip for so long they were probably aching, Thanet thought. Did the fact that she seemed to have relaxed a little betray the extent of her fear that her father would be released and she would be expected to go back to live with him? Briefly Thanet was so filled with pity and anger that his throat closed and he had to swallow hard to speak in anything like his normal tone.

'I expect you're worried about what will happen to you.'

She stopped rubbing her hand and again glanced at Mrs Bonnard. 'Mrs Bonnard said I could stay here.'

Mrs Bonnard took her hand, squeezed it and nodded. 'Of course you can.'

'Yes. You will be able to. For the moment, anyway – and probably indefinitely,' he added hastily as he saw the fear flash back into the girl's eyes.

'Only probably?'

'Almost certainly.' Now it was his turn to glance at Mrs Bonnard. 'I don't know how much Mrs Bonnard has told you about the procedure in circumstances like yours?' He watched Stephanie absorb the implication: she was not a freak, there were other children like her, sufficient indeed for a procedure to have been established for dealing with them.

Mrs Bonnard shook her head. 'Not a lot, I'm afraid. I thought it would be best to wait until you came – beyond telling her that she was welcome to stay here with us, that is.' She glanced at Stephanie and squeezed her hand again. 'I don't think she's really been able to think beyond that.'

'I see.' Thanet became brisk, matter-of-fact. 'The situation has changed, of course, since your father's arrest. But even so, it's all quite simple, really, and I don't anticipate any problems.' *Especially now that I've met you, Mrs Bonnard.* 'When someone is left in your circumstances, Stephanie, and there is no relation to look after you – you haven't any relations, I understand?' He waited for her headshake before continuing. 'Well, in those circumstances, normally the child becomes the responsibility of the Social Services, and is put into care. No!' He held up his hand as panic flashed in Stephanie's eyes. 'I told you, in your case that won't happen, you'll almost certainly stay here.'

'But . . .' she interrupted.

'What?' he said, gently.

'You said, *almost* certainly...'

'Only because there are certain formalities to go through. You see, as I said, because the Social Services are responsible for someone in your circumstances, they really have to be sure that someone like Mrs Bonnard, who offers to look after that child, is a fit person to do so.'

'Fit?'

'Suitable, responsible, someone who will have the child's – your – welfare at heart.' He smiled at Mrs Bonnard. 'And as I'm sure there'll be no problem in Mrs Bonnard's case, I don't think you have anything to worry about.'

'So what will actually happen?' said Mrs Bonnard.

'A social worker will come here to talk to you both, look at the house ... Just to make sure it's a suitable place for a child to live,' he added, as Mrs Bonnard gave an anxious frown. 'And I assure you, from what I've seen you needn't worry on that score. And then you will be made Stephanie's guardian, probably for a trial period. And finally, if everything works out, as I'm sure it will – it's not as if Stephanie is a stranger to you, after all – then eventually you will be made her permanent guardian.' He smiled at Stephanie. 'Does that help?'

She nodded. 'But what...?' She glanced at Mrs Bonnard, bit her lip. 'It's a bit awkward...'

Thanet understood at once what she meant. 'You mean, about the financial side of it?'

She nodded.

'You're afraid of being a burden on Mrs Bonnard, is that it?'

She and Mrs Bonnard spoke together.

'Yes, I don't want to...'

'Stephanie, you really mustn't worry about that. We'll manage, somehow.'

'It shouldn't be as difficult as all that, Mrs Bonnard,' said

Thanet, smiling. 'You will receive Stephanie's Child Benefit and also a Guardianship Allowance.'

'Really?' Her surprise was genuine, Thanet was sure of it. 'I thought we'd probably get the Child Benefit but I'd no idea there'd be any more.'

'It's not that much,' said Thanet, 'but enough to get by.'

'That's all we need,' said Mrs Bonnard, smiling at Stephanie. 'And I can't say it's not a relief. I do work, but I don't earn that much and it's a bit of a struggle sometimes. I'm not qualified for anything better, that's the trouble. That's why I always say to the girls, get yourselves educated. Then you'll always know you'll be able to support yourselves, whatever happens.'

'I agree, absolutely.'

'What will happen to our house?' said Stephanie.

'Nothing, for the moment,' said Thanet. 'There'll be plenty of time to think about that later on.' The Social Services had in fact told him that if Harrow were convicted and imprisoned the house would either have to be sold or rented out, in order to support Stephanie until she was of age. But there was no point in worrying Stephanie with this information at the moment. Let her have time to begin to adjust, first. Which reminded him . . .

'There is one other thing that the social worker will want to discuss with you.' This was delicate ground and again Thanet cast around for the best way to put it. One thing was certain: he must be as matter-of-fact as possible. Above all things Stephanie must not be made to feel bad, or a freak. 'Children in your position, children who have been abused by their parents, usually need help to come to terms with what they have been through.'

Already Stephanie had hung her head, her pale cheeks stained with red flags of shame, and again Thanet had to exert considerable self-control to hide his anger at what this girl had had to suffer. He thought of Harrow's bulging flesh, his sweaty hands, and his flesh crawled. 'They often have to be helped, you see, to understand that what happened was not their fault, that they were not responsible for it, and above all that they are not bad, immoral or different in any way from other children who have not had to suffer as they have.'

He thought of Perdita and the seeds of self-disgust which Harrow had sown in her. Thanet was certain now that it was he who had made her feel a pariah, been the cause of her self-chosen isolation at school. No doubt it was he, too, who was responsible for her dark vision of the world revealed through her art, the sense of impending doom which had so distressed her mother. Had Stephanie been rescued in time? He hoped so, he fervently hoped so. But what about all those others, the secret victims of adult lust and perversion, those too frightened for one reason or another to betray their tormentors? It didn't bear thinking about. He would have to be satisfied that he had perhaps rescued one child from that particular purgatory.

Stephanie had still not raised her head but he could tell by her sudden stillness that she was listening intently. Had he said enough? Should he wait for her to respond, or just quietly leave? He desperately wanted to do the right thing.

She raised her head to look at him and he found he was holding his breath.

'You mean . . . ?' She stopped.

Go on, he silently urged her. *Go on.*

She must have sensed his silent encouragement because she tried again. 'You mean . . . they're not going to blame me?'

Thanet shook his head, filled with rage. What had Harrow said to her? 'No, I'm sure of it. Not in the least.'

'They won't say . . .' She glanced at Mrs Bonnard, who put her arm around the girl's shoulders and gave her a protective hug. Then she looked back at Thanet. '. . . I led him on?'

The desperation in her eyes was almost more than he could

bear. Again he shook his head. 'No, Stephanie, they won't. Believe me, they won't.'

She stared at him for a moment longer and then, the first sign that her rigid self-control was beginning to crack, her lower lip began to tremble. A moment later a solitary tear tracked its way down her cheek and then suddenly her face crumpled and, turning her head into Mrs Bonnard's shoulder, she flung her arm around the older woman with the frantic grasp of a drowning man clutching at a rock, and began to weep.

Thanet knew that, heart-rending as the child's grief might be, it was far better that she should let it out. It was what Mrs Bonnard had been hoping for. She put both arms around Stephanie and began to rock her, to stroke her hair and comfort her as she would a much younger child. Over the girl's head her eyes met Thanet's and she nodded her satisfaction and dismissal.

His mission was accomplished.

He left.

TWENTY-ONE

Thanet awoke, remembered that it was Saturday and he didn't have to go to work, and stretched luxuriously. Yesterday had been hectic, completing all the paperwork inevitable at the end of a murder case, and Joan had been in bed when he got home. Knowing that she would be up early to tend to her mother he had left a note on her bedside table: WEEKEND OFF! As yet they had had no opportunity to talk properly since the case finished and he knew she would be eager to hear all about it. But there was no hurry. The delicious empty space of Saturday and Sunday stretched ahead of them. There would be plenty of time to relax, catch up.

He opened one eye and squinted at the bedside clock. Nine-thirty. Time to move.

He stretched again, sat up and swung his legs over the side of the bed. His nose twitched as he became aware of the beckoning smell of coffee and – yes, surely, bacon! He couldn't remember when they had last had bacon for breakfast, Joan's healthy eating campaign had banned it from their diet, except as the special occasional treat. Suddenly he was very hungry.

He went to the bathroom, showered and shaved. On the way back to the bedroom he paused at the half-open door of

Bridget's room, peeped in. His mother-in-law was sitting up in bed, having breakfast. He went in.

'Morning, Margaret. How are you feeling?'

'Much better, thank you, Luke.'

She looked it, too. The unhealthy greyish pallor had disappeared and her skin had regained a little of its natural colour.

'You look it. Good.'

'I'm sorry to be such a nuisance, though. It's such a lot of work for Joan.'

He sat down on the side of the bed, took her hand. 'Look, the main thing is that you're getting better. If you start worrying about Joan you'll hinder your recovery and defeat the whole object of the exercise. You gave us a nasty fright, you know.'

'I can imagine. Even so ...'

'I'm afraid,' said Thanet smiling, 'that just for once in your life you're going to have to resign yourself to other people doing things for you, instead of the other way around. Think how virtuous you'll make them feel!'

'You always did have the knack of turning things around,' she said, smiling. 'All right, I'll try.'

'Good. Anything you want?'

She shook her head. 'I'm allowed up for a few hours later. Not downstairs, yet, though, I understand.'

'No. Doctor MacPherson said you should wait a week before attempting to climb the stairs, and then only very slowly.'

She grimaced. 'I hate being treated like an invalid.'

'Look at it this way. The more you behave like one to start with, the sooner you'll stop being one.'

She shook her head, smiling. 'You'd better get dressed. By the smell of it your breakfast's just about ready.'

'See you later.'

He called into her room to collect the breakfast tray on the way downstairs. The kitchen was filled with sunshine and appetising smells. Joan turned to greet him, smiling. 'I thought you'd like a lie-in today.'

He put down the tray, went to put his arms around her, kiss her. 'Is the smell of bacon a product of my over-heated imagination?'

She grinned. 'A treat. To celebrate the end of the case. And the fact that it's Saturday. And that for once we've got the whole weekend free.'

Thanet nodded at the table, which was laid for two. 'Ben not here?'

'He left half an hour ago. He's gone into town.'

They ate in a companionable silence and it was not until they were on their second cup of coffee and Thanet had lit his pipe that Joan said, 'Now tell me all about it.'

'About what?' he said, raising his eyebrows in feigned ignorance.

'Luke! Stop teasing. You know perfectly well what I mean.'

'Oh, sorry, you mean the case. Yes, well...' he added hurriedly, seeing her eyes flash with pretended anger. 'Where d'you want to begin?'

He'd already told her the bare facts, of course, that Harrow had confessed, and why the murder had been committed, but very little more.

'Where we always begin. With how you worked it out. That's what always fascinates me. I can never understand how you do it. I'd never have guessed in a million years.'

'Don't exaggerate! You're simply trying to boost my ego.'

'No! I mean it, honestly. You'd told me everything you knew, everything you'd learnt, and I can honestly say the idea would never have entered my head.'.

'That's because you hadn't met the people concerned. You hadn't seen how they behaved, how they looked, how they reacted. If you had –'

'I still wouldn't have worked it out, I'm sure of it. So come on, tell me how you did it.'

He removed his pipe, took her hand with exaggerated courtesy, dropped a kiss on the back of it and bowed his head. 'Your wish is my command.' Then he sat back, frowning. 'Though it's easier said than done. I'll have to think, if I want to get it in sequence.'

'All right then, think. I'll clear these things away – no, you stay there and concentrate on working it out.'

By the time she sat down again he had it all clear in his mind. 'It was after that conversation we had on Wednesday night. You remember? We'd been talking about the case, after supper, and I'd been telling you about Vanessa Broxton's visit to my office, how I'd suddenly realised that there must have been two people involved, not one.' He shook his head. 'I still can't understand why I didn't see that sooner. Anyway, if you recall, we had quite a long discussion about who the second person could have been.'

Joan was nodding. 'I remember.'

'And naturally, that was the question that was paramount in my mind that night, all the time, whatever else I was doing or thinking. Anyway, my back was playing up and you suggested I have a hot bath, so I did. I lay there for ages just thinking about the case, and about Perdita in particular. She was the key to it all, of course. Random violence apart, no one gets himself murdered without good reason. I knew that somewhere in her character, in her life, was something, I'd no idea what, which had brought about her death. So I turned over in my mind everything I'd heard about her from different people . . . I think that what I was trying to do at that point was put aside preconceived ideas, try to find a new way of looking at the case. It's so easy, as you go along, to formulate theories which, if you're not very careful, seem to become fact, which they're not. Then they get in the way.'

Joan was listening intently, nodding from time to time, chin propped on hand, grey eyes fixed unwaveringly on his. A shaft of sunlight falling on her hair turned the soft fair curls to gold. Perhaps it was this talk of Perdita that made Thanet, for the first time in his life, wish that he could paint. How, he speculated, would Perdita have painted Joan? But Perdita had never painted people, only drawn them. Why? he wondered.

He became aware that Joan was waiting for him to continue.

'According to her mother, Perdita never got over her father's death when she was ten. She'd always been a Daddy's girl, apparently, and found it very difficult to adjust to having a stepfather – Harrow had already told me as much himself. Mrs Harrow said she changed a lot, became withdrawn and gloomy and everyone – yourself included – told me how much of a loner she'd been at school. Mrs Harrow told me too that at one time Perdita became obsessed with death and then, a few years ago, when Perdita was having an especially difficult time with her husband, she said something which really shook her mother. She said, "I don't suppose it matters much, does it, Mum? I don't expect I'll have to put up with it much longer." When Mrs Harrow asked what she meant she told her that she'd always thought she'd die young. Mrs Harrow said it was almost as if she knew that she was doomed to die before her time.'

Joan shook her head in sorrow. 'Poor girl.'

'Yes . . . Well, everyone knows that the death of a father will have a profound effect on a child of that age but usually, if the child is reasonably well-adjusted, in time he'll get over it. But Perdita didn't. It seemed to have blighted her life. Not as far as her work was concerned, of course. On the contrary, she seemed to have poured all her emotion into it, which is presumably why it has such a powerful impact. You've seen her paintings, you must know what I mean.'

Joan nodded. 'After our talk on Wednesday night I hunted out an old catalogue I knew I had somewhere, of one of Perdita's local exhibitions.' She got up, disappeared into the sitting room for a few moments. 'Here it is.'

The catalogue was dated 24 October 1985, and there were several illustrations in it. Thanet glanced through them, aware that he was hoping to find a reproduction of the lilies in the garden. But he was disappointed. None of the paintings was familiar to him. All, however, had the same haunting quality. 'What a waste,' he said, shaking his head with regret. 'Think what she might have achieved, if she'd lived.'

'I know. It makes me so angry as well as so sad, when I think about it . . . But what I wanted to say was that looking at those illustrations I found myself for the first time trying to work out *why* they have such a powerful impact. And I agree with you, it must be because of the strength of emotion that went into them.'

'Did you come to any conclusions, as to what that emotion was?'

Joan looked diffident. 'I've thought about it a lot . . . I think, a combination of anger and despair.'

Thanet stared at her. Into his mind had flashed once more an image of the first of Perdita's paintings that he had seen, the one in her sitting room. He remembered feeling the power of that brilliant explosion of colour, noting the violent contrast with the cool neutrality of the colour scheme of the room and thinking that the effect was deliberately contrived to enhance the impact of the painting. He remembered thinking, in the bath, that it was anger which animated it, remembered wondering against what or whom that anger was directed. At the time he had not followed up this line of thought, but now he understood. It was anger at the way life had treated her in her impressionable adolescence, anger at being trapped in a loveless, claustrophobic marriage, anger perhaps also mistakenly turned inward against herself for somehow having been responsible for her stepfather's behaviour. It was no doubt this belief, reinforced later by the discovery of her attraction for men, which had brought about the despair, the darkness which lay beneath.

'Harrow made her feel guilty, didn't he?' he said grimly. 'He made her feel it was all her fault ... And he was doing the same thing to Stephanie.'

He told Joan of Stephanie's fears that the social workers would blame her, think she had led her father on.

'Poor kid. Poor both of them ... And I expect he also made them terrified of telling their mother because of what it would do to her. Her health has been poor for years, you said?'

'Yes. I can just imagine it. "It would kill your mother, if she knew ..." Makes you sick, doesn't it, what these people put their children through.'

'It really does. I assume Harrow will also be prosecuted for child abuse?'

'Yes. It'll all come out at the trial anyway, of course, but in any case Stephanie is determined to go through with it. She wants to be sure that it goes down on his record so that when he gets out of prison he won't ever be able to be employed in a position of authority over children again. It's going to be a tremendous ordeal for her, but she has a lot of courage.'

'She must have. Do you think she'll ever get over all this?'

'I don't know. I hope so. She's lucky, in having Mrs Bonnard to fend for her, but she's been through so much ...'

'Luke ... I wonder ...'

'What?'

'D'you think, if Perdita felt as Stephanie did, that it was somehow her fault, that people would blame her and believe perhaps that she'd encouraged it, that she could almost in some way – subconsciously, I mean – have precipitated her own death?'

'The thought had crossed my mind.'

'She marries a jealous husband, then fans the flame by telling him she wants a divorce ...'

'And fate took a hand by arranging that she break the news to him and go home on the one night when unknown to her

her mother is away and her stepfather is taking advantage of the fact to molest his daughter. D'you realise that if she had chosen any other time, she would still be alive?'

'Not necessarily. And you always say there's no point in saying "if".'

'I think Stephanie overheard Perdita tell him that as soon as she felt her mother was well enough, she would tell her the truth and report him to the authorities . . . He says, of course, that when he went to see her on Monday night, he just wanted to talk to her, to convince her he would never do it again.'

'Do you believe him?'

'I don't know. At this point I don't want to think too deeply about him any more. That's something the jury will have to decide . . . We seem to have got side-tracked.'

'Not really. You were saying you couldn't understand why her father's death seemed to have had such a profound and lasting effect on Perdita.'

'Ah yes, that's right. I couldn't make up my mind. Had it simply been that she couldn't reconcile herself to someone taking her father's place, or had there been some other, deeper reason?

'I then moved on to thinking about something that had really puzzled me all along, which was why Perdita had trained as a nanny instead of going to Art College. If you remember, you suggested it might have been because she wanted her independence but didn't want to hurt her mother by saying so . . .'

'Because her mother assumed that if Perdita studied art she'd go to one of the two local Art Colleges, both of which have a very good reputation.'

'Exactly. So if Perdita went away it would have to be to study something other than art . . . But I still wasn't satisfied. I knew Mrs Harrow was frail and would no doubt have been disappointed if Perdita had gone away, but she struck me as being a very sensible, well-balanced woman. I couldn't see that she would have been so desperately upset by Perdita saying she wanted to go to, say, an Art College in London. I think she would genuinely have wanted what was best for her daughter. No, I was very confused by the whole business. Even if Perdita had another reason for wanting to get away from home, surely she could still have studied art instead of going off on a completely different tack?'

'Perhaps she wanted to be sure that when she'd finished her training, whatever it was, she would have a cast-iron excuse for not living at home again, if her mother wanted her to?'

'Yes, that's possible. I hadn't thought of that. And nannying would be perfect, a live-in job. Yes, that could have been part of it.' Thanet shrugged. 'Anyway, I was still trying to make sense of it and I thought, Let's approach it from another angle. Let's assume that the decision had nothing to do with her mother, that Perdita was desperate to get away for a completely different reason. What if it was simply that she wanted to get away from her stepfather? I knew they didn't get on, her mother had told me so. But even then I still didn't see it. At that point I drifted off to sleep. I can't remember what I dreamt but you woke me up, if you remember, said I was having a nightmare.'

'And you said you weren't. In fact, as I recall, although you looked a bit dazed, you were really rather full of yourself...'

They exchanged reminiscent smiles.

'Well, I was in what we could call a celebratory mood. I suppose my subconscious must have gone on worrying away at the problem while I was asleep and when you woke me it hit me, like a revelation. Do you remember when we met Harrow and Stephanie at the hospital, after we'd been visiting your mother, the way Stephanie flung her father's arm off her shoulders when he was trying to comfort her? As I watched them go I was thinking how sad it was that they didn't seem able to turn to each other for help. I suppose that because of your mother's heart attack I was very aware of how much it meant to have the support of someone close at a time like that. I remember thinking how if – God forbid – it had been Bridget and I in that situation, we would have been depending on each other to see us through. Harrow, I thought, didn't seem to get on any better with his daughter than his step-daughter ... Now, as I say, it hit me. What if Perdita had wanted to get away from her stepfather for the strongest reason of all ... ? What if she had been sexually abused, and what if, when she sought refuge in her mother's house on Saturday night, she found that Stephanie was having to suffer the same torment? Suddenly, it all fell into place. If this was what had happened, it would explain why Stephanie was staying at a friend's house while her mother was in hospital – no doubt Perdita would have insisted on it. And if she had told her stepfather that this time she wasn't going to keep quiet, that as soon as her mother was well enough she would tell her the truth and also inform the authorities, this would certainly give Harrow a powerful motive for the murder. He would not only lose his wife and daughter but his job, too, no one would want to employ an assistant headmaster convicted of sexual abuse. And he must have known his wife's condition was critical, that if he didn't act quickly and she died, Perdita wouldn't hesitate to go straight to the police. And, of course, he knew where Perdita was – she'd had to tell him so that he could get in touch with her if her mother's condition suddenly deteriorated.

'Then I remembered something else. Do you remember that the reason why I suspected that Vanessa Broxton might be guilty was because the one piece of concrete evidence we had was a scrap of blue woollen fibre found inside the polythene bag with which Perdita had been killed, and I'd remembered seeing Vanessa wear a blue woollen jacket on the night of the murder? Well, I then remembered that

Harrow had told me he'd taken a woollen bedjacket in to his wife on the night of the murder, and I recalled seeing Mrs Harrow wearing the bedjacket when I interviewed her in hospital . . . It was blue.'

'And you thought that if he'd gone to see Perdita after visiting his wife that night, he might well have still had in his pocket the polythene bag in which the bedjacket had been wrapped.'

'Exactly! Which was, in fact, what happened. Of course, all this was theoretical until we could check that the fibres matched, but I was sure that this was the answer.'

'I suspected you had something up your sleeve on Thursday morning, when you left for work.'

'I didn't want to say anything until I'd got confirmation of the match, in case I was wrong.'

'But you weren't,' said Joan, smiling. 'Brilliant!'

'You're biased.'

'No, I mean it. I hope Draco was impressed.'

'I think he's too worried about Angharad to be impressed by anything at the moment. I do hope she's going to be all right. I don't know what he'll do if she doesn't get better.'

'No.'

They were both silent for a moment, thinking of the Dracos. Then Joan glanced at the clock. 'My goodness, just look at the time! I must go and help Mother get dressed.'

'Yes, she told me she was getting up later. She's looking a lot better, isn't she?'

'Yes, thank God. I'm not sure how good a patient she's going to be, though.'

'Don't worry, I've been laying down the law on that!'

'Ah, but will she listen?'

'I think so. I certainly hope so. Anyway, you go and see to her and I'll clean up down here.'

Thanet was halfway through the washing-up when the telephone rang. He hurriedly dried his hands and went into the hall, calling 'I'll take it,' up the stairs.

A telephone operator asked him if he would accept a reverse charge call from London. It must be Bridget. 'Certainly,' he said.

A moment later he heard her voice. 'Dad?'

'Bridget!' He was filled with joy.

'You've been very elusive this week. You've been out every time I've spoken to Mum. Been busy on a case, I gather.'

'Yes. I was sorry to have missed you.'

'How's it going? The case?'

'All finished.' He heard the ring of satisfaction in his voice and so did Bridget.

'Brilliant!' she said, unconsciously echoing her mother. 'That didn't take long. Was it an interesting one?'

'I'm not sure how I'd describe it. Anyway, enough about me. How about you? How are you settling in?'

'Fine.'

But he at once detected the reservation in her voice. 'Are you sure?'

'Yes, really.'

Now he was sure of it. Joan had been right. Something was wrong. 'Sprig,' he said, using her old nickname, 'what's the matter? Your mother told me she wasn't too happy about you. What's wrong?'

There was a brief silence, then a sigh. 'I might have known I couldn't fool you two.'

'Is it serious?'

'No.' This time she sounded more positive. 'I'll sort it out in time, I'm sure.'

'What's the problem, exactly? Are you homesick? It would be perfectly natural, you know, it's nothing to be ashamed of. In fact, we half expected it. It's the first time you've actually lived away from home, after all.'

'No, it's not that. Not really. At least, it wouldn't be, if . . . It's the other girls, really.'

Thanet was astonished. Bridget had always been sociable,

had never had any serious problems in relationships with either fellow-pupils at school or colleagues at the restaurant where she had worked for the past year. 'In what way?'

'It's just that, oh, I don't know, they're so different from me. Most of them are much better off, for a start, they seem to spend money like water – not that that worries me in the usual sense. I mean, please don't think I'm complaining about being hard up or anything like that, I have all I need. It's just that, well, I suppose most of them come from such different backgrounds from me and they have such a different attitude to life. For instance, when they go out in the evening they seem to take it for granted that they'll go to a pub and spend the evening there, drinking and smoking ... Oh, that sounds terrible, it makes them sound positively depraved, and they're not, it's just that that's not the way I want to spend either my money or my time, and it makes things a bit difficult, that's all.'

What it boiled down to was a clash of values, Thanet thought. And if Bridget was in the minority it wasn't going to be easy for her. 'Yes, I can see that. But surely all the girls aren't like that?'

'No. There is one girl, she comes from Yorkshire ... And I'm sure there'll be others. It just takes time to find out, that's all. There's so much to take in all at once.'

'I'm sure you're right. And you've only been there a few days.'

'Yes. You mustn't worry about me. I wasn't going to say anything ... How's Gran?'

'Much better. Hold on a minute.'

Joan had appeared at the top of the stairs, arm in arm with her mother, who was wearing a dressing gown. 'Is it Bridget?'

'Yes.'

'Tell her her grandmother'll have a word with her.'

Thanet nodded and the two women turned and made slow

progress towards the door of Thanet and Joan's bedroom, where there was an extension.

'You can talk to her yourself,' he said into the receiver.

'She's up?'

'For limited periods, yes.'

He heard his mother-in-law's voice, firm, loving, reassuring as always. 'Bridget?'

'Gran! How lovely to hear you! How are you?'

Gently, he replaced the receiver, leaving the two women, one old, one young, to work their alchemy of love upon each other. He was happier about Bridget now. She would cope.

He returned to the kitchen. The washing-up water had gone cold and he pulled out the plug, watched the dirty suds swirl away. Then he squirted more liquid detergent into the sink and ran some fresh water. A few bubbles had escaped and he watched them float towards the window, iridescent in the sunlight. Like them he felt buoyant, light as air.

Life was good.

WAKE THE DEAD

To Margaret and Brian,
whose courage and devotion were
an example to us all.

ONE

They were all three pretending to watch television while they waited. It was a sitcom, but none of them was laughing.

Thanet glanced at his watch. Eight-thirty. Enough was enough. 'Come on, let's eat.'

Ben jumped up with alacrity. 'Good. I'm starving.' He followed Joan into the kitchen.

'I'll open the wine.' Thanet crossed to the window for one last glance down the empty street before going into the dining room where the bottle of 1986 Chablis Leclos which he had been saving for just such an occasion stood in the cooler on the festive table. Snowy-white tablecloth, best cutlery and crystal glasses had been brought out for this special meal to celebrate the end of Ben's O level examinations. Where on earth were Bridget and Alexander, this new boyfriend of hers they'd heard so much about?

By now anger at their lateness was beginning to give way to anxiety. They should have been here long since – between seven and eight, Bridget had said. How safe a driver was Alexander? On a Friday evening the motorway from London was always crowded, but surely by now the traffic should have eased. Thanet hoped the meal was not spoiled. Joan had taken so much trouble over it. With Bridget a newly fledged Cordon Bleu professional cook working in the directors' dining room of a firm of London stockbrokers, her mother always felt she had to try to match her daughter's standards on occasions such as this.

The phone rang. Thanet got there first.

'Dad? It's me. Alexander's only just arrived, he got held up at the office. We're leaving now, so we should be there between half past nine and ten. Thought I'd better let you know, in case you were worried.'

'Right.'

Something in his tone must have alerted her. 'There's nothing wrong, is there? Dad?'

'No, not at all.'

But try as he might the note of false assurance came through. And Bridget, of course, knew him only too well.

'You haven't waited supper for us, have you? Oh, don't tell me Mum cooked a special meal!'

Thanet knew he shouldn't say it, but he couldn't stop himself. 'Well, Ben took the last of his O levels today . . .' There was no need to say any more. Bridget, he knew, would immediately envisage the whole scenario.

'Oh, no . . . Dad, I am sorry.'

'We should have told you. But you were so sure you'd be here between seven and eight . . .'

'And of course, Mum wanted it to be a surprise.'

Thanet now felt guilty at having made Bridget feel guilty. It wasn't her fault, after all. He tried to ignore the small, critical voice which insisted, *She could have rung earlier*. 'Never mind. As long as you're all right. We were just beginning to get a bit concerned, I must admit.'

'Oh Dad, I'm sorry, I really am. I should have rung earlier. It's just that I thought there wasn't much point until Alexander actually got here.'

'Not to worry. We'll keep something hot for you.'

'No, don't do that. It'll be so late. Alexander said we'll pick up something on the way.'

'Right. See you later, then.'

Thanet recounted the conversation to the others.

'She could have let us know earlier,' grumbled Ben.

'She realises that now. She said so.'

'And why couldn't Alexander have rung her, if he knew he was going to be late?'

'Food!' said Joan, whisking plates into the dining room.

The prospect cheered them all up, the reality completed the process. Joan had excelled herself and Thanet couldn't help wishing that Bridget had been here to appreciate the fact: home-made pâté with wafer-thin curls of crisp melba toast; baked salmon stuffed with monkfish mousse in lobster sauce; bite-sized new potatoes in their jackets; mangetout peas, fresh broad beans and a delicious *mélange* of peppers, courgettes and mushrooms; then, to crown it all, a summer pudding stuffed with raspberries, blackcurrants and redcurrants, served with that most delectable of forbidden delights, fresh cream. And the wine was, they all agreed, superb.

By the time they heard a car pull up outside the mellowing process was complete.

'There they are.' Ben jumped up and went to the window. 'Wowwwww,' he breathed, his eyes opening wide in astonishment and admiration.

Thanet and Joan looked at each other with raised eyebrows. Ben was at an age when it was considered sophisticated to remain unimpressed by more or less everything.

'What?' Curiosity drove them both to join him at the window.

Ben was still gaping. 'A Porsche! She didn't tell us he had a Porsche!'

Thanet blinked. Ben was right. There it was, a sleek red low-slung schoolboy's dream, parked incongruously in their suburban drive behind the modest Astra provided for Joan by the Probation Service. And just getting out were Bridget and the much-vaunted Alexander. Thanet had no more than a fleeting impression of someone tall and fair before Joan tugged both him and Ben away from the window. 'Come on, stop goggling, you two! Your eyes are sticking out like chapel hat-pegs!'

They all went into the hall to greet them and a moment later the two young people came in in a flurry of apologies.

Hugs all round from Bridget and introductions made, Alexander handed Joan the tall gift-wrapped package he had been carrying in the crook of one arm. 'I'm terribly sorry to have inconvenienced you, Mrs Thanet. Brig tells me you cooked a special dinner.'

A plummy accent, Thanet noted, as Joan's eyes lit up with surprise and pleasure. And 'Brig'! Thanet suppressed the irrational spurt of indignation that this boy had already coined a special nickname for Bridget.

Alexander listened to Joan's It-really-doesn't-matter murmurs before turning to Thanet. 'I really must apologise, sir. Something came up at work and it simply couldn't wait until Monday.'

Sir! Thanet couldn't recall ever having been addressed thus before by the various young men Bridget had brought home over the past eighteen months. His hand was taken in a firm grip and two piercingly blue eyes met his in a gaze of unwavering sincerity. He could see why Bridget was so taken by Alexander. He was tall, well built and undeniably handsome, with regular features, fresh complexion and a thatch of golden curls. His clothes were casual but elegant: designer jeans and Boss T-shirt. He was older than Thanet had expected, twenty-seven or -eight, perhaps. Thanet suppressed a qualm of unease: altogether too experienced and sophisticated for Bridget, surely? He murmured an appropriate response.

Alexander turned to Ben. 'I do hope we didn't ruin your celebration. You took your last O level today, I gather?'

Bridget waited for Ben's reply and then said, 'Go on, Mum, open it!'

They all watched while Joan removed the wrapping paper. 'Oh, look!' she breathed. 'Isn't it beautiful!'

And there was no denying that it was, a handsome deep blue hydrangea with five blooms so perfect that they looked almost unreal.

Bridget and Alexander beamed.

'I've got a plant pot exactly that colour,' said Joan. 'It's in the cupboard under the stairs.'

The pot was produced, the hydrangea placed ceremonially in the centre of the hall table and then they all moved into the sitting room. Coffee was poured and they settled down to talk. Over the next hour or two Thanet's misgivings intensified. Alexander was patently out of their class. He was, as Thanet knew, a stockbroker, and it now emerged that he had been to Winchester and Oxford, having taken a year out (financed by 'the parents', as he put it) to travel around the world. You name it and it seemed that Alexander had done it, from crossing the Sahara in a jeep to backpacking in the Andes. Thanet watched Bridget listening to these traveller's tales with shining eyes and wondered: was this self-possessed and confident young man what he wanted for his daughter? Not, he acknowledged with an inward sigh, that it would make any difference what he wanted. Bridget would make up her own mind and they would have to go along with it.

Are you kind? he said silently to Alexander. *Are you considerate? Would you be faithful to her, good to her when things go badly? What sort of values have you got?*

He confided his unease to Joan later, when they were in bed.

'You're rather jumping the gun, aren't you?'

'I can't help thinking that way, whenever she brings someone home.'

'There's no reason to believe they're serious. To be honest, he struck me as the sort of young man who enjoys having a good time. I shouldn't think he'd be ready to settle down yet. And Bridget is only nineteen, far too young to be thinking about getting married.'

'And that's another thing. He's much older than I expected.'

Joan rolled over to kiss him. 'Stop worrying!'

'You haven't told me what you thought of him, yet.'

She sighed. 'I can understand what she sees in him, of course, but . . .'

'So there is a "but"!'

'Can't we talk about this in the morning, Luke? I'm so tired.'

He was immediately contrite. Joan had worked all day, then produced that wonderful meal . . . 'I'm sorry, love. Of course. At least I haven't got to go to work tomorrow, so I won't disturb you getting up early. You can have a lie-in.'

'I've heard that one before,' she said sleepily.

But for once it looked as though his free weekend really was going to be free. They all got up late, had a leisurely breakfast, then Bridget and Alexander announced that they were going to Rye for the day. Ben had plans of his own and Thanet and Joan had arranged to go along that afternoon and support the annual village fête in Thaxden, where Joan's mother lived. She had made an excellent recovery from her heart attack the previous year and as usual was helping on a stall.

'Wonderful day for it,' said Joan as they set off.

And it was. The sky was an unbroken blue and the July sun sufficiently strong for heatwaves to shimmer above the tarmac.

Thanet nodded. 'They should get a lot of people there.'

The Thaxden Fête was held annually at Thaxden Hall, home of the local MP, Hugo Fairleigh. As village fêtes go it was an elaborate affair, and usually raised large sums of money. The previous year over four thousand had been donated to various local charities and this year they were hoping to exceed that sum. Thanet thought they had a good chance; the proposed hospice in Sturenden was a popular cause.

By the time Thanet and Joan arrived at 2.30 the fête was in full swing. No-parking cones lined the road through the village and a uniformed policeman was directing the traffic into a large field opposite the Hall. Hundreds of cars were already parked there and more were arriving all the time. Families were heading purposefully for the tall gates across the road, where gaily coloured bunting fluttered above a huge sign slung from tree to tree over the entrance. 'THAXDEN FETE. IN AID OF THE STURRENDEN HOSPICE APPEAL.' The blaring music of a fairground organ added to the general air of festivity.

'Looks promising,' said Joan.

'Certainly does. What time did it start?'

'Two o'clock. Jill Cochrane was opening it.'

Jill Cochrane was a well-known local television personality who was always generous of her time in supporting charitable events.

Pausing for a moment to admire the gaudily painted organ which stood just inside the gates, they strolled up the drive towards the front of the house, whose originally classic Georgian façade with five windows above and two either side of the porticoed front door below had, in Thanet's view, been spoiled by the later addition of two wings of unequal size at each end. He said so, to Joan. 'If it were mine, I'd have them down.'

'I don't suppose you would, you know. Very few people will actually sacrifice existing space, unless they have to.'

'Possibly. I don't know . . . Look at that!'

In front of the house a lovingly restored World War Two Spitfire was surrounded by an admiring crowd. Its owner stood alongside, answering questions. Two old metal fire-buckets stood nearby and people were tossing coins into them. Thanet admired the plane for a while, added his contribution, and then he and Joan began to work their way around the stalls and sideshows which encircled both lawns on either side of the drive and spread around the back of the house.

'Look, there's Mum.' Joan waved and headed for the WI stall, where Margaret Bolton and two other women were doing a brisk trade in home-made cakes, biscuits, jams and chutneys.

'Just as well I saved one for you,' she said, bending down to pick up a luscious-looking chocolate gâteau. 'We've practically sold out of cakes already.'

'Wonderful!' said Joan. 'Makes your mouth water to look at it, doesn't it, Luke?'

'Mmm?' Thanet was abstracted. He had just spotted Hugo Fairleigh, who was clearly fulfilling the host's duty of escorting Jill Cochrane around the fête.

'She looks stunning, doesn't she?' said Joan, following his gaze.

Jill was wearing a beautifully cut sleeveless linen sheath in a pale cucumber green.

'Yes.' Thanet's reply was automatic. Eye-catching though she was, it wasn't Jill who had captured his attention. He was wondering why Hugo Fairleigh was looking so – what was the word? – disconcerted, yes, that was it. The MP was watching someone or something intently and Thanet tried to work out who or what it was, but it was hopeless, there were so many people milling about.

Joan was handing over money for the cake. 'Could you hold on to it for me, Mum?'

'Yes, of course.'

'See you afterwards, then.'

They had arranged to go to Mrs Bolton's house for supper.

Half an hour later Thanet was trying his hand, unsuccessfully, at the coconut shy.

'Inferior *biceps brachii*,' murmured a voice in his ear, just as he released his last ball.

It went wide of its mark.

'Thanks a lot!' he said, turning around. He knew who it was, of course.

Doctor Mallard, the police surgeon, and Helen his wife were standing beside Joan. All three were smiling.

'I challenge you to do better!'

Mallard shook his head. 'I'm past it, I'm afraid. Twenty years ago I'd have taken you up on that. But now, well, a nice cup of tea would be more in my line. What do you say?'

Joan and Helen consulted each other with a glance, smiled and nodded. 'Lovely.'

'Good.'

The small marquee where the teas were being served had been erected on the back lawn, presumably so that water was readily available from the Fairleighs' kitchen, and tables and chairs had been set up in front of it.

'Looks as though we'll have to wait,' said Thanet. 'They're all full.'

'No, look.' Joan pointed. 'Those people there are just going. And the table's in the shade.'

'We'll go and sit down,' said Helen. 'You get the tea.'

'What would you like to eat, love?' said Mallard.

'Oh, just a scone, I think. What about you, Joan?'

'The same.' She grinned. 'But you two men can indulge yourself in cakes, if you like.'

There was a short queue and Mallard insisted on paying. 'My invitation, my treat.'

They carried the tea tray across to the welcome shade and settled themselves with the women. Mallard took an appreciative sip. 'Ah, this is the life,' he said, sitting back in his chair. 'Beautiful day, beautiful surroundings . . .' He glanced from Joan to Helen. 'Beautiful women . . .'

'My word, you are in a good mood today, James,' said Joan, smiling.

'And why not? What more could I want, I ask myself?' He patted Helen's hand and they exchanged smiles.

So did Thanet and Joan. They never ceased to marvel at the transformation in Mallard since his second marriage. During the years following the death of his first wife from a slow, lingering cancer, they had wondered if Mallard would ever recover. The cheerful, dapper little man who sat with them this afternoon was scarcely recognisable as the testy, scruffy figure who at that time seemed certain to live out his life entrenched in a bitterness from which nothing could save him.

Until Helen had come on the scene, that is. Thanet, who had known Mallard since childhood, would always be grateful to her for rescuing his old friend – and grateful, too, for what she had done for Bridget. Helen Mallard was a well-known writer of cookery books and throughout Bridget's adolescence had helped and encouraged her in her ambition to follow a career in cookery.

It was as if she had tuned in to his thoughts.

'How's Bridget?' she asked.

Thanet noticed Hugo Fairleigh come out of the house and hurry on to the lawn, looking about him purposefully. He seemed agitated.

It was Joan who answered. 'Home this weekend, as a matter of fact. With the latest boyfriend.' Joan pulled a face. 'Luke's not too keen.'

'Why?' said Mallard. 'What's wrong with him?'

Thanet shrugged. 'Too –' He broke off. Fairleigh's gaze had focused on Mallard and now he was coming towards them.

Mallard, Helen and Joan turned to see what had captured his attention.

'Doctor Mallard . . .'

Thanet had been right. The MP did look agitated – distinctly upset, in fact.

Mallard rose.

'I'm so sorry to interrupt your afternoon, but I wonder if you could spare a moment?'

'Yes, of course.' Mallard glanced at the others. 'Excuse me, will you?'

Fairleigh put a hand under Mallard's elbow, drawing him away towards the house and stooping to murmur in his ear. Then their pace accelerated.

'Wonder what's wrong,' said Joan.

Helen sighed. 'I knew he shouldn't have said that – about everything being perfect. It was tempting fate.'

'It's one of the hazards of being a doctor, I suppose,' said Joan. She glanced at Thanet. 'Rather like being a policeman. You're never really off duty.'

Helen smiled. 'I know. Even on holiday . . . James never lets on that he's a doctor, you know, not if he can help it.'

'I read an article by a doctor once, on that very subject.' Thanet grinned. 'It said that if there's an emergency on the beach, all the men sitting with their heads firmly down reading newspapers will be doctors. One quick glance to check that it's not their nearest and dearest involved and that's it, they just don't want to know.'

'I can believe it,' said Helen.

'Would you like some more tea, while we're waiting?' Thanet rose, picked up the women's cups as they nodded and said, yes, a good idea. Then he paused. 'Ah, there he is now.' He had just spotted Mallard come hurrying out of the back door, alone. The little doctor looked grim, he noticed. What now?

'Look, I'm sorry about this' – Mallard's gaze encompassed all three of his companions – 'but I'm afraid I'm going to have to ask you, ladies, to excuse both of us.'

'Why? What's happened?' said Thanet. He put the cups down.

All three of them instinctively glanced around to see if they could be overheard and leaned forward as Mallard lowered his voice.

'It's Mr Fairleigh's mother. She died this afternoon.' Mallard patted Helen's arm and glanced from her to Joan. 'This is confidential, of course, but . . .' He looked squarely at Thanet. 'There's no doubt in my mind that she's been murdered.'

TWO

As he and Mallard hurried towards the house Thanet had already begun to make a mental list of priorities: call for assistance, contact Lineham, contact Draco, put someone on the gate to take down names and addresses. Thanet groaned inwardly as he tried to estimate how many people were here this afternoon – a thousand, fifteen hundred? Fifteen hundred possible suspects; no, you could cut that down because a lot of them were children, say seven hundred and fifty, then, or . . . He shook his head to clear it. What was he doing, counting suspects? There were a lot of them, that was the point. But before doing anything else and certainly before making an appropriate announcement over the loudspeakers he would have to check for himself that there was a strong possibility that old Mrs Fairleigh really had been murdered. Not that there was any doubt in his mind. The police surgeon was, after all, the very person they normally called in to confirm just that. For himself, he would have taken Doc Mallard's word without question, but he would have to play this by the book. Hugo Fairleigh was an important man and Superintendent Draco might cast off his current lethargy and revert to normal, in which case he would have Thanet's guts for garters if anything went wrong.

*

'You mean to say you informed over a thousand members of the public that you would require them to give us their names and addresses without even bothering to check for yourself that there was good reason?'

'I knew I could rely on Doc Mallard's word, sir.'

'Just listen to me, Thanet. In my patch you never take the word of anyone who is not a trained member of this force without checking. No matter who he is.'

'But –'

'No one is infallible, Thanet, remember that. How did you know he wasn't joking?'

'He wouldn't . . .'

'And it was a hot day, wasn't it? Very hot. Hot enough to give someone sunstroke, especially if, like Doctor Mallard, you happen to be bald.'

'He was wearing a hat, sir. A Panama.'

'I don't care what sort of hat he was wearing! Are you being deliberately obtuse, Thanet? I'm simply making the point that a policeman can't afford to take anything for granted. Ever. Is that clear?'

'Yes, sir.'

They had almost reached the house and with an effort Thanet switched Draco off and stopped. There were one or two points he wanted to get clear before they went in. He noted that there were two doors in the back façade of the house: one at the far end of the central block which was the original house, one in the projecting right-hand wing. This was the one to which Mallard had been leading him and was also the one through which helpers had been going in and out to fetch fresh supplies of water for the tea urns. 'Who did you leave with the body?'

'Don't worry, no one.' Mallard's hand dived into his pocket and produced a key. 'This was in the door, so I used it.' He grinned at Thanet over his half-moon spectacles. 'I watch television too, you know.'

'Where is Mr Fairleigh now?'

'With his wife. We ran into her on our way in and she came up with us.'

'Have you told them what you suspect?'

Mallard shook his head. 'I wanted to have a word with you, first, let you see for yourself.' He pulled a wry face. 'I suppose I was being a bit of a coward, really, wanted some moral support when I broke the news.'

'But you're certain, aren't you?'

Mallard nodded. 'I'm afraid so.'

'How did you explain coming to fetch me?'

Mallard looked shamefaced. 'Just said I wanted to fetch a colleague. Fairleigh seemed to accept it.'

'I'm surprised.'

'I don't think he was thinking straight.'

Fairleigh had looked pretty agitated, Thanet remembered. Even MPs are human, after all, and finding one's mother dead is a shock to anyone. And of course, if he had brought about that death himself, he wouldn't have liked to query anything Mallard suggested, however much he wanted to, in case it brought suspicion upon himself.

'What about locking the bedroom door? Didn't he find that a bit odd?'

'He doesn't know I have – or didn't, anyway. His wife was upset and he took her off somewhere.'

'So how did the old lady die?'

'She was smothered. A pillow over the head, I imagine. She was in bed, of course, and considerably weakened by the stroke Fairleigh told me she'd had about ten days ago. I suppose someone decided it was a good opportunity to finish her off.'

'Any sign of an intruder? Anything taken?'

Mallard shook his head. 'I don't suppose it would have entered Fairleigh's head to check. He seemed to take it for granted that the death was natural – it's the attitude you'd expect him to take whether he did it himself or not.'

So the murderer was almost certainly a member of the family, thought Thanet, as it usually was in such cases. Of course, the police would have to go through the motions, take all those names, conduct perhaps hundreds of interviews, but it would all be a monumental waste of time.

'Right, let's go in.'

The back door opened into a short quarry-tiled corridor leading off to the left. They could hear voices and the clatter of crockery coming from an open door a few yards along. A moment later a woman came out carrying a tray of clean cups and saucers. She frowned when she saw them.

'Can I help you?'

'No, thank you. We're on our way up to see Mr Fairleigh,' said Mallard.

Apparently satisfied she nodded and they flattened themselves against the wall for her to pass.

'Good thing you look so respectable,' said Thanet when she had disappeared through the back door. 'She might have thought we were burglars.'

But it wouldn't have been too difficult for someone to have waited until the coast was clear and then slipped in and up these stairs, he thought as he followed Mallard up a narrow staircase which had once, he guessed, been used exclusively by servants to gain access to the first floor.

He was relieved to find that, strangely enough, he was not experiencing his usual apprehension of the first sight of the corpse. Normally he dreaded that moment, had to brace himself for it to the degree that for several minutes before he was almost incapable of coherent thought. It was a weakness with which he had never quite come to terms and he was grateful that this time he seemed to be getting off lightly. Was it perhaps because he knew that old Mrs Fairleigh's death had involved no obvious violence, that it had apparently appeared sufficiently peaceful to deceive her son – or allow him to hope that he could deceive others – into thinking that it had been natural?

They had almost reached the top of the stairs and Mallard turned. 'To the left,' he whispered, laying a finger on his lips.

Thanet understood at once, and nodded. Mallard didn't want Fairleigh to hear them.

Fortunately this upper corridor was thickly carpeted and their feet made no sound as they moved silently along. There were several doors set at intervals along the right-hand wall and windows spaced out along the left, overlooking the paved terrace and the tea tent on the lawn beyond.

This is ridiculous, thought Thanet. We look like a couple of conspirators. But he could understand Mallard's caution. The police surgeon wanted to be certain that he had the backing of the police before facing Fairleigh.

This was the calm before the storm.

Mallard had the key ready in his hand and now he stopped, inserted it and turned it as quietly as he could.

The bedroom was light and spacious, with pale green fitted carpet and floor-length chintz curtains at the tall sash windows. Thanet had no time for more than a fleeting impression; his attention was focused on the still figure in the high, old-fashioned mahogany bed. He and Mallard advanced and stood side by side looking down at the old woman. The pillow beneath her head, he noted, was slightly askew.

Even in death her strength of character was evident in the firm chin, jutting prow of a nose and deeply etched frown lines on her forehead. She must, Thanet thought, have been a rather formidable person; intolerant, probably, and uncomfortable to live with – ultimately, perhaps, her own worst enemy. Which of her nearest and dearest, he wondered, had finally found her living presence intolerable?

What did you do, or say, that drove someone over the edge? he asked her silently.

What had she thought or felt in those final moments when she must have realised that a familiar face had become filled with murderous intent? If only, he thought, we could wake the dead and hear what they had to tell us. How much simpler it would all be, how much pain could be avoided for those innocent bystanders caught up in the merciless searchlight of a murder investigation.

Apart from the pillow – and its position could so easily be taken for normal that in itself it would certainly not have alerted anyone to a suspicion of foul play – he could see no sign that she had met a violent end, but Mallard was bending forward, pointing out this and that, lifting an eyelid to reveal the burst blood capillaries in the eyes. Thanet's sense of smell had already drawn his attention to a further common sign of suffocation, the voiding of bladder and rectum.

Mallard straightened up. 'So, you see what I mean.'

'Now you've pointed it out, yes. Otherwise I'd never have suspected.' He sighed. 'I wonder just how often murder is committed and no one ever does suspect.'

'More often than we'd care to think, I'm sure, especially in circumstances like this. GPs are busy people, and if a patient has had a major stroke, as she had, death would come as no surprise, her doctor would be half expecting it.'

'So you're saying that if Mrs Fairleigh's own doctor had been called in, instead of you, he would probably have issued a death certificate without a second thought?'

'Highly likely, I should think. Not that I'm casting doubt on the competence of her GP, I don't even know who he is.'

'Unlucky for whoever did this, then, that Mr Fairleigh happened to alight on you. I gather he knew you're a doctor. Did he also know you're a police surgeon?'

'Not to my knowledge. He might, I suppose. I only know him slightly, we've met a few times at local Conservative functions.'

'But why fetch you? Why not send for Mrs Fairleigh's own GP?'

Mallard shrugged. 'I assume he wanted to get a doctor to her as quickly as possible just in case anything could be done, unlikely as that seemed. It was a perfectly understandable reaction, in my view. She was still warm, you see, very recently dead.'

'So you'd say she died within the last hour, say?'

'Yes. I don't think I could narrow it down further than that.'

Thanet glanced at his watch, made a mental note. Four-ten. He made up his mind. 'Right, we'll get going, then. We'd better have some photos before you make any further examination.'

The door had opened as he was speaking and Hugo Fairleigh came in. 'I thought I heard voices.' He gave Thanet a searching look and said to Mallard, 'Who's this? What further examination? What's going on?'

The MP was tall and well groomed, with straight fair hair brushed back and Cambridge blue eyes. He had inherited his mother's firm chin and strong nose. He was immaculately dressed in cream linen suit, white shirt and discreet tie. He possessed, as Thanet knew, considerable charm, which at the moment was conspicuously absent. The blue eyes were frosty, the jutting chin more prominent than usual.

Thanet did not envy Mallard the task of breaking the news.

The little doctor had obviously decided to waste no time

beating about the bush. 'I'm afraid I have some bad news for you, Mr Fairleigh.'

Fairleigh's eyebrows rose.

'I have good reason to believe that your mother did not die a natural death. I therefore felt it my duty to call in the police before proceeding any further. This is Detective Inspector Thanet of Sturrenden CID. I knew he was at the fête, I'd seen him earlier.'

There was a moment's silence. Fairleigh blinked, then his eyes travelled briefly over Thanet's off-duty attire of cotton trousers and pale blue T-shirt.

Something would have to be done about clothes, Thanet realised. He could hardly launch into a murder investigation dressed like this, especially in a house like Thaxden Hall. He must remember to ask Lineham to bring something more appropriate out with him. Fortunately he and the sergeant were roughly the same build.

'You can't be serious.' Fairleigh's tone was icy.

'I'm afraid I am. All too serious.'

Fairleigh glanced from Mallard to Thanet and then advanced to look incredulously down at his mother's body. 'But she was ill. Seriously ill. I told you, she had a severe stroke ten days ago, and we were told then that she could well have another one that could be fatal. So this came as no surprise. A shock, of course, but no surprise.' He turned back to Mallard. 'I'm sorry, I'm afraid I must insist on a second opinion.'

'That is your right, sir,' said Thanet politely. 'But before you proceed perhaps I should inform you that Doctor Mallard is our police surgeon, and is very experienced in such matters. If you could listen, first, to his reasons for having come to this conclusion . . .'

Fairleigh's eyes narrowed and he hesitated.

Thanet watched him closely. He could understand the man's dilemma. If he was himself the murderer he must be kicking himself now for not having called in his mother's own doctor, and especially for having called in one who turned out to be a police surgeon. So what should be the best course of action? Should he play the outraged innocent, make as much fuss as possible, invoke perhaps the influence of higher authorities? Or would it be better to try to hush the whole thing up as far as possible? Guilty or innocent, it would be in his own interest not to antagonise the police, and in either case he would want to be seen as a right-minded citizen, anxious to cooperate with the authorities and detect his mother's murderer as soon as possible.

Yes, Fairleigh would now back-track, Thanet decided.

He was right.

Fairleigh's lips tightened. 'Very well,' he said stiffly. His eyes focused on Mallard in fierce concentration as the little doctor began to talk.

When Mallard had finished Fairleigh turned away and walked across to the window, his hands clasped behind him. The knuckles, Thanet noticed, were white. The man was restraining himself only by a considerable effort of self-control and was no doubt thinking furiously.

Thanet and Mallard waited.

Finally Fairleigh took a deep breath and let it out slowly in a long release of tension. Thanet saw the rigid shoulders relax, the grip of his hands slacken. He turned to face them.

'Very well,' he repeated. 'You've convinced me.' He shoved his right hand in his trouser pocket and began to jingle the coins or keys in it. 'My God, it's against all belief or reason, but you have convinced me. You'd better get on with whatever you have to do.' The chinking sound betrayed his agitation and he must have realised because he snatched his hand out of the pocket and rested it instead on the windowsill. He glanced out at the crowds below. 'You're going to have your work cut out, aren't you?'

The implication was obvious. Fairleigh was trying to ensure that from the outset it was accepted that the crime had been committed by an intruder.

Thanet decided to play along for the moment. It would be to his advantage to allow the murderer, if he were one of the family, to be off guard, think himself safe.

'You may already be too late, of course. I shouldn't think he'll have hung around.'

Thanet became brisk. 'I'll get things moving, then. First, we'll have to put someone on the gate to take names and addresses.'

'Our local bobby is outside, directing traffic,' said Fairleigh.

Thanet nodded. 'Fine, we'll get him to do it. I'll put out an announcement over the loudspeakers, say there's been an accident and we'll be looking for witnesses. Then I'll call in my team. Meanwhile, we'll have to lock this door.'

'Right. If you don't mind using the phone in here for your calls, as you know the way . . . I must get back to my wife. This has all been rather a shock for her, of course, and I can't imagine how she'll react when she hears . . .'

Thanet would have liked to watch young Mrs Fairleigh's reaction himself, but he really had to get someone on the gate as soon as possible, just in case. 'As soon as I've got things organised I'll want to talk to the rest of the family. I'll need to find out if anyone saw anything.'

'Right. We'll be in my mother's sitting room. It's the room next door to this.'

'I'll fetch my bag, and tell Helen not to wait,' said Mallard in Thanet's ear as they followed Fairleigh out of the room. 'She can take the car, no doubt someone will give me a lift home. What about Joan?'

'Ditto. Tell her I'll get Lineham to drop me at her mother's house. If I'm later than 10.30, I'll go straight home.'

There was a buzz of excited conversation after the announcement as people speculated as to the nature of the accident. Then Thanet returned to Mrs Fairleigh's bedroom. It wasn't the place he would have chosen to make his phone calls, with the old lady's body lying there awaiting the indignities to which it would shortly be subjected, but Fairleigh had given him no choice. Spreading a clean handkerchief across his palm before picking up the receiver he rang Lineham first. Fortunately the sergeant was on duty this weekend.

Lineham's whistle down the phone when he heard the news made Thanet's ear ring.

'No need to deafen me, Mike.'

'But Mr Fairleigh's mother! Is this going to cause a stink! Does the Super know yet?'

'No. I'm just going to ring him.'

'Isn't he in London again this weekend?'

Angharad Draco was undergoing treatment for leukaemia, which involved regular trips to a London hospital. Draco always drove her up and fetched her and, whenever possible, stayed there. He adored his wife and the change in the dynamic little Welshman since the diagnosis had been dramatic. The man who had once said that he wanted to know if anyone so much as sneezed in his patch now merely kept things ticking over, an automaton whose attention was more or less permanently engaged elsewhere. More or less, Thanet reminded himself. With the Fairleighs involved this might well be a case of less rather than more.

'I'd forgotten. Yes. I'll give him a ring at the hospital.'

'I'll just get the SOCOs organised, rustle up some reinforcements, and I'll be on my way.'

'Right. Oh, Mike, just one more thing. Could you make time to call in at your house on the way to pick up some clothes for me?'

Lineham understood at once. 'Yes, sure. What would you like?'

'A shirt, a tie, and a lightweight jacket.'

'Trousers OK?'

'They'll do.'

'What colour are they?'

'What does it matter? Fawn.'

'Just wanted to make sure the jacket matched.'

'Mike, I'm not taking part in a fashion parade. Just bring me something more suitable, that's all.'

'OK, sir. I'll see what I can do.'

Thanet tried the hospital but Draco had gone out. He left a message and then went along the corridor to the sitting room. Here he found Mallard, Fairleigh and a third person, a woman. It wasn't Fairleigh's wife, Thanet knew Grace Fairleigh by sight. This was a stranger.

THREE

'Ah, Inspector,' said Fairleigh. 'This is my aunt, Miss Ransome. She and my mother share – shared – this flat. Letty, this is Inspector Thanet.'

No one would ever have taken them for sisters, thought Thanet. Apart from the age difference – Miss Ransome, he guessed, was a good five years younger than Mrs Fairleigh, in her late sixties, probably – this woman would have faded into the background anywhere. She was slight, dowdily dressed in a long-sleeved limp summer dress in floral pastels. She wore no make-up and her straight brown thinning hair streaked with grey was scraped back into a bun, untidy wisps escaping around the sides and at the back of the neck. She was clutching the wooden arms of the chair in which she sat as if to prevent the foundations of her world from rocking. As she glanced up at Thanet and murmured an acknowledgement to the introduction she kept her head down and raised only her eyes, as if expecting to be browbeaten or reprimanded. Had this been her habitual reaction to the woman who lay dead in the next room? Thanet remembered the arrogance of that profile and wondered: had Mrs Fairleigh put down her younger sister once too often?

Miss Ransome had now taken a wisp of lace handkerchief

from the pocket of her dress and was dabbing at the tears which had begun to trickle down her cheeks.

'I just can't believe it. Such a terrible shock. We were half expecting her to go, but to think that someone . . .' She shook her head, looked in despair at the useless scrap of material in her hand and accepted with gratitude the immaculately folded white handkerchief which Fairleigh now took from his breast pocket and handed to her.

'Thank you, dear.'

'Miss Ransome,' said Thanet gently, 'I'm afraid I shall need to talk to you at some point, but I can see that you're very upset at the moment. A little later on, perhaps?'

She blew her nose and nodded. 'Yes, of course.' She glanced up at her nephew. 'Perhaps it would be better if I joined Grace?'

'A good idea. My wife,' he explained to Thanet. 'She has gone to wait in our own drawing room, away from . . .' His eyes flickered in the direction of his mother's bedroom. 'I thought it would be best. Understandably, she is very upset. A friend of hers is with her.' He bent solicitously over his aunt. 'Caroline is with Grace, Letty.' He put a hand under her elbow to help her up. 'Let me take you down to join them.'

'You'll come back up, sir?' said Thanet.

Fairleigh nodded. 'I'll only be a few minutes.' He put an arm around his aunt's shoulders and ushered her gently from the room.

Thanet used the time to fill Mallard in on the arrangements he had made and to look around the room, which was comfortably furnished with faded oriental rugs, curtains and loose covers in floral chintz. There was rather too much furniture for his taste, though, all of it antique and polished to a mirror-like gloss, each piece cluttered with ornaments, pieces of porcelain, photographs in silver frames and table lamps.

The room was on the side of the house and Thanet crossed to look out. The crowds had thinned considerably and one or two of the stallholders were beginning to pack up. Mallard had ensconced himself in an armchair beside the fireplace and seemed quite content to wait, tapping his fingers on the arm of the chair in time to a tune he was whistling softly between his teeth. Thanet had just worked out that it was 'The Skye Boat Song' when Fairleigh returned.

'Oh God,' he said. 'What a day! I still can't believe this is happening.' He sat down and waved Thanet to follow suit. He took out a packet of low-tar cigarettes and offered it around before lighting one. He inhaled deeply. 'Now, what did you want to ask me?'

'If you could just give me a general picture of what's been happening here today? I imagine it's been fairly hectic.'

Fairleigh took another drag at his cigarette and groaned, the smoke issuing from his mouth in a thin stream. 'I don't know why we do this every year, I really don't. We must be mad.'

Thanet thought he knew why. It was because it was good for Fairleigh's public image, to be seen to be prepared to put himself to considerable effort and inconvenience for the sake of charity.

Fairleigh contemplated the glowing tip of his cigarette. 'Well, let me see. It got off to a bad start with the day nurse ringing to say that she was sick and wouldn't be in today. The night nurse had just gone home and the agency couldn't supply another at such short notice so we decided we'd somehow have to manage to look after Mother ourselves.'

'That was at what time?'

'Around 8.15, I should think.'

'And "we" being . . .?'

'Well it had to be my wife, chiefly, as far as this afternoon was concerned. The rest of us – my aunt and I, that is – would be fully occupied. I had to be present at the opening to introduce Jill Cochrane and then to escort her around the stalls and so on, and my aunt was helping to run one of the stalls. We had deliberately left my wife free to deal with any last-minute emergencies that came up, there's always something on an occasion like this. And whereas we'd normally be able to get someone from the village in to help, everyone was involved with the fête. We did manage to find someone to sit with Mother this morning, fortunately, a Mrs Brent, but she was helping with the teas this afternoon, so my wife said she'd take over after lunch. She couldn't stay with Mother all the time, but we decided that if she looked in on her every half an hour or so that should be sufficient. It wasn't as though she needed constant attention.'

'I gather she had a stroke around ten days ago.'

'That's right. On 30 June.'

'Was it serious?'

'Pretty severe, yes. Which was why I wasn't surprised when I looked in this afternoon and found her dead.' He compressed his lips and stubbed out his cigarette with more force than was necessary. 'I never dreamed . . . Anyway, yes, the stroke left her paralysed down one side and unable to make anything but unintelligible noises. She seemed to understand what was said to her, but she had to be fed, washed, looked after like a baby, really. She must have hated the indignity of it all.'

'Did she go into hospital?'

'Oh yes, for the first week. But when there had been no noticeable change in her condition by then, it seemed that it was likely to be a long slow process and she had made me promise that if anything like this ever happened to her, that I would make sure she was nursed at home. She wanted to die in her own bed, she said.' He grimaced. 'Well, she did, didn't she? It would have been better if I'd disregarded her wishes and left her in the hospital. At least there she would have been safe.'

'Had her condition improved, since coming home?'

'A slight improvement only. Over the last day or two she had begun to regain a little movement in her fingers.'

'What about the side that was not paralysed? Was she able to move her arm?'

'Yes. But she didn't, much.' He frowned. 'She just lay there.'

'So she wouldn't have been able to put up much of a struggle, you think.'

The muscles at the side of Fairleigh's jaw tightened as he clenched his teeth and shook his head. 'I shouldn't think so, no.'

Mallard cleared his throat and crossed his legs and Thanet glanced at him, raising his eyebrows in case the doctor had something to say, but Mallard shook his head.

'Perhaps we could go back to this morning, then. What happened after the nurse rang?'

Fairleigh shrugged. 'My wife and I had breakfast, then she went up to see to my mother, I believe my aunt helped her. Mrs Brent arrived at about 9.30 and took over. We had a pretty busy morning, as you can imagine, getting ready for the fête, and I was outside most of the time. Around one we all had a sandwich lunch.'

'All?'

'My wife and I, my aunt, Mrs Brent and Sam.'

'Sam?'

'Samantha Young, our housekeeper. She'd been working outside most of the morning too, she mucks in with everything, she's practically one of the family. Perhaps I should explain that although we all live under the same roof, we run two entirely separate establishments here. My mother and my aunt have their own entrance, their own housekeeper, and take all their meals here in their own wing. We used to see each other, of course, but not much more than if we'd been next-door neighbours.'

'Are there any internal connecting doors?'

'Yes, two, one upstairs and one down, but they are very rarely used . . . Look, is all this relevant, Inspector?'

'I'm just trying to get the general picture. It's important for me to understand how one gains access to your mother's room.'

'Yes, I see. Well as far as this afternoon's concerned, there was only one way.'

Thanet raised his eyebrows.

'Through the door by which you came in, downstairs near the kitchen. For security reasons we always lock the front and back doors of the main house on occasions such as this, and shut the downstairs windows and draw the curtains. It makes sense, don't you agree?'

'Very sensible.' But members of the family would presumably have keys, Thanet thought, and if there was a connecting door upstairs it would have been easy to slip through and into old Mrs Fairleigh's room with none of the women coming and going in the corridor downstairs any the wiser.

'So, you all had lunch at around one. Then what?'

'I went back outside for a last-minute check before going up to change. A few minutes before two Jill Cochrane arrived. At two she opened the fête and after that I was with her most of the time until I came in for a pee.'

Fairleigh was rubbing the side of his nose. Thanet was instantly alerted. This was an unconscious gesture frequently indulged in by someone who was being evasive or, more importantly, lying. And yes, Fairleigh was looking directly at him, holding his gaze as if to demonstrate how transparently truthful he was being.

If they were trying to hide the truth, rogues and villains would often become defiant at this point, as if challenging the interviewer to disprove what they were saying, or else they would find themselves unable to meet his eyes and would look shifty. But many people believed that direct eye contact was tantamount to proof of innocence, unaware that there were other ways in which they were simultaneously betraying themselves. Also, of course, the experienced policeman learned over the years to trust his instinct. Yes, he would certainly have to go into that 'most of the time' in more detail later, thought Thanet. But for the moment he let it pass.

Meanwhile his face betrayed none of his suspicions. 'What time was that?'

Fairleigh thought for a moment. 'It must have been . . .'

There was a knock at the door.

Fairleigh turned his head. 'Come in!'

It was Lineham, Thanet was glad to see, carrying a small suitcase which presumably contained the promised change of clothes. Thanet wished the sergeant could have arrived just a few minutes earlier, to confirm his impression that Fairleigh was lying. He and Lineham had worked together for so long that without the sergeant he felt as though he were operating on three cylinders. Lineham was his extra eyes and ears when his own had too much to assimilate, his second pair of hands in times of crisis, the sounding board against which theories were tested, the stimulation he needed to see possibilities unthought of.

He introduced Lineham to Fairleigh. 'Mr Fairleigh was just telling me what happened this afternoon. You were saying you came in at . . .?'

'About half past three, I suppose, or a little later.'

The blue eyes still held Thanet's, unwavering. If he were lying, was it because he wanted to cover up what had happened before half past three, or after?

'I could have used the downstairs cloakroom, but to be honest I was glad to get away from the crowds for a bit, so I deliberately spun out my time inside by going up to our own bathroom. Then I thought, while I was in I might as well look in on Mother. So I came in through the connecting door and found her' – he shook his head grimly and waved his hand in the direction of the bedroom – 'as you saw her.'

'That would have been, what? Around twenty to four, then?'

'Something like that, yes.'

'During the time that you were in the house, did you see anyone else?'

Fairleigh shook his head.

'Any sign of disturbance, anything in the least unusual?'

'No.' Fairleigh suddenly stood up and took a few agitated steps towards the window before turning. 'I just don't understand it! I suppose he was making for my mother's dressing table, where she kept her jewellery, when he realised she was there. But why do what he did? I mean, it was obvious she was helpless, for God's sake. And with all that din going on outside no one would have been able to hear her if she did call for help.' He took his cigarettes out and lit one with angry puffs. 'The whole thing is my fault, my responsibility. I should have made damned sure that someone was with her all the time.'

If Fairleigh were innocent this was something he would always reproach himself with, Thanet knew. But if not, well, he was putting on a fine show.

'Or if I'd been just a few minutes earlier . . . My wife says she came up to check on Mother at ten past three, and everything was all right then.'

If that were true, the period during which the murder had been committed had now become reduced to half an hour.

'Later on, after the Scenes-of-Crime officers have finished, we'll ask you to check whether or not anything is missing.' Thanet glanced at Lineham. 'I imagine they'll be here soon?'

'Any minute, now, sir, I should think.'

Fairleigh nodded. 'Right.'

'There's just one other point, then. Is there anyone who perhaps had a grudge against your mother? An ex-employee, for example, who might consider himself unfairly treated? Someone whom she might have antagonised in the past?'

Fairleigh looked horrified. 'You're not suggesting this might have been planned, *deliberate*? Good God, Inspector, she was a helpless old woman. Who could possibly have had any reason to wish her harm?'

Who indeed? *Cui bono?* thought Thanet. Who benefits? The old lady might well have been a wealthy woman, and Fairleigh, to his knowledge, her only son and heir – a point he would have to check. And then, however much Fairleigh pooh-poohed the idea, there was another classic motive, revenge. Who knew what harm or injury the old woman might have committed in the past? If someone had long held a grudge against her, what better time would there have been to execute vengeance than now, when she was helpless to defend herself and there was no nurse on duty to act as watch-dog? Sooner or later it was going to dawn on Fairleigh that the police investigation was concentrating on the family, and Thanet had no doubt that that was when the storm would break. But for the moment it would be easier all round if he allowed the MP to go on thinking that his suggestion of an intruder was accepted by the police as the most likely possibility.

Thanet rose. 'Well, thank you for being so patient, sir.'

'What now, Inspector?'

'First, I'd like to change. Sergeant Lineham has brought me more suitable clothes.'

'There's a bathroom next door.'

'And then I'd like a word with your wife and your aunt. I must check if they saw anything suspicious during the afternoon. They'll have had a little time to compose themselves and think about it.'

If he was right, and one of the members of Mrs Fairleigh's family had seized the opportunity to finish her off, the circle of suspects was small: Fairleigh himself, his aunt, his wife.

He was eager to find out what the other two had to say for themselves.

FOUR

The clothes fitted reasonably well and, feeling more comfortable now, Thanet emerged from the bathroom to find Fairleigh and Lineham waiting for him in the corridor outside. Fairleigh led them to a door which opened on to a broad landing in the main house with a white-painted balustrade overlooking the spacious hall below. The carpet was soft, the walls hung with prints and paintings, the air faintly scented by a huge bowl of pot-pourri on a sidetable and the fresh flowers in an arrangement near the top of the curving staircase. The effect was of carefully maintained luxury. Samantha was evidently an efficient housekeeper.

Fairleigh led them down the stairs and across the hall.

'In here,' he said, pushing open a door.

The room was large, square and elegant and seemed to swim in a dim, sub-aqueous light. The curtains, drawn for the afternoon against prying eyes, had been pulled back only a few inches and the delicate greens, turquoises and creams of curtains and upholstery melted into each other, blurring the outlines of the furniture. The shadowy forms of the three women in the room briefly lost definition as they turned towards the door.

'God,' said Fairleigh, striding across to the windows, 'it's like a morgue in here.' He froze, briefly. 'Sorry,' he muttered. 'Not the best choice of word, in the circumstances.' He fumbled at the side of the curtains and they rolled smoothly back. The movement attracted the attention of a passerby, who turned his head and glanced curiously at Hugo. Beyond him a lorry was backing slowly towards the house, cars and vans edging around it. Fairleigh clicked his tongue impatiently and narrowed the gap between the curtains. Then he adjusted those at the other window, too.

'That's better. Grace, this is Inspector Thanet and Sergeant – Lineham, was it? Yes. Inspector, this is my wife.'

Grace Fairleigh was sitting beside another woman – her friend Caroline, presumably – on the sofa. Caroline had an arm around her shoulders. Thanet had seen the MP's wife before of course, at public functions with her husband, and had glimpsed her here and there earlier on. She was tall and slender, with a cloud of black hair and regular, well-formed features. Her eyes were especially beautiful, large, dark and lustrous. This afternoon she looked very tense, her lips compressed, hands clasped tightly in her lap. She acknowledged her husband's introduction with a tight nod at Thanet.

'And this is Miss Plowright, a friend of my wife's.'

Not 'of ours', Thanet noted. He had seen Caroline Plowright before, too, around and about in Sturrenden. He noticed that Fairleigh made no move to approach his wife and comfort her, seeming quite content to leave her to Caroline's ministrations.

'My aunt, Miss Ransome, you have of course already met. And now, Inspector, if that's all you want of me at the moment, there are a hundred and one things I ought to be attending to outside.'

'By all means go and see to them.'

'If you want me you know where to find me.'

And Fairleigh hurried out with almost indecent haste. Was he being unfair to the man? Thanet wondered. It was true that there must, indeed, be a great deal to see to outside, but nothing, surely, that was so urgent as to prevent a husband staying to give moral support to a distressed wife in circumstances such as these?

Caroline Plowright was watching him with a slightly sardonic expression, as if she knew what he was thinking. She was the complete antithesis of her friend – short, solidly built, with meaty arms and shoulders and legs almost as thick at the ankles as at the calf. Her face was broad, with an almost Slavonic tilt to eyes and cheekbones, her short fair hair cut in a square, uncompromising bob. In contrast to Grace, who was wearing an elegant suit of lemon-coloured linen, Caroline's dress was a straight up and down white shift patterned with huge scarlet poppies. She was not wearing a wedding ring. An interesting woman, Thanet thought, not afraid to be noticed despite her physical disadvantages, and with a mind of her own. Observant, too, and therefore potentially useful.

The question now was, how to proceed? Once again he was faced with the perennial dilemma: how to treat a possible suspect who could well be innocent?

'Mrs Fairleigh, I know you must be very upset by all this and I'm sorry to trouble you but I'm afraid that in the circumstances I have to ask you a few questions.'

It was Caroline Plowright who responded. She was watching Grace Fairleigh's reaction anxiously and spared Thanet only a brief glance. 'Is it absolutely necessary to do this now, Inspector? Can't it wait?'

'It's best to deal with it while today's events are fresh in people's minds, Miss Plowright.'

Grace Fairleigh gave Caroline's arm a dismissive pat. 'It's all right, Caroline, really. The inspector is only doing his job. I don't see how I can help, but . . .' She gestured. 'Please, go ahead. And do sit down.'

Automatically, Thanet and Lineham chose seats where they could see the faces of everyone present.

'If you and Miss Ransome could just fill me in on some background information?'

He gave Letty Ransome a questioning glance and she sat up straighter and nodded. He was pleased to see that she was looking much more composed.

'Of course. Anything we can do, to get this dreadful business cleared up as quickly as possible. Though, like Grace, I don't really see how we can help.'

'I'm just trying to get a general picture of the household, what has happened here today. And of course, I especially want you to try to remember if you saw anything, anything at all, however trivial, out of the ordinary.'

They consulted each other with a glance and shook their heads.

'Well, something might come back to you as we talk.'

Neither of them had yet begun to relax, he thought, as he took them through the events of the morning, Grace Fairleigh sitting bolt upright with hands still clasped in her lap and Letty Ransome tugging nervously at one corner of the handkerchief which her nephew had lent her. They both confirmed what Fairleigh had said. After the phone call from the day nurse and an unsuccessful attempt to get another nurse from the agency, Grace had spent some time ringing around to try and find someone to sit with her mother-in-law during the morning. Eventually Mrs Brent had agreed to come in at 9.30. Grace had then gone across to the other wing to tell Letty what had happened and together she and Letty had attended to the old lady and given her breakfast. As Grace was the only person in the household without a specific task at the fête, she had volunteered to check on her mother-in-law every half an hour or so during the afternoon. Letty had given her sister lunch at 12.30, before going down to join the others for sandwiches at one, in the main house.

Now that they were approaching the time of the murder Thanet's interest quickened.

'So what happened after lunch? Mrs Fairleigh?'

Grace shrugged. 'I went up to change. Then I went along to check that my mother-in-law was all right.'

'What time would that have been?'

'About a quarter to two. I made her comfortable, then left, saying I'd be back in half an hour or so to see if she wanted anything.'

'She understood you?'

'Oh yes, certainly. Not for the first few days after her stroke, perhaps, but then she gradually began to respond to simple questions. She had movement on one side, you see.'

'We'd hold her fingers,' said Letty eagerly. 'And she'd give one squeeze for yes, two for no. And over the last day or two the movement was beginning to come back in her paralysed hand. We all thought she was on the mend.' Tears began to flow again and she wiped them away with the crumpled ball that was now Hugo's handkerchief. She shook her head. 'Oh, I know the doctor said she could have another stroke at any time but this . . . Oh, it's dreadful, really dreadful.'

Was he imagining it, or had she peeped at him over the corner of the handkerchief to see what effect her tears were having on him? If so, was it coincidence, he wondered, that Letty Ransome had broken down just as they were approaching that crucial mid-afternoon period?

Grace rose and went to perch on the arm of Letty's chair, putting her arm around the older woman's shoulders and patting her arm. 'Try not to upset yourself too much, Letty. It won't help us find out who did this, will it? We must try to stay calm.'

Caroline had that sardonic look in her eyes again. Why? Thanet wondered. Was it because she didn't believe Letty Ransome's display of grief to be genuine? Yes, he must arrange to have a private word with Miss Caroline Plowright as soon as possible. If anyone could help him to understand this family, she could.

Letty was blowing her nose and sniffing. 'Yes, yes, you're right, of course you are. I'm sorry,' she said to the room at large. 'Making an exhibition of myself . . .'

'Understandable, in the circumstances,' said Thanet, somehow managing to sound both sympathetic and brisk. 'But I'm sure we all want to clear this up as soon as possible. So if we could go back to what you were saying, Mrs Fairleigh?'

With a final glance to check that Letty was now sufficiently composed Grace returned to her seat beside Caroline.

There was a knock at the door. Reinforcements had arrived, including the SOCOs. Lineham went off to deal with them.

'So,' said Thanet, trying to pick up the threads yet again, 'on that occasion you must have left your mother-in-law at about ten or five to two?'

'At five to. I kept an eye on the time because I wanted to be there for the opening at two. I just made it.'

'So when did you go up next?'

'At 2.30.'

'And Mrs Fairleigh senior was all right then?'

'Yes. Fine – well, just the same as usual. I gave her a drink, plumped up her pillows and so on.'

'So you stayed, what, five minutes or so?'

'Yes. Then I went up again at about ten past three. And yes, she was still all right. I was going to go up again at a quarter to four – in fact I was actually on my way when I ran into my husband, with Doctor Mallard. He told me he'd looked in on her a few minutes before, and found her . . . found her dead. It could only just have happened, he said, she was still warm, so he'd fetched a doctor, just in case anything could be done. I . . . I couldn't believe it, I'd only left her half an hour earlier. So I went up with them. And when I saw her she . . . she looked so peaceful, we had no idea there was any question of . . . anything wrong.' She took a deep breath, let it out in a sigh. 'However prepared you are, death always comes as a shock, doesn't it? And when it's . . . when there's . . .' She shook her head. 'It's difficult to take it in.'

Caroline was watching her friend with a curiously assessing look.

What was she trying to assess? Thanet wondered. The truth of Grace Fairleigh's story, or the sincerity of her reaction to the old lady's death? Isobel Fairleigh couldn't have been the easiest of mothers-in-law, he thought, remembering that proud, arrogant profile, the determined lines etched into the dead face. And although the two households had, according to Fairleigh, existed independently, their proximity must have caused problems at times, made the relationship between husband and wife more difficult. Who knew what humiliations Grace may have suffered in the past, the degree of suppressed resentment she may have bottled up for years? Perhaps the temptation of having the old woman at her mercy had proved too much for her? On the other hand, even if old Mrs Fairleigh had been difficult when active, her stroke would surely have eased the situation. A helpless invalid, though an inconvenience, would have been far easier to deal with than an interfering battle-axe, especially when the day-to-day drudgery of looking after her was dealt with by trained nurses. Watching Grace Fairleigh, he wondered if she was in any case capable of the degree of cold-blooded vindictiveness necessary deliberately to finish off someone unable to defend herself. The same applied, of course, to Letty Ransome.

'And what about you, Miss Ransome?' he said, switching his attention. 'What did you do after lunch?'

She was composed again, had listened intently to Grace's account of the afternoon. She looked startled when Thanet addressed her.

'Me? Oh, I, well, I went straight out into the garden to see if any more stuff had come in for my stall and needed pricing. I was on the white elephant stall, you see, people kept on bringing things in all morning, and it's so difficult to decide how much to charge. Some of it was quite good stuff, but you know what it's like on these occasions, people expect to be able to pick things up for next to nothing, and judging exactly the right amount to ask, well, it takes time.' She flushed, ugly red blotches appearing on the sallow skin of face and neck. 'I'm sorry, you don't want to hear all this . . . Anyway, I went outside and stayed there.'

'All afternoon?'

'Yes.'

Thanet noticed Grace's eyes widen slightly at this unequivocal affirmative. Was Letty Ransome deliberately lying, or had she forgotten some errand which had briefly taken her away from her stall?

'We were very busy,' Letty was saying. 'I don't know how much we made yet, of course, but . . . Oh dear, it all seems so trivial, now, in comparison with what's happened.'

'You said "we". Someone was helping you?'

'Yes. Mrs Bennet. We usually do the white elephant stall together.'

'And neither of you took a break? For a cup of tea, perhaps?'

'No, someone usually brings us a cup, halfway through the afternoon. Oh, just a moment, I forgot. Yes, I did come into the house briefly, to –'

The door opened and Lineham came in.

They had worked together too long for it to be necessary

to speak. *Everything organised?* asked Thanet's slight lift of the eyebrows. *All under control* said Lineham's brief nod.

'Miss Ransome was just telling us that she came into the house briefly this afternoon, Sergeant,' said Thanet. 'What time would that have been, Miss Ransome?'

The red splotches on the scrawny neck were appearing again. 'About . . . um . . . a quarter past three, I should think.'

A quarter past three. Thanet's scalp tingled. If Grace Fairleigh were telling the truth and her mother-in-law had still been alive when she left her at around 3.15, and Fairleigh had found her dead at 3.40 . . . Letty Ransome wouldn't be able to risk lying about the time, of course, not in the circumstances, with hundreds of potential witnesses about. He kept his face impassive, however, as he said, 'Now I want you to think very carefully. This could be important. What, exactly, did you do and see?'

This time the tide of colour which began at the neckline of her dress and spread up into her face was so pronounced as to engulf the red patches completely. Thanet watched with interest. What was coming?

Her reply, however, was a distinct anticlimax.

'I simply went to the cloakroom, just inside the back door, then came out again.'

Could maidenly modesty have been responsible for that blush? wondered Thanet. Was that possible, in this day and age? Just, he conceded. On the other hand, if Letty Ransome had something to hide perhaps that betraying flush was something more than embarrassment. Guilt, perhaps, if she had lied. She didn't strike him as the sort of person who was an habitual liar.

'You didn't go upstairs at all?' he persisted.

She shook her head, one of the escaping wisps of hair floating across her mouth with the passage of air. She brushed it away impatiently. 'No.'

And she *was* lying, Thanet was certain of it now. He could tell by the even more pronounced flash of surprise which crossed Grace Fairleigh's face. She had seen her husband's aunt not only inside but upstairs, Thanet was certain of it. She noticed Thanet watching her and looked away.

'There was something you wanted to say, Mrs Fairleigh?'

She met his eyes squarely. 'No.'

So family solidarity was the order of the day. It looked as though there wouldn't be much point in persisting but he decided to try again. 'You must have been coming away from your mother-in-law's room at around the time your aunt came into the house.'

'I expect she was in the cloakroom as I went by.'

Thanet did not miss Letty Ransome's relief.

'Now I must ask you both to think very carefully. Did either of you see anything or anyone in the least suspicious while you were indoors?'

They shook their heads. But he caught the brief flicker of a memory recalled in Letty Ransome's eyes before she lowered her head and again plucked at the handkerchief.

'Miss Ransome?'

She shook her head again, compressed her lips. 'No.'

So she wasn't going to tell him, not at the moment, anyway. Perhaps she wanted to think about it, first, decide in her own time.

He caught Lineham's eye. No, he hadn't imagined all this. Lineham had seen it too, he could tell. The sergeant's slight shrug confirmed his own opinion. There was no point in pursuing the matter at the moment. Neither woman was going to change her story at this point. Wait, then, for further leverage.

Experience had taught him that sooner or later he would find it.

FIVE

'We looking for anything in particular?' said Lineham, peering into one of the drawers of Mrs Fairleigh's desk.

Thanet shrugged. 'Not especially. Anything and everything.' He leaned forward to try to decipher the signature on an indifferent watercolour of the house. It was signed E. Fairleigh, 1878. Hugo Fairleigh's great-grandmother? He tried to work out the dates, then gave up. What did it matter? He resumed his prowling around the room.

It was much later. The SOCOs had been and gone, the old lady's body had been taken away and Thanet and Lineham had been left in sole possession of this, her most private domain. If Isobel Fairleigh had had any secrets, this must be where she had kept them, thought Thanet, looking around the bedroom. The sitting room shared with her sister was too much a joint territory. He wondered how it had felt for old Mrs Fairleigh to give up being the mistress of the entire house and retire to one small section of it. Had she been angry, resentful, or resigned, accepting? No, never resigned, he thought, remembering that proud, decisive profile. Isobel Fairleigh had not been the type to lie down and let life dictate its terms to her. If she had chosen to withdraw, to abdicate in favour of her daughter-in-law, it could only have been a deliberate choice, the result of careful consideration. So, he wondered, why that particular option? Why not move out altogether, to a cottage in the village, perhaps? He couldn't believe that it was because she hadn't been able to afford to buy another house. No, much more likely that she wanted to stay near Hugo. Thanet doubted that there were any other children. It was always Hugo who gazed solemnly out of the framed school, team and undergraduate groups which hung upon these walls, smiled out of the elaborate silver frames disposed about the room. There were just two exceptions, a head and shoulders shot of an officer in First World War uniform – Isobel Fairleigh's father, he guessed, by the resemblance – and a wedding photograph of Isobel and her husband. Thanet picked this up to study it more closely. They had been a handsome couple, Fairleigh tall and well built with the same sleek fair hair as his son, Isobel a classic English beauty, her abundant hair framing a face in which the glow of youth eclipsed the ominous firmness of jaw and mouth. There was no photograph of Hugo and Grace's wedding, he noted.

'Seems to have been pretty well organised,' said Lineham. He was systematically sorting papers into piles: business correspondence, personal letters, bank statements, chequebook stubs, dividend slips.

'That doesn't surprise me.' Thanet's reply was abstracted. He had picked up an envelope which he had noticed earlier on the bedside table. It had already been opened and he took the letter out and glanced at it. Nothing interesting, just an estimate from a local builder for some proposed decorating. 'This is post-marked yesterday. Someone must have brought it in and read it to her.' He put it back on the table. 'Any sign of a diary, Mike?'

'Not so far.'

'Probably in her handbag.' Thanet looked around. He couldn't see one. Someone had probably tidied it away during the old lady's illness. The obvious place was the wardrobe, an elegant Edwardian serpentine-fronted affair of inlaid satinwood. It was full of expensive clothes crammed in so tightly that it must have been difficult to extricate them. Well-polished brogues and high-heeled shoes of sleek, soft calf were neatly lined up on the floor and the long shelf above the hanging rail was stacked high with hats and handbags. Thanet guessed that the one Mrs Fairleigh had been using when she had had her stroke would have been kept apart from the others. Yes, that would be it, on the floor at one end, a pigskin handbag with single handle. He fished it out and sat down on a chair to open it. And yes, here was a diary.

Lineham glanced across. 'Found it?'

'Mmm.' Thanet was already engrossed. What sort of a life had she led?

A busy one, he discovered. Until the last week or two there were entries for most days, sometimes two or three in a day. There were a number of regular weekly commitments. On Mondays, Wednesdays and Fridays Isobel Fairleigh had helped serve meals on wheels at lunchtime. On Tuesday and Thursday afternoons and on Wednesday evenings she had played bridge. On Friday mornings she had had her hair done. In between she had served on various committees, attended coffee mornings and fund-raising events for charity, gone to WI and NADFAS meetings.

And on the first day of every month, regardless of which day of the week it was, she had written a capital B.

Thanet pointed it out to Lineham. 'Wonder who B is?' He turned to 1 July, the day after Isobel had had her stroke. Yes, there it was, an appointment which had never been kept.

'One of the family might know.' Lineham was running his finger down a piece of paper. He whistled, a long drawn out sound of wonder and awe. 'Just look at this! Half-yearly statement from her brokers. She had close on a half a million tucked away here and there. Is Mr Fairleigh's face going to light up when he sees this! Or perhaps he's already seen it, and thought it might be worth his while to give his mother a helping hand, speed her on her way.'

'Half-yearly statement, you say? Sent out when?'

'Dated 3 July.'

'After her stroke, then. In that case, as it's obviously been opened, someone's seen it, that's certain. I wonder who's been opening her letters for her.'

'And who she's left it all to.'

'Quite. Find out who her solicitor is, Mike. Incidentally, I haven't had a chance to tell you before, but I'm pretty certain Fairleigh was lying earlier, about his movements this afternoon.'

'He wasn't exactly shedding too many tears over his mother's death, either, was he, sir?'

'So far as I could see, nobody was.'

'Except Miss Ransome.'

'I didn't think that was grief, did you?'

'Either shock or panic, you mean? She was definitely lying, wasn't she?'

'About not coming upstairs, you mean? Yes. Through her teeth.'

'Young Mrs Fairleigh knew it, too, didn't she? She must have seen her.'

'But had no intention of giving Miss Ransome away.'

'You think Miss Ransome knew she'd been spotted?'

'My impression was that she didn't. And I think she was concentrating so hard on her own performance and its effect on us to notice Grace Fairleigh's reaction.'

'So d'you think Miss Ransome might have done it, sir?' Lineham tapped the broker's list with his fingernail. 'She's probably had a good look at this, and no doubt her sister will have left her a tidy chunk in her will.'

'I agree. Still, we mustn't jump to conclusions, Mike. You know as well as I do that every time we're involved in a murder investigation we find that people start lying right, left and centre, trying to cover up grubby little secrets which have no bearing whatsoever on the case.' Thanet stood up. 'Come on. Bundle all that stuff up into an envelope and we'll take it back with us, study it at our leisure. I want to have a word with Mrs Kerk before we go home.'

This was old Mrs Fairleigh's housekeeper. She had been working in the kitchen all afternoon, supplying hot water for the teas and supervising the washing-up, and Thanet wanted to ask her if she had noticed anything suspicious. He had assumed she lived in, like Hugo Fairleigh's housekeeper, but she didn't and by the time he got around to asking for her she had already gone home.

The address they had been given was on a small new council estate on the edge of the village, an attractive mix of houses, old people's bungalows and maisonettes which was a far cry from the rows of dreary, identical council houses thrown up all over the country in the post-war years. Some of the tenants had obviously taken advantage of right-to-buy schemes encouraged by the Conservative government, pride in their homes demonstrated by porches, extensions and refinements such as wrought-iron gates.

Mrs Kerk's house sported no such embellishments but the council would no doubt consider her a good tenant: the windows sparkled, paintwork shone and the front garden was neatly mown and ablaze with a dazzling display of summer bedding plants.

An expensive motorbike was parked outside by the kerb and as Thanet and Lineham walked up the path the front door opened and a youth came out carrying an elaborate crash-helmet.

'Mrs Kerk?' said Thanet.

The youth hesitated, then pushed open the front door, which he had been about to close behind him. 'Mum!' he yelled.

There was a brief blare of sound from the television set as a door opened and closed and a woman came out. 'Yes?'

The lad ran off down the path, fastening on his helmet as he went. He jumped on to his bike and kick-started the engine. Thanet waited for him to move off before introducing himself and Lineham.

'Oh,' said Mrs Kerk nervously. She glanced back over her shoulder at the door from which she had emerged, then up and down the street. She stepped back. 'You'd better come in.'

She led them down a short passage into a neat modern kitchen well-equipped with gadgets such as microwave oven and food processor. 'Um . . . Would you like to sit down?' She gestured at the small pine table and chairs.

'Thank you.'

Thanet studied her with interest. Isobel Fairleigh couldn't have been the easiest of employers and he suspected that anyone with too much spirit would quickly have come to grief. Mrs Kerk was middle-aged, buxom, with a round placid face and neatly permed brown hair. She wore no make-up and was wearing a flowered cotton skirt and a short-sleeved white blouse which displayed her solidly fleshed upper arms. She folded her hands together on the table in front of her and waited, only the whitening of her knuckles betraying her tension.

He set out to put her at ease. He might need her co-operation later, when he began to probe more deeply into the relationships within the Fairleigh family, and at this initial meeting he didn't want to frighten her off and make her clam up. 'Just some routine questions, Mrs Kerk, no need to worry, this shouldn't take long. How long have you been Mrs Fairleigh's housekeeper?'

His conversational tone reassured her and they chatted for a few minutes before edging nearer the purpose of his visit.

'There were just one or two small points I wanted to clear up with you. The first is this. What were the arrangements for letters, in the household? How did Mrs Fairleigh get her post?'

The factual nature of the question made her relax further and she became quite voluble.

'All the post for the house was delivered to Mr Fairleigh's side. That Bert – our postman – couldn't be bothered to walk all the way around the back to deliver ours separately. It used to make Mrs Fairleigh so mad, time and again she complained about it and for a few weeks he'd do it, and then he'd go back to delivering it all in one bundle. Said it were the post office that didn't separate it out.' She gave a sniff which expressed scorn for all the people in the world who couldn't be bothered to do their job properly.

'And what happened to it after that?'

'Miss Letty or Mrs Fairleigh would go down and fetch it.'

'And since Mrs Fairleigh has been in bed?'

'Sometimes Miss Letty went down for it, sometimes young Mrs Fairleigh would bring it up.'

'And who would read it to her?'

'I don't know. One or the other of them, I suppose.'

'What happened to it today, do you know?'

'No, I'm sorry. We was all so busy, with the fête . . .'

'Yes, of course . . . I wonder, did Mrs Fairleigh usually tell you where she was going, when she went out?'

Mrs Kerk looked blank, shook her head. 'She'd tell me she was going to be out for lunch or dinner, that's all.'

'Only we've been checking through her diary . . .' He fished it out of his pocket and showed her the entry for 3 July. 'And she seems to have met someone with the initial B on the first of each month. Do you have any idea who that might be?'

Another shake of the head. 'Sorry. I really haven't a clue.'

'Her friends never came to the house?'

'She didn't –' She stopped, abruptly. 'Only for the bridge.'

Had she been going to say, 'She didn't have any friends'? 'And who were they?'

'Well, there was Mrs Fairlawn, Mrs Crayford and Mrs Pargeter, mostly. And sometimes Miss Highstead or Mrs Porter, if one of the regulars couldn't come. But it was mostly them three.'

'And do you know their Christian names?'

'Mrs Fairlawn is Edith, I think, and Mrs Pargeter is Margaret. I don't know the others. Miss Letty might be able to help you.'

'Miss Ransome didn't play bridge herself?'

A smile, for the first time. 'No, not she. Said it was beyond her and she wouldn't dare, they all took it so serious, like. It could get quite nasty at times, she said.'

'Right. There's just one other point I wanted to raise with you. You were working in the kitchen off the downstairs passage all afternoon, I understand?'

'That's right, yes.'

'Now I want you to think very carefully before you answer my next question.'

She immediately looked apprehensive, the broad forehead creasing into vertical lines.

'Did you at any time this afternoon see anyone other than those who were helping you come into the house?'

'I was busy.' She was defensive. 'I didn't have much time to stand around watching comings and goings.'

'Yes, I realise that. I just thought you might have happened to notice? If you could think back?'

Silence, while she considered. And yes, she had remembered something, Thanet could tell.

'There was someone,' she said, slowly.

'Yes?'

'A woman.' She stopped.

'Someone you knew?' Thanet was encouraging.

'No, I'd never seen her before. Said she was looking for the toilet. I told her toilets for the public were outside.'

'There is one, though, isn't there, just inside the back door?'

'Yes, but they wasn't supposed to use that. We couldn't have half the village tramping through the house, could we?'

'Where was she?'

'Coming back along the passage towards the back door.'

'From the direction of the stairs, then?'

'Yes. I'd just been out to collect some crockery to wash up. I came in through the back door and she was coming towards me.'

'And what did she say, exactly?'

'Something like, oh, sorry, I was looking for the loo.' Mrs Kerk hesitated. 'She seemed in a hurry.'

'What do you mean?'

'Well, anxious to get out, like. A bit breathless. I thought she just wanted to go bad, you know, and I did wonder whether to tell her to use the indoor toilet, but I thought no, do it for one and before you know where we are we'll have them queueing up outside the back door. So I didn't.'

'Did she seem upset, would you say?'

The housekeeper shook her head. 'I don't rightly know . . . You're not thinking she had anything to do with Mrs Fairleigh's . . . well . . . with what happened, are you?'

'I'm not thinking anything at the moment, Mrs Kerk. At this stage all I'm trying to do is gather information. This woman, could you describe her for me?'

Mrs Kerk frowned with the effort of recollection, screwing up her eyes and pursing her mouth. 'Not young, but not what you'd call middle-aged, either. Early forties, perhaps? Not slim, not fat, sort of plumpish, I suppose. Dark curly hair.'

'Height?'

'Middling. Bit taller than me. Nicely dressed, but not a lady.'

'What do you mean?'

'Her accent. She was well-spoken, but she didn't speak like Mrs Fairleigh or Miss Letty.'

'What was she wearing?'

'A navy dress with little white flowers on it. Long sleeves.'

'I must congratulate you, Mrs Kerk. You are very observant. That is an excellent description.'

Mrs Kerk looked pleased.

Now for the crucial question. 'What time was this, do you know?'

Another frown. 'Sorry, I don't. I didn't think it was important.'

Pity. 'Of course not. But was it early in the afternoon, or later?'

'Must have been getting on, because we was so busy washing up, and people didn't really get going on the teas till about three. I tell you what, though, it wasn't that long before I saw Mr Hugo come hurrying into the house with another man.'

'A smallish man, with half-moon spectacles and a bald head?'

'That's right!'

Doc Mallard. So whoever the woman was, she had been in the house during the crucial period. 'How much time do you think elapsed between your seeing this woman and then Mr Fairleigh?'

'I'm not sure. We had a bit of a rush on about then.'

'If you could think, I'd be grateful.'

She frowned with concentration. 'Ten minutes?' she said, eventually. 'I couldn't swear to it, mind.'

'But it was something like that.'

She nodded.

'Mrs Kerk,' said Thanet, 'there's no doubt about it. You are a gem.' He waited for her gratified smile before saying, 'Now, are you sure you didn't notice anyone else come in? Miss Letty, perhaps?'

A shake of the head.

'Or young Mrs Fairleigh?'

'Oh, yes, I did see her once, now you mention it. Early on, before we got busy.'

'Mr Fairleigh?'

'Only that once, I told you about.'

Thanet rose. 'Well, perhaps you'd have another think. And if you remember anything else, I'd be grateful if you'd let us know.'

'So,' said Lineham as they got into the car. 'Could this be a case of *cherchez la femme*?'

'Drop me at my mother-in-law's house, would you? I told Joan I'd meet her there . . . Who knows? In any case, with all the people there this afternoon it'll be like looking for a needle in a haystack. All the same, we'll take a good look at the names and addresses taken by the men on the gate, show it around to the family. Someone might recognise a name.'

'If this mystery woman had anything to do with the murder, she wouldn't have hung about. She'd have been gone long before you got that organised.'

'You could say the same of anyone, if it wasn't one of the family.'

'True,' said Lineham gloomily. He brightened up. 'But with all that loot lying around waiting to be inherited, I bet you anything it was.'

Thanet laughed. 'I won't take you up on that, it could prove expensive.'

SIX

'Ah, that's better.' Thanet laid down his knife and fork with a little sigh of contentment. Joan and her mother had eaten long since, but had saved supper for him: thick, succulent slices of ham on the bone, new potato salad with chives, a salad of apple, celery, walnut and yoghurt, and crusty home-made rolls. Now, comfortable in his own clothes again, he leaned back in the capacious basket chair and relaxed.

They were sitting on the little paved terrace at the back of his mother-in-law's house. Margaret Bolton was a keen gardener and the scent of nicotiana and old roses hung in the warm, still air. Although it was ten o'clock it was such a lovely evening that they had all been reluctant to go indoors and shut the windows against marauding insects.

'Delicious supper, Margaret.' Thanet took out his pipe and began to fill it.

Margaret Bolton smiled. 'I should think you were ready for it.' She ran a hand languidly through her hair, raising it a little from her scalp and letting it fall gently back into the soft curls which framed her face. 'Lovely to be able to sit outside so late, like this.'

Joan nodded. 'We could almost imagine we were in France.'

She and Thanet exchanged affectionate smiles, remembering their first joint holiday in France many years ago, on their honeymoon. They had loved the Dordogne, revelled in the delight of lingering outside on many an evening such as this, and had since returned time and again to savour the unique pleasures of rural France.

'Let's hope it lasts,' said her mother. 'More coffee, anyone?'

'Yes, please,' said Thanet.

'Just half a cup for me, Mum.' Joan waited until her mother had poured out the coffee and then said, 'Anyway, how did it go today, Luke?'

'So so. As well as could be expected, I suppose.'

'How are they, the Fairleighs?' said Margaret Bolton.

'Oh, all right. Shocked, of course. But not exactly devastated.' It occurred to Thanet that his mother-in-law might be able to give him an outsider's view of the family. She had lived in Thaxden for years, was a member of the local Conservative Association and no doubt came into contact with them fairly frequently at local events. 'I shouldn't think the old lady was too easy to live with.'

'You can say that again! Her poor sister, the way she bossed her about . . . I don't know how Letty put up with it.'

'Perhaps she didn't have much choice,' said Joan.

'You're right,' said Mrs Bolton. 'She used to keep house for her father and the way I heard it, he was a pretty improvident type. When he died the house had to be sold to pay off his debts and Letty was left with virtually nothing. I don't think she was ever trained to do any kind of job and I expect she was only too glad to accept Isobel's offer of a home.'

'When was that?' said Thanet.

'Oh, ages ago. A couple of years after you were married.'

'Somewhere around 1965, then?'

'I should think so, yes.'

'I imagine the Fairleighs could well afford to have her live with them.'

'Oh, yes. I think they're pretty well off. I don't know how long the family has been living in Thaxden Hall, but for two or three generations, anyway. They had a town house in London, too, but that was destroyed in the Blitz during the war. It was rather tragic, really, Hugo's grandparents were staying in it at the time, and they were both killed. His father was their only son and presumably inherited everything.'

'What was he like?'

'I didn't know him as well as I know his son. He didn't mix in village affairs as much as Hugo. He was also the MP for Sturrenden, if you remember. Hugo followed in his father's footsteps.'

'Yes, I know. Didn't he die unexpectedly, of a heart attack?'

'That's right, two or three years before the Conservatives got back into power in the 1979 election. It was the year before Hugo got married, I do remember that. It was a great shock to the family, he was what was commonly called a fine figure of a man and seemed very fit, walked a lot, played tennis and so on. I believe he was tipped for Ministerial Office, if he'd lived.'

'But Hugo Fairleigh didn't stand for election immediately after his father's death, did he? I seem to recall that we had another MP in between.'

'Yes. Arnold Bates. No, when Hugo's father died Hugo was only just launching into politics. He'd been to Oxford and been called to the Bar and presumably Central Office thought he ought to have some more experience before offering him a safe seat. So they let him cut his teeth on a tough Labour by-election and then, when Arnold Bates also died unexpectedly only a couple of years later, Hugo was selected to fight the Sturrenden by-election. He made a very good showing, got in with a slightly increased majority. That was in 1978. Then the following year there was a General Election and he increased the majority still further. He's been our MP ever since.'

'He's pretty well thought of as an MP, isn't he?'

'I think so, yes. He works hard, and he's very conscientious, listens to what people say and tries to do something about it. I think he's definitely on the way up. And of course, the first time he fought the seat there was a lot of sympathy for him locally. His son died halfway through the by-election campaign and people admired the way he managed to carry on. All the local associations really put their backs into helping him.'

'Ah, yes, I remember now,' said Joan. 'A cot death, wasn't it?'

'Yes. It really was a tragedy. It was the only child they've ever had, and it was a Down's syndrome baby. It was born in the spring of that year, 1978, and died in September. It was a terrible shock for his wife. Despite the fact that it was mentally handicapped she absolutely adored that child and almost had a nervous breakdown when it died. It took her years to recover – in fact, I'm not sure that she ever has, not properly.'

'Was she looking after the baby herself?' said Joan.

'No, there was a nanny. Rita something. There was an inquest of course and she was completely exonerated, but I think Grace always blamed herself, felt that if she had been looking after the baby herself all the time as a proper mother should, it would never have happened. You know how it is in such cases, there's such a lot of irrational guilt around.'

They nodded. Joan as a probation officer and Thanet as

a policeman had both come across cases of sudden infant death syndrome as it was officially called; had had to comfort distraught parents whose immediate reaction, however careful and loving they had been, was to blame themselves for their child's death.

'How did Hugo Fairleigh feel about the baby?' said Thanet. He found it difficult to imagine Fairleigh with a Down's syndrome child. He had a feeling that had the child lived it would have been hidden away in an institution as soon as it was old enough to be separated from its mother. And if Grace Fairleigh had, as Margaret seemed to think, been really attached to the child, there would have been all kinds of problems ahead.

'I don't really know. I'm sure it's been a great disappointment to him, since, that there have been no more children. It always must be, when there's no future generation to inherit a family home like Thaxden Hall.'

'I imagine old Mrs Fairleigh was pleased he won that by-election,' said Thanet.

'Oh, delighted, I'm sure. I think that when her husband died so unexpectedly she just transferred her ambitions for him to her son.'

Now Thanet put the question he had been wanting to ask all along. 'What was she like?' He was fond of his mother-in-law and respected her judgement. He awaited her reply with interest.

Margaret Bolton was silent for a while, considering. 'Well,' she said at last, 'as you've no doubt already worked out for yourself, she was a pretty formidable person, really. Bossy, managing. Liked to get her own way. She was on lots of committees, and usually managed to manoeuvre herself into being chairman and running the show.'

'Doesn't sound as though you liked her much,' said Joan.

'No, I didn't. She always behaved as though the world

should be organised to suit her and was prepared to go to any lengths to make sure it did. And people usually gave in to her because she was so overpowering. Mind, she could be charming when it suited her. She was very manipulative. I've seen her persuade people into doing things they didn't want to do without their ever realising how she'd managed it.'

'She liked power, then,' said Thanet.

'Yes, I've never thought of it quite like that but yes, she did. I remember she once told me her father had wished she was a boy so that she could have gone into politics – he was a politician too, did I say? Though he never got very far.'

'Why didn't she, I wonder? Go into politics, I mean,' said Joan.

Margaret Bolton shrugged. 'Women didn't so much, in those days. Perhaps, as a woman, she was encouraged rather to aim for marrying a promising young politician and becoming the power behind the throne. Well, we all know that happens, don't we? And certainly she was always very much in evidence as the MP's wife.'

'She must have found it hard to take a back seat, after her husband died and before Hugo was elected.'

'Yes, she must. Though she soon adjusted. She simply rechannelled her energies into local organisations and charities. And she's always kept them up, since. She had an amazing amount of energy, you know. It made us weaker mortals feel exhausted just watching her, sometimes.'

Thanet grinned. 'She certainly sounds a doughty old bird. But not the easiest of people to get on with at close quarters. How do you think her daughter-in-law coped?'

Margaret Bolton shrugged. 'I don't really know. I don't know either of them well, only the faces they showed in public. I wouldn't say there was any affection between them, but neither did they show any animosity, either. I imagine

Isobel Fairleigh was a rather difficult person to be fond of, and Grace just made the best of it.'

'Hugo Fairleigh and his wife don't seem particularly close, either.' Thanet knew that he was getting very close to the realms of gossip, of which his mother-in-law fiercely disapproved, and he wondered how she would react to this feeler.

As expected, she gave him a reproving look. 'I wouldn't know. I do think, though, that it must be very difficult for people in their position. They live their lives so much in the public eye that they have to erect a façade behind which they can retain some privacy.'

Thanet held up his hands. 'All right, all right, I stand corrected. Let's change the subject!' He looked from Joan to Margaret. 'I don't suppose either of you saw anything that struck you as odd, this afternoon?'

'We talked about that, over supper,' said Margaret. 'And I'm afraid I was just too busy on my stall to have noticed anything much. But Joan did, didn't you?'

'Well,' said Joan slowly. 'I'm not sure if it's worth mentioning, but there was one little incident I did notice. You wouldn't have seen, you were doing something at a sideshow nearby at the time. I was just standing around waiting for you, near the white elephant stall.'

'Miss Ransome's stall?'

Joan nodded. 'That's right. Well, while I was there a funny little man went around to the back of the stall and whispered something in her ear. She gave him a sharp look, they exchanged a few words, then she glanced at her watch and nodded. He went off and a second or two later she said something to the woman who was helping her on the stall and hurried off towards the house.'

'Any idea what time that would have been?'

Joan shook her head. 'Sorry, no. Some time in the middle of the afternoon. I wasn't exactly keeping an eye on the clock.'

'No, quite.'

'From Joan's description I think I know who the man was, if that's any help,' said Margaret. 'I think it was Ernie Byre, the Fairleighs' gardener and stable hand.'

'That's why I wondered if it was worth mentioning,' said Joan. 'He might well have been on some errand to do with the fête.'

But if so, and as a result Letty Ransome had had to go into the house, why hadn't she mentioned it? Though the fact that she left the stall a few moments after this reported conversation didn't necessarily mean that her departure had anything to do with it. 'You say she went off towards the house?'

'Well, in that direction. But she could have been going to speak to someone about something, pass a message on, whatever . . .'

'Quite. Well, thanks for mentioning it, anyway.'

It was time to go. It was definitely getting cooler now and his mother-in-law, he noticed, was rubbing her bare arms. He stood up. 'You're getting cold, Margaret. Time we were on our way.' He picked up his plate, cup and saucer. 'We'll just give you a hand with these . . .'

'No, leave them. There's hardly any washing up anyway. Joan and I did it earlier.'

As they wound their way home through the quiet country lanes it occurred to Thanet that Joan seemed unusually preoccupied.

'Anything the matter?'

She shook her head half-heartedly.

'Come on, what is it? Not Bridget?'

'Oh no. No, nothing to do with the family.'

'One of your clients?' It was unusual for Joan to bring anxieties about a client home with her, but he knew that even an experienced probation officer occasionally came across a case which was difficult to switch off.

'It's Michele.'

'The battered girlfriend?' Joan had talked about this case before. Michele, who was in her mid-twenties, had first been placed in Joan's care after being picked up joy-riding with her boyfriend. Apart from the fact that she had been driving at the time, she had been well over the limit. As it was a first offence she had been let off relatively lightly, being put on probation and having to attend a drink-driving course once a week for a year. It hadn't taken Joan long to discover that the boyfriend – with whom Michele was living – was regularly beating her up. Thanet remembered their first conversation about her.

'It's a classic case, Luke. She positively invites him to hit her. She provokes him, goads him, until he loses control. And she won't bring charges against him. I think she feels it's only right that he should beat her, that she deserves it.'

'As a punishment, you mean?'

'Exactly.'

'For what?'

'Well, that's what we were talking about today. Apparently, when she was in her early teens, her father walked out on her and her mother. She'd been giving them a lot of trouble at the time – playing truant from school, staying out at night until all hours, the usual sort of thing, and there'd been a lot of rows at home. So when he went she was convinced it was because of her, that she'd driven him out.'

'As you say, a classic case. She's blamed herself ever since, feels a thoroughly bad lot, makes sure everyone else gets the message, and picks a man who'll punish her for being what she is. And is she?'

'A bad lot, you mean? No, I don't think so. In fact, I'm sure she's not. She has a lot of good qualities, only she seems incapable of acknowledging them.'

'Think you're going to get anywhere with her?'

'I can only try.'

Joan had been trying ever since, almost a year, now, and had failed dismally. The girl's image of herself was fixed, and whatever approach Joan tried got her nowhere.

'So, what's happened?'

'You remember I told you her mother died?'

'A couple of weeks ago. Yes.'

'Well, she had a letter from her father yesterday. He wants to see her.'

'Ah. And is she going to?'

Joan was silent for a while, considering. 'She's dithering, of course, but I think she probably will. I don't think she'll be able to resist the temptation.'

'She's never heard from him before, in all this time?'

'No. Of course, it's possible that this could be the breakthrough we need.'

'Unless, of course, she finds she's been right all along. That he did leave because he couldn't take any more from her.'

'Oh come on, Luke. We both know that when two people split up it's very rarely because of the children. It's almost always because the parents' relationship has broken down beyond the point of recall.'

'True. But you have to face the possibility.'

Joan sighed. 'I know.'

They had arrived home. Alexander's Porsche was parked outside and lights were on all over the house.

'They're back, then,' said Thanet. 'And they're still up.' He was tired and had hoped that he and Joan would be able to slope quietly off to bed.

His tone had not escaped her. 'Come on, darling,' she said, getting out the car. 'Better come and be sociable for a little while at least.'

He followed her reluctantly up the path to the front door.

SEVEN

When Thanet left home next morning the rest of the household was still sunk in Sunday-morning slumber. He drove through the deserted streets enjoying his after-breakfast pipe – Lineham hated him smoking in the office and he had long since capitulated except in unusual circumstances. It was another glorious summer morning, the sun hot, the sky a clear, unblemished blue.

As he expected, Lineham was already hard at work. The sergeant was very much an early bird and it was rare for Thanet to be there before him.

'Anything interesting, Mike?'

'Not really. I was just going through this list of people at the fête yesterday.' Lineham waved a batch of closely typed sheets.

Someone had been hard at work last night.

'Nothing rings a bell, though.'

'Didn't think it would. Still, it had to be done and we'll take it with us today, get people to glance through it. Did anyone think to list the helpers?'

'Yes. There's a separate section, at the end.'

'Good.'

'Oh, and a reporter from the *Kent Messenger* rang up.'

The first swallow, thought Thanet. No doubt others

would come flocking along soon enough now. He was glad he'd eventually managed to get hold of Superintendent Draco at the hospital and let him know what was happening, though Draco had obviously been anxious and preoccupied with Angharad's treatment. After a few perfunctory questions he had simply said that he relied on Thanet's discretion and would see him at the morning meeting on Monday, as usual.

There was a knock at the door and Mallard came in.

'You're about bright and early for a Sunday, Doc.'

The little doctor beamed. 'Had an early call, so thought I'd pop in on the way home to breakfast.' He crossed to the window and stood looking out. 'Lovely day, isn't it? Helen and I thought we might go on a picnic.'

Thanet and Lineham groaned.

'Don't rub it in,' said Thanet. 'Anyway, how can you if you're on call?'

Mallard turned around and twinkled at him benevolently over his half-moons. He patted his pocket. 'Beep, beep. The wonders of modern science, Luke. We'll stay within easy reach. Anyway, I thought you might like to know, I had a word with old Mrs Fairleigh's doctor – Dr Beltring, do you know him?'

'Know of him.'

'Yes, well he's a nice chap, good reputation, conscientious. He just confirmed what we already knew, really. He wouldn't have been in the least surprised if Mrs Fairleigh had had another stroke.'

'What did he say when you told him she'd been suffocated?'

'He was shocked, naturally. Couldn't believe it. Said he'd like to see the PM results.'

'He was querying your judgement, you mean?'

'No. Just out of interest.'

'Do we know when the PM is?'

'I managed to fix it for first thing tomorrow morning.'

'Thanks . . . Doc, there really isn't the slightest doubt in your mind, is there?'

At one time Thanet would never have dared ask Mallard such a question. The police surgeon would have gone through the roof. Now, Helen's mellowing influence was such that he just smiled and said, 'I won't take offence, Luke. I know you're just asking me to confirm it again, not implying that I could be wrong.' He held up his hand as Thanet opened his mouth to verify this. 'After all, we can all make mistakes. But in this case, no, I'm certain. The evidence was there, plain as a pikestaff to anyone who knew what to look for.'

Thanet felt bound to justify himself. 'It's just that . . .'

'Really, Luke, say no more. I can just imagine how you-know-who would react if we'd started tossing the word "murder" at people like the Fairleighs without justification. I assume you think that one of them is involved?'

'More than likely, don't you think?'

'But you haven't actually said so to Fairleigh yet?'

'Not yet, no.'

'I'm glad it'll be you not me in the firing line this time.'

'It must have crossed his mind though, surely,' said Lineham.

'True,' said Mallard. 'But crossing his mind is one thing, having it spelled out to him is another. Well, must be off. Let me see, what did Helen say was on the menu this morning? Ah yes, fresh croissants.' He gave a cheery wave as he disappeared through the door. 'Have a nice day' floated back at them.

'All right for some,' said Lineham.

'Come on, Mike. You're a workaholic and you know it. Tell me truthfully, now. Which would you prefer, a day at the beach with the family, or a murder investigation?'

'I don't like traffic jams,' said Lineham with a grin. He nodded at the window. 'And today the roads to the coast will be solid with traffic.'

'Now that we've got that straight, we'd better get on. First thing I want to do is have a chat with Caroline Plowright, get a bit of background on the family.'

'Doesn't miss much, that one,' agreed Lineham.

'Exactly. Think it's too early to ring her?' Thanet glanced at his watch. 'It's nine o'clock.'

'I'd say give it a try.' Lineham was already riffling through his notebook, reaching for the phone.

'I think I'll speak to her myself. Might be more diplomatic. She's not directly involved, after all. What's the number?'

Thanet dialled as Lineham read it off.

She answered on the second ring.

'Detective Inspector Thanet here, Sturrenden CID. We met yesterday at the –'

'Yes, I remember. What can I do for you?'

'I'm sorry to trouble you on a Sunday morning, but I wondered if you could spare us a little of your time.'

'Why?' The monosyllable was uncompromising.

Thanet was equally blunt in reply. 'Because you know the Fairleighs well. I think you might be able to help us.'

'If it's dirt you're looking for, no. Not that there is any anyway, but . . .'

'I'm not looking for dirt, as you put it, Miss Plowright. Just a little straightforward background information.'

She was silent for a moment. 'Very well. But it'll have to be at the shop. I'm just leaving.'

'The shop?'

'Big is Beautiful. In the High Street.'

'Ah yes, I know it. Right. What time?'

'As soon as possible, before I get started on my work. Then I won't have to break off. In fifteen minutes?'

'Fine. Thank you.'

Big is Beautiful was at the Market Square end of the High Street. It had opened a couple of years previously and specialised in clothes for larger women. As Joan was an average size fourteen she and Thanet had never had occasion to go in and he'd had no idea who its owner was.

'Remind me to ask Mr Fairleigh for the name of his solicitor,' he said as he and Lineham left Headquarters.

'We're going out to Thaxden next?'

Thanet nodded. 'I want to talk to them all again, today.' He was enjoying the fresh air and sunshine, and the rare experience of a walk along Sturrenden's picturesque High Street without the crowds which usually thronged it. At this hour it was too early even for the weekend window-shoppers who came to gaze into the antique shops even though they were closed on Sundays.

They paused outside Caroline Plowright's shop.

'Looks as though she's expanding,' said Lineham, nodding at the premises next door. These had been empty for some time and now Thanet noticed that the façade had just been painted to match the green and gold façade of Big is Beautiful. The words 'COFFEE SHOP' had been outlined above the arched windows, some of the letters already filled in by an expert hand. 'OPENING SOON', announced a notice on the door.

'Very clever,' said Thanet. 'Tempt people in with a cup of coffee and hope they'll drift next door to spend.'

'I see you're admiring my new venture,' said Caroline Plowright, unlocking the door to let them in. This morning her generous proportions were masked by a silky straight skirt and shift top with three-quarter length sleeves and flattering cowl neckline. The bold abstract pattern in muted blues, greens and turquoise suited her colouring.

She was a good advertisement for her wares, thought Thanet.

'Come and see. I'm very proud of it.'

'We were just saying what a good idea it is.'

Inside the preparations were virtually complete. A generous archway had been opened up in the wall which divided the two premises and the green and cream colour scheme carried right through. The effect was spacious, elegant and congenial. The coffee shop had a conservatory-like air, with tall plants in big cream ceramic pots, comfortable sturdy wicker chairs designed to accommodate the bulk of prospective customers and glass-topped wicker tables well spaced out to allow the passage of substantial bottoms without embarrassment.

'Very nice indeed,' said Thanet admiringly.

'And good for business, I hope.' Caroline ran her hand lovingly over the smooth cane of a nearby chairback. 'A substantial investment, I can tell you.'

'I can imagine. Still, it'll pay off, I'm sure.'

'I hope so! There are just a few final details to sort out, and we'll be launched. I don't suppose you happen to know any large ladies who are looking for jobs?'

'Large ladies?' said Lineham.

She laughed. 'I still need a couple of new staff and I make it a policy never to employ anyone below a size sixteen. It wouldn't do the egos of my customers much good to be served by young slips of girls with sylph-like figures.'

Sound psychology, thought Thanet. He was right, she was pretty acute, and he was hopeful that this augured well for the coming interview. 'If we think of anyone we'll let you know. Do you always come in on Sundays yourself?'

'Yes, to catch up with the paperwork. I never seem to find time during the week. But that's enough of my business. What about yours? Do sit down. I've made some coffee,' she went on, making for the counter at the back of the coffee shop. 'It's fun playing with the new equipment and I thought we might as well be comfortable. You will have a cup?'

'Please.' Her earlier reservations about the interview seemed to have disappeared, thought Thanet as he and Lineham settled down in two of the new chairs, which were just as comfortable as they looked. Perhaps it was just that she had really enjoyed showing off her new baby. She was obviously very excited about it. It had been lucky for them that they happened to have caught her at the right moment.

Her next words punctured his complacency. 'I'm not dim, you know,' she said as she handed out the coffee. 'I mean, yesterday the Fairleighs were talking as if it were a foregone conclusion that it was a burglar who finished off the old girl. Oh, don't look so po-faced, Sergeant. I couldn't stand the woman and refuse to be hypocritical about it. Anyway, I gather from this visit that the police have a different view of the matter.'

Thanet took a sip of coffee. It was good, hot and strong. 'Delicious coffee.'

'Good.' But she wasn't going to let him get away without replying. She raised her eyebrows at him over the rim of her cup and waited.

Refusing to respond would annoy her and he wanted her cooperation. 'At the moment we have an open mind on the subject.'

'Really. I'm glad to hear it. All the same. I'll be interested to hear what Hugo has to say when he finds out he's a suspect in a murder case, along with his wife and his aunt.'

'He's no fool, Miss Plowright. He must be aware that we have to consider the possibility.'

'Consider it, maybe, but take it seriously . . . I gather you haven't actually broken the joyful news to him yet?'

'Not in so many words.'

'Would I like to be there when you do! He's going to blow his top!'

Thanet grinned. 'You want me to arrange it?'

She gave a rueful smile. 'Well, it would have been fun.'

He decided to risk a snub. 'It doesn't sound as though you're too fond of Mr Fairleigh.'

She shrugged. 'I make no secret of it. We're civil to each other, no more. I've no time to waste playing social games.'

'But you're obviously fond of his wife.'

Caroline lit a long thin brown cigarette and blew out a plume of smoke. 'We go back a long way. To our school-days, in fact. You could say that providing moral support for each other has become a habit.'

Thanet sensed that she was beginning to open up. Her expression had softened, her eyes grown reminiscent. This was the moment to keep quiet and hope that she would begin to talk.

She took another pull on her cigarette and put her head back, this time blowing the smoke out dragon-like through her nostrils. 'I suppose you're thinking, why, especially, did you need it? Moral support, I mean.' She grinned and lowered her head to look him in the eye. 'Everybody does, wouldn't you agree, Inspector? If you're lucky you get it first from your parents, then from your friends and then, if you're very lucky indeed, from your husband or wife. Well, Grace and I were out of luck. We missed out on numbers one and three, so number two was particularly important to us. Still is.'

'Neither of you had parents alive when you were young?'

'Oh they were alive all right, but they didn't do us much good. Quite the reverse, in fact. My mother was so unhappy she spent half her life stuffing herself with food and the other half stuffing me. Added to which neither of us was exactly slim to start with.' Caroline held out her wrist.

'Look at that, Inspector. Big-boned, you see? And did you know it's now been proved that a predisposition to fatness is inherited?' She laughed. 'A fat gene, can you imagine it? I wonder if it's bigger and stronger than its fellows? It must be a bully, because it nearly always wins.' She shrugged. 'When I was fifteen I was fifteen stone, can you imagine? School was hell. Girls can be pretty spiteful. If it hadn't been for Grace . . . She took me in hand, you see. Slimmed me down as far as possible, built up my ego, made me see that there are far worse things than being oversized. It took a long time but eventually I learned that she was right. So long as you're fit and have a modicum of commonsense you can make your way in the world as well as anyone else, whatever your size. And if you can forget the chip on your shoulder other people will forget it too.'

But despite her protestations, Caroline had never quite recovered from those childhood humiliations, thought Thanet. All the more credit to her, then, for having turned her biggest liability into her greatest asset.

'And young Mrs Fairleigh's parents?'

Caroline got up to fetch an ashtray from the counter, tapped off the long thin worm of grey ash which had been in danger of sullying the new carpet. 'Too engrossed in each other, never had time for Grace. She was a late child, her mother was over forty when she was born, and her arrival was rather a shock to them. I don't think they ever wanted children and certainly the only thing they ever wanted from Grace was academic success.' She shrugged. 'Unfortunately, Grace couldn't come up with the goods. Poor kid, she kept on trying and failing, trying and failing until eventually she gave up. And naturally that just made things worse. They couldn't seem to accept that any child of theirs could be anything but brilliant. No, they always made it very clear that they had no time for Grace, that they could get along very well without a child, thank you very much. Grace, of course, was very different and I'm sure that was why . . .' She stopped, as if aware that she was about to stray into matters too private for the ears of policemen.

Thanet could guess what she had been going to say, though. 'Why she was so devastated when her baby died, you mean,' he said gently.

She raised her eyebrows. 'You know about that, then. My, you have been busy, haven't you? But yes, that was what I meant. She absolutely adored that child, despite . . .' She looked at Thanet, read the knowledge in his eyes. 'So you know that it was a Down's syndrome baby, too.'

Thanet nodded.

'Yes, well, most people couldn't understand why she was so attached to it, being mentally handicapped and so on. But I could. Somehow, the very fact that it was handicapped, so much more helpless even than a normal baby, made her feel more protective towards it.' Caroline leaned forward to stub out her cigarette, took another sip of coffee. 'She told me once that one of the reasons why she so longed for a baby was because she'd then have someone of her very own to love, and love her back. You should have seen them together.'

Caroline shook her head and briefly there was a sheen of tears in her eyes. 'She insisted on breast-feeding, and on looking after the child herself. Hugo wasn't too pleased about that, as you can imagine. It was inconvenient, you see, meant that she wasn't always available to accompany him to functions. In the end she gave in and employed a nanny, and of course that was what she never forgave herself for, when the baby died. She was always convinced that if she'd been looking after it herself, that cot death would never have happened. She and Hugo were away that night, you know, at some function in London. And when she heard . . . I saw her next day.' Caroline compressed her lips and shook her head. 'I thought she'd go out of her mind with grief and guilt. I don't think she's ever got over it. If she'd ever had another child, it might have been different, but she never did.'

'You said, "someone of her very own to love". But she had her husband.'

Caroline's lip curled. 'Her husband. Oh, maybe I'm prejudiced, but I can't help it. He was as much use to Grace when she needed him as an empty water bottle in the desert. To be honest . . .' She gave Thanet a considering look.

He knew what she was thinking. *Shall I tell him what I really think?* This was what was so fascinating about interviewing witnesses. If you were lucky and handled it well you could almost see the invisible barriers going down, one by one. And if they did, people would become progressively more and more confiding, tell you things that they had originally had no intention of revealing. Perhaps it was because they were enjoying the relatively unique and seductive experience of having someone listen to them with complete attention and genuine interest. This applied especially to those who lived alone. Did Caroline? he wondered.

But as far as she was concerned, there was more to it than that. Realising that her friend must be a suspect Thanet thought that Caroline's aim in this interview would be twofold: to present Grace in as favourable a light as possible and Hugo as the potential villain of the piece. This was why she had told him so much about Grace's background and why Thanet suspected that she would now not hold back from launching into a character assassination of Hugo.

And yes, she had made up her mind. He could read the decision in her eyes before she spoke.

'To be honest, I think he was relieved when the baby died. I don't think it would have suited his image, especially as the child grew older and its handicap became more evident.'

Now he could risk a question he would never have dared ask earlier. 'Did young Mrs Fairleigh blame him, especially, for their being away the night the baby died?'

'Oh yes, of course she did. With disastrous effect.'

'In what way?'

Caroline rummaged for another cigarette, found one. She took her time in lighting it, then gave a cynical little laugh. 'I always think it's so sad, don't you, when dreams turn to ashes?'

'Dreams?'

'Yes. The irony of it, you see, is that it was always Grace who was keen on Hugo. Even at school . . . Our school and his used to get together for certain events, you see, and of course there was always a lot of excitement about this. Well, you can imagine! We were boy-starved, and Hugo was the one most of us fell for. He was really something in those days – I suppose some people might think he still is. But anyway, Grace thought he was the last word, and worshipped him from afar for ages.'

'He never took any notice of her, then?'

'No. It wasn't until years later that they met again, when he was a practising barrister. It was at a dinner party, at the house of a mutual friend. Grace rang me up the next day. She was so excited, he'd asked her out . . . Anyway, six months later they were married and I'm afraid it was downhill all the way from then on.'

'Why was that?'

She blew out a plume of smoke. 'Basically because there's only one thing that matters to Hugo and that's Hugo. To him, Grace was just a social attribute – she came from a good family, could hold her own in society, was an excellent hostess and as a bonus was highly decorative, as I'm sure you'll agree. She soon found out that there was little more to it than that, and became more and more disillusioned. That was why the baby meant so much to her and why things got so much worse between her and Hugo when the tragedy happened.'

'Did he . . ?' There was no way to put this tactfully. But it wasn't necessary, she understood at once what he meant.

'Did he play around, you mean?' She looked thoughtful. 'I don't think so. Not for years, anyway. He was too busy making his way in the world. But then . . .'

Thanet waited. Here came another of those barriers. Would this one come down too? He guessed that she was trying to decide whether her loyalty to Grace would be compromised by talking about Hugo.

She gave him another considering look. 'I did say, didn't I, that if it was dirt you were looking for, I wasn't prepared to play.'

Thanet nodded. There was no point in putting pressure on her. She would make up her own mind and nothing he could say would influence her. But he was willing to bet that she was going to be unable to resist the temptation.

She was silent for a few moments, smoking thoughtfully and gazing out of the window at the street. There were a few more people about now, he noticed.

'Well . . .' she said, then broke off, frowning.

Someone was tapping at the window. A middle-aged couple was peering in, the woman shielding her eyes in order to get a better view of the interior.

Thanet cursed silently. Just the wrong moment for an interruption. He hoped Caroline would pick up where she had left off.

She rose and went across to the window. The woman outside was pointing at their coffee cups and miming drinking movements. Caroline was shaking her head and pointing to the 'OPENING SOON' notice. Eventually the couple gave disappointed shrugs and turned away.

Caroline came back. 'Perhaps I'd better consider Sunday opening, for the coffee shop. There's nowhere else in Sturrenden you can get a decent cup of coffee on a Sunday. Speaking of which, would either of you like some more?'

Thanet and Lineham shook their heads. She picked up her own cup and went to refill it.

Should he wait for her to take up the thread of the conversation again? Thanet wondered. He decided to risk doing so himself. 'You were saying?'

'What?' She gazed at him blankly for a moment, then remembered. 'Ah yes, the dirt. Shall I, shan't I? Will I, won't I? That's what you want to know, isn't it, Inspector?'

Thanet shrugged. 'It's up to you.'

'What, no strong-arm tactics?' She laughed. 'No, not your style, I can see that. Softly softly catchee monkey, that's more your line. No doubt you've realised that putting pressure on me would merely make me clam up. Now, the question is, do you get a reward for your restraint, or not?'

Thanet said nothing, merely tried to make his expression as non-committal as possible. This, he felt, was the turning point in the interview. If she decided to go on now, they were home and dry. Lineham was aware of this too, he could tell. The sergeant was sitting as still as a statue, almost willing himself into invisibility.

Go on, Thanet urged her silently. *Go on*.

She stubbed out the cigarette and took a leisurely sip of coffee. She was enjoying keeping them in suspense, he could see that.

Eventually she grinned and Thanet glimpsed a spark of malicious satisfaction in her eyes. She was going to enjoy this.

'Well, why not?' she said.

EIGHT

Thanet became aware that he had been holding his breath. He released it slowly, unobtrusively, feeling the ache in his lungs subside.

'After all,' said Caroline, 'what do I owe Hugo? Nothing. Less than nothing, in fact, after the way he's treated Grace. And if I don't tell you, someone else is bound to. I imagine all sorts of skeletons fall out once you lot start poking around in cupboards. Can't say I envy you your job, but I can see that it might have a horrible sort of fascination, for those so inclined.'

Was that how she saw him? wondered Thanet. As someone who enjoyed prising out people's grubby little secrets? He had to admit that there was some truth in the accusation. But it wasn't that he enjoyed the 'dirt', as she called it, for its own sake. A murder investigation was a complex business and he remembered Lineham saying once that it was like trying to complete a really difficult jigsaw without ever having seen the picture. To find another piece was to fill in a little more of the picture and if he found enough pieces and managed to put them together then the crime would be solved, it was as simple as that.

Now Caroline was about to hand him one.

'Of course, this is just speculation,' she said. 'I can't give you chapter and verse. And Grace and I have never actually discussed the matter. She wouldn't. Whatever she feels about Hugo she's never been the type to complain about him behind his back. But my guess is that he met someone about a year ago, and the affair is still going on.'

'What grounds have you for suspecting this?'

Caroline shrugged. 'Nothing specific. Just a lot of little things which add up. A change in his attitude towards her, for a start. When he speaks to her, for instance, he never actually looks at her any more. He very rarely asks her to accompany him to functions now, and that's something he's invariably expected of her. It's always been part of his image, you see, to have his charming wife by his side. And then, he has a flat in London and for years he's usually spent two or three nights a week there, but now he hardly ever comes home during the week and quite often he stays up at the weekend, too.'

'You think he might be contemplating a divorce?'

Caroline frowned. 'That's a tricky one. He certainly wouldn't relish the idea of a scandal, however minor. It could damage his reputation in the constituency, Grace is very well liked down here. And it's difficult to imagine Hugo casting all aside for love, he's much too hard-headed for that. I'd say it depends on the woman. If she's happy to remain his little bit on the side, he'd probably be content to go on like that indefinitely. But I could be doing him an injustice, I suppose. If he really is in love with her I imagine it's just conceivable he'd be prepared to throw caution to the winds.'

'How would his wife feel about that, do you think?'

'I don't think she'd make a fuss, if that's what you mean. Personally, I think it would be the best thing that could happen to her. I can't think of a single benefit she gets from being his wife.'

'A comfortable life-style?'

'She has enough money of her own not to worry about that.'

'What about old Mrs Fairleigh? How would she have reacted to the idea of a divorce, d'you think?'

'Ah. I wondered when we'd be getting around to Isobel.' Caroline pursed her lips thoughtfully. 'To be honest, if he was trading Grace in for a younger model, one who'd be able to provide Hugo with an heir, then I'm sure the old bat would have been all in favour of it. In fact, I gather she's even hinted as much, to Hugo, in the past.'

'You didn't like her, either.'

'She and Hugo were my two unfavourite people.' She grinned. 'I wouldn't like you to think I feel like this about everybody, you know. Letty, for instance, is a poppet. No, on the whole I like people, but those two . . . I suppose I've always resented their making Grace so unhappy.'

'She and her mother-in-law didn't get on?'

'I wouldn't put it quite like that. It was an interesting relationship, really. On the one hand you had Isobel, who was selfish, egocentric and demanding, and on the other Grace, who was compliant, eager to please. I suppose you could say that each supplied something the other needed. So superficially at least they seemed to get on reasonably well. It's just that I could see it was doing Grace more harm than good. She was never going to begin to feel more positive about herself all the while Isobel was constantly making her feel a failure.'

'In what way, a failure?'

'Well, by producing an heir that was flawed, for a start. And then, after the baby died, failing to produce another one at all. Isobel used to watch Grace like a hawk, you know, for signs of her being pregnant again. And when nothing happened she began dropping subtle hints. Then the hints became less subtle and, eventually, reproaches . . .' Caroline shook her head in disgust. 'It used to make me sick. Mad, too. Why couldn't the old bitch see that Grace longed for more children herself, that she had suffered enough over the baby's death and was still suffering over her failure to conceive again, without making it worse by twisting the knife in the wound?'

Thanet was beginning to wonder if there was such a thing as an altruistic killing. Caroline Plowright obviously cared deeply about her friend. What if she had seen the opportunity to bring this tyranny to an end, and had grabbed it?

'This was still going on?'

'Oh no. Grace is forty now. I think even Isobel could see that the hope of another baby was becoming more and more faint with each passing year.'

'You make her sound a very unpleasant person.'

'Oh she was. Believe me, she was. How Letty put up with her I just don't know. Not that she had much choice, poor woman, with no means of her own and no kind of training for a job. The way Isobel used to boss her around . . . She used to behave as if Letty's one aim in life should be to make her own as comfortable as possible. And she never, ever let her forget that she was dependent on her for the roof over her head.'

'What was she like, as a person?' Caroline's view of Isobel would of course be biased, but it always fascinated Thanet to hear how different people saw the same person. He knew that one's view of anyone must be coloured by one's own character, that one automatically sees other people through the filter of one's own prejudices and attitudes. In his work he always had to make allowances for this, but found nevertheless that if he talked to enough people about a murder victim he could gradually attain quite a profound understanding of that person's character. And experience had taught him that in the case of domestic murder such understanding was all-important. After all, barring accidents and ill health, most people live to a ripe old age. But somewhere in the character of those who die an unnatural death lies buried deep the reason for it. His mission was to dig, and keep on digging, until he found it.

'Oh God, I'm not exactly going to give you an unprejudiced opinion, am I?' said Caroline, unconsciously echoing his thoughts. 'All the same, let me see . . . Well, as you'll have gathered, she was entirely self-centred. I think she genuinely saw the world as revolving around her. I'd say she was incapable of seeing anything from anyone else's point of view – even of conceiving that there could be another point of view, apart from her own. She didn't suffer fools gladly – she was very efficient herself, a bit of a perfectionist, and was impatient with people who couldn't attain the standards she set. Quiet, diffident people irritated her, I think that was one of the reasons why she treated Letty so badly. And she was very single-minded. If she set out to do something, she would do it, no matter how much opposition there was.'

'Sounds as though she must have put a lot of people's backs up.'

'Oh she did. But don't let me give you the wrong impression. She could be charming at times, when she wanted her own way. The gloves would only come off as a last resort. And she certainly got results, I'll grant her that.'

'Did she have many friends?'

'Not what I would call friends. There were a few people she played bridge with regularly, but I wouldn't say any of them was close to her. She didn't seem to need other people, not in the way most of us do.' Caroline's forehead wrinkled. 'It was odd, really. I mean, in some respects she didn't care what people thought, so long as she got what she wanted, but at the same time she cared very much about keeping up appearances.'

'In what way?'

'Well, she was very proud. It was important to her, to be a Fairleigh and to live in a house which had come down in the family, like Thaxden Hall. And she was very particular about the way she looked – she was always well groomed, beautifully dressed in expensive clothes, hair immaculate and so on.'

'How did she get on with her son?'

Caroline shrugged. 'As well as she got on with anyone. I wouldn't say that there was any deep affection between them, but there wasn't any open disagreement, either. On the whole Hugo used to go along with what she wanted, he probably found it the easiest thing to do. I think his political career was very important to her – she enjoyed the reflected glory, you see. "My son the MP" and all that.'

Walking back along the High Street, Lineham said, 'Well, that didn't get us very far, did it?'

'Oh I don't know. I thought it was fascinating.'

Lineham's grunt indicated that in his view that didn't stop it being a waste of time. 'Not surprising, by the sound of it, that someone decided to pick up a pillow and finish her off.'

'Maybe not, Mike. But who? And why?' But Thanet was content at the moment not really to give his mind to the subject. He turned up his face to the sun. How he loved the summer! As far as he was concerned this glorious weather could go on for ever. Devotees of the British climate who say that it is good to have variety, that we appreciate the sun more because it doesn't always shine, had got it all wrong, in his opinion. He hadn't heard of those who lived in California complaining.

There were more people about now and a number of cars arriving at All Saints' Church where the bells were pealing out for morning service. The bellringers were improving, thought Thanet, and he counted. Ten bells today, the full complement.

Lineham was being single-minded. 'I wonder if she's right about him having an affair. Because if so . . . No, I suppose not.'

'What?'

'Well, I was thinking. I know an MP earns a decent whack in comparison with us, say, but if you think he's got to keep up that great big house, pay a housekeeper and run a flat in town . . . And if he's got a mistress, he'd no doubt want to wine and dine her, give her presents and so on . . . he could find himself pretty strapped for money. But then I thought, no, I bet he's got a nice fat private income on top of his salary to help out.'

'Not necessarily, I suppose. His father could have left everything to his mother – which could be why she was still living in the house. We really must find out about her will, Mike, go and see the solicitor first thing tomorrow morning.'

By the time they reached Thaxden people were coming out of church. 'The service must start at 10.30 here,' said Thanet.

'Reporters waiting for the Fairleighs, by the look of it.' Lineham nodded at three men and a woman clustered around the lych-gate at the entrance to the churchyard.

Thanet spotted Grace and Hugo Fairleigh talking to another couple as they walked down the path to the lych-gate. Their clothes were sober but not funereal. Hugo was wearing a dark suit and discreet tie, Grace a navy linen suit with a navy and white silk scarf tucked into the neckline. Although the whole village must be buzzing with news of the murder Hugo must have decided that the best way to suppress gossip was to meet it head on, appear in public as if nothing other than the personal tragedy of losing his mother had happened. Thanet was surprised, though, that Grace had accompanied him. Her absence would surely have occasioned no comment – or perhaps it would, in the circumstances. In any case, he wondered what it was that made her continue to behave as a loyal wife, if everything Caroline had said were true.

'There are the Fairleighs,' he said to Lineham.

The sergeant slowed down. 'You want me to stop?'

'No. Use your head, Mike. We don't want to talk to them here. No doubt they'll be coming straight home, once they've got rid of the reporters.'

'Sorry. Wasn't thinking.'

At the entrance to Thaxden Hall a man up a ladder was taking down the big sign advertising the fête, and a lorry half loaded with trestle tables was parked in front of the house. As they awaited an answer to their knock two men carrying tea-urns came around the corner of the house and put them on the lorry. Heading back to the village hall, probably, thought Thanet.

The door opened. This must be the Fairleighs' housekeeper, he guessed.

The girl was in her early twenties, plump, dark and cheerful with cheeks as rosy as a ripe Cox and eyes that sparkled with the buoyancy of youth. She was wearing tight jeans and a T-shirt. Thanet had come across this new breed of housekeeper before. Quick to spot the dearth of high-quality well-trained servants, girls like this went away to expensive colleges to be thoroughly grounded in all the arts of running a house of any shape or size. Then, flourishing their Cordon Bleu certificates, they sailed into the lucrative waters of high-class domestic employment and commanded substantial salaries, along with fringe benefits such as rent-free accommodation, free food and often a car for their own use too. As in this case it seemed a harmonious arrangement, the employers feeling they got value for money. the housekeeper effortlessly blending in with a background often so like her own.

'Miss Young?' he said. He introduced himself and Lineham.

She looked slightly surprised that he knew her name. 'Yes,' she said. She smiled. 'But everyone calls me Sam.'

'We'd like a word with Mr Fairleigh.'

She glanced at her watch. 'He's gone to church, but he should be back any minute now. Will you wait?' Her accent confirmed her middle-class origins.

'Thank you.' They followed her into the drawing room where this morning, with the curtains drawn back, the room was filled with light, the greens and turquoises blending with the backdrop of sky, lawns and trees visible through the tall windows.

'Would you like some coffee while you're waiting?'

Thanet smiled to soften his refusal. 'But if we could just have a word,' he added quickly as she turned to go.

'Sure.' She perched on the arm of a chair. 'Any way I can help. This whole business, it's awful.' She shook her head. 'I still can't believe it's happened. I mean, it seems unreal.'

But she was showing no sign of grief, Thanet noted. Was there anyone who genuinely mourned Isobel Fairleigh's passing? he wondered.

'Look, sit down, won't you?' She waved a hospitable hand.

Thanet gave Lineham an almost imperceptible nod. *You do this one.*

'We understand that you were around most of yesterday,' said the sergeant, choosing the most businesslike armchair he could find, a Victorian piece with scrolled wooden arms and heavily carved legs.

Thanet chose to wander in a leisurely manner around the room.

Sam rolled her eyes. 'Around is the word. It was, to put it mildly, somewhat hectic.'

'You were helping with the fête?'

'Amongst other things, yes.'

'Would you mind running quickly through your day for us?'

She put up her hand, scrunched up a handful of dark curls and tugged at them, as if to activate her memories of the previous day, then launched into a summary of her activities. In between her normal duties she had helped in the morning with setting up the arrangements for the teas and generally lending a hand wherever she was needed. In the afternoon she had run one of the sideshows.

On a table near the window were several photographs in ornate silver frames. Thanet bent to study them, his attention focusing on one of Grace Fairleigh and the baby. It was taken in profile, Grace looking up at the child she was holding in raised arms in front of her, mother and baby smiling at each other with such love and tenderness that Thanet saw at once what Caroline had meant. They seemed to be encircled in an almost visible nimbus of radiant happiness. From this angle the child looked perfectly normal. Thanet wondered that the photograph was still on display, here in the drawing room where Grace Fairleigh would see it every day of her life. He would have thought it would be too painful a reminder of what she had lost.

Lineham was still questioning Sam. 'Did you come into the house at all in the afternoon?'

She shook her head.

'Or see anyone else come in?'

Another shake. 'I was on the lawn at the side of the house. I couldn't see either the front or the back door from there.'

Lineham glanced at Thanet. *Anything else?*

'The post, yesterday, Miss Young . . .'

'Sam, please.'

'All right, Sam. Do you happen to remember how many letters there were?'

She thought for a moment, screwing up her eyes. 'There were some letters, yes, but I couldn't tell you how many. I was in rather a hurry, so I just picked them up, glanced through them to see if there were any for me, and put them on the table in the hall, as usual.'

'Do you remember who they were for?'

'Sorry, no. I never sort them out. There's usually quite a lot of mail, most of it for Hugo – Mr Fairleigh – so he always does that, if he's here. Or Grace, if he's not. I know there were some for him, though, because I saw him go off to the study with them later.'

'We know that Mrs Fairleigh senior received at least one letter yesterday. Did you happen to notice how many letters were left on the table in the hall after Mr Fairleigh had taken his?'

Sam shook her head again. 'No, sorry.'

'And you say you didn't notice who any of them were for, when you were looking to see if there were any for you?'

'No. Why should I? The Fairleighs' mail is their own affair, not mine.' The colour in her cheeks intensified. 'I'm not interested in snooping.'

'I'm sure you're not,' said Thanet, smiling and meaning what he said. 'You have better things to do. All the same, if you do happen to remember, perhaps you could give us a ring.'

The front door opened and closed, and footsteps crossed the hall. Samantha jumped up and ran to open the drawing-room door, relieved no doubt at the excuse to break off the interview. 'Hugo?'

Fairleigh appeared. 'Bloody reporters. They're a pain in the neck.' He must have walked back from church, and his fair skin was flushed, his forehead beaded with sweat. He took out a handkerchief and dabbed at his face. 'Ah, good morning, Inspector. Phew, it's a scorcher today, isn't it? Sam, if we could have some iced lemonade?'

'It's ready in the fridge.' She lifted her eyebrows at Thanet. 'If you've finished with me, Inspector?'

Fairleigh laughed. 'Been giving Sam the third degree have you, Thanet?'

Thanet smiled. Despite the brush with reporters Fairleigh seemed in a good mood today. Thanet wondered how long the MP's affability would last when he realised that the investigation was focusing on the family. 'By all means go and get the lemonade, Sam.'

Fairleigh crossed to the window and raised the sash higher, fanning himself with his handkerchief. He did not take his jacket off, Thanet noted. Strictly schooled in the rules of polite behaviour, no doubt he would consider it incorrect to remove the jacket of a suit in the presence of a third person, even in his own house.

Fairleigh put his handkerchief away. 'So,' he said, turning. 'Have you any news yet?'

Thanet side-stepped the question. 'We'd be grateful if you'd have a look at this, sir, see if any of the names rings a bell. It's a list of everyone who was at the fête yesterday.' It occurred to him belatedly that he should have shown the list to Caroline.

Fairleigh took the typewritten sheets, put on some gold-rimmed half-moon spectacles and half turned to catch the light from the window. He ran his fingers down the pages at considerable speed, rather as one does when looking for a particular name in a telephone directory. Thanet supposed that Fairleigh was practised at skimming quickly through documents, but all the same it seemed to him that there could be more to it than that, that the MP was specifically checking to see if a certain name was on the list. If so, whose could it be?

He watched with interest as Fairleigh reached the end of the list, turned back to the beginning and went through it again more slowly. This time it seemed to Thanet that he paused over a name on the last page. But finally he handed the papers back, shaking his head. Was there relief in his eyes?

'Sorry. I know a lot of these people, of course, many of them are local and my constituents, but no one there has any special significance in connection with my mother. So where do we go from here?'

'There are one or two further questions I'd like to put to you.'

'Go ahead.' Fairleigh sat down on one of the sofas. 'Do sit down, Inspector.'

Sam returned carrying a silver tray bearing three tall glasses and a crystal jug clinking with ice-cubes and filled with a pale, opaque liquid. Fresh lemonade, Thanet was willing to bet. No synthetic bottled stuff for Fairleigh.

She poured a glass for her employer, handed it to him, then looked at Thanet. 'I know you said you didn't want coffee, Inspector, but I thought some fresh lemonade . . .?' She raised her eyebrows, jug poised over a second glass.

Thanet shook his head, catching the flicker of disappointment in Lineham's eyes as he followed suit. He would have loved a glass himself and his mouth watered as he imagined the refreshing tingle of the cool, slightly acid liquid passing over his tongue and down his throat. But he suspected that all too soon now Fairleigh was going to cotton on to the direction Thanet's questions were taking, and an explosion would almost certainly follow. In which case Thanet wanted to avoid anything resembling the atmosphere of a social occasion.

Sam gave a little shrug, refilled the glass which Fairleigh had drunk straight off, and left.

Fairleigh took another long swallow. 'Unwise decision, Inspector. This is delicious. You don't know what you're missing.' He put the glass down, lit one of his low-tar cigarettes and inhaled greedily. 'Well, fire away.' He flicked a quick glance at Lineham, who was opening his notebook and taking out a pen.

'Can you think of anyone your mother knew whose name begins with the letter B?'

Fairleigh looked surprised, then his eyes narrowed. 'Christian name or surname?'

'I'm not sure.'

'Why do you ask?' Fairleigh's tone was cool, his affability rapidly fading.

'Because we've been looking through your mother's diary and . . .'

'You've been *what*?'

'Looking through your mother's diary, sir.' Thanet tried to keep his tone as matter-of-fact as possible.

'For what purpose?' Fairleigh's tone was now positively glacial, his eyes like chips of blue ice.

Here we go, thought Thanet. Out of the corner of his eye he could see Lineham sitting very still. Bracing himself, no doubt.

NINE

The lines of Fairleigh's face had sharpened, as if the flesh had melted away from the bones. His eyes sparked with anger and his mouth was a thin, hard line, his prominent nose more beak-like than ever.

He looked, Thanet thought, like an eagle about to swoop upon its prey. But he himself had weathered far worse storms than the one about to break and now that it had arrived he was glad. It would clear the air.

It was important, though, to get in first, before Fairleigh had launched into a tirade he might later regret.

'Mr Fairleigh,' he said calmly, 'I think it would be sensible, at this point, to face certain facts.'

'What facts?' The words were as staccato as machine-gun bullets. But the long years in politics had taught the MP the value of self-control and he was containing his anger, just, until he knew whether it would be prudent to unleash it.

Thanet was crisp, formal. 'One: that this is a murder investigation. Two: that in such an investigation nothing is sacrosanct. Three: that every avenue must be explored, no matter where it leads. Four: that innocent people are bound to be hurt by what seems to them unnecessary scrutiny. And five: that as there is as yet no evidence whatsoever of an intruder, we would be failing in our duty if we did not investigate the possibility that your mother was killed by someone she knew.' He did not add, *Six: and that someone could be one of your family*. This was self-evident.

Fairleigh stubbed out his cigarette with unnecessary force and stood up, once again betraying his tension by thrusting his hands in his pockets and jingling keys and coins. He crossed to stand looking out of the window.

Thanet and Lineham raised their eyebrows at each other behind his back. Was it possible that Thanet had managed to defuse the situation? He tried to think himself into the MP's position. If Fairleigh were guilty, it wouldn't help to antagonise the police. If the MP were innocent, he would naturally be upset and angry at the prospective invasion of his privacy. Anyone would, after all. But as a public figure Fairleigh had much more to lose. It would be very much in his interest to keep on good terms with the police, try to persuade them to keep the investigation as low-key as possible. So he might, he just might damp down the fires of resentment and present a cooperative face.

He watched the MP's rigid back for the first sign of capitulation and yes, there it was, a slight sagging of the shoulders. Fairleigh sighed and turned.

'Very well, Thanet, I take your point. The important thing is to get this matter cleared up as quickly as possible. Though how you can imagine . . .' He shook his head apparently more in sorrow than in anger, and returned to his seat. 'So. You were saying?'

'That we've been looking through your mother's diary and it seems that on the first day of every month she met someone with the initial B.' Thanet fished the diary out of his pocket. 'Look.'

Fairleigh took the diary and riffled through it, pausing from time to time. 'Yes, I see.' He shook his head again. 'I'm sorry, I can't help you there. I've no idea who it could be.'

'But if you do think of anyone, you'll . . .'

'Yes, of course. I'll let you know at once.'

'And you have no idea where she might have been going, on those dates?'

'I'm a busy man, Inspector. During the week I'm rarely here. Perhaps my wife or my aunt might be able to help you.'

'I'll ask them, of course.'

'Was there anything else?'

'One minor point. I understand that a number of letters were delivered here yesterday.'

Fairleigh looked surprised. 'Yes, that's true. But what . . .?'

'Most of them were for you, I suppose.'

'I do get an enormous amount of mail, as you can imagine. Mostly constituency business. And yes, most of yesterday's letters were for me.'

'And the others?'

Fairleigh shrugged. 'I've no idea. I don't think my aunt receives many letters, so I imagine they were either for my wife or my mother. And as they both have the same surname, I wouldn't notice unless I actually looked at the initial. I just took all the ones addressed to me and left the rest on the hall table.'

'Can you remember how many there were?'

Another shrug. 'Three or four, I think. I really can't remember.'

Thanet rose. 'Thank you, sir. I think that's about it, for the moment.'

'Inspector . . .'

'Yes?'

'That list . . . Could I have another look at it?'

'By all means.' Thanet handed it over.

Fairleigh turned to the last page – the page where, Thanet

remembered, the MP had paused during his second perusal and where all those who had helped at the fête were listed.

Fairleigh put his finger on a name. 'I did just wonder . . . but I didn't mention it, because the man's still in prison.'

Thanet sat down again. 'What?' Was the MP casting around for something, anything, to direct Thanet's attention away from the family?

'I didn't say anything before because I felt . . . But I do realise, now, that one simply can't afford to allow sympathy to get in the way, not when it's a matter as serious as this, and my own mother was . . . She's a widow, you see.'

'Who?'

'Well, this Mrs Tanner, who was helping with the teas . . . You remember you asked me yesterday if there was anyone who might have a grudge against my mother?'

Thanet nodded.

'Wayne Tanner, her son . . . He's her only child and it was my mother's evidence that helped put him behind bars. I know Mrs Tanner is pretty bitter about it still.'

'I'm surprised, in that case, that she was helping here yesterday.'

'Her father's dying of cancer. She's been involved in working for the hospice appeal for some time. I know she helps in the hospice shop in Sturrenden, for example. That's probably why she agreed to lend a hand.'

'What happened with her son?'

Apparently, one night in early autumn last year there had been a serious fire at the village school. Old Mrs Fairleigh, driving home from one of her bridge evenings, had seen two youths climbing over the wall at the side of the school playground. She knew most of the local lads by sight and had recognised them. Wayne Tanner, aged eighteen, was one. As soon as she heard that the school was ablaze she rang the police and told them what she had seen.

It was generally known in the village that Tanner was a trouble-maker. There had been various minor offences – stealing from the village shop, windows broken in an empty house, vandalism in gardens – none of which had been reported to the police because people felt sorry for his mother, whose husband was disabled. But the consensus of opinion was that sooner or later Wayne would find himself in serious trouble and no one was surprised when after the fire he was arrested. The evidence against him was conclusive: his clothes still stank of paraffin, and his fingerprints were all over a door which had survived the fire relatively undamaged. Although it was a first offence it was a serious one. Thaxden Primary School was large, serving several of the surrounding villages, and there had been around sixty thousand pounds' worth of damage. Tanner had been convicted and got twelve months.

Mrs Tanner, by now a widow, had made her bitterness against Mrs Fairleigh plain, causing an unpleasant scene outside the Court. The old lady had endured the encounter with dignity, but Hugo knew that it had upset her. She told him later, however, that she had no regrets about identifying Wayne. In her view, if action had been taken against him earlier over some of his minor misdemeanours, he might have been given a sufficient shock to prevent him from graduating later to more serious crime. Mrs Tanner, in her view, had only herself to blame. She had been too soft with the boy.

It sounded to Thanet unlikely in the extreme that Mrs Tanner should, nine months later, take it into her head to resort to murder in order to take revenge for her son's prison sentence, but one never knew. Stranger things had happened, and if the woman were mentally unstable . . .

He took down Mrs Tanner's address and thanked Fairleigh for the information. 'We'll certainly look into it.'

There was a knock at the door and Sam came in. 'Sorry to interrupt, Hugo, but there's a TV crew at the door. They want an interview with you.'

Fairleigh groaned. 'I suppose I'll have to have a word with them, or they'll never go away.' He stood up. 'If we've finished, then, Thanet?'

'Just one other point, sir. Could I have the name of your mother's solicitor?'

Fairleigh frowned, then shrugged. 'It's Oliver Bassett, of Wylie, Bassett and Protheroe.'

'Thank you.' Good, a local firm. That should help.

At the door the MP hesitated. 'Er, Thanet . . .'

'Yes, sir?'

'I can rely upon your discretion, can't I? I mean, the press are going to be after you too . . . Nothing too sensational, eh?'

'I'm always discreet, sir.' Fairleigh would have to be satisfied with that, thought Thanet. He wasn't going to tie himself down with promises, false or otherwise. Occasionally the help of the media was invaluable, and one never knew when it might be needed. All the same, he was going to do his best to keep out of their way. He hated public exposure, unless it was essential. 'If I could have a word with Miss Ransome now?'

Fairleigh nodded. 'Sam will take you up.'

'No, it's all right. We can find our own way.'

'Through there, then.' Fairleigh pointed to a door at the back of the hall and without waiting went out, closing the front door behind him.

Thanet and Lineham were halfway across the hall when Grace Fairleigh emerged from a door on the right. She hesitated when she saw the two policemen and Thanet stopped. 'Mrs Fairleigh . . .'

Having heard so much about her from Caroline he was

curious to talk to her again, and as an excuse to do so there was one small point that he could raise with her, even if he didn't think there was much point in doing so.

In the past, whenever he had seen her at public functions, he had been struck by her elegance, her poise, her air of dignity and remoteness. She must, he had thought, have always been a naturally reserved person. She and Caroline were a classic example of the attraction of opposites and it was obvious that both had gained much from mutual support and encouragement.

According to Caroline the birth of the baby had transformed Grace and after seeing that photograph in the drawing room Thanet could believe it. The Grace Fairleigh who stood before them now was hardly recognisable as the same woman. How much of that warmth still survived beneath that cool, well-groomed façade? Signs of strain were evident in the bruised flesh beneath her eyes but apart from that there was nothing in her manner or appearance to indicate that anything in the household was amiss.

The carefully plucked eyebrows arched in polite inquiry. 'Yes, Inspector?'

'There was something I wanted to ask you.'

She said nothing, merely tilted her head a little, expectantly.

'When I was talking to you and Miss Ransome yesterday, I had the impression that you were surprised when she said she hadn't been upstairs during the afternoon.'

There was a moment's silence, during which her expression did not change. Then, with a hint of disdain, she said, 'Then you were mistaken, Inspector. And now, if you'll excuse me . . .' She turned away and began to climb the stairs, head held high and back ramrod-straight.

The corners of Thanet's mouth tugged down ruefully. 'Ouch. I suppose I asked for that, didn't I?'

'You didn't really expect her to admit she thought Miss Ransome was lying, did you?'

'How right you are. Mike. No, I didn't. Come on.'

Pushing open the door which Fairleigh had indicated they found themselves in the downstairs corridor of Isobel Fairleigh's flat, near the bottom of the staircase. In the kitchen something sizzled in the oven and one end of the scrubbed wooden table was neatly laid for a solitary lunch, with white tablecloth embroidered with forget-me-nots, knife, fork, spoon and table-napkin in a silver ring.

'Odd lot, aren't they?' said Lineham. 'You'd think they'd have asked her around for dinner next door, in the circumstances.'

'Quite.'

Calling Miss Ransome's name in order not to alarm her by their sudden appearance, they climbed the stairs and tried the sitting room: empty. The bathroom was also empty, its door ajar. Apart from Isobel Fairleigh's bedroom, which was still sealed, the only other upstairs room was along the corridor to the right of the staircase. This must be Letty Ransome's bedroom. They knocked and waited before opening the door to glance inside. It was simply furnished, with narrow brass bedstead, crocheted white bedspread and white curtains sprigged with rosebuds. The few items of furnishing were, Thanet guessed, rejects from the rest of the house: a narrow oak wardrobe with a spotted mirror, a rickety bedside table, a worn Persian rug beside the bed. There was no telephone extension in here, Thanet noticed. The contrast with the other rooms in the flat shouted aloud Letty's position as a dependant. Just how much had she resented that position? Thanet wondered.

On the bed lay a shabby black handbag and a black straw hat which had seen better days.

'Looks as though she went to church too,' said Lineham. 'I wonder where she is.'

'Outside, perhaps?'

They tracked her down dead-heading the roses, trug on the ground beside her. She was wearing a broad-brimmed straw hat fraying at the edges, leather gardening gloves and a heavy-duty canvas apron over her black dress. She straightened up, flustered, as she saw them approaching. Despite the hat she looked hot, cheeks and forehead flushed with the exertion.

'Oh, Inspector . . .' She laid the secateurs in the trug on top of the rose clippings, took off one of the gloves and tucked behind her ear a strand of hair which had fallen across her face. 'I hope you don't think I'm . . . But it was so quiet indoors, without Isobel . . . I had to *do* something, you see.'

She was apologising in case they thought she was being disrespectful to the dead. 'Life has to go on,' Thanet said gravely, aware that in situations like this people find clichés comforting.

She looked relieved. 'Oh, yes. Yes, it does, doesn't it?'

'Could you spare us a few minutes?'

'Of course.' She dropped both gloves into the trug then took a wisp of handkerchief from the pocket of her apron, removed her hat and dabbed delicately at her forehead and upper lip. 'It's so hot today, isn't it?'

'Perhaps we could sit in the shade, over there.' Thanet pointed to a slatted wooden bench under a beech tree.

Letty Ransome nodded agreement, tucked her hat under her arm and removed her apron as they walked, folding it neatly and laying it on her lap when she sat down. Evidently she did not think it proper to be interviewed by the police informally attired.

Thanet sat down beside her and Lineham leaned against the tree.

What was she like, Thanet wondered, beneath that spinsterly façade?

At first it seemed that she had nothing new to tell them. Interestingly enough, she read the list of names in much the same way as Hugo: a swift glance through and then a second, more careful perusal. Had they both been looking for the same name? Thanet wondered.

She dismissed out of hand the idea that Mrs Tanner could have had anything to do with the murder and then, frowning over Isobel's diary, said that to her knowledge Isobel knew no one whose name began with B; the regular entries were a mystery to her. She knew nothing about the previous day's mail, said that it was usually Grace who brought Isobel's letters up and read them to her. 'Such a sweet girl. She used to come up every morning and every evening to read to Isobel. In the morning it would be the newspapers and in the evening *The Forsyte Saga*. Isobel was very fond of *The Forsyte Saga*. I used to come and listen too. Grace reads so beautifully, you know, and she'd just reached the place where Soames and Irene . . . I'm sorry, you won't want to hear all this. But it upset her to see Isobel so helpless – well, it upset us all. Isobel was always so independent.'

'What was she like, as a person, your sister?'

A shadow flitted across Letty Ransome's brow, but she said firmly, 'She was very kind to me. She took me in, you know, gave me a home when Father died. Otherwise I'd have . . . Well, I don't know what would have become of me.' She flushed and said somewhat defiantly, 'Oh, I know people thought she made use of me, but I didn't mind. I felt it was the least I could do, to make life as comfortable as possible for her, in the circumstances. In any case, I think most people misunderstood her.'

'In what way?'

'Well, people thought she was bossy, you know, and overbearing. And it was true, I suppose. But it wasn't her fault she was like that, it was Father's.' She smiled and shook her head indulgently. 'Dear Father, he never really got over his disappointment, you see. He so wanted a son. And when, after me, he was told that Mother couldn't have any more children, he decided that Isobel would have to be the next best thing. I was always too timid, but Isobel, well, she was a bold, headstrong child, and he encouraged her. She was to be strong, determined, even ruthless, if necessary, if she believed herself to be in the right. He disapproved of women in politics – in many ways he was a conventional man – otherwise I'm sure he'd have encouraged her to try for Parliament herself. As it was he told her that she must be ambitious in her choice of a husband, and of course she was. Everyone thought Humphrey was heading for great things.' She sighed. 'We never know what fate has in store for us, do we?'

'I suppose she must have been very pleased when her son became a member of parliament?'

'Oh yes. Delighted. It was what she always wanted for him. And Grace, of course, was the perfect wife. Not like . . .' She stopped dead, as if she had suddenly come up against a brick wall.

Thanet's interest quickened. 'Not like . . .?'

'Oh, just a girl Hugo brought home from Oxford once. But she wasn't suitable.'

So why this reluctance? Because she didn't wish to discuss family matters which she felt did not concern him? No, there was more to it than that, he was sure. He would have to be careful, avoid direct questions, or she would clam up altogether.

'I suppose your sister would have had very strong views about that.'

'Yes, she did.' Letty Ransome's fingers had suddenly become very busy, rolling and unrolling a corner of the gardening apron on her lap.

'It's important for an MP's wife to have the right background.'

'Yes, it is.' She was frowning, scarcely listening to him. Trying to make up her mind about something? Her head was bent and she gave him a quick sideways glance. He could almost see her thinking, *Shall I tell him?*

Tell him what?

He glanced at Lineham who raised his eyebrows and lifted his shoulders.

He decided to use silence. Most people find it uncomfortable, and few can withstand the pressure it puts upon them. Letty Ransome, he guessed, would not be one of them.

Although she kept her eyes down, looking apparently at her fingers which were still busy with the corner of the apron, he knew that she was aware of his steady gaze, and could feel her tension mounting.

'I . . .' she said, and gave him another of those fleeting, sideways glances.

He said nothing.

'Yesterday . . .' she began again. And stopped.

He waited.

She put her hand up to her forehead as if her dilemma were causing her physical pain. Which perhaps it was.

'Oh dear. I don't know what to do, I really don't.' She cast a frantic glance around the garden as if looking for help from an unknown source.

'Why don't you tell me what's worrying you?' he said gently. 'You'll feel much better if you get it off your chest.'

'You think so?' She looked full at him now, as if seeking verification of his sincerity.

'I do.' He was firm, authoritative. He meant it. Whatever

was worrying her would continue to worry her until she had unburdened herself.

Her restless fingers relinquished the apron and she folded her hands together in her lap. She had come to a decision. 'It's about Pamela.'

Thanet's eyebrows lifted. 'Pamela?'

'The girl I was talking about. The one Hugo brought home from Oxford. I . . .' She lifted her chin. 'I saw her here, yesterday.'

'At the fête?'

'Yes. I'm sure it was her.'

'You've seen her often, since the time your nephew brought her home?'

'No! That's the point! Never! That's why I was so surprised to see her. Here, in Thaxden. I'd forgotten all about her, but she really hadn't changed much. She looked older, of course, and she'd put on a little weight. But apart from that . . . I recognised her at once. It was quite a shock.'

'What was she doing?'

'Oh, just wandering around the stalls, like everybody else.'

'By herself?'

'Yes.'

Thanet was remembering that expression he had caught on Hugo Fairleigh's face yesterday afternoon. Fairleigh had looked disconcerted, had been watching someone or something intently, and Thanet had been sufficiently intrigued to try to see who or what it was. Could it have been this Pamela? If so, why had he looked put out? He might have been surprised to see a woman he had been fond of twenty odd years ago, but discomposed? Surely not – unless . . . Several pieces of the jigsaw suddenly clicked together in Thanet's brain. His mind raced. Was it possible that this two and two really did make four?

He betrayed none of his excitement, but Lineham knew him too well. The sergeant had stiffened. Or perhaps he had come to the same interesting conclusion himself.

'What does she look like?'

'Well, she's an inch or two taller than me, and I'm five feet four, with dark curly hair.'

'What was she wearing?'

Letty Ransome frowned. Thanet guessed that she wasn't very interested in clothes and didn't pay much attention to them. But on this occasion she would have been sufficiently intrigued to notice, surely?

Her eyes lit up in triumphant recollection. 'I remember now. A navy dress with little white flowers on it. And long sleeves.'

So in one respect at least he had guessed correctly. This was the woman that Mrs Kerk, Isobel's housekeeper, had seen walking along the passage to the back door from the direction of the stairs, only a little while before Fairleigh and Doc Mallard had come hurrying in. Lineham had made the connection too. The sergeant's eyes were alert with speculation. He looked, Thanet thought with amusement, like a hunting dog which had just caught the scent of the fox.

Now to see if another of those pieces fitted. 'Tell me, Miss Ransome, I couldn't help noticing that when you looked through this list just now, it was almost as if you were looking for a particular name. Was it this Pamela's?'

Letty blushed. 'Oh, you noticed. Yes. But it wasn't there. But then, it wouldn't be, would it – or at least, I wouldn't recognise it, if she's married, that is. And I should think she would be, she's such a pretty girl.'

Hardly the word to describe a woman of forty-odd, thought Thanet. But then Letty Ransome was in her late sixties, so perhaps it was understandable. 'What was her maiden name?'

'Grice.' Letty's forehead wrinkled. 'That was one of the things Isobel didn't like about her. She said it was such a common name, and just showed what sort of background the girl came from.'

'Your nephew was serious about her?'

'Oh yes. They actually got engaged. Pamela came here several times, to stay, and Isobel was charming to her. Gave dinner parties for her, took her about and introduced her to friends . . . I was surprised she took so much trouble over her, considering how much she disapproved of the match.'

Interesting, thought Thanet. He found it surprising too, from what he'd learned of Isobel. He'd have to think about that later.

'So what went wrong?'

'Pamela called it off. Hugo was heartbroken, he really was so fond of her. But she wouldn't change her mind.'

'Did she give any reason?'

A delicate shrug. 'Only that she didn't think they were suited. Isobel was very relieved. And of course, it all worked out for the best in the end, when Grace came along.'

Though perhaps not so well in the long run, thought Thanet, watching the shadow flit across Letty's face as she no doubt thought precisely the same thing. 'Did your nephew know she was here yesterday?'

Letty shook her head. 'I don't know. I've hardly seen him since, and in any case it's not really the sort of thing I'd be likely to mention.'

'You didn't see him speak to her at all?'

Another shake of the head. 'No. Er, Inspector . . .'

'Yes?'

'I don't know whether it's worth mentioning . . .'

'What, Miss Ransome?'

'It's just that, well . . .' She shook her head. 'No, I don't want to waste your time.'

'I'm sure you wouldn't be. What is it?'

'Well, it was a little odd . . .'

This time Thanet just waited.

She looked at him timidly. 'It's just that while Isobel was ill, there were a couple of phone calls.'

'What sort of phone calls?'

'Someone wanting to speak to her.'

'A man, or a woman?'

'I'm not sure. The voice wasn't very clear, a bit sort of muffled.'

'When was this?'

'Well, the first one was during the week after she had her stroke.'

'That would be the week before last?'

'Yes. And the second was a few days ago.'

Both calls had been very brief, apparently. On the first occasion the caller had asked to speak to Isobel, had been told that she was ill and had rung off. The second call had come on the morning when for the first time the fingers on Isobel's paralysed hand had moved a little, and Letty, still excited by this, had told the caller that her sister was much better, though still in bed. Once again, the connection had been cut. On neither occasion had the caller given his/her name. Letty was positive that this person had never rung before, and had had no idea who it could be.

'Of course, Isobel was involved in so many things . . . People were always ringing up and half the time I had no idea who they were or what they wanted. That's why I hesitated to mention it.'

Thanet reassured her that she had done the right thing. Every scrap of information helped, he said, no matter how trivial it seemed. Now, there was just one other question he wanted to ask. 'Miss Ransome, I understand that yesterday, just before you came into the house, a man who works here – I believe his name is Ernie – came to speak to you, at your stall.'

He watched with interest as this time the blush crept up her neck in an ugly red tide which left her cheeks and face glowing. Why the embarrassment? Surely there couldn't be any question of romance between them. Letty Ransome was hardly the type for a liaison with the gardener.

The fingers were at work again, this time plucking at the fraying straw around the brim of her hat. 'Yes, that's right. But I don't see . . .'

'What did he want to speak to you about?'

She shook her head in confusion. 'I can't remember. Something trivial, I'm sure.' Her forehead creased in an apparent effort to remember.

But she did remember, Thanet was sure of it. She was not a good liar.

'I'm sorry. I expect it was something to do with the fête. He was busy with various odd jobs all day.'

Whatever it was, it was sufficiently important for her to stick to her guns. And of course, it might have nothing whatsoever to do with the murder. Thanet decided to leave it at that for the moment. 'Does Ernie live on the premises?'

'Yes. He has a little flat over the stables.'

And although she was relieved that he hadn't pressed the matter she hadn't liked the implications of that question, he noted. He thanked her for her help and they left her sitting on the bench in the shade.

'V-e-r-y interesting,' said Lineham, when they were out of earshot.

'I agree. Very. We'll discuss it later. Meanwhile I want you to nip along to the stables, tackle Ernie himself before she gets to him, try and find out what all that was about.

I'm going to see what Mr Fairleigh has to say about this Pamela business. Join me as soon as you can.'

Thanet headed purposefully back towards the house.

TEN

As he neared the house Thanet's pace slowed. It had just dawned on him that he had been so engrossed in what Letty Ransome was telling him that he had forgotten to query her account of her visit to the house around the time of the murder. Was she perhaps much cleverer than he had given her credit for, deliberately manoeuvring him away from looking too closely at her own movements by telling him about Pamela Grice – if that was still her surname – and about the strange phone calls? He didn't think so, but his judgement was far from infallible. Should he go back?

He hovered near the back door, undecided. It had also occurred to him that perhaps he was being too precipitate, rushing off to tackle Hugo like this. It might be better to discuss the implications of the Pamela/Hugo business with Lineham first. After all, he could hardly come straight out with the questions he really wanted to ask: *Is Pamela née Grice your mistress, and did she murder your mother?*

Besides, it might be better not to let Fairleigh know that they knew about Pamela – if there was anything to know, that is. Her presence here yesterday could have been purely coincidental. Perhaps she happened to be in the area and had simply been satisfying a natural curiosity to see again the house of which she could have been mistress and the man she might have married.

No, he couldn't believe that, in view of the fact that she had been seen near the scene of the murder around the time when it had been committed. And he was still convinced that Fairleigh had been lying in his account of that trip indoors at 3.30.

So, to go back and talk to Letty again, or to alert Fairleigh, or neither? Thanet hesitated. Standing still he became aware of the murmur of voices somewhere over to his left. Straining his ears, he listened. Yes, that was Fairleigh, surely. And then Sam's voice, higher-pitched. They must be out in the garden.

The sounds tugged at him like a magnet. He made up his mind. No, he really couldn't leave without trying to find out if Fairleigh was involved with this woman. But he would have to tread warily, it was a sensitive subject.

Thanet cut diagonally across the courtyard towards the voices.

Fairleigh, his wife and Sam were having pre-lunch drinks in the Victorian conservatory which had been built on to the far side of the house. The glazed doors were hooked back to their fullest extent and at this time of day, when the sun had not yet come around, it was a pleasant place to sit, with cool tiled floor, comfortable white wicker chairs and a wealth of exotic plants in huge terracotta pots. Along the back was a narrow brick-edged border planted with climbers trained against the house wall and along the roof struts, trailing down in brilliant swathes of blue, white and magenta, their scent filling the warm, moist air.

It was a picture of gracious living and Thanet knew what Lineham would have said. *It's all right for some!*

Fairleigh was lounging on one of the broad window seats, smiling at Sam, glass in hand. No one would have believed from his appearance or demeanour that his mother had been murdered yesterday, thought Thanet. And then reproached himself for being unfair. A spurious gaiety often sprang up in such circumstances. It was a way of escaping from grim reality. Who knew what Fairleigh was really thinking or feeling?

Grace was gazing down at her glass with an air of abstraction. She glanced up, startled, as Thanet appeared.

Fairleigh stood up, smile fading.

'Oh really . . . Is there no peace? Not more questions, surely, Inspector.'

'If I could just have a word with you, sir . . .'

'Oh, very well.' Fairleigh drained off his glass and thumped it down irritably on the white wicker table nearby. 'Lunch in ten minutes, you said, Sam?'

'Yes. But . . .'

'Ten minutes,' said Fairleigh emphatically. 'We'll go to my study, Thanet.'

He headed for the door without waiting to see if Thanet was following.

In the study he crossed to look out of the window. 'More bloody reporters arriving, by the look of it. If this goes on we'll be in a state of siege. Can't you do something about it?'

'I'll see what I can do. The trouble is, all the while you're clearing up after the fête the open gates are an invitation for them to come in.'

'That's the last lorry-load out there. As soon as it's gone I'll get Ernie to close them.'

Fairleigh sat down behind his desk as if to ensure that Thanet knew who was in charge around here.

It was a pleasant, masculine room, with book-lined walls, comfortable well-worn leather armchairs and an antique desk as big as a small billiard table, its surface covered with piles of neatly stacked files and papers.

'Well?' said Fairleigh impatiently, lighting a cigarette. 'What is it this time?'

Suddenly, Thanet was fed up with being treated as an inferior being.

When Draco first arrived to take over Divisional Headquarters he was always pontificating about the importance of maintaining good relations with the public. An ambitious man before Angharad's illness, he still went through the motions of insisting that important people in the area should be treated with kid gloves.

Well, in deference to his superior, Thanet had taken care to be polite to this man, and much good had it done him. He had no intention of allowing himself to be manoeuvred into losing his temper, because that would be unprofessional, but he didn't see why he should be hamstrung by an irrational need to be conciliatory, just because Fairleigh was a member of parliament. The man was a suspect, and that was that.

'Your aunt tells me that she saw an old friend of yours at the fête yesterday.'

'Oh?' said Fairleigh, warily.

'A Pamela Grice.' He was watching the MP carefully and yes, although the man's self-control was excellent, there was a fraction of a second in which he froze. 'Did you see her?'

'Yes, I did, as a matter of fact.'

'You spoke to her?'

Fairleigh hesitated.

Thanet could understand his dilemma. If the MP had spoken to Pamela, he must realise that someone could have seen them talking, and he wouldn't want to risk being caught out in a lie.

'Yes. Briefly. I was very busy, as you know.'

'You haven't lost touch, then.'

A lorry engine roared into life outside and Fairleigh half rose to peer over his shoulder out of the window. 'Good, it's going.' He sank back into his chair again.

Thanet wasn't letting him off the hook. He waited, his expression making it clear that he expected an answer.

Fairleigh frowned. 'I really can't see what relevance this has to your inquiries, Thanet. But if you must know, last summer I met her for the first time in many years when I went to present the prizes at the Speech Day of the school in London where she teaches.'

'Do you know why she came yesterday?'

Fairleigh's patience was wearing thin. 'How on earth should I know? Why did anybody come? Why did you?'

'The odd thing is, her name doesn't appear on this list.' Thanet lifted the sheaf of papers he was still carrying.

'Perhaps she left before the list was made.'

'Perhaps.' The thought had occurred to Thanet. The question was, why? Because she knew what had happened, had even had a hand in it, and wanted to get away quickly before the storm broke? 'Or perhaps because she married. Grice was her maiden name, I understand.'

Fairleigh said nothing.

'Did she marry, do you know?'

'Her married name is Raven, I believe.' Fairleigh had attempted a casual tone, but it was obvious that he had been reluctant to give the information.

Thanet experienced a little spurt of elation. Now they had a starting point. He glanced quickly through the list of names. It wasn't there. Should he risk asking for her address? No, it would be best to leave Fairleigh in a state of uncertainty as to whether the police were going to follow this up. It shouldn't be difficult to trace her.

Suddenly Fairleigh leaped out of his chair. 'Oh, my God, look at that!'

A cameraman was trying to take a photograph of the MP through the window.

Fairleigh swept the curtains together, plunging the room into semi-darkness. 'That's it, I've had enough!' He stamped across the room to the door. 'Get rid of them, Thanet,' he snapped. 'I'll get Ernie to close the gates. And for God's sake *do* something about this harassment.'

In the hall Thanet ran into Lineham. 'I was just coming to look for you, sir.'

'Come on,' said Thanet grimly. He could understand Fairleigh's anger and sympathised with it, but he resented being ordered about without so much as token politeness.

He opened the front door and was at once showered with questions, a microphone thrust in his face. A brief statement was unavoidable and he gave it, then told the reporters that Fairleigh would not be coming out to speak to them again and that they were to leave the premises. With much grumbling they began piling into their cars and vans. Thanet and Lineham hurried to their car and followed the convoy down the drive. Ahead, Thanet saw two more cars pulling up. He'd have to arrange for a patrol car to keep an eye on the place, make sure the family wasn't plagued by the press, or he'd have Draco on his back.

Looking over his shoulder Thanet saw a small, elderly man hurrying along behind them.

'Ernie,' said Lineham, with a glance in the mirror.

Outside, the latest arrivals tumbled out of their cars and converged on the police car, waving notebooks.

Thanet wound down his window and shook his head at them. 'Sorry, you've missed the boat. I've already made a statement and there'll be no more at the moment.' But there'd be no peace until they were satisfied. On the spur of the moment he made up his mind. 'Press conference tomorrow morning at nine a.m.'

He wound up the window and Lineham, steering his way determinedly through the crowd, accelerated away.

Thanet put in his request for the patrol car and then settled back into his seat. They drove in silence for a while and then he said, 'So, how did you get on with Ernie?'

Lineham shrugged. 'Got nowhere, I'm afraid.' He assumed a rustic accent. 'Oi were running about here and there all day like a cat with a scalded tail, with messages for this one and that one. Do this, Ernie, do that, Ernie. Proper madhouse it were. How do you expect me to remember whether Oi went to talk to Miss Ransome at her stall?'

Thanet laughed. 'Very good, Mike. You've got hidden talents, I see.'

Lineham gave a sheepish grin. 'He's a bit of a character, sir. Like something out of the nineteenth century.'

'So why d'you think Miss Ransome was so embarrassed when I asked her about him?'

'Search me.' Lineham grinned. 'Perhaps he's her secret lover.'

'Ha ha. Very funny.'

'What about this Mrs Tanner? Think there's anything in it?'

'We can't dismiss it out of hand, of course, but I doubt it.'

'Unless she's a nut-case. Dear little Wayne the pyromaniac is her only ewe lamb, isn't he?'

There were overtones of bitterness in Lineham's voice. He himself had suffered much in the past from being the only child of a possessive mother.

'Quite. We'd better check that he's still inside. You never know, with remission for good behaviour he could be out again by now.'

'We'll go and see Mrs Tanner?'

'No, we'll send Bentley, I think. He's good with older women.'

'And we aren't?'

'I have other plans for us.'

'Ah. Pamela Grice?'

'Pamela Raven now.' Thanet gave a brief account of his interview with Fairleigh.

Lineham listened eagerly. 'So d'you think she's the one he's having the affair with?'

'If he's having an affair at all. We've only got Caroline Plowright's word for it.'

'She seemed pretty certain.'

'But it was sheer speculation, remember. All the same . . .'

'It's pretty fishy, though, isn't it? That she was seen coming from the direction of the staircase to the old lady's bedroom around the time of the murder.'

'We are jumping to a lot of conclusions, remember, Mike.'

'You're suggesting that there were two women in their early forties, of medium height, plumpish, with dark curly hair and wearing long-sleeved navy dresses covered with little white flowers?'

Thanet laughed. 'I'm just saying we don't actually know that it was the same woman, Mike. I agree, it sounds likely.'

'Pretty well a dead cert, I'd say. Especially as Mr Fairleigh apparently wasn't too keen to admit he knew her and talked to her yesterday. For my money, they are having an affair and the old lady found out and didn't like it.'

'No reason to murder her, though, Mike. Unless . . .'

The same thought occurred to them both simultaneously.

'Yes!' said Lineham. They were back at Headquarters and he pulled up with a flourish. 'She threatened to cut him out of her will!'

'If so, the solicitor might know something about it. I

don't know though, Mike. It's a bit far-fetched, isn't it? After all, according to Miss Ransome, Mrs Fairleigh senior made the girl very welcome when Fairleigh brought her home, and it was Pamela who called it off.'

'I thought that was most peculiar, didn't you? That she should have gone out of her way to make Pamela feel at home when she was so much against the engagement?'

'I agree.' Thanet was remembering what his mother-in-law had said about Isobel Fairleigh. *She was very manipulative. I've seen her persuade people into doing things they didn't want to do without their ever realising how she'd managed it.* Was this what had happened with Pamela? If so, he couldn't quite see how.

'All the same, say we're right. Say it is Pamela he's having an affair with. Say she's the love of his life and when he met her last year it all started up again. His marriage has been a great disappointment to him and he decides he'll get a divorce and marry Pamela, and this time nothing will stop him. Say he tells his mother . . .'

'Before his wife?'

'We don't know he hasn't told her, do we?'

'True.'

'So say he tells his mother and she's dead against it. She never did like Pamela, she's not his class, and she's getting on a bit to produce any children. Say Mrs Fairleigh threatens to cut him out of her will, like we said . . . You have to admit it would give him a very good motive.'

'You're right. We have to consider it a serious possibility.'

'Did you tell him Pamela had been seen in the house around the time of the murder?'

'No. I thought we'd keep that one up our sleeve. I'd like to tackle her about it first.'

'Which is why we're going to see her?'

'One of the reasons, yes. If we can find her. Come on, Mike.' Thanet opened the door and got out of the car. 'You'd better get to work, see if you can track her down. I'd like to see her today, if possible.'

'Where does she live?'

'London, I imagine. That's where she works, anyway. She's a teacher.'

'If they are in it together Mr Fairleigh is sure to have rung her to warn her we've been asking questions about her.'

'I know. That's why I want to follow through straight away.'

'Put the wind up them, you mean.'

'Yes.'

'If I find her, do I make an appointment, or is it to be a surprise visit?'

'An appointment. If we're right, she'll have been warned that a visit is on the cards, and we don't want to drive all the way to London only to find she's out. It is a Sunday, after all. She could be anywhere.'

They were back in the office now. The room was hot and stuffy and Thanet made straight for the window, flung it open.

Lineham headed for the row of telephone directories. 'You never know, we might be lucky and she'll be in the phone book.'

'Right, I'll leave you to it, then. I'll go and find Bentley, send him off to interview Mrs Tanner. I'll also get someone to check if Tanner's still inside. And I think I'll get Carson to go and see Jill Cochrane. She opened the fête yesterday and Fairleigh was with her most of the afternoon. She may have seen him talking to Pamela, might even have heard something of what they said.'

They were in luck. By the time Thanet had returned and had checked through the reports on his desk, Lineham had found their quarry. He put down the phone, beaming. 'Four o'clock, sir.'

'So I heard. Well done.' Thanet glanced at his watch. Two-thirty. 'Better make a courtesy call to the Met., let them know we're coming up, then we'll be on our way.'

ELEVEN

At this time of the afternoon traffic on the London-bound carriageway of the M20 was light and they made good time. Later, of course, it would be nose-to-tail with day-trippers returning from the coast.

Pamela Raven lived in a pleasant tree-lined cul-de-sac of Victorian terraced houses. Thanet knew from Bridget's tentative inquiries that such houses have now become fashionable and command high prices. In many cases even the smallest have been divided into flats too expensive for youngsters like her to buy. For the moment she had had to settle for sharing a rented flat with three other girls and he thought that the prospect of her ever being able to afford to buy a place of her own in London remote in the extreme. He and Joan had often teased her, saying that her only hope was to marry a rich man with a house of his own. Now he hoped that that man would not be Alexander.

As Lineham backed the car into a tight parking space Thanet said, 'Did she ask why we wanted to see her?'

'Yes. I was deliberately vague, just said it was about an incident at the fête yesterday.'

'Good. Of course, you do realise we've been taking it for granted that she lives alone?'

'It was P. E. Raven in the phone book,' said Lineham,

edging the front nearside wing in past the rear offside wing of the car in front with only a hairsbreadth to spare.

'Her husband's name could begin with a P too.'

'Well, we'll soon find out, won't we, sir?' The sergeant, who prided himself on his driving skill, gave a triumphant smile as with no further manoeuvring the car slipped neatly into the space, coming to rest an inch or two away from the kerb and precisely parallel with it.

Thanet, who invariably found himself toing and froing to achieve such perfect alignment, said enviously, 'Why can't I ever do that?'

Pamela Raven greeted them with a nervous smile and led them through a narrow hall into a sitting room which ran the full depth of the house. Thanet guessed that two small rooms had been knocked into one. French doors at the far end led out into a small courtyard garden furnished with white wrought-iron chairs and table. They accepted her offer of tea and Thanet looked around while they waited.

The room had that comfortable lived-in air that makes visitors feel instantly at home. There was a green fitted carpet and curtains and chair-covers in cream linen with a stylised floral design. The floor to ceiling recesses on either side of the tiled Victorian grate were filled with books and there was a small unit stacked with tapes and records next to the hi-fi system. A bundle of knitting lay on one of the chairs and the desk in front of the window was covered with what looked like end-of-term exam papers. Pamela Raven had evidently been spending her Sunday afternoon hard at work.

Thanet stooped to look more closely at a couple of photographs on the mantelpiece: one of a teenaged girl sitting alone on a wall overlooking the beach – Pamela's daughter, Thanet guessed by the resemblance, and another of a younger version of the same girl with Pamela and a man. Mr Raven, Thanet presumed. If so, was he still around?

'Here we are.' She came back into the room carrying a tray of tea and biscuits. Balancing it on one hand she pushed some of the papers aside and set it down on the desk.

'Your husband and daughter, Mrs Raven?' said Thanet, nodding at the photograph.

'Ex-husband. We were divorced five years ago. And yes, that's Gwen, my daughter.'

Thanet watched as she poured the tea. She was informally dressed in a bright pink T-shirt and navy cotton trousers splashed with pink flowers, and certainly matched the description given to them by both Mrs Kerk, the old lady's housekeeper, and by Letty Ransome: early forties, medium height and build, dark curly hair.

They had already arranged that Lineham should conduct the interview and Thanet settled back to watch and listen. The sergeant began by saying that they understood Mrs Raven had attended the fête at Thaxden Hall the previous day.

She smiled. 'Yes, that's right.'

'May I ask why?'

She waved her hand at the window and the suburban street outside. 'Surely it's obvious. It's lovely to get out of London at weekends. I was born and brought up in the country and I miss it.'

Thanet had already guessed as much from her accent, a slow, country burr. This, presumably, was what Mrs Kerk had meant when she had said that the woman she had seen in the corridor was 'not a lady'. He personally found it most attractive. In fact, she was a very attractive woman. Her face was lively, expressive, and what she lacked in conventional beauty she made up for in warmth of personality. Thanet thought she would find it difficult to lie. Certainly his first impression was that he and Lineham had got it all wrong. He really could not see this woman plotting to murder a helpless old lady.

But appearances can be deceptive, as he had sometimes learned to his cost. It would depend, perhaps, on how much influence Hugo Fairleigh had over her – always assuming, of course, that it was indeed Pamela Raven with whom he was having an affair. If he were, Thanet could understand why: Grace Fairleigh would appear cold and unappealing by comparison.

'But what made you decide to attend this particular event?'

She shrugged. 'Someone I know happened to mention it.'

'Mr Fairleigh?'

She met his gaze squarely, almost defiantly. 'Yes.'

Interesting. So she and Fairleigh had decided that there was no point in attempting to conceal that there was a relationship of a kind between them.

'It was such a lovely day, and I knew I'd have to spend all day today marking exam papers. I thought it would be fun to go to a real village fête again, that's all.'

'And there must have been a certain natural curiosity, too, I imagine,' said Lineham.

She frowned. 'Curiosity?'

'I understand you stayed at Thaxden Hall a number of times in the past.'

'That was *years* ago.'

'Still, no doubt you wondered if it had changed at all.'

She grinned. 'You're right, of course. The temptation proved irresistible.'

'I mean, if things had turned out differently, it could have been your own home. We understand you were engaged to Mr Fairleigh, once.'

Her smile faded. 'Yes, that's true.'

'May we ask what went wrong?'

Thanet flinched inwardly. *Too soon, Mike. Too soon.* Everything had been going so well – too well, perhaps.

Encouraged by the way Mrs Raven was responding Lineham had gone too far too fast. Perhaps he should have conducted this interview himself. But then Mike was perfectly capable, and how was he ever to gain experience in the more delicate interviews like this one if Thanet never gave him the chance to improve his skills?

Pamela Raven flushed with anger. 'No you may not! I really don't see that it's any of your business.' And she glanced at Thanet as if to say, *Tell him he's gone too far*.

Thanet felt bound to defend Lineham. 'I know that some of our questions must seem impertinent, Mrs Raven, but I assure you we wouldn't ask them if it weren't necessary.'

She was still angry. 'I can't see how something that happened twenty years ago can possibly be relevant to what happened yesterday. And incidentally, you still haven't told me what that was, or how I can possibly be concerned with it in any way.'

This was tricky. As yet they were only guessing that there was anything more than a casual relationship between Pamela and Fairleigh. If there were no close link between them Thanet really did not think that Hugo would have been in touch with her since yesterday and Pamela would be genuinely bewildered by this visit, especially as the story was only just breaking in the media. He wondered if the item had yet been on TV. News broadcasts were less regular on Sundays and if Pamela had been working hard all day she might not yet have heard.

On the other hand, if she and Fairleigh were lovers, he would probably have rung last night to tell her what had happened and she would know that Mrs Fairleigh had been murdered. And he would no doubt have rung again today, to let her know that the police knew she had been seen at the fête.

So, was her apparent ignorance feigned or genuine?

The time had come to tell her about the murder and see how she reacted.

He glanced at the papers on the table. 'You've been working all day?'

She frowned. 'Yes. Why?'

'And you obviously haven't watched television, or listened to the radio?'

'No. Look, what is this all about?'

'Then you won't have heard that Mrs Fairleigh senior was found dead in bed yesterday afternoon. Or that it has become evident that she was murdered.'

She drew in a sharp breath and her eyes opened wide in apparent shock. 'Murdered!'

Had he detected a false note there? He couldn't be sure. 'I'm afraid so.'

'Naturally, I'm appalled! But I still don't understand what it has to do with me. And I certainly can't see why you are asking a lot of questions about matters that are ancient history.'

Was this the moment to tell her she'd been seen in the house at the time of the murder? No, not yet, he decided. He shrugged. 'Where murder is involved we simply gather together as much information as possible and hope that in the end it will become evident what is relevant and what is not.'

'Sounds a bit hit and miss.'

'Perhaps. But it usually works, in the end.'

'Still, I don't have to answer, if I don't want to, do I?'

'No. That is your right.'

She stood up. 'Then I shall exercise it.'

Lineham cast an anxious glance at Thanet. He obviously felt that he had mishandled things badly. But he was evidently also determined to try and salvage what he could. 'Mrs Raven, I apologise. I didn't mean to offend you.'

'There are one or two questions we really have to ask you,' said Thanet gently. 'If not today, then another day . . .'

She hesitated and walked across to the desk, stood for a few moments with her back to them.

Lineham watched her with a worried frown.

Eventually she sighed and returned to her chair.

Thanet could see her thinking, *Better to get it over with, I suppose.*

'Very well, then. If you must.'

'Presumably, from what you say, you've kept in touch with Mr Fairleigh.' Lineham was being careful now, feeling his way.

'Not exactly. We hadn't seen each other for years, until last summer. He came to present the prizes at the school where I teach. Since then we've met occasionally for lunch, usually during the school holidays.'

It was obvious that this was the story she and Fairleigh had decided to stick to, equally obvious that there was no point in pursuing the matter at the moment. Thanet waited anxiously to see if Lineham realised this.

He had. 'I see. And on one of these occasions he happened to mention the fête.'

'That's right, yes.'

'When was this?'

She frowned. 'It must have been at half-term.'

'In June, then?'

'Yes.'

'And you've met since then?'

'Look, Sergeant, what, exactly, is the point of these questions?'

This, Thanet felt, was the moment for Lineham to bring up the fact that she had been seen inside the house. He caught the sergeant's eye. *Now.*

'Mrs Raven, at the fête yesterday you went into the house. Would you mind telling us why?'

If she was disconcerted she didn't show it. She must have been prepared for the possibility that the woman who had seen her might have mentioned the fact to the police. She smiled. 'To answer a call of nature, why else?'

'Toilets had been set up for the public in the car-park field.'

'My feet were hurting, Sergeant. Unwisely I had chosen to wear high heels. It was a long way back to the car park and there were women going in and out of the back door all the time. I thought I would be able to slip into the house unnoticed.'

True or false? At the moment Pamela Raven was wearing trainers, and at school it would be quite in order for her to wear flat shoes. There was no rule, unspoken or otherwise, that said schoolteachers had to look elegant – quite the reverse, judging by the clothes Thanet had seen some of them wearing. And everyone knew that women did suffer from wearing high heels if they weren't used to them.

At the beginning of the interview he had thought she would make a bad liar. Now, he wasn't so sure. Or perhaps she was just being economical with the truth.

'You were seen coming from the direction of the stairs, and there's a toilet just inside the back door,' said Lineham.

She shrugged. 'I thought I could remember the geography of the house. I was mistaken.'

'Did you go upstairs?'

'That would have been impertinent, don't you think?'

'Did you?' Now that he had put all the questions they had arranged to ask Lineham was prepared to press a little harder and risk her anger.

'Look, I don't know what you're getting at, Sergeant, but whatever it is you're way off beam. I wanted to go to the loo and thought I knew where to find one. I was wrong. And that's it, all right?'

It was obvious that she wasn't going to budge and that they weren't going to get anything more out of her at the moment.

They were in the hall on the way out when there was the sound of a key in the lock of the front door. Pamela swung it open. 'Oh, Gwen. You're early.'

She sounded put out. No doubt she had hoped they would be gone before her daughter got home, Thanet thought.

The resemblance between them was still striking. Gwen was around eighteen, Thanet guessed, her dark hair in a fashionably tousled curly mop. She was wearing jeans and a T-shirt with 'I LOVE THE WORLD' emblazoned across her chest. A scarlet mini-rucksack was slung over one shoulder. She glanced questioningly from her mother to the two policemen.

'Goodbye, Inspector,' said Pamela firmly, standing aside.

There was very little space in the hall and Gwen stepped back, outside, to let them pass. Thanet wondered how Pamela was going to explain away their visit. Had she told her daughter that she had been to the fête yesterday? If Pamela was having an affair with Hugo, Gwen must surely know about it. How did the girl feel about Fairleigh? he wondered.

As they walked to the car Lineham said, 'Clever-clogs, isn't she?'

'Well, we knew that, didn't we? Oxford graduate, no less.' Thanet grinned. 'Why d'you think I asked you to take the interview?'

'I really messed it up, though, didn't I?' said Lineham angrily. He slammed the door behind him as he got into the car. This was unusual. Lineham's long-running love affair with cars precluded ill-treatment of any kind. 'You should have done the interview yourself.'

'Nonsense, Mike. As usual, you're overreacting. She was looking for an excuse to get rid of us.'

'Then I shouldn't have given her one, should I?' He stared moodily through the windscreen. 'I know what I did wrong. I rushed it, didn't I? I let the fact that she seemed to have relaxed make me push too hard, too quickly.'

'Yes. So now you've worked out what went wrong, forget about it and write it off to experience.'

'I wonder how many times you've said that before! I know what comes next: "That's how we all learn. By making mistakes."'

'But it's true. We do. What's more, we go on making them, as you well know.'

Lineham was not consoled. He always found it hard to come to terms with avoidable failures. It was, Thanet knew, only because the sergeant cared so much about his work. In any case, he soon bounced back. 'Mike . . . Are we going to sit here all day?'

Lineham manoeuvred the car out of the confined space as efficiently as he had manoeuvred it in and Thanet opened the *A–Z*. 'Let's see if I can find the way back.'

'It's OK, sir. I think I can remember it.'

'I don't know how. One suburban street looks just like another suburban street to me.' But Thanet closed the book and put it back on the shelf. It would do Lineham's bruised ego good to demonstrate his superiority in this respect at least.

It wasn't until they were on the motorway that the sergeant spoke again.

'She didn't actually tell a single lie, did you notice? There was nothing that we could come back to her about and say, that wasn't true.'

'I know.'

'She and Fairleigh are a pair.'

'I liked her, myself. After all, if she's in a tight corner it's understandable that she should protect her interests.'

'You're not saying you couldn't blame them for killing off the old lady!'

'Of course not! But that's far from proven yet.'

'I know, I know. Now you're going to tell me I've got to keep an open mind!'

Thanet laughed. 'No need, is there, when you're obviously aware of it yourself. Come on, it'll do us good to forget about the case for a while. How are the children?'

But this wasn't the happiest choice of topics, it seemed.

Lineham grimaced. 'We're a bit worried about Richard, as a matter of fact.'

'Why? What's the matter with him?'

'I wish I knew. I mean, he's a bright lad, wouldn't you agree?'

'Yes, he is.'

'Then why is he always in trouble at school?'

'What sort of trouble?'

'His form teacher can't seem to make up her mind if he's deliberately perverse or just plain lazy. And disorganised! He can't seem to keep track of any of his belongings for more than two minutes together. He's always in trouble for losing things, or forgetting them . . . Louise says the only way she can think of for him to keep his things together would be to tie them to him!'

'You don't think people are expecting too much of him, because he is bright?'

'I don't know.' They were travelling behind a container lorry. 'Look at that! He's doing over seventy!'

'Not our problem, Mike. We can't turn everyone in the country into law-abiding citizens single-handed.'

Lineham pulled out to overtake, glowering up at the lorry driver as they passed the cab.

'So what are you going to do about it?'

'The school has arranged for him to see a child psychologist, tomorrow afternoon.'

'Bit drastic, isn't it?'

'It was their idea. They say if there is a problem we ought to nip it in the bud.'

'Well, he's always seemed a perfectly normal, healthy child to me.'

'You don't have to live with him! We dithered and dithered before agreeing, but in the end we decided it couldn't do him any harm and it might do some good. We can't go on like this indefinitely, it's driving us mad. Did you ever have any problems like this with Ben?'

'We've had problems, of course,' said Thanet, thinking especially of that terrible time when one of Ben's friends had died of glue-sniffing and they had discovered that Ben had also been experimenting with 'solvent inhalation'. 'But nothing quite like what you're describing.'

They drove for a while in silence and then Thanet said, 'You're right. It'll be a good idea for him to see this chap tomorrow.'

'Woman.'

'All right, woman. If nothing else it'll clear the air, relieve your minds, to feel you're doing something about it.'

'I hope you're right.'

It was late when Thanet got home. Alexander's Porsche had gone, he was relieved to see. Much as he loved Bridget he really didn't feel like socialising tonight. He was tired and his back, which had always been a problem ever since he had injured it some years ago, was aching. He longed to stretch out flat and relax.

He wasn't surprised to find that Joan had already gone to bed. He was thirsty and he took an ice-cold can of lager from the fridge and drank half of it straight off before sitting down at the kitchen table to eat the cold meat and salad she had left for him. Afterwards he went upstairs as quietly as he could, hoping not to disturb her.

As he eased himself into bed she stirred, half woke and then settled into sleep again. He stretched out flat on his back, luxuriating in the relief as tired muscles relaxed into the expensive orthopaedic mattress in which they had decided to invest when it became apparent that this back problem wasn't going to go away.

The windows were open to the summer night and the curtains stirred softly in the breeze. Thanet began to breathe deeply and evenly in the hope that he would quickly drop off to sleep. But he knew that, tired as he was, this was unlikely. Always, at the beginning of a case, there was so much to absorb, so much to assess, that his overactive brain took a long time to unwind.

Thanet believed that, random victims of violence apart, murder victims carried in themselves or in their lives the seeds of their own tragic destiny. Something in their circumstances, past or present, or something in their character had finally led to that moment of ultimate violence, and it was his job to find out what it was.

Isobel Fairleigh's character had, according to her sister, been largely shaped by her father's thwarted desire for a son. What had Letty said? *She was a bold, headstrong child, and he encouraged her to be strong, determined, even ruthless, if necessary.*

Well, she had certainly been well taught, by all accounts. According to Joan's mother – surely as impartial a witness as one could hope to find – Isobel had been bossy, managing, manipulative. Caroline had called her selfish, egocentric, demanding, proud. Her sister Letty was the only person who seemed to make excuses for the old woman's unattractive personality, and Thanet wasn't sure if Letty wasn't just that little bit too good to be true. Surely no one treated as she had been could have been as apparently free of resentment as she was? What had Caroline Plowright said? *How Letty put up with her I just don't know. The way Isobel used to boss her around . . . She used to behave as if Letty's one aim in life should be to make her own as comfortable as possible. And she never, ever let her forget she was dependent on her for the roof over her head.* An image of Letty's sparsely furnished bedroom with its cast-off furniture and spotted mirror flashed through Thanet's mind.

It had already occurred to Thanet that Isobel had probably left Letty something in her will, and that Letty might be aware of this. How much of a temptation would it be, to know that independence was within her grasp for the first time in her life? That, and freedom from a tyranny acknowledged by everyone but herself.

And she had definitely been lying about not having gone upstairs when she went into the house around the time of the murder. On that final visit to the old lady Grace had seen Letty, Thanet was sure of it.

Thanet couldn't imagine Letty planning and plotting her sister's death, but with Isobel helpless, who knows how strong the temptation might have become? She could have tried to justify giving in to it by convincing herself that she would be doing Isobel a favour, releasing her from the dependence and indignities she must have hated. It was even possible that she had told Thanet about Pamela in the hope that suspicion would be diverted away from herself. Perhaps he had underestimated her, and her apparent reluctance to confess that she had seen Pamela at the fête yesterday had been carefully calculated to make him eager to know what it was she was apparently withholding.

Still, it had certainly been a valuable piece of information, explaining much that had come before and opening up an important avenue of inquiry. In Thanet's view Hugo was a much more likely suspect.

Fragments of conversation floated through Thanet's mind. Caroline: *My guess is that he met someone about a year ago, and the affair is still going on.* Letty: *Pamela called it off. Hugo was heartbroken.* Hugo: *If you must know, last summer I met her for the first time in many years . . .* Pamela: *I really don't see that it's any of your business.*

Thanet sighed. Ah, but it is, Pamela, he thought as he grew drowsy. It is very much our business.

For if they were having an affair – which seemed more than likely – and if Hugo had told his mother, and if she had objected, and if she had threatened to cut him out of her will . . . If, if, if! Stop it, he told himself sleepily. What is the point in speculating?

But he had to know, and soon.

First thing in the morning, he promised himself. Oliver Bassett, Isobel Fairleigh's solicitor . . .

TWELVE

As soon as Thanet walked into the office next morning he could tell that Lineham was on to something. The sergeant was seated at his desk surrounded by neat piles of paper and his face as he looked up was triumphant.

'Just listen to this!'

There was an answering twist of excitement in Thanet's stomach. 'What?'

Lineham picked up one of the bundles of paper. Bank statements, by the look of it. 'On the first day of every month a large cheque was paid out of old Mrs Fairleigh's account.'

'How large?'

'A thousand quid a month, for the last six months. Before that, for the previous six months, it was nine hundred. For the six months before that eight hundred . . .'

'I get the picture.'

'Don't you see, sir?' Lineham was brimming over with excitement. 'B day. Bank day. The first day of the month . . .'

'No need to spell it out, Mike. I'm not an idiot.' And then, as Lineham looked crestfallen, 'Well done, Mike. Brilliant, in fact. It was a cheque, you say, not a standing order or direct debit?'

'That's right.'

'When it opens, get on to the bank, make an appointment to go and see them.'

'What d'you think the money was for?' Lineham was reluctant to let the matter go.

'Waste of time to speculate at the moment. Let's wait and see what you find out.'

'Then there's this.' Lineham handed Thanet a sheet of paper in a plastic envelope. 'Anonymous, but sounds as though it'd be worth following up.'

The letter was written in block capitals on cheap, lined notepaper.

ASK ABOUT THE ROW WHEN MRS FAIRLEIGH HAD HER STROKE.

'Envelope?' said Thanet.

Lineham handed over another plastic envelope. 'More block capitals. Addressed to you. Postmarked Sturrenden. Who do you think wrote it, sir?'

'Assuming the old lady was at home when she had the stroke, take your pick, Mike. Hugo Fairleigh, Grace Fairleigh, Letty Ransome, Sam, Mrs Kerk . . .'

'I'd plump for Mrs Kerk, wouldn't you?'

'I agree. Anyway, we'll take the letter with us when we go out to the house later, see what reactions we get.' Thanet was pleased. Two leads already this morning. 'Anything else?'

'Confirmation that Tanner is still inside. And reports from Bentley and Carson, on the interviews with Mrs Tanner and Jill Cochrane.'

'What do they say?'

'Well, Bentley says Mrs Tanner is a bit weird. And definitely very anti the old lady. Called her, what was it?' Lineham flipped through the report. 'Yes, here it it. An "evil old cow, who went around poking her nose into everyone else's business". Says she swears she never went upstairs, was busy in and out all afternoon, "run off her legs" was how she put it, carrying trays of crockery.'

'So she was actually working in the house, not out in the tent.'

'Apparently, yes.'

'And no one would have noticed if she happened to take a few minutes longer on one of those occasions.'

'So do we take it any further?'

'Not at the moment. But we obviously can't rule her out. If we run into a lot of dead ends elsewhere, we'll follow it up, go and see her ourselves. What did Jill Cochrane have to say?'

'Nothing helpful, I'm afraid. She and Fairleigh weren't together all the time. He kept stopping to talk to people and she was duty bound to go around all the stalls, people expect it of the person who opens the fête.'

'Quite. Pity. So she doesn't actually remember seeing him speak to someone of Pamela Raven's description?'

'No.'

Thanet glanced at his watch. Time for the morning meeting. 'Must go or I'll be late. Ring Wylie, Bassett and Protheroe, make an appointment for this morning, if possible, with Oliver Bassett. And ring the bank.'

Morning meetings these days were subdued affairs, a far cry from when they were first instituted. Then, Superintendent Draco had been like a terrier, snapping at the heels of his staff and making sure that no detail was overlooked. Thanet, Boon and Tody had long since given up regular inquiries after Angharad Draco's progress; it merely depressed Draco even further, and her illness had reached a stage when they were afraid of what they might hear. Today Draco looked exhausted, his face drawn, with dark, bruised circles beneath lack-lustre eyes. Even his wiry black hair looked limp and tired, like its owner.

Thanet's report was of necessity the longest. Draco listened carefully, asked a few pertinent questions and then said, 'You'll handle this matter with tact, I'm sure, Thanet. If you run into any problems you know where to find me.'

Gone were the maxims and admonitions which had so irritated Thanet in the past. Now he felt that he would suffer them gladly if only Draco would return to being his former ebullient self. After a brief press conference he returned to his office still feeling depressed on the Superintendent's behalf.

'Mr Bassett will see us at 10.30,' said Lineham, as Thanet walked in.

'Good.'

'And I've arranged an appointment with the bank manager at 11.15.'

'Excellent.'

'Didn't Doc Mallard say he'd managed to fix the PM for first thing this morning?'

'Yes. He should let us have a verbal report later on.'

While they waited Thanet and Lineham went through Mrs Fairleigh's papers again, searching for something to indicate what the large regular payment could be for, but there was no clue. By the time they left for their appointment with Bassett, Lineham was becoming increasingly frustrated. 'There must be something,' he said as they walked along the High Street. 'I can't believe a woman can lay out a thousand pounds a month and there'd not be some reference to it in her papers.'

'Patience, Mike, patience. Perhaps the bank will reveal all.'

Lineham merely grunted.

On this sunny Monday morning Sturrenden was looking

its best, preening itself in the sunshine for the benefit of an artist who had set up his easel in a spot which afforded him the best, much painted view of the church. As Thanet and Lineham passed he was covering the bare canvas with a base colour, applying the paint with sweeping enthusiastic strokes. No doubt he couldn't wait to get started on the painting proper.

'All right for some,' said Lineham as they separated to walk around the easel. 'I bet he's glad he doesn't have to spend his time combing through a load of dusty old papers . . . That's a thought, sir. Perhaps we missed some. Papers sometimes slip down at the back of drawers.'

'You can look when we go out, later.'

They had arrived. This was not their first visit to the offices of Wylie, Bassett and Protheroe. On the previous occasion, some seven years ago, Oliver Bassett had himself been a suspect in a murder case, when a woman had been strangled on the first night of a visit to Sturrenden after an absence of twenty years. Thanet had of course seen Bassett out and about in the town during the intervening period and he thought once again, as Bassett rose to greet them, how little the man seemed to change. The solicitor was now in his mid-forties, tall and well-built, with a jutting nose rather like that of his dead client. The height of his forehead was emphasised by the fact that his hair was beginning to recede and the small, prim mouth was turned up in a welcoming smile which vanished as soon as the greetings were over.

'A terrible business,' he said, when they were all seated. 'What sort of person could murder a helpless old woman in her bed?'

'That's what we intend to find out.'

'I imagine you want me to tell you about her will.'

'Mrs Fairleigh was a wealthy woman. Someone stands to gain by her death, no doubt.'

'That does not necessarily mean that they are implicated.'

'Not necessarily, no. But it is obviously a possibility that we have to consider.'

Bassett pursed his lips. 'I find myself in a difficult position. This firm has always acted for the Fairleigh family and I therefore represent both the victim and those whom you no doubt regard as suspects. I have to ask myself where my loyalties lie, with the dead or the living.'

'Oh come, Mr Bassett. You're a man of the law. You couldn't possibly condone murder, under any circumstances. And in any case the contents of the will must become public sooner or later.'

'True.' Bassett sighed. 'I guessed you would be coming to see me, of course, and I suppose my duty is plain.'

But he still sounded very uncertain about it. Why? Unless . . . Thanet's scalp prickled with excitement. Suddenly he was sure that there was more to Bassett's reluctance than met the eye. The solicitor knew something, but he felt he shouldn't divulge it.

'Would you like some coffee?'

Delaying tactics now, thought Thanet. But he was willing to play along and he accepted.

Bassett's secretary must have been primed. The coffee arrived almost at once and Bassett dismissed her with a word of thanks and began to fuss with coffee, sugar and cream in a spinsterish manner. Watching him, Thanet wondered whether the secret of Bassett's homosexuality, revealed to the police during the course of the earlier case, had yet leaked out into the community. He rather thought not. If Bassett ever indulged his tastes, he was very discreet indeed. Even now, in a small country town like Sturrenden, skirts would be drawn aside and in Bassett's profession a spotless reputation was of paramount importance.

Once the little ceremony was over the silence stretched out. Thanet was content to wait and so, for a while, it seemed, was Bassett. Finally, the solicitor put down his cup and sat back, steepling his hands beneath his chin as if to emphasise that the decision he had made had been reached only after due and judicious consideration. 'The terms of the will are straightforward. The bulk of Mrs Fairleigh's estate goes, as might be expected, to her son Hugo.'

'How much does that amount to?' Thanet already had some idea, from the broker's statement, but Bassett didn't know that and would be expecting him to ask.

'Something in excess of half a million pounds. Death duties, of course, will be substantial, but fortunately I managed to convince Mrs Fairleigh that it would be a good idea to make the house over to her son some ten years ago, so the house itself will be exempt.' Bassett looked smug, as well he might.

'You said, "the bulk of the estate". Where does the rest go?'

'There's an annuity of ten thousand a year for her sister, Miss Ransome. I'm sure that Mr Fairleigh will be happy for his aunt to continue to live in the flat she shared with his mother, but I suppose the old lady thought it would be nice for her sister to know that she wouldn't have to face a poverty-stricken old age.'

That was uncharacteristically careless of Bassett, thought Thanet, more certain than ever that the solicitor's attention was focused on some personal dilemma. 'So Miss Ransome was aware of this bequest.'

Bassett looked disconcerted, suddenly aware that he had given away more than he intended to. 'Certainly. Why not?'

'I agree. Why not, indeed. And Mr Fairleigh?'

'Of course,' said Bassett stiffly.

'Were there any other major bequests?'

'No. There's a small sum for Ernest Byre, her gardener, and one or two items of jewellery for her daughter-in-law, nothing of exceptional value. That's all.' He leaned forward. 'Look here, Thanet, it's out of the question, what you're thinking.' But his tone lacked conviction.

How could he get Bassett to open up? Thanet wondered. This man was no fool, to be manipulated into divulging something he wanted to keep secret. Try a direct approach, then?

'Mr Bassett. There's something you're not telling me, isn't there?'

'I don't know what you mean, Thanet.' The solicitor reached for his cup, drank, replaced it carefully in the saucer and put them down on the desk again, each movement as automatic as that of a Victorian mechanical doll. His eyes met Thanet's squarely, almost defiantly.

Thanet guessed that Bassett was being careful in case later on he found himself in the unsavoury position of having to defend one of his clients for murder. His behaviour indicated that he suspected that this could happen. So, what had given rise to those suspicions? It must be something to do with the will. Thanet remembered the anonymous note. Say there had been a row, and the old lady had threatened to change her will. And say she had made an appointment with Bassett, told him why she wanted to see him? If the solicitor refused to talk, as well he might, in the interests of his clients, Thanet could at least infer the truth by seeing which questions he refused to answer.

'I understand that Mrs Fairleigh had her stroke as a result of a row with a member of her family.'

Bingo. Thanet caught the flash of dismay in Bassett's eyes before the solicitor raised his eyebrows and said blandly, 'Did she?'

'Did you know about this row, Mr Bassett?'

'No.' But Bassett was prevaricating, Thanet could tell.

'Did you guess that there had been one, then?'

'Really, Thanet, what is the point of entering the realms of speculation on such a matter?' Bassett was at his most pompous. And avoiding the issue, of course.

'Mrs Fairleigh was going to change her will, wasn't she?'

'You're guessing again, Thanet.'

But coming far too close for comfort. Bassett's prim lips were clamped together as if he were afraid the truth would escape him unawares.

It was time to press a little harder. 'Did Mrs Fairleigh contact you, to tell you she wanted to change her will?'

The telephone rang. Bassett almost snatched it up in his relief at the interruption.

Thanet cursed inwardly and out of the corner of his eye he saw Lineham's biro stab viciously at his notebook as the sergeant gave unobtrusive vent to his feelings.

'It's for you, Thanet.' Bassett handed over the phone.

'Thanet here.'

'Sir? Carson. Sorry to interrupt your interview, but I didn't know where you were going next, and I wanted to catch you . . .'

'Yes, yes . . .' Thanet tried to prevent his irritation showing.

'There's a young girl here, sir. A Miss Raven. Says she wants to see you about the Fairleigh case. She's come down from London especially, she says.'

Gwen Raven, here. Why? Thanet's disappointment of a moment ago vanished. 'Tell her I'll be along shortly. Give her a cup of tea and make her comfortable.'

'Right, sir.' Carson's relief was evident. Thanet's change of tone had not escaped him.

Thanet put the phone down and said, 'Did she, Mr Bassett?'

'Did who what?' Bassett had recovered his composure. He'd had time to work out his answer now.

'Did Mrs Fairleigh contact you to tell you that she wanted to change her will?'

Bassett stood up. 'I can't imagine what gave you that idea, Thanet.' His tone was mocking. 'And now, I'm afraid I have another appointment.'

And so have I, thought Thanet as they took their leave. It was a pity that he hadn't been able to prise any more out of Bassett but he was eager now to hear what had brought Gwen Raven down to Sturrenden to see him.

THIRTEEN

'She was going to, wasn't she?' said Lineham, as soon as they were outside. 'Change her will.'

'Looks like it.'

'Slippery customer, Mr Bassett.'

'He certainly wasn't giving much away.'

'We're beginning to get the picture now, aren't we? That anonymous letter was right on target.'

'Ah, but there's a snag, Mike. The letter implies that she had the stroke during or after the row. And if so, and if it was because of the row that she was going to change her will, how did Bassett know she was going to? She hasn't been able to speak since.'

'Unless she rang him just before she was taken ill. That's it, sir! She's having this row. She's absolutely fuming, so she goes to the phone, rings Bassett up and tells him she wants to change her will. And she has the stroke *while she's speaking to him*. Later, Bassett discovers what had happened and draws his own conclusions. Only he daren't tell us in case it compromises his client.'

'Sounds feasible. But which client, I wonder?'

'Mr Fairleigh, for my money. I can't see Miss Ransome having a blazing row with her sister, can you? I bet,' said Lineham eagerly, warming to his theme, 'Mr Fairleigh told his mother he was going to get a divorce and marry the woman she was so against him marrying in the first place.'

'According to Miss Ransome, remember. We've only got her word for it that old Mrs Fairleigh was against the match. And, as I said before, even if she had been it looks as though she was prepared to go along with it. She took a lot of trouble to introduce the girl into her own circle, and it was Pamela who called it off, not Hugo.'

'Yes, but as I keep saying, there's another reason why she'd be dead against it now, isn't there? Remember Miss Plowright telling us she thought old Mrs Fairleigh would be all in favour of her son marrying again provided it was someone likely to produce an heir? Pamela Raven is in her forties. Not much chance of an heir there, as I've said before.'

'Women do have babies in their forties, Mike.'

'Yes. And as we've been told often enough, the chances of producing a handicapped child are vastly increased. The old woman wouldn't want to risk that happening again, would she?'

They had arrived at the bank and they stopped. 'I'll see you back at the office, Mike.'

Lineham's eyebrows rose. 'You're not coming in?'

Thanet grinned. 'Other fish to fry. That phone call was Carson, telling me that Gwen Raven is in Headquarters, asking for me. Came down especially, from London.'

'Really?' Lineham's face was alive with speculation. 'I wonder why? Perhaps . . .'

'Enough perhapses, Mike. We'll soon find out.'

Gwen Raven was waiting for him in one of the interview rooms, having been given what amounted to five-star treatment: a couple of women's magazines, some chocolate fingers and tea – in a bone-china cup decorated with tiny roses, Thanet was amused to see. Where on earth had Carson managed to find that? he wondered.

'Miss Raven. I'm sorry to have kept you waiting.'

She shook her head. 'It doesn't matter.'

Once again she was wearing jeans and T-shirt, the ubiquitous uniform of the young. But today she looked apprehensive, and tired, too, with dark shadows beneath her eyes and a dispirited droop to her shoulders.

'How can I help you?'

She ran a hand through her hair. 'I'm not sure I ought to be here, really.'

'But you are here,' said Thanet gently. 'So on balance you must have decided it was the right thing to do.'

'I suppose so.' But she still sounded doubtful.

He had to get her to trust him before she would open up.

He sat back in his chair. 'I have a daughter of my own, of about your age.'

She welcomed the change of subject eagerly. 'Is she at University too?'

'No.' Thanet grinned. 'She's always been mad on cookery. So she took a Cordon Bleu course and now she cooks for a directors' dining room, in the City.'

'So she doesn't live at home?'

'No. She shares a flat with three other girls.'

'That's what I want to do, when I come down.'

Gwen, he learned, was reading French and German at Durham University. She had hoped to get into either Oxford or Cambridge, but hadn't made it.

As they talked she began to relax, as he had hoped she would. They chatted for a while about her future plans and then he said, 'You don't have to tell me anything you don't want to tell me, you know. And if, at any time, you change your mind and want to call it a day, I promise I won't put any pressure on you. I can't be fairer than that, can I?'

'I suppose not.' But the strained look was back in her eyes again. Then suddenly she said angrily, 'I expect you think I'm stupid, coming down here like this and then holding back.'

'I certainly don't think you're stupid. And I imagine you have good reasons for hesitating.' He waited a moment and then said gently, 'Perhaps you feel you're being disloyal to your mother?'

Her mouth twisted. 'Yes. You're right, of course. How did you guess? Oh, now I *am* being stupid. In your job, you must . . .' She ran a hand through her hair again. 'I'm not thinking straight this morning, I hardly slept all night, trying to make up my mind whether to come.'

'And here you are.'

'Yes. Here I am. So yes, you're right again. I suppose, as you said just now, I wouldn't be here if I hadn't made up my mind. So . . .' She took a deep breath. 'As I expect you've already guessed, it's about my mother and Hugo Fairleigh.'

Thanet nodded and said nothing, hoping that he looked as receptive and sympathetic as he felt. The last thing he wanted to do was make her feel she was being cross-examined. That would simply make her clam up again. In any case he was confident that now she had taken the first step she would go on.

'After you'd gone last night Mum told me what had happened – to Mr Fairleigh's mother. I couldn't believe it. An old lady like that, and she was pretty helpless, wasn't she, she'd had a stroke?'

'Yes, she had.'

Gwen's face screwed up in disgust. 'It's horrible. Obscene. But what I don't understand is why you came to see Mum. She told me you were interviewing everyone who was there yesterday and knows the Fairleighs. Is that right?'

'More or less, yes.'

'I knew there'd be trouble if she got mixed up with them again!'

Thanet raised his eyebrows. 'What do you mean?'

'After what they did to her the first time . . .'

'Are you talking about when she was engaged to Mr Fairleigh?'

'Yes.'

'But that was getting on for twenty years ago! Before you were born.'

'You have to understand! My mother and I are – were,' she added bitterly, 'very close. Oh, I know they say teenage girls and their mothers don't get on, that they're always fighting about something, but that's not necessarily true. We've had our arguments, of course, but on the whole, well, I suppose we're more like sisters than mother and daughter. Perhaps it's because I'm an only child. Or because she's always talked to me on equal terms, as long as I can remember. Or because my father really didn't want to know, as far as I was concerned . . . Anyway, for whatever reason, that's the way it was. And one of the things she told me about was the time when she was engaged to Hugo. It was when I had a boyfriend who was pretty serious about me. I was only sixteen at the time and I expect she thought I was too young to have just one boyfriend, but she didn't say so. What she really felt strongly about was the fact that his mother was pretty nasty to me. He was an only child too, you see, and his mother was very possessive. To be honest, I think she would have behaved the same towards any girl he brought home, but that wasn't the point. It made me pretty miserable at the time and I talked to Mum about it. And that was when she told me about Mrs Fairleigh.'

'What about her?'

'Well, Mum came from a working-class background, and of course the Fairleighs are upper middle class. I mean, plenty of money, public school, house in the family for generations, that sort of thing. Mum knew straight away that Mrs Fairleigh didn't approve of her.'

'Did Mrs Fairleigh say so?'

'Oh no, she was much too clever for that. And of course, Mum didn't know what was going on at the time. It wasn't until years later, when she was older and knew much more about life, that she really began to understand what had happened.'

'What do you mean?'

'She realised that what Hugo's mother did was systematically set about demonstrating to Mum how unfit she was to be the wife of someone with Hugo's background. She gave elaborate dinner parties for her, with so many knives and forks that Mum went cross-eyed trying to work out what to eat with what. Everyone had plummy voices and talked about things Mum knew nothing about – hunting and farming and charity balls and God knows what else. And of course, Mum's clothes were absolutely unsuitable – she was scraping along on a grant and clothes were the last thing she could afford to buy. Mrs Fairleigh took her on an endless social round, introducing her to families who lived in elegant country houses with tennis courts and ponies in paddocks and gorgeous daughters who'd known Hugo for years, had been to finishing schools in Switzerland and looked as though they stepped straight out of *Harpers & Queen*. Oh, she was clever all right. She never actually said in so many words, *You would never fit into this world*, but everything she showed her shouted it aloud. As I say, Mum had no idea what was going on. All she knew was that she was very unhappy. She felt inadequate all the time, and in fact the experience undermined her self-confidence for years. It was diabolical.'

Diabolical indeed. Fleetingly Thanet thought of Bridget. If she and Alexander became serious about each other, was this what lay in store for her?

'It was soon after she told me all this that she met Hugo

again. So you can imagine how I felt, when they started seeing each other regularly. I didn't want her to be hurt!'

'You don't like Hugo Fairleigh.'

'No I do not! He's not right for Mum. And don't think it's just because I feel he's coming between me and her. I'd be only too glad if she found someone who's kind. Someone who'd really care about her, make her happy.'

'Perhaps he does care about her. I understand it was she who broke off the engagement, and that he was very upset about it.'

'Maybe. But that doesn't mean he could make her happy. He's so . . . Oh, God, he's so superficial. And so ambitious. All that really matters to Hugo is Hugo!' she cried, unconsciously echoing Caroline Plowright.

'Are you sure you're not being a little unfair? Maybe his career does matter to him, but perhaps your mother matters more. If, as you seem to be implying, he's serious about her, he's obviously willing to go through a divorce and risk alienating his constituents, who by all accounts are fond of his present wife.'

'That's how he feels at the moment, yes. But what happens afterwards? What if it did damage his career? It would be my mother he'd blame and what do you think that would do to her?'

'I'm still not sure why you've come to see me.'

'He's a very determined man,' said Gwen, her mouth setting in a stubborn line. 'Takes after his mother, obviously. She was still against him and Mum getting married, you know.'

'What makes you think that?'

She shook her head. 'Just something Mum said, that made me think so.'

So he and Lineham could be right about the reason for the row, thought Thanet. Hugo Fairleigh had obviously broached the subject with his mother.

'What did your mother say exactly?'

'I can't remember. But that was certainly the impression I got.'

'Let me get this straight. Are you trying to say that you think Hugo Fairleigh killed his mother because she was against this marriage?'

'I don't know!' The girl's anxiety and passion drove her from her chair and she stood behind it, gripping the back so hard that her knuckles whitened. 'But someone did. And even the possibility that it could be Hugo . . . that my mother might be thinking of marrying a murderer! Can't you *see*.'

'Yes,' said Thanet gently. 'Of course I do. Come on, sit down again and try to calm yourself.'

He waited until she had settled down again, then said, 'Now, let's try and be rational about this. Have you anything specific to tell me, to back up your suspicions?'

She was silent, thinking, leaning forward in her chair and frowning down at her hands. The nails, Thanet noticed, were bitten down to the quick. Finally she shook her head. 'No,' she said. She sounded exhausted, defeated. 'Nothing specific.' She looked at him squarely, her eyes full of determination. 'But if there is, believe me, I'll be on to you like a shot.'

Thanet escorted her to the main entrance. Lineham was just coming in and together they watched her walk away across the forecourt, shoulders drooping.

'She doesn't look too happy. What did she have to say?'

Thanet told him as they walked together up the stairs.

'So that explains why Mrs Fairleigh apparently took so much trouble to introduce Pamela into her social circle. Talk about devious!'

'Yes. My mother-in-law said that she was very manipulative, that she'd seen Mrs Fairleigh persuade people into doing things they didn't want to do without their ever realising how she'd managed it. Sounds as though this is a classic case in point.'

'Well at least we now know that we were right about Mr Fairleigh wanting a divorce. And it does sound as though we were right about the row, and the stroke, too. So I bet we're also right about the will. And you must admit, sir, that half a million is one hell of a motive.'

'True. Well, we'll have to see. You're looking pleased with yourself, Mike. What did you find out at the bank?'

'Ah, well, listen to this. Those thousand pounds were drawn out *in cash* by Mrs Fairleigh herself, each month.'

'In cash!'

There was a knock at the door and Doctor Mallard came in. He glanced from Thanet to Lineham and said, 'Do I detect a somewhat electric atmosphere in here?'

Thanet grinned. 'Not much escapes you, does it, Doc? We've just discovered that the old lady has been drawing out a thousand pounds a month in cash.'

The little doctor's mouth pursed in a silent whistle. 'Not exactly chicken feed. What was it for, d'you know?'

'Your guess is as good as ours. The obvious answer is blackmail, of course. The withdrawals go back for – how long, Mike?'

'At least five years. Her bank statements only go back to then.'

'But who? And why?'

'Quite. There doesn't seem to be a clue anywhere in her papers. Though it's just occurred to me – you remember those phone calls Miss Ransome told us about, Mike?' Thanet explained to Mallard.

'Yes!' said Lineham. 'The timing is right, too, if they were from the blackmailer. He'd be wondering what had happened to his money.'

'Or she, Mike.'

'Didn't Miss Ransome say if it was a man or a woman?' said Mallard.

Thanet shook his head. 'She couldn't tell. The voice was muffled.'

'The B could still be an initial, of course,' said Lineham.

'You've lost me,' said Doc Mallard. 'What B?'

Thanet explained. 'It was obviously important to her. She's entered it in her diary on the first day of the month right through the year.'

'Does she know anyone whose name begins with the letter B?'

'Not that we've discovered so far.'

'Intriguing,' said Mallard. He perched on the edge of Thanet's desk and looked thoughtful. 'What else could it stand for? What on earth could an old woman find to spend a thousand a month on?'

'Clothes?' said Thanet, remembering the wardrobe crammed with expensive coats, suits, dresses. 'No, it's just too much. And always a regular sum.'

'Anyway, she always paid for clothes by cheque,' said Lineham. 'She used to note it down on the cheque stub – you know, hat, dress, skirt and so on.'

'Perhaps she was a secret gambler,' said Mallard, with a mischievous grin. 'B for Betting.'

Thanet and Lineham laughed.

'You may laugh,' said Mallard, 'but she always was keen on the gee-gees, I believe. And a surprising number of these doughty old ladies do get hooked on form.'

'Well, we'll look into it,' said Thanet. 'Drawing the money out on the first day of the month could imply settling up some monthly account. But in cash?'

Mallard shrugged. 'If it was gambling, maybe she wouldn't have wanted the bank to know, by paying by cheque.'

'I can't really see her trotting into Sturrenden Turf Accountants with a thousand pounds in her handbag every month, can you?' said Lineham.

'She could have got someone to do it for her,' said Mallard.

The same thought struck Thanet and Lineham at the same time.

'Ernie!' they chorused.

'The Fairleighs' gardener-cum-handyman,' Thanet explained to Mallard.

'No one would look twice at him going into a betting shop,' said Lineham.

'True.' Thanet frowned. 'But I still think it very unlikely. The sums are too regular. If she were paying off gambling debts I've have thought they'd vary wildly.'

'Unless she was a very strong-minded type and allowed herself so much a month and no more,' said Lineham.

'Difficult, for a gambler, by the nature of the beast,' said Mallard.

'I still think blackmail's the answer,' said Thanet. 'All the same, send Bentley along to the bookie's, just to make sure. And we'll have a word with Ernie when we go out to Thaxden later.'

'Odd,' said Mallard, 'I feel an almost proprietorial interest in this case.'

'If it hadn't been for you there wouldn't be a case!' said Thanet. 'Talking of which . . . I gather the PM report confirmed your diagnosis?'

Mallard nodded. 'Yes. No surprises at all, in fact. Evidence of stroke as expected, and yes, cause of death was asphyxiation.'

Thanet had not doubted Mallard but he was relieved. He could just imagine the fuss that Fairleigh would have made if the old lady had died a natural death after all.

'So,' said Mallard. 'Have there been any other developments?'

'One or two. Though we still have to confirm a lot of the stuff we've learned.' Thanet filled him in on Fairleigh's intended divorce, the row, the stroke and what they suspected about the proposed change of will.

'Well, well, well. Curiouser and curiouser.' Mallard slid off the desk and straightened his jacket. 'Just goes to confirm once again that skeletons lurk in the cupboards of even the best-ordered families. Keep me posted, won't you, Luke. You'll be getting a written report in due course. Must dash now.'

With the loss of Mallard's brisk presence the room settled back into normality.

'So,' said Lineham. 'What next?'

'About these cash withdrawals,' said Thanet. 'I've been thinking. We'll keep an open mind, of course, but I think we ought to concentrate on the possibility of blackmail. Now, assuming that this was what the money was for, how would it have been paid?'

'In person?'

'Unlikely, don't you think? A secret rendezvous every month. And if it was blackmail, I can't see old Mrs Fairleigh agreeing to regular meetings. I think she'd have wanted to make it as impersonal as possible.'

'By post, then. A parcel, to an accommodation address.'

'A possibility, I agree, though it's a great deal of money to risk sending by mail. And where would she send it from?'

'Different post offices every month.'

Thanet frowned. 'If it were just one payment, or two, perhaps. But as it went on month after month for at least five years . . . Even assuming she used a different post office each time, that's an awful lot of parcels. Village postmasters get to know everybody's business, I shouldn't have thought she'd want to risk it. We'll put a couple of men on to it, just in case, but I would have thought she'd prefer a really anonymous method.'

'But how? The blackmailer wouldn't have wanted to risk having it paid into his – or her – account. Too traceable.'

'I wonder if there is a method of bank payment which couldn't be traced? Give the manager a ring, Mike, and ask.'

It didn't take Lineham long to find out that there was. Apparently, provided that Isobel Fairleigh had the sorting code and account number of the payee, money could be paid into that account at any branch of any bank. Her own anonymity could be preserved either by leaving the 'paid in by' space blank, or by filling in a false name. Provided money was being paid in and not withdrawn no bank was going to bother overmuch with the name of the depositor.

'Neat,' said Thanet. 'I bet that's what she did. Assuming, of course, that we're right about the blackmail. We'll have to do a bit of digging.'

'We're going out to Thaxden now, sir?'

'Yes. And I think we'll pay another visit to Pamela Raven this evening. I'm sure she knows a lot more than she's telling us. Make another appointment, Mike, then we'll grab a sandwich in the canteen before we leave.'

FOURTEEN

The close-cropped green lawns of Thaxden Hall were covered with black spots, as if they had developed melanoma overnight. Ernie, wheelbarrow beside him, was busy filling in with peat and sharp sand the various indentations made by stalls and sideshows at the fête on Saturday. He straightened up as Thanet and Lineham approached.

'You've got quite a job on there,' said Thanet.

Ernie scowled. 'Bloody fête. Same every year.'

He must be in his seventies, Thanet thought, short, thin and wiry with face and stringy forearms tanned to the colour of old leather by constant exposure to the vagaries of the English climate. His sparse brown hair was peppered with grey and there was a large wart on the tip of his bulbous nose.

'You've been with the family a long time, then.'

'Nigh on fifty years.'

'Stone the crows!' said Lineham. 'Fifty years!'

Ernie grinned, revealing a row of blackened stumps which would have made any self-respecting dentist blench. 'You won't find many people as can say that these days.'

'You certainly won't!' said Thanet. 'You must have seen a lot of changes in that time.'

'Some.'

'And you must have known old Mrs Fairleigh pretty well.'

Ernie looked wary. 'What d'you mean?'

'Simply that you must have had a lot of dealings with her, over the years.'

'Ar.'

Thanet took this archetypally rural monosyllable for assent. 'Fond of horses, was she?'

'Damn good seat, she had. No one to compare, hereabouts.'

'Used to hunt, I suppose?' Thanet could imagine the old lady, back straight as a ramrod, leading the field.

'That she did.'

'And follow form, too, I suppose?'

Ernie squinted up at Thanet suspiciously. 'Form?'

'Well, being fond of horses . . . I suppose she was interested in bloodlines and so on.' If that was the right expression. He wasn't too sure of racing terminology.

'Not so far as I know.'

'Liked a little flutter too occasionally, I expect.'

Something subterranean happened to Ernie's face. The skin rippled and bulged and then he suddenly erupted into a great roar of laughter. He doubled up with mirth, shoulders heaving. He shook his head from side to side and gasped, '"Flutter"!'

Thanet and Lineham raised eyebrows at each other and waited for the paroxysm to pass.

Finally, leaning on one hand on the wheelbarrow as if the spasm of mirth had depleted his strength, Ernie fished a red-spotted handkerchief out of his trouser pocket and wiped his streaming eyes. A glance at their faces almost set him off again, but he blew his nose instead.

'The idea seems to amuse you,' said Thanet mildly, deliberately understating the effect the suggestion had had upon this odd little gnome of a man.

'If you'd knowed her . . . She were dead against gambling. It was her father, I heard tell. A great gambler, he was, by all accounts.' Ernie shook his head, face splitting once more into a huge grin. '"Liked a little flutter"!'

But there was something in that grin that Thanet couldn't pin down, something unexpected and disconcerting. What was it?

Ernie picked up his shovel decisively and plunged it into the peaty mixture. 'Well, can't stand here talking all day. Got a lot to do.'

As they walked away they heard a chuckle escape him, like gas bubbling up from underwater. '"Flutter",' floated after them.

They grinned at each other.

'Looks as though we needn't have bothered to send Bentley to make inquiries at the bookie's,' said Lineham.

'I don't know, Mike. Didn't you think there was something a bit, well, excessive, about his reaction?'

'Not really, no. What are you getting at?'

'I don't know. I'm not sure.' Thanet shook his head. 'Well, I don't suppose it matters.' But the idea niggled away at the back of his mind as they were admitted to the house by Sam.

Hugo Fairleigh, it seemed, was out. 'He's gone to London,' she said. This morning her dark hair was tied up in a ponytail with a red ribbon and she was wearing a crisp red and white striped blouse with her jeans. A wicker shopping basket stood on the hall table beside a tan leather shoulder bag and some car keys. 'And I'm just going out too, I'm afraid.'

'Never mind. We want a word with Miss Ransome, as well, and Mrs Fairleigh.'

'Mrs Fairleigh's not here either. Sorry. She should be back soon, though.'

'Good. Has Mr Fairleigh gone to the House of Commons?'
'I imagine so. I don't know.'
'Will he be back tonight?'
'No. Tomorrow evening, he said.'
Perhaps Fairleigh planned to see Pamela tonight, Thanet thought. It would probably be the first time they had met since Saturday. They would have a lot to discuss, he thought grimly.
'If there's nothing else . . .' said Sam, slinging her bag over one shoulder and picking up the basket and keys.
'Just one point. I understand that just before her stroke old Mrs Fairleigh had an argument with someone here in the house.'
'Oh?'
This was news to her, Thanet was sure of it. Her eyes were without guile as she frowned.
'You don't know anything about it?'
She shook her head. 'Sorry.'
'Were you here, that day?'
'No. I was out, shopping. I heard about Mrs Fairleigh's stroke when I got back.' She glanced at her watch. 'I'm sorry, I really must go.'
'Miss Ransome's here, at any rate?'
'So far as I know, yes.'
'We'll find our own way, then.'
Thanet wanted a word with Mrs Kerk first, to test his theory that it was she who had written the anonymous letter. They found her in the kitchen of Isobel Fairleigh's flat. She was frying pieces of stewing steak in a Le Creuset casserole dish, familiar to Thanet as Bridget's favourite cookware. On the draining board was a small pile of prepared vegetables: onions, carrots, parsnips. She glanced up apprehensively as they came in but did not stop what she was doing.

'Smells good,' said Thanet with a smile.

'Miss Ransome's supper.' She continued to turn over the pieces of meat with what Thanet considered to be excessive concentration. He decided to broach the matter directly.

'We received an anonymous letter this morning.'

Her hand jerked and fat splashed on to it. She released the wooden spatula and rubbed her hand against her apron. Then she picked the spatula up again.

'If you would just turn off the gas for a moment . . .' said Thanet.

Reluctantly she complied and almost at once the sizzling diminished as the flame went out. She turned to face them but gave him only a fleeting, nervous glance before dropping her eyes. He became more certain than ever that it was she who had sent that letter.

'It mentioned a row that Mrs Fairleigh had with someone and implied that this was why she had the stroke.'

She said nothing, but folded her arms protectively across her chest.

'Which means, of course, that it must have been written by someone present in the house at the time. Were there any visitors, that day?'

She shook her head, reluctantly.

'Which in turn means that it could have been written by only a very few people.'

She was chewing the inside of her lip, fingers nervously pleating the skirt of the old-fashioned crossover apron she was wearing.

'Presumably,' he went on, 'the argument was with a member of her family, and as they are bound to feel a certain loyalty to each other, I think we can assume that none of them was responsible for sending the letter. Which leaves Sam, and you. And Sam was out at the time.'

She was staring at him, as if mesmerised by his logic.

He waited a moment or two for what he had just said to sink in and then said gently, 'Why did you write it? Why didn't you just tell us about it?'

He knew why, of course. She had been hoping to avoid being questioned like this.

'It was Cyril said I ought to send it,' she said. 'My husband. I didn't know what to do.' Her lips tightened and her chin lifted defiantly. 'I know I didn't like her, not many people did, but it upset me, to think . . . I mean, she was helpless, wasn't she? Couldn't put up any sort of fight or struggle . . . It doesn't bear thinking about . . . No one deserves to die like that, whatever they're like. So I talked it over with Cyril and he said look, if it's worrying you, put it in a letter. Then they'll know about it but you won't be getting yourself involved.'

'Yes, I understand,' said Thanet. He smiled reassuringly at her. 'Know what, exactly?'

'I heard them arguing,' she admitted. Then, quickly, 'And don't go thinking I'm the sort who listens behind doors all the time, because I'm not.'

Pity, thought Thanet.

'I was cleaning the stairs, see, and they were in the sitting room.'

'Who?'

She shook her head. 'I'm not sure. I could hear her, all right – Mrs Fairleigh. She had a very, well, penetrating sort of voice. And I could tell she was angry.'

'What was she saying?'

'I couldn't make the words out. They were sort of blurred. This house is built solid, and it was more the way she was speaking than what she said. I thought, Lord, she's going to be in a mood after this, all right. So as soon as I got to the bottom of the stairs I shut myself in the kitchen and turned the radio on. I don't like rows,' she added defensively. 'They upset me.'

Disappointing. Thanet had hoped for more. 'So what happened after that?'

'Nothing, for about half an hour. Then Mr Hugo came and told me that his mother had had a stroke.'

'Did he say anything about how or when it happened?'

She shook her head. 'Just that the ambulance would be arriving soon and that was why.'

'Did you have the impression that it was Mr Fairleigh she'd been arguing with?'

'Yes. At the time. But thinking about it, later, that was only because it was him who came and told me. But she could have had the stroke after the argument, couldn't she, and Miss Letty could have found her. And the first thing she would have done was go to Mr Hugo for help. So I don't know, you see.' Her voice was rising in the effort to convince him. 'I really don't.'

'It's all right, Mrs Kerk. Don't upset yourself. I believe you.'

'Pity,' said Lineham as they went in search of Letty Ransome. 'If only we could have *known* it was him. Perhaps we can get Miss Ransome to tell us.'

'We can try. But I doubt it.'

Letty Ransome was in the sitting room, chewing a pencil and gazing thoughtfully at the folded newspaper on her knee.

Evidently a crossword addict, Thanet thought.

'Oh, Inspector . . .' She bundled the newspaper on to the seat beside her and stood up, a little stiffly, he noticed. Too much gardening yesterday, probably. She was also, he saw to his surprise, blushing again. Why, this time? Because she was unused to receiving male visitors, official or otherwise? Hardly. She had seemed comfortable enough with Hugo. But perhaps he didn't count, being a relation and therefore familiar to her.

To begin with, it looked as though she had nothing useful to tell them. She denied all knowledge of the row, though Thanet was pretty certain she was lying: that tell-tale blush was much in evidence again. She had been working in the garden, she said, when Hugo came to tell her that Isobel had had a stroke.

Her astonishment when Thanet began to question her about the large sums of money Isobel had been withdrawing each month was evident.

'A thousand pounds? Oh, good gracious me, what a lot of money! Whatever could Isobel have been . . . I just don't know what to say, Inspector. I'm astounded, I really am.'

'You have no idea what the money could have been for?'

'No, not at all. Absolutely not. Such an enormous sum! Oh, but just a moment. On the first of every month, you say? Wasn't that when you said . . . Could it have any connection with the B you were asking about? Oh! I wonder if that's it?' She stared at him, cheeks pink with excitement this time, eyes open so wide that the whites showed clear around the irises.

'What?' said Thanet.

'B day,' she said. 'Bank day! Perhaps that's the explanation! Perhaps she put the B in her diary every month to make sure she didn't forget to go to the bank!'

'Possibly. But even if that were true, it still doesn't tell us where the money went.'

'Of course,' said Lineham. 'The B could stand for something else. An initial, for example, as we suggested yesterday. Or it could be B for Blackmail.'

'Blackmail?' Letty's eyes stretched wide with shock and the very hairs on her head seemed to quiver with indignation as she said, 'What a . . . a preposterous idea. What possible reason could anyone have to blackmail Isobel?'

'We even wondered if those two mysterious phone calls

you had, asking for your sister, could have been from the blackmailer.'

'Oh, surely not. They couldn't have been! They could have been from anyone, anyone at all. Isobel was involved with so many organisations, so many committees . . . Forgive my saying so, Sergeant, but you really have no idea what you're talking about. If you'd only known my sister . . . Isobel was such an upright person, she devoted her whole life to the public good. The idea of blackmail is unthinkable.'

'No need to upset yourself, Miss Ransome. We're just exploring possibilities.' Lineham glanced at Thanet. *How d'you think she'll react to our last suggestion, then?* He grinned to take the sting out of his next words. 'We even wondered if it could stand for Betting.'

'Betting!' For some reason this idea seemed to upset her as much or even more than the last. She put her hand up to her throat and the colour in her cheeks intensified. She shook her head vehemently. 'Oh no, not Isobel. She was dead against gambling in any shape or form.'

'So we gathered, from Ernie,' said Thanet. 'We sent someone around to the bookie's, of course, to check, but it looks as though we needn't have bothered. Still we have to follow up every . . . Miss Ransome, what's the matter?'

The tide of colour had vanished as quickly as it had come, leaving her deathly pale. She swayed and put up a hand to her head. 'I feel . . .'

'A glass of water, Sergeant, quickly. Put your head down, Miss Ransome, between your knees.' Thanet steadied her with one hand on her shoulder, hoping she wasn't going to pass out on him.

Lineham was back in less than a minute. He knelt beside her. 'Here, Miss Ransome, drink this.'

She sipped obediently and slowly her skin lost its unnatural pallor. 'I'm sorry . . .'

Thanet shook his head. 'Please, don't apologise.'

She straightened her shoulders and glanced timidly at him. 'Inspector . . . I can see I shall have to tell you.' She paused, evidently plucking up courage.

'I have a confession to make.'

FIFTEEN

Thanet waited. What now?

Letty Ransome, having begun, seemed at a loss for words. She shifted uneasily in her chair and the newspaper crackled. She glanced down at it, picked it up, laid it on her knee and flattened it out. Then to his surprise, still without saying anything, she held it out.

He took it. One glance was enough to explain her confusion when they came in. Crossword, indeed! It was a copy of the *Daily Telegraph*, open at the racing pages. The schedules of runners were heavily marked with underlinings, question marks, exclamation marks. Isobel may have been against gambling because of her father's addiction but Letty had evidently shared it. A number of small pieces of the jigsaw clicked into place in Thanet's mind. Ernie's immoderate laughter, for instance. That, of course, was what had been puzzling about the old man's reaction; Ernie had been enjoying the irony of the police suspecting Isobel of being a secret gambler when he had no doubt been involved in keeping Letty's activities from her.

Thanet handed the paper to Lineham.

He stated the obvious. 'Your sister didn't know about this?'

She shook her head wordlessly.

'And Ernie helps you?'

She nodded.

'Was that what he went to see you about, on Saturday afternoon, at the fête?'

Another nod.

'He had a tip for one of the afternoon's races?'

'The . . .' She cleared her throat, tried again. 'The Northumberland Plate.'

Thanet raised his eyebrows.

'It's . . . It's a big betting race in the North of England.'

'I've heard of that!' said Lineham. 'A friend of mine comes from up North. Popularly called the Pitmen's Derby, isn't it, because it's held at the time of the miners' annual holiday?'

She nodded, a spark of enthusiasm loosening her tongue. 'Ernie knows someone who works . . . who had some inside information. We'd been waiting all day for him to ring.'

'What time was this race?'

'Three-twenty.'

'And it was around 3.15 when Ernie came to speak to you. Didn't leave you much time, did it?'

'No. I came straight up to ring the Turf Accountant.'

'The one in Sturrenden?'

'Yes.'

'You have an account with him?'

'Yes.'

So that's why she was 'confessing'. Bentley's inquiries would have revealed that she was a regular client.

'Did the horse win?'

She smiled for the first time, her face lighting up. 'Yes.'

'Did you make a lot of money?'

'A modest amount. I know what I'm doing, Inspector. I never bet more than five pounds, and always on sensible odds, six to four, something like that.'

'You told me you didn't come upstairs when you came into the house on Saturday afternoon.'

'Yes. I'm sorry.'

'Miss Ransome, I don't want to be unreasonable about this, but you are making our job rather difficult, aren't you? First you say you didn't come indoors at all during the afternoon. Then you say, oh yes, you forgot, you did come in to go to the loo, but you certainly didn't go upstairs. Now you tell me you did go upstairs, to ring the bookie. You must see that I am beginning to wonder what else you haven't told me.'

'Nothing!' she said. 'Well, I did see Grace, coming out of Isobel's room, but you knew about that, she told you herself that she'd been in there around then. And I couldn't say so at the time because you'd have wanted to know what I was doing upstairs and I couldn't think of a good excuse . . . I wasn't sure if she'd seen me or not.'

'The fact still remains that your sister was killed between 3 and 3.45 that afternoon. And by your own admission you were here. Upstairs. In the very next room.' Thanet was polite but implacable. Bullying old ladies was not his style, but it had to be faced: in the circumstances Letty Ransome was a prime suspect.

Letty's lips began to tremble and she put up her hand and pressed it to them. 'I didn't see anyone else, Inspector, really I didn't. I was in a hurry to get back.'

Thanet's humanitarian instincts were urging him to reassure her, to accept what she was saying and leave. But reason held him back. After seeing Grace come out of Isobel's room Letty Ransome would have known that her sister would be unattended. It would have taken only a matter of minutes to slip along the corridor, pick up that pillow and guarantee herself independence and financial security for the rest of her life. Because she had, all unwittingly, handed the police a further motive on a plate.

'We have only your word for that, haven't we? And as I've just pointed out, you have already lied to us a number of times. Why should we believe you now?'

'Because it's true! It is, really. Oh, what can I do to make you believe me?'

'Look, Miss Ransome, I think you have to recognise that you are in a serious position. I repeat, you were close by when the murder was committed. The means, the pillow, was to hand, and –'

'Inspector! You don't . . . You *can't* be implying that I had anything to do with Isobel's murder. Me, personally?' She was aghast, her eyes filled with horror at the enormity of the idea.

If she were guilty she was a brilliant actress, thought Thanet. 'I'm not implying anything, I'm afraid, Miss Ransome. I am stating a fact. In the circumstances we have to consider you a suspect.'

She stared at him, speechless, for a seemingly interminable length of time. Even a minute's silence can appear endless in an interview like this. Then she said, 'But why? Why should I do something so . . . so dreadful as to . . . to kill my own sister? What possible reason could I have?'

'Under your sister's will you stand to inherit a substantial annuity. Many people would consider ten thousand a year an extremely powerful motive.'

She was shaking her head. 'I don't believe it. I can't believe it. I'd willingly give up any prospect of inheriting a penny if it would bring Isobel back. People who have never been alone don't realise . . . And as you get older . . . I know Isobel was difficult, but she was all I had.'

Thanet understood what Letty was trying to say. All too often he'd seen the surviving partner of an apparently unhappy marriage go to pieces. This didn't always happen, of course, far from it, but it did seem that some people found it preferable to be downtrodden, abused or even perpetually locked in conflict than to be alone, with no one to care whether they lived or died. Though this wasn't strictly true in Letty's case. 'You have your nephew, and his wife.'

Another shake of the head. 'Not the same, Inspector. Isobel and I . . . How can I explain? We had a shared past. Despite our differences this was the bond between us and we both knew it.'

There was nothing more to be said at the moment.

Lineham waited until they were out of earshot. He had recognised Letty's possible further motive, too. 'That's all very well, but the fact remains that she's really hooked, isn't she? And gambling, well, like any other addiction, it can easily get out of hand. What if she's tired of placing piddling little bets, would like to bet twenty quid instead of five, or even fifty, a hundred . . . And as you say, she did know about the annuity. Ten thousand a year isn't peanuts. And sir!' He stopped as a thought struck him. 'We've only got her word for it that she didn't know about that row. Say she did hear it, or hear some of it, anyway, heard her sister say she was going to change her will . . . Or, even better, say the row was with her! Say her sister found out about the gambling, and that was what the argument was about! And then Isobel threatened to cut her out of her will altogether! That gives her an even better motive.'

'I know.' Thanet was reluctant to believe this. He liked Letty Ransome. But she obviously had hidden depths. Who would have suspected her of being a secret gambler? And Lineham was right. A passion for gambling can be a deeply destructive force. To feed their obsession men have been known to put the whole future of their family at risk. Letty Ransome had little else to enliven her dreary life of ministering to her difficult sister's moods and needs. If Isobel had found out and threatened perhaps to cut off the meagre allowance she gave her as well as cancelling the promised annuity, might the temptation to ensure that this did not happen have proved too great? People have a tremendous capacity for self-deception, if it serves their ends. And as he had told himself before, in her own mind Letty might even have justified the killing by convincing herself that it was an act of kindness, that dear Isobel must have hated being a helpless dependant, subject to all the indignities which a severe stroke can involve.

He said as much to Lineham.

'Exactly! Anyway, I'll just nip along and check that no papers have fallen down the back of Mrs Fairleigh's desk.'

'Right. I'll wait on the landing in the main house.'

Lineham wasn't long. He shook his head as he joined Thanet. 'Nothing.'

Down below the front door opened to admit Grace Fairleigh. Thanet hurried down the stairs to meet her. 'Mrs Fairleigh, I was hoping for a word . . .'

Apart from that brief and somewhat mortifying encounter yesterday morning, he hadn't spoken to her properly since Saturday afternoon. Somehow other matters had always taken precedence. But of all the people in the house at the time she was the only one known to have been in Isobel Fairleigh's room around the time of the murder. They only had her word for it that the old lady had been alive when she left her around 3.20. She had to be a prime suspect.

She had put her shoulder bag down on the hall table and now she led them into the drawing room and invited them to sit down.

'How are your inquiries going?'

She was evidently inclined to be more cooperative today. Elegant as ever, she was wearing silky black trousers and a loose black and white top in a complicated geometric design, caught in at the waist by a wide belt which accentuated her narrow waist. Her hair had been swept back into an elaborate pleat, accentuating the classic beauty of her bone structure. She would still be beautiful at eighty, Thanet thought, though lacking warmth and animation it was a beauty which did not appeal to him.

'We are making progress, I think.'

'I gather you've found out about my husband's mistress. Or should I call her his fiancée? Can he have a fiancée, while he's still married to me, I wonder?'

'Has he discussed this with you?'

'What, exactly? That he wanted a divorce and was planning to marry her? Or that she was down here on Saturday, viewing her future home? The answer to the first question is yes, and to the second no. I could see that something had upset him after your visit yesterday and when his aunt told me she'd seen this Pamela woman down here at the fête on Saturday and that she felt she'd had to tell you, I realised what it was. Naturally he wouldn't want her involved in all this.'

'You seem remarkably calm about this proposed divorce, Mrs Fairleigh.'

And it was interesting that she hadn't confided in her friend Caroline.

She shrugged. 'Our marriage was over in everything but name long ago, Inspector. To be honest, I'm past caring.' She looked away, out of the window, and he could almost hear her unspoken thought. *About anything, in fact.*

Caroline was right, Thanet thought. Something in Grace Fairleigh had died along with the child that had meant so much to her, and had never come to life again. He had occasionally come across women like this before, women who had never recovered from a miscarriage or an ill-considered abortion, for example, who many years later still grieved as if the loss had happened only yesterday. On the face of it Grace Fairleigh had much that many women hungered for: exceptional beauty, wealth, a successful husband and a beautiful home. But the beauty was an empty shell, the money meant nothing to her, the marriage was a sham and the house a mere stage set for a barren life.

'How did your mother-in-law feel about the divorce?'

'I've no idea. I don't know that my husband ever discussed it with her.'

'I understand that she was a fairly conventional person. She might not have liked the idea. Especially in view of the fact that she didn't approve of the lady first time around.'

'My husband is a grown man, Inspector. He's long past the stage when his mother's approval or disapproval would have affected such a matter.'

Unless it meant being disinherited, thought Thanet.

'I understand that when your mother-in-law had her stroke, it was because of a serious argument with someone here in the house.'

She was either a good actress or this was news to her. The beautifully plucked eyebrows arched in surprise. 'Who told you that?'

'Is it true?'

'I've no idea. Just what are you implying, Inspector?'

'You were here, at the time?'

The brief flicker of curiosity had already died. She didn't pursue the matter. 'When she had the stroke? Yes.'

'In this part of the house?'

'I was in my bedroom changing to go out when my husband came to tell me that she'd been taken ill and he'd rung for an ambulance.'

It was obvious that, true or not, this was her story and she would stick to it. Thanet decided to leave, but at the door he remembered that he had forgotten to ask her about the letters delivered on the day of the murder. She seemed surprised that he should be interested, but said yes, since her mother-in-law's illness she had been in the habit of taking her letters up and reading them to her. She herself had received a couple of letters that morning and there had been one for her mother-in-law, an estimate from a local builder for some decorating. She'd been so busy during the morning that she'd forgotten about it until after lunch.

Mentally Thanet shrugged. One more loose end tied up.

'I was thinking,' said Lineham as they crunched across the gravel towards the car, 'if this was a detective novel it would have to be her.'

'Because she's the most unlikely candidate, you mean? That doesn't necessarily count her out, though, does it?'

'But what motive would she have?'

'The old lady wasn't the easiest of mothers-in-law, by all accounts.'

Ernie was still busy with his shovelfuls of peat. The lawns looked worse than ever. Idly, Thanet wondered how long they would take to recover. Leaning against the car, he took out his pipe and began to fill it.

Lineham frowned.

Thanet grinned. 'Don't worry, Mike, we'll keep the windows wound down.' He lit the tobacco, tamping it down with his forefinger as it flared up. Long habit had deadened the nerves in his fingertip. It took a second match and then a third before it was drawing properly and out of consideration for Lineham only then did he get into the car. There was always far more smoke when he was first lighting up.

'Even so,' said Lineham as they set off down the drive, 'this would hardly be the time to knock the old lady off, would it? It sounds as though she wasn't going to be her mother-in-law much longer.'

'True.'

A few moments later they passed a row of little terraced cottages. A woman was sweeping the concrete path in front of one of them with brief, angry strokes, as if she had a grudge against the world in general and dirt in particular. The words incised in a stone tablet over the centre cottage caught Thanet's eye. 'Webster Cottages 1873.' The name rang a bell.

On impulse he said, 'Stop the car, Mike. Webster Cottages. Isn't that where Mrs Tanner lives – you know, the woman whose son was put away because of old Mrs Fairleigh's evidence?'

Lineham's forehead wrinkled. 'I believe it is.'

'I wonder if that's her.'

Both men turned to look over their shoulders. The woman was walking back up the path to the front door.

'Let's go and see,' said Thanet, getting out of the car.

'I thought you said we wouldn't bother to interview her ourselves unless something turned up to make you change your mind,' said Lineham as they walked back along the narrow pavement.

Thanet shrugged. 'We might as well, as we're passing.'

There were five cottages in all in the row. The gardens of two were a riot of cottage garden flowers – rosemary, lavender, pinks, alchemilla, hollyhocks and nepeta. Two more had neat pocket-handkerchief lawns surrounded by narrow beds containing a mixture of hybrid tea and floribunda roses. The fifth, the one in which the woman had been working, proclaimed a profound dislike of gardening. Apart from a skimpy bed along the front wall of the house planted with alternate orange tagetes and scarlet salvias the whole area had been paved over. There was not a weed to be seen. The effect was bleak, grudging, as if the owner conceded that a garden was a place in which plants should be displayed but was determined to show nature who had the upper hand.

'What makes you think she lives here?' said Lineham as he knocked at the door.

'Just a hunch.'

The door opened almost at once, as if the woman had been waiting to pounce on intruders.

'Yes?'

She was in her early forties, short and whipcord thin, as if the fierce emotion which emanated from her in waves had burned away all surplus fat. Her brown hair was short, cut in an uneven line. Thanet could imagine her cutting it herself, resigned to a necessary task but not caring about the final effect. She was wearing a cheap nylon overall over a cotton dress.

'What do you want?' The grey-blue eyes, hard as water-smoothed pebbles, moved from one to the other with undisguised hostility.

'Mrs Tanner?'

She gave a tight nod.

Thanet introduced himself and Lineham.

'You've been around once already. I've got nothing more to say.' She turned away, closing the door, but Lineham put out his hand and held it open.

'D'you mind?' Her glare intensified.

'I'm afraid we do.' Thanet was at his most benign. He glanced to right and left. Next door a lace curtain twitched. 'I see your neighbours are interested. Do you really want to talk here on the doorstep?'

Pushing between the two policemen she took a few steps down the path and shook her fist at the window. 'Why can't you mind your own bloody business?' she shouted. She turned back to Thanet. 'You'd better come in, I suppose.' She glanced at the pipe in his hand. 'And you can put that thing out, for a start. I'm not having smoking in my house.'

Without a word Thanet tapped out the pipe on the heel of his shoe, earning himself another glare as shreds of charred tobacco fell upon the path she had just swept. He checked that it was out and put it in his pocket before following her inside.

They stepped straight into a small square sitting room, which was hot and stuffy, as if fresh air was only ever allowed into it when the door was opened. It was spotless but sparsely furnished with a couple of small tables, two wooden-armed easy chairs upholstered in faded green moquette and a fawn carpet from which the floral pattern had almost been worn away. There was a rental television set in the corner beside the fireplace but no evidence of any other activity whatsoever, not a newspaper, a book, a magazine, a bundle of knitting, anything. What did she do when she wasn't watching television? Thanet wondered. Clean things and brood, by the look of her.

Had she always been like this, simmering with suppressed fury like a kettle about to boil over? he wondered. Perhaps not. Her present attitude to her neighbours would scarcely endear her to them and yet village opinion had apparently been behind her at the time of Wayne's earlier misdemeanours. Even now, difficult as it was to believe after having met her, there was a softer side to her nature, as she apparently did voluntary work for the Hospice fund. A growing bitterness would be understandable, if she had had a difficult time with her disabled husband, and it couldn't have been easy, after Tanner died, to raise a teenage boy alone. Wayne had apparently been her Achilles heel and it must have been his imprisonment which had triggered off the anger which seemed to crackle in the air around her.

Briefly he wondered what it was that made people react so differently to adverse circumstances. He had seen women carry intolerable burdens and yet emerge the stronger, had met people who had survived the most appalling tragedies apparently unscathed by the experience. Was it some genetic factor which imparted inner strength, or a personality which had been nurtured by a secure background and parental love?

Whatever it was, it was clear that it had been lacking in Mrs Tanner's life. And it was ironic that it was through the son upon whom she had squandered her meagre hoard of tenderness that she had suffered the cruellest blow of all.

She walked across to the fireplace and turned to face them, folding her arms across her flat nylon chest. 'This is a complete waste of time. I told you, I've nothing to add to what I said before.' She obviously had no intention of inviting them to sit down.

'We have to be thorough. Murder is a serious matter.'

'I can't see what it's got to do with me.'

'Oh come, Mrs Tanner. You must realise that we have to look very closely at everyone known to have a grudge against Mrs Fairleigh.'

She gave a harsh bark of laughter, an unpleasant sound. 'You're going to have your work cut out then, aren't you?'

'What do you mean?'

'Always poking her nose in where she wasn't wanted, wasn't she? You'd think she owned the bloody place.'

'Did she seriously upset anyone else in the village, apart from yourself?'

'Ask around, you'll soon find out. Good riddance, I say. Whoever did her in deserves a medal, if you ask me.'

'Do you deserve that medal, Mrs Tanner?' said Thanet softly.

She unclasped her arms as if unleashing her anger and wagged a forefinger at him. 'Oh, no you don't! Don't think you're going to pin that one on me! I've got more sense than to put my head in a noose because of her!'

'You were there, though, weren't you, in the house that day.'

'Like a dozen other people, yes. Why don't you go and bother them?'

'I see you watch television, Mrs Tanner.' Thanet glanced at the set in the corner. 'So I'm sure you must be familiar with the fact that when the police investigate a murder they look for someone with motive, means and opportunity. You had the motive, the means were to hand, and you also had the opportunity.'

She clenched her fists as if she would have liked to fly at him and hammer at his chest. 'When?' she demanded. 'I was run off my feet, like everyone else.'

'But nobody was watching you. You were in and out all the time with trays, collecting crockery from all over the place. It would have taken only a minute or two to slip up the stairs near the kitchen and do what you had to do.'

'Well I didn't!' Her sallow skin had suddenly taken on an unhealthy greyish tinge, as if she had only just become fully aware of the danger of her position. 'And no one can prove otherwise.'

'Not yet, Mrs Tanner. Not yet. Look,' he added more gently, 'we are not in the business of wrongly accusing people, but –'

'But you are, aren't you! You're accusing me!'

He shook his head firmly. 'No. I'm not.'

'But you said –'

'I did not accuse you. I simply said that we have to take a close look at everyone who had a grudge against her. You are one of those people. You also had the means and opportunity. That's all I said.'

'You're twisting words! Oh, it would suit them, wouldn't it, them up at the big house, if one of us was charged, one of the *common* people. What do we matter, after all? They're the ones with the power, aren't they? It's the same old story, one law for the rich and another for the poor. Money can buy anything these days . . .'

'But it can't buy justice,' said Thanet, raising his voice to stop the tirade. 'That is a fact.'

'Tell me another one! You can't open the paper these days without hearing of some policeman who's been taking backhanders!'

Lineham stirred beside him and Thanet hoped the sergeant was not going to lose his temper. He could feel his own anger rising. *Keep calm. Call her bluff.* 'Do you wish to lay charges against me, Mrs Tanner?' A polite inquiry. The message, *You can't get to me like that.*

She backpedalled at once, as he knew she would. 'I didn't say that,' she said sulkily. And then, in a different tone, almost pleading, 'You're not going to arrest me, then?'

'I'm not arresting anyone yet. I just wanted you to understand the seriousness of your position and to tell you that it might be wise to tone down your attitude towards the old lady a little. She is dead now, after all.'

She stared at him, rubbing her forearms as if, despite the heat of the room, she suddenly felt cold.

'Don't you see?' he said. 'Carrying on like this does you no good, no good at all.'

'Yes,' she said grudgingly. 'I suppose you're right. I . . . I'm sorry.' She frowned and clamped her lips together, as if the apology had caused her physical pain.

'You certainly put her in her place, sir,' said Lineham as they walked back to the car.

'Made a real hash of it, didn't I?' Thanet was depressed. He should have been able to handle the woman better, without trampling all over her like that.

'I think you were brilliant! I'm glad I wasn't doing the interview, I can tell you. I'd have lost my temper at one point.'

'Pity I didn't stick to my original plan. We didn't learn a single thing we didn't know already.'

'I disagree,' said Lineham stoutly. 'I can just imagine her sneaking up the stairs and gloating as she put the pillow over Mrs Fairleigh's head.'

'Perhaps.' Thanet wasn't convinced.

'Finish your pipe, sir.'

Lineham suggesting that he should light up?

Thanet took out his pipe, looked at it, then glanced at the sergeant and grinned. 'Put my dummy in, you mean?'

The tension dissolved as they both started to laugh.

SIXTEEN

Bentley had obviously been looking out for their return. He caught them at the door of Thanet's office.

'Sir!' His round, placid face was unusually animated.

Thanet sighed inwardly. In the past he, too, had discovered nuggets of interesting information only to find that his superior was there before him. But it was just one of those disappointments policemen learned to live with.

'Sorry, Bentley, I think I know what you're going to say. It's about Miss Ransome, isn't it?'

Bentley's face fell. 'Yes, sir. She's a regular client at the bookie's. Has been for years.'

'I know. She told us herself. Large sums?'

'Never more than a fiver, sir. She's careful, chooses sensible odds. Wins a bit more than she loses, that's all.'

Thanet nodded. 'Thanks. At least that confirms what she said.'

Lineham waited until Bentley had gone and then said, 'Sir, d'you mind if I give Louise a ring? She should be back by now.'

Of course. The interview with the child psychologist. Thanet was ashamed that he had forgotten about something so important to Lineham. The sergeant must have been on tenterhooks about it all afternoon and there wouldn't be time for him to go home before they left for London to see Pamela Raven. 'Go ahead.'

He busied himself with papers while Lineham made the phone call, but couldn't help overhearing.

'Louise? How did you get on? *What*? Oh, no.' A long silence while he listened, then, 'I see. Yes . . . Yes. How's Richard? . . . Yes, I suppose so, Oh God . . . Yes, we'll talk about it tonight.'

Lineham put the phone down and sat staring into space. He looked stunned.

'Mike, what is it? What's happened?'

Lineham's eyes focused again. 'Richard is dyslexic.'

'Oh, no. Are they sure?'

Lineham shrugged. 'They seem to be.' He put his head in his hands.

'Mike . . .' Thanet was at a loss for words. He didn't know enough about dyslexia to discuss the subject sensibly. He got up and went to sit on the corner of Lineham's desk. 'Look, it's a blow, yes, and I know it's not much consolation, but at least you now know there's a reason for the way he's been behaving. Do they really think that this would account for it?'

'Apparently. I'll know more later. They've given Louise some stuff to read . . . But it's bound to affect his future. How's he ever going to pass exams if he's got reading problems?'

'It's bound to cause difficulties, yes, there's no point in pretending otherwise. But it doesn't stop people being very successful. You know that series in one of the Sunday magazine supplements, the one about famous people who have something in common? There was one quite recently about people who were dyslexic. Susan Hampshire, for example. And there were lots more.' Thanet wished he had paid more attention to that particular article. Would the magazine have been thrown away, he wondered? He'd have to look.

Lineham shook his head. 'I didn't see it.' But he was looking marginally less miserable.

'Well try not to get into a state about it until you've found out a lot more. So much research has been done into these things nowadays, there's all sorts of help available. Isn't there a Dyslexic Society?'

'I don't know. I expect they'll have told Louise. She said they'd given her a whole pile of literature.'

'How's she taking it?'

'She's upset, of course. But you know Louise. She's a great one for finding out about things and getting things done. And they made all sorts of practical suggestions about helping Richard on a day-to-day basis.'

'Such as?'

'She didn't say.'

'Look, would you prefer to go home? I can take Bentley to London with me instead.'

'I don't know.' Lineham was clearly torn. The sergeant loved his work and jealously guarded the privilege of being Thanet's chosen companion on such excursions. He was silent for a while, thinking, fiddling with a paper clip that he had picked up from his desk. Finally he tossed it into the wastepaper basket. 'I don't suppose a few hours is going to make much difference. And the appointment with Mrs Raven is at seven, we shouldn't be too late getting back.'

'It's up to you. I'll quite understand if you want to opt out.'

But the sergeant's mind was now made up. He shook his head firmly. 'No. I'll come.'

By 5.30 they were on their way. The journey should take only an hour or so, but they had to allow for rush-hour traffic further into London. Thc other carriageway of the motorway was even more congested than it had been on Sunday, with commuters streaming out of London in an endless nose-to-tail queue, but heading in to the capital the traffic was relatively light until they left the M20. Lineham grew fidgety as the hands of the clock crept nearer and nearer the hour of their appointment. He drummed his fingers on the steering wheel as once again they found themselves creeping along at a snail's pace. 'Come on, come on!' he muttered.

'No point in getting worked up about it, Mike. It won't get us there any more quickly. I don't suppose it'll matter if we're a few minutes late.'

In the event they made it with five minutes to spare. 'I wonder if Fairleigh will be there,' said Thanet as they got out of the car.

He was, looking very much at home, smoking a cigarette and lounging in an armchair. 'Good evening, Inspector. We thought we'd give you a little surprise.'

Thanet wondered where Gwen was, and whether she had told her mother of her visit to Sturrenden to see him. He doubted it.

'No surprise, Mr Fairleigh. When we heard you'd gone to London we rather expected to find you here.'

'We decided to come clean, you see.' Fairleigh smiled and tapped away the long worm of ash on his cigarette.

'Ah, did you.'

'Do sit down, Inspector,' said Pamela Raven, perching on the broad arm of Fairleigh's chair. Tonight she was more formally dressed in a navy pleated skirt and navy and white polka-dot blouse. Unlike Fairleigh she looked tense, nervous.

Fairleigh was obviously aware of this. He gave her a reassuring smile and took her hand. *Don't worry, everything's under control. I'm here.*

Thanet chose an armchair and Lineham seated himself at the desk near the window, adjusting the angle of his chair so that he could see everyone in the room and pushing aside a pile of exercise books to make room for his notebook.

'It was obvious you were going to find out about us sooner or later, so we thought we might as well get in first. We've nothing to be ashamed of, after all, nothing to hide.'

Pamela was wearing open-toed sandals and, alert for small, betraying signs, Thanet noticed her toes curl up. People could school themselves to control facial expressions but it was much harder to prevent giving themselves away by the movements of feet and hands. So these two did have something to hide. What? he wondered. For the first time he contemplated the possibility that they might have been in it together.

'Good. Then you won't mind answering a few questions.'

Fairleigh waved his cigarette in an expansive gesture before leaning forward to stub it out. 'Not at all,' he said genially. 'Go ahead.'

But Thanet noticed that almost immediately the MP lit up again. So he, too, was nervous, though he was hiding it well.

'Mr Fairleigh. You knew Mrs Raven intended coming to the fête on Saturday?'

'No.' They spoke simultaneously.

Fairleigh twisted his head to smile up at her and nodded. *You first.*

'It was entirely my idea. Hugo knew nothing about it. I told you last time, I was curious.'

'About what, exactly?'

'To see what the place was like. Whether it had changed. And, well . . .'

'Perhaps I should make it quite clear, Inspector. Mrs Raven and I intend to marry. Thaxden is her future home. And as, at the moment, it is rather difficult to take her there . . .'

With your present wife in residence, supplied Thanet.

'. . . well, it's understandable that she should have taken this opportunity to look at it.'

That wasn't how you felt on Saturday, thought Thanet, remembering how disconcerted the MP had looked when he spotted her – for by now he was convinced that this was what had caused the look which had aroused his curiosity. And it was that look, he realised, which had probably subconsciously prevented him from considering the conspiracy theory.

'When did you make the decision to go down to Thaxden, Mrs Raven?'

'Well, after Hugo told me about the fête, first of all I toyed with the idea. But as the date came closer it took hold more and more. It was as if . . . Oh, it's difficult to describe . . . As if something was tugging at me, urging me to go. Perhaps it was sheer curiosity, to see if the place had changed at all, or perhaps because I knew that one day I should be living there, as Hugo says . . .' She shook her head. 'Anyway, I'd more or less made up my mind by Saturday, and then when I woke up it was such a lovely day . . . The thought of getting out of London into the country was so tempting . . . I knew there were always a lot of people at the fête, and I just intended to mingle with the crowd, take a quick look around and then come away. But then I found I was enjoying it so much . . . I thought I was quite safe, that no one but Hugo would know me . . . But I'd forgotten about his aunt.'

Fairleigh's lips tightened.

'Let me clarify this,' said Thanet. 'I gather, from my conversation with Miss Ransome when she told me she'd seen you, that she is still unaware of the fact that you two are back together again?'

'She was until yesterday,' said Fairleigh, bitterly. 'We saw no point in telling her just yet. She's very fond of my wife and she's also rather strait-laced. She wouldn't have approved of a divorce.'

'But she'd have had to find out eventually.'

'In time, yes. But we didn't feel the right moment had come.'

'But she knows now.'

'My wife told her. I gather she and Letty were talking about the . . . about Saturday, and she mentioned she'd seen Pam at the fête. Then, of course, Grace realised why I wasn't in too good a mood after seeing you yesterday and felt she ought to put Letty in the picture.'

'And how did she react?'

'I haven't seen her since. But I imagine I'm not exactly her blue-eyed boy at the moment.'

Nor she his favourite aunt, Thanet guessed. Fairleigh was no doubt furious with her for having given away Pamela's presence on Saturday and had probably deliberately been avoiding her.

He returned to his questioning.

'You knew old Mrs Fairleigh was ill, of course, Mrs Raven?'

'Yes. Hugo told me.'

'And you knew about the living arrangements of the two households.'

'Yes.'

She could see where his questions were leading, he could see her bracing herself.

'Did you know that the day nurse had failed to turn up on Saturday?'

The question had caught her unprepared. She hesitated and her eyes flickered down at Hugo.

Seated as they were, they were ill placed for silent collusion.

'No, Mrs Raven, there is no need to consult Mr Fairleigh. Surely the question is straightforward enough?'

She sighed. 'Yes. Hugo rang me on Saturday morning.'

'Especially to tell you?'

'Don't be ridiculous, Inspector!' Fairleigh exploded. 'Why on earth should I ring Pamela to tell her something like that? It was merely a . . . well, a social call. I often ring her, as you can well imagine.'

Thanet ignored this outburst and addressed himself to Pamela. 'And did Mr Fairleigh also tell you what arrangements had been made for looking after the old lady during the day?'

'Well, yes . . . I asked him how they were going to manage, as they were all so tied up with the fête, and he told me his wife was going to look in every half an hour or so during the afternoon.'

'Right, that's enough!' Fairleigh was on his feet. 'Pam, you're not to answer any more questions. I'm going to ring my solicitor.'

Thanet was surprised at this reaction. Surely Fairleigh must have realised that Pamela would be questioned along these lines, especially as she must have told him she had been seen in the house. It occurred to him now to wonder why, in fact, Fairleigh had not insisted that this entire interview be conducted in the presence of his legal adviser. Perhaps Fairleigh's natural arrogance had encouraged him to assume that together he and Pamela could pull the wool over the eyes of the police, that they would be able to reveal just what they chose to reveal and no more. Fairleigh was learning a valuable lesson, he thought: never underestimate your opponent. It was surprising that as a politician he hadn't learned it long ago.

'It is 7.30 in the evening, sir. You won't be able to get hold of him now.'

Fairleigh shot Thanet a contemptuous look. *That's what you think*. He took out a pocket diary and began to leaf through it.

Only people like Fairleigh would have the home number

of their solicitors in their pockets, thought Thanet resignedly. Ah well, pity, just when they were beginning to get somewhere.

Fairleigh began to dial.

'No, Hugo, stop!' Pamela was tugging at his sleeve.

He ignored her, twitching his arm to shake her off.

She grabbed it again. 'Hugo, please!'

He turned his head to look at her and a silent battle of wills took place. But Thanet was sure that the argument was not just about whether to ring Bassett or not. There was another issue involved, something they were afraid he would find out if he went on questioning Pamela. He wished he could see their faces properly.

It was Pamela who broke the silence. 'It's no good, Hugo. We'll have to tell them.' Her voice was flat, resigned.

'For God's sake, Pam,' hissed Fairleigh through clenched teeth, shooting a sideways glance at Thanet.

Thanet's face must have told him that it was too late, the damage was done.

'Tell us what, Mrs Raven?' said Thanet softly.

Fairleigh very deliberately replaced the receiver and cast a furious glare at Pamela. *Now look what you've done!*

Pamela was still holding his sleeve. Now she gave it a little tug. 'Don't you see, Hugo. It was bound to come out eventually. Much better that it does. We've done nothing wrong, after all.'

Fairleigh was still glowering at her and now, once again, he shook his arm to cast her off. Then he returned to his chair, slumped down into it and felt in his pocket for his cigarettes.

Pamela remained where she was, watching him with a worried frown, as if awaiting a sign.

Fairleigh lit the cigarette, inhaled deeply and leaned his head back, blowing the smoke out in a long, thin stream.

Then he shrugged, glanced at her and patted the arm of his chair.

Gratefully, eagerly, she went.

Like a little dog, thought Thanet, his dislike of Fairleigh intensifying. Despite her stand of a moment ago there was not much doubt about who called the tune in that relationship.

They both looked at him apprehensively.

'You were saying, Inspector?' said Fairleigh, with an attempt at nonchalance.

The man was a fighter, you had to grant him that.

'Tell us what?' repeated Thanet.

Again, they spoke together.

'That it was –' Hugo.

'It was I –' Pamela.

'Let me tell them,' said Pamela. Taking Fairleigh's silence for assent she took a deep breath.

'It was I who discovered that Mrs Fairleigh was dead.'

'I see.' So despite her earlier denials, she *had* been upstairs. 'Perhaps you'd better tell us exactly what happened.'

'I know I shouldn't have gone up to see her, of course. I wish to God I hadn't!'

They heard the front door open and shut.

'Oh no, there's Gwen!'

Hugo frowned. 'I thought you said she was going to be out this evening.'

'She told me she was!'

They all looked at the door.

It swung open. Gwen stopped dead on the threshold. 'Well, well,' she said, 'quite a reception committee.' Her eyes flicked an anxious, interrogatory glance at Thanet. *Have you told her?*

He shook his head imperceptibly.

Fairleigh was sharp. His eyes narrowed. *What's going on here?*

Pamela was too disconcerted by her daughter's appearance to have noticed. 'Gwen . . .' she said weakly. 'I thought you were out for the evening.'

'Yes, I thought you thought that. In fact, you were so keen to establish that I *was* going to be out that I began to wonder why. So I decided to come back, surprise you.'

'Well you've seen why now, Gwen.' Fairleigh was obviously trying to prevent himself sounding too impatient with her, but his irritation came through. 'Your mother and I are talking to the police.'

'I'm not an idiot, Hugo. I can see that. And don't treat me like a child. As whatever you're saying is bound to affect me, I'm sure the police won't object if I sit in on this.' And she walked across to a corner, picked up a pile of books from a low stool and dumped them on the floor. Then she plonked the stool down in front of the fireplace and sat down on it, hugging her knees.

How were her mother and Fairleigh going to deal with this? Thanet wondered.

'Gwen,' Pamela protested, 'I'm sure you don't want to hear all this.'

'Oh but I do, Mum. In fact, I can't wait.' Gwen glanced at Thanet. 'Do carry on, Inspector.'

It was Fairleigh's turn to try. 'Gwen! Surely it's obvious that your mother would prefer you not to be present.'

'Tough!' She hugged her knees more fiercely. 'I'm staying. If it concerns my mother it concerns me. So unless you want to physically throw me out . . .'

Pamela tried pleading. 'Darling, it's true that I really would prefer you not to be here. It's all so difficult, so embarrassing . . .'

'I see. It's all right for Hugo to be present, but not for me!'

'I didn't mean that! At least . . .' seeing that she was unable to justify that statement Pamela tried again. 'It's just that I don't want you upset, that's all.'

'Upset! Mum, try and get it into your head that I'm not a little girl to be protected from all the unpleasant things in life, not any more. I'm quite tough enough to be upset and survive, you know.'

'Yes, I know that. But –'

'No! Sorry, Mum. I'm staying.'

Fairleigh and Pamela both looked at Thanet as if to implore him to exercise his authority. The trouble was, as usual, he could see all sides. Pamela genuinely wanted to save her daughter distress and at the same time did not want to lose face in front of her. Fairleigh merely found the girl's presence an embarrassing irritation. And Gwen herself was, beneath all that bravado, genuinely concerned for her mother. True, she was no doubt partly motivated by a dislike of Hugo, but after all she was, as she said, beyond the age when she should be protected by adults for her own good. How would Bridget feel in the circumstances? he wondered. She, like Gwen, would be desperate to know what was going on. There was nothing worse than uncertainty in a situation like this. If Pamela were innocent Gwen would be relieved and delighted. If not, somehow she would have to come to terms with the fact, learn to live with it. And in either case it would not help her to be treated as a child.

'I think Gwen is sufficiently sensible to stay, if she wishes.'

Gwen smiled and ducked her head at Thanet in gratitude. Hugo scowled and Pamela sighed, her mouth tugging down at the corners.

Still, thought Thanet, the decision really should not be his alone. This particular issue was a family matter. Much as he himself would regret having to cut the interview short at this point, perhaps Pamela ought at least to be given a choice.

'However,' he added, 'there is a possible alternative. If you wish, Mrs Raven, you could come down to Sturrenden with us and make your statement there.'

He sensed Lineham stir in protest, and it was true that this would not be an ideal solution. Much of the impetus of the present interview would be lost. Pamela had obviously not intended to tell them what she had been about to tell them, and would not have prepared her story. If she chose the way out he had offered her she would have plenty of time to rehearse herself on the way down. He hadn't thought of that. He was an idiot to have suggested it.

Fairleigh had obviously come to much the same conclusion. 'Good idea,' he said, rising and putting out his hand to pull Pamela to her feet. 'I'll drive you down.'

But she did not respond. 'No, wait . . .'

They all looked at her expectantly.

After a moment she said reluctantly, 'Gwen's right. She isn't a child any more and all this does concern her.'

'But Pam . . .' said Hugo.

Gwen jumped up and crossed to put an arm around her mother's shoulders. 'Thanks, Mum.'

Fairleigh scowled. 'Pam! I really don't think this is a good idea.'

She looked up at him and shook her head. 'I'd like to get it over with.'

He stared at her in exasperation and glanced irritably at the two policemen.

Thanet was sure that if they hadn't been present the MP would have put pressure on her to change her mind. Time to intervene. 'Right,' he said pleasantly. 'That seems to be decided, then. If you'd just sit down again,' he added, glancing from Fairleigh to Gwen, 'we can proceed.'

Fairleigh hesitated and seemed about to argue further but apparently decided that there was no point. He sat down ungraciously, face set, refusing to look at Pamela who was watching him anxiously.

Gwen shot him a triumphant glance and sat down on the stool again.

When they were settled Thanet said, 'I'll just fill you in, Gwen. Your mother was just telling us that it was she who discovered that old Mrs Fairleigh was dead.'

'What?' Gwen stared incredulously at her mother. 'But how? Why?'

'That is precisely what we were about to find out,' said Thanet. 'And perhaps I could just add one condition to your being present. No interruptions. Understood?'

She gave him a mutinous look but nodded reluctantly.

'Right, then, Mrs Raven. Perhaps you would continue.'

'Well . . . I certainly hadn't planned to see her, or to go into the house at all for that matter. But it was true, what I told you last time. I did want to go to the loo, and I was wearing high heels and my feet were hurting, and I couldn't face trailing all the way back to the car park. I knew there was a loo just inside the back door. Before the house was split up it was the one we all used when we were playing tennis, it was so convenient. So I thought there'd be no harm in using that. But when I got inside, although I could hear voices in the kitchen there was no one about and I knew the stairs were only just along the corridor . . . It was just one of those things you do on impulse . . . Oh, it was so stupid of me! It's just that I was curious to see what Hugo's mother looked like after all these years, and to find out how ill she really was.'

Gwen stirred and opened her mouth but Thanet shot her a warning glance and she subsided again.

Pamela looked nervously at her daughter and said

defensively, 'If she was going to be my mother-in-law I felt . . . Well, I suppose I felt I had the right. If she was severely incapacitated I might well have to take my turn in looking after her . . . I just wanted to see for myself, that's all.'

She glanced down at Fairleigh, who by now had apparently decided that it would be politic to make the best of the situation. He gave her an encouraging nod. 'Perfectly understandable.'

'Crazy, if you ask me,' muttered Gwen.

'I thought we agreed no interruptions,' said Thanet.

'Oh, I see! *He* can say whatever he likes, but I'm not allowed to say a word!'

'Precisely!' said Thanet. 'I am interviewing your mother and Mr Fairleigh. He is entitled – indeed, I wish him to make any comments he chooses to make. But if you want to stay you *will* remain silent. Understood?'

She gave a sulky nod.

'Please go on, Mrs Raven.'

'There's not much more to tell. When I went into the room I thought at first she was asleep. Then I realised she wasn't breathing, that . . . that she was dead.' Pamela stopped, her face reflecting what she had felt at that moment: shock, disbelief.

'Did you touch her?'

'No! I just . . . Well, I panicked, I suppose. I went straight off to find Hugo. That was when I ran into the woman who must have told you she'd seen me, in the downstairs corridor.'

'Pam came to me in the garden,' said Hugo. 'She was upset, naturally, and I told her I thought she ought to go home. At that point, of course, I didn't know that there was anything . . . unnatural about my mother's death, I just assumed she'd had another stroke. I hurried up to her room to check, then I remembered seeing Doctor Mallard only a few minutes before and thought I'd better get him to take a look at her, just in case there was anything to be done. One hears of these cases when one assumes someone's dead and they're not . . .'

'Did you touch your mother?'

'Just felt for her pulse, that's all.'

'Or anything else?'

'I told you. No. On the way back in with Doctor Mallard we met my wife and told her what had happened. She came with us. Well, the rest you know, you've heard it all before.'

'And you, Mrs Raven, left immediately after speaking to Mr Fairleigh?'

'Yes.'

Which explained why her name had not been on the list compiled at the gate.

'I understand that your mother wasn't too pleased about your proposed divorce and remarriage, Mr Fairleigh.' This was a gamble, but a gamble worth taking. There was still no confirmation that that row had been with Fairleigh and, if it had, what it had been about. It would be interesting and possibly revealing to see his reaction.

'I really don't think that that's any business of yours, Inspector.'

'Don't you? You and she had a row about it, didn't you.' It was a statement, not a question.

Fairleigh stared at him and Thanet could see him trying to make up his mind: was Thanet guessing? Had someone overheard? Would it be best to deny it, and risk being proved a liar, or to admit it and find himself having to answer further questions?

Pamela frowned. 'Is that true, Hugo?'

Fairleigh's shoulders twitched in irritation. It was obvious that, used to getting his own way, he resented being forced into replying against his will.

She took his silence for assent. 'Why didn't you tell me?'

'I didn't want to upset you.'

So it was true. Thanet decided to press his luck a little further. 'It was because of that row that she had her stroke, I understand.'

'Hugo!' Pamela was on her feet, staring down at him. Either this was all news to her or she was a very good actress.

It was too much for Gwen. She too jumped up, and confronted her mother. 'You see?' she shouted. 'I told you Hugo would bring you nothing but trouble, but you wouldn't listen! That wretched old woman! She made you suffer last time and now it's happening all over again!'

'Oh, for God's sake keep out of this!' said Fairleigh, standing up and pushing his way between the two women.

Gwen tried to elbow him aside. 'Why should I?' she shouted. 'She's my mother, isn't she? Why should I just stand by and see her hurt?'

'Gwen . . .' said Pamela. 'Hugo . . .'

'That's enough!' said Thanet. 'I will not have this interview reduced to a family brawl.'

'Don't worry!' Gwen flung at him. 'I've heard enough, thank you. But believe me,' she said to Fairleigh, 'I'll have plenty more to say in the future!' And she marched out, slamming the door behind her.

They heard her run upstairs, another door slam.

'See what you've done?' said Fairleigh, turning on Thanet. 'If you hadn't allowed her to stay . . .'

'Sit down, Mr Fairleigh,' said Thanet quietly.

'It was obviously a ridiculous idea . . .'

Thanet raised his voice a little. 'Mr Fairleigh. Sit down, please.'

'It's all your fault!'

'Is it?' said Thanet coldly. 'I think not. And I repeat.

Please sit down. Or are you going to flounce out of the room too?'

His deliberate choice of verb achieved the desired effect. Fairleigh could not now leave without feeling that he had been made to look ridiculous. He shot a furious glance at Thanet before seating himself again.

'Mrs Raven?'

Thanet was interested to see that this time she did not return to the arm of Fairleigh's chair but sat on the stool which Gwen had vacated.

'Now,' said Thanet. 'I believe we're getting somewhere. It would of course have been a great deal easier on everyone if you had both volunteered all this information instead of having to have it dragged out of you. And it does, naturally, make me wonder if there are still things you haven't told me.' He noted the flicker in Fairleigh's eyes. No doubt the MP was thinking of his mother's threat to change her will. Was this the right moment to bring that up? No, he decided, he would keep that card up his sleeve for future use. Pamela's expression remained unchanged. Fairleigh obviously hadn't told her about that, either.

'What, for instance?' said Fairleigh, already regaining his aplomb.

'You tell me,' said Thanet.

Fairleigh shook his head. 'No, there's nothing else. It should give you great satisfaction, Thanet, to know that you have succeeded in dragging, as you put it, everything out of us. You can return home knowing that your work is well and truly done.'

'For the moment, perhaps. But I'm sure you understand that you are both in a somewhat difficult situation.'

'Oh come, Inspector! You are surely not suggesting that I killed my own mother just because she was against my proposed remarriage!'

Thanet rose. 'Your suggestion, not mine, Mr Fairleigh. But murder has been done for much less.' *And for much, much less than half a million pounds.* 'I would ask that neither of you makes plans to go away in the immediate future.'

Fairleigh jumped up. 'But that's ridiculous! My work takes me all over the place.'

'I see no reason why your work should not continue as normal, provided that you notify us of your whereabouts – and provided that you don't leave the country, of course.'

For once Fairleigh was speechless.

SEVENTEEN

'Luke, what on earth are you doing?'

Thanet was on his knees in the hall, surrounded by piles of newspapers. When he arrived home he had been disappointed to find that Joan was out. He'd forgotten that it was the second Monday in the month, Victim Support Group night. He'd eaten the supper which she had left for him and then dived into the cupboard under the stairs, where they kept discarded newspapers until the Scouts collected them for charity.

He sat back on his heels. 'You remember that article in one of the Sunday supplements? On famous dyslexics?'

'Yes. Why?'

'It's Richard, Mike's son. They've been having a lot of problems with him. Louise took him to see a child psychologist today, and he's been diagnosed as dyslexic.'

'Oh, no. What a shame. He's such a bright lad.'

'I know. Mike's feeling pretty low about it, as you can imagine. I tried to cheer him up, but I don't really know enough about it to be of any help. Anyway, I remembered that article and thought I'd try and look it out.'

'It was some time ago, I think. I'm afraid it'll have gone.'

'Looks like it. I've nearly finished going through these.'

Joan was feeling the soil in the pot of Alexander's

hydrangea. 'This is a bit dry. I must remember to water it in the morning. I'll make some coffee. Or would you prefer tea?'

'Tea, please. I won't be long.'

But the magazine was not there. Thanet rose stiffly, careful of his aching back, and put the newspapers away before joining Joan in the kitchen.

'I remember Susan Hampshire was in it. She wrote a book about dyslexia, didn't she?'

'Yes.' Joan frowned, thinking. 'Let me see, who else was mentioned? There was Jackie Stewart . . .'

'The racing driver?'

'Yes. And Christopher Timothy. And Beryl Reid . . . Oh, and Richard Rogers, the architect. I can't remember any more, I'm afraid. But there's a lot of help available now, from the Dyslexic Association.'

'So I gather. They gave Louise stacks of information at the clinic. Thanks.' Thanet took the cup Joan handed to him and followed her into the sitting room. He lit his pipe and relaxed, easing his stiff back muscles into a comfortable position. They went on talking for a while about Richard and then Thanet gave Joan a brief résumé of his day's activities.

'We're not getting very far, I'm afraid. The trouble is they were all there, in the house, at around the time of the murder. So they all had the opportunity. And the means, of course, was to hand.'

'And most of them had motives, too, by the sound of it. Hugo Fairleigh and his aunt because they both knew they'd benefit under her will . . .'

'Yes. And Hugo an even more powerful motive if the old lady was threatening to cut him out of it.'

'You don't really know that yet though, do you?'

'No. But I'm pretty certain of it, judging by Bassett's behaviour when we talked to him.'

'What about the woman he's in love with, Pamela Raven? Could she have done it, d'you think?'

'Well, there again she had the means and the opportunity, and if Hugo had told her that the old lady was against the marriage . . . I'm pretty certain, judging by her reaction, that she didn't know they'd actually had a row about it and certainly she was pretty shocked when she heard that it was that argument which had caused the old lady's stroke, but even so Hugo might have told her that his mother was threatening to disinherit him . . . Pamela might have thought this would make Hugo call the whole thing off, and could have seen his mother as the sole obstacle to their marriage all over again. Oh, I forgot to tell you. Her daughter came to see me this morning.'

Briefly, Thanet recounted what Gwen had told him of the subtle way old Mrs Fairleigh had gone about undermining Pamela's confidence in her ability to cope with Hugo's life-style.

Joan frowned. 'Nasty. And it worked, apparently. It was Pamela who broke it off, you say?'

'According to Gwen. Took her mother years to get over it, she said.'

'So you think Pamela might still bear a grudge?'

Thanet shrugged. 'I don't know. She seems a nice woman, I liked her. But you can never tell, can you? Old wounds go deep, as we both know, we've seen it often enough in our work. And she did know that the old lady would be unattended, except for Grace's half-hourly visits; Hugo told her. So she'd only have had to watch out for Grace coming back out of the house into the garden and she'd have known the coast was clear. But if she did do it, I wouldn't think she planned it. Maybe, as she says, she just wanted to have a look at old Mrs Fairleigh out of sheer curiosity. And then, when she saw her lying there, the temptation was too great . . .' Thanet shook his head, raised his hands helplessly. 'I just don't know,' he repeated. 'It even crossed my mind that they might have been in it together, but I think that's a bit of a non-starter. I really don't think I can see Pamela Raven sitting down and plotting it all with Hugo. And I'm pretty certain he was telling the truth when he said he had no idea she was coming to the fête.'

'What about this Mrs Tanner? She sounds pretty unbalanced to me.'

'I agree. And I certainly don't think we can rule her out. She was there, on the spot, and of all the people I've met in the case she's the one who is most outspoken about her hatred of the old woman.'

'Isn't that a good reason for thinking she must be innocent? I mean, if she'd done it, surely she'd keep quiet about how she felt?'

Thanet frowned. 'I'm not sure. She's not very bright.'

'And what about Grace Fairleigh? You haven't mentioned her yet.'

Thanet grinned. 'Ah yes. Grace. Mike suggests she's bound to have done it, on the grounds that according to the rules of detective fiction she's the most unlikely person!'

But Joan took the suggestion seriously. 'Not so unlikely, surely. It sounds to me as though anyone having to put up with Isobel Fairleigh as a mother-in-law might be tempted to finish her off if the opportunity to do so presented itself. And Grace is the only person who actually admits to being there in the room around the time of the murder.'

'I know. But I just can't see it, somehow. She doesn't seem to care enough about anything to commit murder for it. And if she's managed to put up with the old lady all these years, why kill her now, when it's pretty obvious she'd never be the same again, after such a severe stroke? And in any case Grace wouldn't have had to put up with her much longer, in view of the proposed divorce. No, it just doesn't add up.'

Suddenly Thanet was sick of talking about the case. 'Anyway, that's enough about me. What about you? What have you been doing today?'

Joan grimaced. 'Well I'm not getting very far either. Not with Michele, anyway.'

The battered girlfriend again, the one whose father had walked out in her teens, who was convinced that it was her bad behaviour that had driven him away and had been trying to punish herself ever since.

'Ah, yes. You said her mother had died a couple of weeks ago and she'd heard from her father again. He wanted to see her and she was trying to make up her mind whether to agree.'

'That's right. Well she did. See him, I mean. Yesterday. And it's had an absolutely devastating effect on her.'

'Why?'

'She's discovered that it wasn't her father's fault the marriage broke up, it was her mother's. He didn't abandon them, it was her mother who more or less threw him out. When Michele asked him why, in that case, he had just walked out like that, without telling her he was going and why, he said he couldn't bring himself to do it, he was afraid he would break down. And that he'd left her mother and her in their flat so that she, Michele, wouldn't suffer too much from the break-up by losing her home as well as her father.'

'It sounds as though he did care about her, then. But if so, why didn't he keep in touch?'

'Said he thought it was best to make a clean break, that it would be easier for her to adjust.'

'So how did she take all this?'

'Well that's the point. As I say, she's devastated. She's

spent all these years blaming herself for the break-up – and I must say, her behaviour at the time does sound pretty extreme, enough to drive any parent up the wall – and now she finds she's been looking at the whole thing the wrong way around. She's completely disorientated.'

'But she'll adjust, surely. It's a very positive thing, to have discovered for certain that she wasn't to blame. As we said when we were talking about her the other day, this could be the breakthrough you were hoping for.'

'True. No doubt, in time, it's bound to be all for the good, especially if she and her father now keep in touch.'

'Does he want to?'

'Apparently. But the thing she's finding so hard to deal with is her anger with her mother. She and her mother got on reasonably well. I wouldn't say they were close, but at least her mother was always there. But now Michele simply can't forgive her for allowing her to think all those years that her father just walked out on them. And the awful thing is, her mother's dead, she can't have it out with her, so this anger is going to stay unresolved.'

'You can only hope she'll come to terms with it eventually.'

'I know. It would help if she didn't spend all her time thinking about it, if she had something positive to focus on, a job for instance. But with her record of unemployment . . .'

'What about the drinking?'

Joan shook her head. 'That was never a problem, really. I know she was drunk when they picked her and her boyfriend up joy-riding, but I really do think she was just unlucky there. He's a bad influence on her. I'm sure she'd never have stolen a car on her own account and she's not an alcoholic, never has been.' Joan sighed. 'If only I could get her to smarten herself up and lose some weight she'd be quite presentable. She eats to compensate, you see, and I think she feels there's no point in dieting, no one will ever give her a job anyway.'

Thanet had an idea. 'Is she grossly overweight?'

Joan's eyebrows rose. 'Not grossly, no. Not really. Why?'

Thanet told her about Caroline's coffee bar and her policy of employing no one under size sixteen. 'She's recruiting staff now. In fact, she actually asked us if we knew of anyone suitable.'

Joan was enthusiastic. 'D'you think Caroline Plowright is the type to employ someone like Michele?'

'Quite possible, I should think. She's had her own problems and she might well be sympathetic. And it's not as though Michele is a thief or a con-artist.'

'I'll mention it to Michele, then, and if she's interested, go and have a word with your Caroline, see if she'd be prepared to consider taking her on. Thanks, darling, that's a brilliant idea.' Joan yawned and stretched. 'Well, I think I'm about ready to go up, are you?'

'Yes.' Thanet knocked out his pipe on the stout ashtray kept for that purpose, and stood up. 'Ben isn't in yet, though. Where is he?'

Joan glanced at the clock. 'He's been to the cinema with Chris and Mike, and then they were going to have a pizza. He should be back any minute now.'

As if on cue the front door banged and a moment later Ben came in.

'Hi!'

'Good time?' said Thanet.

'Great.' Ben grinned. 'I still can't believe it. No more exams! And the summer holidays ahead!'

Thanet smiled. It was good to see Ben looking so carefree. 'Enjoy it!' he said. 'We're just going up. You coming?'

'No, there's something I want to watch on the box.'

Thanet refrained from saying, 'At this hour?' At the moment parental restraint was definitely not the order of the day. 'Don't forget to unplug the set.' An oft-repeated maxim in the Thanet household ever since some friends of theirs had had a serious fire through omitting to do just that.

Ben grinned. 'Yes, Daddy,' he said in a little-boy voice.

In bed, Joan said, 'Odd, isn't it, how misconceptions and distorted memories can influence personality and behaviour for years, when they have no basis in reality.'

'Darling, give it a rest, will you? Switch off. We go to bed to sleep, remember?'

'Amongst other things,' said Joan teasingly, rolling over and putting her arms around him.

Thanet wasn't going to argue about that.

Next morning Lineham was late and still hadn't arrived by 8.45, the time of the morning meeting. This was so unusual that Thanet couldn't help feeling concerned. But there was no message, so presumably the sergeant wasn't ill.

The meeting was not a success from Thanet's point of view. A lack-lustre Draco listened in silence to Thanet's report, asked a few pertinent questions and then said, 'So you haven't got a single lead at the moment?'

'No, sir.'

'Has forensic come up with anything yet?'

Thanet shook his head. 'The trouble is that three of our suspects, Fairleigh, his aunt and his wife, were all in and out of that room regularly, so we're unlikely to come up with anything useful as far as they're concerned. And the same applies to Mrs Raven, who admits to being in the room even though she claims that the old lady was dead by then. Of course, if there were any evidence to prove that Mrs Tanner had been in there, that would be a different matter.'

Draco frowned. 'Better try and hurry forensic up, then, hadn't you. Sure you're not barking up the wrong tree altogether, Thanet?'

'What do you mean, sir?'

'Concentrating on the family. Oh, I know, I know,' and Draco held up his hand as Thanet opened his mouth to protest, 'it usually does turn out to be one of the nearest and dearest in a case like this. But we mustn't ignore the fact that there were a couple of thousand other people around at the time, and by your own admission it would have been relatively easy for any one of them to sneak in unseen. What have you been doing about them?'

'As soon as the list of names and addresses was typed up I put a couple of men on to it, and they've been working their way through it systematically. I've been keeping an eye on the reports they've been putting in each day, but there's been nothing of interest so I haven't bothered to mention it.'

Draco scowled. 'Sounds to me as though you're going around in circles. We really do want to get this one cleared up, or before we know where we are we'll have Fairleigh complaining of police harassment. Get on with it, Thanet, get on with it.'

All very well, thought Thanet gloomily as he climbed the stairs back up to his office. But what was there to get on with at the moment?

Lineham still hadn't turned up. Where was he?

Thanet put his head into the main CID room. 'Any message from Mike?'

Apparently not. Thanet returned to his office and sat down, still smarting from Draco's rebuke. He rang the forensic science laboratory and was told that they were doing their best. They weren't miracle men and his wasn't the only case they had to deal with. Thanet put the phone down and felt for his pipe. As Lineham wasn't here he would console himself with a smoke, put off the unwelcome moment which was, reluctant as he was to admit it, upon him.

When a case ground to a standstill, as this one apparently had, there was only one thing for it, to settle down and go conscientiously through every scrap of information which had come in and make absolutely certain that every lead had been followed up. He had learned from past experience that this could be an invaluable exercise. When you were deeply immersed in a case it often became impossible to see the wood for the trees and during a report-reading session sometimes an unexpected overall picture emerged, obscured until then by the day-to-day trickle of information. Connections hitherto missed could be spotted, new angles become evident.

His pipe was burning steadily now and with a sigh he took out the first file and opened it.

He was coming to the end of the report on the interview with Caroline Plowright when feet pounded up the stairs and Lineham came in with a rush.

'Sorry, sir. I thought I'd never get here! I had to take Richard to school and go in to see his teacher, explain to her what the psychologist had said. Louise was going to do it, but her car wouldn't start. I didn't think it would take so long, or I'd have rung in.' Lineham coughed and glanced reproachfully at Thanet's pipe.

Thanet laid it down in the ashtray. 'I know, I know. Open the window wide and leave the door ajar for a few minutes, the smoke'll soon clear.'

Lineham flung the window open and watched the coils of smoke drift out. He grinned. 'Let's hope they don't call out the fire brigade.'

'You sound a little more cheerful this morning, Mike. Tell me what Louise had to say about Richard.'

Lineham perched on the corner of Thanet's desk. 'Well, dyslexia is apparently a sort of umbrella term covering problems with visual and auditory memory, and the sequencing of sounds, letters, numbers and so on. They gave Louise a lot of tips on how to cope with the everyday aspect of it. It all sounds pretty intimidating, I must say. Apparently dyslexics find it very difficult to be organised so we have to try to make it easier for Richard by, for instance, marking every single item he takes to school. All his shoes have to be marked with an R and an L, so that he knows which foot they go on. And we have to check every morning that he has everything he needs to take with him and every evening that he's brought it all home again, whether there are any letters from the school in his pockets or lunchbox. When we ask him to do things we've got to be specific. It's no good saying, "Tidy your room", we have to say, "Pick up all the books and put them on the shelves, pick up your toys and put them in the cupboard" – that sort of thing.'

'What about learning difficulties?'

'Hard to generalise, apparently. They vary from one dyslexic to another. Some cope pretty well. We just have to wait and see. But it should be easier for Richard now that the school knows he's not just being lazy or bloody-minded.'

Lineham stood up and began to wander restlessly around, picking things up and putting them down without really seeing them. 'There's no point in denying we're worried, especially about his future. And it's going to involve a pretty big adjustment all round. It's funny, there you are, going along as normal and then something happens which shakes you rigid. And the extraordinary thing is, the situation existed all the time. It hasn't changed, but your perception of it has, and you feel, well . . .' Lineham paused, groping for words. 'It's as if there's been a minor earthquake in your life. You look around and everything's the same but different.' He shook his head. 'I'm not explaining this very well. It's a hell of a shock.' He glanced at Thanet. 'What's the matter, sir?'

Thanet shook his head. 'Sorry, Mike. I am listening, and I do understand what you're trying to say, but I've just got to think for a minute . . .' He put his elbows on the desk and closed his eyes, lowering his head and clasping his hands over the top of it to contain his excitement. Without warning, tumblers were clicking over in his brain. He had experienced this sensation before, a surge of exhilaration and a sense of dawning enlightenment which was virtually indescribable. He waited, scarcely daring to breathe, for the turmoil in his mind to ease and then suddenly, with a kind of sweet inevitability, that elusive last piece of the jigsaw fell into place and he had it, the whole picture, clear and true. Was it possible? His mind raced, testing, checking, and yes, he was certain now. He raised his head. Lineham was staring at him. 'Mike, you're brilliant!'

'I am?'

Galvanised, Thanet jumped up, unable to contain his excitement. 'Yes! What you just said!'

'What did I just say?'

'Listen!' Thanet began to explain, watching the dawning understanding on Lineham's face, the beginnings of enthusiasm and finally an excitement which matched Thanet's own. Almost. 'There're an awful lot of assumptions there, sir.'

'Maybe. But you must admit, it fits. Everything fits. Doesn't it?'

'Well, yes . . .'

'I'm right, I know it, you'll see. Meanwhile, there are things to do.' Thanet shoved away the stack of files with an impatient hand and grabbed a piece of paper. 'I'll make a list.'

EIGHTEEN

Thanet's mood had changed. On the two-hour drive back to Sturrenden he had had plenty of time to think and his initial exhilaration, boosted further by the interview just conducted, had dwindled to a mere spark as they approached the next stage in the inquiry.

During the course of a murder investigation he was always obsessed by one question: who had committed the crime? Every thought, every effort was directed to this end, and it was as if, beyond this point, the future did not exist. It was only when he had found the answer that he began to think ahead and ask himself, what now? What effect would the arrest have upon the other people involved in the case and, worse, had the murder even perhaps been understandable? Not forgivable, no. In Thanet's book murder could never be justified. Often, of course, there was no problem. If the crime had been particularly brutal, if mindless violence or sadistic enjoyment had been involved, his feelings of triumph were unalloyed and he would find nothing but fulfilment and satisfaction in bringing the criminal to justice. But he did sometimes find, as in this case, that dangerous compassion for the murderer could creep in and he could even ask himself, if I had found myself in that position, would I have behaved as he or she did? He knew that he should not, could not allow such thoughts to influence his behaviour, but there was no point in denying that they didn't help him to be as single-minded as he ought to be.

No, he was not looking forward to the coming confrontation; confrontation and, with any luck, arrest.

For there was no doubt about it, luck would be needed. As Lineham had pointed out, they had no shred of evidence that would stand up in court. If they failed to extract a confession then that would be that. Even feeling as he did, he refused to allow himself to consider the possibility that this might happen.

So as the now-familiar gates of Thaxden Hall loomed ahead his stomach clenched. He wanted to get this over with. What if the suspect were out? He glanced at his watch. The various inquiries they had had to make during the day had taken longer than he hoped, but perhaps this would now work to his advantage. At 6.30 in the evening most people were at home.

Lineham, too, looked tense, his hands gripping the steering wheel more tightly than usual. They entered the drive and gravel crunched beneath their wheels.

As they stepped out of the car silence enfolded them and Thanet became aware that it was a perfect summer evening. All day he had been so wrapped up in their various activities that he hadn't even noticed the weather, but now, despite his preoccupation, the peace and beauty of the old house and grounds claimed his attention. The mellow rose-red brick glowed in the early evening sunlight and as they approached the front door Thanet noticed for the first time that the borders along the front of the house were planted exclusively with white and silver plants. The mingled scents of white roses, white phlox, night-scented stocks and nicotiana drifted to meet them.

Lineham seized his arm as they waited for the door to open. He pointed at the sky. 'Look!'

They moved out beyond the shelter of the portico for a better view. High above the trees over to their left a huge bird was circling. Thanet had never seen anything like it before.

'What d'you think it is, sir?'

'No idea.' He turned as Sam opened the door, beckoned and pointed. 'What's that?'

She moved out to join them. 'That's Carvic.'

'Carvic?'

'He's a heron. There's a big pond over in the trees, he often comes there to fish.'

'Strange name.'

She laughed. 'It's a private joke.' She was more formally dressed tonight, a Laura Ashley frock by the look of it, thought Thanet, knowledgeable about such things by now after years of a teenage daughter.

The heron swooped down, disappearing into the trees, and Thanet turned reluctantly away. 'We've come to see Mrs Fairleigh.'

She glanced at him sharply. Something in his tone had made her uneasy. She frowned and led the way into the house. 'She may be changing for dinner. Would you wait here, please, while I go and see?'

Thanet wondered whether Grace Fairleigh changed for dinner every evening, even when she dined alone. But Fairleigh had said that Sam always ate with the family. Perhaps that was why she was wearing a dress.

'Just a moment, Sam, before you go. One small point . . . Could you tell me if there have been any letters for old Mrs Fairleigh either today or yesterday?'

She shook her head firmly. 'No.'

'You're sure? Only when I last spoke to you about the letters you said you never bothered to look at who they were for, once you'd checked that there were none for you.'

'I know, but yesterday and today I did, perhaps because you'd been asking questions about them. There were definitely none for Hugo's mother.'

Thanet nodded his satisfaction. Just as he expected.

He and Lineham were silent while they waited, both preoccupied with thoughts of the coming interview. Thanet had already decided to play it by ear, but now he ran over in his mind the various points that he must bring up.

Sam appeared on the landing and leaned over the balustrade. 'You can come up.'

She led them to a door at the far end of the right-hand corridor and opened it. They went in and she closed it behind them. In the silence Thanet could hear her soft footfalls receding along the landing.

It was a small sitting room with windows on two sides on the front corner of the house – small by the standards of Thaxden Hall, that is, but still larger than Thanet's sitting room at home. Evening sunshine poured in through the tall sash window facing him, momentarily dazzling him. He blinked a couple of times to clear his vision.

Grace Fairleigh was standing by one of the windows on the left. 'Did you see it?' she said. 'The heron?'

'Yes. I'd never seen one before.'

'I watch out for him every evening. He doesn't always come.' She turned away from the window. 'What can I do for you, Inspector, Sergeant? Sit down, won't you.'

It was an attractive room, graceful, feminine, with a green and cream colour scheme which seemed to merge with the tranquil rural views through the windows. On a wing chair near one of these lay a tapestry frame with a half-worked design stretched on it. On the floor nearby was an open workbag with a jumble of wools spilling out. There were books on the shelves in the fireplace alcoves, a television set and a compact disc player. This, evidently, was the room

Grace Fairleigh used in preference to the formal drawing room downstairs and interestingly enough it reminded Thanet to some extent of the sitting room of Pamela Raven's flat in London. Perhaps, underneath, the two women were not so different after all. He looked at Grace more closely, noting that as ever she was immaculately groomed, hair in a smooth chignon, make-up perfectly applied. She was wearing a short-sleeved sheath dress in pale blue linen, its elegant simplicity proclaiming its cost more clearly than any label. She looked as beautiful, unattainable and unreal as the models who float down the catwalk of the international fashion shows. And there, of course, lay the difference between the two women. Thanet thought now, as he had thought the first time he met Pamela Raven, that he could understand why Fairleigh had turned from his wife to his mistress. Who would not prefer a living, breathing woman to an empty shell, however beautiful?

She was watching him expectantly and he sighed inwardly. Better get on with it. 'Mrs Fairleigh, there is no point in pretending that this interview is going to be pleasant.'

Her perfectly plucked eyebrows arched slightly.

'We know, you see, what happened on Saturday afternoon.'

'Really?' She sounded no more moved or interested than if they had been discussing the weather.

'We have just returned from a visit to your former nanny, Rita Symes. She's Rita Kenny now, and lives in Suffolk. But of course you know that, don't you?'

Her composure did not falter and she made no response, but for the first time a hint of some emotion showed in her eyes. What was it? Not fear, nor apprehension. But comprehension, yes, and a touch of resignation, perhaps?

It had taken some hours of intense activity to track the

woman down and find out her present whereabouts. When, finally, they had succeeded, there had followed some tense moments while they waited for her to answer the telephone. Would she be out? Away on holiday and inaccessible? But she was neither, and a triumphant Lineham had finally put the phone down and said, 'Three o'clock this afternoon!'

They hadn't known what to expect but the substantial four-bedroomed detached house on a new housing estate had come as no surprise. Rita Kenny, after all, had enjoyed a substantial private income. A new Metro was parked in the driveway.

'She has a very comfortable life-style, as you can imagine. But I can't say that she was exactly pleased to see us.'

An understatement. After fourteen years Rita must until recently have felt that she was safe for ever. She had armoured herself in hair-spray and heavy make-up, but her close-set eyes had been reluctant to meet his and her mouth was pinched with anxiety.

They had had no proof of what he suspected, of course. Thanet could only hope that the bluff he had planned would be successful.

He began formally. 'You are Rita Kenny, formerly Rita Symes, employed in 1978 as nanny to the infant son of Mr and Mrs Hugo Fairleigh of Thaxden Hall, Thaxden, in Kent?'

As he had hoped, this approach, with its formal overtones of courtroom procedure, intimidated her. He saw her throat move in an involuntary swallow of fear.

She glanced from one to the other. 'Yes.'

'You probably know, from reports in the newspapers and on television, that Mr Fairleigh's mother, Mrs Isobel Fairleigh, was found dead last Saturday, and that she had been murdered. Naturally the police were called in and during the course of our investigation we found this.'

He took an envelope from his pocket. This was an enormous gamble. He didn't know if it was the right colour or even the right shape. Guessing that she would have wanted it to be as inconspicuous as possible they had finally chosen a white envelope of standard size and quality. He held it up briefly, careful to allow her no more than the briefest glimpse of the printed capitals on the front – even more of a gamble, then tapped it from time to time on the palm of his left hand to emphasise the points he was making. He shook his head. 'Very careless of you, I'm afraid, Mrs Kenny. Blackmailers should never commit themselves to paper. Especially when what they say implicates them in a much more serious crime.'

She managed to summon up some bravado. 'I don't know what you're talking about.' But her fear was growing. He saw the sheen of perspiration on her forehead and could tell that the palms of her hands were sweating too: she was rubbing them on her thighs, forward and back in unconscious self-betrayal. And she had said nothing about the envelope. They must have guessed correctly. The bluff was working.

'Oh, I think you do, Mrs Kenny. And if you don't now, you certainly will when you're standing in the dock accused of being an accessory to murder and the jury read this letter to prove it.'

She abandoned her pose of incomprehension and jumped up, back of hand to mouth. 'That's not true! I didn't do a thing!'

'Ah, but you did, Mrs Kenny, didn't you? You committed a criminal act, and compounded it by following up with another. You stood by and did nothing, knowing that an innocent child in your care had been murdered, and then for years you profited from that knowledge by blackmailing the murderer. You call that nothing?'

That was the point at which she had broken down and he knew that they had won. It took some time but in between the bursts of self-justification and hysteria they had eventually managed to get the whole story from her.

Grace was staring at him as if mesmerised, waiting for him to continue. He braced himself, knowing that he must go on, knowing too that what he had to say next would sound brutal. Trying to cushion the blow he spoke gently. 'She told us what happened, the night your baby died.'

She flinched as if he had struck her and her eyes filled with a pain which had not diminished with the passage of the years.

'It was a terrible thing to happen. Please believe me when I say I'm sorry, I'm very sorry to . . .'

'What did happen?' she interrupted, her voice harsh, almost unrecognisable. 'I want to know.'

'Mrs Fairleigh . . .'

'I want to *know*! Can't you see? I have to *know*!' Her voice broke and tears spilled over and began to roll down her cheeks. She brushed them away with a fierce, impatient gesture.

'Mrs Fairleigh, I really don't think . . .'

'I must!' She stood up, as if impelled by an invisible force, and took two rapid steps towards the window before turning. 'All these years, I thought . . . And then to find out . . . I can't bear it! I've thought of nothing else since Saturday, lying awake at night imagining . . . Please, Inspector, tell me!' She sat down again, on the very edge of her chair, leaning forward and fixing him with an imploring look which pierced him with dread and compassion.

Beside him Lineham cleared his throat and shifted uncomfortably. The sergeant was finding this as harrowing as he was.

'Very well. If you're sure.'

'I am.'

Slowly, choosing his words with care, Thanet told her what they had learned. She listened in silence, and then, when he had finished, buried her face in her hands, struggling but failing to keep back the tears. Thanet longed to go to her, to put his arm around her shoulders and comfort her, but Lineham's presence inhibited him and besides his task was not yet done. He felt a monster, contemplating what he had to do next. He took a clean handkerchief from his pocket and laid it on her lap.

She fumbled it up, began to wipe her face, shook her head. 'I'm sorry . . .'

'Please, don't worry about it.' An inadequate response, but what else could he say?

She was drying her eyes, wiping her face again, more thoroughly. Finally she blew her nose and gave a shaky little laugh. 'I'll have to buy you a new handkerchief, Inspector.'

The unexpected touch of humour broke the tension and Thanet heard Lineham give a little sigh of relief. Surely the next stage of the interview couldn't possibly be worse than the last?

Her composure was returning and now she sat back and gave a wry smile. 'I assure you I don't make a habit of airing my feelings in public like this.' There were still streaks of mascara on her face. The mask of perfection which she had always presented to the world had gone and she was different, more approachable, more human.

'I know that.'

'And thank you. I appreciate that it couldn't have been easy for you to tell me. But I can't tell you what a relief it is, to know, at last.' She gave him an assessing look. 'I suppose you now want to talk about what happened on Saturday.'

He nodded.

'Well, I'm not going to be difficult. I'm not going to protest my innocence, stand on my rights or call a solicitor. To be honest, it'll be a relief to get it over with. I'm not cut out for this sort of thing and I don't think my conscience would have allowed me to go on lying in my teeth much longer . . . Aren't you going to charge me, first?'

He could hardly believe it. Was she going to confess, with no further ado? It scarcely seemed possible.

'Caution you, yes.' He nodded at Lineham and the sergeant delivered the familiar words.

Then he sat back to listen.

NINETEEN

Joan fastened her seatbelt with a little sigh of contentment. 'I'm looking forward to this.'

'So am I.'

They were going to dinner with Doc Mallard and his wife, and Helen's meals were always memorable. Thanet had accepted the invitation with alacrity.

'Helen's bursting with curiosity about the Fairleigh case, you see,' Mallard had said. 'So she thought she'd bribe you with good food.'

'Helen can bribe me with her cooking any time she likes!' said Thanet.

'I've never known her to be quite so interested before,' said Mallard. 'It's because she was there at the beginning of it, I think. She's felt more involved.'

By then, of course, everyone knew that Grace Fairleigh had confessed and had been charged with the murder of her mother-in-law.

'You know what women are like,' Mallard went on. 'They need to know the ins and outs of everything.' He grinned. 'And I don't mind admitting that I'd like to hear the whole story myself.'

Thanet didn't talk about his work to outsiders, never had and never would, but the Mallards were different. Doc

Mallard was one of the team and Helen's discretion could be relied upon. When Thanet told Joan about the invitation she had said that she would wait until Saturday too, to hear the details. Thanet had in any case been very busy dealing with all the administration attendant upon the winding up of a murder inquiry and there had been no opportunity to talk at length.

He glanced at his wife, cool and summery in a deep blue cotton dress splashed with white flowers. Her face and arms were tanned and she looked fit and relaxed. He took his hand from the steering wheel and laid it briefly over hers. 'Did I tell you how gorgeous you look?'

Joan gave him a teasing smile. 'No, but I knew you'd get around to it sooner or later.'

'Don't be smug!'

It was another lovely evening and Doc Mallard led them through to the conservatory which he and Helen had built on to the back of their bungalow a couple of years ago and which the Mallards used as a summer dining room.

Joan exclaimed with delight. 'Isn't this beautiful!'

It was a miniature version of the conservatory at Thaxden Hall. Exotic plants in massive Chinese ceramic pots stood about on the floor of terracotta tiles, climbing plants in bloom were trained up the walls and across the roof-struts, and the delicately arched windows framed views of the garden. Beyond, the evening sky was flushed with turquoise, rose and amber. Birdsong drifted in through the open double doors, together with the mingled scents of roses and of the herbs which Helen grew in pots on the patio outside.

Helen was pleased. 'We love this room. I spend most of my free time out here.'

They had a leisurely drink and then moved across to the table. The first course was iced cream of watercress soup, served with hot, crusty home-made garlic rolls.

They all tasted it. 'Delicious!'

They had agreed that they would not discuss the case until after dinner and Helen began by asking again after Bridget. She was very fond of her and had got to know her well because of their shared interest in cookery. Bridget had spent many a holiday afternoon at the Mallards' bungalow helping Helen to experiment with new recipes she was devising for her books. 'At the fête you were just going to tell us why you didn't like this new boyfriend of hers, when James was called away by Mr Fairleigh.'

'Ah, yes, Alexander.' Thanet pulled a face. 'Well, perhaps I'm being unfair, but he just doesn't seem Bridget's type.'

'Why not?'

'He's obviously very well off, drives a Porsche . . .'

'A Porsche!' said Mallard, eyebrows going up.

'Ben was most impressed,' said Joan.

Mallard grinned. 'I can imagine.'

Joan laughed. 'Alexander took him out for a short drive in it on Sunday morning. Ben was hoping his friends would see him, but no luck, I'm afraid.'

'Right,' said Mallard. 'So he's got plenty of money and drives an expensive motorcar. Is that a bad thing?'

'Not necessarily,' said Thanet. 'But it's his background, too.' He thought of the problems that Pamela Raven had had with Hugo's life-style. 'His parents are obviously very well off. Alexander went to public school and seems to have been everywhere and done everything. Travelled half around the world, it seems.'

'So have a lot of young people these days,' said Mallard. 'It's very much the done thing.'

'And then, he's so much older than her, about twenty-seven, twenty-eight, I should say.'

'One foot in the grave!' said Helen.

Thanet gave a shamefaced laugh.

'Isn't a certain amount of experience a good thing?' said

Mallard. 'It means he's that much better equipped to deal with the nasty little shocks life throws at us from time to time. And a lot of people would be delighted that he would be able to provide for their daughter in an even better style than that to which she is accustomed. No, come on, Luke, so far you haven't given us one good reason to disapprove of him. All right, so they come from different backgrounds. But Bridget's an intelligent girl and a sensible one. She could adapt, if necessary.'

Helen was nodding.

'I don't know why we're all talking as if this is necessarily going to be a permanent relationship,' said Joan. 'Bridget's always changing boyfriends. And some of them have been a good deal less acceptable than Alexander. Remember the one with the hair, the black leather jacket covered with studs and the great big motorbike? I nearly had a heart attack every time he roared off with Bridget on the pillion!'

'True.'

'And you haven't told us yet what he's like as a person,' said Helen.

'Well, the evening they came down Joan had cooked a special meal to celebrate the end of Ben's O levels. They were supposed to arrive between seven and eight and it was nearly ten by the time they got here. Alexander had been held up at work, some crisis or another, and it was 8.30 before he even bothered to ring Bridget to explain.'

'But he might genuinely have been unable to get away to make a private phone call until then,' said Joan. 'And he did apologise profusely. And they didn't know I'd prepared a special meal for them, did they?'

'No . . .'

'He even apologised to Ben, for spoiling his celebration dinner. In fact, he went out of his way to be nice to Ben, as I've said.'

'Yes . . .'

'And he bought me a gorgeous present, the most lovely hydrangea – *and* wrote a thank-you note, afterwards. It's the first time any boyfriend of Bridget's has done that.'

'And what was his attitude to Bridget?' said Helen.

Thanet glanced at Joan. 'You'd know more about that. I hardly saw him after that first evening, because of the case.'

'He seemed thoughtful and considerate. Consulted her wishes and so on.'

'So in fact,' said Mallard. 'You really can't find a single thing to say against him.'

'Yet!' said Thanet, reluctant to admit that he had perhaps been wrong. He realised that he'd been so engrossed in the conversation that his soup was gone almost without his having tasted it. He watched regretfully as Helen stood up and began collecting the soup plates.

Mallard rose too. 'I'll give you a hand.' He picked up the soup tureen then gave Thanet a penetrating look over his half-moon spectacles. 'Honestly, Luke, it sounds to me as though you're being prejudiced for no good reason. Maybe you won't like me saying so, but perhaps you ought to ask yourself if you'd feel the same about any boyfriend Bridget brought home.'

Mallard was one of the very few people from whom Thanet would take such personal criticism. He was upset, however. He had always been proud of the way he and Joan had managed to nurture Bridget and Ben towards independence. But it was true that he and Bridget had always been very close. Was he, in the last resort, unable to let go?

'I've never had any children of my own, of course,' Mallard went on, 'so it's easy for me to say, but it seems to me that most parents feel that no one is ever quite good enough for their son or daughter. They want the perfect mate for them, but the truth is, as you know only too well, Luke, no one is perfect.' And with this pronouncement Mallard bore the tureen off into the kitchen.

There was an uncomfortable silence. Thanet glanced at Joan, but she was avoiding his eye, staring at a piece of roll which she was crumbling between her fingers.

'You agree with him, don't you?' he said in a low voice.

She looked at him now, uneasily. 'Don't you?'

Thanet sighed. 'Perhaps.' But he knew it was true. For Bridget he wanted a paragon, and Mallard was right, paragons did not exist. There was the difference in background, yes, but again he had to agree with Mallard. Bridget was intelligent, sensible, adaptable. She would learn to cope, if necessary. And apart from that he really couldn't think of any way in which Alexander fell short. The boy couldn't help having been born into a solid middle-class background. Could it be that Alexander, with his public-school education and traveller's tales, had made him, Thanet, feel inadequate and therefore prejudiced? It was an uncomfortable thought.

'Maybe I have been unfair.'

Joan smiled and reached out to squeeze his hand. 'A little, perhaps.'

Helen came in ceremonially bearing a long oval platter. On it was an exquisitely presented cold salmon on a bed of frilled green lettuce leaves, decorated along its entire length with slices of cucumber so thin as to be almost transparent.

'That looks wonderful!' said Thanet, abandoning his unpalatable insight with relief.

'Seems a pity to spoil it by cutting it up,' said Joan, as Helen began deftly to dissect the fish.

Mallard was depositing vegetable dishes on the table: tiny new potatoes steamed in their jackets, buttered and sprinkled with finely chopped parsley; crunchy mangetout peas; and the *pièce de résistance*, a *confit* of baby vegetables braised, as Helen told them later, in a sealed pot with chicken stock, butter and rosemary and served in little nests of lightly cooked spinach.

This was followed by a *mélange* of fresh raspberries and strawberries steeped in Cointreau.

'A perfect meal for a summer evening,' sighed Joan as she laid down her dessert spoon.

'What I'd like to know,' said Thanet to Doc Mallard, 'is how you manage to stay so slim on Helen's cooking.'

'Ah, well she secretly starves me most of the time, you know.' Mallard gave Helen an affectionate glance. 'All this is just to throw people off the scent.'

Helen laughed. 'Coffee, everybody?'

Mallard stood up. 'No, from now on you're not moving from your chair. I'll do it.'

When at last coffee and liqueur chocolates had been distributed and they were settled the Mallards looked expectantly at Thanet.

'Now,' said Mallard. 'As our transatlantic cousins put it, shoot!'

'Where d'you want me to begin?'

Joan waved a hand. 'At the beginning, where else?'

TWENTY

Thanet sipped his coffee, marshalling his thoughts. Then, for Helen's benefit, he filled in the background to the case, sketching each of the personalities involved and the complexities of their relationships, past and present.

'So the problem was, you see, as I said to Joan the other night, all the suspects had the opportunity, and the pillow was there to hand. It would have taken only a few minutes for any of them to slip along to Isobel Fairleigh's room, commit the crime and return to whatever they were doing without having been away long enough for anyone to have noticed their absence. And they all, except apparently for Grace Fairleigh, had a motive. It was, of course, the first murder which led to the second, but we didn't know that at the time.'

'That's what I want to know,' said Mallard. 'What on earth put you on to that?'

This was usually the difficult part: how to get people to understand that final intuitive leap which led him to the solution? Thanet sighed. 'I'll try to explain. It began, of course, as it always does in a murder of this type, with trying to understand the people involved, and especially the character of the victim. Isobel Fairleigh was, as I've already said, a difficult woman. That was obvious from the start.

But gradually a fuller picture emerged. She was ruthless, for a start, and saw the world as existing to serve her needs, always a dangerous combination. So I had to ask myself what those needs were. What had she wanted most out of life? Her father was much to blame, according to her sister Letty. He encouraged her to believe that she could get or do anything she wanted, and what she wanted at first was vicarious power, through her husband, who was a promising politician. But her ambition was thwarted when he died relatively young, and so she transferred her hopes to her son. She was determined to ensure that Hugo would achieve what his father had failed to, and she worked very hard on his behalf in the constituency. She managed to avert an undesirable early marriage by some particularly unpleasant manipulation, and approved wholeheartedly when he married a more suitable girl, of his own class and admirably equipped to be the wife of a successful politician.

'The first thing that went wrong was that Grace, instead of providing Hugo with a healthy heir, produced a Down's syndrome child. This didn't suit Isobel at all. A lolling idiot, as she saw the baby, would as he grew up increasingly become an embarrassment to Hugo in his public career, would be incapable of handling the family home and fortune which he would inherit or of fathering suitable future heirs and, worse, would constantly reflect adversely upon Isobel herself. Self-image was very important to her and the thought of having to parade a mongol grandson didn't appeal to her one little bit. She was a perfectionist herself and had to have the perfect son, the perfect family, the perfect home. She must almost at once have decided what she was going to do when the opportunity arose, and hid the revulsion she must have felt towards the child. I don't think she saw him as a human being at all, but simply as an obstacle to be removed. I imagine that as she saw it, this particular brand of lightning rarely strikes twice. Grace would soon get over losing the baby and produce other, healthy children. Unfortunately this never happened. As I said, Grace was passionately devoted to the baby and never really recovered from its death.'

Helen shivered. 'It's horrible. How could Isobel Fairleigh do such a thing? A helpless little baby . . .'

'She could and she did. Her determination must have been strengthened when, having acquitted himself well on a tough Labour by-election, a few months after the baby was born Hugo was selected as Conservative candidate for Sturrenden on the death of the current MP, Arnold Bates. It was what Isobel had always hoped for. Sturrenden was a safe seat and there was little doubt that Hugo would get in. So she bided her time, watching for her opportunity. It came halfway through the by-election campaign, when the baby was about six months old. He had a cold and both Grace and Hugo were to be away for the night. But she hadn't taken Grace's concern for the child sufficiently into account. Grace was very reluctant to leave the baby as it wasn't well, and at first said she wouldn't accompany Hugo to the function in London as planned. But Hugo was angry and kicked up a fuss, so eventually Grace did agree to go, but only after making the nanny, Rita Symes, promise to look in on the baby a couple of times during the night. Isobel, of course, didn't know any of this. The baby had for some time been sleeping right through the night and she knew that Rita wouldn't normally go into the nursery until around seven, by which time the baby would have been long dead.'

'I don't know whether I can bear to listen to this,' said Joan. 'Can we skip the details?'

Helen nodded. 'I agree.'

But those details were engraved on Thanet's mind.

Rita had dutifully set her alarm for two o'clock, when the

baby had been all right. He had been snuffling, but there had been nothing that she could do to make him more comfortable and, leaving his door ajar, she had gone back to bed, setting her alarm for five.

This time she entered the nursery to find Isobel Fairleigh turning away from the cot, holding a small pillow in both hands. One glance told Rita that the child had stopped breathing. She had thrust the older woman aside and administered the kiss of life, but her efforts were in vain. Isobel had stood by, watching, until Rita had finally straightened up.

The nanny had turned on her.

'You monster! How could you! I'm going to ring the police.'

Isobel had caught her by the arm as she turned towards the door. 'Wait! I don't think you've thought this through.'

'What is there to think about?'

She had attempted to shake her arm free, but Isobel's grip had been like iron, her face implacable.

Thanet became aware that the others were waiting for him to go on. 'Let's just say that, having been caught in the act, Isobel set out to convince Rita that it would be in her own best interests to keep quiet. First of all she threatened that if Rita insisted on going to the police she would blame the nanny for the child's death.'

'If there's an investigation, it would be your word against mine, wouldn't it?'

'What do you mean?'

'I could say that I was worried about my grandson because he had a cold, that I came in to find you holding a pillow over his face . . .'

'You wouldn't! You couldn't!'

'Try me! And who do you think they'd believe? Me, a

respected pillar of the community, or you, a nobody from nowhere?'

Appalled, Rita had stopped struggling to free herself from Isobel's grip and stared at the old woman. Isobel meant every word she said, she could see that. What was she to do?

'And then,' said Thanet, 'Isobel threw in an added inducement. Money. Substantial amounts of it.'

She had swooped in for the kill. 'Besides, this could all turn out to be to your advantage.'

'Advantage? How?' Rita had renewed her efforts to tug herself free. 'You're out of your mind, d'you know that? Crazy.'

'Advantage. Yes. Do you really enjoy this work, Rita? Wiping the bottoms of other people's babies, being at the beck and call of your employers day and night? Just think, you need never work again.'

'What do you mean?'

Rita had begun to waver and Isobel was swift to recognise the fact. Taking her to another room she had begun to talk, persuasively. The baby had been handicapped, its quality of life would have been poor, Isobel had positively done it a favour by putting it out of its misery. Its death would benefit everybody. Hugo would not have to endure the humiliation of parading a mongol child in public and Grace was young, she would soon get over this and have other, healthy children. No one would ever suspect what had happened. Cot deaths were common, the child had a cold, everyone knew that Down's syndrome babies were especially vulnerable to infections. She, Isobel, was quite prepared to carry out her threat of blaming Rita if Rita insisted on dragging the police into it. She would argue that Rita herself had called the police in order to give credence to her story and cast suspicion away from herself. But she really would prefer to avoid any unpleasant and unnecessary fuss, and if Rita agreed she was prepared to make it worth her while. She, Isobel, was wealthy, and could see her way to making Rita a generous allowance, far more than she could ever hope to earn as a nanny.

'An initial payment of five thousand pounds, to be precise,' said Thanet, 'a lot of money in those days, followed by regular monthly payments which would increase along with inflation. The temptation was too much and Rita gave in. Isobel told her what her story should be. Rita would say that her second visit to the child had been at 4.30, not 5, and that the child had still been alive. The next time she checked, at 6.30, he was dead. She had attempted resuscitation through the kiss of life, but without success. She had then rung the doctor and gone to wake up Isobel, tell her what had happened.'

'But how could she hope to get away with it?' said Joan. 'There's always a post mortem in cases of cot death, isn't there?'

They all looked at Mallard, who shook his head sadly. 'I'm afraid that unless there is reason for suspicion, the PM of a cot death is very much a formality. The pathologist would look for bruises, broken bones – reasons to suspect child abuse, in fact – and also do a routine examination of heart, lungs, tissue, brain and so on for obvious medical causes for the death. But if, as in this case, there had been no abuse and the baby had been snuffly or a bit chesty, and especially in the case of a Down's syndrome child who is very susceptible to infections, well, I don't think he'd look any further. Sad, but true. I think they'd get away with it all right – well, they did, didn't they?'

'They certainly did,' said Thanet grimly. He had read the reports of the inquest. 'There's no doubt about it, if it hadn't been for Rita's untimely arrival Isobel would have been home and dry.'

'It's appalling,' said Helen.

'But surely,' said Mallard, 'it's extraordinary that a woman like Isobel Fairleigh, if she was as ruthless as you say, should have been content to go on paying out large sums of money to someone like that year after year without a murmur?'

'Yes,' said Helen. 'What could the girl have done, if Isobel had simply stopped paying up?'

'Quite,' said Joan. 'She couldn't have given Isobel away to the police without incriminating herself.'

'I know. She knew that too, and so did Isobel, I'm sure. But she also knew Isobel,' said Thanet. Just as I do, he thought. After only a few days he felt he knew the arrogant, self-centred old lady as well, perhaps better, than had her own family. 'She knew Isobel would never risk it. Isobel was a proud woman, proud of her son, proud of her family name and above all proud of herself. Her self-image really mattered to her, more than almost anything, I would say.'

'In that case, I'm surprised she didn't take the other way out,' said Mallard. 'Don't they say that murder is easier the second time around? Frankly, I find it surprising that the nanny is still with us.'

'Ah, there's a simple explanation for that. Rita Symes is no fool. She was well aware of the threat to her own safety, so she long ago took the precaution of depositing with her solicitor a letter setting out all the facts, to be opened only in the case of her own death by anything other than natural causes. And of course she made sure that Isobel knew about it.'

'They really were a delightful pair, weren't they!' said Helen, with a grimace of distaste.

'Anyway, you still haven't explained how you got on to all this,' said Mallard.

'Well, it was chiefly something that Joan said, together with a remark that Lineham made, next day.'

'You didn't tell me that,' said Joan. 'Something I said? What?'

'As I recall, I more or less told you to shut up at the time . . .'

'Tut tut,' said Mallard. 'Disharmony in the Thanet household? I don't believe it!'

'It was when we were in bed, after we'd been talking about Michele. Remember?'

Joan was shaking her head, looking blank.

'You said, as nearly as I can recall, that it was odd how misconceptions and distorted memories can influence personality and behaviour for years, when they have no basis in reality.'

'Good grief!' said Mallard. 'Is that the kind of pillow talk you indulge in? I wonder the marriage has lasted so long! We're much less intellectual, aren't we, Helen?'

He and Helen smiled at each other. 'Oh yes, much!' she said.

'All right,' said Thanet. 'Forget the double act. Do you want to hear this or not?'

Mallard pulled an exaggeratedly contrite face. 'Sorry. Of course we do. Would you mind repeating that deep thought of Joan's again?'

Thanet did so.

'Yes,' said Mallard. 'Now that I've had a chance to absorb it, very profound.' He held up his hand as Thanet opened his mouth to protest again. 'I'm serious, Luke. It is. But what I still don't understand is how it advanced your thinking on the case.'

'Well as I say, it didn't click at the time, but then next day . . . You know Richard Lineham has been diagnosed as dyslexic?'

They nodded, their faces solemn now.

'Lineham's very upset about it, naturally, and when we were talking about it next morning he said that discovering something like that really shakes you rigid. The extraordinary thing, he said, is that the situation existed all the time, that *it* hadn't changed but *your perception of it had* and that this is what is so shattering.'

'That's exactly what happened to Michele – my client,' Joan explained to the others.

Thanet nodded. 'Yes. I suppose my subconscious had been chewing away on that all night, so when Lineham said much the same thing, suddenly I knew at once that this had some relevance to the case.'

'But how?' said Helen. 'I just can't see how. That's what's so fascinating.'

Thanet frowned. How to explain? 'Well, let's put it on a personal level. You know how, sometimes, when someone makes a remark, or perhaps when you read something in a book, you relate it to yourself and you think, Yes! That applies to me and I never realised it before!'

They were nodding.

'It's a moment of revelation, of insight, when you perceive a truth which had been there all the time, waiting to be discovered. The point is, you know in a flash that it's true. Well, there often comes a point in a case when this happens to me.'

'The famous policeman's intuition,' said Mallard with a grin.

Thanet shrugged. 'Whatever you like to call it, it happens.'

'It is fascinating, I agree,' said Joan. 'And we've often talked about it, haven't we, Luke? I see it as similar to the process that takes place in the mind of anyone who is seeking to solve a problem, whether it's a mathematician, or a scientist, or even a creative person such as a writer.'

'That's right,' said Thanet. 'I think that what happens is that all the time we are operating on two levels. The conscious mind is busy collecting together all the information needed to solve the problem and all along the subconscious is assimilating, sifting, considering, seeking to make sense of it all. And then someone says something, or something happens and suddenly, deep down, the connection is made. It's a very exciting moment because my conscious mind knows it's happening. It's an actual physical sensation, as if something is trying to push itself up through the layers of consciousness. And I know that if only I stay quite still and allow it to happen it will surface. And then, when it does, it really is like a revelation and everything slots into place, click, click, click. And I just know that I'm right, that this is true. Perhaps I'm not explaining this very well.'

But the others were nodding.

'So go on,' said Mallard. 'What you're saying is that you suddenly realised that what Lineham was saying could apply to one of your suspects.'

Thanet was nodding. 'I got that sensation I've just described in my head. A certain situation had existed all along, some event had occurred which had been radically misunderstood by the murderer, an event which had had a profound effect upon him – or her, of course. Then something had happened which had in a flash changed his perception of it, revealed the truth. And the experience had been so shattering, so mind-blowing, that he had committed murder.

'Well, there was one suspect who *had* experienced a traumatic event from which she had never recovered. Grace Fairleigh. Everyone had told me how she had doted on that baby, what a profound effect its death had had upon her. But how could this relate to Isobel? Unless . . . Unless Isobel had murdered the baby and Grace had somehow found out.'

Thanet paused. His listeners were spellbound.

'And that was when everything fell into place. If this were true, it would explain everything – why Isobel was being blackmailed, and by whom, and how Grace had discovered the truth. I knew, you see, that Isobel couldn't have paid the latest blackmail instalment because she always drew the money out on the first of the month and she had her stroke on 30 June. So by the time the murder was committed ten days later the blackmailer was no doubt becoming impatient. I strongly suspected that two strange phone calls asking for Isobel which Letty Ransome had answered were from the blackmailer.' Thanet glanced at Mallard. 'If you remember, I mentioned them to you the other day, when we were discussing the case with Mike Lineham. So I now surmised that having failed to get through to Isobel by telephone, the blackmailer had decided instead to write. If I was right, of course, the blackmailer could only be one person, the baby's nanny, Rita Symes. I also knew that it was Grace who usually took Isobel's letters up and read them to her, and that she had done so that day. It all fitted, you see.'

'But if Rita knew that Isobel had had a stroke . . .' said Helen.

Thanet was shaking his head. 'That was the point. She didn't. Both those phone calls were very brief. On the first occasion the caller had rung off immediately when Letty Ransome said that her sister was ill, and on the second occasion Letty, excited by the fact that Isobel had that morning for the first time shown some signs of being able to move the fingers on her paralysed side, had simply said that her sister was much better, though still in bed. So the caller would have had no idea that it was a stroke Isobel had suffered. So Rita assumed that Isobel would read the letter herself.'

'But surely she wouldn't have risked giving herself away in a letter?' said Mallard.

'It was stupid, I agree. But she wanted that money. If you're used to a thousand a month coming in and it suddenly stops, you miss it! What she didn't know, of course, was that the postman was in the habit of delivering the letters for both households to the main house, but even so she took the precaution of printing the envelope, just in case Grace saw it lying around and by any remote chance remembered what Rita's handwriting looked like. But she didn't do the same with the letter.'

'So that was it!' said Joan. 'Grace recognised the handwriting! After all those years?'

'Well, she didn't recognise it immediately. But you must remember that for Grace, everything to do with the baby has remained engraved upon her mind. As soon as she started reading the letter she realised who it was from.'

'What did it say? Have you seen it?'

Thanet shook his head. 'Grace destroyed it. And no, I don't know precisely what it said. I'm sure Rita wasn't foolish enough to spell out what she and Isobel had done. But whatever she said, it was enough to cause Grace to realise the truth.'

Grace's account of what had happened had been painful to listen to.

'At first I couldn't take it in. I was sitting by Isobel's bed, reading the letter aloud. Then, as it dawned on me who the letter was from and what the implications were, it was as if I was suddenly outside myself, and it was someone else's voice I was listening to. I looked at Isobel lying there. She couldn't speak, as you know, but she could understand all right and she could see that I knew what she had done. Her eyes . . . She was in a panic, I could tell. She put out her good hand towards me in an imploring gesture, but I ignored it. All I could think of was what had happened to my baby. I could see that same hand poised above him, holding a pillow, and I saw it come down, cover his little face. I'm not making excuses when I say that then I just blanked out. The next thing I was aware of was standing over Isobel, pressing a pillow down over her face. I lifted it away and saw that she was dead. I was quite calm. There seemed to be a kind of poetic justice in the fact that she had died in the same way as he did. I raised her head and replaced the pillow. Then I went back out into the garden.'

'Poor woman,' said Joan. 'What a shock it must have been.'

'What would have happened if she hadn't confessed?' said Mallard. 'You had no actual evidence against her, did you?'

'No. We would have been stuck, no doubt about that. But to be honest, although my professional pride required me to bring the case to what might be termed a successful conclusion, I think I would have been relieved. She's suffered enough.'

'So what will happen to her?' said Helen. 'Will she be convicted, d'you think?'

'Oh yes, I should think so. She has confessed, after all, and I can't see her changing her story. But I'm sure her counsel will plead emotional stress and claim that she was temporarily unbalanced by the shock of discovering that her baby had been murdered, so it will probably be on the grounds of manslaughter with diminished responsibility.'

'So what sort of sentence would that mean?'

'Well, on those grounds it couldn't be more than two years, and it's more than likely that she'll either get a suspended sentence or be put on probation.' Thanet pulled a face, remembering. 'D'you know what she said to me, after she'd told me what happened? She said, "I won't ask you what will happen to me now, because frankly I don't care. One prison is much the same as another."'

The other three were silent. Outside, dusk had fallen while they were talking and the birds had stopped singing. Beyond the trees at the far end of the garden the sky was still stained with streaks of red, apricot and pink from the reflected glow of the sun which had long since set. The brighter flowers in the garden seemed to have vanished, receding into the background with the passing of the light, but the paler ones loomed ghostly on their stems, as if suspended from invisible wires.

Mallard rose and began switching on the lamps.

'Better close the doors, darling,' said Helen. 'It seems a pity, but the moths will all be coming in. I'll make some more coffee, shall I?'

At the door she turned. 'What about the nanny? She won't get away scot-free, will she?'

'I hope not,' said Thanet grimly. 'We'll have to put the case up to the Director of Public Prosecutions, but under Section 4 of the Criminal Law Act of 1967 she might well get up to ten years.'

'On what grounds?'

'Helping to conceal the crime of murder by giving false evidence at the inquest.'

'I see. And what about the blackmail?'

'A bit more complicated. But we're working on it.'

Next morning, Sunday, Thanet was in the kitchen making an early morning cup of tea for Joan when the telephone rang. He went into the hall to answer it.

'Dad?'

'Bridget! How are you? What are you doing ringing at this hour on a Sunday?'

'You weren't still in bed, I hope?'

'Certainly not! I was making a cup of tea for your mother.'

'She tells me the case is over. Well done!'

'That's right.'

'You don't sound too pleased about it.'

'It wasn't a very pleasant case.'

'Are they ever? Anyway, that's why I was ringing. You were so busy we hardly saw you last weekend. We tried to ring last night, but you were out.'

'Yes. We went to dinner at the Mallards'. Helen was asking for you.'

'I must go and see her next time I'm down for a weekend. But as far as today is concerned, Alexander is suggesting that we drive down and he takes us all out to lunch. What d'you think?'

'Ben too?'

'Yes, of course. Dad?' There was a touch of anxiety in Bridget's voice now. 'You did like him, didn't you?'

Thanet glanced at the hydrangea. It looked healthy, expensive, handsome. Just like its donor, he thought. He remembered that uncomfortable moment of insight, the thought that his prejudice against Alexander might have arisen from his own feelings of inferiority. The Mallards were right. He couldn't think of a single reason why Alexander should not be a suitable suitor for Bridget, should it ever come to that. He took a deep breath. 'Of course I did. He's a very nice young man.'

'I thought you would.' Her relief came over loud and clear. 'So what d'you think, about today?'

'It's a lovely idea,' said Thanet. 'Your mother will be delighted at not having to cook Sunday lunch.'

'That's what we thought. Good. We'll be down about 12.30, then. Can we leave it to you to think of a nice place to go and book a table?'

'Of course. We'll look forward to it.'

And he meant it.

NO LAUGHING MATTER

To Keith and Olwyn

I wish to express my gratitude to Stephen Skelton for allowing me to visit the award-winning vineyard at Tenterden, Kent, where he is wine-maker, and especially to his assistant Chris Nicholas, who was so generous with his time and expertise at the busiest period of the year.

ONE

Thanet drummed his fingers on the steering wheel, scowling at the stationary line of tail-lights which curved away ahead of him. He glanced at the dashboard clock. Twenty to eight already. Bridget's train was due in ten minutes and he wanted to be there, waiting on the platform, when she arrived. He thought he had allowed plenty of time – at this hour of the evening the streets of Sturrenden were usually relatively deserted. There must have been an accident.

The approaching wail of an ambulance siren confirmed his guess. And yes, ahead of him, rhythmic pulses of blue light irradiated the sky, reflecting off the windows of the houses on the other side of the street, on the bend. Perhaps he should do a U-turn, make his way to the station by another route? Come *on*, he breathed. Move!

Miraculously, almost at once the furthest tail-lights disappeared around the curve in the road as the line of cars began to crawl past the scene of the accident. There was no time for Thanet to catch more than a glimpse of the Ford Cortina slewed across the road, the motorcycle half under its front wheels, the dazed figure sitting head on hands on the kerb and the stretcher already being loaded into the ambulance. Ben ought to be seeing this, thought Thanet grimly. Perhaps he'd stop nagging us to allow him a moped.

He arrived on the platform with a minute to spare, his mind now entirely focused on Bridget again. What was wrong? For the hundredth time their brief telephone conversation ran through his mind.

'Dad? Look, is it all right if I come home for a few days?'

'Yes, of course. But . . . Are you all right? Is anything wrong?'

'I'll be down on Friday evening, then.'

'What time? I'll meet you.'

'Lovely. I'll catch the 6.15. Thanks, Dad. See you then.'

And the phone had gone down, cutting off further inquiries.

It must be something to do with Alexander, thought Thanet. This was Bridget's wealthy, successful ex-public school boyfriend. She had been going out with him for over a year now and Thanet's initial misgivings over the difference in their backgrounds had gradually given way to acceptance. But he still had reservations. It was evident that Bridget was head over heels in love with Alexander but Thanet wasn't so sure of Alexander's feelings for her. He was fond of her, yes, but sufficiently fond to make a commitment? Thanet doubted it, and in one respect this was a good thing. At twenty Bridget was still very young. But if Alexander had broken it off . . . Thanet couldn't bear the thought of the heartache she would suffer. It was all very well to say that once your children were grown up they were no longer your responsibility and had to fend for themselves. They were still a part of you, always would be, and their joys and sorrows would always be yours, to a greater or lesser degree. And in

Bridget's case . . . Ah, here came the train. Thanet steeled himself. Yes, there she was. He walked briskly up the platform to meet her. She looked pinched and pale, he thought, diminished somehow, and in his opinion inadequately clad for a raw October evening in cotton trousers, T-shirt and thin cardigan.

She attempted a smile, kissed his cheek and handed over her psychedelic green and orange squashy bag.

'All right?' he said, trying to avoid too searching a scrutiny of her face.

Her eyes met his, briefly, then slid away as she nodded.

Well, he had no intention of pressing her. She could confide in them – if she chose to confide in them at all – in her own good time. They drove home in silence.

Joan heard the car and opened the front door to greet them. In response to the question in her eyes Thanet shook his head. *Nothing, yet.*

Joan gave Bridget a quick hug. 'Have you eaten?'

'I had a sandwich at Victoria.'

'Coffee, then?'

'Yes, lovely.'

They spent the next couple of hours watching television, trying to pretend that nothing was wrong, the air full of unspoken questions. When the ten o'clock news came on Bridget stretched and stood up. 'I think I'll go up, if you don't mind. It's been a pretty hectic week.'

Bridget, going to bed at ten p.m.? Unheard of! They concealed their dismay behind understanding nods and smiles.

'I think I'll burst if we don't find out soon,' said Joan as they listened to their daughter climb the stairs, her dragging footsteps a painful betrayal of her state of mind.

'The last thing she'll want is to be bombarded with questions.'

'Really, Luke, I meant no such thing. But a little parental concern . . .'

'She knows we're concerned! Give her time. She just needs a breathing space, that's all.'

The phone rang. Joan pulled a face. 'Must be for you, at this time of night. I'll make some tea.'

Thanet went to answer it reluctantly. He felt sluggish, depressed about Bridget, disinclined to do anything but have a hot, soothing drink and fall into bed.

As he picked up the phone Ben came in, slamming the front door behind him. At sixteen, already an inch taller than his father and with a physique to match, he seemed incapable of doing anything quietly.

'Sis home?'

Thanet pointed up the stairs and flapped his hand for silence, pressing the phone closer to his ear. 'Sorry, what did you say?'

'It's Pater, sir.'

Despite his lethargy of a moment ago, Thanet's scalp pricked. The Station Officer wouldn't bother him off duty unless it was important.

'Yes? Oh, hold on a moment, will you?' Thanet covered the receiver, exasperated. 'How d'you expect me to have a telephone conversation with all this noise going on?'

Joan had emerged from the kitchen. Ben was already halfway up the stairs and she was calling after him. 'She's tired. She's gone to bed.'

Ben looked astounded. 'At this hour? Anyway, I'm only going to say hi.' He took the rest of the stairs two at a time and they heard him knock on Bridget's door, the murmur of voices.

Joan shrugged and went back into the kitchen.

'Sorry, Pater,' said Thanet. 'Go on.'

'Patrol car responding to a 999 call has just radioed in for assistance. Suspicious death, sir. Could be murder.'

'Where?' Already the adrenalin was starting to flow.

'Sturrenden Vineyard. It's out on the –'

'I know where it is. Any more details?'

'Not yet, sir.'

'Right, I'm on my way. SOCOs notified?'

'Yes, sir. And Doc Mallard.'

'DS Lineham?'

'I'll ring him next, sir. And the rest of the team.'

Thanet put the phone down, went to the kitchen door.

Joan was screwing the top on to the Thermos flask. 'All right, I heard.' She handed him the flask. 'I wonder how many times I've done this.'

Thanet grinned and kissed her. 'I shouldn't start counting, it'll only depress you.'

Sturrenden Vineyard lay four miles west of the town, on the Maidstone road. As Thanet drove through the quiet streets he tried to recall what he knew about it. Very little, he realised, except that it was there and had become an increasingly thriving business. The Thanets drank very little and had never actually bought any wine there, nor had either of them gone on any of the vineyard walks or guided tours. Just as well, perhaps? He would be approaching the place with a completely open mind . . . No, not true, he realised. There was something he'd heard about the owner, what was his name? An odd name, but he couldn't recall it. Anyway, it was something unsavoury, he was sure . . . He frowned into the darkness. No, it was no good, the memory eluded him.

Ten minutes later the first notice appeared. 'STURRENDEN VINEYARD 100 YDS ON R.' and shortly afterwards the illuminated sign came into view, a curved arch spanning the entrance. Thanet paused to look at it.

STURRENDEN VINEYARD

AWARD-WINNING ENGLISH WINES. FREE TASTINGS.

VINEYARD TOURS.

Details of opening times were given below in print too small to be legible at night. Bunches of grapes linked by vine leaves decorated each end of the board.

A car was approaching from behind as Thanet swung across the road and through the wide entrance gates. The car flashed its lights and followed suit. Lineham's Escort, Thanet realised. In the car park they pulled up side by side next to Mallard's old Rover. There were a number of other cars in the extensive parking area – a couple of police cars and several which presumably belonged to the vineyard.

'Nice white Mercedes over there,' said Lineham wistfully. 'This place is doing all right, by the look of it.' He and Thanet had worked together for so long that by now greetings were superfluous.

Thanet nodded. Lineham was right. The Mercedes aside, even by night all the signs of substantial reinvestment were there: fresh tarmac, new fencing and a general air of order and prosperity. Over to the right, set well back behind a tall, dense yew hedge, was a sizeable period farmhouse, lights blazing out their message of crisis from every window. Ahead, their roofs a looming darkness against the night sky, was a substantial cluster of farm buildings. Between two of the nearest barns there was a lorry-width gap in which stood a uniformed constable, clearly visible in the light streaming from the buildings on either side. As they drew closer Thanet could see that the one to the left had been converted into the vineyard shop, the one to the right the office.

'Evening, Tenby,' he said. 'Which way?'

The man half turned to the left and pointed. 'In that big building there, sir. The bottling plant. He's in the laboratory.' He paused, swallowed. 'It's a bit of a mess, sir.'

Thanet's heart sank. He always dreaded the first sight of the corpse. There was something so poignant about the newly dead, separated by so short a span of time from those who still lived and breathed. Although he had succeeded remarkably well in concealing this weakness from his colleagues Thanet always had consciously to armour himself against that first, awe-full moment. And if the death had been really violent, if there was a lot of blood and 'mess', as Tenby put it, the ordeal was ten times worse, Thanet's over-active imagination visualising those last agonising minutes before the victim was released to merciful unconsciousness. But forewarned was, to some extent, forearmed. 'In what way?' he said calmly.

'Looks as though the victim fell through a window, cutting his throat in the process. There's a lot of blood about. And glass everywhere.'

Bad, but it sounds as though I've seen far worse, thought Thanet. 'Do we know who he is yet?'

'Owner of the vineyard, sir. Chap called Randish.'

Of course! Randish, that was the name. And Thanet remembered now where he'd heard it. He wondered if Lineham would.

The sergeant had, of course. 'Randish,' repeated Lineham as they walked through the wide passageway into a big yard some sixty feet square, surrounded by buildings. 'That's the bloke I told you about, remember? A couple of years ago? Louise was worried about one of the mothers in Mandy's playgroup, she'd noticed bruises, usually in places where they weren't easily spotted, and she suspected the husband was knocking her about. She'd tried to get the woman to open up, but she wouldn't and Louise wanted to know if there was any way we could help her.'

'Yes, I remember. And we said no, there wasn't. If the wife chose not to lay a complaint against her husband, there was absolutely nothing we could do about it.'

'So. Interesting,' said Lineham. 'Incidentally, what did Tenby mean, "laboratory", sir? What do you need a laboratory for, on a vineyard?'

Thanet shrugged. 'No idea.' He had come a halt and was looking around, trying to absorb the geography of the place. There was a lot to take in.

The whole of the right-hand side of the yard was taken up by the building PC Tenby had pointed out, the bottling plant. This was a relatively new construction, presumably purpose-built. Huge sliding doors stood open, spilling light into the yard. Thanet caught glimpses of tall stainless-steel vats, complicated machinery and, to the right, some of his men moving around near an open door to an inner room, the laboratory, presumably.

Straight ahead on the far side of the yard was an open-sided building. Harsh strip-lighting shone down upon a cylindrical stainless-steel structure some twelve feet long – a press, perhaps? – standing to one side, opposite a couple of trailers. A tractor, with a third trailer still attached, stood in between. Obviously the grapes were driven straight into this area from the vineyard beyond. Of course, at this time of the year they must be in the middle of the grape harvest, their busiest period. The floor glistened wet, as if newly hosed down.

Thanet became aware that Lineham was shifting from one foot to the other, trying to contain his impatience to get on and into the heart of the activity behind them. He was aware, too, that although he genuinely felt it important to take time to absorb his initial impressions of a place, part of the reason for this delay was his reluctance to proceed to the next stage. But it couldn't be put off for ever; he might as well get it over with. With a quick, comprehensive glance at the other buildings, at whose use he couldn't even begin to guess, he sighed and turned. 'All right, then, Mike. Come on.'

Lineham set off with alacrity, Thanet trailing behind.

Inside, the huge space was divided lengthwise by a plate glass wall, on the far side of which was the bottling plant, its tiled floor and walls spotless, the machinery of the plant itself gleaming hygienically. To the left of the double doors stood the row of vats which Thanet had glimpsed earlier, and two shorter rows of huge oak barrels supported by stout, crossed stretchers. The open door to the laboratory was in an inner wall to the right of the double doors and Thanet's stomach gave an uneasy heave as he noticed a pool of vomit nearby. A couple of SOCOs were talking to two patrolmen. As Thanet and Lineham approached a flash went off inside the laboratory.

'Bit tricky in there at the moment, sir,' said one of the SOCOs to Thanet. 'Never seen so much broken glass in my life. We took all the shots we needed of the body and then thought we'd finish taking the floor first so we could sweep up a bit.' He handed Thanet and Lineham some heavy-duty plastic overshoes.

They put them on.

'We'll be careful,' said Thanet. 'Just take a quick look.' He turned to the patrolmen. 'Who discovered the body?'

'Chap called Vintage. He's the assistant winemaker here.'

'Appropriate name,' said Lineham, with a grin.

Thanet shot him a quelling glance. *This is no laughing matter*. At once, he regretted it. He was being unreasonable.

Amongst policemen an apparently inappropriate levity was often a safety mechanism against the sordid reality of much of their work. He was too tense. The sooner the next few minutes were over, the better. 'Where is Vintage?'

'Down at the house, sir, with the victim's wife.'

'Right. Doc Mallard's still here, I gather?'

'Should be nearly finished by now.'

'Good.' He couldn't put it off any longer. Thanet took a deep breath and stepped inside, glass crunching beneath his feet. His brain photographed the scene, fixing it indelibly in his memory: an oblong room with high wall-benches swept virtually bare; and broken glass, everywhere, in chunks, shards and splinters, mostly colourless but with here and there a glint of green.

And blood.

Blood spattered on the floor, blood glistening on pieces of glass, blood smeared on the wall beneath the window, blood saturating the shirt-front of the man who lay in a half-seated position slumped against that wall, head at an awkward angle. Above him yawned a huge, jagged hole in the window. Despite the fresh air streaming in there was a slightly acrid underlying smell of fermenting grapes. The atmosphere seemed still to reverberate with echoes of the violent scene which had played itself out in this white, clinical room so short a time ago.

Behind him, Lineham whistled softly. 'Someone lost his temper here, all right.'

Lineham was right. Only a furious, ungovernable rage could have created this kind of wholesale destruction.

Mallard, crouched near the body, looked up. 'Bit of a mess, eh, Luke?'

Thanet nodded, bracing himself for a closer look, and

picked his way through the glass to stand beside the little police surgeon. And yes, there it was, that familiar twist in his gut, that painful pang of – what? Pity? Regret? Anger? Fear? Dread? A complex mixture, perhaps, of all of them. No one in the prime of life, as this man had been, should expect to die like this, in the familiar, apparent safety of his day-to-day working environment. Randish couldn't have been more than thirty-five, and looked tall, well-built and healthy. He had been good-looking, too; handsome, even, with thick dark curly hair and regular, well-formed features. Very attractive to women, probably, Thanet thought, and remembered Louise's suspicions. True or false? And, even if true, what were the circumstances which lay behind it all? Thanet knew that in the next days and weeks he would sooner or later find out; that Randish, until now no more to him than a stranger's name in a casual conversation, would come alive in a unique and extraordinary way. For, unlike the living, the dead have no means of safeguarding their secrets.

'What d'you think happened?' he asked Mallard, in no real expectation of an answer. Mallard invariably refused to be drawn on matters non-medical.

The little doctor peered up at Thanet over his half-moon spectacles, their gold rims glinting in the harsh bright light, and put out his hand. 'Give me a heave, will you? I couldn't kneel because of the glass and I think I've seized up.'

Thanet obliged.

'Thanks.' Mallard peered down at the body. 'You'll have to work that out for yourself. Not my province. But I can most certainly pronounce him dead and as you can see for yourself there's little doubt as to cause. The jugular vein was severed and there's so much blood about it's almost certain that the carotid artery was, too. I'll stick my neck out and say he bled to death. It would have been very quick, a matter of minutes. We won't be able to confirm until the PM, of course, but I'd say it was most unlikely to be anything else.'

'Look as though someone used him as an Aunt Sally,' said Lineham, 'chucked everything he could lay his hands on at him. Randish backs towards the window, probably holding up his arms to protect his face, then he treads on something – a bottle, perhaps – which makes him lose his balance. He falls backwards, twisting sideways, and goes through the window, slicing through that artery in the process. Then he gradually collapses, the weight of his body dragging him down into a sitting position.'

'Quite feasible,' said Mallard.

'How long ago?' said Thanet.

Mallard puffed out his lips, expelled air softly and shook his head. 'You don't give up, do you, Luke? You know as well as I do that it's impossible to be accurate.'

Thanet grinned. They went through this charade every time. 'Oh come on, Doc, just give us some idea.'

Mallard considered, head on one side, and then said reluctantly, 'Some time in the last three hours? And earlier in that period, rather than later.'

Thanet glanced at his watch. Ten-thirty. Between 7.30 and 9.30. then, probably. 'Thanks. You've finished here, now?'

Mallard snapped his bag shut. 'I have. It's off to my nice warm bed for me.'

'Don't rub it in. I'll walk you to your car.'

'Don't bother.'

'It'll be good to get some fresh air.'

Outside, Thanet gratefully inhaled the clean, moist air, anxious to rid his nostrils of the smell of death, the taint of murder. As they emerged from the passageway he saw that the ambulance had arrived at last and some more cars were pulling in.

'Draco won't be here, I suppose,' said Mallard. 'Didn't Angharad have another test this week?'

'Yes. On Wednesday. They went up today for the result.'

In the early years of Superintendent Draco's reign in Sturrenden he had galvanised the place into becoming the most efficient Division in the South-East. He was ubiquitous and his men never knew when he would suddenly materialise, breathing down their necks. But a couple of years ago his beautiful and much-loved wife Angharad had had leukaemia diagnosed and overnight Draco had become a changed man. Gone were the light of enthusiasm in his eyes, the hectoring tone in his voice, the infuriating bounce from his step. Although his men had all complained bitterly at the way the Super had harried and chivvied them, they had grown to admire, respect and even to like him, and there was not one of them who would not have suffered the worst of harassments to see Draco back on his original form. There were signs that Angharad's condition was improving, but she was still trailing up to London regularly for bone-marrow tests and Draco's staff always knew when another test was coming up: for days beforehand he would become increasingly abstracted and morose. He always accompanied his wife both for the test and for the results two days later and for the last six months or so had got into the habit of taking her away to a hotel for a day or two afterwards.

Mallard sighed. 'Living through all that is not an experience I'd wish on my worst enemy.'

Thanet glanced at the little doctor, aware that Mallard was remembering his own bitter years. The Thanets and the Mallards were good friends, Thanet having known the older man since childhood. He and Joan were very fond of Helen, Mallard's second wife, and grateful to her for rescuing the little doctor from the years of depression which had followed the lingering death of his first wife from cancer. Thanet was saved from a reply – for what could usefully be said? – by the approach of the two ambulancemen, carrying a stretcher. He knew them both by sight.

'Sorry we took so long, Inspector. Been a spate of accidents this evening.'

Thanet shook his head. 'There's no hurry with this one. Anyway, it's all clear now. Just check that the SOCOs have finished and you can take him away.'

Hard on their heels came more of his men. He sent them to find Lineham. 'I'll be with you in a few moments.'

At the car Mallard turned. 'How's Bridget these days? Helen was saying the other day we hadn't seen her for ages. I know she misses their cookery sessions.'

Helen Mallard, a well-known cookery writer, had encouraged Bridget in her choice of career and at one time the two of them regularly used to spend afternoons together concocting new dishes for Helen's latest project.

'She's down for a long weekend, as a matter of fact. I picked her up at the station earlier this evening.'

Something in Thanet's tone must have alerted Mallard to his concern.

'Nothing wrong, is there?'

'We don't know for certain, yet. But she seems pretty down in the mouth.'

'Alexander?'

'More than likely, I should think.'

'Who'd be young again?' said Mallard, unlocking his

car. He patted the old Rover affectionately. 'There's a lot to be said for growing old together. So much more comfortable.'

Thanet laughed. 'So far as I can recall, at the age of twenty it wasn't comfort I was looking for!' He watched Mallard drive off and then set purposefully off back to the laboratory. Action was now called for: get the men organised; then interview the chap who had discovered the body, Vintage.

He was eager to get on with it.

TWO

The yew hedge was tall, dense, thick, planted no doubt as an evergreen screen to preserve the Randishes' privacy in winter and summer alike. Living over the shop, so to speak, must have certain disadvantages, thought Thanet as he followed Lineham through the tall arched wrought-iron gate which fitted snugly into a clipped opening in the hedge.

Though this house would compensate for most.

It was Tudor, black and white, the marriage of beams and plasterwork a delight to the eye. The curtains were drawn in the room to the left of the front door but lights still blazed from most of the windows, illuminating the neat front cottage garden. This was past its best now but still sported clumps of flowers here and there, their colours indistinguishable in the dim light. The path of ancient paving stones was bordered by a dwarf lavender hedge which in summer must release its sweet scent as visitors brushed by.

Thanet waited for the inevitable remark from Lineham. Anything larger than the sergeant's own modest dwelling invariably provoked a comment.

Lineham did not disappoint him.

'Not exactly on the breadline, are they?' said the

sergeant as they approached the massive front door with its shallow medieval arch. 'Where's the doorbell?'

'Is this it?' Thanet grasped the curlicue on the end of a piece of stout wire dangling to the right of the door, and tugged. In the distance a bell tinkled.

'Sounds like it,' said Lineham. 'This place really is the genuine article, isn't it? Be interesting to see what it's like inside.'

'We're not house-hunting, Mike.' But Thanet's tone was mild. He, too, would be interested to see the interior. People's houses were very revealing, he found.

Footsteps approached, unseen hands fumbled with a latch, and the door opened. The man was broad-shouldered, with a thatch of thick, white hair.

'Detective Inspector Thanet and Detective Sergeant Lineham, Sturrenden CID,' said Thanet.

'Owen Landers.' The man stood back. 'Come in.' He closed the door behind them. 'Randish is – was – my son-in-law.'

They were in a narrow hall, the patina on its panelled walls a mute testimony to centuries of polishing. The floor was of flagstones, partly concealed by the rich subdued colours of a red and blue Persian rug.

Thanet offered his condolences and then said, 'We understand that it was a Mr Vintage who found the body and we were told he was here.'

Landers would be in his late fifties, Thanet thought, and a farmer, at a guess. That ruddy, weatherbeaten complexion could only be the result of years of exposure to the caprices of the British climate, and his clothes were what Thanet thought of as top quality country gear – cord trousers, cable-stitch sweater and brogues.

'Yes.' Landers gestured to a half-open door. 'Come in.'

A wave of heat greeted them as they stepped inside. It

was the kind of room often seen in the pages of glossy magazines: beamed, low-ceilinged, with casement windows on three sides and a huge inglenook fireplace. There were more Persian rugs on the floor of polished brick, linen curtains and upholstery in glowing colours and several pieces of fine antique furniture, all displayed to advantage by the light of strategically placed table lamps. The three people in it looked up apprehensively – a middle-aged woman, a woman in her thirties and a slightly younger man.

'My wife, my daughter and Vintage,' said Landers. He introduced Thanet and Lineham and then added, 'They want a word with you, Oliver.'

Vintage was standing in front of the fireplace, his back to the wood-burning stove. 'Yes, of course.' He was young, twenty-seven or twenty-eight at a guess, and whipcord thin with a shock of straight black hair which flopped across a high, bony forehead. He looked, Thanet thought, like a man on the verge of collapse. His shoulders drooped, his hands hung limply by his sides, his eyes were dull in their deep-hollowed eye-sockets, his skin tallow-white. His clothes were as creased and stained as if he had worked and slept in them for weeks. Indifference, overuse or simple neglect? Thanet wondered. In any case, it was clear that, the murder aside, Vintage was a man who had been under stress for some considerable time.

And a man under stress can snap.

'You can use the dining room,' said Landers.

After the first apprehensive glance Mrs Randish had ignored them. Hunched on the edge of her chair, hands outstretched to the stove, she seemed oblivious of their presence, sunk in private misery. Her tear-stained face and swollen eyes told their own story. The older woman's attention was focused on her daughter. Perched on the arm of the chair beside her she watched her steadily with a fierce, protective gaze.

Thanet was glad to get out of the room. Dressed in his outdoor clothes he felt he couldn't have stood the heat in there much longer. He was relieved to find the dining room cooler, but he and Lineham still took off their raincoats before sitting down at the round oak gate-legged table.

Vintage remained standing.

'Do sit down, Mr Vintage.'

'If I do I shall never get up again.' Nevertheless, apparently unable to resist the temptation, he sat, slumping in the chair as if his muscles no longer had the strength to hold him upright. After a moment he straightened his shoulders and sat up a little, presumably to brace himself for the interview.

'It must all have been a terrible shock,' said Thanet.

'Yes it was, of course. But it's not just that. I've been working flat out for weeks now. It's the busiest time of the year. It's OK while you keep going, but when you stop it hits you, you know?'

Thanet nodded sympathetically. 'Pretty long hours, I imagine.'

'I don't usually get to bed till two or three and then I'm up again to get here and start work at 7.30.'

'You actually make the wine?'

'With some supervision from Zak – that's Mr Randish, yes.'

Zak, thought Thanet. What an outlandish name. Short for Zachariah, perhaps?

'He's the winemaker, I'm his assistant,' Vintage was explaining. 'He's been training me for the last four years so in practice most of the time he leaves me to get on with it.'

'Just the two of you make the wine?'

'Yes. But he's also the winemaker for another vineyard, at Chasing Manor, and he divides his time between the two. So a lot of the time I'm here by myself. It's pretty hectic because we not only press the grapes from this vineyard but from a lot of smaller vineyards in the area. Most don't have their own presses, you see.'

'So you were here by yourself today?'

'Zak was here for a couple of hours this morning, as usual, before going to Chasing.' Vintage's tone was guarded.

'Anything unusual happen?'

'No.'

But he was lying, Thanet was sure of it. 'What did you do?'

'Discussed yesterday's work, today's arrangements. Made one batch of wine.'

What could the man be hiding? 'Together?'

'Yes.'

'Was that usual?'

'Not unusual.'

It all seemed innocuous, but Thanet was still convinced there was more to it than this. It would keep, however. He pressed on.

'And how long does a batch take?'

'Two and a half hours.'

'So Mr Randish left at – what? Ten?'

'Nearer half past, I should think.'

'And what time did he get back?'

The routine during harvest was that Randish usually got back from Chasing Manor vineyard at about six, had a bite to eat and then came up to the press where Vintage was working. They would sort out any problems that had cropped up during the day and then work through the evening, sometimes together, but more often than not individually. Randish would divide his time between laboratory and office.

'There's a lot of paperwork, then?' said Thanet.

Vintage passed a hand wearily over his forehead. 'Oh God, yes, you wouldn't believe it. Everything, but everything, has to be catalogued for the Customs and Excise. If you sneeze, they want to know it.'

'What sort of information do they require?'

'They have to know exactly what happened, what date, what went where, how many ounces of sugar you used with each batch, how much yeast went in. They want to know every movement from tank to tank, every single fluid ounce you've got in there, how much you lost after fermentation when you rack a tank off, all your losses through the process.' Vintage put his head in his hands. 'How I'm going to manage to do all that as well as the winemaking, I just don't know.'

It certainly sounded a mammoth task for one man. 'Perhaps you'll be able to get someone in to give you a hand.'

'Where from? Anyone who'd be of any use is working flat out at the moment, like me.' He shook his head in despair. 'Sorry, Inspector, not your problem, is it?'

'You say Mr Randish usually divided his time between the office and the laboratory. What would he be doing in the laboratory?'

'Checking sulphur levels, sugar levels, fermentation, Ph, acidity and so on and then noting it all down, putting it on computer.'

'And would you see him during the evening? Would you have to go over to the laboratory or the office for anything?'

A shrug. 'Sometimes. Depends.'

'And tonight?'

'No. I had a lot of other things to do.'

Vintage was holding back again. What had been going on? No doubt they'd find out, sooner or later.

'So exactly what did happen this evening?'

According to Vintage he and Randish had followed their usual routine. They had worked together from 6.30 to 7, doing the turnaround between batches, which involved a lot of manual work that always went more quickly if there were two of you. Randish then went across to the office and that was the last Vintage saw of him until 9.30, when the next batch finished. That was when he went to the laboratory and found him dead.

'Did you go in?'

'Just a couple of steps inside the door.' Vintage grimaced. 'I didn't need to go any further.'

He had gone straight to the phone in the office next door, rung the police and Mr Landers, then hurried down to the house to warn Mrs Randish of their arrival, and the reason for it. She had insisted on coming to see her husband's body for herself.

'I tried to stop her, but she wouldn't listen. Short of physically restraining her, there was nothing I could do to stop her.'

No wonder she was so upset, thought Thanet. The shock of a husband's sudden death is enough, but to see him in that condition . . . 'Did she go into the room, touch anything?'

'Just a couple of steps, like me. Then she came to a dead halt, stood staring for a minute, then went outside and was sick. I'm not surprised.'

They had then returned to the house, by which time Mrs Randish's parents had arrived. They lived less than a mile away.

'So that would have been, let me see, at about ten to ten?'

Vintage thought. 'Something like that, yes. And the police arrived about five minutes later.'

'Did Mr Landers go up to the laboratory?'

'Yes. He wanted to see for himself, as well. I don't think any of them could believe it, really.' This time Vintage anticipated Thanet's question. 'But he only went just inside the door, too.'

'So no one actually touched the body?'

Vintage shook his head.

Thanet considered. 'Was there anyone else working here this evening?'

'No.' Vintage pulled a face. 'Drops me in it, doesn't it?'

'Should it?'

'What do you mean?'

'Did you have any reason to kill Mr Randish?'

'No!'

But again, it didn't ring quite true.

'Do you realise you haven't shown the slightest sign of regret over his death?'

'Haven't I?' Vintage rubbed his hands nervously together. 'I don't suppose it's sunk in yet. But believe me, I'd rather have him alive than dead.'

'Why?'

'Purely selfish reasons. Because it really does leave me in a hell of a mess here. And also, in the long term, because I still had a lot to learn from him. He was a bloody good winemaker.'

'I notice you don't say anything about liking him or missing him as a friend.'

'You don't have to like someone to work with him.'

No, but it helps, thought Thanet, glancing at Lineham who was to him almost indispensible. The sergeant was listening intently, making the occasional note. There was one other question that had to be put. Let Lineham ask it. 'Do you have any further questions to put, Sergeant?'

Lineham glanced down at his notebook, as if consulting it. 'You say you were working here alone all evening, Mr Vintage. Did you see anyone else around, at any time?'

'No! Oh, hang on . . . Yes . . .' Vintage stopped.

It was obvious that he'd suddenly remembered, had said so without thinking and then had second thoughts. Why?

'Yes, or no?' said Lineham.

'Yes,' said Vintage reluctantly, aware no doubt that retracting now could lead to all sorts of complications. 'I'd forgotten because it was early on, soon after Zak went across to the office.'

Lineham waited expectantly.

'Reg Mason came up. He'd been to see Mrs Randish, he said.'

'Who's he?'

'A local builder. He's been converting a complex of farm buildings on their land into holiday cottages.'

'What did he want to see her about?'

'He didn't say. Why should he? It's none of my business.'

Thanet sighed inwardly. Vintage was not a good liar.

Lineham wasn't prepared to let the matter go. 'So why did he come up to see you?'

'Search me. Just to say hullo. Perhaps he just felt like a natter.'

'So did he stay talking long?'

'No, just a few minutes. He could see I was busy.'

'Did you see him leave?'

'Yes.'

'You're sure he didn't go into the bottling plant?'

'No, he didn't!'

'The press is that stainless-steel machine underneath the open-sided shed at the far side of the yard?'

'Yes.'

'Then you'd have had a clear view of the big doors into the bottling plant all evening. No one would have been able to go in or out without your seeing them.'

Vintage laughed. 'You must be joking! If I'd stood there beside it like a dummy all the time then yes, that would be true, I grant you. But I was all over the place, shifting things about, swilling out, hosing down, moving supplies of sugar, batches of waiting grapes, cleaning out some of the fermentation vessels in an adjoining shed . . . Shall I go on?'

'I think you've made your point. So it would have been easy for someone to slip into the laboratory without your seeing them.'

'Right!'

'Did you hear anything, then? Cars arriving or leaving?'

'If you'd heard the noise the press makes when the compressor comes on you wouldn't be asking me that, either.'

Thanet couldn't make up his mind if Vintage was deliberately being unhelpful, or whether he was just trying to make it clear that although he had been alone here there had been ample opportunity for anyone else to get in if they had watched for the opportunity.

Lineham glanced at Thanet. *I don't think we're going to get any further.*

Thanet nodded. 'Well, I think that's all for the moment, Mr Vintage. We'll need to talk to you again tomorrow, and you can make a formal statement then. But you can go home now, try and get a decent night's sleep for once.'

'Will I be able to go on pressing tomorrow?'

Thanet shook his head. 'I'm sorry, that's out of the question.'

'But I have to! We've got four batches booked in, from small vineyards, and more the next day. And the day after that! We can't just not deal with them. This is these people's livelihood, Inspector, they work all year for this. We've just got to go on.'

'I'm sorry,' Thanet repeated, 'but I can't have people tramping around all over the place tomorrow. The vineyard will have to be closed. But I do understand what you're saying and I'll do my level best to make sure you're able to go on the following day.'

Vintage compressed his lips but could see that it was pointless to argue. With an ill grace, he left.

THREE

Lineham tossed his notebook on to the table. 'He knows more than he's telling, doesn't he?'

'Yes. But is it relevant? That's the point.' People were, Thanet knew, prepared to go to astonishing lengths to preserve their privacy and even in a murder investigation would tell the police only what they felt they ought to know. Understandable but infuriating. All the same, he was intrigued by Oliver Vintage. 'I wouldn't mind betting there's more to his condition than just plain tiredness.'

'He's ill, you mean?'

'Not ill, but . . . Well, I'd say he's a man with a problem, a problem that's really getting him down. And he's having an especially hard time coping with it at the moment, because of the demands his work is making on him.'

'You think Randish was the problem?'

'Could be. If so, no doubt we'll find out sooner or later.'

It was, he thought, an extraordinary way to earn a living. Here he sat, in a dead man's chair at a dead man's table, trying to feel his way into a dead man's life. If anyone had asked him why he did it he supposed he'd say, well, someone has to. And if asked to elaborate, even knowing that he risked sounding grandiose, he'd say that some of us have to try to balance the scales of justice, or evil would flourish unchecked and the world would descend into anarchy. His own contribution towards the struggle might be small, but it was what gave meaning and purpose to his life.

'Pity they all went tramping into the laboratory,' Lineham said.

'I know. No doubt they'll all have glass embedded in their shoes, so we won't be able to eliminate any of them that way.'

'Except Mrs Landers.'

'True.'

'So, what now, sir?'

'We'd better have a word with Mrs Randish, if she's up to it. Let's go and see.'

As soon as they entered the sitting room Thanet could sense the tension in the air. It showed in Landers' aggressive pose in front of the hearth, chin thrust forward, legs apart and hands clasped behind his back; showed too in Mrs Landers' worried expression and in the rigidity of Alice Randish's back. Alice was still huddled on the edge of her seat as close to the woodstove as she could get, stretching out her hands to its warmth and rubbing them together from time to time. With her long fair hair falling forward to hide her face and her slight, almost girlish figure, she could easily have been taken for a teenager, Thanet thought. Her mother was still perched on the arm of the chair beside her.

What had they been arguing about? Thanet wondered. 'Mrs Randish,' he said, 'I really am very sorry to have to trouble you at a time like this. I mean that. But it would help us enormously if you could answer just a few questions.'

'Can't it wait till morning?' snapped Landers. 'I've sent

for the doctor. Alice will need something to help her sleep tonight. I thought we'd take her home with us. The children too, of course. It'll mean waking them up, but that can't be helped.'

'Daddy, do stop fussing,' Alice said wearily, without looking up. 'I told you, I'll be perfectly all right.'

Was this the cause of the disagreement? Thanet doubted it. Whether Alice should go or stay was surely not a sufficiently emotive issue. He said nothing, simply stood, waiting, and in a moment Alice did glance up.

'Do sit down, Inspector.'

'Alice . . .'

'Daddy, please!'

Thanet took a seat on the opposite side of the hearth, wishing that it weren't so hot in here. Already he could feel sweat pricking at his back.

'How old are the children?' he said, hoping to break the ice.

Landers answered for her. 'Eight and six.' He was still standing in front of the hearth, a physical barrier between Thanet and Alice.

Thanet had had enough of this. 'Would you mind taking a seat, sir? And if you'd like to stay –'

'Of course I'm staying!'

'Then I'd be grateful if you would refrain from interrupting. Otherwise I'm afraid I shall have to insist on seeing Mrs Randish alone.'

Landers didn't like it but with an ill grace retreated to a sofa at the far side of the room.

Thanet guessed that Alice was an only child and had probably been both over-protected and over-indulged. He wondered how Landers would have felt if he knew that Randish had been knocking his beloved daughter about. That was a thought. Perhaps he had known. Somehow

Thanet had to find out if there was any foundation for Louise's suspicions and if there were, whether Landers had been aware of the situation.

But not yet. Such delicate matters could not be rushed.

He turned back to Alice. 'Now, Mrs Randish, I understand that your husband was away for most of the day.'

For the first time she lifted her head and looked at Thanet properly.

Her eyes were astonishing, he thought, a deep cornflower blue, fringed with long lashes. Her features were regular, the bone structure delicate, its underlying beauty unmarred by the superficial marks of grief. She was aptly named, he thought, remembering Tenniel's famous illustrations for Alice in Wonderland.

'Yes, that's right,' she said. Her tone was heavy with despair and he felt a surge of pity for her.

Be careful, said a small voice in his head. She could have done it herself. He had a lightning vision of the slender figure before him galvanised with fury, the flower-like face contorted with rage, that ladylike voice hurling imprecations at Randish. It would have taken no strength at all to sweep bottles, test tubes, flasks off the benches, to seize and hurl some of them at her husband.

Thanet shook his head to clear it. He needed all his wits about him to tread the tightrope he always had to walk when interviewing a bereaved husband or wife. Statistics make it more than likely that you are talking to the murderer, but this can never be taken for granted. And you are in any case addressing a person whose private world has been destroyed for ever.

Noticing that her lower lip had begun to tremble and her eyes to fill with tears he tried to make his tone as matter-of-fact as possible. 'What time did he leave this morning?' *I hate this.*

'I don't know. I was out on Rosie. My horse.'

'And what time did he come back?'

'Just before six, as usual.'

Her voice was steadying, Thanet noticed with relief.

'We always eat early during harvest, so that he can work right through the evening without stopping.'

'So you had supper, and then?'

'He left to go up to the winery, about 6.30.'

'Did you see him again during the evening?'

She bit her lip and shook her head, the long hair swaying from side to side.

'What did you do after he left?'

'Put the children to bed, read them a story. Watched television.'

'So you were alone for the rest of the evening?'

Suddenly tension was back in the air. She glanced at her father, hesitated. 'No.'

Her mother also looked at Landers, somewhat apprehensively, Thanet thought.

What was going on?

'I was here for a while, Inspector,' said Landers.

Thanet was intrigued. So a father had called to see his daughter. Why this reaction? There could be only one reason. The visit must have a possible connection with the murder, in their opinion at least.

'Why was that?' Thanet asked Alice, but she was avoiding his eye, it seemed, staring fixedly at the woodstove and twisting a lock of hair round and round a forefinger.

Mrs Landers had suddenly become engrossed in scraping at an invisible spot on her skirt with her thumbnail.

'Mrs Randish?' Thanet persisted. 'What was the reason for your father's visit?'

'Oh, for God's sake!' Landers exploded. He jumped up and strode across the room towards them. 'Do I have to have a reason to call on my own daughter? You don't think I have to ring up and make an appointment, do you?'

What was it that Landers was trying to prevent her saying? The answer to what had originally been a casual enquiry had become important. Thanet noticed with amusement that Lineham had stopped writing and was staring fixedly at Landers as if trying to read his mind, his nose pointing like a gundog on the trail.

This, clearly, was what the argument had been about. Landers had wanted to hold something back from the police, his daughter had disagreed with him.

'Mrs Randish?' Thanet said again.

Alice looked at her father. 'Oh, what's the point, Daddy? Can't you see you're just making matters worse? I told you they'd be bound to find out sooner or later.'

Very neat. Landers was no match for his daughter, thought Thanet. Alice was obviously skilled at getting her own way. She hadn't openly gone against his wishes but had yet managed to manoeuvre him into the position where it had become obvious that he had something to hide.

Landers was understandably looking baffled and exasperated.

Thanet glanced from one to the other. 'Know what?' He guessed who would be the one to reply.

'Oh, very well!' said Landers. He took up his original position in front of the hearth, unconsciously betraying his agitation by shoving his hand in his pocket and jingling some coins. 'It's just that it's a private matter and rather complicated and as it had been resolved anyway it seemed pointless to mention it, especially as it has no bearing whatsoever on what happened here tonight.'

Thanet said nothing; waited.

Landers shifted from one foot to the other. 'My daughter and her husband have been having some work done by a local builder.'

'Reg Mason,' said Thanet, remembering Vintage's evasiveness on the subject. Perhaps he was now going to find out what all that was about.

They all looked startled.

'Yes. How did you . . .?'

'Mr Vintage told me he'd called to see Mrs Randish this evening.'

Alice shot a triumphant glance at her father. *You see?*

'Go on, Mr Landers.'

It was the sort of sad little tale which had become all too familiar during the recession years. Landers was patently reluctant to tell it and Thanet had to prompt and probe in order to get the details.

Reg Mason's firm was small and he tended to take on only one big project at a time. In the boom years of the late eighties when there had been so much work about that builders could pick and choose and virtually name their own price, he had, like many people, overstretched his resources by buying a much bigger house, with a correspondingly huge mortgage padded out by a bank loan. At that time the future seemed golden, the supply of work endless and confidence was high. Then in '90 and '91 everything went wrong. The bottom fell out of the property market, building work virtually ground to a halt, interest rates shot up. The mortgage became crippling and there was no money coming in. Reg had realised he must retrench. He had put his house on the market but no one could afford to buy it at the price he had to ask. He had reduced it, repeatedly, to no avail. He had had to lay off some of the small team of workmen he had employed for years.

Then Randish's project came along, the conversion of a group of farm buildings into holiday cottages, and Mason had jumped at the chance to tender for it. Randish's credit was good and Mason saw it as a safe enterprise which would keep his firm ticking over until the economic situation improved. Work had started about eighteen months ago and to begin with there had been no problems, Randish paying up reasonably promptly once a month, as agreed. Mason could not afford to pay his suppliers without a regular income from his client.

As always with such work the most expensive months were the last, when floors were tiled, central heating put in, kitchens and bathrooms installed, and it was when these larger bills started to come in that the trouble began. Randish disputed them, claiming that they were far beyond the original estimate. Mason said that this was because Randish had altered the initial specifications, choosing more expensive finishes and introducing additional features. The dispute had been put into the hands of solicitors and had been running for over six months.

Until the matter of the disputed bills, which over three months amounted to a sum of some sixty thousand pounds, Mason had managed to limp along. But after that the situation had become increasingly desperate. His building merchants, unpaid, refused to provide further supplies, thus preventing him from taking on other work until the matter was settled. Both bank and building society pressed progressively harder as unpaid mortgage and interest payments mounted up. A month ago they had lost patience and today he had received a letter from the building society's solicitors saying that they were seeking a court hearing with a view to repossession. The situation was exacerbated by the fact that Mason's wife had a heart condition which was being adversely affected by the strain and anxiety.

Mason had come tonight to make one more attempt to persuade Randish to pay at least a part of the sum owing, much of which was well within the original agreed estimate. Alice had advised him against attempting to talk to her husband that evening. Zak was tired and overworked and would not be in a receptive mood. But she felt sorry for Reg, whom she had known since she was a child, and she promised to do her best to try to persuade her husband to change his mind. Knowing, however, that this was most unlikely, when Reg left she had decided to ask her father's advice. She had rung Landers and asked him to come over.

Thanet could understand why Landers hadn't wanted all this to come out. Mason was obviously a desperate man. His anger and resentment must have been building up for months, justifiably so far as Thanet could see. Even if his bills had been extortionate, most of the money had apparently legitimately been owed to him. In view of Mason's dire financial position Randish could, in all decency, at least have paid him that sum and taken legal action only over the excess amount. The letter informing Mason that repossession was imminent must have been the last straw. That scene of destruction in the laboratory spoke eloquently of an explosion of anger. Mason now seemed a prime candidate and Landers must know it. But it was obvious from the way that Landers had spoken of Mason and presented his story that he was very much on the builder's side. They had probably been boys together and old loyalties die hard. It was equally obvious that Landers had not been fond of his son-in-law and wasn't sorry to see the last of him.

'So,' Thanet said to Alice, 'you had the impression that Mr Mason was going to do as you suggested and not attempt to see your husband tonight?'

'Yes.' She frowned. 'But if Oliver saw him he must have gone up to the winery.'

'Yes, he did. But he didn't see Mr Randish. Mr Vintage says he only stayed a few minutes, then left.'

Landers looked relieved.

'However,' Thanet added, 'Mr Vintage has also made it clear that although he was working at the winery all evening he was moving about a lot and anyone could have got into the bottling plant without being seen.'

'You're not suggesting Reg came back, are you?' said Landers sharply.

'It's possible.'

'No!'

Without warning the door swung open and they all turned towards it, startled.

On the threshold stood a miniature version of Alice Randish, bare-footed and wearing a Snoopy nightshirt. Bridget used to have one exactly like it, Thanet remembered. The little girl blinked at the unexpected sight of a roomful of people.

Her appearance galvanised Alice Randish into action. 'Fiona!' She was across the room in a flash, stooping to put her arms around her daughter. 'Darling, what's the matter?'

'I was thirsty, Mummy. I called, but you didn't come.' Her eyes travelled from face to face. 'Where's Daddy?'

There was a brief, pregnant silence. What would Alice Randish do? Thanet wondered. Break the news of Randish's death to her daughter now, when she herself was at her most vulnerable and least fit to cope with Fiona's reaction? Or wait until morning?

The decision was taken out of her hands. Landers stepped in. He crossed to his granddaughter and swung her up into his arms. 'Grandad will get you a drink, sweetheart. And then we thought it might be fun for you all to come and stay with us for a few days. Would you like that?' Without waiting for an answer he bore Fiona away.

Having told her father she would prefer to stay at home, Alice was understandably looking irritated at his high-handedness. Her lips tightened and she glanced at her mother, who shook her head resignedly. *What did you expect?*

So far, Thanet realised, Mrs Landers hadn't said a single word. He wondered if her relationship with her husband was always so overshadowed by that between him and Alice.

She spoke now. 'Actually, your father's right, dear. Apart from anything else it will be very disturbing for the children to be here over the next few days. There's bound to be a lot of activity, isn't that so, Inspector?'

'Inevitably, I'm afraid.'

'And it really would be better for you, too, to be away from all this. Do reconsider.'

Alice was silent for a few moments, then she sighed. 'I suppose you're right.' She pulled a face. 'I'm just being feeble, I suppose. The thought of organising the packing . . .' She ran a hand through her hair and gave a defeated shrug. 'I just can't seem to think straight.'

Her mother put an arm around her shoulders. 'That's not surprising. Don't worry, I'll see to all that. We won't need to take much tonight, anyway. We can come back tomorrow.'

In the hall a bell tinkled.

'That'll be the doctor,' said Mrs Landers.

There was a sudden flurry of activity: the doctor was admitted; Thanet and Lineham retired once more to the dining room. As they were crossing the hall Landers returned with Fiona and handed her over to her grandmother, who bore her off upstairs. Thanet asked Landers to accompany them. Clearly reluctant, he complied.

'You seem very certain that Mason couldn't have come back,' said Thanet, as if their conversation had not been interrupted.

The phone rang in the hall.

Thanet cursed as Landers jumped up with alacrity. 'I'd better answer that.'

He closed the door behind him and Thanet heard him murmuring responses. A moment or two later he returned, looking stunned. He slumped down into his seat. 'My God,' he said. 'I just don't believe it.'

FOUR

'Bad news, sir?' said Thanet.

'I don't believe it,' Landers repeated. 'They say lightning never strikes twice in the same place. That was my daughter's sister-in-law – Zak's sister. They were very close. She's a widow, and older than him and . . . Well, anyway, she's got two children, twins, a boy and a girl. She was ringing to say the girl, Zak's niece, died this evening. She was only twenty. She's been in hospital for some time, but even so . . .'

The same age as Bridget, thought Thanet, with a pang of sympathy for this unknown woman.

Landers jumped up and began pacing about. The shock seemed to have loosened his tongue. 'I don't know how Alice will take this, especially after what's happened here tonight. She was very fond of her niece. They've always been close, ever since Karen and Jonathan came to stay here for a few days when their mother was in hospital. That was years ago, just before Fiona was born. In fact, Karen seemed to get on better with Alice than with her uncle. So how Alice is going to react . . .' He stopped pacing and turned to face Thanet. 'Oh, you may have thought Alice was calm enough just now, but I know her and believe me, she's just hanging on by the skin of her teeth. She was besotted with that husband of hers. I expect you thought I was coming on a bit strong with her, didn't you? Playing the heavy father? Well that was because I knew it was the only way to stop her falling apart over these first few hours. Give her something to kick against and she'd be OK until the doctor could knock her out. If I'd gone all mushy on her she'd never have been able to cope.'

It all sounded very logical but Thanet wasn't so sure. It wouldn't surprise him to discover that Landers was really talking about himself, that it was he who wouldn't have been able to cope if Alice had 'fallen apart', as he put it. Especially, perhaps, if he had committed the murder himself and was the cause of the disintegration.

'Did you tell Mr Randish's sister about his death?'

'No. Fortunately she wasn't expecting him to come over tonight. She knows he works all hours during harvest, and she asked me to tell him not to. Said she'd just got back from the hospital, she was exhausted and was going to bed. She'd see him tomorrow, she said. I suppose I'll have to go round and break the news of Zak's death to her myself. There's no one else to do it. God knows how she's going to take it.' Landers was obviously dreading the prospect, and Thanet couldn't blame him. Breaking the news of the death of a close relative was high on the list of jobs all policemen hated most.

'We could do it if you like, sir.'

'Oh.' Landers looked taken aback. 'That's very decent of you, Thanet. But no, I think Alice would want me to. Thanks all the same.'

They heard the door across the passageway open and Landers hurried into the hall. There was a brief consultation with the doctor, who had prescribed Alice a sedative, Thanet gathered, and was advising that Mr and Mrs

Landers now took her home and got her to bed. Consulted, Thanet said that there were a few more questions he had to ask Landers before he left. At this point Mrs Landers came back downstairs with Fiona, carrying a younger child, the little boy, swathed in a duvet. It was decided that Mrs Landers, Alice and the children should go on ahead, Mrs Landers driving Alice's car, and that Landers would follow shortly.

When, finally, they had gone, Thanet and Lineham returned to the sitting room with Landers and Thanet put his question for the third time. Perhaps this time he would get an answer.

'You seemed very emphatic, Mr Landers, that Mr Mason couldn't have come back later, after Mr Vintage had seen him leave.'

'That was because Reg and I were together.'

'Really? Where?'

'In the pub, in the village.'

'What time was this?'

Landers ran his fingers through his thick white hair. 'Straight after I left here.'

Patiently, Thanet worked out the timings.

Alice had rung Landers to ask him to come over at around 7.45. Landers and his wife were just finishing their evening meal and he left about twenty minutes later, reaching the vineyard five minutes after that. He knew Mason's van and noticed it in the car park of the village pub as he drove past.

Alice was watching a favourite sitcom when he arrived and they had seen the end of it together before discussing Mason's predicament.

Landers had come up with a possible solution.

'There's an empty cottage on my farm, quite a decent one, detached and with a small garden. I told Alice I'd decided to offer it to Reg, at a nominal rent, until he could get his business back on its feet again.'

'That was very generous of you, Mr Landers.'

Landers looked embarrassed. 'Yes, well, Reg and I go back a long way.'

'You're good friends?'

'I wouldn't say that. But we've known each other since we were boys and we've always been on good terms. He's worked hard all his life and I don't want to see him go under.'

'So you decided to tell him about the cottage?'

'Well, Alice said she'd have one more go at trying to persuade Zak to change his mind about paying Reg at least a proportion of the money owing to him. But yes, we decided that in any case I'd have a word with Reg to reassure him that whatever happened, he'd still have a roof over his head. So that's what I did.'

Landers had left Alice at around 8.45 and seeing Mason's van still in the car park at the pub had called in to have a drink with him and give him the good news. He and Mason had left the pub together at around 9.15 and he, Landers, had arrived home shortly afterwards. Mason had said he was going straight home to tell his wife about Landers' offer.

'That's why I'm so certain Reg didn't come back here later. He was itching to get home and tell Kath, his wife, about the cottage. And in any case, the offer had taken the pressure off him, don't you see?'

They let Landers go. The Mercedes in the vineyard car park was his. They watched its tail-lights disappear down the drive and then Lineham said, 'Mason certainly isn't off the hook, as far as I can see. According to Vintage, Mason left about ten to eight but Vintage didn't actually see him leave the premises. He could easily have sneaked back into the bottling plant without Vintage seeing him. I know Landers says he saw Mason's van parked at the pub when he went by at ten past eight but that was twenty minutes later. And Mason had another opportunity to come back later on, after leaving Landers outside the pub. It's all very well saying the offer of the house had taken the pressure off him, but that doesn't mean he'd stop feeling angry with Randish, who had got him into the mess in the first place.'

'Quite.'

'So do we go and see him, sir?'

'I suppose so.' Thanet peered at his watch. It was just after midnight. He didn't like disturbing people at this hour, but murder was murder. If he left it until morning vital evidence could disappear and Mason would have time to compose himself and get his story straight. No, it would have to be tonight.

The village of Charthurst was only half a mile from the vineyard, just a few minutes away by car, and at this time of night was silent and deserted. Most of the houses were in darkness but lights illuminated the well-kept forecourt of the Harrow, the pub where Landers and Mason had met. Lineham was right, Thanet thought. Twenty minutes would have been ample for Mason to have slipped back into the laboratory, committed the murder and got down here by the time Landers drove past. When Mason first went up to the winery that night, had he told Vintage he wanted to talk to Randish, and why? And had Vintage advised him against it? If so, why hadn't Vintage said so? If this was what Vintage had been hiding, why should he be so concerned to protect Mason? Because he was sorry for him? Felt he'd been ill-treated?

In any case, perhaps Mason had pretended to leave because he would have been embarrassed to be seen going into the bottling plant against the advice of both Alice Randish and Vintage. But if he had waited until Vintage's back was turned, or if he had slipped back later, and if Randish had been particularly tactless or dismissive in his refusal to listen to his plea, then Mason might well have finally snapped, lost control. And there was no doubt about it, whoever killed Randish had been completely out of control. Yes, Mason might well be their man.

Landers had told them where Mason lived and from his description they found the house without difficulty. Even without the 'FOR SALE' sign outside they could scarcely have missed it. The last street lamp in the village illuminated a high brick wall and tall wrought-iron gates flanked by pillars from which two lions gazed haughtily down on passers-by. Someone obviously had delusions of grandeur. Mason, or a previous owner? Thanet wondered.

The house itself was set well back from the road behind large areas of lawn and as they drove up the curving drive a row of security lights spaced out along its façade clicked on. It had been built some time in the last ten years, Thanet guessed, and it was big, a good sixty to eighty feet long, with a four-car garage. Although it was not to his taste Thanet could see why, in the heady years of the housing boom, Mason had been tempted into overstretching himself to buy it. It shouted 'SUCCESS' from every picture window.

Lineham gave a low whistle. 'No wonder he can't sell it. I wonder how much he's asking for it.'

Houses like this, in the higher price brackets, were the last to move in the still sluggish housing market. 'Thinking of putting in a bid, Mike?'

'Ha, ha, very funny. That'd be the day.'

The doorbell sounded unnaturally loud in the darkness and silence.

'I hate hauling people out of bed at this hour,' muttered Thanet. 'Makes me feel like the secret police.'

'Got to be done, sir.'

'Maybe. That doesn't make me feel any better about it, though.'

Above, there was the sound of a window opening and a man's voice called out, 'Who is it?'

Thanet and Lineham stepped back, peered up. 'Sorry to disturb you, sir. It's the police.'

'I'll come down.'

The silhouetted head disappeared and a moment later a light clicked on in the hall. Someone approached the front door inside and there was a brief pause. Thanet guessed that Mason was inspecting them through the spyhole. Finally the door opened on a chain and a hand emerged through the crack. 'Your identification, please.'

Thanet handed over his warrant card and eventually the door swung wide.

'Sorry about that,' said Mason. 'But you can't be too careful these days.'

He was short and stocky, with a squarish head, cropped brown hair and wary brown eyes. He was wearing an old-fashioned woollen dressing gown in a brown and fawn check pattern and striped flannel pyjamas. He led them into a big sitting room where dralon-upholstered chairs and settees were dotted uneasily about on a sea of heavily patterned carpet. There were a couple of occasional tables and an elaborate arrangement of artificial flowers. No books, no newspapers, no magazines, not even a television set, Thanet noted. The effect was as bleak and impersonal as a dentist's waiting room and Mason looked completely out of place in it. It was cold, too, with a damp, penetrating chill. Thanet guessed that the Masons had been forced to economise on their central heating and that this room was no longer in use.

Mason shivered and pulled his dressing gown more closely about him. 'I'll light the fire.'

It was a gas fire of imitation logs and when he had lit it he stood with his back to it, rubbing his arms. 'What's all this about?'

'I understand you went up to the vineyard to see Mr Randish this evening, sir?'

'Yes. Why?'

'He was found dead tonight. In his laboratory.'

Mason stopped rubbing his arms and became quite still. 'Dead?' He looked astounded.

Genuine astonishment or not? Thanet had no idea.

'But how? I mean, he was perfectly all right when I last saw him.'

'When was that, Mr Mason?'

'Yesterday afternoon.'

'You didn't see him tonight?'

'No. I wanted to, yes, but . . . Look, why all the questions?'

'Mr Randish was murdered, sir.'

If Mason was acting he was making a good job of it. His jaw dropped open and he groped blindly for the arm of the nearest chair, sank down into it. 'Murdered? I don't . . .'

The door swung open and a girl of about eighteen came into the room. 'What's going on, Dad?'

She too was short and stockily built, with long dark curly hair, blunt nose and square, determined jaw. Her quilted dressing gown was tightly belted beneath her ample breasts, her solid legs terminating in large feet incongruously thrust into high-heeled mules trimmed with swansdown.

'It's the police, love. Mr Randish . . .' Mason looked helplessly at Thanet. *How can I tell her?*

Her eyes narrowed and she glanced from her father to the two policemen. 'What about him?'

She'd have to know sooner or later, and in any case Thanet suspected she was a lot tougher than her father's attitude would suggest. 'Mr Randish was found dead tonight, Miss Mason. He'd been murdered.'

Her eyebrows shot up. 'Murdered!' She glanced at her father and Thanet had the impression that she was thinking fast, working out the implications. 'Well, well, well!' she said at last, and sauntered towards them, wobbling slightly on the impossibly high heels. 'Good riddance to bad rubbish, I say.'

'Sharon!'

'Don't "Sharon" me, Dad. You know what I thought of that creep! What's the point in being hypocritical about it?' She turned to Thanet. 'All the same, I don't see what you're doing here. What d'you want with us?'

'We understand your father went to see Mr Randish tonight, Miss Mason.'

'So what? Oh I see . . . So that's it! Someone told you about Dad's little problem and bingo, you added two and two together to make five. Typical!'

'Sharon, no one's said anything about –'

'No, they don't need to, do they? Come on, Dad, who d'you think you're kidding? Why else d'you think they've got you out of bed at this hour? Better go and get your clothes on, pack your suitcase or they're going to be dragging you off to the police station in your pyjamas.'

'You're jumping the gun somewhat, Miss Mason. At this stage we simply want to ask your father some questions.'

'Oh, I see, the arrest is the next stage, is it? Well I can

tell you straight off you're barking up the wrong tree. Dad wouldn't hurt a fly. And he didn't even see Mr Skinflint Randish this evening. Did you tell them that, Dad?'

Thanet was getting a little tired of this. 'Your father hasn't had a chance to tell us anything yet,' he snapped. 'All we know so far is what we have heard from other people. That's why we've come to see him.'

'Well go on then, Dad. Tell them.'

And Sharon planted herself in front of the fire, arms folded belligerently across her substantial bosom.

They all looked at Mason.

He shrugged. 'There's not much to tell. I did go up to the vineyard, yes, but I didn't see Mr Randish.'

'Why not?' said Thanet. 'No, begin at the beginning. What time was this?'

Mason's story tallied with what Alice and Vintage had told them. He had arrived at the vineyard at about 7.30 and had spent ten minutes or so talking to Alice Randish, a further ten talking to Vintage. Then he had left.

'Mrs Randish tells us that she advised you not to see Mr Randish this evening, that she thought it would be better for her to speak to him first. So why did you go up to the winery?'

'I thought if Mr Randish knew how serious my position was, he might –'

'And pigs might fly!' said Sharon. 'I told you there was no point in going, didn't I? If you'd listened to me you wouldn't be in this mess now, would you?'

Thanet ignored the interruption. 'So why didn't you speak to him?'

'Because Oliver also advised me not to.'

So Mason *had* told Vintage that he intended to speak to Randish.

'Oh, did he? Why was that?'

'He didn't think it was a good moment to approach him.'

'Any particular reason?'

'Mr Randish wasn't in a very good mood, he said.'

'Did he say why?'

Mason hesitated and before he could reply the door opened again. An older woman this time, Mason's wife, presumably. She stood supporting herself with one hand against the door post. 'Reg? What's happening?'

Mason jumped up and both he and his daughter hurried to assist her.

'Kath, you shouldn't be here . . .'

'Mum, what are you doing up?'

Mrs Mason peered past them at Thanet and Lineham. 'Who's this? What are they doing here? It's nearly one in the morning.'

'And you should be in bed,' said Mason gently, attempting to steer his wife back out of the door again.

She detached her elbow from his grasp. 'Reg, please . . . I want to know what's going on.'

'There's been an accident in the village, Mum,' said Sharon. 'It's the police. They're making some inquiries.'

'What accident? Why is it so urgent? Why can't it wait till morning?'

She was clearly determined not to be fobbed off and they seemed equally determined not to tell her. Thanet now remembered Landers telling him that Mrs Mason had a heart condition. Perhaps he should, after all, have waited until morning to question the builder, when he could have got him on his own.

She was becoming exasperated. 'Reg, for goodness' sake stop treating me like a child and tell me straight what's happened.'

'All right, love. But come and sit down first.'

He glanced at Sharon and some unspoken communication passed between them. Sharon left the room.

Mason led his wife to a settee and sat down beside her, taking her hand. Gently, he broke the news to her.

She drew in her breath sharply and he watched her anxiously.

Sharon came quietly back into the room. She was holding something in her hand. Thanet couldn't see what it was.

Mrs Mason looked up at Thanet. 'I still don't understand what you're doing here. What's it got to do with –' She broke off and turned back to her husband. 'Reg, you went up there tonight. Is that . . .' Her hand flew to her chest as realisation hit her and Sharon hurried forward, stumbling in her haste as one of her heels caught on the edge of the hearthrug. If the look she directed at Thanet and Lineham could have killed, they would have fallen dead on the spot. She dropped to her knees in front of her mother, shaking some tiny tablets out of the pill bottle she was holding.

This was what she had gone to fetch, Thanet realised. She and her father had been afraid this might happen.

She handed a tablet to her mother, who put it under her tongue.

They all watched Mrs Mason anxiously. In a minute or two she began to breathe more evenly and the hand she was pressing against her chest relaxed.

Thanet became aware that he had been holding his breath. He and Lineham exchanged relieved glances.

'It's all right,' she said feebly. 'I'm fine now.' She patted her daughter's hand. 'Thanks, love.'

Sharon stood up, coming to her feet like a released spring. 'I think you'd better go,' she said to Thanet and

Lineham in tones of barely suppressed fury. 'You've done enough damage for one night.'

Thanet was inclined to agree with her. He could finish questioning Mason tomorrow. It was obvious that the builder wasn't going anywhere.

It was not until he was almost home that he realised there was something he had forgotten to do. One of the reasons why he had not wanted to leave the interview with Mason until the next day was that he had intended to take away the shoes Mason had been wearing that night, in case there were fragments of glass embedded in their soles. His concern for Mrs Mason and his relief that she seemed to have recovered had driven this completely out of his mind.

He hoped that at this very moment vital evidence was not being destroyed.

FIVE

Joan was fast asleep when Thanet got home and he was careful not to wake her. Next morning she brought him a cup of tea in bed. Usually it was the other way around.

He blinked himself awake, peered at the clock, sank back with a sigh of relief. Seven o'clock. He hadn't overslept, then. 'What are you doing up at this hour, love? Got to go in to work today?'

Joan was a probation officer and usually had Saturdays off. Occasionally, though, there was some special task to perform.

She drew the curtains back and a grey, mournful light crept into the room. 'No. I just woke up early, that's all. What a miserable day.'

'Is it raining?'

'No.' She peered up at the sky. 'I wouldn't be surprised if it did later, though.'

She sounded uncharacteristically gloomy and looked tired, Thanet thought. 'Do I gather you've found out what's wrong with Bridget?'

'Yes. We had a talk last night, after you'd gone.' She came back, sat down on the bed, a dispirited slump to her shoulders. 'It's as we thought. Alexander has broken it off.'

'Just like that.'

'Just like that?'

'No warning, no hint of what was coming?'

'Apparently not. Oh, I suppose there must have been signs, but if there were, Bridget didn't see them. Or didn't want to see them, perhaps.'

'Did he give any particular reason?'

'Only that he doesn't feel ready for a long-term commitment yet.'

Thanet experienced a spurt of anger. How dare this handsome, privileged, debonair young man float into Bridget's life and then toss her aside, careless of any damage he might have inflicted? 'How's she taking it?'

'Well, you saw for yourself.'

'Quite. Well, I don't suppose there's much we can do for her at the moment, except give her moral support. Anyway, let's try to look on the bright side. She's still young, she'll get over it eventually, I suppose.' He hoped.

'Maybe. But I'm afraid she's going to have a bad time for a while. She really was very fond of him. And inevitably she's asking herself where she went wrong.'

'If we could help her to see that it was Alexander's problem, not hers . . .'

'I know. Oh Luke, it's such a shame. He was such a nice young man.'

'Maybe. But I never did think he was right for her, as you know.'

'I never really understood why.'

Thanet leaned forward and kissed her. 'Darling, much as I'd love to have a deep and earnest conversation on the merits or otherwise of Alexander as a suitor for our daughter, if I don't get up soon I shan't want to get up at all.'

She laughed and stood up. 'I'll go and get you some breakfast.'

'No need. I can do it myself.'

'I know that. But I thought I'd cook something for a change.'

Thanet wasn't going to argue with that. Cooked breakfasts were a rare treat nowadays, indulged in only occasionally at weekends.

Neither Bridget nor Ben put in an appearance and they had a leisurely breakfast *à deux*. Fortified by bacon, egg, toast and marmalade, several cups of freshly brewed coffee and a pipe, Thanet arrived at the office feeling ready to tackle anything. As usual, Lineham was already at work. Thanet could never be sure whether the sergeant invariably arrived early because he loved his job and couldn't wait to get to his desk each morning, or whether he found the early-morning chaos of life with a young family so trying that it was a relief to escape from it. In any case, he suspected that by now it was a matter of pride to Lineham to arrive before his boss.

'Morning, Mike. Anything new?'

'The *Kent Messenger*'s been on the phone, sir. And TVS.'

Thanet groaned. He hated the public relations side of his job, but forced himself to take it in his stride. Occasionally the police really needed the cooperation of the media and he was careful not to antagonise them. After all, like him they were only doing their job. 'Tell them I'll give them a statement this evening but that there'll be nothing until then. Perhaps that'll keep them from being underfoot all day.'

'In time for the six o'clock news, sir?'

'I suppose so. Anything else?'

'PM's arranged for later on today.'

'Good.' Thanet glanced at his watch. Time for the morning meeting, a ritual instituted by Draco when he first arrived, and which they had kept up whether he was there to take it or not. 'Look, while I'm at the meeting get a message out to the vineyard. The regular staff will no doubt be turning up for work as usual. Make sure they're not allowed home until they've all been questioned. Get Carson and Bentley out there to do it. And give Reg Mason a ring. I want to talk to him again, but not at home. I don't want a repeat performance of last night with Mrs Mason. Ask him to come in to Headquarters, as soon after nine as possible.'

At the meeting Chief Inspector Tody, who acted as Draco's deputy in his absence, confirmed that Draco had intended taking his wife away for the weekend after getting the results of her latest test the previous day.

'Let's hope the news is good,' he said.

On the way back upstairs Thanet ran into DC Wakeham, hovering outside his door. This was a recent recruit to Thanet's team, keen as mustard but still unsure of himself. Thanet always kept a close eye on new arrivals. It was very interesting to see how they settled in – important, too. Nothing was as disruptive to teamwork as disharmony between its members. Wakeham would do, he thought. The DC was feeling his way carefully, trying to learn and to pull his weight without treading on anyone's toes.

'You've got something for me, Chris?'

Wakeham wore a worried frown. 'I'm not sure, sir. I don't even know if I ought to mention it, when . . .'

'Come on in. Let's hear it all the same.'

Inside, Wakeham looked if anything even more worried. 'I hope I'm not jumping the gun, sir. I mean, I don't even know if there's any point in mentioning it at the moment . . .'

'Chris,' said Thanet patiently, 'you've said that once,

already. But you're here now, so just get on with it, will you?' Then, as Wakeham still hesitated, 'Well come on, man, spit it out. It's obvious you'll go on worrying about it until you do.'

'It's just that I've been looking at the photographs. Of the murder victim, sir. And I'm sure I've seen him before.'

'Where? And when?'

Wakeham looked downcast. 'Well, that's why I wondered if I ought to mention it at the moment, sir. I can't remember.'

Thanet laughed. 'I know the feeling, Chris, I know the feeling. We all do, for that matter. But don't worry, it'll come to you. And when it does, let me know. Meanwhile my advice is try to forget about it. Let your subconscious do the work for you. Sooner or later it'll come up with the answer.'

'Right, sir. Thank you.'

Wakeham was almost at the door when Thanet called him back. 'There's a little job I'd like you to do. One of the suspects in the Randish case is a chap called Reg Mason. He's coming in for questioning this morning and when he leaves I'd like you to go home with him and pick up the clothes he was wearing on his visit to the vineyard last night. Especially the shoes. Get all the stuff sent off to the lab, asking them particularly to look out for fragments of glass embedded in the soles of the shoes. And then I want you to do a little digging about those shoes, just to make sure he's given you the right ones. Talk to Vintage, the assistant winemaker at the vineyard, see if he can remember what shoes Mason was wearing last night. Also, have a word with Randish's father-in-law and the landlord at the pub. Anyone, in fact, who might have noticed. Use your initiative.'

Wakeham went off looking like a Labrador who had just spotted an especially juicy bone.

'That should distract him all right,' said Thanet with a grin.

'He's a good lad,' said Lineham. 'A bit too much of a worrier at the moment, but only because he's so anxious to do the right thing. He'll get over that.'

'I agree. Now, what did you fix up with Mason?'

'I missed him, sir. He'd already left.' Watching Thanet's face, Lineham grinned. 'But before you explode, let me say it's only because he was already on his way here, of his own accord. In fact, he should be arriving any minute now.'

'Check, will you?'

Mason was already waiting downstairs and it was arranged that Lineham would question him today.

Slumped at the table in an interview room in a brown leather jacket which had seen better days, Mason looked tired and depressed. Thanet guessed that he hadn't slept much the previous night. His eyes were weary, the skin beneath them slack and puffy.

'How's Mrs Mason?' Thanet asked.

'All right. But I didn't want her upset again, so in case there was anything else you wanted to ask me I thought I'd come in, so you didn't have to come to the house.'

'A good idea,' said Lineham. 'There were one or two points . . .'

'Fire away, then.' Mason leaned back in his chair, shoving his hands into his pockets. He looked resigned, as if unpleasant experiences had become the norm for him of late.

'You realise that you're in a very difficult position, Mr Mason.'

The builder gave a short, unamused bark of laughter.

'You can say that again! In fact, you might say things couldn't be much worse.'

'We understand that because of the dispute with Mr Randish, there's a question of your house being repossessed.'

'That's what I meant.'

Lineham frowned. 'Don't play games, Mr Mason. It wasn't what I meant, as I'm sure you're aware. But I'll spell it out. I'm referring to Mr Randish's murder. You obviously had a grudge against him and you were there, at the vineyard, at the time when the crime was committed. What's more, when you went up there last night you must have been feeling pretty desperate.'

'OK, OK.' Mason waved a weary hand. 'So I was feeling pretty desperate. That doesn't mean I knocked him off, does it? If we all went around bumping off everyone we felt angry with, pretty soon there'd be no one left, would there?'

'All the same, you must have been very determined to see him, make one last appeal to his better nature, shall we say.'

That short bark of laughter again. 'You must be joking. Better nature! What better nature?'

'You didn't like him, did you? In fact you hated his guts.'

Suddenly, Mason leaned forward. 'Wouldn't you?' he spat. 'If someone wouldn't pay you what he rightfully owed you and as a result *your* family was going to be out on the street, wouldn't you hate his guts?' He subsided, indignation already fading. 'No, I don't deny it, I did hate him for what he's done to me, to us. But that still doesn't mean I'd commit murder just to get my own back.'

'Maybe you didn't go up there intending to. Maybe you just wanted to have a reasonable, rational discussion with him, man to man. But what if he wouldn't play ball? What if he just told you to get lost, or worse, just laughed at you? What then? Wouldn't all your good intentions fly out the window? Come on, Mr Mason, why not admit it? It's so easy to snap, isn't it, when you've been under a strain for a long time, as you have, so easy to lose your temper, pick up a bottle and throw it at him in sheer frustration. Then another and another, and before you know where you are, it's too late, he's dead . . .'

Mason's jaw had dropped. 'You must be out of your tiny mind! Look, ask anyone, anyone who knows me, anyone who's ever known me. OK, I might get a bit irritable from time to time, but I bet you won't find a single person who's seen me lose my temper, not ever.'

'They say that every man has his breaking point, Mr Mason. Perhaps you'd reached yours.'

'No! I never even saw him, I told you!'

Lineham leaned forward. 'We find it very difficult to believe that. Try to look at it from our point of view. You're frantic about losing your home. You go up there to make one last appeal. You see Mrs Randish. She says she'll speak to her husband on your behalf and suggests you don't approach him again until after she's done so. So what do you do? Go home? No. You came intending to see Mr Randish and see him you will. So you go up to the winery and ask Mr Vintage where Randish is. And then, surprise, surprise, where Mrs Randish has failed to convince you, Mr Vintage succeeds. You take his advice and off you go, like a little lamb. So what we want to know is why? Why listen to him and not to Randish's wife, who presumably knows her husband best?'

'I told you last night! Because Mr Randish was in a bad mood, Oliver said, and he thought it would do my case more harm than good to tackle him last night.'

Thanet wasn't surprised to learn that, as he had suspected when he last spoke to Mason, Vintage had indeed known why Mason wanted to see Randish and had been reluctant to say so to the police because he was in sympathy with the builder's cause. No doubt the dispute was common knowledge in the village, as such things are in a small community. But it still didn't explain why Mason had taken his advice.

'Yes, I know you told us that,' said Lineham. 'But he must have put forward some very convincing argument, to get you to listen to him. What was it?'

Once again Mason hesitated, as he had last night.

Mason shrugged. 'It was enough, to know he was in a bad mood. I mean, what was the point of putting his back up?' But his tone lacked conviction.

He was definitely holding something back, thought Thanet. And he was beginning to waver. *Go on Mike, press home your advantage.*

Lineham was shaking his head, 'Not good enough, Mr Mason. Look, I don't think you realise the seriousness of your position. You were there, on the spot, when a man you hated was murdered. If you refuse to be frank with us and fail to give us a convincing reason why you gave up and went away without seeing him, you can't blame us for drawing our own conclusions.'

'But I didn't go near him, I swear it!'

Lineham said nothing, just gazed steadily at Mason, whose eyes eventually fell away. 'It was because they'd had a row,' he muttered.

Lineham must have been pleased at Mason's capitulation, but he didn't show it. 'Who had a row? Mr Randish and Mr Vintage?'

Mason nodded.

'Then why on earth didn't you say so before?'

Thanet could guess why. Mason had hesitated to point the finger of suspicion at Vintage for the same reason that Vintage had been reluctant to talk about Mason's visit: they had evidently both been ill-treated in some way by Zak Randish and had not wanted to implicate a fellow-sufferer. What had the row between Vintage and Randish been about? he wondered.

Mason had not replied, just shook his head, and Lineham sounded exasperated as he said, 'Well, what was the row about?'

'None of my business, I'm afraid. I didn't ask.'

That didn't mean that Vintage hadn't told him, though, thought Thanet. But by the stubborn line to Mason's lips he guessed that Lineham wasn't going to succeed in getting him to say any more on this subject. He was right. The sergeant tried various tacks and then, recognising that it was a hopeless task, went on to question Mason about the rest of the evening. Mason's account tallied with what Landers had told them.

'And when you left the pub at 9.15 with Mr Landers?'

'I went straight home to tell my wife about Mr Landers' offer. I knew she'd be relieved to know we had somewhere to go.'

And Lineham could not shake him.

They watched him depart with DC Wakeham and then Lineham said, 'So, the plot thickens. Mr Vintage was keeping very quiet about that row, wasn't he?'

'Wouldn't you, if you'd had a row with someone and a couple of hours later he was found murdered?'

Lineham laughed. 'Put like that, yes, I suppose I would. Anyway, d'you think Mason was telling the truth?'

Thanet pursed his lips. 'Some of it, yes. All of it? I'm not sure. In any case, Vintage certainly has some explaining to do. Let's go.'

SIX

The first drops of the rain which Joan had forecast spotted the windscreen as Lineham turned into the entrance to the vineyard.

Alice Randish and Fiona were just getting into a Range Rover. They were both wearing corduroy trousers, roll-neck sweaters and Puffa waistcoats, Fiona's outfit a scaled-down version of her mother's. Alice, Thanet remembered, owned a horse and Fiona probably had a pony. Livestock had to be attended to whatever crisis its owners were going through. Thanet raised a hand in greeting and Alice acknowledged it with a tight nod as she drove away. Her face was set, as if she were hanging on to her self-control by the most slender of threads. Thanet wondered if she had been told about her niece's death yet.

The rain was coming down more steadily now and with increasing force. Lights were on in the shop and two women inside turned curious faces as Thanet and Lineham hurried past to the bottling plant.

Inside the big double doors they took off their raincoats and shook them before the water could soak into the fabric. Carson had come to meet them and he now led them into the office, where he gave them an update on the various searches and inquiries that were going on. Most of the staff had been interviewed and allowed to go home, but two of the women had been held back. One of the girls who served in the shop had told him that Oliver Vintage had been 'in a mood' the previous day, though she didn't know why. She usually worked in the shop only on Saturdays, but had come in to help out yesterday because the regular girl was ill, so she knew nothing of what had been going on at the vineyard during the days leading up to the murder. The manageress was a different matter. Both Carson and Bentley were sure that she knew more than she was telling, but had failed to get her to open up.

'Has Vintage shown up yet?' said Thanet. 'I told him I'd want to see him again this morning.'

'Yes, some time ago. He went off into the vineyard to look at some grapes,' said Carson. He glanced at the rain, which was now beating relentlessly against the windows. 'I shouldn't think he'll stay out long, in this.'

The manageress's name was Mrs Prote and she was waiting in the shop.

'Prote. What sort of name is that?' said Lineham.

While they waited for Carson to fetch her Lineham prowled around the office, coming to a halt in front of the computer. The sergeant had been hooked on computers ever since he'd done a course a few years back. 'Nice computer system, sir.'

Thanet wasn't interested. 'Really?'

'Yes. Expensive. New, by the look of it. And a laser printer. I'm surprised he didn't get something cheaper, for a business of this size.'

Carson was back. 'Mrs Prote, sir.'

The manageress was in her late thirties, tall and dark, with horn-rimmed spectacles and hair swept back into a neat French roll. The pleats in her navy blue skirt were crisp, her shoes highly polished. She looked as if she were used to having everything under control and her expression was apprehensive and somewhat bewildered – hurt, even, as if life had unexpectedly let her down. As she came in she cast a proprietorial glance around the office as if to check that these interlopers had not been tampering with her arrangements. She sat down primly, knees together, feet neatly aligned.

She had worked at the vineyard for four years, Thanet learned, and was in charge of the hiring of staff and of the administration of both vineyard and tea shop, leaving Randish free for his work as winemaker and consultant.

'What sort of consultant?' said Lineham.

'He advises people who are setting up their own vineyards on the types of grapes to plant, explains to them the various advantages and disadvantages of the two main systems of growing, and also acts as agent for winemaking equipment. Anything, really, to do with the growing of grapes and the making of wine. He's – he was, very much respected as a winemaker.'

'How did you get on with him, Mrs Prote?' said Thanet.

Interesting, he thought. A toe on her right foot had twitched. Feet were often a giveaway. People could school themselves to control their facial muscles, but their extremities seemed to have a life of their own. She had obviously had reservations about her employer.

'All right.'

'You don't sound too enthusiastic.'

'We got along perfectly well as employer and employee. I know my job, I'm reasonably good at it, I think, and he was satisfied with my work. Otherwise I wouldn't have stayed as long as I have.'

'What about Mr Vintage?'

Extraordinary things, eyes, thought Thanet. Fascinating, how they reflect one's inner feelings and attitudes. Mrs Prote did not blink, nor did her expression alter even slightly, except for her eyes. There, it was just as if a shutter had closed. And her right toe twitched again.

'What about him?'

'How do you get on with him?'

'Fine. Though we don't actually have a lot to do with each other. He works outside and I work inside and our responsibilities don't often overlap.'

'What do you think of his work?'

'He's hardworking and conscientious, anxious to learn. I know Mr Randish thought he was becoming a very good winemaker.'

She had relaxed a little, pleased to present Vintage in a good light. Time to try to get under her guard.

'What was the row about, between Vintage and Mr Randish?'

She blinked and this time she twisted her right foot around her left ankle. 'What row?'

Thanet sighed. 'Look, Mrs Prote, I'm not going to insult your intelligence by playing games. I'll be frank with you. One of your members of staff has told us that Oliver Vintage was "in a mood" all day yesterday, and we know from another source that Vintage and your employer had a row last night . . .'

'Last night?' At once, she looked as though she wished she hadn't spoken.

'You're surprised. Interestingly enough, not by the fact that they had a row at all, but by the fact that it was last night. Why is that?'

She shook her head to convey – what? Confusion? Reluctance?

'What can I say to convince you that you have to be frank with us? This is, I must stress, a murder inquiry. If you know anything, anything at all, which could help us, it really is your duty to say so.'

But duties could conflict, as Thanet knew only too well, and people frequently chose to give their loyalty to people rather than to the abstract cause of justice.

'There's really not much point in hiding anything, you know,' Thanet added softly. 'We always find out, sooner or later, I assure you. I can see we are talking about someone you obviously like and respect and I can understand your reluctance to tell us anything you feel might incriminate him. But surely it's better that we learn anything there is to be learnt from someone who is on his side.'

'I doubt that you'd find anyone who isn't. Not that he is in need of such support, of course.'

'Nevertheless . . .'

Thanet let the silence stretch out, aware of its power to exert pressure where words have failed.

Mrs Prote had turned her head and was gazing out of the window as if seeking the answer to her dilemma in the familiar view outside.

She had come to a decision. Her lips tightened.

She's not going to tell me, thought Thanet.

She shook her head. 'I'm sorry, Inspector, I can't help you. But I will say this. I've worked with Oliver Vintage for four years now and I honestly do not believe he could have anything to do with what happened here last night.'

Thanet could see that there was no point in pursuing the matter. Her mind was made up and that was that. He sent Lineham to find Vintage.

While he waited he stared out of the window at the view which had greeted Randish every day of his working life. What had the man been like? So far he hadn't even begun to understand what made him tick. They seemed to have been plunged at once into suspects and motives. But it was Randish who was the key to the mystery, Randish whose behaviour had for some reason hurled someone into a fit of ungovernable rage. Thanet realised he should have discussed him at greater length with Mrs Prote, but he had been so intent upon trying to get her to talk about the row with Vintage that he had let the chance slip. He could always see her again, of course, but meanwhile he wasn't going to make the same mistake with Vintage.

The heavy shower had eased off and the sky was lightening. Perhaps it would clear up later after all. Vintage, however, had obviously caught the worst of it. His old waxed jacket streamed with water and his hair was plastered to his scalp, accentuating the skull-like effect imparted by the deep eye-sockets and the hollows beneath the cheekbones. The early night didn't seem to have done him much good. He still looked bone-weary.

He took off his coat, dropped it on the floor and perched on the edge of a desk, taking out a green-spotted handkerchief to mop his face. 'Bloody rain. We could do without this, on top of everything else.'

Thanet leaned back in a relaxed manner and said, 'Tell us about Mr Randish. What was he like?'

'Like?' Vintage frowned. 'In what way?'

Thanet waved a hand. 'Any way.'

'Well, he was ambitious. Always looking for ways to expand his business, to make more money. But hard-working, mind.'

'Ruthless, perhaps?'

'A bit, yes, I suppose. All successful businessmen are, aren't they?'

'Go on.'

Vintage frowned. 'It's difficult, when you work with someone every day. You don't stand back and look at them, you tend to take them for granted.'

'Try.'

'Well, he had a very good opinion of himself.'

'Egotists are by definition very self-centred.'

No response.

'They tend to be somewhat dismissive of other people's feelings.' And that shot had gone home, Thanet thought. Vintage's eyes had dropped and he had compressed his lips.

Vintage shifted uncomfortably. 'I don't really like talking about him like this.'

'Speaking ill of the dead, you mean?'

'Yes.'

'Understandable, but really rather pointless, don't you think? I'm not asking you to spread malicious gossip, just to give me your own frank, personal opinion of him. Nothing you can say will harm him now and it might help us to understand what happened last night.'

'I don't see how.'

'Just take my word for it, Mr Vintage.'

Vintage slid off the desk and walked to the window, stood looking out, with his back to them. 'I still can't quite take it in, that he's dead. He was so very much alive, if you see what I mean. Always full of energy, always looking for new avenues to explore.'

Vintage was prevaricating, Thanet realised, while he tried to make up his mind how much to tell them. Thanet was happy to go along with this if it would encourage Vintage to open up. 'Yes, I understand he had a number of strings to his bow. He must have had a lot of contacts. I believe his sister lives locally, so I imagine he grew up in the area.'

'Yes he did, I think.'

'How did he get into vine-growing, do you know?'

Vintage returned to his perch, settled down again. 'I think he was always interested in farming, used to work on farms in the school holidays and joined the Young Farmers' Club. That was where he met Mark Benton, I believe – Mark's father, James Benton, owns the other vineyard where Zak is – was – winemaker, at Chasing Manor. That was where Zak really became interested in vines, through going out to the vineyard with Mark. He started working there during the holidays after that, instead of on a farm. Mr Benton was winemaker there at the time, of course, but by the time he retired Zak had had quite a lot of experience and I suppose it was natural for him to take over. Mr Benton still owns the vineyard, though.'

'Mark Benton didn't take over when his father retired?'

'No. He went into something completely different. He's an accountant.'

'His father must have been disappointed.'

'Zak told me Mark was never interested in the vineyard. You can't force these things.'

'No. Presumably Mr Randish went to college to study – what do you call it, the study of vine-growing? Viticulture?'

'That's right, viticulture. No, he couldn't. At that time there was no such course at any college in the country. Now, there is a course in vine-growing and winemaking, at Plumpton. It started a few years ago. Oddly enough, it was to Plumpton Agricultural College that Zak went. No, like me, Zak went to some workshop courses at Alfriston, run by the Agricultural Training Board. It was the only way to learn viticulture at the time. But I was lucky. My old man could afford to pay for me to go to

Australia. The vineyards out there are amazing and I got in a couple of years' very useful experience, learnt a hell of a lot.'

'You're saying that Mr Randish's family couldn't have afforded to send him to do something like that?'

'Well I could be wrong but that's certainly the impression I've got.'

'So how did he acquire this place?' Though Thanet suspected he could guess.

'I really don't know.'

'How did he meet his wife, do you know?'

'In the Young Farmers', I believe.'

Yes, a good place for an impecunious and ambitious lad interested in farming to meet a prospective bride, thought Thanet. Or was he being unfair to Randish? 'How did they get on?'

'Oh, for God's sake! If you want to discuss his marriage, you'll have to ask his wife.'

Thanet didn't know what made him then ask, 'Are you married, Mr Vintage?' He watched a bleakness seep into Vintage's expression. What was wrong there?

'Yes. But what's that got to do with it?'

'Just wondered. Been married long?'

'Two years.'

Thanet filed away a question mark over Vintage's marriage, for further investigation later if necessary. 'How did Mr Randish get on with his father-in-law, Mr Landers?'

Another hit, it seemed. Once again there was an evasive look in Vintage's eyes. 'None of my business.'

'But you must have had an opinion.'

'I thought you weren't asking for gossip. My personal opinion of Zak's character, you said you wanted.'

Vintage was getting annoyed. Good. Thanet hadn't

deliberately set out to needle him, but anger frequently led to loss of control and hence indiscretion. Time to edge towards the main point of the interview.

'Why didn't you tell us about Reg Mason's dispute with Mr Randish?'

Vintage blinked at the sudden change of tack. 'That was none of my business, either.'

'I'm getting a little tired of people trying to protect other people. It's understandable, but misguided and completely pointless. As I was saying to Mrs Prote a moment ago, we always find out sooner or later. She, of course, was trying to protect you.'

Vintage's eyebrows went up, but Thanet could tell that his surprise was not genuine and there was even a touch of resignation in his voice as he said, 'Me?'

'Yes, you, Mr Vintage.'

Suddenly, Thanet was fed up. Interviewing was the part of his work that he enjoyed most. He enjoyed planning tactics, drawing on his accumulated experience in order to coax information out of reluctant witnesses. But just occasionally he became tired of all the manoeuvring. He sighed. 'How on earth can I get it into your head that there really is no point in trying to hide things from us?' He leaned forward, allowing his frustration to show. 'I honestly don't think you realise the seriousness of your position. Your employer was killed here yesterday. This is a murder investigation, and in a murder investigation everyone, but everyone connected with the victim comes under a searchlight and especially those who are known to have quarrelled with him. You all seem to think you live in little worlds of your own, but those worlds overlap, all the time. People see things, they hear things, and even if they don't want to tell us about them through misguided but perhaps understandable loyalty, sooner or later the truth will come out. As it has in your case. We *know* you had a row with Mr Randish yesterday and we want to know what it was about. So I suggest you stop pretending you don't know what I'm talking about, and tell us.'

Had he got through? Thanet wondered. If not, which tack should he try next? He was aware of Lineham's waiting stillness, of the almost palpable tension in the room.

Vintage's face was expressionless but Thanet guessed he was thinking furiously. His eyes were narrowed as he stared at Thanet and bunched cheek muscles betrayed clenched teeth.

At last he took a deep breath, blew the air out softly between pursed lips. 'I suppose you're right. You're bound to find out sooner or later, so you might as well hear it from me.'

SEVEN

Vintage slid off the desk again and went to look out of the window. 'It takes years to build up a place like this,' he said. 'I wonder what'll happen to it now.' He glanced at Thanet. 'How much do you know about English wines?'

'Virtually nothing.'

Vintage turned to face them, resting his buttocks on the windowsill. 'Well, before I explain about yesterday, just let me give you a little bit of background. It'll help you to understand what happened.

'If you want to produce a good wine, having the technical knowledge is important, of course. You've got to understand soil structure and soil management, know about the correct use of fertilisers and disease and pest control. But say you have that knowledge, say you've made a major investment, bought the land, planted your wines, tended them for years, picked your first harvest and got a pretty good wine from it, what then? The trouble is, English wine is not cheap and represents only about a third of a per cent of all the wine that's drunk in England. We don't get any of the grants the French and Germans get. So this is where you come up against your main problem: selling. With all other agricultural crops you have a ready-made market, but with wine you have to go out and sell your product and the competition is incredibly stiff. So, even assuming you employ all the right marketing techniques, if you really want to take off you still need something to make your wine stand out from all the rest. A major award, for example.'

Here, Thanet realised, was a true enthusiast. Vintage's eyes were glowing, the words flowed off his tongue as fluently as if he were giving a lecture he had delivered many times. This was a subject which he had pondered, discussed and studied from every angle.

'Of course, it's perfectly possible to make a moderate commercial success of a small vineyard and it has become an increasingly popular thing to do. You need so little land, you see. The reality is that if you have ten acres, once you're up and running, most years you will get thirty to forty thousand bottles of wine. But as I say, the problem is you have to shift it or you're going to end up with barns full of wine and no money to live on. Somehow you have to build up a demand for your product. You also have to decide whether you're going for quality or for a cheaper, more commercial proposition. A good wine-maker like Zak, of course, only ever goes for quality, and his reputation matters. He can do a lot to influence the way the wine turns out; he really holds the strings.

'I'm telling you all this because although I work a lot of the time here at Sturrenden, I've also been getting my own vineyard going. I told you how generous my father was, in sending me to Australia for a couple of years. Well, when I got back and he saw how keen I still was, he bought me a cottage with thirty acres to set myself up. I'm an only child, my mother died years ago, and he said I might as well have the money now, when I needed it, than wait until after he was dead to inherit it. Right at the outset I decided I was going for quality. If I could only win a couple of awards I'd be on my way.

'Well, I've done fairly well in a modest sort of way. I picked my first grapes two years ago and I've managed to shift quite a bit of my stock. But this year I knew I was going to get my big chance. This year, for the first time ever, I had perfectly ripe Pinot noir grapes, as perfect as they get them in Burgundy. The weather conditions were excellent and as the summer went on I was getting more and more excited about them. Believe me, the amount of care I put into looking after those grapes . . . Anyway, I was going around telling everyone how great this wine was going to be, and finally, just over a week ago, we picked them and brought them over here for pressing. We put them into plastic picking bins and stacked them. You then leave them for a week and the natural yeast in the grapes starts to ferment. You don't actually add anything. You can only do this if you have a good summer, with really ripe grapes – it's how they make wine in Burgundy.

'So, we covered the bins with sheets and left them to stand, stirring every day by hand. In the beginning the juice was very light in colour but as the days went on it got darker and richer and I got more and more excited. Every night I said to Zak, let's press it, let's press it, but no, every night he kept saying, we'll leave it one more night, one more night. I could have done it myself but I didn't want to. I wanted those grapes to get every ounce of Zak's expertise. Finally he decided we would press it on Thursday night but we got a bit late with the previous load so he promised he'd stay on here late next morning – yesterday – and we'd do it together.'

'Which you did,' said Thanet. 'I remember you telling me you'd pressed a load together.' He also remembered being certain at the time that Vintage was not telling the whole story. Though he didn't see where all this was leading.

'Which we did.' Vintage was nodding, but his expression was sour. 'The problem was, when I got in yesterday I discovered that one of the bins had split.'

'Ah . . . You lost all the juice from it?'

'Yes. There it was, all over the floor. My special, potentially award-winning wine! If Zak hadn't kept on putting it off and putting it off . . . I've told you all this because it was no secret, everybody knew about it and I'd rather you heard the story from me than from anybody else.'

No wonder Vintage had been 'in a mood' all day yesterday. 'So you had a row with Randish.'

'I wouldn't put it quite like that. I couldn't afford to really let fly. I was still dependent on Zak's skill to see me through making the rest of the batch, wasn't I?'

'You mean you were afraid that if you had a real bust-up with him, he might deliberately spoil it?'

Vintage shook his head vigorously. 'Oh no. His professional pride wouldn't allow him to do that. But he might have, well, taken a little less care over it, shall we say. Not even deliberately, perhaps. But your concentration is never very good after a row, is it? Apart from which, I didn't want to lose my job here. Zak was my employer, after all, and I still had a lot to learn from him. No, I couldn't take the risk. Anyway, Zak apologised, handsomely. So that was that.'

'I see.' Thanet did. Unable to give full vent to his anger, Vintage had bottled it up all day. The perfect recipe for the kind of explosive situation in which Randish had met his death. It also explained why Mrs Prote had been surprised to hear that Vintage and Randish had had a row in the evening – if, indeed, they had. No doubt she would have known about yesterday morning's disaster and assumed, by the fact that the two men had proceeded to press the batch together, that the matter had been settled between them.

'But the impression we got from Mr Mason was that you had a row with Mr Randish last night.'

Vintage was shaking his head. 'To be honest, I deliberately misled him. I told him I didn't think it would be a good idea to have another go at Zak last night because I'd had a row with him myself earlier and he wasn't in a very good mood. Which was true. I didn't say when, deliberately. I thought Reg would do his cause more harm than good if he tackled Zak when he was tired and on edge.'

And Vintage stuck to his story: he had been fully occupied with the load he was pressing. He had not seen Randish between 7 and 9.30, when he had gone across to the laboratory to tell him the load was finished, and had found him dead, nor had he seen anyone else enter or leave the bottling plant.

'You realise you're in a very difficult position,' said Thanet, 'entirely alone here all evening, apart from the brief conversation with Mr Mason.'

'No need to rub it in,' said Vintage wearily. 'I'm not an idiot. But I repeat, I didn't do it, so you'll never be able to prove otherwise.'

And there, Thanet agreed, was the rub. Lack of proof. And if Vintage were guilty, he didn't see how they would ever get it. The man must have been in the lab thousands of times, so scientific evidence of his presence there wouldn't help. They'd check his clothes, of course, for bloodstains, but Thanet didn't think the murderer would have been standing close enough to have been splashed with blood. Randish's throat had been cut by broken glass as he lost his balance and fell backwards through the window. Still, you never knew. Past experience had shown that it was surprising what might turn up.

Vintage was anxious to see if he could recruit someone who could at least help him out with the manual work involved in pressing when the vineyard resumed working next day, and Thanet let him go.

'God knows how we're ever going to catch up,' said Vintage gloomily as he went off.

Thanet and Lineham watched him walk to the car park and get into a mud-spattered Land-Rover.

'What d'you think, Mike?' said Thanet.

Lineham closed his notebook with a snap. 'I really don't know. I mean, it's all very well for him to say "that was that" after Randish apologised, but how could he have just put it out of his mind? Working alone all day like that he'd have had plenty of time to brood, plenty of time for his sense of grievance to grow . . . Maybe he had intended to let the matter rest, but suppose that during the evening he had to go across to the lab for some reason and Randish said or did something to trigger him off? It wouldn't have taken much, I shouldn't think. And the rest of his wine was safely pressed by then, remember, so he wouldn't have had that to make him hold back as he did in the morning.'

'Quite.'

'So what now, sir?'

'Keep digging, I suppose. While we're here we might as well take a look at Randish's papers, in case there are any more skeletons in his closet.'

They spoke to Mrs Prote again first, but learnt nothing of interest. She refused to be drawn into giving a personal opinion of Randish's character and was adamant that to her knowledge, apart from the long-running dispute with Mason, there had been no disagreement or conflict in his business life which could possibly have led to last night's tragedy. 'If there had been, I'd have known about it.'

A quick skim through the files of correspondence in the office seemed to bear this out, and Thanet and Lineham next went down to the house, to see if they could turn up anything more interesting there.

Randish's study overlooked an uninspired back garden, an oblong patch of lawn surrounded by bedraggled flower-beds. The room was small and square and most of the space was taken up by a wing chair and an oversized pedestal desk, but attempts had been made to give it a masculine air: the wing chair was covered in dark green leather and there were hunting prints on the walls.

They worked their way quickly down through the desk drawers, Thanet on one side, Lineham on the other, finding only the usual odds and ends which seem to accumulate in any desk, together with stationery, bank statements (healthy without being remarkable), old cheque-book stubs and household bills and receipts. Lineham reached the bottom drawer first, Thanet having been held up by a perusal of the bank statements.

'Hullo, this one's locked,' said the sergeant on an optimistic note. 'Lucky we kept those keys.' He fished out of his pocket the keyring which had been found in Randish's pocket last night and which they had held back for just this type of eventuality.

There were a number of keys on the ring but only three small enough to be possible. The second one Lineham tried turned smoothly in the lock. He slid the drawer right out and put it down on top of the desk. 'Letters,' he said. He opened a cardboard box in one corner. 'And photographs.'

The photographs were all of girls, mostly taken alone, sometimes with a younger, slimmer Randish, and in all sorts of situations: sitting on bicycles, perched on gates, seated on walls, sprawled on grass, leaning against trees.

'Wild oats,' said Lineham. 'Quite a Don Juan, wasn't he?'

Thanet was shuffling through the photographs again. There was something . . . some message which his brain was trying to pick up, here. He shook his head. It was no good, he couldn't think what it was.

They picked up the bundles of letters and began glancing at them.

'These are all from girls, too,' said Lineham. 'You can see why he wouldn't want his wife to read them.'

'Ancient history, though,' said Thanet. 'They seem to date mostly – exclusively, in fact – from the time when he was away at college.'

'Even so . . . And look at this lot.' Lineham had picked up the fattest bundle. 'I've glanced at one or two. They're written over a period of three years, mostly headed Trews Farm, Charthurst and signed Alice. From his wife, no doubt, before they were married.' He handed them to Thanet.

'So he was going out with her then.'

'All the time he was away, by the look of it.'

Thanet flicked through the bundle. Some of the envelopes were addressed to Randish at Plumpton Agricultural College, some to c/o Mr K Darks, Wentley Farm, Nr Hassocks, Sussex, the rest to c/o Mrs Wood, Jasmine Cottage, Plumpton, Nr Lewes, Sussex. This latter batch had foreign stamps, Thanet noticed. He peered at them. Switzerland. 'Looks as though Mrs Randish was away at finishing school during his last year at college.'

'And he was two-timing her, that's the point, for the whole three years. Or should I say three-timing her, or even four, five or six. No wonder he kept this drawer locked.' Lineham was picking envelopes up at random, peering at postmarks. 'These others are from all over the place, Bradford, Plymouth, Norwich, from heaven knows where, as well as from Plumpton. And all sent to an address in Sturrenden.'

Thanet was trying to decipher the dates on postmarks. 'Written to Randish during college holidays, by the look of it.' He wondered how Alice Randish was going to feel when she came across these, as she must, eventually. Would it make it easier or harder for her to come to terms with his death?

'If he was two-timing her then,' said Lineham, 'then I bet he was two-timing her now.'

'The thought had crossed my mind. But if so, with whom?'

They stared at each other, thinking.

'Did you notice,' said Thanet slowly, 'that Vintage seemed a bit cagey, when I asked him how long he'd been married?'

'Yes, I did. I definitely had the impression there was something wrong. You're suggesting his wife . . . and Randish?'

'Could be. Perhaps we'll pay her a little call later on this morning.'

'In any case, it does open up interesting possibilities, doesn't it, if he was a ladies' man? A leopard doesn't change his spots, as they say.'

'Very profound, Mike. But I agree. If it's not Mrs Vintage, it could be someone else.'

'I wonder how Mrs Randish's father would have taken that, sir. I mean, if Randish was in the habit of playing around. And especially if what Louise suspected was true, and Randish got a bit rough with his wife from time to time. Landers certainly wouldn't have liked that.'

'Quite. We certainly can't count him out, I agree. Which is one of the reasons why I want to see him next. I'd like another word with Mrs Randish too. With any luck we'll catch her there.' He glanced at his watch. 'We'd better get a move on.' He began to stack the letters back in the drawer and Lineham joined in. 'Make sure you lock these up again. And then we'll be on our way.'

EIGHT

Landers and his wife lived on the far side of Charthurst. Most of the village lay just off the main road and although Thanet had passed through it on a couple of occasions he had never looked at it properly before. Last night, of course, it had been dark, but even by daylight it was unremarkable, typical of the hundreds of villages scattered all over Kent, with a nucleus of older houses, mostly brick and tile-hung, weather-boarded or Tudor black and white, a sprinkle of Victorian cottages, a rash of new houses squeezed in wherever possible and the ubiquitous council estate. There was a church, a dilapidated village hall, a pub, a post office-cum-stores and a village school, which like so many had unfortunately long since been converted into a house. That, no doubt, mused Thanet as they drove past it, was where the bonds of rural loyalty between Landers and Mason had been forged. Landers had probably been sent away to school later on, but to begin with he and Mason would have shared a classroom, perhaps even a desk. The amalgamation of so many small schools like this one was, he believed, one of the many factors responsible for the decline in rural life. Ferried by school bus or by accommodating parents, children were taught from infancy to look away from their communities for their activities, hobbies and satisfactions. It was scarcely surprising that when they grew up they either moved to the towns or regarded the villages as little more than dormitories.

By daylight Mason's house still looked as if it were trying to proclaim the prosperity of its owner, an impression marred by the fact that the sole vehicle parked in the drive was an old pick-up truck which looked as though it were on its last legs – the only transport Mason was now able to afford, Thanet presumed.

Trews Farm was about a mile beyond the village and looked prosperous – probably was, thought Thanet, remembering the Mercedes. The house itself was about four hundred yards from the road and the surface of the long drive was smoothly tarmacked, the verges mown, the hedges well trimmed. On one side were orderly rows of raspberry canes trained on wires, on the other an orchard which had recently been picked; the branches were bare of fruit and the windfalls had been raked into little piles at the end of each line of trees. If first impressions were anything to go by, Landers was to be congratulated. Farmers, Thanet knew, had been having a very bad time. Over the last few years there had been more bankruptcies and more suicides in the farming industry than there had ever been before and Kent had been badly hit. But it looked as though Landers was efficient enough – or perhaps lucky enough – to have escaped the worst of the recession. Perhaps he had weathered the storm by having long-standing contracts to supply some of the larger supermarket chains.

In any case, Thanet guessed that the packing sheds, cold store and other, larger agricultural buildings associated with the work of the farm were elsewhere; the cluster of buildings at the end of the track was too picturesque to be businesslike on the scale which successful modern fruit farming demanded. It was characteristically Kentish: a brick and tile-hung farmhouse, an oast house with conical roof and white-painted cowl, a wooden barn and a range of open-fronted cart-sheds in which were parked the Range Rover Alice Randish had been driving earlier and a trim little silver-blue Rover Metro.

'Glad it's stopped raining,' said Lineham as they got out of the car.

'Mmm.' Thanet was watching Mrs Landers, who was crossing the yard with the little boy they had last seen bundled up in a duvet. He was riding a bright red tricycle which reminded Thanet of one Ben had had when he was that age. They were accompanied by a golden Labrador which now came bounding across to investigate the newcomers, sending up sprays of water as it splashed through the puddles.

'Good boy,' said Lineham placatingly, putting out a slightly nervous hand to pat the dog's handsome head as it skidded to a halt. He flinched and shuffled backwards as it sat down and lifted a friendly but very wet and muddy paw to greet him.

'Timon, here!' called Mrs Landers, and the dog trotted obediently back to its mistress.

'He's well trained,' said Thanet with some relief as he and Lineham approached her. He liked dogs as long as they were kept under control. Like postmen, policemen all too frequently have to suffer from the unwelcome attentions of badly behaved pets watched admiringly by their doting owners.

Last night Mrs Landers had taken so little part in the conversation that he had not paid her much attention. Now he looked at her properly. She was, he guessed, used to being overshadowed by her husband, and her unremarkable physical appearance matched the unobtrusive role she habitually played: neatly styled greying hair, clothes chosen for comfort and serviceability rather than elegance or style. Her eyes were a faded version of her daughter's. But Thanet remembered the fierce, protective stare with which she had watched Alice last night and reminded himself not to underestimate her; there was steel beneath that misleadingly innocuous exterior.

'I don't like badly behaved dogs,' said Mrs Landers, her expression softening as she glanced at the Labrador. 'Especially big ones. If you don't train them properly your friends soon stop calling.'

'And what's your name?' said Lineham, smiling down at the child.

'Malcolm,' said the boy shyly. He had his father's sturdy frame, thick dark curly hair and regular features.

'I've got a little boy like you,' said Lineham, squatting. 'Well, a bit older, I suppose. He's called Richard.'

'Has he got a tricycle?'

'He used to. But he's got a bicycle now.'

'When I'm a bit bigger Daddy's going to teach me to ride a bicycle.'

A shadow fell over the conversation.

Thanet and Lineham glanced at Mrs Landers, who shook her head. 'We've told them, but he hasn't taken it in.'

'He'll need time,' said Thanet.

They all turned as a car approached at speed up the drive: Landers' white Mercedes. It slowed as it entered the yard and rolled neatly into one of the sections of the cart-shed. Landers got out, looking grim.

Of course, Thanet remembered, this morning Landers had had the unenviable task of breaking the news of her brother's death to Randish's sister, whose daughter had also died last night.

The dog had gone bounding to meet him, followed by Malcolm on his tricycle, and Landers stooped to pat one and smile at the other before coming on. He nodded a greeting at Thanet and Lineham and said, 'Excuse me for a moment, will you?' He took both his wife's hands and drew her aside. 'You won't believe this, Dulce . . .' The dog was nuzzling at his hand and he said, 'Stop it, Timon. Lie down.'

The dog subsided obediently on to the ground.

'What?' said Mrs Landers, watching her husband's face. 'Not more bad news, surely? There just can't be.'

'When I got to Rachael's house there was no reply. So I went next door. The neighbour told me Rachael was still at the hospital. Because' – and Landers gave his wife's hands a little shake, as if warning her to brace herself for what was coming – 'because *Jonathan* had an accident last night.'

'Oh, no . . . I don't believe it. Poor Rachael!'

'Apparently the police came around last night shortly after she got back from the hospital – it must have been just after she rang Alice's house and spoke to me – to tell her. She went straight back and she's been there all night.'

'So how is he? You went to the hospital?'

'Yes.' Landers shook his head. 'It's not good, Dulce. He's still unconscious.' Landers released his wife's hands. 'Jonathan is Zak's nephew,' he said to Thanet, 'the twin brother of the girl who died last night. He and his sister have always been very close.' He turned back to his wife. 'Apparently Jonathan was with Karen when she died. Rachael says she can only assume that he was so upset he was driving carelessly. And of course, on a motorcycle you're so vulnerable.'

'So how badly hurt is he?'

Landers shrugged. 'No bones broken, but he's seriously concussed. As I say, he hasn't regained consciousness yet. He's just . . . lying there.'

Poor woman, thought Thanet. He'd occasionally come across this type of situation before, when someone seemed to suffer a positive avalanche of disaster. The resilience of the human spirit never failed to amaze him. He'd often wondered how people could bear it when they lost their entire family at one fell swoop, in a fire, perhaps, or a car crash. How did they cope, when suddenly there was not a single member of their family left to turn to for consolation? This lad was not dead yet, of course, and with any luck would survive, but even so, Randish's sister must meanwhile be in a pretty parlous state.

'So how is Rachael taking it?' said Mrs Landers. 'Did you tell her about Zak?'

'Yes. I didn't want to, mind, but I thought, if I don't she'll only read about it in the papers or hear it from a neighbour or on television and I didn't want to risk that. But I think she's in such a daze about Karen and Jonathan she didn't really take it in. She just stared at me, didn't say a word.'

'I'll have to go to her.'

'We'd better tell Alice about Jonathan, first.'

'Do we have to, for the moment? She's still reeling from hearing about Karen, after last night.'

'I suppose we could leave it until tomorrow, when there might be better news. Where is she?'

'Lying down. Ever since she and Fiona got back from seeing to the horses.'

Landers turned to Thanet again. 'Sorry about all this, Inspector.'

'No need to apologise! I'm only sorry to hear that you've had yet more bad news.'

'It's not as though we're especially close to Zak's sister, but she is all alone and you can't help feeling sorry for her. And we're naturally concerned as to how our daughter will take it . . . Are you just leaving, or arriving?'

'Arriving, I'm afraid. There are some more questions I really must ask you.'

'We'd better go in.'

'Did you want me for anything, Inspector?' said Mrs Randish. 'Because if not, I'd really like to go down to the hospital.'

Thanet shook his head. 'Go, by all means.'

'Thank you. Fiona's in the playroom, Owen. I'll take Malcolm along to join her. If you could just look in on them from time to time, while Alice is lying down . . .'

She went off upstairs with her grandson.

'I could do with a cup of coffee,' said Landers. 'Would you like one?'

They accepted the offer and followed him to a door at the end of the wide corridor which served as a hall, the Labrador padding along behind.

The kitchen was big, with a huge pine table in the centre and a dresser at one end, and had a pleasantly lived-in air. Thanet guessed that it had been modernised recently, but the alterations had been cleverly done: the pine units looked mellowed by time, as though they had always been there. Landers filled a kettle and put it on the Aga. In what seemed a matter of seconds it had boiled, the coffee was made and they were seated at the table, the dog sitting down beside Landers and watching its master expectantly.

He caressed its broad head absent-mindedly and took a long swallow of coffee. 'So,' he said. 'Go ahead.'

Landers seemed in a much more cooperative mood this morning, thought Thanet. Good. Perhaps it was because he was no longer trying to protect Reg Mason, or perhaps because he was pleased that his daughter was back under his roof. And possibly, from what they were learning about Zak Randish, because he was relieved that his son-in-law was permanently out of the picture. That, Thanet reminded himself, was what they were here to find out: what had been Landers' attitude towards Zak Randish? 'I was hoping you'd be able to fill me in a little on Mr Randish's background, sir.'

'In what way?'

'Anything you care to tell me. I gather he's known your daughter a long time.'

Landers' lips tightened. 'Since she was sixteen.'

'How did they meet?'

'Look, what possible relevance can this have? It's ancient history now.'

'Believe me, Mr Landers, anything I can learn about Mr Randish will help, anything at all. Bear with me, will you?'

Landers was reluctant to talk but little by little an amplified version of what Vintage had told them emerged. Alice and Randish had in fact met when Randish was fruit-picking on Landers' farm during the school holidays.

'It doesn't sound as though you were too keen on the relationship,' said Thanet.

'Alice was too young to have a steady boyfriend – any steady boyfriend.'

It took all Thanet's skill to extract any further information, but he gathered that for Landers' precious only daughter the fruit farmer had wanted an altogether more advantageous match. Randish's background was undesirable – his father had been a mere labourer on the roads and the family had lived in a council house.

'Any father wants the best for his children,' said Landers defensively.

And he was right, of course. Any father did. Thanet did. But people's ideas as to what 'the best' was varied enormously. Landers had disapproved of Randish because of his humble background, Thanet had disapproved of Alexander because of his privileged one. Which of them was right? Neither, thought Thanet. We're both judging by the wrong criteria. He tucked the thought away for future examination. 'Of course,' he said.

'And Zak never was "the best" as far as you were concerned, was he, Dad?' Alice was standing in the doorway and her tone was bitter.

Thanet wondered how long she had been listening.

She walked across to stand with her back to the Aga, holding out her hands to the warmth as she had to the woodstove last night. A sleepless night had bruised the delicate skin beneath her eyes and the long fair hair hung lank and lustreless on her shoulders. 'Why don't you tell the Inspector some of the good things about him? Yes, his background was poor, his father a drunken lout and his mother pathetic, downtrodden, but it was the fact that he was able to rise above all that and put it behind him that made him so special. And you certainly couldn't complain that he was lazy. He worked like a slave to get the vineyard where it is today and you know it.'

'Alice . . .' Her father got up, followed by the dog, and went to put an arm around her shoulders. 'I know all that. It's just that . . .'

She shook his arm off and put her hand up to run her fingers through her hair. The loose sleeve of her blouse fell back and all three men saw it, a large discoloured patch on the tender flesh of the inside upper arm.

Thanet and Lineham exchanged glances. There was

only one way that such a bruise could have been inflicted in that particular position. Louise had been right.

And Landers had seen them noticing. Not realising that he was offering the policeman a weapon to use against him, he was unable to resist casting a triumphant glance at Thanet. *You see what I mean?*

Intent on her grievance Alice was unaware of what she had unintentionally revealed. '"It's just that" what?' she said. 'It's just that it really doesn't matter any more if you come out into the open and say what you really think of him? It's just that he's been such a thorn in your flesh for so long you're merely relieved he's gone? You never did like him, did you, Dad, and I bet you're delighted you'll never have to set eyes on him again!'

The Labrador was standing watching them, tail drooping, clearly unhappy about this argument between two of its people.

'Alice . . .' Landers attempted to put his arm around her shoulders again but once more she shook him off.

'Don't "Alice" me!' she cried. And rushed out.

Landers' glance at Thanet and Lineham somehow contrived to be apologetic, humorous, indulgent and rueful, all at once. He returned to his seat. 'She's upset,' he said, the understatement intended as a joke.

The dog pushed its nose into his hand, seeking reassurance that all was now well and again he patted it automatically.

'She's very loyal,' said Thanet, unsmiling.

'She's always been the same, as far as Zak was concerned.'

Time to stop pussy-footing around, thought Thanet. 'How long have you known that he was ill-treating her? And don't pretend you don't know what I mean. We all saw that bruise and it was obvious you realised its significance.'

'I've known for years,' said Landers bitterly. 'Have you got any children, Inspector?'

Thanet nodded. 'Two.'

'Either of them married?'

'No.'

'Just wait,' said Landers grimly. 'I hope, for your sake, that you like the partners they choose. Because believe me, there's nothing you can do about it. If you disapprove and say so, you risk losing them altogether. You just have to stand by and watch it happen, hope it'll all work out for the best in the end.'

'Which is what you did with your daughter.'

'Didn't have much choice, did I? I've only got one child, more's the pity. And I had to stand by and see her throw herself away on that . . . on Randish. I did my best to smooth the way for her, of course, but when it comes down to it there's nothing you can do about their day-to-day relationship. You just have to let them get on with it.'

'And did it get to the stage where you'd had enough of letting them get on with it?'

'Did I go up there last night and shove him through that window, you mean? No, I didn't. She had me over a barrel, you see.'

'What do you mean?'

'Alice thought the sun shone out of him,' said Landers. He looked bewildered and his tone was almost plaintive as he went on. 'I could never understand why. But from the moment she first set eyes on Randish she was besotted. I thought, when it first dawned on me that he was knocking her about, that she'd come to her senses. I waited and waited, but no, he could always get her eating out of his hand. And if you love someone, really love someone, you want what's best for them, however you feel about it.

You see my dilemma? If I got rid of Randish – and I'll admit there have been many occasions when I could cheerfully have thrown him through a window – I'd be depriving her of her greatest happiness, incomprehensible though that was to me. So my hands were tied. No, you'll have to look elsewhere for your murderer, Inspector. Sorry.'

'D'you know if Mr Randish was playing around?'

'Was he having an affair, you mean? Not so far as I know.'

But Landers was lying, Thanet was certain of it. The fruit farmer might have been caught out once, but he wasn't going to hand Thanet another motive on a plate, even if it might point the finger of suspicion in another direction.

'Do you know of anyone apart from Mr Mason who might have had a grudge against Mr Randish?'

The mention of Reg Mason's name made Landers scowl. 'I told you, you can leave Reg out of it. He just isn't the type to lose his temper and whoever caused that mess up there last night was beside himself with rage, as I'm sure you'll agree. But no, Zak might have trodden on a few toes, but I can't think of anyone who'd hate him to that degree.'

'Mr Vintage told us that your son-in-law also made the wine for another vineyard, at Chasing Manor. How did he get on with the people there?'

'The Bentons? Fine, to my knowledge. They've known him since he was a teenager and I hardly think James Benton would have let Zak take over the winemaking there if there'd been any problems between them.'

'They could have arisen recently.'

'I doubt it. Anyway, you'll have to ask him.'

'Don't worry, we intend to.'

As they walked to the car, Lineham asked, 'Are we going to Chasing Manor next?'

'Let's have a look at the map.'

They held it out between them.

'As I thought,' said Thanet. 'Vintage's house is on the way. Let's pay a call on Mrs Vintage first, see what's going on there. If she was Randish's current girlfriend I'd like to know.'

NINE

The hollow sensation in Thanet's stomach reminded him that it was a long time since breakfast, so they pulled in at the pub in the village.

'We can check Mason's alibi, such as it is, at the same time.'

Although it hadn't started raining again the sky was still overcast and the air was damp and raw. Thanet shivered as they crossed the car park and decided he would eschew his usual sandwich and have something hot.

'Shepherd's pie, I think,' he said with satisfaction, scanning the bar menu. One of his favourites.

'Me, too,' said Lineham.

While they were waiting for the food they questioned the landlord. He had been on duty the night before and although he couldn't be certain of the precise time at which Mason arrived, he confirmed that Landers had later joined him and that the two men had left together about half an hour after that. He also said that although Mason had seemed depressed before Landers arrived, by the time they left he had looked considerably more cheerful.

'Because Landers had offered him the house, presumably,' said Thanet as they carried their drinks to a table in the corner. 'All of which confirms what they've both told us.'

'Still doesn't alter the fact that Mason had the opportunity both before and after he was in here.'

'True.'

When it arrived the pie was excellent, generous helpings with plenty of meat and real, not substitute, potato on top.

'We'll have to come here again,' said Thanet.

While they were eating they discussed the morning's interviews.

'Don't seem to have made much progress, do we?' Lineham was uncharacteristically gloomy.

'Oh, I don't know. I think we're getting there, slowly.' A picture of Randish was, Thanet felt, gradually beginning to emerge: a man whose driving ambition had been forged by his deprived childhood, who saw even his wife, perhaps, as a means to an end; a man powerless to prevent himself repeating in his own marriage the pattern of violence which Thanet suspected Randish's 'drunken lout' of a father had inflicted upon his 'pathetic, downtrodden' mother; a man, Thanet was beginning to believe, for whom other people's feelings did not exist. Well, it looked as though he had trampled on someone else's sensibilities once too often.

Enough of the case, for now. Thanet laid down his fork and patted his pockets, feeling for pipe, pouch, matches. Out of consideration for Lineham he waited until the sergeant had finished eating before lighting up. Then he sat back, puffing contentedly. 'How's Louise getting on?'

Lineham's wife was a trained nurse and until the children came along had been a staff nurse at Sturrenden

General. She had then devoted herself to full-time motherhood and had found it a great strain. Eventually she had taken a part-time job, looking forward to the day when Richard started school and she would be free to resume her career. But like so many women, when that day finally arrived she found that she had lost her confidence. Eventually she had been persuaded to take a retraining course for working mothers and she was now halfway through it.

'Fine,' said Lineham. 'Progressively better and better, as a matter of fact, as she gets her confidence back. The course is very well designed, she has one day in the classroom and one in the wards, and she's expected to do half a day's studying as well. And the hours are so convenient, especially tailored to the needs of mothers with children at school. If only we could get Richard sorted out everything in the garden would be lovely.'

'But I thought he'd seen the – what did you call her? The dyslexic support teacher? – and had an assessment and a special programme worked out for him.'

The previous year Lineham's son Richard, now aged eight, had been diagnosed dyslexic. Lineham and Louise had been worried about him for some time, realising that something was wrong but unable to put their finger on the problem. The diagnosis had been a shock but there had also been a measure of relief: at least now, they thought, something constructive could be done, at once.

They were wrong.

Help was theoretically available, but in practice, they discovered, it took a long time to arrive. Kent County Council was getting itself increasingly organised to provide specialised tuition for children like Richard, but resources were as yet inadequate to provide the degree of help each child needed. Richard had had to take his place in the queue and for three months nothing had happened while his application was being 'processed'. There was only one dyslexic support teacher for the entire area and she was grossly overworked. At last, however, she had seen him for his assessment and Lineham and Louise had had high hopes of the results.

'Yes, she did see him, and he is working on the programme she set up for him.'

'So why the gloom?'

'Guess how much special tuition he's getting.'

'I've no idea. A couple of hours a week?'

'Try again,' said Lineham grimly.

'One hour, then.'

'And again.'

'Not less than an hour, surely.'

'He gets, believe it or not, twenty minutes a week.'

'Twenty minutes a *week*! But that's hopeless!'

'Quite. The trouble is, there just aren't enough special support teachers around. There are thirty-two between eighty-five schools. And Richard's dyslexia is apparently not as severe as some, so he doesn't qualify for as much help. Another problem is that because the dyslexia provision has only been set up relatively recently there's still a backlog of children who were late being diagnosed and are desperately behind, so they naturally come first.'

'So there's nothing you can do?'

'We've tried everything, believe me. But it's like banging your head against a brick wall. The school takes the attitude that it's doing its best, but that if the help simply isn't available, there's nothing to be done about it.'

'Have you taken it up with the Education Authority?'

'Yes. But it's the same old story. It takes for ever to get any kind of response, and when we do they simply say that everything that can be done is being done, but that they simply haven't the funding to provide adequately for every single child with special needs. There is a very good special unit, at the Malling School near Maidstone, but children can't go there until they're eleven, even if they're lucky enough to get in. It's so frustrating!'

'How's Richard reacting to all this?'

'I think he's coming to believe more and more that he's just plain stupid. And how can we convince him otherwise, when as far as he's concerned all the apparent evidence is to the contrary? To make matters worse, he's just gone up a form and from what he tells me I suspect his new teacher is one of the old school, who privately thinks dyslexia is just a fancy label to hang around the neck of a pupil who is really either stupid, lazy or just plain difficult.'

'I thought that attitude had gone out with the Ark.'

'Unfortunately, no, it seems. Old habits die hard, I'm afraid.'

'It must be very depressing for you, not finding any way of doing something constructive to help him.'

'You can say that again! And we're not alone, believe me. You wouldn't credit the number of times we've heard this story over and over again from other parents of dyslexic children. Still, we haven't given up yet. At the moment we're enquiring about private tuition. The trouble is, there are so few people qualified to give it.'

Outside it had started raining again and they had to make a dash for the car. As he drove Lineham was unwontedly quiet – brooding, Thanet suspected, on Richard's predicament. Thanet had always been grateful that Bridget and Ben had been normal healthy children, and the courage and devotion of those parents who were not so fortunate never failed to arouse his heartfelt admiration. Would he have been able to find such reserves of strength in himself, had he been called upon to do so? He doubted it. But then, perhaps one never knew, unless one was actually put to the test. Richard, of course, appeared in every way a perfectly bright healthy child, but in one respect this made things even more difficult: people were less inclined to make allowances for him.

Usually Thanet enjoyed a drive through the countryside but this afternoon there was little pleasure in it. The foliage was beginning to turn colour and on a sunny day the woods and hedgerows would have been splashed with gold, streaked with scarlet, but the blanket of lowering cloud and flurries of driving rain cast a pall over everything. There were puddles in the furrows of newly ploughed fields and tree branches drooped, heavy with the weight of water in their sodden leaves.

It took about fifteen minutes to get to Vintage's house. This was a much more modest set-up. There was a simple signboard announcing 'AMBERLY VINEYARD, WINES FOR SALE', and a short drive up to a pretty weather-boarded house. Looking about him, though, Thanet could see the potential of the place: ample space for a big car park and two substantial barns for storage. The neat rows of vines had a well-tended air.

'I think I'm in the wrong job,' said Lineham. 'How big did he say this place is?'

'Thirty acres.'

'And how much wine a year did he say could be produced off ten? Thirty to forty thousand bottles, wasn't it?' Lineham screwed up his face, calculating. 'So on thirty acres that's – no, wait a minute, I'm getting lost in all the noughts . . .'

'Mike! We're not here to do mental arithmetic. You can amuse yourself with that when you're off duty. Anyway, don't forget what he said. The main problem is selling it.'

Thanet was pleased to see that there was a car parked in front of one of the barns, an old green Morris Traveller. Mrs Vintage was probably in, then. The house, however, had a neglected air. The windows were dirty, streaked with grime from the morning's rain, and some of the curtains were drawn, some not. There was an accumulation of leaves around the front door as though it hadn't been used for some time. Perhaps it hadn't, thought Thanet as they knocked. Farming people often habitually use the back door because of all the mud that is carried in. Someone was in, anyway: inside a radio or television set was blaring out, almost but not quite drowning another sound, that of a baby crying.

No reply.

They knocked again, harder; still no response. Thanet was becoming uneasy. There was something wrong here, he could sense it.

Lineham evidently felt the same. 'Don't like the look of this, sir.'

'Perhaps she hasn't heard because of the noise.'

'Do we go around the back?'

Thanet nodded.

On the way past the window to the right of the door he stooped to peer in between the half-drawn curtains. This was the room with the television set. It stood in the corner beside the fireplace and opposite, at right angles to the window, slumped on a settee, was a woman, her profile masked by her hair. Thanet tapped at the window, but she gave no indication of having heard. He knocked harder and called Lineham back, knocked again, still with no response.

At last, as they peered in together, to Thanet's intense relief, the woman stirred. Slowly she turned her head to look at them. Her eyes were blank, incurious, and although she couldn't have been more than a few feet away, the sight of two strange men peering in at her initially produced no reaction whatsoever.

'Mrs Vintage?' Thanet called. 'Police.' He fished out his warrant card and held it up to the glass.

She continued to stare at him as if he were speaking in a foreign tongue and then slowly, very slowly, as if she were walking through water, she rose and approached the window. She was wearing a dressing gown, Thanet realised, and slippers. She'd been ill, perhaps, or still was. She was very pale, with dark circles beneath her eyes, and her long brown hair hung lank and greasy as if it were long overdue for a wash.

She was now close enough for them to speak to her. They had arranged that this time Lineham should take the interview and he also pressed his warrant card against the windowpane. 'Could we have a word, Mrs Vintage?'

Thanet half expected her to say no or at least to indicate that she would dress, first. It seemed to take a few moments for Lineham's request to penetrate but then, without a word, still with that curious trancelike motion, she turned and left the room through a door at the far side.

Thanet and Lineham looked at each other, eyebrows raised, mouths tugged down at the corners.

'Drugs?' said Lineham.

They returned to the front door but when there was no sound from inside hurried around to the back. She was waiting for them, leaning against the edge of the half-open door, a tabby cat weaving around her bare legs.

'What is it?' she said. Her voice was hoarse, as if she had a cold, and she cleared her throat.

'We're inquiring into the death of Mr Randish,' said Lineham. 'And we wondered if we could have a few words with you.'

She frowned, and again it seemed to take several moments before the meaning of what he had said penetrated.

Definitely drugged, Thanet decided. Tranquillisers, he suspected.

'Mr Randish? Dead?' The news seemed to have shaken her into a greater awareness and she stood back, held the door wider. 'Come in.'

But why the surprise? Thanet wondered. Why hadn't her husband told her the news before he left for the vineyard this morning?

Inside she glanced about her as if becoming aware of her surroundings for the first time. 'It's a bit of a mess,' she said vaguely, but without real concern.

And that was an understatement if ever he'd heard one, thought Thanet. Every square inch of surface was piled high with opened tins, dirty dishes encrusted with food and used saucepans. The floor hadn't been swept or washed for some time and there was a row of empty saucers beside which the cat had stationed itself, watching its mistress with an optimistic stare. Someone, however, had been at work recently: a huge pile of washing up had been left to drain beside the sink, and on the filthy cooker, standing in a pan of water, stood a baby's bottle full of milk. Two more bottles were lined up nearby. The child must be due for a feed, thought Thanet. Inside the house the noise of its crying was much louder and it sounded frantic. Mrs Vintage, however, made no move to turn on the heat under the saucepan.

'We'll go in the other room.' She led the way. The baby was upstairs and in the hall the noise it was making intensified. How could any mother ignore such a desperate appeal for attention? Thanet wondered. Lineham, he could tell, was thinking the same.

In the sitting room she made no move to turn down the volume on the set, simply returned to her seat and sat down, tugging the edges of her dressing gown together across her bare legs. The shoulders, Thanet noticed, were encrusted here and there with little patches of dried vomit, where the baby had brought up wind.

'Do you mind if we have the TV off, ma'am?' said Lineham.

She shook her head.

The sound of the baby's cries seemed magnified in the ensuing silence.

'We don't mind waiting, if you want to attend to the baby,' said the sergeant.

'He'll be all right for a few minutes.'

Then, shockingly, she got up and shut the door, reducing the sound to a distant wail. She returned to her seat.

Thanet and Lineham exchanged glances. What could they do? You couldn't force a mother to look after her baby.

'Didn't your husband tell you about Mr Randish?'

She shook her head. 'I was asleep when he got home last night. And when he left this morning.'

Her voice had lost its hoarseness and Thanet suddenly realised why. It had been the roughness not of illness but of disuse. With a sudden flash of comprehension he glimpsed what this woman's life was like. By the sound of its cry the baby was very young and therefore very demanding. The first weeks of a child's life were always exhausting for the mother, a time when she herself was not fully restored to health and needed help to cope with the extra demands upon her time and energy. Vintage had told them that the harvest was the busiest time of year, that for weeks now he had been rising very early and not getting to bed until two or three in the morning.

During that period he had probably hardly even spoken to his wife. Mrs Vintage had had to cope alone and clearly the task had been too much for her. Thanet guessed too that there was more to it than that. She was, he was willing to bet, suffering from post-natal depression and had been given tranquillisers to help her cope. Vintage must know that something was wrong, but fully stretched as he was he had probably shut his eyes to the extent of the problem. It was he, probably, who had prepared those bottles for the baby and done that washing-up before leaving this morning.

This, Thanet was sure, was the reason for Vintage's unease when speaking about his marriage. They would have to look elsewhere for Randish's mistress, if he'd had one. Meanwhile, what was to be done about this situation? Theoretically, nothing. It certainly wasn't his responsibility to sort out suspects' domestic problems. On the other hand, there was the child to consider.

Lineham was giving Mrs Vintage a brief account of Randish's death. Outside a car drew up, a door slammed. Thanet rose to look out of the window: Vintage. Here, perhaps, was his opportunity. Unobtrusively, he withdrew to the kitchen. Vintage was just coming in through the back door. He was scowling.

'What are you doing here?' But there was no real aggression in his tone, just a weary acceptance.

No wonder the man looked so exhausted, Thanet thought. He must feel as though his life was completely out of control. 'I'm afraid we turn up everywhere in this sort of inquiry.'

Vintage had registered the baby's frantic crying. He glanced at the cooker, took in the three untouched bottles of baby feed, moved at once to turn on the heat beneath the one in the saucepan of water.

'Where's my wife?'

'In the sitting room, with Sergeant Lineham.'

'Excuse me.'

Before Thanet could say anything Vintage left the room and Thanet heard him trudge upstairs. Briefly, the crying stopped, then started again. He was, Thanet guessed, changing the child's nappy. A few minutes later he returned to the kitchen cradling the baby. It was indeed very young, less than eight weeks old, Thanet guessed. It was scarlet with frustration, its scrap of hair wet with perspiration, its face screwed up in agonised appeal as it continued to wail with every ounce of energy it still possessed. Not for the first time Thanet marvelled that something so small could make so much noise and cause so much disruption.

With his free hand Vintage snatched the bottle out of the saucepan, sprinkled a few drops of milk on the back of his other hand to test the temperature and shoved the teat into the baby's gaping mouth. Its lips clamped around the rubber and it began to suck with desperate urgency. Vintage hooked his foot around one of the chairs, dragged it away from the cluttered table and sat down.

There was a blissful silence.

Both men watched the child without speaking for a few moments. Then Thanet also pulled out a chair and sat down. There would never be a better time to say this, he thought.

'You realise your wife is ill, Mr Vintage.'

Vintage glanced up, briefly. 'It's none of your business.'

'Maybe not. But a child at risk is.'

'She's seen a doctor.'

'Where? Here?' Thanet's glance underlined the chaos in the room. 'Or at the surgery?' He did not add, *where she and the baby would have been dressed and tidied up for public inspection*. The implication was obvious.

'Yes,' admitted Vintage reluctantly.

'Then it's up to you to spell out to him just how bad things are, so that he can keep a close eye on her. Oh, I do realise how difficult it must have been for you, over the last few weeks. But all the same, it can't go on, you must see that.'

Vintage put the bottle down and laid the baby gently against his shoulder, patted its back to bring up the wind. He sighed, a long slow sigh of capitulation. 'I know. You're right. I suppose I didn't want to admit how serious the problem was. I kept saying to myself, if she can just hang on until harvest is finished . . . As it is, I just don't see how I can cope. And this business with Zak has just made things ten times worse, if that's possible.'

'Is there no one who could come and stay, to help look after the baby?' Vintage's mother, Thanet remembered, was dead. 'Your wife's mother, perhaps?'

'She couldn't even begin to manage. She's just out of hospital after a hysterectomy.'

'Brothers, sisters?'

'I haven't got any.' The baby burped obligingly and Vintage set the teat to its mouth again. 'Beth has a sister, but she lives up north and has four children of her own. I don't see how she could possibly leave them for any period of time.'

'There must be someone.'

'That's the trouble,' said Vintage. 'There isn't. Only me.' This time the look he directed at Thanet was one of despair. 'What am I going to do?'

Thanet thought. 'Is there any chance of hiring a nanny for a while, until your wife is on her feet again?'

'We can't afford it. The doctor said it could take months.'

'I appreciate that, but can you afford not to? I'm not sure if you realise just how serious this is. If it were my wife I'd be prepared if not to steal at least to beg or borrow, to help her through it. You may not like the idea, but desperate situations demand desperate remedies. Perhaps you could arrange a loan from the bank. Or would your father lend you the money?'

'He might. But I'd hate to ask. He was so generous in setting us up here that I've spent the last four years trying to prove how independent I can be.'

'Have you actually discussed the situation with him?'

Vintage shook his head. 'No. Anyway, he's been away on business for the last fortnight, in Thailand, and it's only during that period that things have got so bad.'

'When's he due back?'

'Monday.'

'Well, I suggest you swallow your pride and see what he can do. I would have thought that if he appreciates it's a question of his grandchild's welfare, he'd be more than willing to lend a hand.'

Vintage sighed again. 'You're right.'

The teat had slipped out of the baby's mouth and it slept, exhausted and replete. Vintage pushed aside a plate on the table to make room for the bottle and looked down at the child. 'We'll manage something, won't we?' he murmured.

Thanet stood up. 'Good.'

On cue, he heard the sitting-room door open and Lineham appeared.

'All finished?' he asked the sergeant.

Lineham nodded.

Vintage watched them go. 'Thanks, Inspector.'

Thanet grinned. 'All in a day's work!' he said.

TEN

'Did Vintage tell you what the doctor's diagnosis was?' said Lineham.

On their way to Chasing Manor vineyard they had been discussing what they had learnt at Vintage's house. Not a lot, they had decided, and had been silent for a while mulling things over.

'Not in so many words, no. But it's obvious, isn't it?'

'Post-natal depression. Yes. But what I'm wondering is if it's *too* obvious.'

'What do you mean, Mike?'

'Well, you take one look at Mrs Vintage and the set-up there and immediately that's the conclusion you jump to.'

'I still don't see what you're getting at.'

'What if her illness has a completely different cause? What if the reason she's depressed is because she was having an affair with Randish and when she discovered she was pregnant he threw her over? What if the baby is Randish's? Just think what a motive that would give her husband!'

Thanet remembered Vintage's concern for the child, the tenderness with which he had handled it. 'I can't believe that.' He didn't want to believe it, he realised. He was sorry for Vintage and sympathetic to the difficult situation in which he found himself. He would have to be careful. He mustn't allow bias to warp his judgement. 'If you'd seen him with the baby . . .'

'All right. Perhaps I'm wrong about the baby. Or perhaps I'm right and he just doesn't realise it isn't his. But in any case I could still be right about the affair – I say "I", but it was you who suggested it in the first place!'

'I know that. But having seen Mrs Randish I'm not so sure.'

'That's because you're thinking of her as she is now. At her worst. But while I was talking to her I was trying to visualise what she'd look like in good health, with make-up on and so on, and I bet she'd turn heads any day of the week.'

'Maybe. All right. Let's say she and Randish were having an affair. What, exactly, are you suggesting, Mike? That Vintage has known about it all along? In which case, why do nothing until last night? Or are you suggesting he's only just found out?'

'That he's only just found out.'

'How?'

'No idea. Perhaps someone told him. Perhaps something was said which made him put two and two together.'

'And come up with five, most likely! No, sorry, Mike, I'm still sceptical. In any case, there's one big objection to the idea that his wife might have been Randish's mistress.'

'What's that?'

'When we told her Randish was dead, don't you think we would have got more of a reaction?'

'But she was doped up to the eyeballs, we could both see that! All her reactions were about as low-key as they could get! And if Vintage did somehow find out last night, he would fit the bill perfectly. For one thing, he was there alone most of the evening, and for another, whoever killed Randish just exploded with rage, didn't he? Just think about it! Vintage was very tired, exhausted in fact, which means his self-control would be at its lowest. Also, because of Randish he'd just lost a substantial portion of the very special wine he was hoping would launch him on the road to success. Then he learns his wife had been having an affair with the man! It's enough to make anyone snap!'

'Mike, this is pure speculation and you know it.' Thanet's tone was indulgent. Lineham's enthusiasm was one of his more endearing qualities and Thanet was used to the fact that the sergeant sometimes got carried away.

'That doesn't mean it can't be true.'

'No, just that we have to wait until we have some hard evidence to support the idea before we can take it any further. So let's drop it for the moment, shall we? Anyway, isn't this the vineyard coming up?'

Lineham slowed down. 'Looks like it.'

The signboard for Chasing Manor vineyard had been designed to look like a wine label, the label which no doubt was put on their bottles. In the centre was a cameo of the vineyard, a sketch of a classic Georgian house set in well-ordered rows of vines.

'I'm beginning to feel as though we're on a tour of the vineyards of Kent,' said Thanet. 'I never knew there were so many.'

'Oh yes, there are dozens of them. There's one at Tenterden, one at Biddenden, one at Frittenden, one at Leeds, one at Bearsted . . .'

'All right, Mike. I didn't ask for a catalogue. Anyway, how do you know so much about it?'

'I've got a neighbour who's a wine buff. His favourite

pastime at weekends is touring vineyards. This one doesn't look as though it's doing too badly.'

Thanet looked around. Over to his right, set well back behind a brick wall and a generous front garden, was the house on the signboard, translated into bricks and mortar. It was a classic example of Georgian architecture: front door in the centre, two sash windows to right and left, five above. For once the architect had got the proportions exactly right and not even the grey light of a damp October afternoon could dim the beauty which had mellowed through the centuries. Sitting serenely in its setting of well-kept lawns and flowerbeds it seemed to encapsulate so much of what people envisage when they think of the beauty of rural England. What must it be like to live in a house like that? Thanet wondered.

'A real hive of activity, in fact,' said Lineham.

Thanet tore his eyes away from the house. The sergeant was right. There was a coach in the car park and a number of cars. Machinery hummed and there were people moving about. As they walked towards the buildings ahead the noise got louder and they met a group of people leaving the shop, carrying bottles and packs of wine. The coach party, probably, thought Thanet, and by the laughter and chatter he guessed that they had probably attended a wine-tasting session before making their purchases.

The noise intensified. It sounded like the spin on a giant washing machine. It was emanating, they discovered, from a cylindrical stainless-steel wine press identical to the one at Sturrenden.

Lineham raised his voice to make himself heard. 'That must be what Vintage meant, when he talked about the noise the press makes when the compressor comes on.'

Thanet nodded. 'Probably.'

There were in fact two presses, one on each side of a wide covered area, but only one was working at the moment. Preparations were in progress for starting off another batch in the other press: a man on a tractor was backing a trailer-load of grapes up to a smaller bin-shaped trailer of sturdy green plastic which had been connected to the press by a thick corrugated hose about 5 inches in diameter. Another man was standing by, watching, and a third man was hosing out a huge black plastic barrel. As they approached he picked up a broom and began to sweep the water towards a runnel leading to a drain.

Although Benton had retired Thanet guessed that in the circumstances the former winemaker would have stepped in to do Randish's job. He picked out the man watching as the most likely candidate. He had an air of authority about him. Thanet raised his voice to make himself heard. 'Mr Benton?'

The man turned. 'Yes?'

Warm brown eyes regarded him with affable curiosity. If Benton was in his early sixties he was very well preserved, with thick brown curly hair untouched by grey and a luxuriant beard.

'Mr James Benton?'

'That's right.'

Thanet introduced himself and Lineham, watching the bleakness creep into Benton's eyes.

Benton half turned, spoke to the man on the tractor. 'Can you manage for a while, Mark?'

'Is that your son, sir?'

Benton nodded. 'Yes, why?'

Randish's childhood friend, now an accountant, according to Vintage. What a bit of luck, thought Thanet. He certainly hadn't expected to find him here today. Presumably the younger Benton had also stepped in to help out in the emergency. With two presses in operation this vineyard must have double the workload of Sturrenden to cope with. 'I'd like him to join us, please.'

Benton frowned. 'We're rather behind here. Would you mind waiting a few minutes while we start this batch off? Then we'll be free for a while.'

'Fine.'

Thanet and Lineham watched with interest. The trailer connected to the press, they discovered, had a huge stainless-steel screw running across the bottom inside, from front to back. When it started to revolve it would feed the grapes into the hose leading to the press. They watched while the grapes were emptied in and the process started, then Benton led the way across the yard and up an outside staircase to an office on the upper floor of one of the barns. He sat down behind the desk and offered Thanet the only other chair. Mark Benton perched on the desk edge and Lineham went to lean against the windowsill.

'We still can't believe it,' said Benton. 'Murder is something you read about in the newspapers or hear about on the radio or television. You just don't think it could ever happen to someone you know.'

Thanet nodded sympathetically. He'd heard this said so many times before, and he could believe it.

'I mean, here we are, perfectly ordinary people leading perfectly ordinary lives and then wham . . . I suppose until now we've been lucky.' He glanced at his son. 'It's just that we've known Zak since he was in his teens.'

'You were fond of him?' Thanet was intrigued. Apart from Alice Randish this was the first time he'd heard anyone speak of the dead man with anything approaching affection.

Benton hesitated. 'I wouldn't say "fond" was the right

word. He'd been around so long he was practically one of the family, wasn't he, Mark? And I suppose my attitude to him was pretty much what it would be to one of my own children. I took his faults for granted.'

Mark Benton grinned. 'Thanks, Dad!'

Mark Benton must take after his mother, Thanet thought. He was shorter than his father and much less robust in appearance, with straight floppy brown hair and gold-rimmed spectacles which gave him a studious look.

Benton waved a hand. 'You know perfectly well what I mean.'

'So what were his faults, would you say?' said Thanet.

Benton frowned, ran his hand through his thick hair, then leaned forward to ease his waxed jacket off. He tossed it on to the floor beside him. 'That's tricky. You never sit down and actually list people's characteristics in your mind, do you? I mean, what usually occurs is that something happens and you think, God, he's an impatient beggar, or he's a heartless blighter, or he'd trample over anyone who got in his way, and so on. D'you see what I mean?'

'Yes. Were you thinking of Mr Randish just then, when you were speaking? Was he in fact impatient, heartless, ruthless?'

Benton shifted uncomfortably in his chair and glanced at his son. 'I suppose I was, to a certain extent. Sorry, Mark, but there's no point in trying to make out that Zak was some sort of saint, because he wasn't.'

'I've never suggested otherwise.'

'And in any case, we would be doing him a disservice if we tried to pull the wool over the inspector's eyes.'

'Don't treat me like an idiot, Dad, I realise that! I don't know what you're going on like this for in any case. You know Zak and I hardly ever saw each other any more.'

'Oh? Why was that, sir?' Thanet was interested.

Mark shrugged. 'We just drifted apart. Our paths divided, I suppose, and we went different ways. I don't actually work on the vineyard, I reneged and became a white-collar worker.'

'An accountant, I believe.'

Mark looked surprised and a little wary. 'That's right. You're very well informed, Inspector.'

'But you had known Mr Randish a long time.'

'As my father said, since we were in our teens, yes.'

'And – correct me if I'm wrong – but I had the impression, just now, that it wasn't just because your ways divided that you didn't see much of each other any more, but also perhaps because you didn't like him as much as you once did.'

'Yes, that's true. But – look, I hope you're not about to suggest that I went over to Sturrenden last night and bumped him off, are you?'

Mark Benton's tone was jocular, but his father jumped in before Thanet could respond. 'Don't be ridiculous, Mark! The inspector's suggesting no such thing.'

'Quite right, I'm not suggesting anything of the sort. It's just that I'm trying to find out as much as I can about Mr Randish, and the only way I can do that is to ask questions of the people who knew him. And you, Mr Benton, are in a position where you could be especially useful to us. You've known him a long time but you're not so close to him now that you can't stand back a little and give us a more impartial view than people he was involved with on a day-to-day basis.'

'I was, as I'm sure you realised, Inspector, joking. Anything I can do to help . . . Ask away.'

Much of what Mark Benton told them simply confirmed what they had already heard. Randish had met

Alice when he was fruit-picking on her father's farm during the school holidays and it was she who introduced him to the Young Farmers' Club, which was where he met Mark.

'She was absolutely crazy about him. All the while they were together, even in a crowd, she'd hardly take her eyes off him. It was as if the rest of us simply didn't exist.'

'Did he feel the same about her?'

'He was keen, certainly, but not to that degree. I think he just went along with it, to begin with, at least.'

'And then?'

Mark Benton looked uncomfortable. 'Well, to be honest, I think it dawned on him that he might be on to a good thing.'

'Because she was an only child, you mean, and her father had a large farm.'

Mark nodded reluctantly. 'Yes.'

Benton intervened. 'I don't know if what Mark is saying is true, Inspector, it well might be. In fact, it wouldn't surprise me in the least. All the same, I do feel that we might be giving you the wrong impression. Zak had many good qualities, or I wouldn't have employed him to take over here when I retired. He was reliable, very hard-working and as far as I was concerned absolutely trust-worthy.'

'Oh come on, Dad, don't be a humbug! Who was apologising to me a few minutes ago for being too frank about Zak? I don't like saying these things about him any more than you do, especially when he can't defend him-self, but let's face it, people don't get themselves killed because they're reliable, hardworking and trustworthy. They get themselves killed, presumably, because they've treated someone badly – very badly.'

'All the same, I think it has to be said. Zak worked

incredibly hard to get where he did, and when you consider his background . . . His father was a drunken brute, Inspector, who used to beat his wife and children without any excuse at all. There was some very nasty publicity once, when a neighbour reported him to the NSPCC. I imagine the whole family heaved a sigh of relief when he got drunk one night and landed up in the river. Fortunately he couldn't swim. There was no foul play, there were plenty of witnesses around. Zak was around fourteen then, I believe.'

'I had the impression that Mr Landers wasn't too keen on Mr Randish's association with his daughter,' said Thanet.

'Can you blame him, with a background like that?' said Benton senior. 'If Mark had had a sister I wouldn't have been too keen on Zak as a prospective suitor for her, I can tell you. And not because I'm a snob, either. The poverty of his background wouldn't have worried me if his parents were good people. But bad blood is a different matter.'

And so was an undesirable example. Had the Bentons known or suspected that Randish was beating his wife, as his father had beaten his mother?

'And would your anxiety have been justified, sir?'

'What do you mean?'

Benton was looking puzzled, but Mark had understood, Thanet could see it in his face. 'Are you married, sir?' he asked the younger man, on a sudden inspiration.

'Yes. Why?'

'Just wondered.'

'It was through Alice that Mark met Zoë – his wife – as a matter of fact,' said Benton. 'She and Alice were at the same finishing school in Switzerland, and Alice invited her to stay when they left.'

That explained a lot, thought Thanet. If the two girls were friends and the two young men had known each other for a long time, no doubt they had seen quite a lot of each other in the early years of their marriages. And if Randish had started knocking Alice about, Zoë – like Lineham's wife, Louise – might well have noticed, or guessed. In which case, even if the two young women had kept up their friendship, Mark Benton might well out of distaste have allowed his friendship with Zak to lapse. 'It was during Mr Randish's final year at college that Mrs Randish – Miss Landers as she was then – was away in Switzerland, wasn't it?'

'Yes. I think Landers sent her away in the hope that separation might break the relationship up. A vain hope, I'm afraid. The experiment was a dismal failure. The minute Alice got back she and Zak were inseparable again. Not long afterwards they announced their engagement.'

'Mr Landers gave his consent to the marriage?'

'Well, Alice was nineteen by then. Strictly speaking she didn't need it.'

But that wouldn't have suited Randish's plans at all, thought Thanet. He needed Landers' blessing.

'What happened,' said Mark, 'was that Mr Landers agreed, provided they waited two years before getting married. If they still wanted to go ahead at the end of that time, he would not oppose it.'

'I suppose he thought that if they were still determined then, he might as well give in gracefully,' said Benton. 'Which, of course, is what happened.'

'I assume he set them up in the house and vineyard?'

'It was his wedding present,' said Benton.

So Randish's patience had been amply rewarded.

Lineham shifted from one foot to the other and Thanet

could hear his unspoken comment. *Some wedding present!*

'And meanwhile Mr Randish was working here?'

'Yes. I told you, I couldn't fault him in that respect. He learned fast as he had a real flair for winemaking. Some have got it and some haven't. He did.'

'You were saying,' said Thanet to Mark Benton, 'that Mr Randish was never as keen on his wife as she was on him.' He paused, choosing his next words carefully. 'Do you know if he had other girlfriends at the same time, while he was away at college, for instance?'

'Good God, yes!' said Mark Benton. 'His attitude was that he should make hay while the sun was shining.'

'Didn't Miss Landers suspect?'

'I can't think how he got away with it, but he seemed to. It must have been some juggling act, during his second year at least, because her father gave her a car for her seventeenth birthday and once she passed her test there was no holding her, she was off to Plumpton every weekend.'

'Hence the finishing school during Zak's final year there, I imagine,' said Benton.

'He had a particularly torrid affair while she was away, I remember,' said Mark. 'With his landlady's daughter, I believe. I met her once. Interestingly enough, she looked a bit like Alice, except that she was dark instead of fair. She was the same type, I suppose – small, slight, rather fragile-looking.'

Of course! thought Thanet. That was what had been eluding him when he was looking at those photographs. All Zak's girlfriends had been the same physical type. 'And did his attitude change after he was married?' he said, arriving at last at the point up to which he had been leading.

'Ah,' said Benton. 'Now there, I certainly can't help you.' There was a brief silence. He glanced at Mark.

'So that's what you've been getting at,' said Mark. 'You're thinking in terms of a jealous husband, or lover.'

'It's a possible explanation.'

'Well, all I can say is that I do know for a fact that Zak wasn't exactly the most faithful husband in the world. But whether or not he had a current girlfriend, mistress, whatever, I'm afraid I have no idea. And that's the truth.'

'So,' said Lineham as they walked back to the car. 'Surprise, surprise, we're back to "*cherchez la femme*".'

'You've been working on your French accent, Mike.'

'Shouldn't be too much of a problem, sir, should it, to round up all the small, slight, fragile-looking girls in the area and find out which of them was Randish's mistress?'

'Ha ha. Very funny.'

Lineham cocked his head. 'Isn't that the car radio?' He hurried off.

Thanet's shoelace was undone and he stopped to fix it. The call was brief and by the time he arrived at the car Lineham was replacing the handset.

The sergeant leaned across to unlock the passenger door. He was grinning from ear to ear.

'What's up?' said Thanet.

'You won't believe this!' said Lineham.

ELEVEN

Thanet got into the car. 'Believe what? Well, come on, Mike, stop grinning like a Cheshire cat and spit it out.'

'It looks as though we've found the *femme*!'

'Oh?' Thanet was wary. He wanted to hear more before he started rejoicing.

'That was a message from DC Wakeham. You remember he was saying this morning that he was sure he'd seen Randish before? Well, he remembered where. It was at a restaurant in Lenham. Randish was with a girl and they were very engrossed in each other. Wakeham especially noticed them because he fancied the girl. Anyway, and this is the point, the friend Wakeham was with knew who she was. He works in computers and so does she. You remember the new system I commented on, at the vineyard? I bet that was how Randish met her.'

'Could be. When was this, that Wakeham saw them?'

'Couple of weeks ago, sir.'

'But he didn't know the name of the girl? Or the firm she works for?'

'No. But he's trying to get hold of his friend, to find out.'

'Good. Well, let's hope you're right.' It all sounded feasible and if so it was a lucky break. It wasn't often that an answer fell into their laps almost before they'd asked the question.

'Where now, sir? Back to Headquarters? You promised that statement to the press.'

Thanet groaned. 'I suppose so.'

It was nearly 9.30 before he at last reached home. Joan and Bridget were watching a film on television.

'Your supper's in the oven,' Joan said. 'Side salad in the fridge.'

'Thanks, love.' In the kitchen the table was laid for one. Thanet turned off the oven, took an oven-cloth and removed the dish inside. A mouth-watering aroma rose to greet him. As he expected it was one of Bridget's specialities, salmon and prawn lasagne. Bridget was a Cordon Bleu cook, a freelance professional who cooked for directors' dining rooms in the City. The effortless ease with which she produced delicious meals never failed to arouse her mother's envy and admiration and invariably, when she was home, despite Joan's protests that it was no break for her, she cooked for the family. Thanet inhaled appreciatively, suddenly realising how hungry he was. He was glad to see that they'd left him a generous helping.

As usual, at the end of a long day, his back was aching and he adjusted himself into the most comfortable position before beginning to eat. Gradually, as he enjoyed his meal, the strains and tensions began to seep away and by the time he'd finished, cleared away and lit his pipe he was feeling a new man. He put his head around the sitting-room door. 'Tea, coffee, Horlicks, cocoa, chocolate?'

Briefly they turned smiling faces towards him. They both wanted tea.

He returned to the kitchen, made tea for three. The front door slammed and Ben wandered into the kitchen.

'Hi.'

'You're early for a Saturday night.'

'Yeah. Got a training session in the morning. Have to get up early, groan, groan.'

'Want some tea? I've just made some.'

'Think I'll really live it up, have some chocolate instead. Don't worry, I'll make it myself. Saw you on the box tonight, by the way. Great performance, Dad. We'll make a star of you yet.'

'No comment,' said Thanet, departing with the tray of tea.

The play was just finishing.

'Well timed, darling,' said Joan.

'How are things?' said Thanet.

Bridget pulled a face. 'Not exactly great.'

'Oh?' Thanet was surprised. Surely Bridget wasn't going to talk about Alexander here, now, with Ben about to come in?

Joan had guessed what he was thinking. 'It's Karen, Luke. You remember Bridget's friend Karen, the one with anorexia?'

Thanet was nodding.

'Well, she died last night.'

Thanet stared at her as wheels clicked in his brain. Karen. He heard Landers' voice. *Zak's niece died this evening. She was only twenty. She's been in hospital for some time.*

Joan glanced uneasily at Bridget, who was staring down at her hands, her expression grim. 'And that wasn't all.'

Thanet knew what was coming next. Landers' voice again: *Jonathan had an accident last night . . . the twin brother of the girl who died . . . he and his sister have always been very close . . .*

'Bridget went around to Karen's house,' Joan was

saying, 'and there was no one in. But the next-door neighbour heard her knocking and came out. She told her about Karen, then said that Karen's mother was still at the hospital because Karen's brother Jonathan had had an accident . . .' Joan stopped. 'You're not looking surprised,' she said.

'I'd already heard. I'm sorry about your friend, Sprig,' he said to Bridget. He rarely used her childhood nickname these days but this time it just slipped out.

Bridget looked close to tears. 'It was such a shock,' she said. 'I knew she wasn't getting on very well. Last time I was home she'd gone down to five stone again. But I didn't think . . . And then, Jonathan, too. I rang the hospital and he's still unconscious.'

'Who's still unconscious?' Ben came in carrying a mug and a triple-decker sandwich.

No one commented on the latter. They were used, by now, to Ben's late-night snacks.

'Jonathan Redman,' said Joan. Quickly, she filled Ben in on what they had been saying.

'A motorbike accident!' said Ben, glancing at his father.

Thanet nodded. With what he considered superhuman restraint he refrained from saying anything. The question of a motorbike was a bone of contention between them and he hoped that Ben would have enough sense to draw his own conclusions. He remembered thinking the same thing last night when he'd passed the scene of that accident. It struck him now that it might well have been Jonathan Redman on the stretcher.

'But how did you know about all this, Luke?' said Joan.

'This murder I'm working on. The victim was Karen's uncle, Mrs Redman's brother.'

All three stared at him, taken aback. Joan was the first to speak. 'Oh no!' she said. 'Poor woman! She must be absolutely devastated by all this.'

'I know,' said Thanet. 'I was thinking earlier on that I can't imagine how anyone in her situation even begins to cope.'

'I'll go and see her tomorrow,' said Bridget suddenly. 'In case I can do anything to help.'

'Her brother's mother-in-law, Mrs Landers, was going around to keep her company today,' said Thanet. 'But of course, in the circumstances, she can't stay with her all the time. Mrs Landers' daughter is naturally very upset over her husband's death, and there are the grandchildren to think of.'

'Quite,' said Bridget. 'But Mrs Redman will be feeling so alone. She hasn't got anybody else, to my knowledge. She's incredibly shy and awkward in company and it puts people off. I don't think she has any close friends.'

'I'm not surprised,' said Ben. 'She and Mr Redman were a pair of oddballs, in my opinion. I went there once with you, do you remember, when he was still alive? Mrs Redman wouldn't say "boo" to a goose and Mr Redman gave me the creeps.' He took a huge bite out of his sandwich.

'In what way?' said Joan.

Somehow Ben managed simultaneously to screw up his face in distaste at the memory and masticate energetically. He swallowed. 'Dunno. This was yonks ago. I couldn't have been more than, what, eleven? at the time, so I don't suppose I stopped to analyse what I didn't like about him. All I knew was that I wasn't too anxious to go back there.' He returned to his sandwich.

'I don't blame you,' said Bridget. 'It wasn't much fun going to the Redmans', especially if Mr Redman was there. He was a bit of a religious maniac. Very strict. Like something out of the dark ages, really. He wouldn't allow a television set in the house, or a radio. I'm sure he didn't approve of me. He had very rigid rules about the way they were all supposed to behave, even about how they should dress – Karen wasn't allowed to wear bright colours, short skirts, jeans or T-shirts, and as for make-up, that was absolutely *verboten*.' Like Ben she pulled a face. 'He gave me the creeps too.'

Thanet had a feeling that she could have said more, that there was in fact something specific that she was holding back. He had had a case once in which a similar family was involved, he remembered. And there, too, the extremity of the father's views had led to tragedy. The roots of Karen's anorexia had no doubt lain in the warped relationships within her family.

He said as much to Joan as they were getting ready for bed. 'And I have a feeling that Bridget knows more than she's telling.' He swung his legs into bed and lay down, feeling the tense muscles of his aching back relax into the blissful support of the orthopaedic mattress in which they had invested some years ago.

Joan was patting moisture cream into her face. 'You could be right. She and Karen were very close at one time.' She finished creaming her face and got into bed. She sighed. 'It's such a waste, isn't it, a young girl like that, dying unnecessarily. Anorexia is a dreadful thing and I'm only thankful Bridget never succumbed.'

'As far as she's concerned, the one positive aspect of all this is that it has given her something other than Alexander to think about.'

'Quite.'

'How's she been today?'

'Well, there's no doubt about it, it's been an awful

blow to her self-confidence. She'll bounce back eventually, I imagine, she's pretty resilient, but it's bound to take time. And, of course, hearing about Karen has rather overshadowed everything else. But as you heard downstairs, she is trying to be positive. She's arranged to go and have coffee with Helen tomorrow morning.'

'Helen will be pleased. Doc M. told me only last night that Helen was saying recently that she hadn't seen Bridget for ages. She misses their cookery sessions, he says.'

'And we're going to Mother's for tea.'

Thanet grinned. 'It all sounds rather dull for a twenty-year-old, but highly therapeutic.'

To spend time with people who loved and valued her was just what Bridget needed, he thought next morning, looking at his daughter's drawn face as she came into the kitchen. It wrenched at his heart to see her like this and to feel so powerless to help her. He was standing waiting for the kettle to boil and went to put his arm around her shoulders, give her a hug. 'What are you doing up at this unearthly hour on a Sunday morning?' Almost before the words were out, he knew he shouldn't have asked.

'I didn't sleep very well.'

The opening was there, he had to take it. In any case they couldn't go on avoiding the subject as they had been. 'I was sorry to hear about Alexander,' he said.

She twisted to look up at him; disengaged herself. 'Were you, Dad?' she said bitterly. 'I'd have thought you might be relieved. You never did like him, did you?'

She was hurt and angry, he saw, angry with Alexander, with herself, with life. Now, briefly, her anger had found a focus in him. Well, there was no point in being anything but honest. But how to do it, without inflicting more pain? 'I did like him.' But his reservations showed in his tone of voice, he realised. 'I just wasn't sure he was right for you.'

'Why not?' said Bridget passionately. And then, 'Oh, what's the point in going over and over it? It's finished now, anyway.' And, putting up a hand to dash away the tears which had sprung into her eyes, she rushed from the room.

Thanet was reminded of the scene between Alice Randish and her father yesterday, which had been over much the same issue – parental disapproval of choice of partner – and had ended in much the same way, and he felt a pang of sympathy for Landers. Despite his rationalisation of a moment ago, he was upset. How not to administer comfort, in one easy lesson, he thought wryly.

He made the tea and, before sitting down to breakfast, carried a cup upstairs. Joan, he knew, would still be asleep, she usually had a lie-in on a Sunday morning before going to church. He tapped softly on Bridget's door. 'Cup of tea,' he murmured.

No response.

With a sigh he deposited it on the floor and went back downstairs. She would come around, he knew. Meanwhile the memory of the brief and uncomfortable little scene lodged like a splinter in his consciousness. It would, he knew, lie there festering all day. It was rare indeed for him to be on bad terms with Bridget, however briefly.

He had little appetite for breakfast but knowing how uncertain meal times were when he was working on a case made himself eat some cereal. Outside, however, the sun was trying to break through, his pipe consoled him a little and by the time he arrived in the office he was feeling marginally more cheerful. It was depressing therefore to find that the usually ebullient Lineham, there before him as usual, was looking gloomy.

Reluctantly, Thanet removed his pipe out of consideration for the sergeant and tapped it out in the stout ashtray which stood on his desk for that purpose. 'It can't be as bad as that, surely, Mike.'

Lineham tossed the report he had been reading on to his desk. 'Nothing!' he said. 'Nothing of any use, anyway. And if there's nothing coming in at this stage, what's it going to be like later?'

'Oh come on, stop being so pessimistic. You know perfectly well one can simply never tell what's going to turn up next. You've said yourself that's one of the things you like about this job.'

'True.'

'So? There must be something to report, surely, even if it's all negative.'

'The PM report is in, but it doesn't tell us anything we didn't already know.' Lineham passed it over and Thanet glanced through it. Randish had apparently been in very good shape and in layman's terms had, as they surmised, quite simply bled to death as a result of the gash in his throat.

'What about the girl DC Wakeham saw?' said Thanet. 'Has he tracked down the friend who knows her, yet?'

Lineham shook his head. 'Couldn't get hold of him last night, sir. Not surprising, as it was Saturday night. Wakeham's gone off to have another go. If he fails, we could always make inquiries at the vineyard. If Randish did meet her through the firm who sold him his new computer system Mrs Prote would know who they are. If she's not at work today – and it is Sunday, after all – we've got her address. She might even know who the girl is. As I said, it's an expensive system and the firm might well have sent this girl to work at the vineyard for a couple of days to make sure their clients knew how to handle it. They often do. In which case, come to think of it, Vintage probably met her too.'

'You're assuming a lot, Mike. It might be pure coincidence that she works in computers. Randish could have met her in a dozen different ways. Still, I agree, it would be worth a try. Has Wakeham sent Mason's shoes off to forensic?'

'Yes. But they say they're snowed under and can't promise to come back to us for several days, at least.'

'Surprise, surprise.'

The morning meeting was brief again, Thanet's report once more being the longest. There was still no news of the results of Angharad's latest test. They all hoped that in this case no news did indeed mean good news. They should know tomorrow morning, when Draco returned.

Back in the office Thanet found Mallard waiting for him, alone. Lineham had evidently gone off on some errand.

'Morning, Luke. Don't suppose you've got any queries about the PM, it was all pretty straightforward, but I thought I'd pop in just in case.'

Thanet shook his head. 'Don't think so, thanks. It's all crystal clear.'

'He would have been good for another forty or fifty years, you know, barring accidents.'

'So I gathered.'

'How's it going?'

'We're feeling our way, as usual, not getting very far at the moment.'

'Actually, I really called to ask how Bridget is. I don't know if she told you, but she's coming around for coffee with Helen this morning. Is Alexander the problem?'

'I'm afraid so.' Briefly, Thanet gave Mallard a summary of the situation. 'We're hoping Helen will cheer her up.'

'She's very good at cheering people up,' said Mallard. 'Look what a good job she did on me!'

'True,' said Thanet smiling.

Thoughts of his own past must have reminded Mallard of Draco's present. 'Any news of Angharad?' he asked.

Thanet shook his head. 'We're keeping our fingers crossed.'

'So am I,' said Mallard grimly. 'This is a really important test, you know.'

'More so than the last? Why?'

'How much do you know about leukaemia?'

'Only snippets I've gathered here and there. I used to think it was invariably fatal, but we've all been astounded to see how Angharad has picked up over the last year.'

After the diagnosis they had all watched fearfully as Angharad had become a shadow of her former self. She had lost all her wonderful red hair and scorning a wig had taken to wearing exotic turbans. The ghost of her former, exceptional beauty had lingered only in the bone structure of her face. And then, miraculously, she had begun to improve. Little by little she had put on weight: had even, eventually, discarded the turbans and emerged like a freshly hatched chick with a fine frizz of hair the colour of a new-minted penny. Colour had begun to return to her cheeks and vitality to her movements.

'As you know,' said Mallard, 'Angharad has acute myeloid leukaemia. It was diagnosed two years ago. So you'll understand just how astounding that improvement is if I tell you that the average outlook is two years of life from diagnosis, with one or more remissions, each shorter than the last because of the disease becoming resistant to treatment. The first remission is on average one year, the second six months, the third – and you might not get one – four weeks. If someone recovers, it is always during first remission. If you have a second remission you will die unless you have a transplant, and that's a very risky business.'

'You're saying that Angharad is still in her first remission?'

'Yes. So far she's been one of the lucky ones.'

'I'd no idea. To begin with I think we were all afraid to talk to the Super about it, for fear of making him more depressed. No, to tell you the truth, I think we were just too cowardly, in case the news was bad and we wouldn't know what to say.'

'Understandable,' said Mallard.

'And then of course, when she seemed to start getting better I think we felt that to comment on the improvement would somehow be tempting fate. So we just stood by and kept our fingers crossed that it would continue.'

'Yes. Well, I'm afraid we're not out of the wood yet. Patients can do extraordinarily well and survive several years without relapses, but only about ten per cent of the total are cured and never relapse. After five years without a relapse you can be pretty sure. This particular test is important because for the first two years you have tests every two months and this is the last of the series. If she's clear it'll be a major landmark in her recovery.'

'But even if she is, they'll still have three more years to go before they can really begin to feel safe.'

'Yes. But if it is clear this time, she'll at least be in with a chance. From now on, all being well, it'll be every three to four months between tests, for a further two years. Then every six months for a couple of years. Then every year.'

Thanet had always shied away from imagining too vividly what it must be like for a relatively young woman of thirty-seven like Angharad to live with the shadow of death always hovering over her, to have to summon up over and over again sufficient courage to live through yet another course of debilitating chemotherapy. He fervently hoped that for the Dracos the worst of the nightmare would now be over.

Lineham hurried into the room. The spring was back in his step, his eyes alight with enthusiasm. 'We've got it, sir! Oh, sorry, Doc, morning.'

Mallard acknowledged the sergeant's greeting with a nod, an indulgent twinkle in his eye.

'Got what, Mike?' said Thanet.

'The girl's name. DC Wakeham just rang in. It's Elaine Wood. Wakeham's friend wasn't sure which firm she works for, though. He met her at some conference.'

'This is Randish's latest girlfriend, apparently,' Thanet explained to Mallard. 'Or could be.'

'Well, don't mind me. I'm just off anyway.'

'Right. We'll go out to the vineyard, then, Mike, test this theory of yours and see if they can tell us where to find her.'

'Want a bet on it, sir?'

'A pint, at lunchtime?'

'Done!'

'Tut, tut,' said Mallard. He clicked his tongue in mock disapproval. 'Gambling in the ranks. What would Superintendent Draco say?'

TWELVE

With the resumption of work Sturrenden vineyard had come to life. The car park was surprisingly full for this hour on a Sunday morning and there were a number of customers in the shop.

'Murder is always good for business,' muttered Lineham cynically as they got out of the car.

Thanet grunted. The prurient attitude of the public towards anything to do with murder never failed to disgust him. Heads turned and necks craned as they went past.

Lights were on in the office but it was empty. Perhaps Mrs Prote wasn't in and they'd have to talk to Vintage instead.

In the covered yard the press was in operation and hoses of different thicknesses and colours snaked off in all directions. Vintage had evidently found someone to help him out: a young man Thanet had never seen before was hosing down the pressing area. He was wearing a long black rubber apron and wellington boots. As they picked their way towards him he dropped the hose, picked up a bass broom and began to sweep the water vigorously towards a central drain. Reflections of the neon lights above fragmented and reformed as the water rolled across them. A strong fruity smell hung in the air.

'Sturrenden CID,' said Lineham. 'Is Mrs Prote in today?'

The young man stopped sweeping. He was about twenty, with cropped black hair and an incipient beard. There was a sheen of perspiration on his forehead. 'Who?'

'Mrs Prote. The manageress.'

'I've just come in for the day, to help out, so I don't know people here. What does she look like?'

'Tall, dark, horn-rimmed glasses.'

'Yes, she's about somewhere.'

'There she is, Mike,' said Thanet.

Mrs Prote was descending the outside staircase from the Tea Room, which was in the upper floor of the barn housing the shop. As they crossed the yard Thanet said, 'Let's hope she's less prickly than she was yesterday, or you'll have your work cut out.'

Lineham, they had agreed, was to take this interview.

They waited for her at the bottom of the staircase. Once again she was immaculate, not a hair out of place in the smooth French pleat, blouse pristine white, dark green skirt and cardigan an exact match, shoes gleaming like polished chestnuts. She didn't look too pleased to see them: the brown eyes behind the horn-rimmed spectacles were hostile, resentful. 'I hope this won't take too long. I've got a lot to do today.'

'We weren't sure if you'd be in, as it's Sunday,' said Thanet.

She made no comment, simply led them into the office and sat down behind her desk, taking up the same pose as yesterday: knees together, feet side by side, hands folded in lap.

No doubt about it, thought Thanet, she would like life to be equally neat, well organised, under control. Maybe her hostility towards them stemmed from the fact that she didn't know how to deal with it when it became messy. And murder was invariably messy, in more ways than one.

'May we?' said Lineham, putting a hand on one of the other two chairs.

'If you must. As I said, I hope this won't take long.'

'We'll be as quick as we can.' Lineham swung the chair around to face her and Thanet moved the other one across to the window. This was Lineham's idea, Lineham's show.

'Nice computer system,' said Lineham. 'New, isn't it?'

Her eyebrows arched in surprise. 'Relatively, yes.'

'How long have you had it?'

'Three months or so.'

'Which firm did you buy it from?'

Her shoulders twitched impatiently. 'Look, is this relevant? I don't want to be rude, but . . .'

'If it wasn't relevant, Mrs Prote, I wouldn't be asking about it.'

She frowned. 'I really don't see how . . .'

Lineham sighed and said wearily, 'Mrs Prote. Do you want your employer's murderer to be found?'

'Well of course I do! What a ridiculous question!'

'Then perhaps you could be just a little more cooperative.'

'But I am being cooperative!'

'Are you? We obviously have different ideas of the meaning of the word. As far as we're concerned you weren't particularly cooperative yesterday and you're not being particularly cooperative today. First you say you've got a lot of work to do so you'd like this interview to be as brief as possible and then you prevaricate, thereby prolonging it.'

'I wasn't prevaricating!'

She glanced at Thanet, as if expecting him to back her up. He folded his arms and stared back at her, his face unresponsive, making it clear that he agreed with Lineham.

'I just don't see what computers have to do with Mr Randish's death.'

The point had been made. She was on the defensive now and Lineham recognised this. His tone was patient as he said, 'Mrs Prote, we are the ones who are investigating Mr Randish's death. Perhaps you'd allow us to judge what is or is not relevant.'

There was a brief silence, then Lineham went on. 'So, would you now answer my question: which firm did you buy it from?'

'Compu-Tech, in Sturrenden.'

'I haven't heard of them. They're a small firm?'

'Yes.'

'Were you pleased with the service they gave?'

'Very.'

'Was this the first computer system you've had here, or did you have a less sophisticated one before?'

'No, this is the first.'

'So I suppose the firm supplied you with someone to work beside you for the first day or two, while you got used to it?'

'Yes. It was one of the reasons why we chose that particular firm.'

'Was the person they sent a man or a woman?'

'A woman. Why?'

Lineham ignored the question.

'What was her name?'

'Elaine.'

Thanet could tell that Lineham was longing to flick a

triumphant glance at him. *Told you so!* But the sergeant restrained himself.

'Elaine what?'

'I've no idea. She just called herself Elaine, you know how these girls do.'

'A girl, you said. How old was she, would you say?'

Mrs Prote thought. 'Mid-twenties, perhaps?'

'But she looked younger?'

'Yes, on a first impression. She was small, slim, dark.'

Just Randish's type, according to his friend Mark Benton, thought Thanet. He could see Lineham thinking the same thing. And she matched Wakeham's description.

'Did she give Mr Randish tuition too?'

'Yes. It was part of the package. We both need – needed – to use the computer, if for different reasons.'

'How did Mr Randish get on with this Elaine?'

Mrs Prote was looking wary. 'All right.'

She didn't ask why, Thanet noted.

'Did he take any special interest in her, did you notice?'

'What do you mean?'

'To put it bluntly, did he fancy her?'

Her lips tightened. 'How would I know?'

'Mrs Prote, are you trying to tell me that you stayed here in this room with the pair of them for – how long? A day? Two days?' Lineham paused, waited pointedly for her answer.

'Two days,' she said reluctantly.

'And you didn't notice Mr Randish's attitude towards her?'

She was chewing the inside of her lip. She didn't reply.

Lineham sighed and sat back in his chair, folding his arms. 'I really don't know why you're making this such hard work,' he said.

'I just don't believe in idle gossip, Sergeant,' she said primly. 'Nor do I think one should speak ill of the dead.'

'Idle gossip!' said Lineham explosively. 'How *can* you sit there so self-righteously and say that? A man has been *murdered*, Mrs Prote. In my book that is a far worse crime, a far worse sin, if you like, than speaking ill of the dead. And no one could ever convince me otherwise.'

She stared at him, apparently silenced. Then she blinked. 'I hate this,' she said in a low voice, and took off her spectacles, as if this would help her to avoid seeing something she didn't want to look at. Without them she looked several years younger and vulnerable, as if her protective armour had been removed. 'I absolutely hate it.'

'I can understand that,' said Lineham. 'No one likes getting caught up in a murder investigation.'

'But don't you see?' she cried, with more feeling than she had shown so far, 'that's just a fine-sounding generalisation! "No one likes getting caught up in a murder investigation." It doesn't even begin to tell you what it *feels* like! It's horrible, as if everything is . . . contaminated.' And she shuddered, crossing her arms and hugging herself as if to try to contain her revulsion.

He had never heard it put quite like that before, but Thanet knew she had summed up how people in her position felt. Their lives had been touched, however briefly, by the most evil of crimes, the taking of human life, and nothing would ever be quite the same again. They would go on living, carry on in much the same way as they always had, but there, lurking in the back of their minds, would always be the long shadow cast by murder.

He decided to step in. 'Mrs Prote, you must believe us when we say we do understand that. I'm sure you feel that we are poking and prying gratuitously, but we're not, I assure you. Sergeant Lineham is right. Murder is the worst crime in the book and we need every ounce of help we can get, from people like yourself, to try and clear the matter up. I can understand that you don't like going against the principles by which you normally live your life, but you have to accept that these are not normal circumstances and normal rules do not apply.'

While he was speaking she had put her spectacles back on, he noticed. When he had finished she nodded slowly. Then she sighed. 'I can see that. All right. I'll try.'

Lineham waited a moment, then said, 'So was Mr Randish attracted to her, do you think?'

She sighed again. 'Yes, he was. Very much so.' A faint flush crept up her neck. 'It was positively embarrassing at times.'

'Do you think he might have taken her out?'

'That's what you've been getting at, isn't it? You think they might have had an affair? To be honest, I just don't know. I never saw them together. And even if they did, I can't see how it would matter, now.'

'Do you *think* they did?' persisted Lineham.

'Well . . .' She stopped.

'What?'

She hesitated.

Old habits die hard, thought Thanet.

But she stuck to her decision to be open with them. 'Well, as I said, I just don't know. And it doesn't seem fair, to guess. But for what it's worth, I do believe he was the sort of man who did. Have affairs, I mean.'

'Why do you say that?'

Had he made a pass at Mrs Prote? Thanet wondered. No. Not his type.

'Occasionally I've seen him with other women. And it

was obvious, from the way he was behaving, that it had gone past friendship.'

'Did his wife know?'

'I've no idea.'

'Or his father-in-law?'

She shook her head. 'Sorry.'

She wrote the address of Compu-Tech down for them.

Outside they hesitated, and Lineham said, 'Do we still want to see Vintage? We've got all we need from Mrs Prote, haven't we?'

'There's just one point,' said Thanet.

'What?' said Lineham automatically. He was tucking away in his notebook the piece of paper which Mrs Prote had given him. 'That's funny. This address is in a residential area.'

'Mrs Prote said they were a small firm. Perhaps they work from home. Small firms often do. Good. That means we'll be able to go and see them today.'

'What were you saying about Vintage, sir?'

'Well, you remember when I asked him how Randish and Mr Landers got on together, he was a bit evasive?'

'Yes. Why?'

'Well, I'm wondering if he'd overheard something.'

'Some argument, you mean?'

'Well it's possible, isn't it? It doesn't sound as though Randish was all that discreet. If Mrs Prote saw him with other women, Landers could have, too. I'm sure he was lying when he said he didn't know if Randish was having an affair. It might have happened just once too often for his liking and he decided to tackle Randish about it.'

How would he feel himself, Thanet wondered, if Bridget were married and he discovered her husband was cheating on her? Furious, he imagined. Any father would. It cheapened what he held most dear. In his own case, if he hadn't been relieved that Alexander had broken it off he would be pretty angry with him now, for rejecting Bridget – as a matter of fact he still was, Thanet realised, for causing her to suffer like this.

'If only we didn't have to drag all this information out of people!' said Lineham. 'It makes the whole process so laborious.'

'What?' Thanet tore his attention away from Bridget's unhappy situation. 'Oh . . . I don't know, Mike. We grumble about it, yes, but just think how boring it would be if everybody told us everything we wanted to know straight off.'

'It'd certainly make our job easier, though, wouldn't it! Anyway, do we see Vintage, or not?'

'Might as well, while we're here.'

There was no sign of either Vintage or his temporary helper in the yard and they went back to the office to ask Mrs Prote where he might be.

'Probably cleaning out the vats, in that barn,' she said, pointing.

They walked across the yard. Thanet paused at the door and called out. 'Mr Vintage?'

The barn was apparently empty. Machinery hummed faintly and there was a swishing noise from somewhere. Along one wall there was a row of tall stainless-steel vats with circular doors in front like those on automatic washing machines, but larger. Two of the doors stood open and to Thanet's surprise a head now poked out of each, as if a giant tortoise had just woken up. One of them belonged to Vintage. He saw the look on their faces and grinned.

'We're cleaning the vats out. This is the only way to do the job properly.'

It was the first time he'd seen Vintage smile, Thanet realised. It made him look much younger.

Vintage climbed out and said, 'You carry on, Steve, won't be long.'

He was, Thanet thought, definitely looking better today. The dark circles were still there beneath his eyes but the dragging weariness which had permeated his every movement had gone and there was an air of buoyancy about him. It was amazing what a couple of good nights' sleep could do.

'What are they?' Lineham waved a hand at the tanks.

'Fermentation and storage vats.' Vintage went on explaining while Thanet began to edge unobtrusively towards the door. As he hoped, Vintage followed. He thought the winemaker might talk more freely if they couldn't be overheard – though just how much would be audible from inside one of those vats he had no idea. 'How's your wife today?' he asked, when Vintage had finished.

Vintage looked shamefaced. 'I owe you one for yesterday, Inspector. To be honest, when you started dishing out advice I was pretty angry. But I really needed someone to come along and give me a kick up the backside. Beth and I had a long talk last night and we've decided to hire a nanny, for however long it takes for her to come out of this. When my father comes back tomorrow I'll ask him for a loan. I'm pretty sure he'll help us out but if not I'll borrow from the bank. Beth's a lot happier already, now we've decided on a positive course of action. I think she'd more or less given up hope that things would ever improve.'

'Good.' Thanet couldn't help feeling a glow of satisfaction. It wasn't often that anyone handed out bouquets in his line of work.

'So,' said Vintage. 'What did you want to see me about?'

Despite what Thanet had said to Lineham, it was a relief to know that for once he wasn't going to have to work for the cooperation of a witness. 'When we were here yesterday I asked you how Mr Randish got on with his father-in-law. You weren't keen to talk about it. But since then we've learned that he wasn't exactly the most faithful of husbands and apparently didn't bother too much about being discreet. It doesn't take much imagination to work out that Mr Landers might well have found out and become pretty angry about the way his daughter was being treated. And that you were aware of this.'

Vintage thrust his hands in pockets and looked away, as if seeking guidance from somewhere. 'I heard them arguing,' he said eventually, with obvious reluctance. 'I went over to the laboratory one evening to ask Zak something and Mr Landers was there.'

Thanet felt a spurt of satisfaction. He was right. Landers had been lying. 'When was this?'

'A few days ago. Tuesday or Wednesday. Wednesday, I think.'

'What were they saying?'

'I didn't hear much. I'm not in the habit of eavesdropping. The door was open and I just caught a few words as I approached. When I heard what was going on I came away.'

'So what, exactly, did you hear?'

Vintage compressed his lips. 'Mr Landers was . . .' He stopped and his mouth now set in a stubborn line. He shook his head. 'It's no good, I can't tell you. You'll have to ask him yourself.'

'Was it that incriminating?'

'No! It's just that habits of a lifetime die hard. I know I said I owe you one, but I still don't think that gives you the right to ask me to go against the principles I live by.

And telling tales about someone I like and admire is one of them. If that makes me sound like an insufferable prig, then that's just too bad, it's how I feel. Anyway, I really can't believe that Mr Landers had anything to do with Zak's death.' He glanced at his watch. 'If you want to talk to him about it, he should be here in ten minutes or so. He said he'd be over about 12.30, to see how things were going.'

Thanet had no option but to let Vintage go.

'That'll teach me to think an interview is going to be plain sailing!' he said to Lineham as they returned to the car to wait for Landers. 'Anyway, what do you now think about your theory that Mrs Vintage's depression could be over Randish breaking off an affair with her?'

'I still haven't changed my mind,' said Lineham stubbornly. 'It's still possible, in my view. If he'd ditched her when he found out she was pregnant, he'd have been on the lookout for a replacement when this Elaine came along.'

'Hmm. I don't know. I feel we're only just beginning to scratch the surface of this case.'

'There's Landers, sir. He's early.'

Landers' Mercedes was pulling into the car park and they went to meet him.

THIRTEEN

The strain was beginning to tell on Landers, Thanet thought. His shoulders sagged beneath the well-cut tweed jacket and he looked as though he hadn't got much sleep last night: his eyelids drooped as if he were having difficulty in keeping them open. Anxiety on Alice's behalf? Thanet wondered. Or guilt?

He suggested they go across to the Randishes' house and Landers led the way without comment. The central heating had been left on and the house struck warm as they entered. Landers took them into the sitting room, where there was a faint, acrid smell of stale woodsmoke.

He took up the same slightly belligerent stance as last night in front of the cold woodstove. 'Well, what is it this time?'

Thanet wasn't going to allow him to take the initiative. 'Why did you lie to me yesterday, Mr Landers?'

'Lie? About what?' An unconvincing pretence at surprise.

'I asked you if you knew whether your son-in-law was having an affair. You said no.'

'What about it?'

'You were overheard having a row with him about precisely that.'

'Ah.'

Disappointingly, Landers did not seem over-concerned at having been caught out. 'Nobody likes having his dirty linen washed in public.'

'Don't try to minimise the importance of this, Mr Landers. We now know that you had two reasons for being very angry with your son-in-law. He was knocking your daughter about and being unfaithful to her as well.'

'You can be angry with someone without resorting to violence.'

'Without *intending* to resort to violence, yes. But if something triggers that anger off . . .'

'Such as?'

Thanet shrugged. 'I've no idea. It could have been a dozen things. You could have issued an ultimatum to him when you had that row with him on Wednesday, and found that he had ignored it.'

'Perhaps you saw him with this woman on Friday,' said Lineham, 'and decided to have another go at him.'

'Or maybe you noticed that fresh bruise on your daughter's arm when you came over to see her at her request on Friday evening,' said Thanet.

'Or perhaps,' said Lineham, 'she herself told you he'd been ill-treating her again.'

'And if you did go up to see him for any of these reasons after leaving her,' said Thanet, 'he may have reacted to what you were saying in a way which made you see red.'

'He could have laughed at you, for instance. Imagine how that would have made you feel, in the circumstances!'

'All right, all right,' said Landers irritably. 'You can stop the double act. I get the scenario. But it's all in your imagination. I told you, I left here after talking to Alice and went straight to the pub.'

'But you have absolutely no way of proving it,' said Thanet.

'And neither have you!'

'Yet,' said Thanet succinctly. 'But believe me, if that was what happened, Mr Landers, we'll find a way.'

'Think what you like,' snapped Landers, 'but you'll never prove it because it didn't happen.'

They left together and Landers strode angrily off in the direction of the pressing area.

'Well,' said Lineham gloomily. 'That didn't get us very far.'

Thanet grinned. 'Cheer up, Mike. Remember Bruce and the spider.'

'Very funny.'

'I think you need refuelling. We'll call in at the pub again, before paying Compu-Tech a visit.'

Three-quarters of an hour later, considerably refreshed, they were driving slowly through one of the older suburbs of Sturrenden, looking out for the premises of Compu-Tech at number 15A White Horse Lane. The houses here had been built in the 1930s when space was not at a premium and they were set well back from the road in generous gardens, some of which had recently been divided to provide new building plots. Thanet guessed by the address that this was what had happened with Compu-Tech. He would have thought that this was too far from the centre of town to run a successful business, but evidently he was wrong, perhaps because there were so many cowboys around in computers that reliability and efficiency were what people were looking for. Word-of-mouth recommendation was important and if all Compu-Tech's customers were as satisfied as Mrs Prote no doubt the word had soon got around.

He spotted a white signboard. 'I think that's it, Mike.'

Lineham slowed to check, then turned into the driveway.

Inside the gate the drive divided, one arm snaking around behind the substantial stockbroker-Tudor-style house to the right, the other turning sharp left into an attractive parking area of block paving laid in a herringbone pattern in front of a neat one-storey building.

'I suppose the bloke who lives in the house runs his business from here,' said Lineham. 'Looks as though he's doing all right.'

The place had a prosperous air. The parking area was embellished with terracotta pots filled with variegated ivy and there was not a dead leaf or a scrap of litter to be seen. Compu-Tech's premises were relatively new; paintwork sparkled, windows shone and despite yesterday's rain the ramp of non-slip tiles leading to the front door was unsullied.

Ramp?

Thanet looked about him with new eyes. There was a handrail alongside it, he noted, and the door was unusually wide. He pointed this out to Lineham. 'If the chap who runs the firm is handicapped, maybe that's why his office is here rather than in the town.'

'Could be,' said Lineham. 'In any case, is there any point in knocking here? Perhaps we ought to go over to the house instead.'

'We're just assuming the owner lives in the house. We'll try here first. If there's no reply, we'll go across.'

They knocked twice, with no response.

They were just turning away when they heard footsteps approaching along the side of the building and a moment later a young woman rounded the corner.

'Can I help you?'

She was absolutely beautiful, thought Thanet, tall and

slender with abundant black hair and dusky skin almost the colour of a ripe aubergine. She was wearing jeans and a brightly patterned sweater and on her hip she carried an enchanting little girl of about five. Four velvet-brown eyes stared at him as he explained who he was and presented his identification.

'We wanted to have a word with the owner of Compu-Tech, in connection with a case we're working on.'

'Is he in trouble?'

'No, not at all. We just want some information from him.'

'He's out to lunch, but he said he'd be back about a quarter past two. What time is it now?'

A Kentish accent, Thanet noted. Second generation immigrant background, then.

Lineham checked his watch. 'Five to.'

She hesitated, then said, 'I'm his housekeeper. You can come into my place and wait, if you like.'

Thanet accepted with alacrity. This was an unexpected bonus.

'The owner of Compu-Tech doesn't live in the big house, then?' he said as they trailed behind her to the far end of the long, low building. 'We rather wondered if we were knocking at the wrong door.'

She shook her head and flashed a smile at him over her shoulder, her teeth dazzlingly white and even. 'His parents live there. Giles – Mr Fester – built this place with the compensation money from his accident.'

'His accident?'

She had left her blue-painted front door standing ajar and they followed her through a tiny hall into a small square sitting room. The overwhelming impression was of colour, but of daring colour harmonies rather than of garishness. The carpet, which was scattered with toys, was neutral but the curtains were a kaleidoscope of pink, purple, and magenta with, here and there, touches of red which should have clashed but somehow didn't. There was very little furniture: one sturdy low coffee table with a portable television set on it, two armchairs with loose covers, one pink, one purple, and a child's wicker armchair. On the long blank wall opposite the window hung a sizeable appliqué picture of what Thanet immediately recognised as Sturrenden High Street. Fascinated, he went to look more closely at it. There it was, executed in a wealth of different fabrics – wool and cotton, velvet and taffeta, silk, brocade, and lace – and in a variety of embroidery stitches, down to the last picturesque detail: antique shops, church, pubs, market square and beyond, the silvery sheen of the river Sture, its tiny waves stitched in shiny metallic thread.

She had gone off to fetch a kitchen chair and when she came back he said, 'Did you do this?'

She nodded, smiling. 'Yes. It's my hobby.'

'It's amazing. How long did it take?'

'Several months, working in the evenings. I don't go out much.'

She wasn't wearing a wedding ring, Thanet noticed as they sat down. A single parent, then, whose life and choice of work would be dictated by the needs of her little girl. But it looked as though she had been lucky here. A council flat, often in a high-rise building, was as much as most young women in her position could hope for.

'It's very kind of you to allow us to wait here, Mrs . . .?'

'Miss,' she said, with a wry smile. 'Miss Patel. But call me Kari. And this' – she hugged her daughter, who had climbed on to her lap – 'is Jemima. Jem for short.'

Thanet smiled at the child. 'Hullo, Jem.'

'You were saying your employer – Mr Fester, was it?' said Lineham.

'Mr Fester, yes.'

'You were saying he'd had an accident.'

Her smile faded. 'Yes. A bad one. I didn't know him then, of course, this was seven or eight years ago, I believe, but he was in a car crash and he's been in a wheelchair ever since. He's paralysed from the waist down. He's an amazing man, when you think what he's achieved in spite of his handicap.'

The warmth with which she spoke of him made Thanet wonder if she felt more than admiration for her employer. 'Yes. The clients we talked to spoke very highly of his firm.'

'It has a very good reputation in the area. But then, he's got a real talent for his work, or so I'm told. I don't understand much about computers myself.'

'What does he do, exactly?'

Apparently deciding that the two strangers offered no threat Jem slipped off her mother's lap and knelt on the floor by a weird and wonderful creation in Lego bricks. She scooped up some more bricks and automatically her mother held out cupped hands to receive them, then began to hand them one by one to her daughter as she used them. It was obviously a well-worn routine.

'Anything to do with computers,' said Kari, watching Jem. 'He's an agent for some of the well-known makes and he's written a couple of very successful word-processing programmes. But the thing he enjoys most is inventing computer programmes to suit clients' special needs. And then he dabbles in computer games as well.'

'Wow,' said Lineham, obviously impressed. 'He must be a genius!'

She laughed. 'Not far off it, I imagine.'

'And you presumably look after this place for him and cook his meals?'

'Yes. I clean, tidy, wash, cook. He can do most of those things for himself but he prefers to spend his time on other things. Like basketball, for instance.' She smiled at their surprise. 'Before his accident he was a great sportsman and it's lucky he found a sport he can still play. He's in the Kent team and spends a lot of time practising and working out in the gym in Sturrenden.'

'He certainly does sound pretty amazing,' said Thanet.

She smiled. 'I told you. He is. I was very lucky to get this job.' She dropped a caressing hand on to Jem's curls. 'It suits us down to the ground.'

'Is it a very big firm?' said Lineham.

'No. There's just Giles, a girl called Elaine, who's also qualified in computers, and a receptionist-cum-secretary.'

The way she said 'a girl called Elaine' gave her away. Thanet was sure now that he'd been right about her feelings for her employer. She was definitely jealous of Elaine, or at least resented her for some reason. Perhaps Fester was the man in Elaine's life?

Probing further he learned that Elaine lived in Sturrenden and had worked for Giles Fester for two years – and that it was Elaine he had taken out to lunch. She would be coming back here with him afterwards and would probably spend the afternoon with him. He glanced at Lineham. *Take over, Mike.* He wanted to think.

The reason why they had pursued this particular line of inquiry was because they had wondered if Randish's current mistress could lead them to a jealous husband or boyfriend lurking in the background, and it had obviously also occurred to Thanet that Elaine's employer could be the man they were seeking. When he had learnt that Giles

Fester was confined to a wheelchair he had dismissed this idea but Kari's reaction, coupled with the fact that the relationship between Elaine and Fester was obviously more than a working one, had made him think again. Fester seemed an unlikely candidate, true, but was he as unlikely as all that?

Lineham was asking if Fester and Elaine spent much of their time off together.

'A fair amount,' said Kari.

It was obvious that she did not like the turn the conversation had taken. Now she cocked her head in relief. 'I think that's them now.'

'Just one more question, Miss Patel,' said Lineham quickly as she jumped up, taking Jem by the hand.

'What?'

Already at the door she half turned, poised for flight.

He stood up. 'Was Mr Fester out on Friday night?'

Her expression hardened. 'I've no idea. I spent the evening with a girlfriend. Jem came with me.'

She turned and hurried on ahead, Jem running to keep up with her. Behind her back Thanet and Lineham exchanged rueful glances.

'Sorry,' Lineham murmured. 'Mucked that up, didn't I?'

Thanet shook his head. 'Don't worry about it. She wouldn't have told you anyway.'

'Perhaps not. Pretty keen on him, isn't she?'

They caught up with her at the parking area. With Jem settled on her hip again she was talking through the car window to the man in the driver's seat of a BMW with a disabled sticker in the back. He turned his head to watch them as they approached.

Kari turned away – reluctantly, Thanet thought, and went off down the side path again.

'Sorry to disturb you on a Sunday afternoon, sir,' said Thanet. He introduced himself and Lineham and smiled at the girl who was getting out of the passenger seat.

She smiled back at him. 'Elaine Wood.'

She looked familiar. Thanet had probably seen her around the town. It wasn't surprising that Wakeham had noticed her, he thought. She was eye-catching enough to attract any man's attention, though her regular, Barbie-doll features, fashionably tousled shoulder-length dark hair and immaculate make-up were too magazine-coverish for his own taste. But she was certainly Randish's type – small, slender and exuding femininity. She was wearing tight jeans and an expensive soft suede jacket in a pale mint green. And, no doubt about it, that smile had been tinged with nervousness. She knew why they had come.

'Have I done something I shouldn't?' said Fester with a grin.

Without waiting for an answer he swung open the car door, revealing the fact that he was sitting not in a conventional car seat but in a wheelchair.

Thanet's doubts over the safety of this arrangement were quickly dispelled. Fester leaned first to one side then the other and with a series of sharp tugs revealed that the wheelchair had been securely bolted to the floor. Thanet and Lineham watched fascinated as Fester then pressed a switch which caused a small platform to slide out beside the driver's door. In no time at all he had manoeuvred his electric wheelchair out on to the platform, activated concealed hydraulics which lowered the platform to the ground, wheeled himself off it and returned it to its original position.

'That's an ingenious arrangement you've got there, sir,' said Lineham in obvious admiration.

Fester laughed. 'We had some teething troubles, but I think we've got them cracked.'

He was a handsome young man of about thirty with a mop of curly hair and a luxuriant beard. He was wearing chestnut-coloured corduroy trousers and a thick white Aran sweater. His shoulders were broad and his arms powerful. His parents must have been heartbroken when an accident had put him in a wheelchair for the rest of his life, thought Thanet.

'Did you design it yourself?' said Lineham.

Fester was enjoying the sergeant's interest. 'Yes, I did, as a matter of fact.'

'You ought to patent it. You'd make a fortune.'

'I'm afraid you'd need a small fortune, to buy one! I don't think the DHSS would be too keen on it as a standard modification.'

Swinging around, Fester set off up the ramp to the front door, followed by Elaine. Inside they passed through a reception area and along a short corridor with two office doors opening off to the left. At the far end was another door and Fester took a plastic key-card from his pocket and inserted it into a slit beside it. The door clicked open. 'Extra security,' he said with a smile.

They followed him in and found themselves in an open-plan hall/living room/kitchen with a wide door at the far side leading probably to a bedroom and en suite bathroom, Thanet thought. The kitchen area had been designed with low work-surfaces and the living area was comfortable, attractive and obstacle-free, with colourful floor-length curtains in a masculine, geometric design of black, red and grey, and black leather settee and armchairs on an off-white carpet. One wall was covered in bookshelves from floor to ceiling and there was an expensive CD system with racks of CDs alongside.

Fester waved a hand. 'Do sit down, Inspector, Sergeant. I'm most intrigued by your visit. Would you like some tea or coffee?'

Thanet refused and he and Lineham sat down. Elaine remained standing.

'I expect you want to talk to Mr Fester privately,' she said.

Thanet smiled at her. 'Oh no, not at all. In fact, the only reason why we came here was to try to find out where you lived. We thought that as your employer Mr Fester would know.'

'Me?' she said nervously. She glanced apprehensively at Fester.

She's been two-timing him, Thanet thought. The question was, had Fester known?

'So please, Miss Wood, sit down, won't you?'

FOURTEEN

Elaine sat down in one of the armchairs, the black leather accentuating the darkness of her hair and eyes, the soft luxurious paleness of her suede jacket. She had recovered her composure and looked relaxed, knees folded sideways, one hand in her lap, the other lying carelessly along the arm of the chair. It was a studied pose – too studied to be natural, Thanet thought. In his experience even the most innocent members of the public were tense and nervous when interviewed by the police for the first time. What did she have to hide? he wondered. If she had concealed her relationship with Randish from Fester, perhaps she was still hoping that she could bluff her way out of this.

Thanet reminded himself not to fall into the familiar trap of equating glamour with lack of intellect. Elaine Wood was a trained computer expert, an intelligent woman. It would be best to establish at the outset that they were aware of her connection with Randish.

'As you, Miss Wood, have no doubt realised, we are investigating the murder of Mr Randish, the owner of Sturrenden Vineyard.'

'A terrible business,' said Fester. 'We were talking about it over lunch. But . . .'

Thanet acknowledged the comment with a nod before going on. 'Miss Wood, I must confess I was somewhat taken aback by your reaction just now, when I said we'd come here to try and trace you through your employer. A number of witnesses have confirmed that you were going out with Mr Randish and it seems that you didn't exactly try to hide the fact. You must surely have been expecting us to interview you.'

She flicked a glance at Fester, who raised his eyebrows at her. But Thanet was sure that his surprise was feigned, not genuine.

She gave a resigned sigh. 'Half expecting it, I suppose you might say.'

'You seem surprised, Mr Fester.'

'Why shouldn't I be?'

'You didn't know about this relationship?'

'I resent that word, Inspector,' said Elaine. 'You make it sound much more serious than it was.'

'Did you know about it, Mr Fester?' Thanet persisted.

'No. Miss Wood's private life is her own affair.'

'Except that it does seem to overlap with yours.'

'Why should that concern you?'

'I should have thought it was fairly obvious.'

'Not in the least.'

'Then think about it, sir.' Thanet turned back to Elaine. 'When did you last see Mr Randish, Miss Wood?'

'On Tuesday.'

'Where did you go?'

'We went out for a pub lunch, at the Barley Mow on the Cranbrook Road.'

'I suppose it must have been difficult for you to meet in the evenings lately, it was the busiest time of year for him. Did you see anyone you know?' Thanet was thinking of Landers. If Landers had seen them having lunch together on Tuesday that would account for his having had a row with Zak about it on Wednesday.

'No.'

'Anyone Mr Randish knew?'

'Not to my knowledge. But I really haven't the faintest idea whether we did or not. He must have known loads of people I didn't. He grew up in the area.'

'And you didn't?'

'No. I was brought up in Sussex.'

'So you never met Mr Randish until you went out to the vineyard to work with him on the new computer system?'

'No.'

'You knew he was married?'

'Naturally. I could hardly fail to know, considering his wife and family live on the premises.'

Thanet wasn't here to question her morals. 'You don't seem exactly heartbroken that he's dead.'

'Why should I be? I was upset when I heard the news, of course I was, I'd be upset if I heard anyone I knew had been murdered – wouldn't you? But don't get it wrong, Inspector. It wasn't exactly the love affair of a lifetime. Zak was attractive, yes, fun to be with, and he gave me a good time. But that's all.'

'That may be true. But it might not have looked that way to other people . . . to Mr Fester here, for instance.'

'What do you mean?' she said.

'Well, as I was pointing out a moment ago, you do go out with him as well.'

'So?' said Fester.

'Don't pretend that you don't understand, sir. The fact is that a man has been murdered. We don't yet know why, but as I'm sure you're aware, there are a limited number of motives for a crime like this. And one of them is jealousy.'

'Jealousy!' Fester gave an ironic laugh. 'How you can look at me, look at this' – his gesture encompassed the wheelchair, his useless legs – 'and talk about a crime of passion, I just don't know.'

'Don't treat me like an idiot! Do you think I don't know that someone in your situation is as capable of experiencing powerful emotion as the next man?'

'Not much point in having feelings if you can't do anything about them, though, is there, Inspector?'

Fester's tone was flippant, but Thanet's question had gone home, he could tell. 'Maybe,' said Thanet softly, 'that very fact would make the situation even more explosive.'

'How can you talk to Giles like that?' interrupted Elaine. 'With him being . . . as he is?'

'Strangely enough, Elaine,' said Fester, 'I don't actually mind. In an odd way the inspector is actually paying me a compliment.'

'A compliment! You call accusing you of murder a compliment!'

'Yes. He's ignoring the fact that I'm a cripple and treating me just like anyone else. It's practically a unique experience for me. All the same, Inspector, you're still wrong.'

'Giles and I are just good friends,' said Elaine. 'I know the phrase is a bit of a joke, but in this case it's true. We just enjoy each other's company, that's all.'

Thanet caught the flicker of pain in Fester's eyes. That may be true on your side, Miss Wood, he thought, but it's far from being true on his. And don't pretend you're not aware of it, either. 'Let's go back to Friday night,' he said to her. 'What did you do?'

'Believe it or not, I stayed in. Watched television, had a bath, washed my hair, went to bed early. Very boring, I'm afraid.'

She was hiding something. 'There's something else, isn't there? Something you're not telling me.'

'I assure you I'm telling you the truth, Inspector. That was what I did – stayed in, all by myself, and had a thoroughly domestic evening.'

'I'm not querying the truth of what you're saying, simply questioning that you've told me all there is to tell.' She had darted a quick, uneasy look at Fester, Thanet noticed. And Fester was listening intently, eyes narrowed.

Thanet tried to think. What if Fester had asked her out on Friday evening and she had put him off, ostensibly because she wanted to have a quiet evening at home, but in fact because she had arranged to meet Randish? She would now be reluctant to admit it in front of Fester because she wouldn't want to be caught out in a lie. All the same, it would be interesting to see her reaction. 'You had a date with Mr Randish, didn't you?'

The quickly suppressed glint of surprise in her eyes and her too-swift denial confirmed his guess. Thanet suspected that Fester's thought processes had paralleled his own and that he too had seen through her reaction – his hands had clenched on his knees and a fleeting expression of disillusionment had crossed his face, vanishing so quickly that Thanet might have missed it if he hadn't been watching him so closely. Had Elaine seen it, he wondered? There was no doubt about it, her composure had slipped. Her tension showed in the painted fingernails tapping against the arm of the chair. She saw him looking and hastily put her hand in her lap, folding it into the other. He decided it was worth pursuing the subject a little longer. 'What time had he arranged to come, Miss Wood? Late in the evening, perhaps, as he was so busy?'

'I told you, Inspector, you're barking up the wrong tree.'

She had no intention of retracting, that was obvious.

Thanet gave her a sceptical look, making sure she knew he didn't believe her. 'Do you live in a house, a flat?'

'A flat.'

'Where?'

'Landway House in Beecham Road.'

Thanet knew it, a new block of flats on the site of a former warehouse near the river. 'Did you see or speak to anyone on Friday evening?'

She shook her head. 'Not that I can remember, unfortunately.'

He turned to Fester. 'And what about you, Mr Fester? What were you doing on Friday evening?'

Fester smiled. 'You'll think us a very dull pair, I'm afraid, Inspector. I, too, spent the evening at home, watched television etc., etc. Though I didn't wash my hair, I must admit.'

He was being flippant again – too flippant, for a man who had just been informed he could consider himself a murder suspect. And he was watching Thanet's reaction too closely. It was obvious, however, that he wasn't going to change his story without good reason either. Thanet decided to leave it for the moment. He caught the brief flash of relief in Elaine's expression as he stood up. Simple relief because the interview was over, he wondered, or was she hiding something else? Perhaps there was a question which she had expected but which he had failed to ask? He hesitated a moment, racking his brains, but it was no good. No doubt about it, they'd have to look into this further, come back later.

He said so to Lineham, outside.

'They were both lying in their teeth, if you ask me,' said the sergeant as they got into the car. 'I bet she'd given him the brush-off for Friday evening because she had a date with Randish, and didn't want to lose face by admitting it. Where now, sir?'

'Back to the office, I think. Mmm. I'm not sure there wasn't more to it than that. But yes, I agree, that's what I thought. Though according to what Vintage said about the workload at the vineyard, I wouldn't have thought Randish would have had much time for his love life during harvest.'

Lineham started the car and pulled out. 'Perhaps she was getting fed up with never seeing him in the evenings, made a fuss about it, and to shut her up he agreed to take her out for a quick drink or something.'

'Possible, I suppose. Though in that case you'd think she'd have rung his office to find out why he hadn't turned up.'

'Perhaps she did, before Vintage discovered the body at 9.30, and got no reply.'

'True.'

'But Fester is a different matter, in my opinion. I mean, if you'd told me I'd ever suspect a bloke in a wheelchair of committing this murder I'd have thought you were joking. Now, I'm not so sure.'

'He's certainly pretty taken with the delectable Miss Wood,' said Thanet.

'Who wouldn't be! Just think what it must be like to be in his position, working with a girl you really fancy, day in and day out, and to feel you can't make a real play for her because it wouldn't be fair on her to ask her to marry a cripple.'

'Able-bodied people do marry handicapped partners, Mike.'

'I know that. But you have to be a pretty special person to take on someone handicapped to that degree. And Elaine, well, she just didn't strike me as the type.'

'I agree. Underneath that porcelain exterior I'd say she

was pretty tough and calculating. Ambitious, probably, too.'

'Yes. But she is most definitely the sort of girl a bloke might go crazy over. And if Fester had had a pretty clear field until Randish came along . . .'

'Quite.'

'And he's pretty remarkable isn't he? I mean, look at what he's made of his life despite his handicap. You can't help admiring him. Honestly, sir, I really do hope he's not the one we're after. But to be realistic, it's obvious that he's the type who really goes for what he wants and usually gets it. And if what he wants is Elaine . . .'

'I agree. There's another point that occurred to me too, Mike. The actual method of the murder ties in uncomfortably close with the limitations Fester's condition imposes on him.'

'What do you mean?'

'Well, if you actually try to visualise what happened in that laboratory, you begin to realise that there are certain things we already know about this murderer.'

'Such as?'

They had arrived back at Headquarters. There were various things to attend to and they waited until they were back in Thanet's office before taking up the conversation where they had broken off.

'What were you saying about the murderer, sir?'

'Well, I think we can assume, for a start, that this was an unpremeditated murder. Right?'

'Right.'

'An accidental murder, even?'

'I'd go along with that.'

'That what happened was that someone who was very angry with Randish went along to have it out with him and the whole thing got out of hand.'

Lineham was nodding.

'Well, have you given any thought as to what that person must be like?'

'Not really. There's been so much to take in . . .'

'Well think about it now.' Thanet was longing to smoke. Of its own volition his hand emerged from his pocket holding his pipe. Becoming aware of this he shoved it back in again. He was addicted and he knew it. Part of him was ashamed of the fact but the far larger part was realistic: if he smoked he was a happy man and functioned well; if he didn't he was just plain miserable and his work went to pieces. But he had come to appreciate that it was misery for Lineham if he lit up in his presence, so he really made a big effort these days to be considerate about this.

Lineham noticed. He occasionally had pangs of conscience about Thanet's self-imposed restraint. 'Go on, sir, light up if it'll help you to think.'

'Thanks.' Thanet took out his pipe and pouch with alacrity. 'You can open the door and the window if you like.' He couldn't help smiling to himself. Sometimes he and Lineham functioned like an old married couple. He had occasionally had to work with a substitute and it was never the same. He and Mike were on the same wavelength and that was all there was to it. They were so used to each other that their communication was frequently unspoken: all it needed was a glance, a nod, a shake of the head. He watched indulgently as Lineham half opened the window and propped the door ajar with a box file. Cool air filtered into the room and the papers on Thanet's desk stirred in the draught. He finished filling his pipe and lit up before speaking again.

'As I was saying, Mike, just think about it. Imagine for the sake of argument that the murderer is a man. Now, in normal circumstances – leaving aside your armed criminal, that is – if a man has a row with another man and one of them loses his temper, what is the most likely thing for him to do?'

'Go for him. Sock him on the jaw, probably.'

The improvised ventilation system, though somewhat uncomfortable, was effective. The through draught was whisking the clouds of smoke away, out of the open window. 'Quite. But in this case?'

'He chucked something at him.'

'So what does that tell us about him?'

'Either that he was afraid of what he would do if he lost control of himself, or that he was afraid of Randish.'

'Physically, you mean?'

'Yes. Randish was a big man and pretty fit. So our murderer was much smaller, perhaps. Or . . . I see what you mean about Fester. Yes. He wouldn't have gone for Randish in the usual way but he's very adept at manoeuvring himself about in that wheelchair. Also, all that basketball must have given him pretty powerful arms and shoulders.'

'There's a further possibility, too, Mike.'

'What? Oh, yes. That it could have been a woman, you mean.'

'Exactly.'

'So where does that get us?'

Thanet struck another match. His pipe wasn't drawing properly yet. 'Think of our suspects, Mike, in the light of what we've been saying. Take Landers first.'

'Too big.'

'Vintage.'

'He's fairly slight. Possible.'

'Reg Mason?'

'Ditto.'

'And Fester, of course, as we said. Then there are the women. Alice Randish, her mother . . .'

'I didn't know we were considering Mrs Landers, but I suppose you're right. Are we counting Elaine Wood, too?'

'Why not? The more the merrier, it seems to me.'

'So what we were saying doesn't get us very far, does it? Except for Landers they're all still in the running. Do we definitely count him out, now?'

'Certainly not, Mike. We were only theorising. It was considering Fester as a suspect that set me off. No, what we really need now is some hard evidence.'

'Not much prospect of that at the moment, is there? D'you want me to get a house-to-house going, see if we can find anyone who might have seen Fester go out that night?'

'Yes. Ditto Elaine.' Thanet was silent, puffing steadily and gazing up absent-mindedly at the sinuous movements of the smoke swirling away into the gathering dusk. 'You know, Mike, I can't help feeling that there's something we've overlooked.'

'Something we heard when we were interviewing Fester and Elaine, you mean?'

'I don't know. But there is something, I'm sure.'

'Take your own advice, sir. Stop thinking about it and you'll remember.'

Thanet grinned. 'It's easier to give advice than to take it.'

FIFTEEN

As he opened the front door Thanet sniffed appreciatively. A delicious aroma was wafting along the hall to greet him. The kitchen door was ajar and he could hear voices and laughter. All the way home he had been thinking about the case and trying to recall what it was that had triggered off his uneasy feeling of having missed something, but now he could feel the cares rolling off his shoulders. He put his head into the kitchen. 'That smells good.' He kissed them both, in turn. Bridget looked a lot more relaxed, he was thankful to see, their morning disagreement apparently forgotten.

'Supper in ten minutes,' said Joan.

It was good to have his family united around the table for once, thought Thanet as they all sat down. It was a rare experience these days. Bridget was not usually here, of course, and Ben seemed to snatch his meals between activities, often eating earlier or later than his parents. It was also a great pleasure to see Bridget and Ben behaving like adults – most of the time, anyway. The childish squabbles of old seemed to be a thing of the past, civilised conversation the order of the day.

The savoury smell had emanated from an elaborate fish risotto and they all tucked in enthusiastically.

'Great!' said Ben, after the first mouthful. 'How's Jonathan?'

'He's recovered consciousness, I'm glad to say, and he's been moved out of intensive care.'

Joan had obviously heard the news before and she glanced at Thanet. 'That must be a tremendous relief for his mother, mustn't it?'

'It certainly must,' said Thanet. 'Did you see her?' he asked Bridget.

'Yes. D'you know, she still hasn't been home since Friday night! She's been sitting beside his bed ever since!'

'I can understand that,' said Thanet. 'If you or Ben were in a coma . . .'

'Don't!' said Joan with a shudder. 'It doesn't bear thinking about. Anyway, it's wonderful that Jonathan's come round. Sometimes you hear of these motorcycle accident victims being in a coma for months.'

She hadn't looked at Ben and Thanet didn't think the remark had been directed at him, but Ben obviously didn't see it that way. 'All right, Mum! No need to rub it in. I've got the message.'

'He's still very dazed, though,' said Bridget. 'He doesn't remember a thing about Friday evening.'

'That's not unusual after an accident,' said Thanet. 'In fact, some people never do remember the circumstances surrounding it.'

'Yes, but I'm not just talking about the accident itself. The worst thing is, he doesn't even remember that Karen is dead.'

'Oh, no!' said Joan. 'You didn't tell me that.'

'Poor Mrs Redman,' said Bridget. 'She's absolutely dreading breaking the news to him all over again.'

'I can imagine,' said Thanet. 'You went in to the hospital yourself, I gather.'

'Yes. I didn't stay long, though, there wasn't much point. Jonathan wasn't up to talking and Mrs Redman was so tired I thought she'd fall asleep where she was.'

'She could go home and get some rest now, though, couldn't she?'

'Yes, she could, but she wants to wait a bit longer first. Jonathan's all she has left now, and I don't think she could bear to leave him.'

'Bridget's been playing the good Samaritan,' said Joan with a smile. 'She took Jonathan's clothes home, fetched various things he and Mrs Redman needed, fed the cat . . .'

'I thought there was something different about you this evening,' said Ben to his sister. 'It's the halo.'

'Don't tell me the cat hadn't been fed since Friday!' said Thanet.

'Oh no. Mrs Phillips, their neighbour, had been looking after him,' said Bridget.

No doubt about it, thought Thanet, all this buzzing about had done Bridget good. Far better for her to be actively engaged in something than moping around at home.

All in all she seemed to have had a busy day. Conversation turned to her visit to the Mallards this morning and then to the joint trip she and Joan had made out to Thaxden, to have tea with Joan's mother.

After they had cleared away the first course and stacked the dishes in the dishwasher Bridget brought in the dessert.

'Oh boy!' said Ben, his eyes lighting up at the sight of the raspberry pavlova she had made. 'I can put up with this treatment as long as you like!'

'You'd better make the most of it,' she said. 'I'm going back tomorrow evening.'

'So soon!' said Thanet. 'And I've hardly seen you.' He'd been afraid this might happen, which was why he'd made a special effort to get home early this evening.

'And not likely to, with a murder case going on,' said Bridget. 'Don't worry, Dad, I do understand. Anyway, I was wondering if you could give me a lift to the station. Mum's got a meeting. It doesn't matter if you can't, I'll walk.'

'Of course I will, if I can.'

His back gave him trouble all evening and it was again a relief to get into bed and allow tense muscles to relax. He closed his eyes and at once, with the distraction of what was happening around him shut out, started worrying again about what it was he couldn't remember. What was the precise moment at which he had become aware of it? Joan's voice broke into his thoughts.

'Luke?'

It was obvious from her tone that she'd tried to catch his attention before. He opened his eyes.

She was taking off her dressing gown. 'Ah, so you are still awake.'

'I was thinking.'

'So was I. About that poor woman.'

'Mrs Redman, you mean?'

'Yes.' She switched off the overhead light and slid into bed beside him. He put his arm around her and she snuggled into his shoulder with a sigh of contentment. 'We're so lucky.'

'I know.'

'When I think of what she must have been through ... D'you know what Bridget told me today?'

'What?'

'She's known for years, apparently – Bridget, I mean. But she's never said anything before, she promised

Karen . . . But now Karen's dead I suppose she feels released from that promise . . . Well, I don't know. Perhaps she doesn't. Perhaps it was because she's still so upset about Karen . . . And she knows I won't talk about it to anyone else. Except you, of course.'

'Darling,' said Thanet. 'Come to the point. What did Bridget tell you?'

'It really shook me, I can tell you. And as you know, I'm not easily shaken.'

In her work as a probation officer Joan saw plenty of the seamy side of life.

'I suppose it's because it happened to one of Bridget's friends . . .'

'Joan!'

'All right! Well, as you know, Karen has been anorexic for years. Ever since she was twelve, in fact. What I didn't know until today was why.' Joan pulled away a little and twisted her head to watch Thanet's reaction. 'When she was twelve she had a baby.'

'At twelve!'

Joan nodded. 'At the time, no one knew about it. Bridget didn't know Karen at the time, it was the summer before they both started at Sturrenden High. But that autumn Bridget and Karen became friends and she stuck to her faithfully through the bad times, as you know, always visited her when she was hospitalised. It was during one of those periods, when the girls were about seventeen and Karen was at a very low ebb, that she told Bridget about the baby.'

'She actually had the baby?'

'Yes. It was adopted. But apparently Karen was five months' pregnant before her mother realised! Incredible, isn't it? I mean, I've read about such cases, even about girls actually having the baby without their mothers' knowledge, but it is difficult to comprehend. Though I suppose it's less surprising in that household than it would be in most. I gather nudity was considered so taboo that even when the children were tiny they never shared baths or saw each other naked. Anyway, by the time her mother found out it was too late for Karen to have an abortion and even if it hadn't been I gather her parents would never have allowed it, it would have been against their principles. So they sent her away to some home for unmarried mothers and put out a story that she was visiting relations. Her absence covered the period of the long summer holidays, apparently, so no one was ever the wiser. The whole thing came as a terrible shock to Karen. She'd no idea she was going to have a baby. You wouldn't believe it could still happen in this day and age, but Bridget says that Karen's mother was so inhibited about sex that she never talked to her about it and Karen was unbelievably ignorant, she only knew what she'd picked up at school. She'd only had one period, a very slight one, and she'd heard that periods were often irregular to begin with, so when she didn't have any more she didn't think anything of it. But she did notice she'd begun to put on weight, so without telling anyone she began to diet.'

'And that was how her anorexia started.'

'Yes. The dieting, of course, was one reason why no one noticed she was pregnant. But naturally she found that no matter how little she ate, she was still getting fatter.'

'But she realised why that was, surely? When she did find out she was pregnant?'

Joan was shaking her head. 'Intellectually yes, she knew that was why she was putting on weight. But emotionally, by then she was powerless to stop herself believing otherwise.'

'But later on, then, after she'd had the baby, when things got back to normal . . .?'

'That was the tragedy. They never did get back to normal. By then the idea that she was overweight was so entrenched in her mind that she simply couldn't shake it off.'

'Poor kid. And the baby's father?'

Joan was nodding. 'Yes. I can see you've guessed, after what the children were saying about him yesterday. Bridget is pretty certain it was Karen's father. Though Karen never actually admitted it. Perhaps she was too ashamed. It would fit in with the continuing anorexia, though, wouldn't it – I mean with the theory that for various reasons the anorexic is reluctant to grow up.'

'What theory is that?' Thanet didn't know much about anorexia.

'That for whatever reason, she wants to "deny her womanhood", as the jargon puts it. One of the results of starving yourself is that you stop having periods; not having periods means you're not becoming a woman. Not eating is therefore how you achieve the desired result. That's the idea, anyway.'

'And it was all hushed up, he got away with it.' In Thanet's work he saw all too often the results of such abuse, the lifetime of suffering to which the innocent victims were frequently condemned. He'd had a case not so long ago in which the murder victim had been in that position, a talented artist whose death had been the direct result of such childhood torture. In that instance the abuser had finally been brought to justice, but Redman, perhaps equally guilty of his daughter's death, had died unpunished for his sins.

'If he really was responsible then yes, I'm afraid so.'

Joan was quickly asleep but Thanet lay awake for

some time, staring into the darkness and thinking back over the hectic activity of the last couple of days. It was always the same at the beginning of a case. There was so much to do, see, assimilate, that it was essential to stand back from time to time and try to make a cool, detached assessment of the situation. It was easy to get so bogged down in personalities, cross-currents and speculation that it was impossible to see what was really going on. Especially when, as now, he was beating his brains out trying to remember something. He clenched his hands in frustration under the bedclothes and then told himself not to be so stupid. There was no point in getting worked up about it. He would remember, sooner or later, and Lineham was right: he ought to put it clean out of his mind, forget about it, and let his subconscious get to work. Perhaps, by morning, the miracle would have happened and he would wake up to find that all had become clear.

Unfortunately, this was not the case. The alarm went off as usual at 6.45 and he staggered half awake into the bathroom, aware that the knowledge was still eluding him. He hadn't got to sleep until the early hours and he felt tired and depressed. Why do I do this job? he asked himself. Why do I beat my brains out, like this? Why not choose something less demanding, where I don't have to struggle and fight every inch of the way? His temper was not improved by the fact that he cut himself shaving. When he went downstairs Joan took one look at his face and said, 'Oh dear. Like that, is it?'

'Like what?' he snapped.

'Never mind. Here, have some cereal. You'll feel better after you've had something to eat.'

'I've come to a decision.'

'Oh?'

'I think I've reached a mid-life crisis. I'm going to

apply to be a postman. Just think what it must be like to do a job where people are actually pleased to see you when you knock on their doors!'

She came to sit down with him, a rare event in the morning, and buttered a slice of toast. 'I gather the case isn't going too well? I'm sorry, there seemed to be so much to talk about that I didn't even ask last night.'

'No, no, it's going along much as usual.'

'But?'

Thanet shook his head. 'Nothing, really.'

Joan looked sceptical.

'Oh all right. It's just that I'm trying to remember something, and can't. It's so frustrating! And don't say "put it out of your mind and you'll remember." I've tried that and it didn't work.'

'Then there's absolutely nothing you can do about it, is there?' she said calmly.

Toast popped up and she went to fetch it, poured him some coffee. She obviously thought he needed pampering, he thought wryly, usually he did these things for himself in the mornings. And she was right. It was ridiculous to allow himself to be thrown by something beyond his control. He felt himself begin to relax. He watched the Flora melt on his toast and spread the marmalade with a lavish hand. It was grapefruit marmalade, he realised, his favourite, and an expensive brand usually reserved for a weekend treat. He grinned, then began to laugh.

'What's the matter?' she said, an answering smile spreading across her face.

He held up the marmalade. 'You're treating me like a spoilt child – and, let's face it, you're absolutely right, I'm behaving like one.' He leaned across to kiss her. 'Sorry, love!'

'We're all entitled to be bad tempered occasionally.

Just remember that, the next time I start behaving like a bear with a sore head.'

'I will! Promise!'

The letterbox clattered.

'Post's early this morning,' said Joan, and went out into the hall, returning a few moments later. She flipped through the letters and put two beside Thanet's plate.

He glanced at them. One was an electricity bill, by the look of it, the other was his own handwriting. Some tickets he'd sent away for, probably. Nothing interesting, then, and they could both wait until later.

So why did he have this uncomfortable sensation in his head?

He glanced at Joan, who was reading one of her letters, and took another bite of toast, staring at the handwritten envelope. There *was* something. What was it?

Suddenly it came to him.

He stopped chewing and stared unseeing into space. Perhaps it hadn't been so important after all. No, it really would be too much of a coincidence, if . . . But then, coincidences happened in real life which would never be believed in fiction, and there was at least one fact to back up the idea. And if he was right . . .

Joan became aware of his immobility. 'Luke? What's the matter?'

He looked at her, a broad smile spreading slowly across his face, and kissed her again. 'You're a gem.'

She raised her eyebrows. 'Why, precisely? I mean, it's a great boost to the morale when your husband starts showering you with kisses and paying you lavish compliments at 7.30 on a Monday morning, but it would be nice to know what I've done to deserve it.'

'You made me switch off, stop trying to remember. And, of course . . . bingo!'

Joan laughed. 'I can't believe it worked as quickly as that. It certainly doesn't in my experience.'

'Magic!' said Thanet. It was the handwritten envelope which had really done the trick, of course, but he wasn't going to spoil things by mentioning that.

'So come on, tell. What was it?'

He shook his head. 'Just a small thing. And I can't make up my mind if it really was important, or not. Let me think about it a bit more first. Anyway, I haven't told you enough about the case yet for you to understand its significance, if it has any.'

Thanet had always talked to Joan about his work. It was so demanding both on him and on their marriage that he felt it was essential she didn't feel excluded. She had always appreciated this, he knew – and on more than one occasion had helped him to see his way to a solution.

'I know. There's been so little time, with Bridget being here. We'll try to talk tonight, shall we? Oh, no, I've got that meeting. Still, with any luck it won't go on too late.'

'See you then,' said Thanet. Quickly he cleared away the dishes, stacked them in the dishwasher and felt for his pipe. He was eager to get to work and discuss his idea with Lineham.

Outside the day matched his new mood, bright and breezy. Puffy white clouds chased each other across the sky and there was an invigorating freshness in the air, more like March or April than late October. He hoped that Lineham hadn't chosen this morning of all mornings to come in later than usual.

He gave Pater, the Station Officer, a brisk greeting.

'Everybody seems to be looking cheerful this morning,' said Pater. 'Must be the weather.'

Thanet paused. 'Who's "everybody"?'

'The Super, for one.'

'Really?'

The two men looked at each other, aware of what this might mean. Pater lowered his voice. 'Good news about Mrs Draco, d'you think, sir?'

'Let's keep our fingers crossed.'

Thanet took the stairs two at a time. Lineham, he was relieved to see, was already at his desk, frowning over a report. 'Heard anything about Angharad Draco, Mike? Pater says the Super seems in a good mood this morning.'

'So I understand. I haven't actually seen him myself. But it sounds promising.'

'No doubt we'll find out at the morning meeting.' Thanet sat down.

'Any particular reason why you're looking so pleased with yourself, sir?'

'Could be. You know I said last night that I was sure there was something we'd overlooked?'

'Yes. Have you remembered what it was?'

Thanet nodded, smiling.

'And?' Lineham leaned forward eagerly as Thanet began to talk.

SIXTEEN

'It was simply a matter of making a connection,' said Thanet.

'Between . . .?'

'You remember those letters we came across, in the locked drawer of Randish's desk?'

'The love letters, you mean?'

'Yes. Specifically, the ones from Randish's wife. They were addressed to him care of his landlady, if you remember.'

'Yes, I do.'

'Do you by any chance remember her name?'

Lineham thought, deep frown lines creasing his forehead. 'It was short, I remember that, but . . . No, I can't.'

'It was Wood,' said Thanet.

Lineham stared at him. 'Are you suggesting there's some connection between her and Elaine Wood? Be a bit of a coincidence, wouldn't it?'

'Yes it would, agreed. But Elaine did tell us she'd been brought up in Sussex, and Plumpton's in Sussex.'

'But what connection? Randish's landlady couldn't be Elaine Wood's mother, surely?'

'Well, it's not out of the question, is it? It's only, what, fifteen or sixteen years ago. Mrs Wood could have had

Elaine in her late teens and only have been in her early thirties at the time. And some young men enjoy having affairs with older women. But no, I don't think so. Don't you remember Mark Benton told us that Randish had a particularly torrid affair with his landlady's daughter?'

'Yes, I do. So what you're suggesting is that this Mrs Wood was Elaine's grandmother?'

'Yes.'

'It's a bit far-fetched, isn't it? Wood's a very common name.'

'Maybe. But there's another thing, too. When I first saw Elaine I thought she looked familiar. I decided at the time that it must be because I'd seen her around, in the town, but now I wonder if it could be because she resembled one of the young women in that batch of photographs of Randish's girlfriends.'

'It could simply be because, as we know, Randish always seemed to go for the same physical type. You could equally well say that Elaine looked familiar because she looks like Alice Randish. Which she does, except that one is dark and the other's fair.'

That was true. Perhaps Lineham was right. The whole thing was too tenuous.

'Anyway, I'm not sure what you're suggesting, sir. Say you're right about all this. If Elaine's name is Wood and her grandmother's name was Wood, that means her mother must have been unmarried. Elaine can't be Randish's daughter, she's too old, she must have been, what, ten or eleven at the time.'

'I know. I agree, her mother must have been single.'

'Well, say all this is true. Say Elaine did know Zak when she was a child. Say she recognised him when she went out to the vineyard to install the computer system. So what?'

'So then he gets himself murdered, that's what!'

Lineham was shaking his head. 'I still think it's all too far-fetched. All right, we both know coincidences happen . . .'

'Not that much of a coincidence, Mike. People do run across each other by chance, years after they first met.'

'But they don't necessarily murder each other!'

Thanet was becoming exasperated. Lineham was only expressing many of the doubts he felt himself but the more the sergeant argued the more he found himself defending the theory. 'But they might! If there was good reason! In any case, there's only one way to find out.'

'Go to Plumpton, you mean?'

'Yes. It'll only take us an hour to an hour and a half.'

Lineham's face showed clearly that he thought this would be a waste of time.

Thanet sighed. 'Go on, Mike. You might as well say what you're really thinking.'

'Well, it's just that I think we ought to be trying to find out a lot more about some of the other suspects. We've hardly given a thought so far to Alice Randish or her father, for instance, let alone the most likely one of all, Reg Mason.'

'Did you have any specific action in mind?'

'Well, no, but we haven't really put our minds to it, have we?'

'True, but there's no rush, is there? We'd only be gone for a few hours. None of them is going to run away, they'll still be waiting when we get back.'

Lineham said nothing, just set his lips, stubbornly.

'Oh come on, Mike, admit it. These hunches of mine often turn out to be worth following up.'

'True,' Lineham said grudgingly.

'And it's not as though we'd be neglecting something

we really ought to be doing, is it? There are no promising leads we urgently need to follow up.'

'There was one thing. This came in this morning.' Lineham picked up a report and handed it to Thanet. 'Fester said he didn't go out on Friday night.'

Thanet scanned it quickly. A woman who lived opposite Giles Fester reported seeing him leave the house and drive away at around 7.15 that evening.

'So he was lying. Interesting,' said Thanet. 'I agree, we'll have to see him again. Well, if you're really keen to do that, we can split up. I'll go to Plumpton, take someone else with me, Wakeham perhaps . . .' Thanet knew Lineham wouldn't like this suggestion and he was right. The sergeant immediately capitulated.

'No, no, Fester isn't going anywhere either, after all. We can see him later.'

'True. If we leave for Plumpton straight after the morning meeting we can be back by early afternoon.' Thanet glanced at his watch and jumped up. 'And talking about the morning meeting . . . If the Super is on form again he'll expect us to be there on the dot.'

As Thanet hurried down the stairs he felt thoroughly disgruntled. He was annoyed with Lineham and annoyed with himself for being annoyed. The truth was that despite his own doubts he had really been hoping that Lineham would fall upon this idea with enthusiasm. He knew he was being unreasonable. Both he and Lineham were used to the other playing the devil's advocate, it was a useful way of seeing if a theory held water. But this time, for some reason, it had got under his skin. Perhaps it was because underneath, despite all the arguments against it, he just *felt* he was right. There was something about Elaine that had left him feeling uneasy and he wasn't sure why. He remembered now his impression that she had been relieved at the end of the interview, that there was a question he should have asked, and hadn't. Now he wondered: was it relief that her previous connection with Zak – if there was one – hadn't come out?

For his own satisfaction he had to know and a trip to Plumpton was the only answer.

He decided not to mention any of this at the meeting in case it came to nothing. After all, even if he were right and there was a connection between Elaine and Randish's former landlady, it might have absolutely nothing to do with Randish's murder.

At the bottom of the stairs he ran into Inspector Peter Boon of the uniformed branch, his long-time friend and colleague.

'Thirty seconds to go!' said Boon with a grin.

They hurried along the corridor to the door of Draco's office and as Thanet knocked Boon stood ostentatiously gazing at his watch whispering a count-down. 'Fifteen, fourteen, thirteen, twelve . . .'

'Come in!'

Thanet and Boon grinned at each other. It was a relief to hear something of the old vigour back in Draco's voice. 'Sounds in good form today,' said Thanet.

Draco glanced at the clock and waved a hand at them. 'Sit down, sit down.'

Chief Inspector Tody was of course already there, clipboard at the ready.

One look at Draco was enough to tell Thanet that the news about Angharad must indeed be good. Her husband's appearance had over the last two years acted as a barometer of her progress. Draco was a fiery little Welshman of barely regulation height, with dark Celtic eyes, sallow skin and wiry black hair which in his livelier moments seemed almost to crackle with electricity. During the first year of his wife's illness Draco had lost all his bounce and restless vigour, his eyes had dulled and even his hair had become limp and lifeless. During the second year there had been a slow, almost imperceptible improvement and today the transformation was complete. Draco's shirt collar was crisp, his tie tightly knotted, his trouser creases sharp as a knife, his shoes burnished to a gloss which even a sergeant major on parade would have found difficult to criticise.

Thanet was amused to find himself straightening his tie and running a hand over his hair.

'Right,' said Draco. 'Let's get on with it.'

The murder was still the most important investigation in hand at the moment and in view of Draco's previous absence, Thanet's report was lengthy and detailed. Draco listened intently and at the end peppered him with questions.

'Right,' he said eventually. 'You seem to be doing a pretty good job, as usual, Thanet. If there are problems or queries, of course, you know where to find me.'

'Yes, sir.' Draco's praise was so rarely given that it invariably produced a warm glow in the recipient. Thanet was amused to notice that he himself was no exception and Boon's ironic twinkle showed that he too was aware of what they privately called 'The Draco Effect'.

Draco squared up the piece of paper on which he had been making notes in the dead centre of his immaculately tidy desk. 'Right, gentlemen, I think that's about all for today . . .'

This was the signal for them all to rise and they were doing so when he said, 'Except . . .'

They subsided, each of them optimistic that Draco was now going to give them the news they were hoping to hear. Briefly, Thanet's mind flashed back to a similar scene two years ago, but then Draco's demeanour had been lack-lustre, his voice dull with despair.

I had hoped it wouldn't come to this, but . . . I'm afraid, however, that it looks as though I am going to have to make somewhat heavier demands than usual upon you . . .

And then had come the bad news.

Now, Draco's voice was full of barely suppressed joy, his Welsh accent more noticeable than usual. 'As you know, my wife has just had another test, as she has every two months over the last two years. What you may not have realised was that this was an especially important one, the last of that series. From now on, the interval between tests will be greater. And so far, the prognosis is good. She is still in remission. We've got a long way to go yet, but we seem to have cleared the first and most important hurdle.'

The other three all started to speak at once.

'That's great news, sir . . .'

'Wonderful news, sir . . .'

'That's terrific, sir . . .'

Draco was beaming, his face split almost in two by an enormous, delighted grin. 'Thank you, thank you . . . I haven't said anything until now about her progress because I had an almost superstitious dread that if I did something would go wrong. And I must emphasise that even now we are far from out of the wood . . .'

According to Mallard, by at least three more years, thought Thanet.

'But I felt that I owed it to you all to tell you what was going on.' Draco paused, picked up an elastic band and began to fiddle with it, winding it around his fingers. 'I have never actually said so before, but I want you all to know just how much I appreciate your support over the last two years. You've often had to carry my workload as well as your own, and it can't have been easy. But not once, by word or gesture, have any of you complained.'

Thanet saw to his horror that Draco the fierce, Draco the fiery, the Welsh Dragon as they had called him behind his back when he first arrived, was on the verge of tears. He sent up a silent prayer: *Don't let him cry!* And then reproached himself. Why shouldn't men cry, if they wished? No one could ever, under any circumstances, call Draco unmanly, and certainly none of the three men here this morning would think any the worse of him for it.

But Draco was mastering his emotion. He shook out an immaculately laundered white handkerchief, which would have been a superb advertisement for any washing powder, and blew his nose loudly. 'Angharad has especially asked me thank you too on her behalf. She says that it has helped her enormously to have me there when she needed me, and she knows I couldn't have done that without you.'

'We were glad to be able to help, sir,' said Tody.

Thanet and Boon were nodding.

'Yes, maybe,' said Draco with a twinkle. 'But this business isn't over yet, remember. I hope you can still say that in a couple of years' time.'

'I'm sure we shall, sir. And allow me to say . . .'

Tody was overdoing it as usual, thought Thanet.

'. . . and I'm sure I speak on behalf of everyone in your sub-division, how delighted we are. Please give your wife our good wishes for her continued progress.'

'Thank you, Tody. All being well, of course' – Draco stood up and the others followed suit – 'the demands upon you should now diminish somewhat.'

'Great!' said Boon, outside. 'We'd better go and spread the good news.'

'I don't think we'll need to do much spreading,' said Thanet.

And it was true. By the curious osmosis endemic to small communities, the news seemed to have permeated the entire building already. It showed in the tone of voice of snatches of conversation, in a burst of laughter here and there, in a general liveliness which seemed to pervade even the corridors. There was no doubt about it, the influence of the man at the top was crucial to an establishment of this size, thought Thanet. Like a school whose tone is set by the headmaster, so much depended on the superintendent of a sub-divisional headquarters. Thanet would never have believed, when Draco first burst upon them in all his missionary fervour, that he could ever have felt like this about the man. And even now, of course, he had to admit that despite the affection and respect he felt for him, there were times when Draco drove him up the wall.

He gave Lineham the good news and they set off for Plumpton, calling briefly at the vineyard on the way to pick up the address of Randish's former landlady. Curious to see if his memory was playing tricks on him, Thanet also collected the cardboard box of photographs. Back in the car he put it on his lap and began to shuffle through them. It didn't take him long to find the one he wanted. 'Got it. Yes, this is the one I was thinking of, definitely.' Though he had to admit that the resemblance wasn't as striking as he remembered. The girl was smiling into the camera, leaning against a five-barred gate, wearing jeans and a T-shirt. Her hair was tied back in a pony-tail and she didn't look a day over twenty. If Thanet was right, she had at that time a daughter of ten or eleven and must have been least twenty-four or twenty-five, minimum. Was it possible that he was wrong after all, and this was a wild-goose chase? Well, if so, at least he would be satisfied that he had found out for certain.

He waited until they were on a straight stretch of road empty of traffic and held the photograph up so that Lineham could risk a quick glance at it.

'I can't really tell, without a proper look,' said Lineham.

'Take my word for it. The resemblance is there,' said Thanet, aware that he was trying to convince himself as much as his sergeant. Because, glancing through the other photographs, he also had to admit that Lineham's suggestion was equally feasible and it could simply be that Elaine was the same physical type. The girls were, without exception, small and slight, their height often betrayed by the scale of their surroundings. The one who perhaps was Elaine's mother, for example, couldn't have been more than five feet tall; the top rung of the five-barred gate was just below her shoulder.

Slipping that one photograph into his wallet Thanet sat back to enjoy the drive. It was, he thought, one of the loveliest in the south-east. Via Cranbrook, Hawkhurst, Etchingham and Burwash the road ran through beautiful rolling countryside which at this time of year was a glorious patchwork of autumn colour.

'Louise would love this,' said Lineham as they came into the pretty village of Burwash, with its tree-lined pavements and picturesque old houses.

'Bateman's is only a little way further on,' said Thanet. 'Rudyard Kipling's house. We had a family outing down this way once, there's lots to see.'

'We're hoping to do more of that sort of thing when the children are bigger. They're a bit young yet.'

Soon after Ringmer they passed the Glyndebourne turning and the bare sweeping curves of the South Downs reared up on their left.

Most of the way the sun had been shining but as they drove down the long hill into Lewes Thanet noticed a heavy bank of cloud ahead. The bursts of sunshine became shorter and shorter and at less frequent intervals.

'Looks as though the heavens are going to open,' said Lineham.

'I hope not. I haven't got my raincoat.' In his hurry to get to work this morning Thanet had forgotten it.

'There's an old anorak you can borrow in the boot, if the worst comes to the worst.'

'Thanks. Turn right, up the High Street, and right again, at the top.'

Lineham concentrated while he negotiated the heavy traffic through the centre of the old town then said, 'Actually, sir, I was thinking. We really should have rung, first. If she's out we'll have a wasted journey.'

'I thought of that. But even if she is out I thought we could make some inquiries, talk to neighbours.' The truth was that he hadn't wanted there to be a reason for not going. He wanted to fill in another blank in Randish's life, see the place where he had spent a number of years, talk to more people who had known him.

'She might have moved away.'

'True.'

'Or even be dead.'

'In the normal way of things, the odds are that she isn't. I worked it out and she's probably in her mid sixties.'

Soon afterwards Plumpton was signposted.

'Turn left here,' said Thanet. 'It's only a couple of miles, now. I don't suppose it's a very big village. We shouldn't have too much difficulty in finding the house.'

A rash assumption, he soon realised. Not long afterwards they came to a sign saying Plumpton half a mile. They passed a pub, then the Agricultural College on the right. Then came a couple of houses, then open countryside again. Lineham slowed down. 'Is that it?'

'Looks like it.'

Plumpton, they discovered, was a very scattered community with no proper centre and after asking directions they got lost twice before eventually managing to find Jasmine Cottage, which was not as picturesque as its name. It was Victorian and semi-detached, built of ugly red brick, with a square bay window to the left of the front door.

As they got out of the car it started to rain, huge coin-sized drops which spotted the road surface.

'I'd better borrow that anorak, Mike.'

Thanet raised his eyebrows at the garment Lineham produced. It was not just old but distinctly tatty, with stains down the front and a long tear in one sleeve.

'Sorry, sir, it looks even worse than I remembered. I keep it to use in emergencies – you know, for changing tyres in the rain and so on.'

'It looks like it!'

'Borrow my raincoat,' said Lineham magnanimously, beginning to take it off.

'No, no. Give me the anorak, quickly.' The rain was coming down steadily now. 'I'll just put it over my head.'

The front gate was broken, propped open with a brick, and the garden was neglected: the lawn was shaggy, the narrow flower borders choked with weeds. The long new season's growth of a rambler rose beside the door had not been tied in and thorns clutched at Thanet's sleeve as he rang the bell.

'Did it work?' said Lineham. 'I didn't hear anything.' He turned his collar up against the increasing downpour.

Thanet lifted the letter-box flap and banged it a few times. The sound reverberated through the house but there was still no response. The front door of the cottage next door opened and a woman came out, peering suspiciously at them from beneath an umbrella with two broken spokes.

'What d'you want?' She was middle-aged and grossly overweight, her legs and ankles so swollen that the flesh hung over the sides of her shoes.

Lineham stepped away from the shelter of the house, hunching down into his collar. 'We wanted to talk to Mrs Wood.' He fished his warrant card out of his pocket and held it up.

She reached across the dilapidated picket fence which divided the two gardens, took it from him and peered at it. 'Just a minute.' She waddled off indoors.

Lineham shrugged at Thanet. 'Looks as though Mrs Wood still lives here, anyway.' The rain was tipping down now and for shelter the two men huddled as close to the house wall as they could get – an unwise move, for a moment later without warning a blocked gutter above them overflowed, and water cascaded down upon them.

As they jumped back Thanet noticed that the net curtain at the bay window behind Lineham was moving. A small round blob had appeared at the bottom and one corner of the curtain was being raised a few inches. 'Look behind you, Mike!' he hissed.

Lineham turned, but the curtain had dropped and there was nothing to see. 'What?'

The blob had been the end of a walking stick, Thanet guessed. Which meant that Mrs Wood was probably immobilised and couldn't reach the curtain any other way. Hence the care being taken by her neighbour.

The woman had come out again. 'You can't be too

careful these days!' she said as she handed Lineham's card back.

'Quite right!' said Thanet.

Mrs Wood, it appeared, was bedridden with severe arthritis. The key to the front door was kept under an upturned flower pot nearby, so that regular visitors could get in.

'Not exactly the most original hiding place,' said Lineham as he retrieved it. 'It'd be the first place a burglar would look, especially if he knew a key was left out.'

They let themselves in and stood, dripping, on the doormat just inside. The house struck chill and the narrow hall was gloomy, with dark red floor tiles and brown paintwork on doors and banisters. Ahead, a passageway beside the staircase led to another door.

Thanet shivered. 'Better take our coats off.'

They draped them over an old-fashioned hall-stand to the right of the door.

'It's freezing in here!' said Lineham. 'And my feet are soaking.'

'Stop grumbling, Mike. Look at me!' The anorak had afforded little protection. Thanet's trouser legs and feet were also wet and he had an uneasy feeling that the water had run down and soaked the bottom of the back of his jacket, too.

He raised his voice and called, 'Mrs Wood?' then knocked at the door on the left, confident that that was where he would find her.

SEVENTEEN

Thanet put his head around the door. 'May we come in, Mrs Wood? Don't be alarmed, it's the police. We showed our identification to your neighbour and she told us where to find the key.'

'Come on in.'

The figure in the bed by the window was so thin and frail that she barely made a hump in the bedclothes. He must surely have been wrong in his estimate of her age, thought Thanet. This woman was in her seventies. She must have borne her daughter much later than he had guessed. Her straight white hair had been cut short by an inexpert hand and her skin was so pale as to be almost translucent. Her hands were pitifully swollen and gnarled with disease. On top of the bedspread lay a lightweight aluminium walking stick and beside the bed was a cluttered bedside table, a walking frame and a commode. The room was large and had evidently once been a sitting room, but the temperature in here didn't seem to be much higher than it was in the hall; a solitary bar glowed on the electric fire which had been put in the middle of the floor, facing the bed. A portable television was running and an advertisement was urging viewers to book now for a winter sunshine holiday.

Mrs Wood invited them to sit down. A couple of chairs had been placed near the bed, for visitors.

When they were settled, Thanet said, 'I don't know if you've heard, but a former lodger of yours died the other day . . .'

An extraordinary change came over Mrs Wood's face. Her eyes glittered and a tide of red, startling against the colourless hair and washed-out nightgown, flowed up towards her hairline.

If her physical condition had allowed it she would have clenched her hands into fists, Thanet thought, watching the misshapen fingers curl. There *was* something, then. His scalp prickled with excitement.

The colour had ebbed as swiftly as it had appeared, leaving her skin more devoid of colour than ever. 'Zak Randish, you mean,' she said. 'Oh yes, I heard about that all right. Murdered, wasn't he.' And she smiled, a small, cold, satisfied smile.

There was somehow something shocking about this pathetic old lady displaying such vindictiveness, thought Thanet, though why that should be he wasn't quite sure. 'I wonder,' he said, 'would it be possible to turn the television off for a while?'

The remote control was to hand and after a couple of abortive attempts, Mrs Wood managed to stab the correct button. 'It's no more than he deserved, I'm sure,' she announced loudly into the ensuing silence.

While they waited for her to turn the set off Thanet had noticed that on the bedside table, with their backs to him, were a couple of photographs. Would one of them be of Elaine? he wondered. How could he get a look at them? 'You obviously didn't like him,' he said, half his attention on the photographs and aware that this was an understatement if ever there was one.

'I hated him!' she said vehemently. 'He killed my daughter!'

She wasn't even looking at them to gauge the effect of this announcement but was gazing fiercely into space, focused upon some inner vision that had nothing to do with their presence here. Thanet and Lineham raised eyebrows at each other and shrugged. Neither of them believed she had meant it literally. Then she seemed to become aware of her surroundings again and her eyes wandered over the bed, her pathetic hands, the single-bar electric fire and finally Thanet and Lineham. 'I wouldn't be stuck here like this now, all alone, if it wasn't for him. I'd still have my Jill to look after me.'

'How is that?' said Thanet. He recognised the signs. People who lived alone, especially those who were elderly and incapacitated, were almost invariably eager to talk, usually about whatever it was that they spent their time brooding upon – their health, a grievance, their memories. Once launched, the occasional question here and there was all that was necessary to prompt them into further elaboration. He sensed Lineham beside him going into what he thought of as the sergeant's invisible mode; over the years, when Lineham judged that a witness was about to open up, he had developed the knack of fading into the background. Still as a statue, only the occasional blink betrayed the fact that he was alert and absorbing everything that was going on. Whenever Thanet was stuck with an inexperienced officer who fidgeted, coughed, scribbled ostentatiously and generally distracted the witness he thought longingly of this trick of Lineham's and wished that it was part of standard training procedure.

Her tale was much what he expected. A boyfriend had 'taken advantage' of Jill when she was fifteen and had dropped her flat when he heard she was pregnant. Not long before that a neighbour had had an abortion that had gone wrong and been desperately ill, so Jill had refused even to consider having one. Around that time her father died and she and her mother had had to think of some means of earning money. They had decided to take in students from the nearby agricultural college. A number of local people did this, and it would mean that Jill could stay at home and look after the baby when it arrived. In fact, later on, when Linny went to school, Jill got a job in a shop in Lewes.

Thanet pricked up his ears, wished again that he could take a look at those photographs. This was the first time the child's name had been mentioned, its gender even hinted at. Linny sounded like a girl's name and could well be an abbreviation of Elaine. He would ask later if necessary. The old lady was well launched and he didn't want to interrupt the flow.

All went well until Zak arrived, at the beginning of the third and final year of his course. During his first year he had been in college residential accommodation; during his second he had been living on the farm on which he had been doing his year's practical experience. Until then Jill, wary of men after that early, disastrous experience, had not taken much interest in the opposite sex, but reading between the lines Thanet gathered that one look at Zak had changed all that. According to Mrs Wood, of course, it was Zak who had made all the running.

'Promised to marry her, he did,' she said bitterly.

Wishful thinking, thought Thanet. In view of Zak's long-term plans for the future he very much doubted Randish had ever had any such intention. Alice Randish, with her father's spreading acres, would be a much more enticing proposition.

'She couldn't believe it when, after he left, she didn't

hear a single word from him. She waited and waited, wrote him time and time again, but never a word from him did she hear. She was beside herself. It was awful to see her watching and waiting for the postman every day, I got so that I'd wake up in the mornings feeling sick to think of her disappointment when there was no letter for her yet again. In the end she said to me, "There's nothing for it, Mum, I'll just have to go and see him. Perhaps he's ill, perhaps he's broken his arm and can't write . . ." And perhaps pigs might fly, I thought to myself. I didn't say so, of course, it wouldn't have done any good, but I saw from the first what he was like, with his smarmy ways. A real ladies' man, that's what. If he ever got married I bet his wife had a terrible time of it. Anyway, I did try to persuade Jill not to go. I guessed it would end badly. But she wouldn't listen, go she would. So she went. And I never saw her again.'

'What happened?' said Thanet, startled into a direct question.

'She crashed the car on the way home, on that big hill the other side of Etchingham. She was killed instantly, they said.'

'Are you suggesting it wasn't an accident?'

'No one knows.' Mrs Wood was shaking her head, the tears coming to her eyes. 'No one will ever know.' She groped blindly for a box of tissues on her bedside table and Thanet handed them to her. Clumsily she pulled one out, dabbed the tears away. 'Thanks. But it makes no difference, don't you see? Whether it was a genuine accident or whether she . . . she did it on purpose, it was him what killed her. If it was an accident, it was because she was so upset after seeing him. She was a good driver, careful . . .'

Even the best of drivers can have accidents, Thanet

knew, but he could see that there was no point in saying so. Mrs Wood's ideas were too deeply entrenched for a brief conversation with a stranger to alter them even slightly. And after all, it was quite likely that she was right. Even if Jill Wood had not intended to kill herself, her concentration may well have been poor after a final rejection by Zak. 'I expect your granddaughter was a comfort to you,' he said, pleased that his patience had been rewarded and he had at last been able to introduce the subject which had brought them here.

And as he had hoped her response confirmed that the child had been a girl.

'She was only ten! What can you expect from a child of that age, especially when she's so upset herself? Still, you're right. She was a comfort. Until she went away to college, that is. Mind, I wouldn't have wanted to hold her back. She's done very well.' Mrs Wood began to grope for one of the photographs. 'That's her, there.'

Thanet leaned forward with alacrity to help her. As he turned the photograph around a thrill of triumph shot through him. There was no doubt about it, this was Elaine Wood, a little younger, perhaps, but instantly recognisable. He held it out for Lineham to see. 'She's a beautiful girl.'

Mrs Wood fumbled for the other photograph. 'And that's her mother.'

Further confirmation. This was definitely the girl he had thought might be Elaine's mother. 'They're very alike.' He passed the second photograph to Lineham, who held them side by side to compare the two young women. 'I suppose your granddaughter is very much the same age now as your daughter was when that was taken.'

'Yes, she is. She's doing very well. Works with them new-fangled computer things.'

'How did she get on with Mr Randish when he was here?'

'Oh, all right. He went out of his way to worm himself into her good books, so she wouldn't make things difficult for him with her mum. And, of course, she'd never had a father, so she did tend to make a beeline for the men. But after Jill died I made sure Linny knew it was all his fault Oh yes, I made sure of that all right.'

'Does she come to see you often?'

'Whenever she can get away. It's difficult for her, she doesn't work locally. She works in . . .' Mrs Wood broke off, stared first at Thanet, then at Lineham, then at Thanet again. At first welcoming the distraction of visitors and then becoming engrossed in her story, until this moment she had not really questioned the reason for their presence. Now, perhaps, she had sensed danger for the first time. 'Where . . . Where did you say you were from?'

'From Sturrenden. We are investigating Mr Randish's murder.'

'Why have you come to see me?'

She had talked so freely until now that Thanet was certain she had no idea that her granddaughter had been involved with Randish. If he told her, he would perhaps cause her a great deal of unnecessary distress. If it turned out that Elaine had in fact killed Zak then that distress would be unavoidable. Meanwhile it would be best to keep her in ignorance. 'Naturally,' he said, 'we are trying to talk to everyone who knew him.'

He stood up and watched her relax a little at the thought that they were leaving. 'It's a pity your granddaughter doesn't live nearer. She might have been able to help you more.' Why wasn't Elaine doing more for her grandmother, anyway? With her qualifications there would surely have been plenty of jobs available in Lewes or Brighton. Not that it was any of his business, but still . . .

The old lady had sensed his unspoken criticism and was shaking her head. 'I'm here because I want to be. I always said I didn't want to go into a nursing home, I'd die in my own bed. And that's what I'm going to do.'

'It must be very difficult for you.'

'I manage.' She waved a hand. 'People come. I get meals on wheels, and the district nurse comes in to bath me.' She scowled at Thanet. 'I wouldn't want Linny ruining her life for my sake. You're only young once, and you should be free to enjoy it.'

Outside Thanet was thankful to see that it had stopped raining.

Lineham said, 'You got into her bad books there, sir. Daring to hint at criticism of her precious Linny.'

'I did it on purpose, to distract her, as I've no doubt you realised, Mike. Anyway, I don't know about you, but my feet have gone numb.'

'Mine too.'

'Early lunch, I think. I wonder if that pub back there has a fire. What was it called?'

'The Half Moon.'

'That's right. Let's go and find out.'

They were in luck. As soon as they stepped through the door a blissful warmth enveloped them. The Half Moon had not one fire but two, a woodstove at one end, near the dartboard and billiard table, and an open fire at the other. Best of all, there was an empty table near the latter.

'What d'you think that means?' Lineham nodded at the

smoke-blackened concrete lintel over the fire, on which some words had been chiselled.

WOOD FEEDS FIRE WORDS IRE.

'Ire means anger, doesn't it?' said Thanet.

'Ah. I see. Life would be pretty boring if we all took a vow of silence, though, wouldn't it?' Lineham stretched out his feet to the welcoming warmth. 'Wish I could take my socks off!'

'I don't think you'd be too popular with the landlord!'

They contented themselves with eating something hot – home-made moussaka – and allowing the heat to soak into their bones. Afterwards, Thanet sat back and lit his pipe, watching his wet trousers steaming gently. 'That's better.' He waited until his pipe was drawing properly and then said, 'Well, Mike?'

'OK, sir, so I owe you an apology. You were right. But I'll tell you this. Although I didn't like Elaine Wood and, frankly, I wasn't too keen on her grandmother, either, I do hope she's not our murderer. She's all the old lady's got.'

'I think it must be advancing years that are turning you soft, Mike. First you say you hope it wasn't Fester, now you say you hope it wasn't Elaine. Are there any other candidates you'd like to put out of the running?'

'Oh, all right, sir. So I'm going soft. You may not be saying so, but by your past record I bet you feel exactly the same underneath.'

Thanet laughed. 'Touché. But in any case, you have to admit now that Elaine does have a motive.'

'A real classic, isn't it: revenge for the death of her mother. Yes. I'm sure old Mrs Wood would have missed no opportunity over the years to make sure Elaine had got the message. And Elaine would have recognised Randish the minute she saw him, don't you think? Between their twenties and their thirties people don't change all that much.'

'She might have realised who he was before that, Mike, if she'd heard his name before she went out to the vineyard, which is quite likely. It's pretty unusual, after all.'

'So she might have been on her guard. The question is, would he have recognised her?'

'She would have changed a lot, between ten and twenty-five. If he did, it would be because of her resemblance to her mother.'

'As you pointed out, sir, she is very much the same age as her mother was when Randish knew her.'

'Quite.'

'Her surname might have rung a bell, too.'

'If he heard it, Mike. You know how informal people are these days. She was probably only referred to as Elaine. And that wouldn't have meant anything to him if he only knew her as Linny.'

'Perhaps he did recognise her, sir. Perhaps it added spice to the situation, as far as he was concerned.'

'Possibly, yes. In any case, if either of them did recognise the other, I wonder if they let the other person know. Quite an intriguing situation, really. What d'you think?'

Lineham considered. 'I'd say that he might have, but she probably wouldn't have.'

Thanet tapped his pipe out on the ashtray. 'Come on, let's go and find out.'

EIGHTEEN

On the way back to Sturrenden the weather was at its most capricious: periods of brilliant sunshine followed by heavy outbursts of rain. On one occasion visibility became so poor that Lineham pulled in to the side of the road until the worst was over.

The heater was on in the car but both men were still uncomfortably aware of damp feet, and Thanet decided that before going to Compu-Tech to interview Elaine and question Fester about the lie he had told it would be sensible to go home and change. He would collect his raincoat, as well.

They called at Thanet's house first, Lineham electing to wait in the car. In the hall Thanet almost fell over a pair of discarded trainers lying in the middle of the floor – Bridget's, presumably. He picked them up to move them out of the way. It looked as though she had been caught in a downpour too. They were sodden, the patterned soles caked with mud and embedded with pieces of gravel and even a splinter of glass. What on earth had she been up to?

'Dad! What are you doing home? For a minute I thought we had burglars!'

Bridget had appeared at the top of the stairs, a towel wound around her head.

'We got soaked, like you.' Thanet waggled the trainers at her.

'Oh, sorry. I was going to put them in the kitchen to dry as soon as I'd changed. I wasn't expecting anyone else home for hours yet.'

'I'll put them on the mat by the back door.' Thanet did so, first picking out the fragment of glass in case Bridget didn't notice it and cut herself. He dropped it in the waste bin, then hurried upstairs.

A minute or two later she appeared at his bedroom door as he was pulling on some dry trousers. 'Got time for a cup of coffee?'

'No, sorry, love, Mike's waiting in the car outside and we're on our way to an interview. It's just that I knew I'd be in trouble with your mother if I spent the rest of the day with wet feet.' Thanet was tugging on fresh socks as he spoke.

'Quite right, too,' said Bridget with a grin.

Thanet slipped on some dry shoes and wiggled his toes. They felt blissfully cosseted and comfortable. 'That's better!'

Bridget followed him as far as the top of the stairs. 'Still all right for tonight?' she called down after him.

'So far.' Thanet raised a hand in farewell. 'The 8.05, you said?'

'That's right.' Her ''bye' floated after him as he closed the door.

After a brief halt at Lineham's house they set off again.

'Think we ought to call in at the office?' said Lineham.

Thanet shook his head. He was eager now to get to Compu-Tech.

'Which of them are we going to talk to first?'

'Fester, I think. It shouldn't take long. Frankly, I don't think we're going to get anywhere with him.'

'Why not?'

'I think he'll simply continue to deny that he went out that night. He'll realise it's the witness's word against his and challenge us to prove he's lying. And of course, we won't be able to. End of story.'

'There must be something we can do, to get him to admit it.'

Thanet shook his head. 'I don't see how, at this stage. Unless . . .'

'What?'

'Hold on a minute, Mike. I'm thinking.'

Perhaps it would be better to interview them together. Then, if Fester saw that Elaine was in difficulties he might be driven to indiscretion himself in order to bail her out. But it was going to be difficult enough anyway to get Elaine to talk freely and if Fester were present she would be even less likely to open up. 'No, that won't work.'

'What?'

Thanet explained.

'I see what you mean.'

'No, we'll have to see them separately, do the best we can.'

At Compu-Tech Kari was sweeping up sodden leaves in the paved parking area and shovelling them into a wheelbarrow. The sky was still heavily overcast and in the dreary grey light she was a welcome splash of colour in bright red wellies and anorak. Her flowing hair was tied up into a pony-tail which swung as she worked. She paused as they got out of the car, leaning on the handle of her broom. 'It's a never-ending job at this time of the year.'

'I didn't know you were the gardener as well.'

She grinned and gestured at the ivy-filled terracotta

pots. 'If you can call looking after those being the gardener, then yes, I suppose I am. But I do like to keep the place tidy.'

Kari had called herself lucky the other day, thought Thanet, but it was not all one-sided. Fester was lucky too. He had struck gold here.

There was a silver Peugeot 205 parked next to Fester's BMW.

'His and hers,' said Lineham in a low voice as they walked up the ramp to the door. 'I bet that's Elaine Wood's. Just the car I'd have expected her to choose.'

'Could belong to a client. She might be out on a job.'

Lineham shook his head. 'It'll be hers.'

Privately, Thanet agreed with him. At first, however, it looked as though the sergeant was wrong. The office was empty except for a receptionist typing busily.

'Can I help you?' She was young and pretty, with beautifully cut very short black hair and a wide smile.

To Thanet's relief Fester and Elaine were both in. They were in Fester's office and the receptionist rang through. A moment later Elaine emerged. Not surprisingly, she didn't look too pleased to see them and Thanet did not miss the glint of relief in her eyes when he asked to speak to Fester.

Fester's office was strictly functional, the walls bare of the certificates, diplomas and photographs considered obligatory by so many. It was predictably uncluttered, the only furniture being four low armchairs grouped around a coffee table on one side of the room and on the other an interesting desk, custom-made by the look of it. It had been built on a shallow curve and ingeniously designed without legs at the two front corners, to allow easy access to Fester's wheelchair. Not surprisingly in view of the nature of Fester's business, there seemed to be a lot of sophisticated electronic equipment. This, presumably, was where he did a great deal of his creative thinking.

Fester rolled forward to greet them. Here, at the very heart of the success he had forged out of disaster, he looked confident and assured, in expensive casual trousers of a silky grey-green fabric with a slight sheen to it and a roll-neck cashmere sweater of exactly the same shade. 'Another interrogation, Inspector?' A joke, his smile said.

'Yes, as a matter of fact.' The armchairs were, Thanet noted, lower than Fester's wheelchair and not wishing to feel at a disadvantage he strolled across to the window and leaned against the sill.

'I can't persuade you to sit down? No?' Fester's smile had faded and as if to reassert his authority in his own domain he wheeled himself behind his desk and picked up a slim gold pen which had been lying on the open file in front of him. He began to slide it to and fro through his fingers. 'How can I help you, then?'

He had addressed his question to Thanet and looked slightly surprised when it was Lineham who moved forward to position himself squarely in front of him and, using the confrontational opening upon which he and Thanet had agreed, said, 'You lied to us the other day, sir. And we'd like to know why.'

Fester's eyes narrowed. 'What do you mean?'

Lineham did his best but as Thanet had predicted Fester flatly denied that he had been out that evening. The neighbour was mistaken, he claimed, had probably confused Friday with Thursday, when he had indeed gone out, to the gym in Sturrenden.

Nothing would shake him so Thanet asked if they could borrow his office to interview Elaine again.

With an ill grace he agreed, and used his intercom to ask the receptionist to send her in. 'I hope this won't take too long, Inspector. It's very inconvenient. I do have work to do, you know.'

'I realise that, sir. We'll be as quick as we can, I assure you.'

Fester left the room looking distinctly put out and Thanet noticed that instead of turning right towards the main office he turned left towards his living quarters.

A moment later Elaine came in and they all sat down. As they did so there was an almost inaudible click from the direction of the desk. Thanet was nearest to it and he glanced at the others to see if they had heard it. Evidently not. Lineham was fishing a pen out of his pocket and Elaine was settling herself in her chair. Earlier on Thanet's position by the window had given him a clear view of Fester's equipment and now the curve of the desk still allowed him an angled view of part of it. A red light on the intercom had come on, a different one from that which had lit up earlier when Fester spoke to the receptionist in the outer office.

Thanet realised what had happened. Despite the remarkable way in which he coped with his handicap Fester's mobility was still restricted and he had installed an elaborate intercom system which enabled him no doubt to communicate with any part of his establishment either from here or from the flat next door. Fester was, Thanet was convinced, in love with Elaine and no doubt part of his bad temper of a moment ago had been due to the fact that he was being excluded from this interview and wouldn't know what was going on. This was why he had turned left to his living quarters when he went out of the office just now. He must have realised almost at once that if he was quick about it he could listen in if he wished, and had hurried next door to switch the intercom on.

Thanet was pleased. With any luck now, his own problem was solved: Elaine would talk as freely as they could persuade her to, without being inhibited by Fester's presence, and Fester could possibly be provoked into playing the knight in shining armour and giving himself away on Elaine's behalf. It would make the interview rather complicated but Thanet enjoyed a challenge. He would see what he could do.

He became aware that Elaine had said something and that she and Lineham were both watching him expectantly. 'Sorry, I was thinking. Now then, Miss Wood, I feel we ought to tell you that we are rather better informed than we were last time we interviewed you.'

'Oh?' Her eyes were wary. She had managed to combine the glamour-girl look – immaculate make-up, carefully contrived casual hairstyle – with an air of efficiency. Her hyacinth blue suit and crisp white blouse with matching blue coin-sized spots were both stylish and businesslike.

'Did Mr Randish recognise you, when he first met you again, a few months ago?'

A flash of alarm, quickly suppressed. 'Recognise me?' she said, carefully.

'Oh come, Miss Wood, don't pretend you don't understand what I mean. But to spell it out, I'll tell you that we have just returned from Plumpton, where we had a very interesting conversation with your grandmother.'

She stared at him. Then, unexpectedly, he saw a spark of amusement in her eyes. Her lips curved in a wry smile. 'Ah,' she said.

He waited, interested to see what she would come up with next.

'You have been busy, haven't you, Inspector.'

'Evidently.' His tone was dry.

She crossed her legs, nylon whispering against nylon. 'So, what of it? It's all ancient history now. I don't see how something that happened fifteen years ago can possibly have any bearing on Zak Randish's death.'

'Don't you? I find that very difficult to believe. But let's go back a little. When did you first realise who he was?'

'As soon as I heard his name, naturally. I wasn't certain, of course, not until I saw him. But it is a very unusual name. I've never come across it at any other time, before or since.'

'That would have been when?'

'About four months ago. Tracey – our receptionist – told me that a Mr Randish had rung to enquire about a computer system and she'd told him I'd ring back.'

'You, not Mr Fester?'

'No. I handle sales and installation.' She glanced at the desk with its bank of equipment. 'Giles does the more creative stuff.'

'How did you feel, when you realised who Mr Randish might be?'

'It was a bit of a shock, naturally.'

'Did you mention that you might have met him before, either to Tracey or to Mr Fester?'

'No, of course not. It would have meant giving explanations, and I wasn't prepared to do that.'

Thanet wondered what Fester was making of all this. By now his curiosity must be at boiling point. 'And when you saw him, you knew at once that it was the same man?'

'Yes. He seemed scarcely to have changed at all.'

'Which brings me back to my original question. Did he recognise you?'

She shook her head. 'I was only ten when I knew him.

It doesn't take too much imagination to see that I must have changed a great deal since then. I did wonder if my name would ring a bell but nobody ever called me Elaine at home and Wood is a very common surname, you only have to look in the directory.'

'You are very like your mother, though.'

'Not sufficiently like, apparently.'

'So did you tell him who you were?'

'No.'

'Why not?'

'Because it would have been too awkward, of course! I knew I'd have to spend a couple of days in his office while he and that po-faced manager of his got the hang of the computer and I just thought it would be much easier if I said nothing.'

'Did he ever find out?'

'No!'

'No,' echoed Thanet softly. 'But not telling him led to a further complication, didn't it? You found he was attracted to you.'

She put up one hand to toss back her hair in a coquettish gesture. 'I'm used to that. I can handle it.'

'But you responded, all the same.'

She lifted her shoulders. 'Why not?'

'Why not, Miss Wood? Because according to your grandmother he was responsible for your mother's death, that's why not!'

'We don't know that, do we?'

'No, we don't *know* that. But what we do know is that he treated her very shabbily indeed, giving her good reason to believe he was going to marry her and then walking out on her and never contacting her again. I would have thought he'd be the last man on earth you'd choose to go out with, in the circumstances.'

'I told you! That was all ancient history!' But her composure was slipping, he was glad to see. If he could just make her say what she had really thought, really felt . . .

'Ah, but it wasn't really ancient history at all, was it? It could have been, I agree, if your grandmother had let it rest, but she didn't, did she? She couldn't. In her eyes, Randish killed your mother and that was all there was to it – and she told us, in no uncertain terms, that she had made sure you knew it. So are you really asking me to believe that when you met him again you were able to put all that aside and not only forgive him but actually enjoy going out with him?'

He was deliberately goading her, watching her closely for the signs that her control was about to snap, and now he was rewarded.

'All right!' she said, clutching at her head with both hands and jumping up. 'All right, all right, all right!'

Her agitation took her to the window where she stood with her back to them, leaning on the sill with both hands, arms rigid, head down and shoulders hunched in tension. After a few moments she lifted her head and took a couple of long, steadying breaths. They saw her shoulders relax before she turned. 'You're quite right, of course. It was impossible to forgive him. How could I? My grandmother probably told you that my mother was the only parent I ever had.'

'So why did you agree to go out with him?'

'To make him pay, of course.' Her tone was flat, weary. She returned to her chair. 'I could never bring her back, but I could make him suffer what she suffered.'

There had been no sound from the next room and Thanet wondered how Fester was taking all these revelations. 'Suffer how, exactly?' he said.

Her eyes gleamed with malice as in reply she smoothed

her skirt over her thighs and then ran the fingertips of one hand caressingly over one shapely, silky knee. 'I should have thought that was obvious, Inspector.'

Her smile mocked not only Thanet but Lineham, Randish, all men. How can you look at me and ask that question? it said. You are but putty in the hands of a woman like me.

'Spell it out for me,' Thanet said, face and voice carefully neutral. He saw Lineham shift uncomfortably and knew that the sergeant was sharing his distaste.

'Very well. It's quite simple, really. I intended to do everything in my power to make him fall for me.' Her tone was light, almost playful, but now it suddenly changed, became venomous. 'And then, when he had, to leave him flat, as he left her.'

Thanet again thought of Fester, listening next door, and couldn't help feeling sorry for him. Any illusions he had had about Elaine must be crumbling fast. 'I see. And I assume that you would claim he died before you were able to finish carrying out your plan.'

'Unfortunately, yes.' There was a wry glint in her eyes as she said, 'I must confess that I wish whoever killed him had waited just a little longer.'

Thanet caught Lineham's eye and knew what he was thinking. *Charming!*

'So let's go back now to Friday. You weren't telling the truth, were you, when you denied having arranged to meet Mr Randish that evening?'

'No.' She sighed. 'That was because Giles was there, of course. He didn't know I was going out with Zak. It won't have escaped you that he's rather keen on me and with him in his condition, well, let's just say I don't like to upset him if I can help it.'

Thanet flinched inwardly, thinking of Fester listening

next door. The mixture of indulgence and condescension in her tone must have made him wince.

'So when he asked me to go out with him on Friday I refused, told him there were various things I'd planned to do at home that evening.'

'What time did you and Mr Randish arrange to meet?'

'He said he couldn't give me a specific time, it all depended on when he could get away. And then he'd probably only be able to stay for half an hour or so. To be honest, I was pretty fed up about it. It meant I'd have to waste the evening hanging about waiting for him to turn up, unable to settle down to anything else. But he was dead keen, so I had to go along with it. He'd been so busy with the harvest lately that he'd hardly seen me. In the event, of course, he didn't turn up at all.'

'So what did you do?'

'Nothing. Why should I? I couldn't have cared less – except that, as I say, it meant a wasted evening.'

'You didn't try ringing the vineyard?'

'No.'

'And you didn't go out there?' A pointless question really, but it had to be asked. Thanet was convinced that Elaine had been telling the truth. Her idea of revenge rang true in the light of what he now knew of her character.

'No!'

'So you say.' Thanet was still conscious of their unseen listener, though in view of what Fester had heard it was highly unlikely that he would be as anxious to jump to Elaine's defence as he might have been half an hour ago.

She remained unruffled. 'So I say. And you'll never be able to prove otherwise because what I've told you is the truth.'

'Well,' said Thanet, rising, 'we shall see.'

Elaine stood up. 'That's all? I can go?'

'For the moment, yes.' Out of the corner of his eye he saw the light on the intercom go off and heard the click for which he had been listening.

He saw at once that Elaine had heard it too. She had been turning towards the door but now she froze and her eyes went towards the desk.

From where she stood, Thanet realised, she couldn't see the face of the intercom panel, so she wouldn't know whether it had just been switched on or off, whether the click meant that Fester had overheard the entire interview or had just switched on because he was about to speak. She waited a moment, presumably to see if he was going to, and when he didn't calmly walked to the desk and leaned forward for an unobstructed view of the panel.

She had to know whether or not Fester had been listening, Thanet realised, couldn't have left this room without knowing.

She registered the absence of lights and straightened up, stood for a moment thinking, then with set face crossed the room and opened the door.

Fester must have moved fast. He was outside, waiting.

Thanet wished that he could see their faces as they looked at each other in the light of their new knowledge. He felt sorry for Fester, and guilty over the pain he must have caused him. On the other hand it was not he but Fester who by eavesdropping had brought about this situation and it was perhaps just as well that the man's illusions about Elaine should have been destroyed. Nothing but heartache would have awaited him along that road. Perhaps now he would be free to look for a more worthwhile relationship. Remembering Kari, Thanet thought that Fester might not have to look far.

Lineham was looking puzzled. 'What's going on?' he whispered.

Thanet shook his head. 'Tell you later,' he murmured as Elaine moved away in the direction of the main office and Fester rolled forward into the doorway, blocking their path. 'Could I have another word, Inspector?'

'By all means.'

This time, by unspoken mutual agreement, they arranged themselves around the low table.

Fester gave Thanet a searching look. 'Am I right in thinking you know what I did just now?'

Thanet nodded. 'I heard the click at the beginning of the interview. And from where I was sitting I could see the light come on. But I'd better just explain to Sergeant Lineham. He wasn't as well placed.' Briefly, Thanet did so, watching Lineham take in all the implications.

'I assure you I don't make a habit of it,' said Fester, 'and I can't pretend I'm proud of myself. Quite the opposite, in fact.' He gave a wry smile. 'I suppose I deserved all I got. They say that eavesdroppers never hear anything good about themselves, don't they?'

'You didn't hear anything bad.'

'It depends what you mean by "bad". Nothing derogatory, no, but it was a bit of an eye-opener, as I'm sure you realised.'

'If it's any consolation, you're not the first to be taken in by an attractive woman, and you won't be the last. And Miss Wood does seem to be something of an expert. Look how she deceived Mr Randish.'

Fester gave a shamefaced grin. 'Thanks. Anyway, I think I owe you an explanation. Before, I was prepared to lie. Now, I'm not. Not that I have any great revelation to put before you, don't think that. I'm not about to confess and hold out my wrists for the handcuffs.'

'I didn't think you were,' said Thanet smiling. 'In fact, I think I can guess what you're going to tell me. So, to save you the humiliation of actually doing so, let me see if I'm right. On Friday evening, suspecting that Miss Wood was not telling you the truth – that in fact she had a date with someone else, you decided to keep an eye on her. Am I right?'

Fester gave a resigned nod.

'You couldn't own up the last time we spoke to you because she was present and you didn't want her to know you'd been watching her.'

'Yes. I left here about 7.15 as your witness claimed, drove to the car park behind Elaine's block of flats and parked where I could see both her garage and the entrance to the flats. I stayed there until around ten, then came home.'

'So you'll be able to tell us for certain whether or not she went out that night,' said Lineham.

'Quite,' said Fester. 'And she didn't.'

'You're sure of that, sir?'

'Positive.'

That seemed to be that. There was nothing more to be learned here.

Back in the car Lineham said, 'If he's telling the truth, they're both in the clear. And you believe him, don't you?'

Thanet nodded. 'Don't you?'

'Yes,' said Lineham reluctantly. 'So where does that leave us?'

Thanet sighed. 'Back at square one, I'm afraid.'

NINETEEN

They drove in silence for a few minutes and then Thanet banged his knee with a clenched fist in frustration. 'What a waste of time!'

'Not at all,' said Lineham. 'We've done some eliminating, if nothing else.'

Small consolation.

Silence again. Thanet was sunk in gloom. He'd thought he was so clever, with his ingenious theory of revenge for past wounds! He was only thankful that he'd said nothing of all this at the morning meeting. He could imagine Draco's reaction now.

> *Yes, well I'm not surprised. We have to keep our feet on the ground, you know, Thanet, not allow ourselves to be carried away. Perhaps it would be as well to remember in future that good police work is always based on fact, not fancy.*

Thanet realised that he was close to grinding his teeth. Had he been doing so? He glanced at Lineham, but the sergeant was concentrating on his driving. Thanet gazed moodily out of the window. Even the weather was being perverse; now that they were equipped for rain, the sun had come out and the roads were already almost dry.

Lineham pulled up to allow a stream of schoolchildren to cross the road. The lollipop lady, as the traffic controllers on such crossings are invariably called, smiled her thanks at him as she waved him on. The school day must be over already. Thanet glanced at his watch. Yes, it was half past three. He groaned. What a waste of time, he thought again.

'Come on, sir. Cheer up. You were right, after all.'

'About what?'

'About the connection between Elaine and Randish's former landlady. Honestly, I don't know what you're looking so gloomy about.'

'Hurt pride, I suppose, Mike, if the truth be told. It's always a blow when it turns out that you're not as clever as you thought you were. Serves me right.'

'Well, if you ask me you're over-reacting. I don't know what you expected. That Elaine would say, "Yes, it's a fair cop, guv. I done it because of what he did to my mum"?'

Thanet gave a shamefaced grin. 'If I'm absolutely honest then yes, I suppose I did rather hope for something like that. I certainly thought I'd cracked it. As it is, well, I suppose I should just be thankful my hunch proved right. I could have been way off beam, after all. We could have found that Elaine had absolutely no connection whatsoever with old Mrs Wood.'

'Exactly.'

'Not that it gets us very far to find out that she did. I suppose that's why I'm so angry with myself. I feel I've been self-indulgent, and wasted the best part of a day. I just wanted to prove that my theory was right and to hell with everything else.'

'What else, for example?'

'Well . . .' Thanet thought, but couldn't come up with anything.

'Exactly. You could only say you've wasted the time if we could have been usefully employed elsewhere and as you said yourself this morning there wasn't really anything else to follow up – apart from the fact that Fester had been lying about not having gone out that night, and we've dealt with that anyway.'

Lineham was not only right, but in view of his reluctance to go to Plumpton today, was being very generous. Thanet glanced across at the sergeant's familiar profile and experienced a surge of gratitude and affection. 'Thanks, Mike. What would I do without you?'

Lineham went pink. 'I dare say you'd survive, sir,' he said.

They had arrived. Back in the office they checked on messages and information that had come in while they were away.

'Nothing in the least bit promising,' said Lineham despondently.

'Never mind.' Thanet was brisk, spirits restored. 'It's obviously time to do a rethink. After all, it's not as though we haven't got any suspects. If anything we've got too many.'

Lineham sat back, stretching out his legs and folding his arms across his chest. 'So who would you put your money on, sir? Reg Mason?'

'I'm not sure.'

'He's the one who Randish was hurting most, after all. From the way Mrs Mason reacted the other night it's obvious that she can't put up with too much stress. If you ask me, Mason might well have ended up losing his wife as well as his home. But now, well, I should think it quite likely that Mrs Randish will at least pay off the original sum agreed for the work done and Mason's problems will be over.'

'It's true that he probably benefits most in the short term.'

'And a man in his position is bound to have a pretty short fuse. Let's face it, he had motive, means, opportunity, the lot. He really does fit the bill.'

'Maybe. But what about Landers? He was pretty browned off with the way Randish was treating Alice, wouldn't you say? I know how I'd feel if I discovered Bridget's husband was not only knocking her about but regularly being unfaithful too. It's all very well for him to protest that he couldn't have killed Randish because Alice would be heartbroken to lose her husband. I should think he could pretty easily convince himself that she'd get over it in time, wouldn't you?'

'Are you saying you think Landers went up to the lab that night deliberately to kill Randish? I thought we'd agreed that this murder was unpremeditated.'

'No, I'm not. But he's obviously fond of Reg Mason. It's much more likely that after hearing about the repossession and despite his decision to offer Reg a cottage if the worst came to the worst, he went up to the winery to make one last attempt to persuade Randish to pay up at least a part of the disputed sum. Randish could have been dismissive or rude or just plain insulting, and all Landers' grievances against him could suddenly have rolled together and erupted.'

'But you said you thought Randish must have been killed by someone much weaker or smaller than he was, because of the way it happened. If Landers lost his temper with Randish he wouldn't have started throwing things at him, surely, he'd have gone for him.'

'True. Unless, as you suggested yourself, whoever killed Randish – let's just assume it was Landers – was so angry with him that he was afraid that if he started a fight he might completely lose control.'

'And lost it anyway, you mean?'

'Perhaps. Yes.'

'It's possible, granted. But personally, if we're going to discount Reg Mason, I'd go for Vintage. If anyone's living on a knife edge, it's him, and he had the best opportunity of anybody. He had the whole evening at his disposal.'

'True. But you could say the same of Alice Randish. She not only fits the bill perfectly as far as motive, means and opportunity are concerned but statistically she's the most likely suspect. In fact, the more I think about it, Mike, the more I wonder if we've been pretty remiss in not looking at her more closely.'

Lineham considered the idea. 'If Randish had been unfaithful once too often . . . Maybe she found out about Elaine. Maybe her father told her, hoping to disillusion her! Yes! What if Landers hoped that by telling her about Elaine she could be persuaded to divorce Randish? Landers would just love to have her and the children under his control again, wouldn't he? Actually, sir, if you think about it, that's an added motive for him, don't you think?'

'Yes. I hadn't thought of that.'

'What if he told her about Elaine that evening, when he came over to see her about Reg Mason? And then, after he'd gone, she felt she had to know, she had to find out if it was true. She couldn't bear the prospect of waiting until her husband came back, he was always so late at harvest time, so she decided to go up to the winery and tackle him then and there. And suppose he admitted it but refused to stop seeing Elaine – or worse, laughed at Alice, asked her what she proposed to do about it . . . Those are exactly the circumstances in which she might have lost her temper, picked up the nearest thing to hand to throw at him and then, having started, found she couldn't stop.'

Thanet was nodding. He could see it all too clearly. 'There's just one snag, though, isn't there? If Alice did do it, why did she insist on going back up to the winery with Vintage, to look at the body? And would she have been sick if she'd seen it before?'

'Maybe she didn't realise he was dead. Maybe she threw everything she could lay her hands on at him and then turned and ran just before he went through the window?'

'She'd have heard the crash, surely,' said Thanet. 'And gone back to investigate?'

They were both silent for a while, thinking, then Thanet stirred. 'Well, all this speculation isn't getting us very far. In fact, I don't suppose we are going to get much further unless we can come up with some concrete evidence. Still, we ought to go through the motions, so . . .'

'Don't tell me,' said Lineham, pulling a face. 'We ought to go through the files.'

They both hated this stage in a case, when there was no obvious way forward. Equally, they both knew how valuable it could be to stand back and take a fresh look at what had already come in. Details which may have seemed unimportant when they first emerged could later on, in the light of new information, prove significant. And as their knowledge of the people involved in the case became more extensive, discrepancies in behaviour initially dismissed as irrelevant could stand out as being worthy of further scrutiny.

The phone rang and Lineham snatched it up eagerly. 'Yes? I see. Right, Sister. Yes, of course. Certainly. We'll come along right away.'

He put the phone down, beaming. 'Saved by the bell.'

'Sister?' said Thanet.

'Sister Benedict. No she's not a nun. She's the sister in charge of the ward where Randish's nephew is recuperating after that motorcycle accident.'

'Jonathan Redman.'

Lineham's eyebrows went up. 'I didn't know you knew his surname.'

'It's a long story. I forgot to mention this before, it didn't seem relevant. But to be brief, he and his twin sister – the girl who died – are friends of Bridget's. She's been to visit him in hospital.'

'Well, apparently he's asking to see you.'

'Me, specifically?'

'Well, the detective in charge of the Randish case.'

'I wonder why.'

As they hurried down the stairs like schoolboys excused from a particularly tedious piece of homework, Thanet told Lineham the little he knew about the boy.

'And Bridget says he doesn't remember anything about the accident?'

'When she saw him yesterday he hadn't even remembered his sister was dead. Bridget said his mother was dreading breaking the news to him all over again.'

'Poor kid. I can imagine. So perhaps his memory has come back. Perhaps, before he had the accident that night, he'd been driving along the road past the vineyard and saw something significant – someone leaving, whatever . . .'

'We'll soon find out. But I shouldn't get too excited, Mike. I don't suppose it's anything very important.'

'Anything's better than nothing,' said Lineham.

In the hospital Lineham set off briskly along the corridors with the air of someone who knows where he is going. He had become familiar with the sprawling, labyrinthine mass of Sturrenden General Hospital in the days when Louise had been working here full-time. Thanet trailed along behind.

Sister Benedict was evidently on the look-out for them; the moment they set foot in the entrance to the ward she appeared and asked them to step into her office. She was young and pretty, with a shining cap of hair the colour of burnished copper, a sight to gladden the heart of any sick person, Thanet felt. Her manner was brisk, businesslike, but there was no doubt about her concern for her patient.

'You might as well know that I don't think this is at all a good idea,' she said sternly. 'Jonathan had a really nasty motorcycle accident a couple of days ago and was unconscious for the first twenty-four hours. He didn't come out of intensive care until yesterday, so I really do not want him upset.'

'I do understand,' said Thanet. 'I know a bit about him, as a matter of fact. He's a friend of my daughter's and she's been in to visit him.'

'The pretty girl with fair hair?'

Thanet nodded, with the small inner glow of satisfaction he always experienced when anyone paid Bridget a compliment.

'Well, you'll know what I'm talking about, then. But he seems so determined to speak to the police I didn't think he'd settle until he had.'

'What does he want to see us about, do you know?'

She shook her head.

'When did he start asking for us?'

'After his mother left, about an hour ago.'

'She's been here all day?'

'No. I understand she didn't leave his side for the first forty-eight hours. Then last night we managed to persuade her to go home and try to get some rest. I don't think she did, though. Poor woman, she's having a terrible time ... There's this awful murder, for a start and then ... But, of course, you'd know about her daughter, Karen, Jonathan's twin?'

'Yes, Karen and my daughter have been good friends for years.'

'You'd know that Jonathan and his sister were very close, then. He was with her when she died, apparently, and his mother thinks that it was because he was so upset, afterwards, that he was driving carelessly and had the accident. Your daughter may have told you that he has partial amnesia, which is quite common, of course, after an accident, but the awful thing is that in this case it also extended to the period just before, and he had forgotten that his sister was dead. His mother was absolutely dreading breaking the news to him again.'

'You're using the past tense. I gather he's now been told?'

'She told him this afternoon. She came back late this morning and we had to tell her that as he was feeling so much better, Jonathan was urging us to put him in a wheelchair and let him go and visit his sister. In fact, that's the reason he's still in bed. We felt that the minute we allowed him up it would be difficult to keep on finding excuses for not letting him do so. But that situation couldn't be allowed to go on indefinitely, obviously, and although we very much sympathised with Mrs Redman we felt we had to make this clear to her. We did offer to break the news of Karen's death to Jonathan for her, but she said no, she'd rather do it herself.'

'So how did he take it?'

Sister Benedict lifted her hands in a gesture of surprise. 'Astonishingly well, I gather. She said he just went very quiet, seemed to go off into a trance. Patients never fail to surprise us. You can simply never tell how how they're going to react. Anyway, she was a lot happier when she went off just now – if you can use that word, in her present circumstances.'

'And how does he seem now?'

'Quiet. But then, he's been quiet all along.' She gave a rueful smile. 'But not docile, mind. As I said, he was absolutely determined to see you.'

'Did his mother also tell him about his uncle's death, or did he hear about it in some other way – radio, television, newspaper?'

'He hasn't been out of bed yet,' said Sister Benedict, 'and the television is in the day room. And he's not been feeling well enough to read or listen to the radio on the head phones. After a crack on the head like that you need rest and quiet. No, I think she must have told him. We did discuss whether he should be told or not and although she was reluctant to do so, she did realise he might otherwise hear about it in the media. I don't think she was too worried about breaking the news to him, actually. I got the impression he wasn't particularly close to his uncle. It was telling him about his sister's death that was worrying her much more.'

While they had been talking she had relaxed but now the stern look with which she had met them returned. 'I'll take you in to see him now but please remember what I said. I really do not want him upset. As I say, if he hadn't been so insistent I would have refused to ring you, made him wait until tomorrow.'

'We'll do our best, Sister, I promise.'

She led them right down the ward to the far left-hand corner. Thanet always hated walking the length of a hospital ward. He never knew whether to smile to right and left, acknowledging those patients who were conscious as if he were visiting royalty, or to ignore them. At least on this occasion, with Sister Benedict marching purposefully ahead, he didn't have to scrutinise each one in search of a familiar face. Which was probably just as well. He may have met Jonathan Redman in the past, amongst all the other young people Bridget brought home, but he didn't think he'd know him when he saw him.

But he was wrong. Sister Benedict had stopped and the face on the pillows before them was at least vaguely familiar. Although Karen and Jonathan had been non-identical twins there was still a strong resemblance. And it was obvious that the lad had recognised him.

Thanet had been prepared, obviously, for Jonathan to look ill, but he was still shocked by what he saw. Jonathan's face was paper-white, his head was still swathed in bandages and his hands lay limply on the bed-cover. Like Karen he had always been slight in build and his body seemed scarcely to mound the blankets.

Sister Benedict glanced from one to the other. 'Well, here are your policemen, Jonathan. No need to introduce you, I see. I'll leave you to it.'

With a last, warning look at Thanet she swept the curtains around the bed, creating a false illusion of privacy, and left.

Thanet and Lineham seated themselves on the stools provided for visitors.

'Well then, Jonathan,' said Thanet smiling. 'What's all this about?'

TWENTY

'But before you tell me,' Thanet went on, 'let me say how very sorry Mrs Thanet and I were to hear about Karen.'

Jonathan pressed his lips together and turned his head away. Thanet was dismayed to see tears roll down the boy's cheeks. Jonathan looked so young, he thought, more like sixteen than twenty, and desperately vulnerable. Perhaps he shouldn't have mentioned Karen? But how could he have spent some time talking to the lad without saying a word about her? He watched helplessly as Jonathan wiped the tears away and mumbled an apology. With three people in it the tiny enclosed world of the curtained cubicle suddenly seemed claustrophobically small and on impulse Thanet leaned across and murmured in Lineham's ear. Jonathan might feel more comfortable alone with someone he knew. Discreetly, Lineham withdrew.

'Thanks, Mr Thanet.' But despite the expression of gratitude Jonathan didn't look any more at ease.

Thanet decided it would be best to press on, let the boy get off his chest whatever it was that was worrying him. Conscious of the fact that there was another patient in a bed only a few feet away, he moved his stool closer to Jonathan and said in a low voice, 'So, why did you ask to see the police?'

'You are in charge of my uncle's case?'

'Yes.' Jonathan wasn't merely uneasy, Thanet realised, he was very much afraid, and in the split second before the boy spoke again he experienced a tremor of premonition.

'I wanted to tell you I killed him.'

Thanet felt as though he had run into a brick wall that had materialised from nowhere. He stared at Jonathan, astounded.

Jonathan's fingers clutched convulsively at the bedclothes and his tone was despairing as he said, 'This may sound crazy, but I didn't remember anything about it until a couple of hours ago, when Mum told me about . . . about the murder.'

In a blinding flash of comprehension Thanet suddenly saw it all. 'It was Karen, wasn't it? She told you, before she died?'

There was no need for him to spell it out. They were both on the same wavelength. Jonathan nodded, eyes full of misery. 'So you know about the baby.'

'Yes.' Thanet was uncomfortably aware that he knew only because of a confidence between Bridget and her mother.

'I suppose Bridget told you. I expect she thought it didn't matter, now Karen is dead.' There was no condemnation in Jonathan's voice. He just sounded inexpressibly weary, defeated.

Still, Thanet felt bound to defend his daughter. 'I wouldn't put it like that. She's known for years and has never said a word. I think it's only because she was so upset about Karen that she told her mother now. And naturally, my wife told me. We had no idea who the father was, of course.'

'Neither did we. Karen never would tell us, I don't

know why. To be honest, I suspected . . . I feel awful about it now, but . . . Oh, God . . .' He put up a hand, rubbed his forehead as if to ease the pain of knowing. 'In the beginning Mum tried to get it out of her, but . . . I didn't know much about it at the time, of course. In fact, I don't think anyone ever actually spelled it out to me, that my sister was having a baby. Mum finds it difficult to talk about things like that. But later, when Karen's anorexia got worse – did you know the theory was that the pregnancy triggered off the anorexia?'

'Yes, I did.'

After a halting start Jonathan was now well launched into his story. It was, no doubt, the first time he had ever talked about this to anyone outside the family and it would probably be an immense relief to him to get it off his chest. All Thanet now had to do was lend a sympathetic ear and make the occasional appropriate response.

'Well later, when this came out, I was much older of course, and Dad was dead. Mum didn't have anyone else to talk to, and she was so sick with worry about Karen she just had to talk to someone, so she talked to me. And she told me that at the time it was almost as if, all along, Karen would never really accept that she was actually having a baby. Mum said it was impossible to talk to her about it. She wouldn't even acknowledge your question, she'd just ignore it, change the subject. In the end Mum gave up. And afterwards, after the baby was born, I think all we wanted to do was forget about it as quickly as possible, put the whole thing behind us. I think we might even have managed to pretend it had never happened if it hadn't been for Karen's anorexia. But on Friday . . . On Friday, I think she knew, knew she was going to die. And I think I knew it, too. And I couldn't bear the thought that I would never, ever know who'd done this to her. So

I pressed her to tell me. I'd never done that before and I suppose she could see how important it was to me. So she told me.'

Jonathan shook his head, slowly, as if even the slightest movement hurt. 'I still don't understand why she never told anyone before. You'd think she'd have wanted people to know, wanted him punished. I can only think it must have been because she knew how upset Mum would be. Mum thought the sun shone out of Uncle Zak, still does – did. I don't think they had much of a life with their parents and this made a pretty strong bond between them. I know she did all she could to encourage him to get a decent education. From things she's said I suspect that while he was away at college she regularly used to send him money from the little she earned, and I think she always felt she'd contributed to his success. And I must admit he's always been decent to her. He's helped us out ever since Dad died . . . Looking back, I suppose that was conscience money,' he added bitterly.

Brisk footsteps tapped their way down the ward and Sister Benedict put her head around the curtain. 'Everything all right?' She gave Jonathan a penetrating look and, apparently satisfied by his appearance and their reassurances, left them alone again.

'The really awful thing,' said Jonathan into the ensuing silence, 'is that I was there when it happened – oh, not present of course, I don't mean that. But around, somewhere.'

'When he . . .' Thanet found he couldn't say 'raped'. Not to this grieving boy and not in these circumstances. He resorted to the common euphemism. 'When he abused her, you mean?'

'Yes. For the last hour or two, ever since Mum told me Karen had died – I'd forgotten, can you believe that? Forgotten, that my twin sister was dead!'

'The mind plays odd tricks,' said Thanet. 'Sometimes we "forget" what we don't want to remember. And as I'm sure they've told you, amnesia of varying degrees is very common in cases of head injury.'

'Well anyway, ever since she told me, and it all came back to me in a rush – what Karen had said, and what I'd done afterwards – I've been lying here struggling to block out those last pictures of what happened to Uncle Zak by trying to remember. It was when we were twelve. Mum had to go into hospital for some minor op . . . She was only away for a couple of days, and for some reason Dad couldn't look after us – I think he was away on business or something. Anyway, Uncle Zak took us out to stay with him and Auntie Alice, at the vineyard. That was when it happened, apparently. It was just that once.' Jonathan gave Thanet a miserable glance and shook his head. 'It doesn't bear thinking about, does it? A few minutes' pleasure and he'd signed Karen's death warrant.'

It sounded melodramatic but it was the simple truth, thought Thanet. 'Look, Jonathan, you're not trying to say you feel responsible, are you? That you should have protected Karen, prevented it happening? Because that simply isn't true.'

'Isn't it?'

'No! A boy of twelve can't be his sister's self-appointed guardian twenty-four hours of the day, every day, year after year. Because we're not just talking about the time you spent at the vineyard. Karen was equally vulnerable at any time, before or since.'

Jonathan said nothing.

'You really must not torture yourself like this,' said Thanet.

Still Jonathan remained silent. But he must have been

considering what Thanet had said because eventually he sighed, plucked at a loose thread on his pyjama cuff and said, 'I suppose you're right.'

'I am,' said Thanet, with all the certainty he could muster.

'Anyway,' said Jonathan with a sudden spurt of energy, 'that doesn't alter the fact that he thought he'd got away with it, the filthy pig! God, how he must have squirmed, when he learnt Karen was pregnant – as I assume he must have – in case she gave him away! But as time went on and nothing happened he must have felt more and more safe. And all the while, Karen was slowly dying . . . When she told me, on Friday, all this seemed to sort of explode in my head. I didn't show it, of course. I didn't want to upset her. She died soon afterwards.' Jonathan bit his lip to stop it trembling. 'And when she did . . . I couldn't bear to stay there, in the same room, and look at her. All I could think of was having it out with him, telling him what I thought of him, *making* him understand what he'd done to her . . .' Jonathan shook his head in wonderment. 'I assume I must have got on my motorbike and driven out to the vineyard, but I don't remember a thing about that. The next thing I remember is barging into his laboratory.'

Even though he knew what he was going to hear Thanet was conscious that his breathing had become shallow, his pulse had speeded up. Now, at last, he was approaching the heart of the mystery.

'He was standing at the bench, doing something with test tubes. I wanted to go for him but I made myself stop. I wanted him to *know* what he'd done.'

'Jonathan! What the hell do you mean, bursting in here like –'

'Shut up! She's dead, you bastard, and you killed her!'

'What do you mean? Who's dead? What are you talking . . .?'

'Karen! Karen's dead! Oh, what a relief that must be for you! Now no one will ever know!'

'Know what? Really, Jonathan, you –'

'Don't "really, Jonathan" me! I'll spell it out for you, shall I? I've come straight from the hospital, where my sister Karen has just died. And before she died she told me that it was you – you, who raped her when she was a kid of twelve – only a few years older than Fiona. How would you feel if Fiona has a baby when she's twelve because some filthy pervert couldn't keep his hands off her? Yes, that got to you, didn't it?'

'Jonathan. Calm down. I'm sorry to hear about Karen . . .'

'Are you? Are you sorry? Like hell you are!'

'I repeat, I'm sorry to hear about Karen. But I really cannot see how that makes me responsible for her death.'

'Oh you can't, can't you? Well that's because you haven't been living with her for the past eight years, seen her dying by inches because when she was pregnant with your bastard she got it into her head for once and for all that she was too bloody fat!'

'Fat!'

'And he thought that was *funny*!' Jonathan shook his head in despair. 'Funny! When it was thinking she was too fat that killed her! The bastard grinned. He actually grinned! And that did it. I went for him.'

David and Goliath, thought Thanet. He could visualise it all too vividly: the slight figure hurling itself in fury against the tall, well-muscled Zak Randish.

'But he was so much stronger than me. He just put up his hands, got hold of my forearms and held me off. Oh God, it was so humiliating . . .'

'Jonathan. Calm down and back off, will you?'
'Let me go. Let me go, you pervert!'
'All right, I will.'

'And he just sort of threw me back against the wall. I fell over and as I got up I noticed some full bottles of wine lined up on the floor under one of the benches. I grabbed one and, without thinking, threw it at him. He ducked and I missed. The bottle smashed through the window behind him and . . . I don't know how to describe what happened next. It was as if the sound of breaking glass triggered off something in my head, as if I actually felt something snap in my brain . . . Honest, Mr Thanet, I'm not trying to make excuses, just trying to tell you how it was.'

'I know that, Jonathan.'

The boy shook his head. 'I suppose I just went berserk. I just chucked everything I could lay my hands on at him. I didn't mean to kill him, I just, well, I suppose I just wanted to get that awful . . . rage out of my system. I can't tell you exactly what made him lose his balance and go over backwards, but he did. One moment he was standing there and the next he'd crashed through the window. The blood . . . It was horrible. And then he just sort of slid down into a sitting position. There was blood everywhere, and it was really gushing out, pouring down his neck and front . . . He . . .'

'All right, Jonathan. No need to go on. I get the picture.'

'I couldn't move. It was as if I was paralysed or something. It seemed only a matter of seconds before he slumped sideways and I could see he was dead. So I ran.'

And you were so distraught that on the way back you had the accident, thought Thanet. Once again he wondered if it had been the site of Jonathan's accident he had passed on the way to the station to meet Bridget, Jonathan on the stretcher he had seen being loaded into the ambulance.

'Jonathan,' he said, 'I have to ask you this, because others will do so. Why didn't you ring for an ambulance?'

'But he was dead! There was no point!'

'Did you check?'

'No, but it was obvious.'

'What do you mean?'

Jonathan frowned, remembering, and trying to work it out. 'It was his eyes,' he said at last. 'If people are just unconscious they have their eyes shut. His sort of . . . glazed over, and stayed open.'

'Yes, I see. All the same, it might have been a good idea, just in case.' A fatuous statement, really. Jonathan had obviously been incapable of rational thought.

'I suppose so. Oh God, what a mess. I don't know how Mum's going to react. What on earth am I going to say to her?'

'She'll have to know. And know why you did it, too. Or perhaps you've already told her it was your uncle who was responsible for Karen's pregnancy?'

Jonathan shook his head. 'When it all came back to me I was too shocked to tell her anything, in case I said the wrong thing. Does she *have* to know it was him?'

'Oh come on, Jonathan,' said Thanet gently. 'How else are you going to explain what happened? In any case, she's bound to find out eventually.'

'It'll come out in Court, you mean. Oh God, I don't think I can face it. Unless . . .' He looked up, his eyes gleaming.

'Unless what?' By the way Jonathan was looking at him Thanet had a feeling something tricky was about to come up.

'I don't suppose . . . No, I can't ask you.'

Thanet refrained from asking 'What?' He thought he could guess.

Jonathan waited a moment and when Thanet didn't respond said desperately, 'Have you told anyone else about Karen and the baby?'

'Of course not!'

'Well, no one else knows. If you didn't tell anyone, I wouldn't have to either, would I? I mean, I could just say I did it because I was angry with Uncle Zak.'

'About what?'

Jonathan waved a hand. 'I'd think of something.'

'No. Sorry, Jonathan, I couldn't agree to that.'

'But why not? Bridget told Mrs Thanet in confidence, didn't she? And Mrs Thanet told you. If you tell anyone else Bridget will be furious with you.'

'I know,' said Thanet grimly. 'But the fact is that I simply cannot withhold evidence which has come into my possession. And if Bridget realises, and I would make sure she did, that knowing *why* you killed your uncle would probably have a profound effect upon the kind of sentence you're likely to get, I think she'll probably forgive me. I really am sorry, Jonathan, but I can't do it. In any case, as far as your mother's concerned, just remember you're all she has left now. I think you'll find it's more important to her to understand why you did this than to preserve your uncle's reputation.'

'Do you think so?'

'I do. And what's more, in the circumstances, I think Karen would, too.'

'But I promised her I wouldn't tell anyone, ever!'

'Circumstances have changed, you must see that. Do you think she'd want you to spend years and years in prison?'

'I will anyway, surely.'

'Your chances will be improved, if the jury can be given good reason why you lost control as you did. It's no good, Jonathan. You really can't keep quiet about this.'

Jonathan remained silent, lips set in a stubborn line.

'Look,' said Thanet, with an inward sigh. 'Would it help if I told your mother for you? At least then you will, strictly speaking, have kept your word.'

It was a compromise, a less than satisfactory solution, but Jonathan seized on the suggestion eagerly. 'Would you? Would you really?'

What have I let myself in for? thought Thanet as he walked back down the ward. I must be mad.

Lineham was sitting on a chair outside Sister Benedict's office. She must have been watching out for Thanet through the glass panel which gave her a view of what was going on in her ward, because she came out as he approached. 'How is he?' she said.

Lineham stood up, joining them as Thanet said, 'Happier in his mind, I think. Would you excuse me just for a moment, Sister?'

He felt he owed it to Lineham to break the news to him first. When he did so, the sergeant looked as stunned as he himself had initially felt.

'And you believed him?'

'Yes, Mike, I did. Look, I'll explain it all to you in a minute, but I have to square things with sister, first.'

Sister Benedict, too, reacted with incredulity and once again Thanet had to explain that he was taking the confession seriously. 'I'm afraid we shall have to cause you a certain amount of disruption. I know he's not going anywhere at the moment but I shall have to put someone on guard here and of course we shall have to take a formal statement. He'll need to see his solicitor, too.'

After the initial shock Sister Benedict had made a swift recovery. 'From what you're saying, I assume I can take it that he is no danger either to my staff or my patients?'

'Absolutely not. I can guarantee it.'

'Right. Well, in that case, one of the side wards is vacant. We'll put him in there.'

'An excellent idea.'

She put her office at their disposal and arrangements were swiftly made.

'Right,' said Lineham, as they left. 'I can't wait to hear this.'

'I'll tell you on the way.'

'Where to?'

'To see Jonathan's mother. And believe me, I'm not looking forward to it.'

TWENTY-ONE

Thanet decided that it would be best to sit in the car in the hospital car park to talk. Explanations would be complicated and he wanted Lineham's undivided attention. Lineham listened in silence and when Thanet had finished said, 'Poor kid.'

'Jonathan, you mean? Or Karen?'

'Both of them.'

'Well, I never thought the day would dawn, but at last it has!'

'What day?'

'The day when you were actually sorry for someone who has committed a murder!'

Lineham looked sheepish. 'Well, these are rather unusual circumstances, sir.'

'Murders frequently are committed in unusual circumstances. No, Mike, there's no doubt about it. What I said the other day is true. You are definitely going soft in your old age.'

At thirty-four Lineham was able to smile at the idea.

Thanet sobered. 'Unfortunately, so am I, if in a rather different way.'

'What do you mean?'

'Because the idea that Jonathan could have done it never even entered my head!'

'But how could you possibly have known?'

'Well, I don't see how *you* could have worked it out, certainly – and don't look like that, Mike! I'm not in the habit of insulting you, am I? I'm about to explain why! The point is that in order to have done so you really did need one or two essential pieces of information – or rather, three, to be precise: that Karen had had a baby when she was twelve; that no one ever knew who the father was; and that it was her pregnancy which triggered off the anorexia that killed her. You had none of them, but I had them all.'

'Even if you did, I don't see how you could have guessed.'

'Not guessed. Worked it out. Yes I could! Think about it. The clues were all there.' Thanet began to tick them off on his fingers as he spoke. 'Landers told us that Alice Randish had been particularly fond of Karen ever since the twins came to stay at the vineyard for a few days when their mother was in hospital, and *that it was just before Fiona was born*.'

'Why is that so significant?'

'For two reasons. One, Fiona is eight. Now, I knew that Karen was twenty, because she is the same age as Bridget. And I later learnt that Karen was twelve when she had the baby.'

'So you could have worked out that it was around the time when they went to stay at the vineyard that Karen became pregnant – and therefore, that Randish might have been responsible.'

'Exactly.'

'And the second reason?'

'Because if it was just before Fiona was born, Randish

might well have been suffering from sexual frustration. And he was always a man who needed women.'

'And Karen just happened to be around at the time, you mean?'

'Quite.'

'Nasty.'

'He was a pretty nasty character, by all accounts. And that in itself was important, too. Only a nasty character would have taken advantage of his twelve-year-old niece.'

'Go on.'

'Landers also told us that Karen seemed to get on better with Alice Randish than with her uncle.'

'Nothing unusual about that. Everyone's got relations they like better than others.'

'You're missing the point, Mike. The point is that the fact has significance only if you take other factors into consideration.'

'So, what other factors?'

'A major one was Randish's taste in women.'

'Small, slight, you mean.'

'Invariably, yes.'

'I see what you're getting at. As Karen would have been. Not quite the same thing, though, is it? A twelve-year-old girl?'

'Perhaps not. But has it occurred to you that possibly that was where Randish's taste truly lay? That he picked his women because physically they were the nearest thing to pubescent?'

'That's a thought, sir. Do you think he might have tried it on with Elaine Wood? She was ten at the time. Perhaps that's another reason why she was so determined to get her own back on him.'

'Possibly. If so, I don't suppose we'll ever know. And of course I could be doing him an injustice in suggesting it.'

'He must have got the fright of his life when he heard Karen was pregnant. Perhaps that's what has kept him on the straight and narrow ever since.'

'So far as we know. Quite. Anyway, the other thing that ought to have put me on to Jonathan, of course, was the coincidence of two deaths and a major accident in one family within the space of only a couple of hours. Just think what the odds must be against it! There *seemed* to be no connection between them but I really should have realised that there must be – or at the very least have considered that there might be. If I had, all these other things would have begun to fall into place. I just assumed that Jonathan had had an accident because he was so upset after being with his sister when she died. But if I'd checked the time at which he left the hospital along with the time of his accident, I might have begun to wonder if he hadn't been upset for another reason, such as witnessing or even committing a murder.'

'There seemed to be such a tenuous connection . . .'

'But the connection was there, that's the point. And knowing all these other facts, I should have spotted that it was more important than we assumed. In fact, I ought to know by now that you shouldn't assume anything, in this game, ever.'

'I think you're being unduly hard on yourself.'

'I haven't finished yet! There's one other, further point, which came up only this afternoon. It was just a small thing, but it should have given me cause to think . . . You remember when we called in at my house, for me to change? Well, Bridget was there. She'd got soaked too, and I nearly fell over her trainers. She'd left them on the mat in the hall, so I picked them up. They were in an awful state – caked with mud. And there was a fragment of glass embedded in the sole of one of them.'

'So? I don't see what you're getting at.'

'Glass, Mike! Think!'

'I'm beginning to feel distinctly dim, sir. I can't see any possible connection between Bridget's trainers and Jonathan's guilt.'

'No, you're not being dim, Mike. I'm not being fair to you. Once again, I'm in possession of the facts and you're not. Will it make a difference if I tell you this? When Bridget went to visit Jonathan yesterday she discovered that Mrs Redman hadn't left Jonathan's bedside since she first arrived at the hospital after the accident. There were various things that needed to be done, so Bridget volunteered to do them – and this included taking Jonathan's clothes home. The clothes he was wearing on the night of the murder.'

'I see . . . You're saying that Jonathan might have picked up some splinters of glass either in the soles of his shoes or elsewhere in his clothes and that when Bridget was handling his things, some of them might have fallen out and she trod in them?'

'Possibly, Mike, yes. Oh, I do realise that she could have picked that bit of glass up anywhere, that it could be pure coincidence. But you saw what a state the laboratory was in. Glass must have been flying about all over the place. Anyway, forensic might be able to verify – provided I can rescue the piece of glass from our kitchen waste bin. I actually put it there myself! In any case, whether that was what happened or whether she picked it up somewhere else, by chance, it was one more thing which should at least have given me pause for thought, a nudge in the right direction. No, Mike, there's no doubt about it. I've been shamefully slow on the uptake.'

'Well, I still think you're being too hard on yourself. And in any case, we'd no doubt have got there in the end.'

'When forensic identified Jonathan's fingerprints on pieces of glass picked up in the laboratory, you mean? I'd like to think so, yes – if it would ever have occurred to us to take his prints in the first place, to compare them.'

'It would have,' said Lineham confidently. 'You'd have added two and two together sooner or later. I'm sure of it.'

'I wish I agreed with you.'

'If you don't mind me saying so, sir, I think what's really bugging you is that Jonathan got in first with his confession and beat you to it.'

'Ouch. You're probably right. And if you are it'll do me good to be brought down a peg or two.' Thanet grinned. 'The trouble with you, Mike, is that you know me too well.' He glanced at his watch. 'Anyway, we'd better make a move. I want to get this over with.' He gave Lineham Mrs Redman's address.

'I assume we're going to see her to break the news of Jonathan's confession,' said Lineham as he started the car.

'There's a bit more to it than that, I'm afraid.'

Thanet explained his agreement with Jonathan and Lineham groaned. 'Great! Honestly, sir, you do land yourself in it, don't you?'

The Redmans lived on a big council estate on the far side of town. It was five o'clock and despite the much vaunted one-way system which had been installed some years ago, the roads were clogged with home-going traffic. Patiently, Lineham settled down to work his way through the endless sets of traffic lights.

Although he wasn't looking forward to the interview, by the time they arrived Thanet found that he was feeling increasingly curious about Mrs Redman. So far she had been a shadowy figure, ever-present but always in the background, out of sight. He had met her a couple of times briefly, years ago, at school functions, but she was very quiet and they had scarcely exchanged more than a few words.

She had certainly had more than her share of misfortune, he thought: an unhappy childhood with a 'drunken brute' of a father, a difficult marriage with a rigid, unyielding man who had given both Bridget and Ben 'the creeps', and then all the pain of seeing a daughter who was no more than a child bear a child herself as the result of rape and thereafter spend the remaining years of her short life in and out of hospital under the cloud of anorexia. Then, to cap it all, had come the events of the last few days.

And he, Thanet, was about to deliver the *coup de grâce* – no, not a *coup de grâce*, because he wouldn't be putting Mrs Redman out of her misery but increasing it tenfold. What on earth had he been thinking of, actually to volunteer for a task like this? he asked himself as the car slid smoothly to a stop outside her house. He glanced at Lineham, who pulled a face. 'Good luck, sir. I'd rather you than me. Do you want me to come in with you?'

Thanet shook his head. 'It'll be easier alone.'

The sky had become overcast again and lights had been switched on in some of the houses. The Redmans' house and garden were well cared for but all the curtains had been drawn and the place looked deserted, forlorn, as if the life had bled slowly out of it and all that was left was an empty shell.

Thanet told himself not to be fanciful. He walked briskly up the concrete path, noting the regimented rows of newly planted wallflowers, and knocked at the front door. There was no reply. He knocked again, stepped back, scanned the house, glanced over his shoulder at Lineham, who gave an exaggerated shrug. He knocked once more, still with no response. He was about to give up, walk away, when there was a sound from above. The curtain had been pulled aside and the window opened a crack. A face peered out. 'Yes?'

'Mrs Redman? It's Inspector Thanet, Bridget's father. Could I have a word?'

'I'll be right down.' The window closed.

She had no doubt been having a rest, thought Thanet, feeling guilty at having disturbed her. The past few days must have been exhausting beyond belief. He shifted his weight from one foot to the other as he waited, thinking that breaking bad news to people was the part of his job he hated most, and how this time was even worse because he knew everybody involved.

He didn't have to wait long. In a few moments the door opened. She had put on a plaid woollen dressing gown which was so long it touched the floor and looked as though it might once have belonged to her husband. She was still tying the twisted two-coloured cord at her waist. 'Is it Jonathan?' Her face was knotted with anxiety, as if she were bracing herself for the worst. She was, as he remembered, a little wisp of a woman who scarcely reached his shoulder. Unless she had married or had children very late indeed she must be about the same age as he and Joan, but she looked many years older. Long-term suffering and anxiety had left their mark, scoring deep furrows between her eyes and draining away any vitality she might once have possessed.

'Jonathan's fine,' said Thanet. 'I've just left him, as a matter of fact. But I do need to talk to you.'

She peered back at him anxiously, over her shoulder, as she led him into the room at the front of the house, switching the light on as she went in. With daylight still seeping in around the edges of the drawn curtains the artificial light cast a sickly glow over the sparsely furnished room. Randish's so-called generosity to his sister's family certainly didn't show in here, thought Thanet, noting the scuffed carpet and worn loose covers. The room, though shabby, showed evidence of care – it was scrupulously clean and someone, Jonathan perhaps, had recently given the walls a coat of emulsion paint. There was a small twelve-inch television set on a table in the corner. Evidently, since Mr Redman's death, some of the household rules had been relaxed.

She sat down on the very edge of a chair, tucking the dressing gown around her legs as if even a glimpse of ankle would be improper. 'Is it about the accident?'

'No, it's not.' Thanet took a deep breath. There was no way that this was going to be easy. Nothing could cushion the blow. He hesitated, seeking the right words. 'I'm afraid it's rather more serious than that.'

'It's about my brother, then? About his . . . death.' The last word was barely audible.

'Yes, it is. And I'm sorry. You've had a lot to bear these last few days, Mrs Redman. My wife and I were so upset to hear about Karen.'

She stared at him and he saw she was fighting to hold back the tears. The prospect of what he was about to do appalled him, but it had to be done. Perhaps in the circumstances it was not a good idea to be too sympathetic. Deliberately, he made his tone brisk. 'Yes, as I say, it does concern your brother. But I'm afraid, in connection with Mr Randish's death, it also concerns Jonathan.'

Surprise helped her to regain her self-control. 'How?'

Thanet put into words what he had been thinking a moment ago. 'Mrs Redman, there is no way I can soften this blow. But I was at the hospital because Jonathan asked to see me. Specifically, he asked to see the officer in charge of the investigation into your brother's death. Because he wanted to confess.'

She blinked, and it was a moment or two before her lips moved. 'Confess?' The word emerged as a whisper.

Thanet nodded.

'You mean . . .' It was no more than a thread of sound.

'I'm sorry. Yes.' He had to spell it out, make sure that there was no misunderstanding. 'Jonathan has confessed to his uncle's murder.'

She was shaking her head. 'There must be some mistake. He wouldn't. He couldn't have.'

'There's no mistake, I'm afraid.'

Her head was still moving from side to side in rejection of what he was saying.

'Mrs Redman. Please. Listen. I have got to tell you.'

Suddenly she was still, intent. He waited a moment until he was certain she was concentrating and then said, 'This is what Jonathan has said. He told me that he went out to the vineyard on Friday night, that he had an argument with his uncle, that he lost his temper and started throwing things at him. Your brother slipped and crashed backwards through the window. That was how he died. Jonathan had no intention of causing his death, of course. He was so shocked that on the way back he had the accident. He must have been incapable of driving safely. I have to add that his account of the incident corresponds in every detail with what happened, details he couldn't possibly have known unless he had been there.'

She was staring at him, a fixed and desperate stare, as if every ounce of intelligence she possessed was being directed towards attempting to understand the incomprehensible. 'It can't be true. Why hasn't he told me? Why hasn't he said a word about it till now? And why, why should he have such a violent argument with his uncle in the first place?'

'If you think about it you'll realise why he hasn't said anything about this before. As you know, until this afternoon, he didn't even remember that Karen . . . what had happened to Karen. Not until you reminded him. But when you did, it all came back to him in a rush. He didn't say anything to you about his uncle then because it was such a shock to him to remember what he had done that at first he couldn't even begin to think straight.'

'But why? You still haven't explained why? I can't see any possible reason . . .' She had wound the loose ends of the waist cord around her hands so tightly in her agitation that her fingers were beginning to turn white. 'It must all be in his imagination. It's the blow on the head that's done it.' The idea drove her to her feet, twisting her hands to release them from the constricting cord. 'Yes. That's what it is.' She stood looking down at him, her eyes frantic, panting in her terror, agitation and anxiety to convince.

Thanet was cursing himself for not having had the commonsense to bring a policewoman with him. Was there no end to his blunders in this case? He stood up and grasped her hands. 'Please, Mrs Redman, sit down, and I'll explain.' Gently, Thanet coaxed her backwards into her chair. This time she sat well back, arms laid along the chair arms, fingers gripping the ends as if she needed to anchor herself to something solid.

Now came the crunch. 'The reason why Jonathan went rushing out to the vineyard on Friday evening was because before she died, Karen told him something.' He paused, hoping that she would now have an inkling of what he was going to say, but her expression didn't change.

'He told me he had never asked her before, but he sensed that she was slipping away and he felt he couldn't bear never to know who had . . .' Thanet struggled to find the right words, conscious that even angels would find it difficult to tread such delicate ground without giving pain. 'Who had fathered her child. So he pressed her to tell him. And she did.'

He watched understanding dawn in her eyes. Slowly, her lips parted. 'Zak?' she whispered.

He nodded, thankful that it was over, done, but apprehensive now of her reaction.

Her eyes glazed and then she was frowning at her lap, gazing down as intently as if she would find there explanations of all that had so mystified her in the past. She was, Thanet realised, reinterpreting all that had happened, rewriting her family's history. Only the whiteness of the knuckles across her clenched fists betrayed how painful the readjustment was. He hadn't known what to expect – tears, hysterics, denials, perhaps – but not this silent suffering which was so painful to watch.

At last she looked up. 'What will happen to Jonathan now?'

He hadn't realised that he had been holding his breath and he released it in a long, slow sigh of relief that she had accepted the truth of what he had told her. He was relieved too that she was thinking now of Jonathan's future, of the living, not the dead, and thankful that she had not questioned how he had come by his intimate knowledge of Karen's past. Perhaps she simply assumed that Jonathan had told him, and he certainly wasn't going to disillusion her.

With any luck, the worst was over.

TWENTY-TWO

Bridget appeared in the hall as Thanet let himself into the house. She looked fresh and pretty in trim jeans and a dark green Dash sweatshirt with a colourful floral design on the front. She had twisted her newly washed hair up into a knot high on the back of her head. 'Hullo, Dad, you're earlier than I expected. Your supper's in the oven. I'll get it.'

She was still feeling low about Alexander, Thanet could tell, but the fact that she had made an effort over her appearance was a good sign, he felt. The girl who had arrived on Friday evening couldn't have cared less what she looked like. He hung up his coat. 'No, don't worry, I'm not hungry at the moment. I'll have it when I get back from the station. Ben in?'

Despite the heavy workload which was the inevitable result of the end of a case, Thanet had made a special effort to get home early in the hope of catching Bridget alone. Joan's car had gone, so he assumed she had left for her meeting.

'Doing his homework, upstairs.'

'Good. I want to talk to you.' Seeing her expression change, become wary, he realised she assumed he meant he wanted to discuss the situation with Alexander. 'About Jonathan,' he hastened to add.

Her eyebrows arched. 'About Jonathan?' She led the way into the sitting room and they both sat down, Thanet careful of his aching back, which was playing up again.

'Yes. I assume you haven't been in to see him this afternoon?' Thanet eased himself into a more comfortable position.

'No. I went in this morning. They seem to have endless visiting hours there. Why?'

'This afternoon, his mother broke the news of Karen's death to him. The shock seemed to act as some sort of trigger, and his memories of Friday night came flooding back.'

'That's great! I told him it would happen, sooner or later.'

'Yes. It's good in one way . . .'

'What do you mean?'

'This afternoon the sister in charge of his ward rang the office, saying that Jonathan wanted to speak to me – that is, to the officer in charge of the Randish case, which of course happened to be me.'

'Really? But why on earth . . .?'

'Just listen, love. So I went to the hospital. Where Jonathan told me that it was he who had killed his uncle.'

Bridget's eyes stretched wide. 'What?'

For the second time that day Thanet had to tell Jonathan's story, thankful that this time it wasn't such a traumatic experience for his audience. Bridget was shocked, yes, upset, but the news obviously didn't have the same emotional impact on her as it had on Mrs Redman. Her final reaction was the same as Lineham's.

'Poor Jonathan. And poor Mrs Redman, too. How is she taking it?'

'Very well, considering. It was an awful shock at first, of course.'

'Is anyone with her? I told you before, she just doesn't seem to have any friends. Perhaps I ought to go around, put off going back to London until tomorrow.'

'No, it's all right. Mrs Landers is with her – her brother's mother-in-law. She's a very nice woman, she'll look after her. She went to see her on Saturday, in the hospital, as soon as she heard about Jonathan's accident.'

'What will happen to Jonathan?'

'I imagine his legal representatives will persuade him to plead not guilty to murder but guilty of manslaughter, on the grounds of provocation and diminished responsibility.'

'Diminished responsibility, presumably, because the shock of his sister's death . . .'

'His *twin* sister's death . . .'

'. . . and of learning that his uncle was morally responsible for it, temporarily unhinged him.'

'That's right, yes.'

'And provocation?'

'Because, as I told you, when Jonathan tried to make his uncle understand why he was so angry with him, tried to explain precisely why he felt Randish was responsible for Karen's death, he laughed at him. That was really what made Jonathan snap, and in the circumstances it would certainly be considered provocation, I think.'

Bridget shivered. 'He must have been a horrible man.'

'Yes, he wasn't exactly an admirable character.'

'So what difference will it make, if the jury does find Jonathan guilty of manslaughter? He'll still go to prison, surely?'

'The difference is that the judge has much greater flexibility in sentencing. It's even possible that, if the judge is sympathetic, in the circumstances Jonathan might get away with a suspended sentence.'

'Oh I do hope so! After all they've been through . . . It'll be bad enough as it is, having all their private family affairs broadcast in Court.'

'I know.'

'And then there's Mr Randish's family. Think how they're going to feel when all this comes out! He's got a wife, hasn't he?'

'And two young children, yes.' Thanet sighed. 'That's often the way with murder cases, I'm afraid. So many innocent people get hurt, and the effects go on and on for years.'

'I've often wondered how you feel when you have a case like this one, and the murderer turns out to be someone you really feel sorry for, someone who never intended to commit the crime in the first place.'

'That's a difficult one. There's no doubt you feel quite different if the murder was deliberate, or the result of mindless, wanton violence. But in cases like this . . . Well, there is some satisfaction, I suppose, in having brought the thing to a conclusion. But in this particular instance I can't even claim to have done that. If Jonathan hadn't confessed he might never have been found out.'

'I don't believe that. You'd have got there in the end, I'm sure.' Once again, Bridget was echoing Lineham.

'Your faith is touching, love, but I'm afraid it's misplaced.'

'I don't believe that. Come on, Dad, admit it. When you're working on a case you're like a dog with a bone. You can't leave it alone. You go on worrying away at it, worrying away at it until you get there. I've lived with you nearly all my life, remember, and I've seen it happen over and over again!'

There was a sudden thunder of feet on the stairs: Ben in a hurry. The door burst open. 'Oh, hi, Dad, thought I heard you come home. Just nipping over to Tim's. Got a bit of a problem with my Maths. You off soon, Sis?'

'Any minute now,' said Bridget, smiling.

'See you, then.' He hesitated.

He probably wanted to offer comfort over Alexander, but didn't know how to do it, thought Thanet.

'Been nice to have you home,' Ben said awkwardly. And fled without waiting for a response.

There was a brief silence. It was obvious that Bridget, too, recognised what Ben had been trying to do. She flicked a glance at Thanet and gave an embarrassed laugh. 'Good to be appreciated.' Then she looked at her watch. 'Time to be off, Dad.'

Her green and orange squashy bag was already packed, waiting in the hall. Thanet picked it up and slung it over his shoulder. 'Of course,' he said as they walked to the car, 'it goes without saying that all this is in the strictest confidence. Only you've been so involved with Karen, in the past, and with Jonathan, over the last few days, that I felt I owed it to you to explain what happened.'

'I appreciate it, Dad. And, of course, I shan't say a word, to anyone.'

A few minutes later they were approaching the scene of Jonathan's accident. Earlier, curiosity had made Thanet check and yes, there was no doubt about it, it was Jonathan he had seen on that stretcher on Friday night, being loaded into the ambulance. He pointed the place out to Bridget.

'You actually saw the accident?'

'No, I arrived just afterwards. Naturally I had no idea who was involved. I'm afraid I was more concerned with being held up and not getting to the station in time to meet your train.'

It seemed a lifetime away. So much had happened in

those few short days. He had penetrated deep into the lives of those who on that Friday evening had still been strangers to him, equally unaware of his existence. For him the Randish case would one day be no more than an interesting memory, but for them the effects would, as he had said to Bridget, linger on, reverberating into the future. How was Jonathan going to live with the fact that he had killed a man? How was his mother going to come to terms with the fact that her much-loved brother had not only violated her young daughter but ultimately caused Karen's death and made her twin a murderer? Then there was Alice. She would find it very hard, having been so fond of Karen, but her passion for Zak had survived both physical abuse and repeated infidelities and eventually she would, he felt, forgive her dead husband his transgressions as she had forgiven him so many in the past. But what about the children, Fiona and Malcolm? Would their mother and grandparents always be able to keep from them the truth about their father's death?

'What's the matter, Dad?'

'Nothing in particular. Why?'

'You sighed. You're not worrying about me?'

It was the first time, since she had been so angry with him yesterday morning, that either of them had broached the subject. He was tempted to tell her the truth, that he had been thinking about the case, but he couldn't let the opportunity pass. Instead, he avoided a direct answer. 'I am concerned about you, naturally. We all are.'

He glanced at her, but it was difficult to make out her expression. Despite the occasional streetlamp the light in the car was dim. Then, briefly, the flare of passing headlights illuminated her face. She was, he realised with surprise, looking contrite.

'I've been wanting to say . . . I'm sorry I snapped at you yesterday morning,' she said.

'I hope you haven't been worrying about that! I'd forgotten all about it.' Not true, but he wasn't going to tell her that.

They had reached the station and he pulled into a parking place. Neither of them moved, unwilling now to leave unfinished business between them.

'I was thinking about it, afterwards,' said Bridget slowly. 'And I guess I was angry with you because I couldn't forgive you for being right about Alexander.'

Thanet knew how much that double admission must have cost her. But he was glad, too, that she had been able to make it. It was the first, important step back towards recovery. He put out his hand and touched hers, lightly. 'I'm sorry, love. I really mean that. I can't bear to see you unhappy.'

'I know.' Suddenly she was brisk again. 'It's all part of growing up, I suppose. But I must admit, it's a part I could do without.' She opened the door and got out.

Satisfied now that the healing process had begun, he followed suit.

They walked together on to the platform and waited for the train. It arrived on time and he saw her in, waved her off. He watched until its lights had vanished in the distance and then went back to the car. As he pulled away his mind moved ahead, to later on that evening when Joan would come home and he would be able to tell her all about the case.

Not for the first time he felt sorry for all those lonely, divorced or separated detectives in fiction.

As far as he was concerned, there was no substitute for having a wife to go home to.

PUPPET FOR A CORPSE

Dorothy Simpson

On the face of it, Dr Pettifer had everything to live for – a thriving country practice, a beautiful (and very pregnant) wife, rude good health in both body and bank balance. Everyone swore there was no reason why he should have taken an overdose.

That's what they all say, murmured Inspector Thanet, knowing how high was the suicide rate among the medical profession. Stress, overwork, worry – all took there toll.

But he had to admit there were some curious features about this case, little things that aroused his suspicions. For a start, would-be suicides didn't normally arrange for their cars to be repaired, or book expensive holidays for themselves only hours before they reached for the tablets …

'A whodunnit in the fine tradition of the puzzle game'
The Times

'The sort of book you curl up in bed with on wet days … good, lazy reading'
Literary Review

LAST SEEN ALIVE

Dorothy Simpson

It was all of twenty years since Alicia Parnell last saw Sturrenden. While she was still a schoolgirl a jilted boyfriend had killed himself, and her parents had tactfully moved away from that corner of Kent. Nevertheless the old crowd were delighted to welcome her when she turned up out of the blue one day. Just why she'd come back, though, no one could guess.

But within hours Alicia was found strangled in her room at the Black Swan. And for Inspector Thanet – who had known all of them since his youth – there were special problems. Could he have lived most of his life alongside someone who harboured a grudge so strong that only Alicia's death could settle the matter? Or would his investigations turn up fresh scandals, a murky undercurrent to life in that placid old market town of which even he had been blissfully – and tragically – ignorant?

'A seamless crime story that offers a startling and believable surprise ending'
Publishers Weekly

'Well organised ... a cunningly contrived plot'
TLS

CRIME

SUSPICIOUS DEATH

Dorothy Simpson

ACCIDENT, SUICIDE … OR MURDER?

The woman in the blue sequined cocktail dress was dragged from her watery grave beneath a bridge. A highly suspicious death – and Inspector Thanet is called in to investigate.

The more he learns about the late Marcia Salden, mistress of Telford Green Manor, the less likely a candidate she seemed for suicide. A successful self-made woman with a thriving business, she had everything she wanted, including the mansion she had coveted since childhood. She also had a knack for stirring up trouble …

As Inspector Thanet attempts to unravel the complex sequence of events surrounding her death, he discovers that if Mrs Salden hadn't managed to get herself murdered, it wasn't for want of trying …

'As good a Dorothy Simpson as we have seen for some time'
TLS

'Tantalising …'
She

CRIME

DEAD BY MORNING

Dorothy Simpson

On a snowy, February morning, Leo Martindale is found dead in a ditch outside the gates of his ancestral home – apparently a hit and run victim.

After an absence – and a silence – of twenty-five years, he had just returned to Kent to claim his vast inheritance. Is his death an accident? Or is it, as Inspector Thanet of Sturrenden CID begins to suspect, murder?

As his investigation proceeds, Thanet finds a profusion of suspects – all glad to see the last of Leo Martindale, and more importantly, all with opportunity to kill him. In a fog of conflicting suspicions, Inspector Thanet struggles to solve one of his toughest cases …

'Well-rounded characters, a satisfying mind-teaser, the best of British'
The Observer

'A thoroughly traditional detective story'
Today

CRIME

Other bestselling Warner titles available by mail:

☐	The Night She Died	Dorothy Simpson	£3.99
☐	Six Feet Under	Dorothy Simpson	£5.99
☐	Puppet For a Corpse	Dorothy Simpson	£4.99
☐	Last Seen Alive	Dorothy Simpson	£5.99
☐	Suspicious Death	Dorothy Simpson	£5.99
☐	Dead by Morning	Dorothy Simpson	£5.99
☐	Doomed to Die	Dorothy Simpson	£5.99
☐	Wake the Dead	Dorothy Simpson	£5.99
☐	No Laughing Matter	Dorothy Simpson	£5.99
☐	First Inspector Thanet Omnibus	Dorothy Simpson	£10.99
☐	Second Inspector Thanet Omnibus	Dorothy Simpson	£10.99
☐	Third Inspector Thanet Omnibus	Dorothy Simpson	£10.99

The prices shown above are correct at time of going to press. However, the publishers reserve the right to increase prices on covers from those previously advertised without prior notice.

WARNER BOOKS

WARNER BOOKS
P.O. Box 121, Kettering, Northants NN14 4ZQ
Tel: 01832 737525, Fax: 01832 733076
Email: aspenhouse@FSBDial.co.uk

POST AND PACKING:

Payments can be made as follows: cheque, postal order (payable to Warner Books) or by credit cards. Do not send cash or currency.

All U.K. Orders — **FREE OF CHARGE**
E.E.C. & Overseas — 25% of order value

Name (Block Letters) ____________________

Address ____________________

____

Post/zip code: ____________________

☐ Please keep me in touch with future Warner publications

☐ I enclose my remittance £__________

☐ I wish to pay by Visa/Access/Mastercard/Eurocard

Card Expiry Date ____________